A TEXT BOOK OF

MECHANICS
OF
SOLIDS

FOR
SEMESTER – III

B.E. DEGREE COURSE IN CIVIL ENGINEERING

Strictly According to New Revised Syllabus of
ANNA UNIVERSITY, CHENNAI
(R – 2013)

ALSO USEFUL FOR SRM UNIVERSITY, KATTANKULATHUR

Dr. SURESH R. PAREKAR
M.E. Ph.D. (Structures)
Associate Professor and Head,
Civil Engineering Department,
AISSM's College of Engineering, PUNE.

NIRALI
PRAKASHAN
ADVANCEMENT OF KNOWLEDGE

N 3484

MECHANICS OF SOLIDS SEM. III CIVIL (ANNA UNIVERSITY)   ISBN 978-93-5164-593-1

First Edition : June 2015
© : Author

Published By :   POLYPLATE

NIRALI PRAKASHAN
Abhyudaya Pragati, 1312, Shivaji Nagar,
Off J.M. Road, PUNE – 411005
Tel - (020) 25512336/37/39, Fax - (020) 25511379
Email : niralipune@pragationline.com

☞ **DISTRIBUTION CENTRES**

PUNE

Nirali Prakashan : 119, Budhwar Peth, Jogeshwari Mandir Lane, Pune 411002, Maharashtra
Tel : (020) 2445 2044, 66022708, Fax : (020) 2445 1538
Email : bookorder@pragationline.com, niralilocal@pragationline.com

Nirali Prakashan : S. No. 28/27, Dhyari, Near Pari Company, Pune 411041
Tel : (020) 24690204 Fax : (020) 24690316
Email : dhyari@pragationline.com, bookorder@pragationline.com

MUMBAI

Nirali Prakashan : 385, S.V.P. Road, Rasdhara Co-op. Hsg. Society Ltd.,
Girgaum, Mumbai 400004, Maharashtra
Tel : (022) 2385 6339 / 2386 9976, Fax : (022) 2386 9976
Email : niralimumbai@pragationline.com

☞ **DISTRIBUTION BRANCHES**

JALGAON

Nirali Prakashan : 34, V. V. Golani Market, Navi Peth, Jalgaon 425001,
Maharashtra, Tel : (0257) 222 0395, Mob : 94234 91860

KOLHAPUR

Nirali Prakashan : New Mahadvar Road, Kedar Plaza, 1st Floor Opp. IDBI Bank
Kolhapur 416 012, Maharashtra. Mob : 9850046155

NAGPUR

Pratibha Book Distributors: Above Maratha Mandir, Shop No. 3, First Floor,
Rani Jhanshi Square, Sitabuldi, Nagpur 440012, Maharashtra
Tel : (0712) 254 7129

DELHI

Nirali Prakashan : 4593/21, Basement, Aggarwal Lane 15, Ansari Road, Daryaganj
Near Times of India Building, New Delhi 110002
Mob : 08505972553

BENGALURU

Pragati Book House : House No. 1, Sanjeevappa Lane, Avenue Road Cross,
Opp. Rice Church, Bengaluru – 560002.
Tel : (080) 64513344, 64513355,Mob : 9880582331, 9845021552
Email:bharatsavla@yahoo.com

CHENNAI

Pragati Books : 9/1, Montieth Road, Behind Taas Mahal, Egmore,
Chennai 600008 Tamil Nadu, Tel : (044) 6518 3535,
Mob : 94440 01782 / 98450 21552 / 98805 82331,
Email : bharatsavla@yahoo.com

niralipune@pragationline.com | www.pragationline.com

Also find us on 🅕 www.facebook.com/niralibooks

PREFACE

The subject '**Mechanics of Solids**' is a foundation stone for any Engineering Course. Today, Engineering applications are mostly interdisciplinary, involving basics of various fundamental subjects. One such subject of vital importance is "**Mechanics of Solids**". The present text is aimed at catering the needs of students appearing for Sem. III B.E. Degree Course in Civil Engineering. This book is strictly written as per the new revised syllabus of ANNA UNIVERSITY, CHENNAI (R – 2013).

Also this text book covers the Syllabus of SRM UNIVERSITY, KATTANKULATHUR.

The text gives fundamental and simple treatment to the subject with a clear and distinct presentation of theoretical concepts and well graded numerous examples.

Main features of this book are **Complete Coverage** of the new syllabus revised in June 2015 with large number of **Worked (Solved) Examples** and **Numerical Problems** given at the end of each chapter.

I am sincerely thankful to **Shri. Dineshbhai Furia, Shri. Jignesh Furia, Mrs. Nirali Verma, Shri. M. P. Munde** and the entire team of Nirali Prakashan who really have taken keen interest and untiring efforts in publishing this text.

I am also thankful to Mrs. Deepali Lachake (Co-ordinator), Mrs. Shilpa Kale and Mrs. Roshan Khan for their kind co-operation throughout the work.

I take this opportunity to express my deep sense of gratitude towards all the dear friends and students for their direct or indirect help in making this venture a success.

In spite of having taken all the precautions, it is possible that some errors may have escaped my attention. The readers are kindly requested to bring to my notice such corrections for being rectified in the next edition.

13th June 2015   **Dr. S. R. Parekar**

SYLLABUS

Unit I : Stress And Strain (9)

Stress and strain at a point, Tension, Compression, Shear Stress, Hooke"s Law, Relationship among elastic constants, Stress Strain Diagram for Mild Steel, TOR steel, Concrete, Ultimate Stress, Yield Stress, Factor of Safety, Thermal Stresses, Thin Cylinders and Shells, Strain Energy due to Axial Force, Resilience, Stresses due to impact and Suddenly Applied Load, Compound Bars.

Unit II : Shear And Bending In Beams (9)

Beams and Bending- Types of loads, supports, Shear Force and Bending Moment Diagrams for statically determinate beam with concentrated load, UDL, uniformly varying load. Theory of Simple Bending, Analysis of Beams for Stresses, Stress Distribution at a cross Section due to bending moment and shear force for Cantilever, simply supported and overhanging beams with different loading conditions - Flitched Beams.

Unit III : Deflection (9)

Double integration method - Macaulay's methods - Area moment method - conjugate beam method for computation of slopes and deflections of determinant beams.

Unit IV : Torsion (9)

Torsion of Circular and Hollow Shafts, Elastic Theory of Torsion, Stresses and Deflection in Circular Solid and Hollow Shafts, combined bending moment and torsion of shafts - strain energy due to torsion - Modulus of Rupture, Power transmitted to shaft, Shaft in series and parallel, Closed and Open Coiled helical springs, Leaf Springs, Springs in series and parallel, Design of buffer springs.

Unit V : Complex Stresses And Plane Trusses (9)

2 D State of Stress, 2 D Normal and Shear Stresses on any plane, Principal Stresses and Principal Planes, Mohr's circle - Plane trusses: Analysis of plane trusses - method of joints - method of sections.

CONTENTS

Unit - I

Chapter 1 : Simple Stresses and Strains   1.1 – 1.56

1.1	Introduction	1.1
1.2	Loads and their Classification	1.2
1.3	Stress	1.3
	1.3.1 Types of Stresses	1.3
	1.3.2 Sign Convention and Unit of Stress	1.4
1.4	Strain	1.5
	1.4.1 Types of Strains	1.5
	1.4.2 Sign Convention and Unit of Strain	1.6
1.5	Poisson's Ratio (μ)	1.6
1.6	Hooke's Law and Modulus of Elasticity (E)	1.6
1.7	Modulus of Rigidity or Shear Modulus (G)	1.7
1.8	Volumetric Stress and Volumetric Strain	1.7
1.9	Bulk Modulus (K)	1.8
1.10	Stress-Strain Curve	1.8
1.11	Allowable Stress and Factor of Safety	1.9
1.12	Relation between Modulus of Elasticity (e) and Modulus of Rigidity (g)	1.9
1.13	Relation between Modulus of Elasticity (E) & Bulk Modulus (K)	1.11
	• Solved Examples	1.12
1.14	Generalised Hooke's Law	1.17
1.15	Axial Flexibility (F)	1.22
1.16	Axial Stiffness (S)	1.22
1.17	Stress & Elongation Produced in a Bar due to its own Weight	1.22
1.18	Elongation of Conical Bar due to its own Weight	1.23
1.19	Linearly Varying Sections	1.24
1.20	Compound Sections	1.24
1.21	Temperature Stresses	1.36
	• Exercise	1.51

Chapter 2 : Thin Cylinders and Shells   **2.1 – 2.32**

2.1	Thin Cylindrical and Spherical Vessels	2.1
2.2	Stresses Induced	2.1
2.3	Evaluation of Stresses	2.2
	2.3.1 Circumferential or Hoop Stress	2.2
	2.3.2 Longitudinal Stress	2.3
	2.3.3 Shear Stress	2.3
2.4	Evaluation of Strains	2.4
	2.4.1 Circumferential Strain, e_c	2.4
	2.4.2 Longitudinal Strain, e_L	2.4
	2.4.3 Area Strain $\dfrac{\delta A}{A}$	2.5
	2.4.4 Volumetric Strain, $\dfrac{\delta V}{V}$	2.5
	2.4.5 Thickness Strain $\dfrac{\delta t}{t}$	2.5
2.5	Evaluation of Deformations	2.6
	2.5.1 Increase in Diameter, δd	2.6
	2.5.2 Increase in Length, δL	2.6
	2.5.3 Increase in Cross-sectional Area, δA	2.6
	2.5.4 Increase in Volume, δV	2.6
	2.5.5 Decrease in Thickness, δt	2.6
2.6	Effects of Compressible and Non-Compressible Fluid Injected Under Pressure	2.7
	2.6.1 Compressible Fluid	2.7
	2.6.2 Incompressible Fluid	2.7
	• Solved Examples	2.7
2.7	Thin Spherical Shell under Internal Pressure	2.19
2.8	Thick Cylinders	2.23
	2.8.1 Lame's Assumption	2.23
	2.8.2 Derivation of Lame's Formulae for Radial Pressure and Circumferential Stress	2.23
	2.8.3 Evaluation of 'a' and 'b' in Lame's Equations	2.25
	2.8.4 Evaluation of f_{max} and f_{min} when $p_{min} = 0$	2.25
	• Exercise	2.28

Chapter 3 : Strain Energy   3.1 – 3.44

3.1	Introduction	3.1
3.2	Strain Energy due To Axial Force	3.1
3.3	Proof Resilience	3.2
3.4	Modulus of Resilience	3.2
3.5	Stress due to Various Types of Axial Loads	3.3
	3.5.1 Gradually Applied Load	3.3
	3.5.2 Suddenly Applied Load	3.3
	3.5.3 Impact Load	3.4
	• Solved Examples	3.5
3.6	Combined Actions	3.19
	3.6.1 Bending and Torsion	3.19
	3.6.2 Axial Force and Torsion	3.21
	3.6.3 Axial force, Bending and Torsion	3.21
	• Solved Examples	3.22
3.7	Strain Energy due to Torsion	3.34
3.8	Theories of Failure	3.36
	• Exercise	3.40

Unit - II

Chapter 4 : Shear Force and Bending Moment (Part – A)   4.1 – 4.34

4.1	Introduction	4.1
4.2	Types of Supports	4.1
4.3	Types of Loads	4.2
4.4	Reactions	4.3
4.5	Types of Beams	4.4
4.6	Shear Force and Bending Moment	4.4
	4.6.1 Sign Conventions for Shear Force and Bending Moment	4.6
4.7	Shear Force and Bending Moment Diagrams (SFD and BMD)	4.6
4.8	Relationship between Load, Shear and Bending Moment	4.7
	• Solved Examples	4.8
	• Exercise	4.31

Chapter 5 : Shear Force and Bending Moment (Part – B) **5.1 – 5.16**

5.1 Relationship between Load, Shear and Bending Moment 5.1

• Solved Examples 5.2

• Exercise 5.14

Unit - III

Chapter 6 : Deflection of Beams and Conjugate Method **6.1 – 6.62**

6.1 Introduction 6.1

6.2 Assumptions 6.1

6.3 Slope, Deflection and Radius of Curvature 6.2

6.4 Methods of Displacement Analysis 6.3

6.5 Macaulay's Method 6.3

6.6 Boundary Conditions 6.5

6.7 Sign Conventions 6.6

6.8 Bending Moment Equations for Macaulay's Method 6.6

• Solved Examples 6.7

6.9 Moment Area Methods – Mohr's Theorems 6.16

  6.9.1 Sign Conventions 6.19

6.10 Application of Moment-Area Method to Cantilever Beams 6.21

• Solved Examples 6.22

6.11 Application of Moment-Area Method to Simply
Supported and Overhanging Beams 6.26

• Solved Examples 6.28

6.12 Conjugate Beam Method 6.34

6.13 Support Conditions 6.36

• Solved Examples 6.38

• Exercise 6.56

Unit - IV

Chapter 7 : Torsion **7.1 – 7.58**

7.1 Introduction 7.1

7.2 Basics of Torsion 7.1

7.3 Method of Section 7.1

  7.3.1 Torsional Moment Diagram 7.2

7.4 Theory of Torsion 7.4

  7.4.1 Assumptions in Deriving the Torsion Formulae 7.4

  7.4.2 Derivation of Torsion Formula 7.4

7.5	Important Terms	7.6
	7.5.1 Torsional Stiffness	7.6
	7.5.2 Torsional Flexibility	7.6
	7.5.3 Torsional Rigidity	7.6
	7.5.4 Torsional Section Modulus	7.6
	7.5.5 Power Transmitted by Shaft	7.7
	• Solved Examples	7.8
7.6	Design of Shafts	7.12
7.7	Solid and Hollow Circular Shafts for the Same Torque	7.12
7.8	Shafts in Series	7.24
7.9	Statically Indeterminate Problems	7.32
	7.9.1 Shafts Fixed at Both Ends	7.32
	7.9.2 Shafts in Parallel	7.33
	• Exercise	7.54

Chapter 8 : Helical and Leaf Springs — **8.1-8.10**

8.1	Introduction	8.1
8.2	Closed-Coiled Helical Spring With Axial Load	8.2
8.3	Close-Helical Spring With Axial Twist	8.3
8.4	Open-Coiled Helical Spring	8.4
8.5	Laminated Spring	8.5
	• Solved Examples	8.7
	• Exercise	8.10

Unit - V

Chapter 9 : Complex Stresses and Plane Trusses — **9.1 – 9.48**

9.1	Introduction	9.1
9.2	Transformation of Plane Stress	9.2
9.3	Principal Stresses	9.4
9.4	Maximum Shear Stress	9.5
	• Solved Examples	9.6
9.5	Mohr's Circle	9.27
9.6	Theories of Failure	9.39
	• Exercise	9.45

SIMPLE STRESSES AND STRAINS

1.1 INTRODUCTION

The group of studies known as mechanics may be divided and classified in many ways, one of which is indicated below :

Mechanics $\begin{cases}\text{Particle and Rigid Bodies} \\ \text{(Applied Mechanics)} \\ \text{Deformable Bodies}\end{cases}$ — $\begin{cases}\text{Elastic (Strength of Materials)} \\ \text{Plastic (Advanced Course in Plasticity)} \\ \text{Fluid (Hydraulics, Fluid Mechanics, Aerodynamics)}\end{cases}$

In the usual Applied or Engineering mechanics, all the bodies studied are considered to be particles or rigid bodies - particles when the dimensions of the body are neglected, rigid bodies when the dimensions are considered but the deformations are neglected.

There are many cases in which the distortions of different dimensions of the body must be considered. Structural members, machine parts and springs are usually made of solid materials that deform considerably under the action of external loads, but regain their original shape after the load is removed. Such materials are said to be *elastic*.

In all the studies to follow, the free body concept as used in earlier studies in mechanics, will be found indispensable, as well as equations of equilibrium, because the subject "Strength of Materials" is built upon previous knowledge of mechanics with the addition of only a few new concepts. To illustrate the distinction between the problems of Applied Mechanics and those of Strength of Materials, consider the beam of Fig. 1.1.

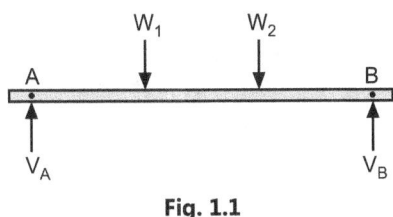

Fig. 1.1

In Applied Mechanics, we learned how to apply the equations of equilibrium to the free body in order to determine the unknown reactions V_A and V_B, having given the magnitude and spacing of loads. Although the beam does deform due to applied loads, the changes in the dimensions are so small that it has no appreciable effect on the reactions. That is, we consider the beam to be a rigid body.

In Strength of Materials, we shall continue to neglect these deformations while determining the reactions, but we shall be concerned with these deformations while doing other calculations like we may wish to determine how much the beam will deflect or we may be interested in the deformations as a step in determining the internal stresses. Magnitude of these internal stresses must be known in order to proportion a member for a given length and loading.

Throughout this text, we study the principles that govern two fundamental concepts, strength and rigidity. In this first chapter, we start with the simple axial loading, later we consider bending loads, twisting loads and finally we discuss simultaneous combinations of these three basic types of loadings.

1.2 LOADS AND THEIR CLASSIFICATION

Loads may be classified in two ways :

(a) According to manner to their application : As per this classification, loads may be classified as (i) Dead load, (ii) Live load, (iii) Wind load, (iv) Seismic loads, (v) Temperature loads, (vi) Impact loads, (vii) Erection loads, etc.

(b) According to effect they produce : Variety of loads acting on structural member produce different types of effect. For convenience these forces are resolved into components that are normal and tangential to the cross-section as shown in Fig. 1.2. The origin of the reference axis is always taken at the centroid of the cross-section. Each of these components have different structural effect and produces different structural deformation.

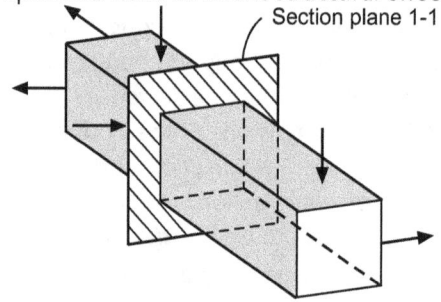
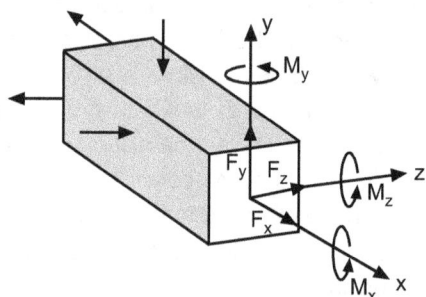

(a) General loading on member	**(b) Internal forces at cross-section 1-1**

Fig. 1.2

Various components and their structural names are as follows :

   (i) F_x : Axial Force : The force acting *normal to the cross-section and passing through CG* is called as axial force. The primary effect of axial force is to change the length of member. Axial force may be tensile in nature (pull) which causes increase in the length of a member or compressive in nature (push) which causes decrease in the length of a member.

   (ii) F_y ; F_z : Shear Forces : The force acting *tangential to the cross-section* is called as shear force. The primary effect of these forces is to cause sliding of one cross-section with respect to other.

   (iii) M_x : Torsional Moment : Net moment vector acting *normal to the cross-section* is called as torsional moment or torque or torsion. The primary effect of torsional moment is to cause rotation of different cross-sections of member with respect to each other about polar axis. This rotation is called as twist.

   (iv) M_y ; M_z : Bending Moment : Net moment vector acting *tangential to the cross-section* is called as bending moment. These moments cause bending of the member about an axis parallel to the cross-section and ultimately produce slopes and deflection.

The subject Strength of Materials is the study of all above structural actions, corresponding deformations and stresses produced by an individual action or combination thereof.

1.3 STRESS

When as elastic body is subjected to loads, it undergoes deformation. While undergoing deformations, the particles of the material offer a resisting force. When this resisting force equals the applied loads, equilibrium is attained and further deformation stops. This internal resistance is called as *stress*. The resistance per unit area is called as intensity of stress. Generally, the word stress refers to *intensity of stress*. Thus, stress is *resistance per unit area*.

1.3.1 Types of Stresses

Stresses are of two types : (i) Normal Stresses and (ii) Shear Stresses.

Stresses which act normal to the section are called as normal stresses while that acting tangential to the section are called shear stresses. It should be noted that *axial force* produces *uniform normal stresses* over the section while *bending moment* produces *linearly varying stresses* over the section within elastic limit, as discussed later in the text. Shear force and torsional moment produces shear stresses over the section. Thus, type of stress produced depends on the type of action the cross-section is subjected to.

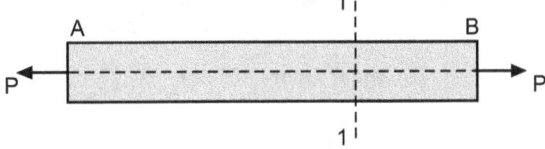

(a) Member subjected to axial tension (Pull)

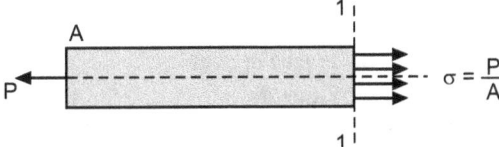

(b) Uniform normal tensile stresses produced by axial pull

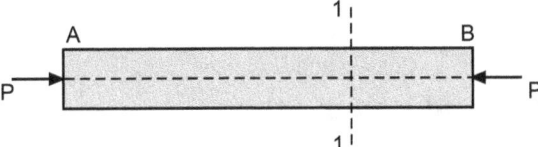

(c) Member subjected to axial compression (Push)

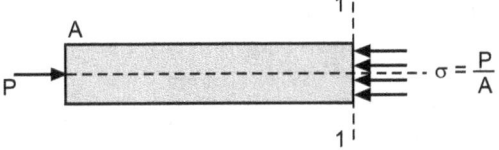

(d) Uniform normal compressive stresses produced by axial push

Fig. 1.3

Normal stresses can further be classified as tensile or compressive in nature, depending on kind of deformation the member undergoes.

Fig. 1.3 (a) shows member subjected to axial tensile force. Consider section 1-1 and FBD of part of the member as shown in Fig. 1.3 (b). For equilibrium, cross-section must offer a resistive force = applied force = P. This resistive force per unit area is called as **normal stress**.

Thus, for axial force, normal stress $= \sigma_n = \dfrac{P}{A}$ 　　　　　　　　　　... (1.1)

where, A = cross-sectional area of member.

Fig. 1.3 (c) and 1.3 (d) respectively show compressive force and corresponding normal stresses.

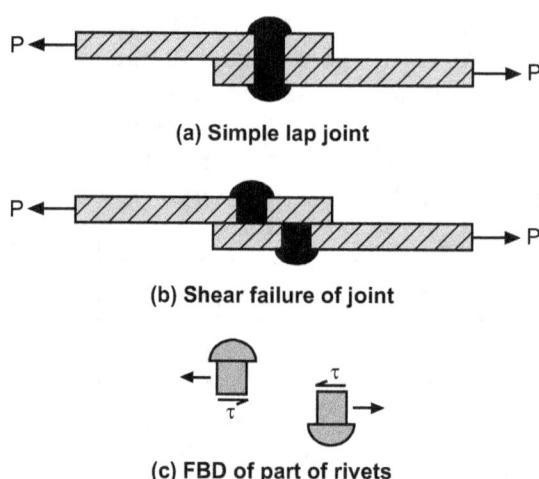

(a) Simple lap joint

(b) Shear failure of joint

(c) FBD of part of rivets

Fig. 1.4

Fig. 1.4 shows a simple riveted lap joint and its shear failure. It should be noted that, the force which causes failure of rivet is acting tangential to its cross-section and hence produces shear stress (τ).

$$\text{Shear stress} = \tau = \frac{\text{Shear force}}{\text{Cross-sectional area}} \qquad ... (1.2)$$

1.3.2 Sign Convention and Unit of Stress

Normal tensile stress is considered positive while normal compressive stress is considered negative.

Shear stress 'τ' which produces clockwise couple is considered positive and that producing anticlockwise couple is considered negative as shown in Fig. 1.5.

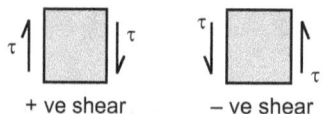

+ ve shear 　　　　 − ve shear

Fig. 1.5

Unit of stress is MPa or GPa (mega or gega Pascal).

Note :
$$1 \text{ MPa } = 1 \text{ N/mm}^2$$
$$1 \text{ GPa } = 1 \text{ kN/mm}^2$$
$\therefore$
$$1 \text{ GPa } = 10^3 \text{ MPa}$$

1.4 STRAIN

When an elastic body is subjected to loads, it undergoes deformation. Strain is a *measure of deformation produced by application of external forces*.

1.4.1 Types of Strains

Strains are of two types : (i) Linear strain and (ii) Shear strain.

(i) Linear Strain : It is the ratio of alteration in any dimension of the body to the respective original dimension.

Thus,　Linear strain = ε = $\dfrac{\text{Change in dimension}}{\text{Original dimension}}$ 　　　　... (1.3)

In case of an axial force, linear strain produced along the length is called as **longitudinal strain** while that produced along cross-section is called as **lateral strain**.

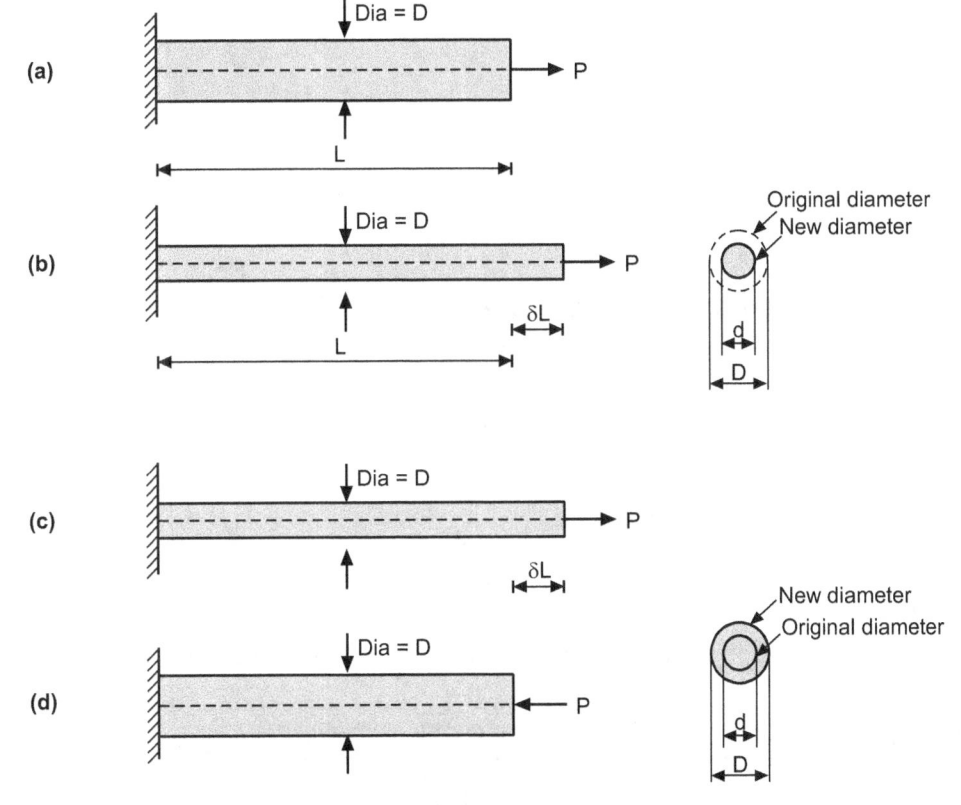

Fig. 1.6 : Longitudinal and Lateral strains

Linear strain may be tensile or compressive in nature. Axial pull causes increase in length while decrease in cross-sectional dimensions and axial push causes decrease in length while increase in cross-sectional dimensions as shown in Fig. 1.6.

Thus,

$$\text{Longitudinal strain} = \varepsilon_L = \frac{\text{Change in length}}{\text{Original length}}$$

$$\therefore \qquad\qquad \varepsilon_L = \frac{\delta L}{L} \qquad\qquad \text{... (1.4)}$$

$$\text{Lateral strain} = \varepsilon_{Lt} = \frac{\text{Change in cross-sectional dimensions}}{\text{Original cross-sectional dimensions}} \qquad \text{... (1.5)}$$

For the example of circular bar considered in Fig. 1.6,

$$\text{Lateral strain} = \varepsilon_{Lt} = \frac{\text{Change in diameter}}{\text{Original diameter}}$$

(ii) Shear strain : If an element ABCD shown in Fig. 1.7 is subjected to shear stress τ on faces AB and CD, then it undergoes angular deformation ϕ as shown.

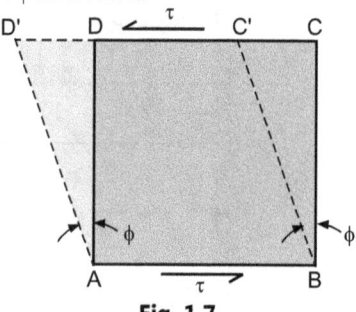

$$\text{Shear strain} = \gamma = \tan\phi = \frac{DD'}{AD} \qquad \text{... (1.6)}$$

Shear strain being very small,

$$\tan\phi \approx \phi$$

Fig. 1.7

1.4.2 Sign Convention and Unit of Strain

Linear strain tensile in nature is considered positive while that compressive in nature is considered negative.

Shear strain sign convention is same as explained in article 1.3.2.

Strain does not have any unit.

1.5 POISSON'S RATIO (μ)

It is the ratio of lateral strain to linear strain.

Thus, $$\mu = \frac{\text{Lateral strain}}{\text{Linear strain}} = \frac{\varepsilon_{Lt}}{\varepsilon_L} \qquad \text{... (1.7)}$$

The value of Poisson's ratio depends on type of material and for most metals it is 0.25 to 0.35.

1.6 HOOKE'S LAW AND MODULUS OF ELASTICITY (E)

By experiment it has been established for many structural materials that, within elastic limit, the elongation of the bar is proportional to tensile force. This linear relationship between the force and the elongation produced by it was formulated by Robert Hooke and hence known as Hooke's law.

If bars of same material but different lengths and different cross-sectional areas are experimented, it is observed that its elongation is proportional to tensile force, length and inversely proportional to the cross-sectional area.

Thus,
$$\delta L \ \propto \ \frac{PL}{A}$$

OR
$$\delta L \ = \ \frac{PL}{AE} \qquad \qquad \text{... (1.8)}$$

where, E = constant for any given material and is called as **Modulus of elasticity or Young's modulus.**

From equation (1.8), we can further write,

$$E \ = \ \frac{\sigma_n}{\varepsilon_L} \qquad \qquad \text{... (1.9)}$$

as
$$\sigma \ = \ \frac{P}{A} \quad \text{and} \quad \varepsilon_L \ = \ \frac{\delta L}{L}$$

Thus, Hooke's law states that **stress is proportional to strain.** It should be noted that unit of Modulus of elasticity is same as that of stress.

1.7 MODULUS OF RIGIDITY OR SHEAR MODULUS (G)

The shear stress (τ) is proportional to shear strain (γ) as long as proportional limit in shear is not exceeded.

Thus,
$$\tau \ \propto \ \gamma$$
i.e.
$$\tau \ = \ G\gamma$$

or
$$G \ = \ \frac{\tau}{\gamma} \qquad \qquad \text{... (1.10)}$$

where,
$$G \ = \ \text{Modulus of rigidity or Shear modulus}$$

It should be noted that the unit of modulus of rigidity is same as that of stress.

1.8 VOLUMETRIC STRESS AND VOLUMETRIC STRAIN

When an elastic body is subjected to three mutually perpendicular equal direct stresses as shown in Fig. 1.8, it undergoes a change in volume without distortion of shape. Such a stress is called as *volumetric stress (σ_V)*. Such a state of stress occurs when a cube is at a large depth in a liquid. The intensity of compressive pressure will have the same magnitude on all the faces. Such a state of stress is also called as *hydrostatic* state of stress.

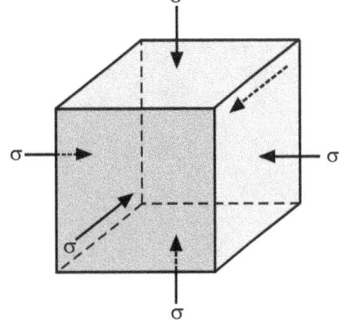

Fig. 1.8

The ratio of change in volume to original volume of a body is called as volumetric strain.

$$\varepsilon_V = \frac{\delta V}{V} \qquad \qquad \text{... (1.11)}$$

where, δV = Change in volume

V = Original volume

Let L, b, and d be the length, width and depth of an elastic member subjected to external force.

$$\text{Original volume} = V = L \cdot b \cdot d$$

$$\text{Change in volume} = \delta V = \delta L \cdot bd + \delta b \cdot L \cdot d + \delta d \cdot L \cdot b$$

$\therefore$ $$\text{Volumetric strain} = \varepsilon_V = \frac{\delta V}{V}$$

$$= \frac{\delta L \cdot bd + \delta b \cdot L \cdot d + \delta d \cdot L \cdot b}{L\,b\,d}$$

$$\frac{\delta V}{V} = \frac{\delta L}{L} + \frac{\delta b}{b} + \frac{\delta d}{d} \qquad \qquad \text{... (1.12)}$$

Volumetric strain is thus equal to algebraic sum of linear strains of the three sides.

Thus, for axial loading,

$$\varepsilon_V = \varepsilon_L + \varepsilon_{Lt} + \varepsilon_{Lt}$$

$$= \varepsilon_L - \mu\,\varepsilon_L - \mu\,\varepsilon_L$$

$$= \varepsilon_L\,(1 - 2\mu) \qquad \qquad \text{... (1.13)}$$

It should be noted that, lateral strain is of opposite sense to that of longitudinal strain.

1.9 BULK MODULUS (K)

It is defined as the ratio of volumetric stress (σ_V) to volumetric strain (ε_V).

Thus, $$\text{Bulk modulus} = K = \frac{\sigma_V}{\varepsilon_V} \qquad \qquad \text{... (1.14)}$$

It should be noted that, the unit of Bulk modulus is same as that of stress.

1.10 STRESS-STRAIN CURVE

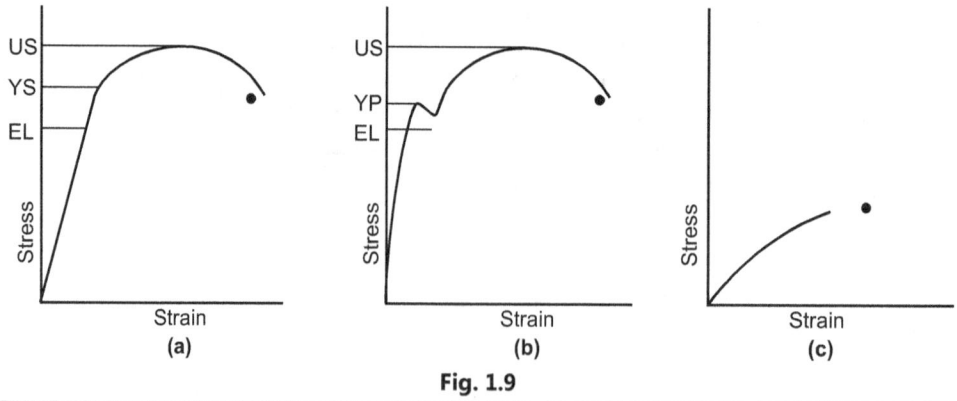

Fig. 1.9

In Fig. 1.9, typical stress-strain curves are shown for several common materials. Such curves are obtained by loading a specimen of the material in tension and recording simultaneous observations of both load and elongation. From these readings, stresses and strains are computed and curves are plotted.

The Elastic Limit (EL) is that stress below which the ratio of stress to strain is constant. See Fig. 1.9 (a) and 1.9 (b). More precisely we have defined the proportional limit or proportional elastic limit but the words are often used interchangeably.

The Yield Point (YP) is that stress at which elongation continues without increase in the load. See Fig. 1.9 (b). Low carbon steel is one of the few materials which exhibits a true yield point. For the majority of ductile materials, those which do not exhibit this characteristic, a corresponding value called yield strength is determined.

Yield Strength (YS) is that stress at which a predetermined permanent set is produced. See Fig. 1.9 (a). The yield point or yield strength each indicates the stress below which a given increment of stress will produce a small strain and above which the same increment of stress will produce a very much larger increment of strain.

The **Ultimate Strength (US)** is the ratio of maximum load sustained during a tensile test divided by the original cross-sectional area.

One or the other of the curves of Fig. 1.9 (a) and 1.9 (b) is a representative of most structural materials. However, the brittle materials, such as concrete and ordinary cast iron, usually exhibit tensile curves similar to Fig. 1.9 (c), breaking with negligible elongation.

The values of yield point, elastic limit and modulus of elasticity are generally determined from tension tests, the results may be applied to problems of compression as well.

1.11 ALLOWABLE STRESS AND FACTOR OF SAFETY

The factor of safety allows for errors in estimating design loads, some variations in material quality and perhaps most important of all, errors in the assumptions used in the design calculations. There are two ways of defining factor of safety :

  (i)   **Based on ultimate stress :** It is the ratio of ultimate stress to working stress.

  (ii) **Based on yield stress :** It is the ratio of yield stress to working stress.

It is obvious that the factor of safety based on ultimate stress has larger value than that based on yield stress.

The factor of safety may vary depending upon the judgement of designers and depending upon their experience.

1.12 RELATION BETWEEN MODULUS OF ELASTICITY (E) AND MODULUS OF RIGIDITY (G)

Consider an elementary rectangular block ABCD of unit thickness, having shear stresses 'τ' acting on faces AD and BC as shown in Fig. 1.10. Assuming AD to be fixed, block ABCD will deform to AB'C'D. Let ϕ be the shear strain.

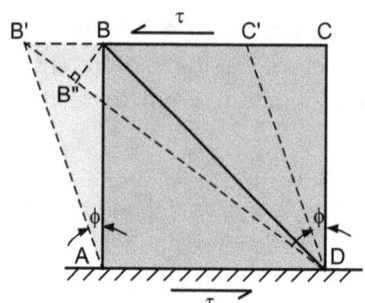

Fig. 1.10

$$\text{Linear strain of diagonal BD} = \frac{DB' - DB}{DB}$$

$$= \frac{B'B''}{DB}$$

$$= \frac{(BB')\cos 45}{\sqrt{2}\ AB}$$

$$\varepsilon_{BD} = \frac{1}{2}\left(\frac{BB'}{AB}\right) = \frac{1}{2}(\phi) \text{ (Tensile)} \qquad \qquad \dots (1.15)$$

Similarly, the linear strain of the diagonal AC is also $\frac{1}{2}(\phi)$, but it is compressive in nature.

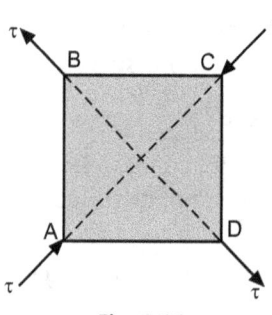

Fig. 1.11

Linear strain of diagonal BD can also be derived by considering direct tensile stress τ across the plane AC, accompanied by the direct compressive stress across the plane BD as shown in Fig. 1.11. This is an equivalent of stress system considered in Fig. 1.10. The combined effect of the two direct stresses on diagonal BD will therefore be tensile strain of magnitude

$$\varepsilon_{BD} = \frac{\tau}{E}(1 + \mu) \qquad \qquad \dots (1.16)$$

This linear strain is already found to be $\frac{1}{2}(\phi)$.

∴   Equating equations (1.15) and (1.16), we get

$$\frac{\tau}{E}(1 + \mu) = \frac{1}{2}(\phi)$$

$$\frac{\tau}{E}(1 + \mu) = \frac{1}{2}\left(\frac{\tau}{G}\right)$$

∴ $$\mathbf{E = 2\,G\,(1 + \mu)} \qquad \qquad \dots (1.17)$$

1.13 RELATION BETWEEN MODULUS OF ELASTICITY (E) & BULK MODULUS (K)

Consider a cube of side 'L' with its faces subjected to direct stresses of intensity (σ) as shown in Fig. 1.12.

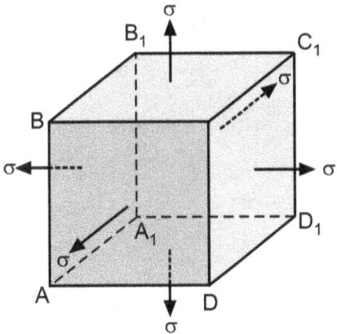

Fig. 1.12

The linear strain in any one direction is given by generalised Hooke's law,

Thus,
$$\frac{\delta L}{L} = \frac{1}{E}(\sigma - \mu\sigma - \mu\sigma)$$

$$= \frac{\sigma}{E}(1 - 2\mu) \qquad \text{... (1.18)}$$

where, μ = Poisson's ratio

Original volume of cube, $V = L^3$

∴ $\delta V = 3L^2\, \delta L$

∴   Volumetric strain $= \varepsilon_V = \dfrac{\delta V}{V}$

$$= \frac{3L^2\, \delta L}{L^3} = 3 \cdot \frac{\delta L}{L} \qquad \text{... (1.19)}$$

Substituting for $\dfrac{\delta L}{L}$ from equation (1.18), we get

$$\varepsilon_V = 3 \cdot \left[\frac{\sigma}{E}(1 - 2\mu)\right] \qquad \text{... (1.20)}$$

Bulk modulus, $K = \dfrac{\sigma}{\varepsilon_V} = \dfrac{\sigma}{\dfrac{3\sigma}{E}(1 - 2\mu)}$

∴ $E = 3K(1 - 2\mu) \qquad \text{... (1.21)}$

From equations (1.17) and (1.21), the relation between four elastic constants is given by

$$E = 2G(1 + \mu) = 3K(1 - 2\mu) \qquad \text{... (1.22)}$$

SOLVED EXAMPLES

Example 1.1 : *A 2.8 m long member is 60 mm deep and 40 mm wide in cross-section. It is subjected to axial tensile force of 210 kN as shown in Fig. 1.13. Determine (i) Change in length, (ii) Change in cross-sectional dimensions, (iii) Change in volume. Assume E = 200 GPa, μ = 0.3.*

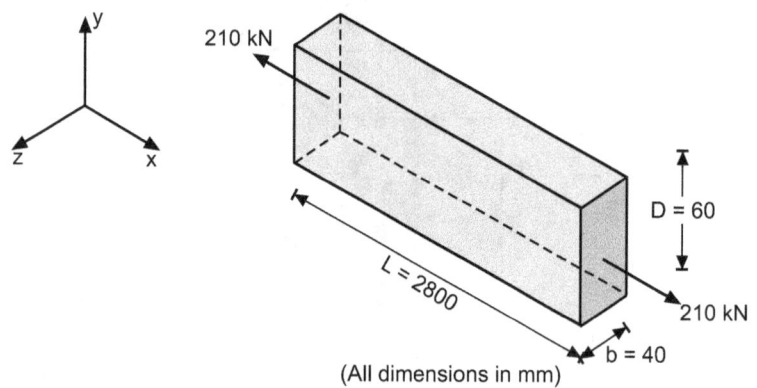

(All dimensions in mm)

Fig. 1.13 : Given member

Data : As shown in Fig. 1.13, E = 200 GPa, μ = 0.3.

Required : δL, δb, δD, δV.

Concept : Standard formulae.

Solution : (i) Geometric properties :

$$\text{Cross-sectional area } = A = 60 \times 40 = 2400 \text{ mm}^2.$$

(ii) Stresses and strains :

$$\text{Normal stress } = \sigma = \frac{P}{A} = \frac{210 \times 10^3}{2400} = 87.5 \text{ MPa (Tensile)}$$

$$\text{Longitudinal strain } = \varepsilon_L = \frac{\sigma}{E} = \frac{87.5}{200 \times 10^3} = 4.375 \times 10^{-4} \text{ (Tensile)}$$

$$\text{Lateral strain } = \varepsilon_{Lt} = \mu \cdot \varepsilon_L = 0.3 \times 4.375 \times 10^{-4}$$

$$= 1.3125 \times 10^{-4} \text{ (Compressive)}$$

(iii) Change in dimensions :

$$\text{Change in length, } \delta L = \varepsilon_L \cdot L$$

$$= 4.375 \times 10^{-4} \times 2800$$

$$= \textbf{1.225 mm (increase)}$$

$$\text{Change in depth, } \delta D = \varepsilon_{Lt} \cdot D$$

$$= 1.3125 \times 10^{-4} \times 60$$

$$= \textbf{0.0078 mm (decrease)}$$

Change in width, $\delta b = \varepsilon_{Lt} \cdot b$

$$= 1.3125 \times 10^{-4} \times 40$$

$$= \mathbf{0.0052\ mm\ (decrease)}$$

(iv) Change in volume :

     Volumetric strain $\varepsilon_v = \varepsilon_x + \varepsilon_y + \varepsilon_z = \varepsilon_L + \varepsilon_{Lt} + \varepsilon_{Lt}$

$$= \varepsilon\,(1 - 2\mu)$$

$$= 4.375 \times 10^{-4}\,(1 - 2 \times 0.3)$$

$$= 1.75 \times 10^{-4}$$

$$\delta V = \varepsilon_v \cdot V = (1.75 \times 10^{-4})\,(2800 \times 60 \times 40)$$

$$= \mathbf{1176\ mm^3\ (increase)}$$

Example 1.2 : *Determine the change in volume of 25 mm cube of aluminium (E = 70 GPa)*
and $\mu = \dfrac{1}{3}$ when dropped at a distance of 8 km in the ocean.

Assume density of water = 10 kN/m³.

Data : Cube size : 25 mm, E = 70 GPa, $\mu = \dfrac{1}{3}$, γ_{water} = 10 kN/m³, h = 8 km

Required : Change in volume.

Concept : Water pressure = Volumetric stress = $\sigma_v = \gamma h$

     Bulk modulus $= K = \dfrac{E}{3\,(1 - 2\mu)}$

     Volumetric strain $= \varepsilon_v = \dfrac{\sigma_v}{K}$

Solution : (i) Volumetric stress :

$$\sigma_v = \gamma h = 10 \times 8000 = 8 \times 10^4\ kN/m^2 = 80\ MPa$$

(ii)   Bulk modulus (K) :

$$K = \dfrac{E}{3\,(1 - 2\mu)} = \dfrac{70 \times 10^3}{3\left(1 - 2 \times \dfrac{1}{3}\right)} = 70 \times 10^3\ MPa$$

(iii) Change in volume (δV) :

     Volumetric strain $= \varepsilon_v = \dfrac{\delta V}{V} = \dfrac{\sigma_v}{K}$

$\therefore$ $\delta V = \dfrac{\sigma_v}{K} \cdot V$

$$= \dfrac{80}{70 \times 10^3} \times (25)^3$$

$$= \mathbf{17.85\ mm^3\ (decrease)}$$

Example 1.3 : *A bar of certain material is 60 mm × 60 mm in cross-section is subjected to an axial pull of 230 kN. The extension over a length of 120 mm is 0.07 mm and decrease in each side is 0.007 mm. Calculate all the elastic constants for material.*

Data : Cross-section of member = 60 mm × 60 mm, P = 230 kN (Tensile)

δL = 0.07 mm increase, L = 120 mm, δb = 0.007 mm (decrease)

Required : Elastic constants.

Concept : Standard formulae.

Solution : (i) Geometric properties :

Cross-sectional area,   A = 60 × 60 = 3600 mm²

(ii)   Stresses and strains :

$$\text{Normal stress} = \sigma = \frac{P}{A} = \frac{230 \times 10^3}{3600} = 63.89 \text{ MPa}$$

$$\text{Longitudinal strain} = \varepsilon_L = \frac{\delta L}{L} = \frac{0.07}{120} = 5.83 \times 10^{-4}$$

$$\text{Lateral strain} = \varepsilon_{Lt} = \frac{\delta b}{b} = \frac{0.007}{60} = 1.167 \times 10^{-4}$$

(iii) Elastic constants :

$$\text{Young's modulus,} \quad E = \frac{\sigma}{\varepsilon_L} = \frac{63.89}{5.83 \times 10^{-4}} = 109.58 \times 10^3 \text{ MPa} = \textbf{109.58 GPa}$$

$$\text{Poisson's ratio,} \quad \mu = \frac{\varepsilon_{Lt}}{\varepsilon_L} = \frac{1.167 \times 10^{-4}}{5.83 \times 10^{-4}} = \textbf{0.2}$$

$$\text{Shear modulus,} \quad G = \frac{E}{2\,(1 + \mu)} = \frac{109.58}{2\,(1 + 0.2)} = \textbf{45.66 GPa}$$

$$\text{Bulk modulus,} \quad K = \frac{E}{3\,(1 - 2\mu)} = \frac{109.58}{3\,(1 - 2 \times 0.2)} = \textbf{60.87 GPa}$$

Example 1.4 : *When a metal tube of external diameter 20 mm and internal diameter 15 mm was subjected to an axial load of 23 kN, the extension on gauge length of 60 mm was 0.05 mm and decrease in outer diameter was 0.005 mm. Find Young's modulus of elasticity (E), Poisson's ratio (μ) and change in volume (δV) assuming length of tube = 700 mm.*

Data : D = 20 mm, d = 15 mm, P = 23 kN, δL = 0.05 mm for gauge length of 60 mm,

δD = 0.005 mm (decrease), Length of tube = L = 700 mm.

Required : E, μ, and change in volume (δV).

Concept : Standard formulae.

Solution : (i) Geometric properties :

Cross-sectional area, $A = \frac{\pi}{4}(D^2 - d^2)$

$$= \frac{\pi}{4}(20^2 - 15^2)$$

$$= 137.44 \text{ mm}^2$$

(ii) Stress and strain :

Normal stress, $\sigma = \frac{P}{A} = \frac{23 \times 10^3}{137.44} = 167.34 \text{ MPa}$

Longitudinal strain, $\varepsilon_L = \frac{\delta L}{L} = \frac{0.05}{60} = 8.33 \times 10^{-4}$

Lateral strain, $\varepsilon_{Lt} = \frac{\delta D}{D} = \frac{0.005}{20} = 2.5 \times 10^{-4}$

(iii) Young's modulus (E) and Poisson's ratio (μ) :

$$E = \frac{\text{Normal stress}}{\text{Longitudinal strain}} = \frac{167.34}{8.33 \times 10^{-4}}$$

$$= 200.89 \times 10^3 \text{ MPa} = 200.89 \text{ GPa}$$

$$\mu = \frac{\text{Lateral strain}}{\text{Longitudinal strain}} = \frac{2.5 \times 10^{-4}}{8.33 \times 10^{-4}} = 0.3$$

(iv) Change in volume (δV) :

Volumetric strain, $\varepsilon_V = \varepsilon_L (1 - 2\mu)$

$$= 8.33 \times 10^{-4} (1 - 2 \times 0.3)$$

$$= 3.332 \times 10^{-4}$$

Change in volume, $\delta V = \varepsilon_V \cdot V$

$$= 3.332 \times 10^{-4} (137.44 \times 700)$$

$$= \textbf{32.05 mm}^3 \textbf{ (increase)}$$

Example 1.5 : *A bar of cross-section 8 mm × 8 mm is subjected to axial pull of 7 kN. The lateral dimensions of the bar are found to have reduced by 1.5 × 10⁻³ mm. Find Poisson's ratio and Modulus of elasticity, assuming G = 80 GPa.*

Data : Cross-section of member = 8 mm × 8 mm, axial force = 7 kN, change in cross-sectional dimension = 1.5×10^{-3} mm, G = 80 GPa.

Required : Modulus of elasticity (E) and Poisson's ratio (μ).

Concept : Standard formulae.

Solution : (i) Stresses and strains :

Normal stress, $\sigma = \frac{P}{A} = \frac{7 \times 10^3}{8 \times 8} = 109.375 \text{ MPa}$

Longitudinal strain, $\varepsilon_L \;=\; \dfrac{\sigma}{E} \;=\; \dfrac{109.375}{E}$

Lateral strain, ε_{Lt} = Change in c/s dimension / Original dimension

$$= \frac{1.5 \times 10^{-3}}{8}$$

$$= 1.875 \times 10^{-4}$$

(ii)   Modulus of elasticity and Poisson's ratio :

We have, $\varepsilon_{Lt} \;=\; \mu\,\varepsilon_L$

$$1.875 \times 10^{-4} \;=\; \mu \times \frac{109.375}{E}$$

$E \;=\; 583.33 \times 10^3\,\mu$ ... (i)

Also, $E \;=\; 2G\,(1 + \mu)$

∴ $E \;=\; 2 \times 80 \times 10^3\,(1 + \mu)$

$$= 160 \times 10^3\,(1 + \mu)$$ ... (ii)

Equating equations (i) and (ii),

$$583.33 \times 10^3\,\mu \;=\; 160 \times 10^3\,(1 + \mu)$$

∴ $\mu \;=\; 0.377$, put in (i)

$E \;=\; 220.47 \times 10^3$ MPa

$$=\; \mathbf{220.47\ GPa}$$

Example 1.6 : *A solid cylinder 100 mm high and 50 mm in diameter is inserted in another cylinder of 50 mm inner diameter and the surfaces of the two cylinders in contact are glued together. If the ultimate shear stress of the glue is 2.6 N/mm², calculate the ultimate load under which the joint will fail.*

Data : h = 100 mm, for outer cylinder inner diameter d = 50 mm,
for inner cylinder, d = 50 mm, τ_{max} = 2.6 N/mm²

Required : Ultimate load.

Concept : Shear stress.

Solution : (i) Geometric properties :

Area under shear $= 100 \times \pi \times 50$

$$= 5000\,\pi\ \text{mm}^2$$

(ii)   Ultimate load :

Ultimate load   = Area under shear $\times \tau_{max}$

$$= 5000\,\pi \times 2.6$$

$$= 40840.7\ \text{N}$$

$$= \mathbf{40.84\ kN}$$

Example 1.7 : *A forked end carries an axial pin 25 mm diameter which is in double shear. Calculate the ultimate and safe loads for this pin if the ultimate shear stress of the material is 200 MPa and the ratio between the ultimate and safe stress is to be 5 : 1.*

Data : $\phi_{pin} = 25$ mm, $\tau_{max} = 200$ MPa, $\dfrac{\tau_{max}}{\tau_{safe}} = \dfrac{5}{1}$

Required : Ultimate and safe loads for the pin.

Concept : Normal and shear stress.

Solution : (i) Geometric properties :

$$\text{Cross-sectional area of the pin, } A_p = \frac{\pi}{4}(25)^2$$

$$= 490 \text{ mm}^2$$

(ii) $\qquad$ Area under shear $= 2 \cdot A_p$

$$= 2 \times 490 = 980 \text{ mm}^2$$

(iii) $\qquad$ Ultimate load $= 980 \times 200$

$$= 196 \times 10^3 \text{ N} = 196 \text{ kN}$$

(iv) $\qquad$ Safe load $= \dfrac{196}{5} = \textbf{39.2 kN}$

1.14 GENERALISED HOOKE'S LAW

When an elastic body is subjected to normal stresses in x, y and z directions as shown in Fig. 1.14, the corresponding strains in these directions are given by

$$\left. \begin{aligned} \varepsilon_x &= \frac{1}{E}(\sigma_x - \mu\,\sigma_y - \mu\,\sigma_z) \\[4pt] \varepsilon_y &= \frac{1}{E}(\sigma_y - \mu\,\sigma_x - \mu\,\sigma_z) \\[4pt] \varepsilon_z &= \frac{1}{E}(\sigma_z - \mu\,\sigma_x - \mu\,\sigma_y) \end{aligned} \right\} \qquad \dots (1.23)$$

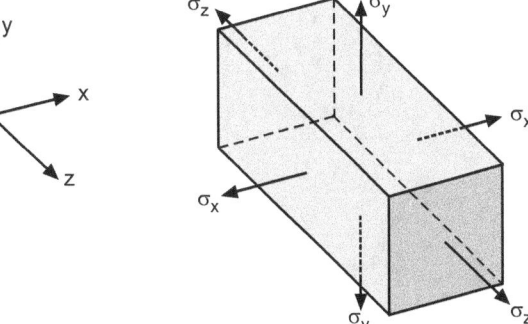

Fig. 1.14

Example 1.8 : *A rectangular bar 200 mm long, 70 mm wide and 20 mm thick is loaded with an axial tensile load of 150 kN; together with a normal compressive force of 1500 kN on 70 mm × 200 mm face and tensile force of 250 kN on 20 mm × 200 mm face. Calculate change in length, width, thickness and volume. Assume E = 200 GPa and μ = 0.3.*

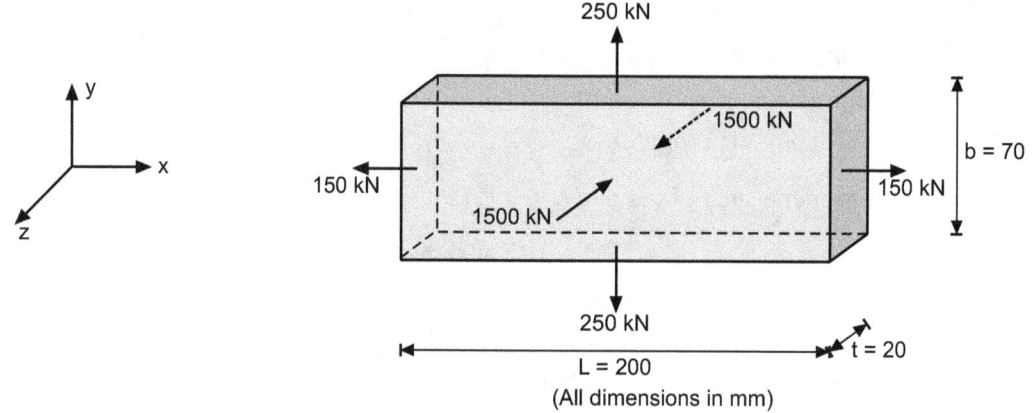

Fig. 1.15

Data : As shown in Fig. 1.15, E = 200 GPa, μ = 0.3.

Required : Change in length, width, thickness and volume.

Concept : Generalised Hooke's law.

Solution : (i) Normal stresses :

$$\sigma_x = \frac{150 \times 10^3}{20 \times 70} = 107.14 \text{ MPa}$$

$$\sigma_y = \frac{250 \times 10^3}{200 \times 20} = 62.5 \text{ MPa}$$

$$\sigma_z = -\frac{1500 \times 10^3}{200 \times 70} = -107.14 \text{ MPa}$$

Note : – ve sign for σ_z is due to its compressive nature.

(ii)   Strains :

$$\varepsilon_x = \frac{1}{E}(\sigma_x - \mu\,\sigma_y - \mu\,\sigma_z)$$

$$= \frac{1}{E}(107.14 - 0.3 \times 62.5 - 0.3\,(-107.14))$$

$$= \frac{120.532}{E}$$

$$\varepsilon_y = \frac{1}{E}(\sigma_y - \mu\,\sigma_x - \mu\,\sigma_z)$$

$$= \frac{1}{E}(62.5 - 0.3 \times 107.14 - 0.3\,(-107.14))$$

$$= \frac{62.5}{E}$$

$$\varepsilon_z = \frac{1}{E}(\sigma_z - \mu\,\sigma_x - \mu\,\sigma_y)$$

$$= \frac{1}{E}(-107.14 - 0.3 \times 107.14 - 0.3 \times 62.5)$$

$$= -\frac{158.03}{E}$$

(iii) Change in dimensions :

$$\delta L = \varepsilon_x \cdot L = \frac{120.532}{E} \times 200$$

$$= \frac{120.532}{200 \times 10^3} \times 200$$

$$= \textbf{0.12 mm (increase)}$$

$$\delta b = \varepsilon_y \cdot b = \frac{62.5}{E} \times 70$$

$$= \frac{62.5}{200 \times 10^3} \times 70$$

$$= \textbf{0.0218 mm (increase)}$$

$$\delta t = \varepsilon_z \cdot t = \frac{-158.03}{E} \times 20 = \frac{-158.03}{200 \times 10^3} \times 20$$

$$= -0.0158 \text{ mm}$$

$$= \textbf{0.0158 mm (decrease)}$$

(iv) Change in volume :

$$\text{Volumetric strain, } \varepsilon_v = \varepsilon_x + \varepsilon_y + \varepsilon_z$$

$$= \frac{1}{E}(120.532 + 62.5 - 158.03)$$

$$= \frac{25.002}{E}$$

$$\text{Change in volume} = \varepsilon_v \cdot V$$

$$= \frac{25.002}{200 \times 10^3} \times (200 \times 70 \times 20)$$

$$= \textbf{35 mm}^3 \textbf{ (increase)}$$

Example 1.9 : *A mild steel bar 250 mm long and 100 mm × 100 mm in cross-section is subjected to longitudinal axial compressive force of 1000 kN. Determine the values of lateral forces necessary to prevent any transverse strain. Also find change in length and volume.*
    Assume E = 200 GPa and μ = 0.3.

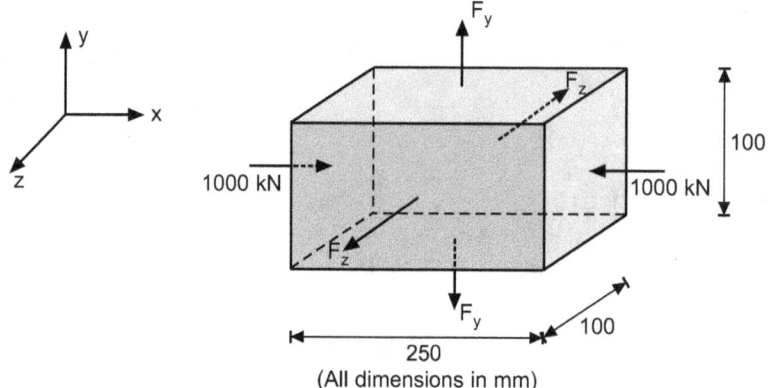

250
(All dimensions in mm)

Fig. 1.16

Data : As shown in Fig. 1.16, E = 200 GPa, μ = 0.3.

Required : Forces F_y and F_z in y and z directions respectively such that there is no transverse strain. Let these forces be tensile in nature as shown.

Concept : Generalised Hooke's law.

Solution : (i) Normal stresses :

$$\sigma_x = \frac{-1000 \times 10^3}{100 \times 100} = -100 \text{ MPa}$$

$$\sigma_y = \frac{F_y \times 10^3}{250 \times 100} = \frac{F_y}{25} \text{ MPa}$$

$$\sigma_z = \frac{F_z \times 10^3}{250 \times 100} = \frac{F_z}{25} \text{ MPa}$$

where, F_y and F_z are forces assumed in kN.

(ii) Strains :

$$\varepsilon_x = \frac{1}{E}(\sigma_x - \mu\,\sigma_y - \mu\,\sigma_z)$$

$$= \frac{1}{E}\left(-100 - 0.3 \times \frac{F_y}{25} - 0.3 \times \frac{F_z}{25}\right)$$

$$= -\frac{1}{E}(100 + 0.012\,F_y + 0.012\,F_z)$$

$$\varepsilon_y = \frac{1}{E}(\sigma_y - \mu\,\sigma_x - \mu\,\sigma_z)$$

$$= \frac{1}{E}\left(\frac{F_y}{25} - 0.3 \times (-100) - 0.3 \times \frac{F_z}{25}\right)$$

$$= \frac{1}{E}(0.04\ F_y + 30 - 0.012\ F_z)$$

$$\varepsilon_z = \frac{1}{E}(\sigma_z - \mu\ \sigma_x - \mu\ \sigma_y)$$

$$= \frac{1}{E}\left(\frac{F_z}{25} - 0.3 \times (-100) - 0.3 \times \frac{F_y}{25}\right)$$

$$= \frac{1}{E}(0.04\ F_z + 30 - 0.012\ F_y)$$

(iii) Magnitudes of F_y and F_z for no transverse strains :

It is given that transverse strains ε_y and ε_z are zero.

$$\therefore \qquad \frac{1}{E}(0.04\ F_y + 30 - 0.012\ F_z) = 0 \qquad\qquad \text{... (i)}$$

$$\frac{1}{E}(0.04\ F_z + 30 - 0.012\ F_y) = 0 \qquad\qquad \text{... (ii)}$$

Solving equations (i) and (ii), we get

$$F_y = -1071.42\ \text{kN}$$

$$F_z = -1071.42\ \text{kN}$$

Note : –ve sign indicates compression.

(iv) Change in length :

$$\varepsilon_x = -\frac{1}{E}(100 + 0.012 \times (-1071.42) + 0.012 \times (-1071.42))$$

$$= \frac{-74.28}{E}$$

$$\delta L = \varepsilon_x \cdot L$$

$$\delta L = \frac{-74.28}{200 \times 10^3} \times 250$$

$$= -0.093\ \text{mm} = 0.093\ \textbf{mm (decrease)}$$

(v) Change in volume :

Volumetric strain $= \varepsilon_v = \varepsilon_x + \varepsilon_y + \varepsilon_z$

$$= \frac{-74.28}{E} + 0 + 0$$

$$= \frac{-74.28}{E}$$

Change in volume $= \delta V = \varepsilon_v \cdot V$

$$= \frac{-74.28}{200 \times 10^3}(250 \times 100 \times 100) = -928.5\ \text{mm}^3$$

$$= \textbf{928.5 mm}^3\ \textbf{(decrease)}$$

1.15 AXIAL FLEXIBILITY (F)

Axial flexibility (f) is defined as the change in length produced by unit axial force.

We have, $\delta L = \dfrac{PL}{AE}$

$\therefore$ $f = \dfrac{L}{AE}$ ... (1.24)

Axial flexibility is directly proportional to length (L) of a member and inversely proportional to product of cross-sectional area and Young's modulus of elasticity called as **axial rigidity (EA).**

Unit of axial flexibility is mm/N or m/N, etc.

1.16 AXIAL STIFFNESS (S)

Axial stiffness (S) is defined as the axial force required to cause unit change in length.

We have, $\delta L = \dfrac{PL}{AE}$

$\therefore$ $S = \dfrac{AE}{L}$ ... (1.25)

Axial stiffness is directly proportional to axial rigidity (EA) and inversely proportional to length (L).

Unit of axial stiffness is N/mm or N/m, etc.

It should be noted that axial flexibility and stiffness are reciprocals of each other.

1.17 STRESS & ELONGATION PRODUCED IN A BAR DUE TO ITS OWN WEIGHT

Let a bar of length 'L' and diameter 'D' be rigidly fixed at the upper end and hanging vertically as shown in Fig. 1.17. Let w be the weight per unit volume of the bar.

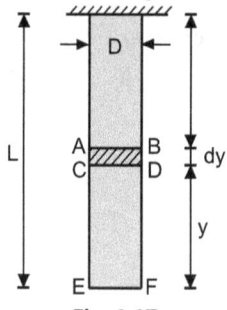

Fig. 1.17

Consider a small strip of the bar between the sections AB and CD at a distance 'y' of thickness 'dy' as shown in Fig. 1.17.

Downward force acting at CD is equal to the weight of the bar CDEF $= \dfrac{\pi}{4} D^2 yw$

Stress at section CD $= \sigma = \dfrac{\text{Force at CD}}{\text{c/s area}}$

$$= \frac{\left(\frac{\pi}{4}\right) D^2 \, yw}{\left(\frac{\pi}{4}\right) D^2}$$

$$\sigma = yw \qquad \qquad \qquad ... (1.26)$$

Thus, stress at any section due to self weight of the bar is directly proportional to y i.e. the distance of the section from the lower end. Stress at the lower end of the bar is zero and at the top it is maximum = wL.

Stresses at the sections AB and CD can be assumed same, since dy is very small. The elongation of length 'dy' $= \frac{\sigma}{E} \cdot dy = \frac{yw}{E} \cdot dy$.

Elongation of entire length of the bar,

$$\delta L = \int_{0}^{L} \frac{yw}{E} \cdot dy$$

$$= \frac{w}{E} \left(\frac{y^2}{2}\right)_{0}^{L}$$

$$\therefore \qquad \delta L = \frac{wL^2}{2E} \qquad \qquad \qquad ... (1.27)$$

Note : Elongation produced by the self weight of the bar is equal to that produced by a load of half its weight applied at the end.

1.18 ELONGATION OF CONICAL BAR DUE TO ITS OWN WEIGHT

A conical rod of length L and base diameter D is rigidly fixed at BC as shown in Fig. 1.18.

Let w be the weight per unit volume of the bar. Consider a small length 'dy' at distance 'y' from A as shown in Fig. 1.18.

$$\text{Weight of portion AFG} = \left(\frac{\pi}{4} d^2 \cdot \frac{y}{3}\right) w$$

where, d = Diameter of cross section FG

$$\text{Stress at section FG} = \sigma = \frac{\text{Force at FG}}{\text{Area at FG}}$$

$$= \frac{\left(\frac{\pi}{4} d^2 \cdot \frac{y}{3}\right) w}{\frac{\pi}{4} d^2}$$

$$\sigma = \frac{wy}{3} \qquad \qquad \qquad ... (1.28)$$

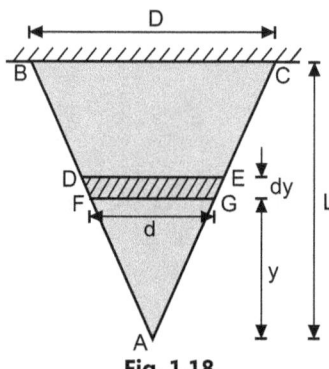

Fig. 1.18

Elongation of length 'dy' $= \dfrac{\sigma}{E} \cdot dy$

$$= \dfrac{wy}{3E} \cdot dy$$

∴   Elongation of the bar due to self weight

$$= \int_{0}^{L} \dfrac{wy}{3E} \cdot dy$$

$$= \dfrac{w}{3E} \left(\dfrac{y^2}{2}\right)_{0}^{L}$$

$$= \dfrac{wL^2}{6\,E} \qquad\qquad\qquad \dots (1.29)$$

1.19 LINEARLY VARYING SECTIONS

For these members, cross-sectional area changes linearly as a function of length of member. Change in length of these members can be computed with the help of integration.

1.20 COMPOUND SECTIONS

When a member consists of *segments or components of different cross-sectional area but of same material,* it is called as compound section. Fig. 1.19 shows a compound section subjected to axial tensile force P.

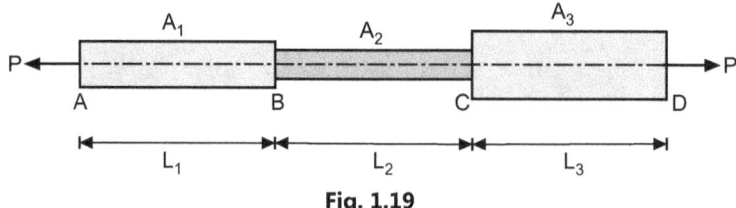

Fig. 1.19

Axial force 'P' is constant throughout the length of member but normal stresses are different because of different cross-sectional areas of components. For these sections, change in normal stresses from one component to other is sudden because of sudden change in cross-sectional areas.

Thus, for the compound section considered,

$$(\sigma)_{AB} = \frac{P}{A_1}$$

$$(\sigma)_{BC} = \frac{P}{A_2}$$

$$(\sigma)_{CD} = \frac{P}{A_3}$$

... (1.30)

Change in length of complete member can be obtained by,

$$\delta L = (\delta L)_{AB} + (\delta L)_{BC} + (\delta L)_{CD}$$

$$= \left(\frac{PL}{AE}\right)_{AB} + \left(\frac{PL}{AE}\right)_{BC} + \left(\frac{PL}{AE}\right)_{CD}$$

Since, axial force P is constant throughout the length of member,

$$\delta L = P\left[\left(\frac{L}{AE}\right)_{AB} + \left(\frac{L}{AE}\right)_{BC} + \left(\frac{L}{AE}\right)_{CD}\right]$$

$$= P \text{ [Sum of flexibility coefficients of components]} \quad ... (1.31)$$

However, material being same throughout,

$$\delta L = \frac{P}{E}\left[\left(\frac{L}{A}\right)_{AB} + \left(\frac{L}{A}\right)_{BC} + \left(\frac{L}{A}\right)_{CD}\right]$$

... (1.32)

Axial Force Diagram (AFD) : It is the *diagram which shows variation of axial force along the length of member.* For knowing axial force in different components, method of section is used. Method of section consists of following steps :

(i)   Take a section which cuts the component of our interest.

(ii) Take algebraic addition of all the forces either to the left or to the right of section with due care of signs. Sign convention to be followed is axial tension positive and axial compression negative. The force going away from the section represents tension, while towards the section represents compression.

The above procedure is explained further with a numerical example as under :

Let, a compound section be subjected to axial forces as shown in Fig. 1.20 (a).

To find axial forces in components AB, BC and CD, consider sections 1-1, 2-2 and 3-3 respectively. It should be remembered that, member as a whole with given external forces and FBD of components with external and internal forces (shown dotted) must maintain the equilibrium.

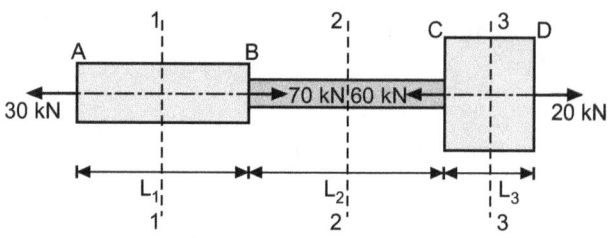

(a) Given member

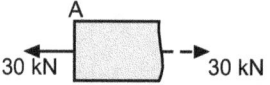

(b) FBD of section 1-1

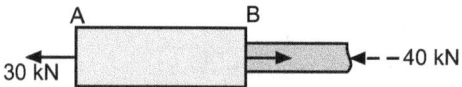

(c) FBD of section 2-2

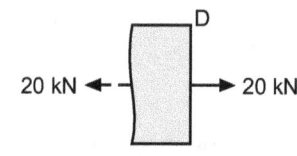

(d) FBD of section 3-3

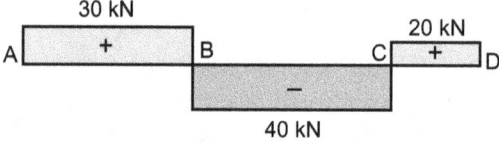

(e) AFD +ve : Tension, –ve : Compression

Fig. 1.20

Thus,   Axial force for component AB   = P_{AB} = 30 kN (Tensile)

Axial force for component BC   = P_{BC} = 30 – 70 = – 40 kN

= 40 kN (Compressive)

Axial force for component CD   = P_{CD} = 20 kN (Tensile)

AFD is as shown in Fig. 1.20 (e).

Example 1.10 : *A compound bar shown in Fig. 1.21 elongates by 0.45 mm when subjected to an axial pull of 150 kN. Calculate Young's modulus of elasticity.*

Data : δL = 0.45 mm, Refer Fig. 1.21.

Required : Young's modulus of elasticity (E).

Concept : $\delta L = \delta L_1 + \delta L_2 + \delta L_3$

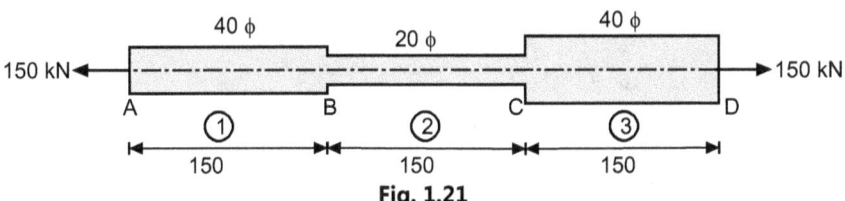

Fig. 1.21

Solution : (i) Geometric properties :

$$A_1 = A_3 = \frac{\pi}{4} (40)^2 = 1256.63 \text{ mm}^2$$

$$A_2 = \frac{\pi}{4} (20)^2 = 314.16 \text{ mm}^2$$

(ii) Modulus of elasticity (E) :

$$\delta L = \delta L_1 + \delta L_2 + \delta L_3$$

$$= \left(\frac{PL}{AE}\right)_1 + \left(\frac{PL}{AE}\right)_2 + \left(\frac{PL}{AE}\right)_3 = \frac{PL}{E}\left(\frac{1}{A_1} + \frac{1}{A_2} + \frac{1}{A_3}\right)$$

Substituting,

$$0.45 = \frac{150 \times 10^3 \times 150}{E}\left(\frac{1}{1256.63} + \frac{1}{314.16} + \frac{1}{1256.63}\right)$$

∴ $$E = 238.732 \times 10^3 \text{ MPa} = \textbf{238.732 GPa}$$

Example 1.11 : *For the compound bar ABC shown in Fig. 1.22, (i) Determine the magnitude of P for equilibrium, (ii) Draw axial force diagram, (iii) Find total change in length, (iv) Find displacement of B with respect to A. Assume E = 200 GPa.*

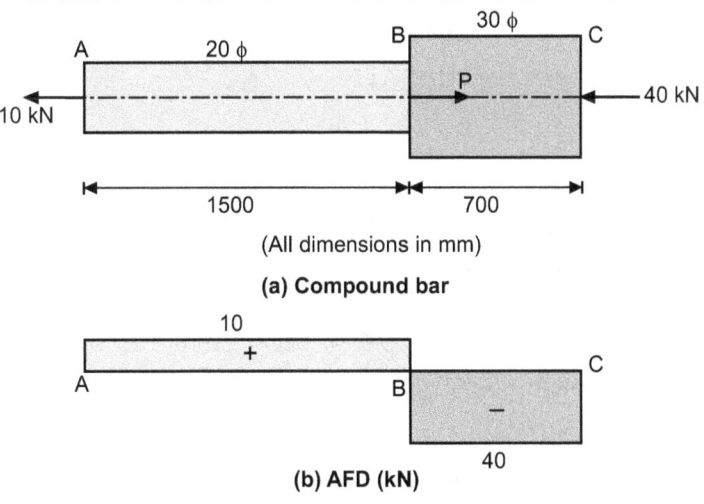

(All dimensions in mm)

(a) Compound bar

(b) AFD (kN)

Fig. 1.22

Data : As shown in Fig. 1.22 (a), E = 200 GPa.

Required : (i) P, (ii) δL, (iii) δB/A.

Concept :   (i) $\Sigma F_X = 0$ gives magnitude of P.

(ii) $\delta L = (\delta L)_{AB} + (\delta L)_{BC}$

(iii) Displacement of B with respect to A = $(\delta L)_{AB}$

Solution : (i) Magnitude of 'P' :

$\Sigma F_X = 0, -10 + P - 40 = 0$

$\therefore$ $P = 50$ kN

(ii) Axial force diagram :

Taking vertical sections for members AB and BC, we get

Axial force for member AB = $P_{AB} = 10$ kN (Tensile)

Axial force for member BC = $P_{BC} = 40$ kN (Compressive)

Axial force diagram is as shown in Fig. 1.22 (b).

(iii) Total change in length :

$$\delta L = (\delta L)_{AB} + (\delta L)_{BC} = \left(\frac{PL}{AE}\right)_{AB} + \left(\frac{PL}{AE}\right)_{BC}$$

$$= \frac{1}{200 \times 10^3}\left[\frac{10 \times 10^3 \times 1500}{\frac{\pi}{4}(20)^2} + \frac{(-40) \times 10^3 \times 700}{\frac{\pi}{4}(30)^2}\right]$$

$$= 0.238 - 0.198$$

$$= \mathbf{0.04 \text{ mm (increase)}}$$

(iv) Displacement of B with respect to A :

$$\delta B/A = (\delta L)_{AB} = \left(\frac{PL}{AE}\right)_{AB}$$

$$= \mathbf{0.238 \text{ mm } (\rightarrow)}$$

Example 1.12 : *For member ABC shown in Fig. 1.23, Find the diameter of portion BC if displacement of C with respect to A is 2 mm. Assume E = 200 GPa.*

Data : As shown in Fig. 1.23 (a), E = 200 GPa, $\delta L = 2$ mm

Required : Diameter of portion BC (ϕ) mm.

Concept : $\delta L = (\delta L)_{AB} + (\delta L)_{BC}$

Solution : (i) Geometric properties :

Cross-sectional area of AB = $A_{AB} = \frac{\pi}{4}(30)^2 = 706.85$ mm^2

Cross-sectional area of BC = $A_{BC} = \frac{\pi}{4}(\phi)^2$ mm^2

(ii) Analysis :

Let H_A ($\rightarrow$) be the reaction at A.

$\Sigma F_X = 0$,

$$H_A + 150 + 75 = 0$$

$\therefore$ $$H_A = -225 \text{ kN} = 225 \text{ kN} (\leftarrow)$$

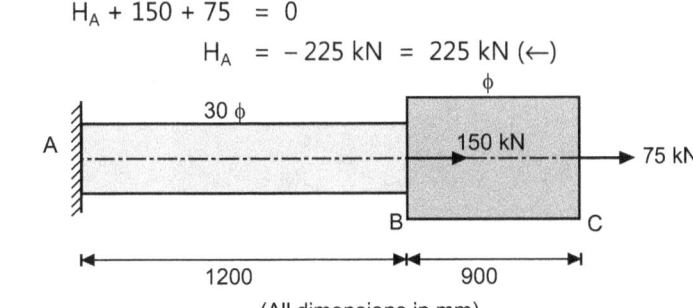

(a) Compound member

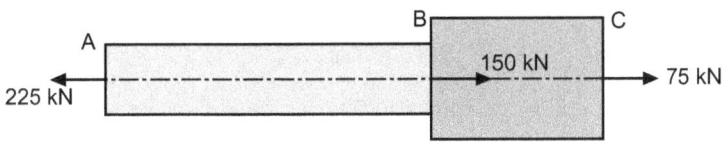

(b) FBD

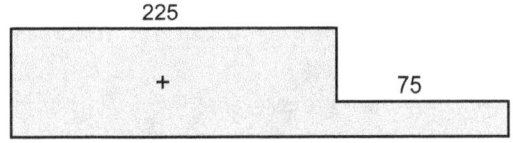

(c) AFD (kN)

Fig. 1.23

FBD of member is as shown in Fig. 1.23 (b).

Axial force diagram is as shown in Fig. 1.23 (c).

Note : Axial forces are obtained by taking sections in portions AB and BC.

(iii) Diameter of portion BC :

$$\delta L = (\delta L)_{AB} + (\delta L)_{BC}$$

$$2 = \left(\frac{PL}{AE}\right)_{AB} + \left(\frac{PL}{AE}\right)_{BC}$$

$$= \frac{1}{200 \times 10^3}\left[\frac{225 \times 10^3 \times 1200}{706.85} + \frac{75 \times 10^3 \times 900}{\frac{\pi}{4}(\phi)^2}\right]$$

$$\phi = \textbf{69.05 mm}$$

Example 1.13 : *A member 36 mmⵁ is subjected to axial forces as shown in Fig. 1.24. Find the total change in length of the bar assuming E = 200 GPa.*

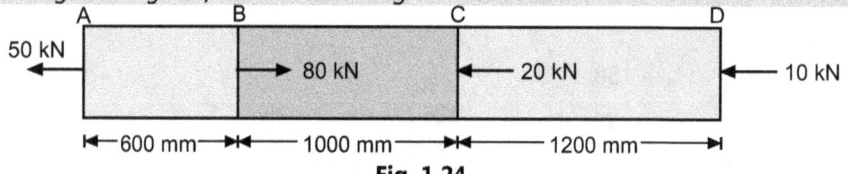

Fig. 1.24

Data : As shown in Fig. 1.24, E = 200 × 10³ MPa.

Required : δl

Concept : Standard formulae.

Solution : (i) Geometric properties :

$$A \;=\; \frac{\pi}{4} \times d^2 \;=\; \frac{\pi}{4} \times (36)^2 \;=\; 1017.88 \text{ mm}^2$$

(ii) Change in length :

$$\delta l \;=\; \left(\frac{Pl}{AE}\right)_{AB} + \left(\frac{Pl}{AE}\right)_{BC} + \left(\frac{Pl}{AE}\right)_{CD}$$

$$=\; \frac{1}{AE}\left[(Pl)_{AB} + (Pl)_{BC} + (Pl)_{CD}\right]$$

$$=\; \frac{[(50 \times 10^3 \times 600) - (30 \times 10^3 \times 1000) - (10 \times 10^3 \times 1200)]}{1017.88 \times 200 \times 10^3}$$

$$=\; -0.118 \text{ mm}$$

∴ $\delta l \;=\; -0.118 \text{ mm} \;=\;$ **0.118 mm (decrease)**

Example 1.14 : *A member is framed by connecting a steel bar to aluminium bar as shown in Fig. 1.25. Assuming that bars are prevented from buckling sidewise, calculate the magnitude of force P that will cause the total length of member to decrease by 0.33 mm.*
$E_{st} \;=\; 210 \text{ GPa}, \; E_{Al} \;=\; 70 \text{ GPa}.$

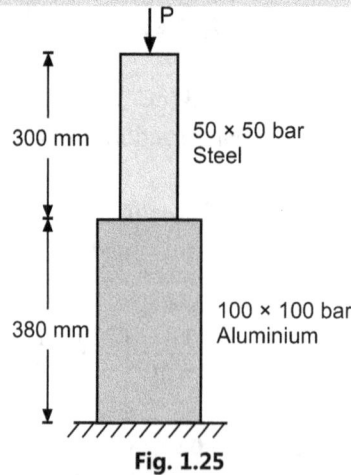

Fig. 1.25

Data : As shown in Fig. 1.25, $E_{st} = 210 \times 10^3$ MPa, $E_{Al} = 70 \times 10^3$ MPa, $\delta l = 0.33$ mm

Required : P.

Concept : Standard formulae, $\delta l = \dfrac{Pl}{AE}$

Solution : (i) Geometric properties :

$$A_{st} = 50 \times 50 = 2500 \text{ mm}^2$$
$$A_{Al} = 100 \times 100 = 10000 \text{ mm}^2$$

(ii) Calculation for P :

$$\delta l = \left(\frac{Pl}{AE}\right)_{st} + \left(\frac{Pl}{AE}\right)_{Al}$$

As both bars are in compression, so there is decrease in total length.

∴ $\delta l = -0.33$

Substituting, $-0.33 = -\left(\dfrac{P \times 300 \times 10^3}{2500 \times 210 \times 10^3}\right) - \left(\dfrac{P \times 380 \times 10^3}{10000 \times 70 \times 10^3}\right)$

∴ $P = \textbf{296.15 kN (Compression)}$

Example 1.15 : *A member ABCD is loaded as shown in Fig. 1.26. Determine (a) total deformation of rod, (b) displacement of 'C'. Assume E = 70 GPa.*

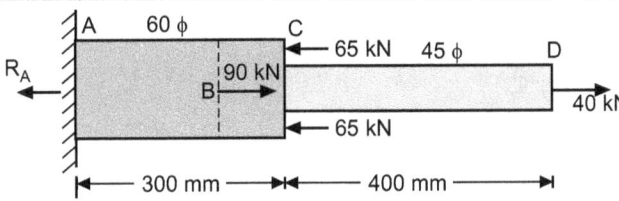

Fig. 1.26

Data : As shown in Fig. 1.26, $E = 70 \times 10^3$ MPa

Required : δl, displacement of C.

Concept : Equilibrium equation, $\delta l = \dfrac{Pl}{AE}$

Solution : (i) Geometric properties :

$$A_{AB} = \frac{\pi}{4} \times (60)^2 = 2827.43 \text{ mm}^2$$

$$A_{BC} = \frac{\pi}{4} \times (60)^2 = 2827.43 \text{ mm}^2$$

$$A_{CD} = \frac{\pi}{4} \times (45)^2 = 1590.43 \text{ mm}^2$$

(ii) Equilibrium equation :

$$\Sigma F_X = 0$$
$$-R_A + 90 - 130 + 40 = 0$$
∴ $$R_A = 0$$

(iii) Total deformation :

$$\delta l = \left(\frac{Pl}{AE}\right)_{AB} + \left(\frac{Pl}{AE}\right)_{BC} + \left(\frac{Pl}{AE}\right)_{CD}$$

Substituting, $\delta l = 0 - \left(\dfrac{90 \times 10^3 \times 200}{2827.43 \times 70 \times 10^3}\right) + \left(\dfrac{40 \times 10^3 \times 400}{1590.43 \times 70 \times 10^3}\right)$

$$= -0.091 + 0.1437$$

∴ $\delta l = \mathbf{0.0527\ mm}$

(iv) Displacement of point C :

As there is no force on AB, so point B remains on the same point and so C will be displaced by 0.091 mm towards left.

Example 1.16 : *A stepped rod is as shown in Fig. 1.27. Find the value of P that will not exceed a maximum overall deformation of 2 mm or a stress in steel of 140 MPa, that in Aluminium 80 MPa and in Brass 120 MPa.*

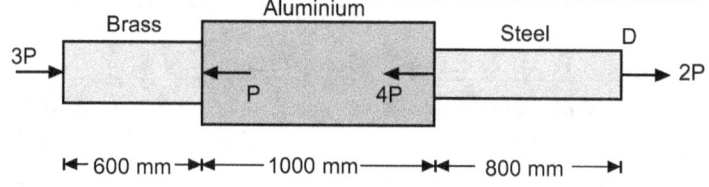

Fig. 1.27

Data : As shown in Fig. 1.27.

Required : P

Concept : Standard formulae.

Solution : (i) P due to Brass :

$$\left(\sigma = \frac{3P}{A}\right)_{Br} \quad \therefore \quad P = \frac{\sigma A}{3} = \frac{120 \times 450}{3}$$

$$P = 18000\ N \hspace{4cm} ...\ (i)$$

(ii)   P due to Aluminium :

$$\left(\sigma = \frac{2P}{A}\right)_{Al} \quad \therefore \quad P = \frac{\sigma A}{2} = \frac{80 \times 600}{2}$$

$$P = 24000\ N \hspace{4cm} ...\ (ii)$$

(iii) P due to Steel :

$$\left(\sigma = \frac{2P}{A}\right)_{Steel} \quad \therefore \quad P = \frac{\sigma A}{2} = \frac{140 \times 300}{2}$$

$$P = 21000\ N \hspace{4cm} ...\ (iii)$$

(iv) P due to overall deformation :

$$\delta l = \left(\frac{Pl}{AE}\right)_{Br} + \left(\frac{Pl}{AE}\right)_{Al} + \left(\frac{Pl}{AE}\right)_{st}$$

Substituting,　　　$2 = \dfrac{3P \times 600 \times 10^3}{450 \times 83 \times 10^3} + \dfrac{2P \times 1000 \times 10^3}{600 \times 70 \times 10^3} - \dfrac{2P \times 800 \times 10^3}{300 \times 200 \times 10^3}$

$2 = 0.048\,P + 4.76 \times 10^{-3}\,P - 0.0267\,P$

$P = 76.745$ kN

$P = 76745$ N　　　　　　　　　　　... (iv)

∴ Value of P = **18000 N = 18 kN**　　　　　[Least of equations (i), (ii), (iii) and (iv)]

Example 1.17 : *A member ABCD is subjected to point loads P_1, P_2, P_3 and P_4 as shown in Fig. 1.28. Calculate the force P_3 necessary for equilibrium if P_1 = 120 kN, P_2 = 220 kN and P_4 = 160 kN. Determine also the net change in length of the member. Take E = 200 GN/m².*

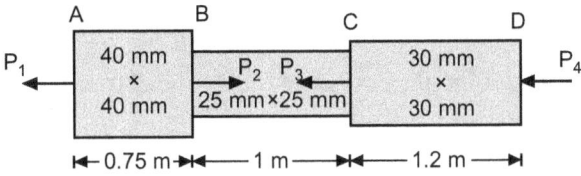

Fig. 1.28

Data : As shown in Fig. 1.28, P_1 = 120 kN, P_2 = 220 kN, P_4 = 160 kN,

E = 200 GN/m² = 200 × 10³ N/mm²

Required : P_3, δl.

Concept : ΣF_x = 0, standard formulae.

Solution :

(i)　　　　　　　$\Sigma F_x = 0$

∴　　　$-P_1 + P_2 - P_3 + P_4 = 0$

$P_1 + P_3 = P_2 + P_4$

∴　　　$120 + P_3 = 220 + 160$

∴　　　　**P_3 = 260 kN**

(ii)　　　　$\delta l = \left(\dfrac{Pl}{AE}\right)_{AB} + \left(\dfrac{Pl}{AE}\right)_{BC} + \left(\dfrac{Pl}{AE}\right)_{CD}$

Substituting,　　$\delta l = \left(\dfrac{120 \times 10^3 \times 750}{40 \times 40 \times 200 \times 10^3}\right) - \left(\dfrac{100 \times 10^3 \times 1000}{25 \times 25 \times 200 \times 10^3}\right)$

$+ \left(\dfrac{160 \times 10^3 \times 1200}{30 \times 30 \times 200 \times 10^3}\right)$

$= 0.28 - 0.8 + 1.067$

∴　　　　δl = **0.547 mm**

Example 1.18 : *Rod AB has diameter 25 mm, length 800 mm and modulus of elasticity E_1, while rod BC has diameter 25 mm, length 550 mm and modulus of elasticity E_2. P_1, P_2 and P_3 are axial forces acting on the rod ABC as shown in Fig. 1.29. When P_1 = 0, P_2 = 20 kN, P_3 = 20 kN, elongation of the rod is 1 mm and when P_1 = 20 kN, P_2 = 0, P_3 = 20 kN, elongation of rod ABC is 1.8 mm. Determine the values of E_1 and E_2.*

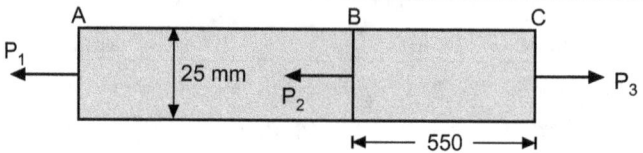

Fig. 1.29

Data : (i) As shown in Fig. 1.29, P_1 = 0, P_2 = 50 kN, P_3 = 20 kN, δl_1 = 1 mm

       (ii) P_1 = 20 kN, P_2 = 0, P_3 = 20 kN, δl_2 = 1.8 mm

Required : (i) E_1 , (ii) E_2.

Concept : $\delta l = \delta l_{AB} + \delta l_{AC}$

Solution : (i) Geometric properties :

Cross-sectional area of AB = cross-sectional area of BC

$$A_{AB} = A_{BC} = \frac{\pi}{4} \times (25)^2 = 490.87 \text{ mm}^2$$

(ii) Modulus of elasticity E_1 and E_2 :

$$\delta l_1 = \left(\frac{Pl}{AE}\right)_{AB} + \left(\frac{Pl}{AE}\right)_{BC}$$

$$1 = 0 + \frac{20 \times 10^3 \times 550}{490.87 \times E_2}$$

$$\therefore \quad E_2 = \mathbf{22409.19 \text{ N/mm}^2}$$

$$\delta l_2 = \left(\frac{Pl}{AE}\right)_{AB} + \left(\frac{Pl}{AE}\right)_{BC}$$

$$1.8 = \frac{20 \times 10^3 \times 800}{490.87 \times E_1} + \frac{20 \times 10^3 \times 550}{490.87 \times 22409.19}$$

$$1.8 = \frac{32595.19}{E_1} + 1$$

$$\therefore \quad \frac{32595.19}{E_1} = 0.8$$

$$\therefore \quad E_1 = \mathbf{40743.99 \text{ N/mm}^2}$$

Example 1.19 : *For a member ABC as shown in Fig. 1.30, find the diameter of the portion BC, if the total deformation of the member is 3 mm. Diameter of AB portion is 30 mm. Use E = 200 GPa.*

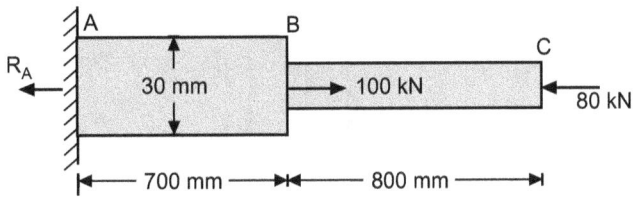

Fig. 1.30

Data : As shown in Fig. 1.30, $E = 200 \times 10^3$ MPa, $\delta l = 3$ mm

Required : Diameter of BC.

Concept : $\delta l = \dfrac{Pl}{AE}$

Solution : (i) Geometric properties :

$$A_{AB} = \frac{\pi}{4} \times (30)^2$$
$$= 706.86 \text{ mm}^2$$
$$A_{BC} = \frac{\pi}{4} \times d^2$$

(ii) Analysis : $\Sigma F_X = 0$

$$- H_A + 100 - 80 = 0$$
$$\therefore \qquad H_A = 20 \text{ kN } (\leftarrow)$$

Note : As BC member has force larger than AB, so there is decrease in total length of the member.

(iii) Diameter of portion BC :

$$\delta l = \left(\frac{Pl}{AE}\right)_{AB} + \left(\frac{Pl}{AE}\right)_{BC}$$

Substituting, $- 3 = \dfrac{20 \times 10^3 \times 700}{706.86 \times 200 \times 10^3} - \dfrac{80 \times 10^3 \times 800}{A \times 200 \times 10^3}$

$\therefore \qquad A = 103.25 \text{ mm}^2$

$\therefore \qquad \dfrac{\pi}{4} D^2 = 103.25$

$\therefore \qquad D = \textbf{11.466 mm}$

Example 1.20 : *A steel bar (E = 200 GPa) is supported and loaded as shown in Fig. 1.31. The cross-sectional area of the bar is 250 mm². Determine the force P, so that the lower end D of the bar does not move vertically when the loads are applied.*

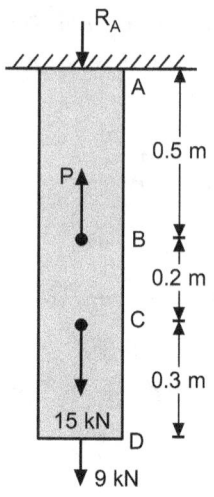

Fig. 1.31

Data : As shown in Fig. 1.31, A = 250 mm², E = 200 GPa, δl = 0.

Required : P.

Concept : (i) ΣF_X = 0 gives R_A, (ii) $\delta l = \dfrac{Pl}{AE}$

Solution : (i) Magnitude of reaction :

$$\Sigma F_X = 0$$

$$- R_A + P - 24 = 0$$

$$\therefore \qquad R_A = (P - 24)$$

(ii) Total change in length :

$$\delta l = 0 = \delta l_{AB} + \delta l_{BC} + \delta l_{CD} = \left(\frac{Pl}{AE}\right)_{AB} + \left(\frac{Pl}{AE}\right)_{BC} + \left(\frac{Pl}{AE}\right)_{CD}$$

Substituting, $\qquad 0 = \dfrac{[-(P - 24) \times 10^3 \times 500] + (24 \times 10^3 \times 200) + (9 \times 10^3 \times 300)}{AE}$

$$(P - 24) \times 10^3 \times 500 = (24 \times 10^3 \times 200) + (9 \times 10^3 \times 300)$$

$$\therefore \qquad \mathbf{P = 39\ kN}$$

1.21 TEMPERATURE STRESSES

When a member is subjected to temperature change, it is likely to expand or contract. This free expansion or contraction (δL) is given by

$$\delta L = \alpha t \cdot L \qquad\qquad \text{... (1.33)}$$

where, $\qquad \alpha$ = Coefficient of thermal expansion

t = Change in temperature

L = Length of member

α is usually expressed in units of per °C.

When this free expansion or contraction is prevented then only member will be subjected to temperature stresses. In other words, only *statically indeterminate systems* will be subjected to temperature stresses. This temperature stress is given by

$$\sigma = \frac{\delta L \cdot E}{L}$$

$$\sigma = \alpha t E \qquad \qquad \text{... (1.34)}$$

It should be noted that, when number is subjected to temperature **rise**, it is likely to expand, and if this expansion is prevented, it is subjected to temperature stress which is **compressive** in nature. Similarly, temperature **fall** will cause **tensile** stresses in a member.

Following are the two situations that we generally come across.

(i) Members of different cross-sectional areas arranged in series and fixed at both ends :

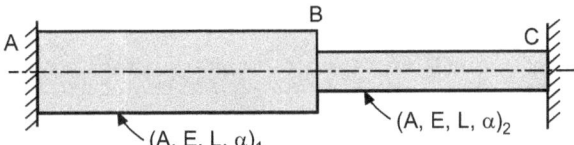

Fig. 1.32 : Members in series

If such a member is subjected to temperature change, free expansion or contraction being prevented, it will be subjected to temperature stresses. To evaluate these stresses is a statically indeterminate problem.

The force of internal resistance developed, to prevent the change in length of member as a whole, must be same for both components.

Thus, equation of statics can be written as :

$$P_1 = P_2$$

i.e. $$\sigma_1 A_1 = \sigma_2 A_2 \qquad \qquad \text{... (1.35)}$$

Equation of compatibility can be written as,

(Free change in length possible) – (Change in length prevented) $= 0$

$$[(\alpha t L)_1 + (\alpha t L)_2] - \left[\left(\frac{\sigma L}{E}\right)_1 + \left(\frac{\sigma L}{E}\right)_2 \right] = 0 \qquad \qquad \text{... (1.36)}$$

($\because$ change in length of a member as a whole is zero.)

Solving equations (1.35) and (1.36), required temperature stresses can be obtained.

In case if any of the support yields, equation (1.36) of compatibility is to be modified as,

$$[(\alpha t L)_1 - (\alpha t L)_2] - \left[\left(\frac{\sigma L}{E}\right)_1 + \left(\frac{\sigma L}{E}\right)_2 \right] = \text{Amount of yielding of support} \qquad \text{... (1.37)}$$

(ii) Members of two or more materials joined in parallel :

(a) Members in parallel

(b) Free expansion of individual members :

(c) Actual expansion of composite member :

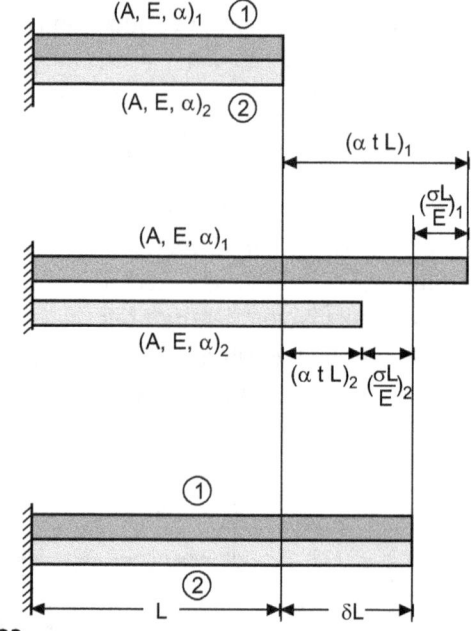

Fig. 1.33

When such a member is subjected to temperature change, actual expansion or contraction of each of the member must be the same.

This actual change in length is different from free change in length as shown in Fig. 1.33.

Hence, members will be subjected to temperature stresses. This is also a statically indeterminate problem.

Equation of statics is the same as that of equation (1.35). Since both the components must undergo equal amount of change in length, equation of compatibility can be written as,

$$(\delta L)_1 = (\delta L)_2$$

$$\left(\alpha t L - \frac{\sigma L}{E}\right)_1 = \left(\alpha t L + \frac{\sigma L}{E}\right)_2$$

The above equation assumes $\alpha_1 > \alpha_2$ as indicated by larger free expansion of member 1 in Fig. 1.43.

Thus, in general, equation of compatibility will be written as,

$$\left(\sigma t L \pm \frac{\sigma L}{E}\right)_1 = \left(\alpha t L \pm \frac{\sigma L}{E}\right)_2 \qquad \qquad ... (1.38)$$

It should be noted that, material having relatively higher value of α will be subjected to compressive stresses, hence the term $\sigma L/E$ for the corresponding material must be assigned –ve sign.

Solving equations (1.35) and (1.38), required temperature stresses can be obtained.

Example 1.21 : *A steel rod 1 m long of uniform cross section is fixed at ends. It is subjected to initial tensile stress of 48 MPa. Find,*

(a)   *Rise in temperature required to make the rod stress free.*

(b)   *Stress in rod if temperature is increased further by 16ºC.*

$\alpha = 12 \times 10^{-6}/ºC$, $E = 200$ GPa.

Data : $L = 1$ m, $\sigma = 48$ MPa , $\alpha = 12 \times 10^{-6}$ /ºC, $E = 200$ GPa.

Required :   (a)   Rise in temperature required to make the rod stress free.

(b)   Stress in rod if temperature is increased further by 16ºC.

Concept : (i) To make the rod stress free, temperature stress = 48 MPa, compressive should be developed. (ii) Temperature stress = $\sigma = \alpha t E$.

Solution : (i) Rise in temperature :

$$\sigma = \alpha t E$$
$$48 = 12 \times 10^{-6} \times t \times 2 \times 10^{5}$$

∴ $t = \textbf{20ºC}$ ...**(Rise)**

(ii)   Stress in rod : $\sigma = \alpha t E$

$$= 12 \times 10^{-6} \times 16 \times 2 \times 10^{5}$$

∴ $\sigma = \textbf{38.4 MPa}$ ...**(Compressive)**

Example 1.22 : *A steel rod 10 mm ϕ and 1 mm long is fixed at ends. If temperature of rod is increased by 50ºC, what will be reaction at supports ? If the rod remains unchanged in length, and if the temperature stress in the rod is to be reduced by 40 %, what should be the yielding of support ? Take E = 100 GPa, $\alpha = 10^{-5}$ /ºC.*

Data : $d = 10$ mm, $L = 1$ m, $t = 50$ºC, $E = 100$ GPa, $\alpha = 10^{-5}$ /ºC.

Required : Reaction at supports; yielding of supports.

Concept : (i) Reaction at supports = Temperature stress in the member × Cross-sectional area of member.

(ii)   Yielding of support causes decrease in temperature stress.

Solution : (i) Geometric properties :

Area of steel rod $= A = \dfrac{\pi}{4} (10)^{2} = 78.54$ mm²

(ii)   Reaction at supports :

$$\sigma = \alpha t E$$
$$= 10^{-5} \times 50 \times 100 \times 10^{3}$$
$$= 50 \text{ MPa (Compressive)}$$

Reaction $= R = \sigma \cdot A$

$$= 50 \times 78.54$$
$$= \textbf{3.9 kN}$$

(iii) Yielding of support :

Stress consumed in yielding of support = 40 % of 50 MPa

$$= 20 \text{ MPa}$$

∴　　Yielding of support $= \Delta L = \dfrac{\sigma L}{E} = \dfrac{20 \times 1000}{100 \times 10^3} = \mathbf{0.2 \text{ mm}}$

Example 1.23 : *Rails of 10 m length are laid on the track in the morning. The atmospheric temperature then was 12°C. A gap of 1.5 mm was kept between two consecutive rails. At what maximum temperature the rails will remain stress free ? If the temperature is raised further by 10°C, what will be the magnitude and nature of the stresses induced in the rails ?*

Take α = 12 × 10⁻⁶ /°C, E = 200 GPa.

Data : L = 10 m, ΔL = 1.5 mm, $\alpha = 12 \times 10^{-6}$ /°C, E = 200 GPa.

Required : Maximum temperature the rails will remain stress free, find magnitude and nature of the stresses induced in the rails when temperature is further raised by 10°C.

Concept : Till the time there is a gap between consecutive rails, no temperature stresses are induced.

Solution : (i) Let t be the temperature at stress free condition.

Extension for individual rail = 1.5 mm

$$\Delta L = \alpha t L$$

∴　　　$1.5 = 12 \times 10^{-6} \times (t - 12) \times 10 \times 10^3$

∴　　　$t = \mathbf{24.5 \ ^\circ C}$

(ii)　　　$\sigma = \alpha t E = 12 \times 10^{-6} \times 10 \times 200 \times 10^3$

$$= \mathbf{24 \text{ MPa (Compressive)}}$$

Example 1.24 : *Data as shown in Fig. 1.34 below. Find the thermal stresses if the temperature rises by 10 K. Assume $L_1 = L_2 = L$, $A_1 = 2A_2$. Take α = 11.7 × 10⁻⁶ /K, E = 200 GPa.*

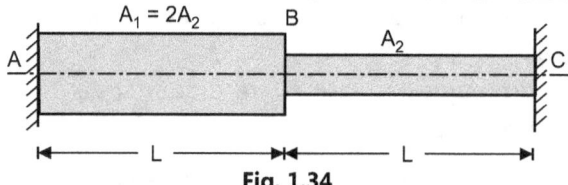

Fig. 1.34

Data : As shown in Fig. 1.34.

Required : Thermal stresses.

Concept : Statically indeterminate : Statics and Compatibility.

Solution : (i) Equation of statics :

$$\sigma_1 A_1 = \sigma_2 A_2$$

$$\sigma_1 (2A_2) = \sigma_2 A_2$$

∴　　　　$\sigma_1 = \dfrac{\sigma_2}{2}$　　　　　　... (i)

(ii) Compatibility :

$$(\alpha\,t\,L)_1 + (\alpha\,t\,L)_2 - \left[\left(\frac{\sigma L}{E}\right)_1 + \left(\frac{\sigma L}{E}\right)_2\right] = 0$$

$\therefore$ $2\,\alpha\,t = \dfrac{\sigma_1}{E_1} + \dfrac{\sigma_2}{E_2}$

$\therefore$ $(2 \times 11.7 \times 10^{-6} \times 10)\,E = \sigma_1 + \sigma_2$

$\therefore$ $\sigma_1 + \sigma_2 = 46.8\ \text{MPa}$ ... (ii)

(iii) Thermal stresses :

Solving equations (i) and (ii), $\sigma_1 = \dfrac{\sigma_2}{2}$ from equations (i) and (ii)

$\sigma_1 = $ **15.6 MPa (Compressive)**

$\sigma_2 = $ **31.2 MPa (Compressive)**

Example 1.25 : *Data as shown in Fig. 1.35 below. If the temperature of the bar is raised through 14 K, find force exerted on supports.*

$\alpha_S = 11 \times 10^{-6}\,/K$, $E_S = 210\ GPa$; $\alpha_B = 20 \times 10^{-6}\,/K$, $E_B = 85\ MPa$.

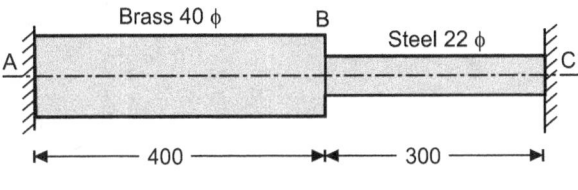

(All dimensions in mm)

Fig. 1.35 : Given member

Data : As shown in Fig. 1.35.

Required : Force exerted on supports.

Concept : Statically indeterminate : Statics and Compatibility.

Solution : (i) Geometric properties :

Area of steel, $A_S = \dfrac{\pi}{4}(22)^2 = 380.12\ \text{mm}^2$

Area of brass, $A_B = \dfrac{\pi}{4}(40)^2 = 1256.63\ \text{mm}^2$

(ii) $(\sigma \cdot A)_S = (\sigma \cdot A)_B$

$\sigma_S \times 380.12 = \sigma_B \times 1256.63$

$\therefore$ $\sigma_S = 3.30\ \sigma_B$ ... (i)

(iii) Compatibility :

$$(\alpha\,t\,L)_S + (\alpha\,t\,L)_B - \left[\left(\frac{\sigma L}{E}\right)_S + \left(\frac{\sigma L}{E}\right)_B\right] = 0$$

$$(11 \times 10^{-6} \times 14 \times 300) + (20 \times 10^{-6} \times 14 \times 400) = \frac{\sigma_S \times 300}{210 \times 10^3} + \frac{\sigma_B \times 400}{85 \times 10^3}$$

$$\therefore \qquad\qquad\qquad 0.1582 = \frac{\sigma_S}{700} + \frac{\sigma_B}{212.5} \qquad\qquad \text{... (ii)}$$

(iv) Thermal stresses : Solving equations (i) and (ii),

$$\sigma_B = 16.79 \text{ MPa (Compressive)}$$
$$\sigma_S = 55.42 \text{ MPa (Compressive)}$$

(v)　Force at supports :　　$F = \sigma_S A_S = \sigma_B A_B$

$$= 55.42 \times 380 \times 10^{-3} \text{ kN}$$
$$= \mathbf{21.059 \text{ kN}}$$

Example 1.26 :　*Data as shown in Fig. 1.36 below. Find the stress in each rod when temperature of aluminium rod only is increased by 50°C.*

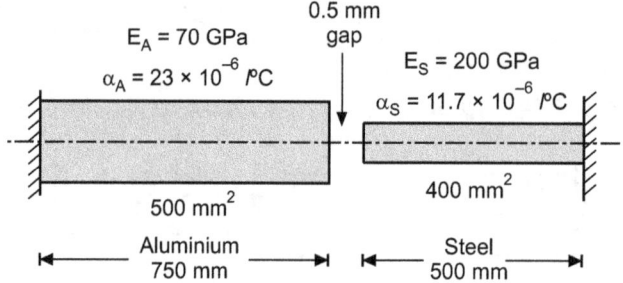

0.5 mm gap

$E_A = 70$ GPa
$\alpha_A = 23 \times 10^{-6}$ /°C

$E_S = 200$ GPa
$\alpha_S = 11.7 \times 10^{-6}$ /°C

500 mm^2　　　400 mm^2

Aluminium 750 mm　　　Steel 500 mm

Fig. 1.36 : Given members

Data : $A_A = 500$ mm², $A_S = 400$ mm², $\alpha_A = 23 \times 10^{-6}$ /°C

$E_A = 70$ GPa, $E_S = 200$ GPa, $\alpha_S = 11.7 \times 10^{-6}$ /°C

Required : Stress in each rod.

Concept : Till the time gap is present, no stresses are developed.

Solution : (i) Equation of statics :

$$\sigma_A \cdot A_A = \sigma_S \cdot A_S$$
$$\sigma_A (500) = \sigma_S (400)$$
$$\sigma_A = 0.8 (\sigma_S) \qquad\qquad \text{... (i)}$$

(ii)　Equation of compatibility :

$$(\alpha\, t\, L)_A + (\alpha\, t\, L)_S - \left[\left(\frac{\sigma L}{E}\right)_A + \left(\frac{\sigma L}{E}\right)_S \right] = 0.5$$

Substituting,

$$23 \times 10^{-6} \times 50 \times 750 - \left[\frac{\sigma_A \times 750}{70 \times 10^3} + \frac{\sigma_S \times 500}{200 \times 10^3} \right] = 0.5 \qquad (\because (\alpha\, t\, L)_S = 0)$$

$$\therefore \qquad 0.3625 \;=\; \frac{\sigma_A}{93.34} + \frac{\sigma_S}{400} \qquad \text{... (ii)}$$

(iii) Thermal stresses :

Solving equations (i) and (ii), σ_S = **32.74 MPa (Compressive)**

$$\sigma_A \;=\; \textbf{26.2 MPa (Compressive)}$$

Example 1.27 : *A compound member is supported as shown in Fig. 1.37 below. Initially the system is stress free. If the temperature is then dropped by 20°K, find (i) stress in each bar if the supports are unyielding, (ii) stress in each bar, if the right hand support yield by 0.1 mm. Assume $\alpha_B = 20 \times 10^{-6}$ /°C, $\alpha_A = 25 \times 10^{-6}$ /°C, $E_B = 90$ GPa and $E_A = 70$ GPa.*

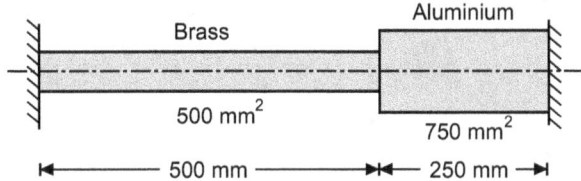

Fig. 1.37

Data : $A_B = 500$ mm², $A_A = 750$ mm², $\alpha_B = 20 \times 10^{-6}$ /°C.

$\alpha_A = 25 \times 10^{-6}$ /°C, $E_B = 90$ MPa, $E_A = 70$ GPa.

Required : (i) Stress in each bar if the supports are unyielding.

(ii) Stress in each bar if the right hand support yield by 0.1 mm.

Concept : Statically indeterminate : Statics and Compatibility.

Solution : (i) Equation of statics :

$$(\sigma A)_B \;=\; (\sigma A)_A$$
$$\sigma_B \times 500 \;=\; \sigma_A \times 750$$
$$\sigma_B \;=\; 1.5\, \sigma_A \qquad \text{... (i)}$$

(ii) Equation of compatibility :

$$(\alpha\, t\, L)_B + (\alpha\, t\, L)_A - \left[\left(\frac{\sigma L}{E}\right)_B + \left(\frac{\sigma L}{E}\right)_A \right] \;=\; 0$$

$$(20 \times 10^{-6} \times 20 \times 500) + (25 \times 10^{-6} \times 20 \times 250) \;=\; \frac{\sigma_B \times 500}{90 \times 10^3} + \frac{\sigma_A \times 250}{70 \times 10^3}$$

$$0.325 \;=\; \frac{\sigma_B}{180} + \frac{\sigma_A}{280} \qquad \text{... (ii)}$$

(iii) Thermal stresses :

Solving equations (i) and (ii),

$$\sigma_B \;=\; \textbf{40.95 MPa (Tensile)}$$
$$\sigma_A \;=\; \textbf{27.3 MPa (Tensile)}$$

(iv) When support yields by 0.1 mm, equation of statics remains the same.

$$\sigma_B = 1.5 \, \sigma_A \qquad \text{... (iii)}$$

(v)   Compatibility :

$$(\alpha \, t \, L)_B + (\alpha \, t \, L)_A - \left[\left(\frac{\sigma L}{E}\right)_B + \left(\frac{\sigma L}{E}\right)_A\right] = 0.1$$

$$0.325 = \frac{\sigma_B}{180} + \frac{\sigma_A}{280} + 0.1$$

$$0.225 = \frac{\sigma_B}{180} + \frac{\sigma_A}{280} \qquad \text{... (iv)}$$

(vi) Thermal stresses :

Solving equations (i) and (iii),

$$\sigma_B = \textbf{28.55 MPa (Tensile)}$$
$$\sigma_A = \textbf{19.03 MPa (Tensile)}$$

Example 1.28 : *Data as shown in Fig. 1.38. The temperature of the combination is increased by 30°C. Calculate the stresses induced in the rod and in the tube. Also find actual expansion of composite member.*

Take $\alpha_S = 12 \times 10^{-6} /°C$, $E_S = 200$ GPa, $\alpha_{Cu} = 16 \times 10^{-6} /°C$, $E_C = 100$ GPa.

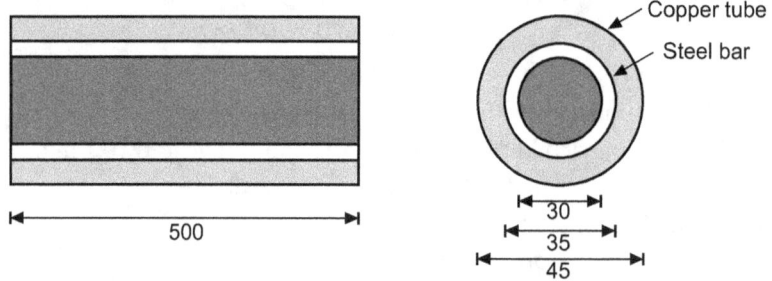

(a) Given member   **(b) Cross section of member**

Fig. 1.38

Data : As shown in Fig. 1.38.

Required : Stresses induced in the rod and in the tube; actual expansion of composite member.

Concept : Statically indeterminate : Statics and Compatibility.

Solution : (i) Geometric properties :

$$\text{Area of steel} = A_S = \frac{\pi}{4}(30)^2 = 706.8 \text{ mm}^2$$

$$\text{Area of copper} = A_C = \frac{\pi}{4}[(45)^2 - (35)^2] = 628.3 \text{ mm}^2$$

(ii) Equation of statics :

$$P_C = P_S$$

∴ $\sigma_C A_C = \sigma_S A_S$

∴ $\sigma_C = 1.124 \, \sigma_S$ ... (i)

(iii) Equation of compatibility :

$$\left(\alpha t L - \frac{\sigma L}{E}\right)_{Cu} = \left(\frac{\sigma L}{E} + \alpha t L\right)_{st}$$

As $\alpha_C > \alpha_{st}$; Cu will be subjected to compression.

$$\left(16 \times 10^{-6} \times 30 - \frac{\sigma_C}{100 \times 10^3}\right) = \left(12 \times 10^{-6} \times 30 + \frac{\sigma_S}{200 \times 10^3}\right)$$

Substituting, $\sigma_S + 2\sigma_C = 24$ ... (ii)

(iv) Thermal stresses :

Solving equations (i) and (ii),

$$\sigma_S = \textbf{7.38 MPa (Tensile)}$$

$$\sigma_C = \textbf{8.31 MPa (Compressive)}$$

(v)   Actual expansion :

$$(\delta L)_C = (\delta L)_{st}$$

$$\left(\alpha t L - \frac{\sigma L}{E}\right)_C = \left(16 \times 10^{-6} \times 30 \times 500 - \frac{8.31 \times 500}{100 \times 10^3}\right)$$

∴ $(\delta L)_C = \textbf{0.198 mm}$

Example 1.29 : *Three wires as shown in Fig. 1.39 are supporting a load of 18 kN. The cross-sectional area of each wire is 150 mm². If the lengths of wires are adjusted so as to share the load equally at 20°C, find the stresses in wires at 50°C temperature.*

Take $E_S = 2 \times 10^5$ MPa, $\alpha_S = 12 \times 10^{-6}$ /°C, $E_C = 1 \times 10^5$ MPa, $\alpha_C = 18 \times 10^{-6}$ /°C.

Data : $P = 18$ kN, $A_S = A_C = 150$ mm².

Required : Stresses in wires at 50°C.

Concept : (i) Statically indeterminate

          (ii) Superposition of stresses.

Solution : (i) Geometric properties :

Area of steel (A_S) = Area of copper (A_C) = 150 mm²

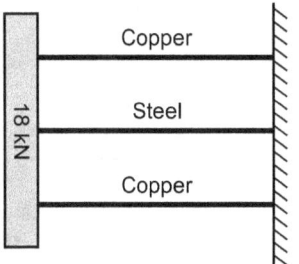

Fig. 1.39

(ii) Equation of statics :

Due to temperature change,

Compressive force in copper wires = Tensile force in steel wire

$$2\,(\sigma_C \times A_C) = (\sigma_S \times A_S)$$

$$2\,\sigma_C = \sigma_S$$

$$\sigma_C = 0.5\,\sigma_S \qquad\qquad \ldots\text{(i)}$$

(iii) Equation of compatibility :

$$\left(\alpha\,t\,L - \frac{\sigma L}{E}\right)_C = \left(\alpha\,t\,L + \frac{\sigma L}{E}\right)_S$$

$$\therefore \qquad 18 \times 10^{-6} \times (50 - 20) - \frac{\sigma_C}{1 \times 10^5} = 12 \times 10^{-6} \times (50 - 20) + \frac{\sigma_S}{2 \times 10^5}$$

$$1.8 \times 10^{-4} = \frac{\sigma_S}{2 \times 10^5} + \frac{\sigma_C}{1 \times 10^5}$$

$$36 = \sigma_S + 2\,\sigma_C \qquad\qquad \ldots\text{(ii)}$$

(iv) Solution of equations : Solving equations (i) and (ii),

$$\sigma_S = 18 \text{ MPa (Tensile)}$$

$$\sigma_C = 9 \text{ MPa (Compressive)}$$

(v) Stresses due to load :

At 20°C, the load is shared equally by three wires.

$$\therefore \qquad \text{Load taken by each wire} = \frac{18 \times 10^3}{3} = 6 \times 10^3$$

$$\therefore \qquad \text{Tensile stress in each wire} = \frac{6 \times 10^3}{150} = 40 \text{ MPa (Tensile)}$$

(vi) Final stresses :

$$\text{Stress in steel} = \sigma_S = 18 + 40 = \textbf{58 MPa (Tensile)}$$

$$\text{Stress in copper} = \sigma_C = -9 + 40 = \textbf{31 MPa (Tensile)}$$

Example 1.30 : *A copper flat 60 mm × 30 mm is joined to another 60 mm × 60 mm steel flat as shown in Fig. 1.40. If the combination is heated through 100°C, determine :*

(i)   Stress produced in each bar,

(ii) The shear force between the flats,

(iii) Shear stress.

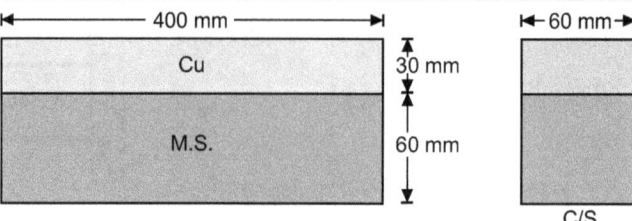

Fig. 1.40

Given : $\alpha_C = 18.5 \times 10^{-6}$ /°C, $\alpha_S = 12 \times 10^{-6}$ /°C, $E_C = 101$ GPa, $E_S = 220$ GPa.

Data : As shown in Fig. 1.40.

Required : Stresses induced in the bar, shear force and shear stress.

Concept : Statically indeterminate : Statics and compatibility.

Solution : (i) Geometric properties :

$$A_{Cu} = 60 \times 30 = 1800 \text{ mm}^2$$

$$A_{MS} = 60 \times 60 = 3600 \text{ mm}^2$$

(ii) Equation of statics :

$$P_{Cu} = P_{MS}$$

$$\sigma_{Cu} A_{Cu} = \sigma_{MS} A_{MS}$$

$$\sigma_{Cu} \times 1800 = \sigma_{MS} \times 3600$$

$$\sigma_{Cu} = 2 \times \sigma_{MS} \qquad \text{... (i)}$$

(iii) Equation of compatibility :

$$\left(\alpha t L - \frac{\sigma L}{E}\right)_{Cu} = \left(\frac{\sigma L}{E} + \alpha t L\right)_{MS}$$

As $\alpha_{Cu} > \alpha_{MS}$; Cu will be subjected to compression.

$$\left(18.5 \times 10^{-6} \times 100 \times 400 - \frac{\sigma_{Cu} \times 400}{101 \times 10^3}\right) = \left(\frac{\sigma_{st} \times 400}{220 \times 10^3} + 12 \times 10^{-6} \times 100 \times 400\right)$$

$$0.74 - 3.96 \times 10^{-3} \sigma_{Cu} = \sigma_{MS} \times 1.82 \times 10^{-3} + 0.48$$

$$1.82 \times 10^{-3} \sigma_{MS} + 3.96 \times 10^{-3} \sigma_{Cu} = 0.26$$

$$1.82 \times 10^{-3} \sigma_{MS} + 2 \times 3.96 \times 10^{-3} \sigma_{MS} = 0.26 \qquad \text{... (ii)}$$

Putting equation (i) in (ii), $\qquad \sigma_{MS} = 26.69$ N/mm²

$\therefore \qquad\qquad\qquad\qquad\qquad \sigma_{Cu} = 53.39$ N/mm²

(iv) Shear force between flats :

$$S = \sigma_{Cu} \times A_{Cu} = 53.39 \times 1800$$

$\therefore \qquad\qquad\qquad\qquad\qquad\qquad S = \textbf{96102 N}$

Example 1.31 : *Rails of 15 m length were laid on the track in the morning when the temperature was 16°C. A gap of 1.8 mm was kept between the two rails. At what maximum temperature the rails will remain stress free ? If temperature is further increased by 15°C, what will be the magnitude and nature of stresses induced in the rails ?*

Assume $\alpha = 12 \times 10^{-6}$ /°C and E = 200 GPa. Assume that rails can expand in one direction.

Data : l = 15 m, δl = $\dfrac{1.8}{2}$ = 0.9 mm (for each)

t = 16°C, t = (16 + 15) = 31°C, α = 12 × 10⁻⁶ /°C, E = 200 GPa = 200 × 10³ MPa.

Required : Maximum temperature for which rails are stress free and stress at 31°C.

Concept : $\delta l = l\,\alpha\,t$ and $\sigma = \alpha\,t\,E$

Solution : Case (i) :

$$\delta l = l\,\alpha\,t$$
$$0.9 = 15000 \times 12 \times 10^{-6} \times t$$

∴   t = Change in temperature = 5°C

∴   Maximum temperature at which rails are stress free = (16 + 5) = **21°C**

Case (ii) : Change in temperature = 31 – 21 = 10°C

∴ $\sigma = \alpha\,t\,E$
$$= 12 \times 10^{-6} \times 10 \times 200 \times 10^{3}$$

∴ σ = **24 N/mm² (Compressive)**

Example 1.32 : *A compound strut consists of a brass portion AB of diameter 75 mm and a steel portion BC 40 mm diameter as shown in Fig. 1.41. Supports at A and C are rigid. If temperature is raised through 140°C, find*

(i) Nature and magnitude of stresses developed in brass and steel.

(ii) Force exerted on the supports and

(iii) The relative movement at the junction B.

Given : α_{Br} = 20 × 10⁻⁶ /°C, α_{st} = 11 × 10⁻⁶ /°C, E_{Br} = 85 GPa, E_{st} = 210 GPa

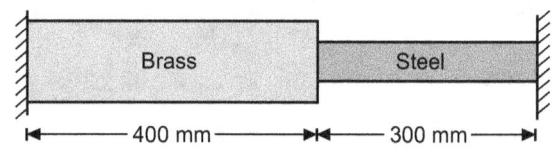

Fig. 1.41

Data : Brass : d = 75 mm, l = 400 mm, α = 20 × 10⁻⁶ /°C, E = 85 GPa,

          Steel : d = 40 mm, l = 300 mm, α = 11 × 10⁻⁶ /°C, E = 210 GPa, t = 140°C

Required : Stresses, reaction and relative movement of junction B.

Concept : Statically indeterminate, statics and compatibility.

Solution :

(i) Geometric properties :

$$A_{Br} = \frac{\pi}{4} \times (75)^2 = 4417.86 \text{ mm}^2$$

$$A_{st} = \frac{\pi}{4} \times (40)^2 = 1256.64 \text{ mm}^2$$

(ii) $(\sigma \cdot A)_{Br} = (\sigma \cdot A)_{st}$

$$\sigma_{Br} \times 4417.86 = \sigma_{st} \times 1256.64$$

$\therefore$ $\qquad\qquad\qquad\qquad\qquad \sigma_{st} = 3.52\, \sigma_{Br}$

(iii) Compatibility :

$$(\alpha\, t\, l)_{st} + (\alpha\, t\, l)_{Br} - \left[\left(\frac{\sigma l}{E}\right)_{st} + \left(\frac{\sigma l}{E}\right)_{Br}\right] = 0$$

$$11 \times 10^{-6} \times 140 \times 400 + 20 \times 10^{-6} \times 140 \times 300 - \left[\frac{\sigma_{st} \times 300}{210 \times 10^3} + \frac{\sigma_{Br} \times 400}{85 \times 10^3}\right] = 0$$

$$0.616 + 0.84 - \left[1.43 \times 10^{-3}\, \sigma_{st} + 4.706 \times 10^{-3} \times \sigma_{Br}\right] = 0$$

$$9.7396 \times 10^{-3}\, \sigma_{Br} = 1.456$$

$$\sigma_{Br} = 149.49 \text{ N/mm}^2$$

$$\sigma_{st} = \textbf{526.21 N/mm}^2$$

(iv) $\qquad\qquad\qquad\qquad\qquad \sigma_{st} = \dfrac{P_{st}}{A}$

$\therefore$ $\qquad\qquad\qquad\qquad\qquad P_{st} = \sigma_{st}\, A = 526.21 \times 1256.64$

$\therefore$ $\qquad\qquad\qquad\qquad\qquad P_{st} = \textbf{661.25 kN}$

Example 1.33 : *The steel wire in Fig. 1.42 is stretched between two rigid supports. The initial stress in the wire is 30 MPa, when the temperature is 20°C. What is the stress in the wire when temperature drops to 0°C ? At what temperature will the stress be zero ?*
$\alpha = 14 \times 10^{-6}/°C$ *and E = 210 GPa.*

Fig. 1.42

Data : As shown in Fig. 1.42, $\alpha = 14 \times 10^{-6}/°C$, E = 210 GPa, $t_1 = 20°C$, $\sigma = 30$ MPa.

Required : Stress at zero temperature, temperature at zero stress.

Concept : Compressive force will be developed due to decrease in temperature and tensile force will be developed due to increase in temperature.

Solution : (i) Temperature drops from 20°C to 0°C.

$\therefore$ $\qquad\qquad\qquad\qquad\qquad \sigma = \alpha t E$

$\qquad\qquad\qquad\qquad\qquad\quad = 14 \times 10^{-6} \times 20 \times 210 \times 10^3$

$\qquad\qquad\qquad\qquad\qquad\quad = 58.8$ MPa

$\therefore$ $\qquad\qquad$ Stress in wire $= -30 + 58.8 = 28.8$ MPa (Compressive)

(ii) $\sigma = 30$ MPa tensile should be developed to neutralize compressive force.

$$\sigma = \alpha t E$$

$$30 = 14 \times 10^{-6} \times t \times 210 \times 10^3$$

$$\therefore \qquad t = 10.2°C$$

When temperature is 9.8°C, stress in bar will be zero.

Example 1.34 : *Determine the temperature change that will cause a compressive stress of 36 MPa in the composite bar shown in Fig. 1.43, if* E_S = 210 GPa, E_A = 70 GPa *and* α_S = 12 ×10^{-6} /℃, α_A = 23 ×10^{-6} /℃.

Data : Compressive stress = 36 MPa, E_S = 210 GPa, E_A = 70 GPa,

$$\alpha_S = 12 \times 10^{-6} /°C \text{ and } \alpha_A = 23 \times 10^{-6} /°C$$

Required : Temperature change that will cause a compressive stress of 36 MPa in the composite bar.

Concept : Standard formula.

Solution : Temperature is calculated to elongated 0.3 mm. Till 0.3 mm expansion, stress will not develop.

$$\delta l_S + \delta l_{Al} = (l\alpha t)_S + (l\alpha t)_{Al}$$

$$0.3 = 250 \times 12 \times 10^{-6} \, t_1 + 300 \times 23 \times 10^{-6} \, t_1$$

$$t_1 = 30.3°C$$

$$\sigma_S \, A_S = \sigma_{Al} \, A_{Al}$$

As area is same, stress is always same. Now aluminium bar touch the other support and displacement is not possible now.

$$(l\alpha t)_S + (l\alpha t)_{Al} = \left(\frac{Pl}{AE}\right)_S + \left(\frac{Pl}{AE}\right)_{AL}$$

$$(250 \times 12 \times 10^{-6} \times t_2) + (300 \times 23 \times 10^{-6} \times t_2)$$

$$= \left[\frac{\sigma_S \times 250}{210 \times 10^3}\right] + \left[\frac{\sigma_{AL} \times 300}{70 \times 10^3}\right]$$

$$\sigma_S = \sigma_{Al} = 36 \text{ MPa}$$

$$9.9 \times 10^{-3} \, t_2 = 0.197$$

$$t_2 = 19.90°C$$

$$t = t_1 + t_2 = 30.30 + 19.90$$

Compressive stress in the composite bar occurs at 50.20°C.

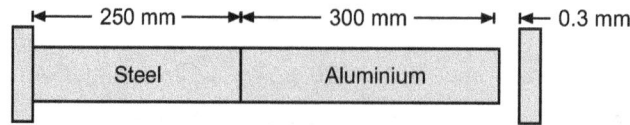

Fig. 1.43

EXERCISE

1. A member 1 m long, 20 mm × 20 mm in cross-section is subjected to axial pull of 20 kN. If modulus of elasticity of material is 200 GPa, find the elongation of member.   (δL = 0.25 mm)

2. Two steel rods AB and BC each 5 m long are connected at B as shown in Fig. 1.44. A load of 200 kN is supported at B as shown.
   (a) Determine the diameter of each member if allowable stress is 100 MPa.
   (b) Determine the vertical displacement of joint B assuming E = 200 GPa.

   (d = 50.46 mm, δB = 5 mm ($\rightarrow$))

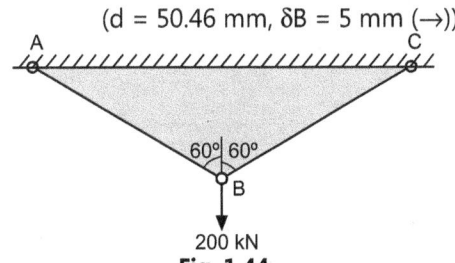

Fig. 1.44

3. A hollow circular member is 3 m long, 300 mm outside diameter and thickness of metal 50 mm is subjected to axial load such that stress produced is 75 MPa. If E = 150 GPa, find (i) magnitude of load, (ii) change in length.

   (P = 2945.2 kN, δL = 1.5 mm)

4. The following observations were made during a tensile test on a mild steel specimen 30 mm diameter and 200 mm long.
   Elongation with 40 kN load = 0.054 mm
   Yield load = 90 kN
   Maximum load = 140 kN
   Length of specimen at fracture = 241 mm.
   Determine (i) Young's modulus of elasticity, (ii) Yield stress, (iii) Ultimate stress, (iv) Percentage elongation.

   (E = 209.56 GPa, Yield stress = 127.32 MPa,
   Ultimate stress = 198 MPa, Percentage elongation = 20.5 %)

5. A prismatic steel bar 800 mm long is stretched by 0.7 mm by axial tensile force 'P'. Find the magnitude of force P if the volume of the bar is 450 × 10³ mm³ and E = 210 GPa.   (P = 103.35 kN)

6. Two steel plates are joined together by 16 mm diameter rivets. If plates are pulled apart by a force of 25 kN, as shown in Fig. 1.45, find shear stress in the rivets.

   (62.18 MPa)

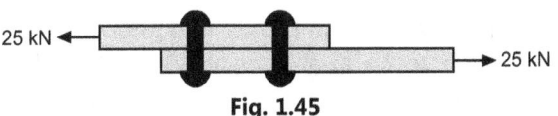

Fig. 1.45

7. A steel rod 30 mm in diameter, 300 mm long is subjected to axial forces alternating between 18 kN compression and 8 kN tension. Find the difference between the greatest and the least lengths of the rod. Take E = 210 GPa.   (0.0524 mm)

8. A short cast iron block of rectangular section 50 mm × 20 mm is subjected to an axial compressive load of 49 kN. Calculate the shear and the normal stresses on a section inclined at 30° to the line of action of load.   (σ = 12.25 MPa, τ = 21.21 MPa)

9. A compound bar ABCD is subjected to an axial compressive load of 30 kN as shown in Fig. 1.46. Find stresses in individual components and total change in length of bar. Assume E = 200 GPa.

(σ_{AB} = 23.87 MPa, σ_{BC} = 95.49 MPa, σ_{CD} = 42.44 MPa, δL = 0.364 mm)

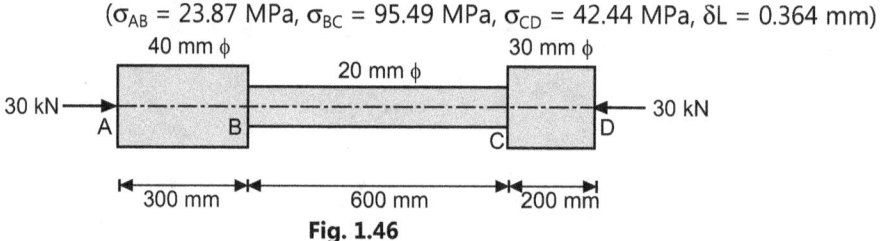

Fig. 1.46

10. A compound bar ABCD shown in Fig. 1.47 is subjected to axial compressive load which causes maximum stress of 100 MPa. Find total contraction of member if E = 150 GPa.   (δL = 0.28 mm)

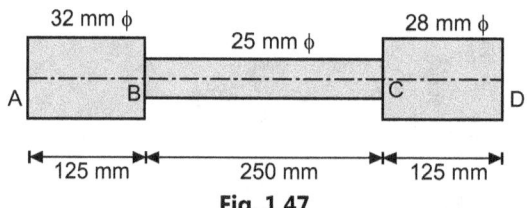

Fig. 1.47

11. A member 36 mmϕ is subjected to axial forces as shown in Fig. 1.48. Find the total change in length of the bar assuming E = 100 GPa.   (0.1178 mm contraction)

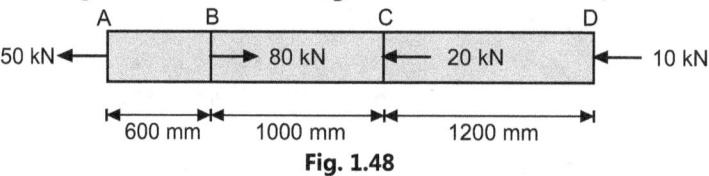

Fig. 1.48

12. A straight bar of steel 3 m long has rectangular cross section which varies uniformly from 100 mm × 12 mm at one end to 25 mm × 12 mm at other end. Find change in length of member when subjected to axial load of 35 kN. Assume E = 200 GPa.

(0.807 mm)

13. A rod tapers uniformly from 40 mm to 22 mm in diameter in a length of 400 mm. If the rod is subjected to an axial load of 40 kN, find the extension of the rod assuming E = 200 GPa.   (0.115 mm)

14. A cylinder 150 mm in diameter, 300 mm in length is subjected to axial compressive load of 180 kN which causes increase in diameter by 0.0952 mm and a decrease in length by 0.64 mm. Compute the values of Poisson's ratio and modulus of elasticity.

$$(\mu = 0.295, E = 4.78 \text{ GPa})$$

15. A member ABCD is subjected to forces as shown in Fig. 1.49. Find force 'P' necessary for equilibrium. Also find total elongation of the bar. Assume E = 210 GPa.

$$(P = 280 \text{ kN}, \delta L = 0.476 \text{ mm})$$

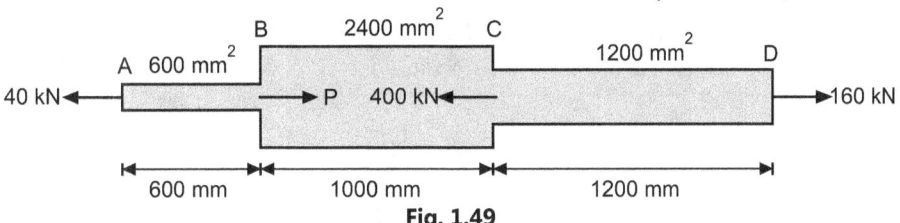

Fig. 1.49

16. A member ABCD is loaded as shown in Fig. 1.50. Determine (i) total deformation of rod, (ii) displacement of 'C'. Assume E = 70 GPa.

$$(\delta L = 0.0528 \text{ mm}, \delta C = 0.09 \text{ mm} (\leftarrow))$$

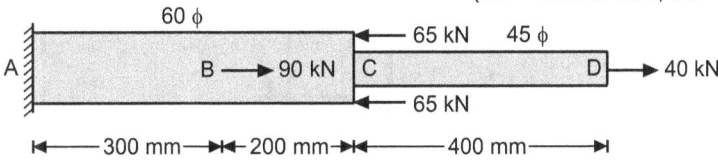

Fig. 1.50

17. A square bar is subjected to axial compressive stress σ_x in the longitudinal direction. The lateral strains in the direction at right angles are completely prevented by suitable external pressure. Evaluate this external pressure.

$$\left(p = \left(\frac{\mu}{1-\mu}\right)\sigma_x , \frac{\sigma_x}{\epsilon_x} = \frac{E}{\mu^2 - 1} \right)$$

18. A short piece of steel pipe is to carry an axial compressive force of 1200 kN with a factor of safety of 1.8 against yielding. If thickness t of the pipe is $\frac{1}{8}$ th of its outside diameter, find minimum required outside diameter. Assume yield stress = 270 MPa.

(153 mm)

19. A metal rod 10 mm diameter when tested under axial pull of 10 kN was found to reduce its diameter by 0.003 mm. Modulus of rigidity for the material is G = 51 GPa. Find other elastic constants. $(\mu = 0.317, E = 134.3 \text{ GPa}, K = 122.3 \text{ GPa})$

20. A steel bar ABC transmits an axial tensile force such that, total change in length is 0.6 mm. Determine for parts AB and BC the changes in length and diameter. Assume $\mu = 0.3$ and E = 200 GPa.

(For AB, $\delta L = 0.232$ mm, $\delta d = 0.00185$ mm; for BC, $\delta L = 0.368$ mm, $\delta d = 0.00286$ mm)

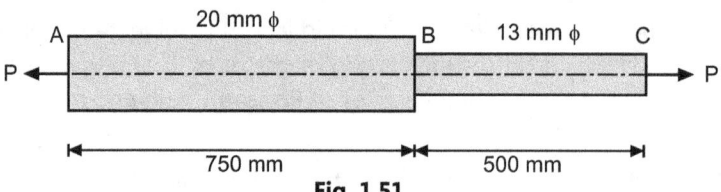

Fig. 1.51

21. A rigid beam weighing 200 N is held in horizontal position by three vertical wires as shown in Fig. 1.52. The outer wires of brass are 1.25 mm in diameter and the central steel wire is 0.6 mm in diameter. If the wires are stress free before the beam is attached, estimate the stresses induced in each wire. Assume E_s = 210 GPa, E_b = 86 GPa.   (σ_b = 63.59 MPa, σ_s = 154.48 MPa)

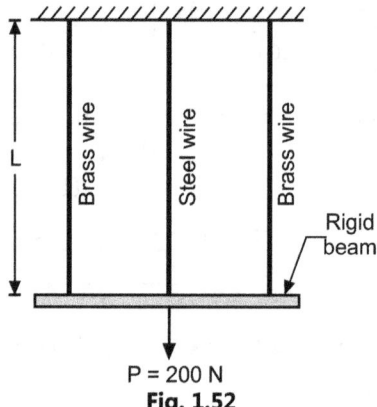

Fig. 1.52

22. A steel rod 15 m long is subjected to temperature change of 50°C. Find the temperature stress produced (i) when the expansion of the rod is prevented, (ii) the rod is permitted to expand by 5 mm. Assume α_s = 1.2 × 10⁻⁶ /°C and E = 200 GPa.

    (120 MPa, 53.33 MPa)

23. A cartwheel of 1.2 m diameter is to be provided with a thin steel tyre. Assuming the wheel to be rigid if the stress in steel is not to exceed 150 MPa, calculate the minimum diameter of the tyre and the minimum temperature to which it should be heated before slipping on to wheel. Assume E = 200 GPa, α_s = 12 × 10⁻⁶/°C.

    (1199.1 mm, 62.5°C)

24. A surveyor steel tape, nominally 30 meters is 12 mm wide and 1 mm thick. Its length is correct when used at a temperature of 16°C and under a pull of 100 N. By how much it will be in error when used at a temperature of 50°C and under a pull of 50 N ? E = 200 GPa and α = 11 × 10⁻⁶/°C.   (10.595 mm longer)

25. A bar of steel and two bars of copper, each of the same area and length, have their ends rigidly connected together when a temperature of 25°C so that the steel bar lies between the two copper bars. When the temperature is raised to 275°C, the length of the bar increases by 2 mm. Determine the original length and final stresses in the bar.

Take E_S = 200 GPa, E_C = 110 GPa, α_C = 17.5 × 10⁻⁶/°C, α_S = 12 × 10⁻⁶ /°C.

(σ_C = 71.98 MPa, σ_S = 143.97 MPa, l = 537.55 mm)

26. A copper flat 60 mm × 30 mm is joined to another 60 mm × 60 mm steel flat as shown in Fig. 1.53. If the combination is heated through 100°C, determine
    (i)   stress produced in each of the bar,
    (ii)   shear force between the flats, and
    (iii) shear stress.

α_C = 18.5 × 10⁻⁶ /°C; α_S = 12 × 10⁻⁶ /°C; E_C = 110 GPa; E_S = 220 GPa.

(σ_C = 57.2 MPa; σ_S = 28.6 MPa, Shear force = 102.96 kN; Shear stress = 4.29 MPa)

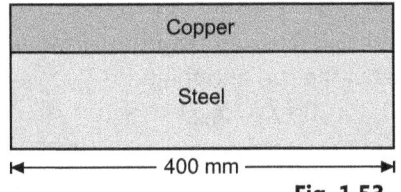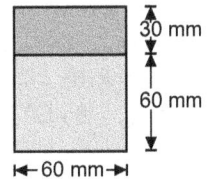

Fig. 1.53

27. A composite bar made up of aluminium and steel is held between two supports as shown in Fig. 1.54. What will be the stresses in the two bars when the temperature is dropped by 30°C if (i) supports are non-yielding, (ii) one of the support yields by 0.1 mm.

E_s = 210 GPa; E_a = 74 GPa, σ_s = 11.7 × 10⁻⁶ /°C; α_a = 23.4 × 10⁻⁶ /°C

(For non-yielding supports ; σ_s = 22.09 MPa; σ_a = 88.38 MPa;

For yielding of supports; σ_s = 16.85 MPa, σ_a = 67.41 MPa)

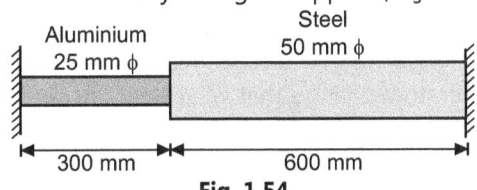

Fig. 1.54

28. A compound bar is made up by connecting a steel member and a copper member as shown in Fig. 1.55.

Take α_s = 12 × 10⁻⁶ /°C; α_c = 15.6 × 10⁻⁶ /°C; E_s = 200 GPa; E_c = 100 GPa.

Estimate the stress induced in the members due to temperature rise of 100°C.

(σ_c = 26.16 MPa; σ_s = 26.16 MPa and 13.08 MPa)

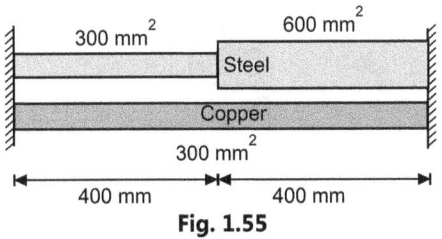

Fig. 1.55

29. A mild steel bar 20 mm in diameter and 300 mm long is encased in a brass tube whose external diameter is 30 mm and internal diameter is 25 mm. The composite bar is heated through 40°C. Calculate the stresses induced in each material.
$\alpha_s = 11.2 \times 10^{-6}$ /°C, $\alpha_b = 16.5 \times 10^{-6}$ /°C, $E_s = 200$ GPa, $E_c = 100$ GPa.
($\sigma_b = 15.77$ MPa, $\sigma_s = 10.84$ MPa)

30. A steel rod, 20 mm diameter, 200 mm long is heated through 120°K and at the same time subjected to a pull P. If the total extension of the rod is 0.3 mm, what should be the magnitude of P ? $\alpha_s = 12 \times 10^{-6}$ /K, E = 215 GPa.   (P = 3.769 kN)

31. A steel rod 25 mm diameter passes through a brass tube of 25 mm internal diameter and 35 mm external diameter. The nut on the rod is tightened until a stress of 15 MPa is developed in the rod. The temperature of the tube is then raised by 60°K. What are the final stresses in the rod and the tube ?
$E_s = 200$ GPa, $E_b = 80$ GPa, $\alpha_s = 11.7 \times 10^{-6}$ /°K, $\alpha_b = 19 \times 10^{-6}$ /K.
($\sigma_s = 39.16$ MPa tensile; $\sigma_b = 40.79$ MPa compressive)

32. A circular section tapered bar is rigidly fixed at both ends as shown in Fig. 1.56. If the temperature is raised by 30°C, calculate the maximum stress in the bar. E = 200 GPa, $\alpha = 12 \times 10^{-6}$/°C.   (126 MPa)

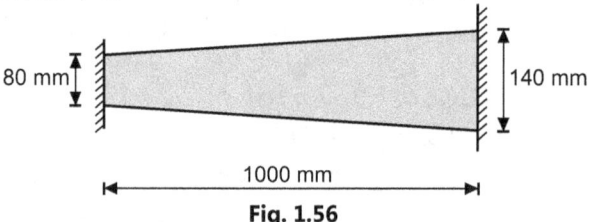

80 mm   140 mm

1000 mm

Fig. 1.56

33. A rigid bar of negligible weight is supported as shown in Fig. 1.57. If W = 80 kN, compute the temperature change that will cause the stress in the steel rod to be 55 MPa. Take $\alpha_s = 11.7 \times 10^{-6}$/°C, $\alpha_b = 18.9 \times 10^{-6}$/°C.   (28.3°C)

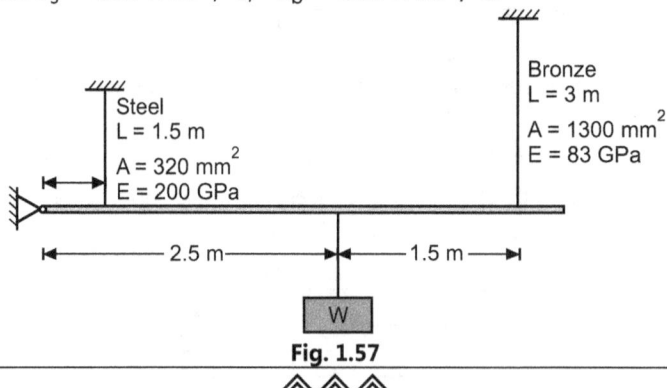

Bronze
L = 3 m
A = 1300 mm^2
E = 83 GPa

Steel
L = 1.5 m
A = 320 mm^2
E = 200 GPa

2.5 m   1.5 m

W

Fig. 1.57

◈ ◈ ◈

THIN CYLINDERS AND SHELLS

2.1 THIN CYLINDRICAL AND SPHERICAL VESSELS

A thin cylindrical or spherical shell is one in which thickness of metal is small as compared with the diameter. If thickness 't' of the metal is equal to or less than d/20, where d is the internal diameter of the shell, we consider the shell as thin, otherwise it is considered as thick.

The different stresses induced in the shell vary across the thickness, but if the cylinder or sphere is thin, the variation in stresses is negligible and we assume these stresses as uniform. These vessels are used either to store or to carry a liquid.

If the size of the shell is large, circumferential or longitudinal joints in the plates are inevitable. This will increase the magnitude of induced stresses. We will restrict our study only to thin walled seamless cylindrical and spherical vessels.

2.2 STRESSES INDUCED

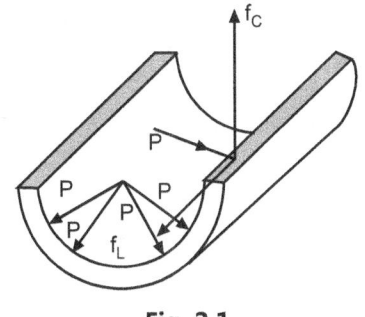

Fig. 2.1

When a thin shell contains any fluid under a pressure 'p', three types of mutually perpendicular stresses are induced at any point in the material of the shell, as shown in Fig. 2.1. They are :

(i) Hoop or circumferential stress, denoted by f_C, directed along the tangent to the circumference of the shell.

(ii) Longitudinal stress, denoted by f_L, directed along the length of the shell.

Circumferential and longitudinal stresses are tensile in nature as increase the diameter (and therefore circumference) and the length of the shell respectively.

(iii) Radial stress, compressive, in nature. Its magnitude is equal to the liquid pressure at the inner surface. As the external face of the shell is open to the atmosphere, the radial pressure is zero for the external surface.

The magnitude of the radial pressure is very small as compared with circumferential and longitudinal stresses. In further analysis, the radial pressure, therefore is neglected.

2.3 EVALUATION OF STRESSES

2.3.1 Circumferential or Hoop Stress

For a thin cylinder as shown in Fig. 2.2,

d = Internal diameter　　　　　　t = Thickness of metal

L = Length of cylinder　　　　　　p = Pressure of the fluid inside the cylinder

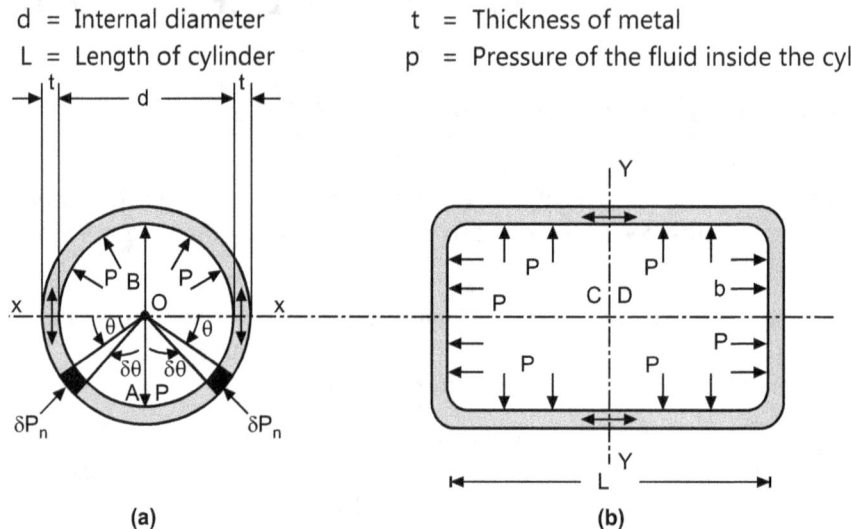

(a)　　　　　　　　　　　　　　　(b)

Fig. 2.2

Consider a longitudinal section X-X passing through the centre O, dividing the cylinder in two halves A and B as shown in Fig. 2.2 (a). Consider two symmetrical elemental strips of the cylinder subtending an angle $\delta\theta$ at the centre, at an angle θ to the horizontal at O. The effect of the radial pressure on each strip is a normal force, $\delta P_n = p\,r\,\delta\theta \times l$, where r is the radius of the cylinder. The horizontal components of these two normal forces balance each other and therefore the resultant of these two normal forces is the sum of their vertical components acting downwards.

$\therefore$　　　　　　　　　$\delta P = (2\,p\,r\,\delta\theta\,l)\sin\theta$

The total bursting force is obtained by summing these vertical components for all such strips in the lower half portion of the cylindrical shell.

$\therefore$
$$P = 2\,p\,r\,l \int_{0}^{\frac{\pi}{2}} \sin\theta\,d\theta$$

$\therefore$
$$P = 2\,p\,r\,l\,[-\cos\theta]_{0}^{\pi/2}$$

$$= 2\,p\,r\,l\,[\cos\theta]_{\pi/2}^{0}$$

$$= 2\,p\,r\,l = p\,d\,l$$

Thus the resultant bursting force on the portion A is a downward force P given by p d l which is the product of the radial pressure p and the projected area on the diametrical plane X-X. The resultant bursting force on the upper half B will be the same force p d l, but acting upward.

The bursting force on the lower half portion A is balanced by the resisting force which acts across the area 2 (t l). If f_c is the uniform intensity of tensile stress, the resistive force will be f_c (2 t l). As the direction of the stress is tangential to the circumference, it is called *circumferential stress* and is denoted by f_c. Equating the bursting force and the balancing force,

$$p \, d \, l = f_c \, 2 \, t \, l$$

$\therefore$
$$f_c = \frac{pd}{2t} \qquad \qquad \text{... (2.1)}$$

2.3.2 Longitudinal Stress

Now consider a section YY normal to the axis of the cylinder dividing it into two parts C and D as shown in Fig. 2.2 (b). The effect of the radial pressure p on the portion C is a bursting force,

$$P = p \frac{\pi}{4} d^2$$

If f_L is the uniform tensile stress set up by the section YY to resist this bursting force, the resisting tensile force will be $f_L \pi d t$. As the direction of the stress is along the length of the cylinder, it is called *longitudinal stress* and is denoted by f_L. Equating the bursting force to the resisting force,

$$p \frac{\pi}{4} d^2 = f_L (\pi d t)$$

$\therefore$
$$f_L = \frac{pd}{4t} \qquad \qquad \text{... (2.2)}$$

It will be seen from equations (2.1) and (2.2) that $f_c = 2 f_L$

2.3.3 Shear Stress

As f_c and f_L are two principal stresses,

$$f_S = \text{Maximum shear stress}$$

$$= \frac{f_c - f_L}{2}$$

$$= \left(\frac{p \, d}{2 \, t} - \frac{p \, d}{4 \, t} \right) \times \frac{1}{2}$$

$$f_S = \frac{p \, d}{8 \, t} \qquad \qquad \text{... (2.3)}$$

The shear stress acts at 45° to the principal plane.

2.4 EVALUATION OF STRAINS

Any point on a thin shell is subjected to a biaxial stress system mutually perpendicular to each other as shown in Fig. 2.3.

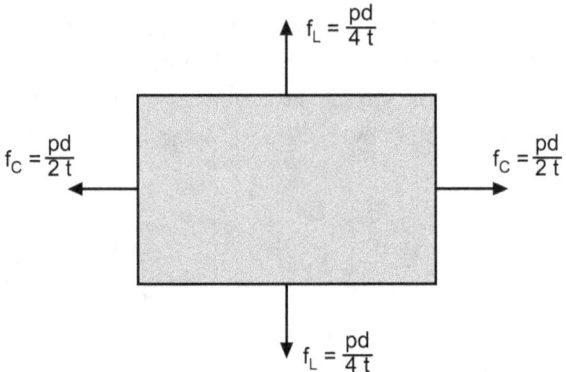

Fig. 2.3

We will find the circumferential and longitudinal strains by applying Hooke's law and Poisson's law for elastic materials. Thus,

2.4.1 Circumferential Strain, e_C

$$= \frac{f_C}{E} - \frac{\mu\, f_L}{E}$$

$$= \frac{2\, f_L}{E} - \frac{\mu\, f_L}{E}$$

$$= \frac{f_L}{E}\, (2 - \mu)$$

$$= \frac{p\, d}{4\, t\, E}\, (2 - \mu) \qquad\qquad \text{... (2.4)}$$

2.4.2 Longitudinal Strain, e_L

$$= \frac{f_L}{E} - \frac{\mu\, f_C}{E}$$

$$= \frac{f_L}{E} - \frac{\mu\, (2\, f_L)}{E}$$

$$= \frac{f_L}{E}\, (1 - 2\, \mu)$$

$$= \frac{pd}{4\, t\, E}\, (1 - 2\mu) \qquad\qquad \text{... (2.5)}$$

With the help of these basic strains, e_C and e_L, we will now find area strain, volumetric strain and thickness strain.

2.4.3 Area Strain, $\dfrac{\delta A}{A}$

$$A = \frac{\pi}{4} d^2$$

$\therefore$
$$\delta A = \frac{\pi}{4} 2d \times \delta d$$

$\therefore$
$$\frac{\delta A}{A} = \frac{\frac{\pi}{4} 2d\, \delta d}{\frac{\pi}{4} d^2} = \frac{2\, \delta d}{d}$$

But
$$\frac{\delta d}{d} = \frac{d\, \pi\, d}{\pi\, d} = e_C$$

$\therefore$
$$\frac{\delta A}{A} = \frac{2\, \delta d}{d} = 2e_C = \frac{pd}{2tE} (2 - \mu) \qquad \ldots (2.6)$$

2.4.4 Volumetric Strain, $\dfrac{\delta V}{V}$

$$V = \frac{\pi}{4} d^2 L$$

$\therefore$
$$\delta V = \frac{\pi}{4} d^2\, \delta L + L \frac{\pi}{4} 2d\, \delta d$$

$\therefore$
$$\frac{\delta V}{V} = \frac{\frac{\pi}{4} d^2\, \delta L + L \frac{\pi}{4} 2d\, \delta d}{\frac{\pi}{4} d^2 L} = \frac{\delta L}{L} + \frac{2\, \delta d}{d}$$

$$= e_L + 2e_C$$

$\therefore$
$$\frac{\delta V}{V} = \frac{pd}{4tE} (1 - 2\mu) + 2 \frac{pd}{4tE} (2 - \mu)$$

$\therefore$
$$\frac{\delta V}{V} = \frac{pd}{4tE} (5 - 4\mu) \qquad \ldots (2.7)$$

2.4.5 Thickness Strain, $\dfrac{\delta t}{t}$

The thickness of a thin shell will decrease as a result of circumferential and longitudinal stress. Applying Poisson's law,

$$\frac{\delta t}{t} = -\frac{\mu\, f_C}{E} - \frac{\mu\, f_L}{E}$$

$$= -\frac{\mu}{E}\left(\frac{pd}{2t} + \frac{pd}{4t}\right)$$

$$= -\frac{3\,\mu\,pd}{4\,t\,E} \qquad \dots (2.8)$$

2.5 EVALUATION OF DEFORMATIONS

2.5.1 Increase in Diameter, δd

$$\delta d = e_C \cdot d = \frac{f_L}{E}\,(2 - \mu)\;d$$

$$= \frac{pd}{4\,t\,E}\,(2 - \mu)\;d \qquad \dots (2.9)$$

2.5.2 Increase in Length, δL

$$\delta L = e_L \cdot L$$

$$= \frac{f_L}{E}\,(1 - 2\mu)\;\cdot L$$

$$= \frac{pd}{4\,t\,E}\,(1 - 2\mu)\;\cdot L \qquad \dots (2.10)$$

2.5.3 Increase in Cross-sectional Area, δA

$$\frac{\delta A}{A} = 2\,e_C$$

$$\therefore \qquad \delta A = 2e_C \cdot A$$

$$\therefore \qquad \delta A = \frac{pd}{2\,t\,E}\,(2 - \mu)\;\cdot\frac{\pi}{4}\,d^2 \qquad \dots (2.11)$$

2.5.4 Increase in Volume, δV

$$\frac{\delta V}{V} = \frac{pd}{4\,t\,E}\,(5 - 4\mu)$$

$$\therefore \qquad \delta V = \frac{pd}{4\,t\,E}\,(5 - 4\mu)\left(\frac{\pi}{4}\,d^2 L\right) \qquad \dots (2.12)$$

2.5.5 Decrease in Thickness, δt

$$\frac{\delta t}{t} = -\frac{3\,\mu pd}{4\,t\,E}$$

$$\therefore \qquad \delta t = -\frac{3\,\mu pd}{4\,t\,E}\cdot t = -\frac{3\,\mu pd}{4\,E} \qquad \dots (2.13)$$

2.6 EFFECTS OF COMPRESSIBLE AND NON-COMPRESSIBLE FLUID INJECTED UNDER PRESSURE

2.6.1 Compressible Fluid

If a compressible fluid under pressure is injected in the container, we have to consider two types of volume changes :

(a) Increase in the capacity of the shell – This is calculated by using the expression

$$\delta V = \frac{pd}{4tE} (5 - 4\mu) \cdot V$$

(b) Decrease in the volume of fluid, given by $-\frac{p}{K} V$, where K is bulk modulus of fluid.

When the pressure is released, the total quantity that will be expelled out will be :

$$\delta V = \left[\frac{pd}{4tE} (5 - 4\mu) V + \frac{p}{K} V \right] \qquad \text{... (2.14)}$$

2.6.2 Incompressible Fluid

In case of incompressible fluid, the volume change $-\frac{p}{K} V$ will be absent. The quantity of the fluid that can be injected will be only

$$dV = \frac{pd}{4tE} (5 - 4\mu) \cdot V \qquad \text{... (2.15)}$$

SOLVED EXAMPLES

Example 2.1 : *A research deep submersible aluminate has cylindrical pressure hull of outside diameter 2.5 m and wall thickness 150 mm. The aluminium alloy has yield point of 450 MPa. Determine the circumferential stress in the pressure hull when it is at operating depth of 5000 m below the surface of the sea. Use mean diameter for the calculations and consider unit weight of sea water as 10 kN/m³.*

Solution : $P = \gamma_w \cdot h = 10 \times 5000$

$\qquad\qquad\qquad = 50,000$ kPa

$\qquad\qquad\qquad = 50$ MPa

Mean diameter $= 2500 - 150$

$\qquad\qquad\qquad = 2350$ mm

$$f_c = \frac{pd}{2t} = \frac{50 \times 2350}{2 \times 150}$$

$\qquad\qquad = \textbf{391.67 MPa}$

As the aluminium alloy has yield point of 450 MPa, the circumferential stress of 391.67 MPa is within permissible limit.

Example 2.2 : *A cylindrical shell of 2 m length, 600 mm internal diameter and 20 mm metal thickness is subjected to an internal pressure of 12 MPa. Compute the values of hoop stress, longitudinal strain and change in the diameter of the cylinder. E = 200 GPa and Poisson's ratio = 0.3*

Solution : 1.

$$f_C = \text{Hoop stress} = \frac{pd}{2t}$$

$$= \frac{12 \times 600}{2 \times 20}$$

$$= \textbf{180 MPa}$$

2.

$$e_L = \text{Longitudinal strain} = \frac{f_L}{E}(1 - 2)$$

$$= \frac{180\,(1 - 0.6)}{2 \times 200 \times 10^3} = \mathbf{1.8 \times 10^{-4}}$$

3.

$$e_C = \text{Circumferential strain} = \frac{f_L}{E}(2 - \mu)$$

$$= \frac{90}{200 \times 10^3}(2 - 0.3)$$

$$= 7.65 \times 10^{-4}$$

$$\delta d = e_C \cdot d = 7.65 \times 10^{-4} \times 600$$

$$= \textbf{0.459 mm (increase)}$$

Example 2.3 : *A cylindrical shell of 2 m length, 600 mm internal diameter, and 10 mm metal thickness is subjected to an internal pressure of 10 MPa. Find the change in the diameter and length taking E = 200 GPa, μ = 0.30.*

Solution :

$$f_L = \frac{pd}{4t} = \frac{10 \times 600}{4 \times 10}$$

$$= 150\ \text{MPa}$$

$$\delta d = e_C \cdot d = \frac{f_L}{E}(2 - \mu)\ d$$

$$= \frac{150}{200 \times 10^3}(2 - 0.3) \times 600$$

$$= \textbf{0.765 mm (increase)}$$

$$\delta L = e_L \cdot L = \frac{f_L}{E}(1 - 2\mu)\ L$$

$$= \frac{150}{200 \times 10^3}(1 - 0.6) \times 2000$$

$$= \textbf{0.60 mm (increase)}$$

Example 2.4 : *A cylindrical pressure vessel is fabricated from steel plates of 20 mm thickness. The diameter of the vessel is 500 mm and the length is 3 m. If the normal stress in the steel is limited to 140 MPa, determine the maximum value of internal pressure for this vessel. Find also the change in the length of the vessel under the maximum pressure. E_{st} = 210 GPa, μ = 0.28.*

Solution : Maximum normal stress = f_c = 140 MPa

As $$f_c = \frac{pd}{2t}$$

$$p = \frac{2tf_c}{d}$$

∴   p = Internal pressure

$$= \frac{2 \times 20 \times 140}{500} = \textbf{11.2 MPa}$$

$$\delta L = e_L \cdot L = \frac{f_L}{E}(1 - 2\mu) \cdot L$$

∴ $$\delta L = \frac{140}{2} \cdot \frac{1}{210 \times 10^3} \times (1 - 0.56) \times 3000$$

$$= \textbf{0.44 mm}$$

Example 2.5 : *A cylindrical pressure vessel of 3.00 m outside diameter used for processing rubber is 10 m long. If the cylindrical portion of the cylinder is made from 24 mm thick steel plate and the vessel operates at 800 kPa internal pressure, determine the elongation in the length and the increase in the diameter caused by the operating pressure. E_{st} = 200 GPa and Poisson's ratio = 0.30.*

Solution :   p = 800 kPa = 0.8 MPa

$$f_L = \frac{pd}{4t} = \frac{0.8(3000 - 2 \times 24)}{4 \times 24}$$

$$= 24.6 \text{ MPa}$$

1. $$\delta d = e_c \cdot d = \frac{f_L}{E}(2 - \mu) \cdot d$$

$$= \frac{24.6}{200 \times 10^3}(2 - 0.3)(3000 - 2 \times 24)$$

$$= \textbf{0.617 mm (increase)}$$

2. $$\delta L = e_L \cdot L = \frac{f_L}{E}(1 - 2\mu) L$$

$$= \frac{24.6}{200 \times 10^3}(1 - 0.6) \times (10 \times 10^3)$$

$$= \textbf{0.492 mm (increase)}$$

Example 2.6 : *Because of corrosion, the thickness of a thin cylindrical shell is reduced by 3 mm. As the effect of this reduction, the hoop stress is increased by 12% under the same internal pressure. Find the original thickness of the shell.*

Solution : The effect of the corrosion will be on the external surface of the thin cylinder. The internal diameter will remain the same.

$$\text{Hoop stress before corrosion} = \frac{pd}{2t}$$

$$\text{Hoop stress after corrosion} = \frac{pd}{2(t-3)}$$

But,

$$\frac{pd}{2(t-3)} = 1.12 \frac{pd}{2t}$$

$$t = 1.12(t-3)$$

$$t = \textbf{28 mm}$$

Example 2.7 : *A boiler made of 12 mm steel plates is 1200 mm in diameter and 2500 mm long. It is subjected to an internal pressure of 3 MPa. Find (a) the hoop stress, (b) the longitudinal stress, (c) the change in the thickness of the plate and (d) the absolute maximum shear stress.*

Solution :

$$f_C = \text{Hoop stress} = \frac{pd}{2t} = \frac{3 \times 1200}{2 \times 12} = \textbf{150 MPa}$$

$$f_L = \text{Longitudinal stress}$$

$$= \frac{f_C}{2} = \textbf{75 MPa}$$

$$\frac{\delta t}{t} = -\frac{3\,\mu pd}{4Et}$$

As values of E and μ are not given, we assume

$$E = 200 \text{ GPa and } \mu = 0.3$$

∴

$$\frac{\delta t}{t} = -\frac{3 \times 0.3 \times 3 \times 1200}{4 \times 200 \times 10^3 \times 12} = -0.0003375$$

$$\delta t = -0.0003375 \times 12 = -0.00405 \text{ mm}$$

$$= \textbf{0.00405 mm (decrease)}$$

4.　(a) Considering biaxial stress system,

$$\sigma_1 = \text{major principal stress} = f_C$$

$$\sigma_2 = \text{minor principal stress} = f_L$$

$$\text{Maximum shear stress} = \frac{f_C - f_L}{2}$$

$$= \frac{150 - \dfrac{150}{2}}{2} = \textbf{37.5 MPa}$$

(b) Considering triaxial stress system, σ_1 and σ_2 as above and $\sigma_3 = 0$,

$$\text{Maximum shear stress } = \frac{\sigma_1 - \sigma_2}{2}$$

$$= \frac{150 - 0}{2} = \textbf{75 MPa}$$

(c) σ_1 and σ_2 as above and $\sigma_3 = p = -3$ MPa i.e. compressive,

$$\text{Maximum shear stress } = \frac{\sigma_1 - \sigma_3}{2}$$

$$= \frac{150 - (-3)}{2} = \textbf{76.5 MPa}$$

$\therefore$ Absolute maximum shear stress = **76.5 MPa**

Example 2.8 : *A thin cylindrical shell of length 2 m and having an internal volume of 2.26 m³ is subjected to an internal pressure of 3 MPa. If the maximum permissible tensile stress in the material is 180 MPa, calculate the change in the internal volume of this cylinder. E = 210 GPa and μ = 0.25.*

Solution : f_C = Maximum permissible stress in the material

= 180 MPa

$\therefore$ $f_L = \dfrac{f_C}{2} = 90$ MPa

$$\delta V = \frac{f_L}{E} (5 - 4\mu) \ V$$

$$= \frac{90}{210 \times 10^3} \times 4 \times 2.26 \times 10^9 \ \text{mm}^3$$

$$= \textbf{3874285.7 mm}^3$$

Example 2.9 : *A cylindrical shell 120 mm in diameter, thickness of metal 5 mm and 840 mm long is filled with an incompressible fluid at atmospheric pressure. If an additional 10 cm³ of fluid is pumped into the cylinder, calculate the pressure exerted by the fluid on the wall of the cylinder and the hoop stress induced in the section. E = 200 GPa and μ = 0.3.*

Solution : V = Volume of the cylinder $= \dfrac{\pi}{4} \times 120^2 \times 840$

$$= 9500176.2 \ \text{mm}^3$$

$$\delta V = 10 \ \text{cm}^3 = 10^4 \ \text{mm}^3$$

$$\frac{\delta V}{V} = 0.001053, \quad \text{but} \quad \frac{\delta V}{V} = \frac{pd}{4 \, t \, E} (5 - 4\mu)$$

$$p = \frac{0.001053 \times 4 \times 5 \times 200 \times 10^3}{120 \, (5 - 1.2)}$$

$$= \textbf{9.24 MPa}$$

$$f_c = \frac{pd}{2t}$$

$$= \frac{9.24 \times 120}{2 \times 5} = \textbf{110.88 MPa}$$

Example 2.10 : *A thin cylindrical container of diameter 1.5 m and length 4.0 m is subjected to internal fluid pressure of 3 MPa. The maximum shear stress in the material is not to excee 37.5 MPa. Find the minimum thickness of the container and change in the volume for the same. E = 200 GPa and Poisson's ratio = 0.25.*

Solution : Maximum shear stress $= \dfrac{f_c - f_L}{2} = \dfrac{pd}{8t}$

$\therefore$ $\qquad \dfrac{pd}{8t} = 37.50$

$\therefore$ $\qquad t = \dfrac{3 \times 1500}{8 \times 37.50} = \textbf{15 mm}$

$$\delta V = \frac{pd}{4tE}(5 - 4\mu) \cdot V$$

$\therefore$ $\qquad \delta V = \dfrac{(37.50 \times 2)}{200 \times 10^3} \times 4 \times \left(\dfrac{\pi}{4} \times 1500^2 \times 4000\right)$

$$= \textbf{10602875 mm}^3$$

Example 2.11 : *A cylindrical shell 120 mm internal diameter, thickness of metal 5 mm and 1000 mm long is filled with an incompressible fluid at atmospheric pressure. If an additional 10000 mm³ fluid is pumped into the cylinder, calculate the pressure exerted by the fluid on the wall of the cylinder and the hoop stress induced in the section. E = 200 GPa and μ = 0.30.*

Solution : $\qquad V = \dfrac{\pi}{4}d^2 L = \dfrac{\pi}{4} \times (120)^2 \times 1000$

$$= 11309734 \text{ mm}^3$$

$\qquad \dfrac{\delta V}{V} = \dfrac{10000}{11309734} = 8.842 \times 10^{-4}$ $\qquad$ ... (i)

But $\qquad \dfrac{\delta V}{V} = \dfrac{pd}{4tE}(5 - 4\mu)$

$$= \frac{p \times 120}{4 \times 5 \times 200 \times 10^3}(5 - 1.2)$$

$$= (1.14 \times 10^{-4})p \qquad \qquad \text{... (ii)}$$

Equating equation (i) and (ii),

$$(1.14 \times 10^{-4}) \, p = 8.842 \times 10^{-4}$$

$\therefore$ 　　　　　　　　$p = \textbf{7.76 MPa}$

$$f_c = \text{Hoop stress} = \frac{pd}{2t}$$

$$= \frac{7.76 \times 120}{2 \times 5} = \textbf{93.12 MPa}$$

Example 2.12 : *A thin cylindrical steel vessel has hemispherical ends. Overall length of the vessel is 500 mm. The outside diameter of the cylinder is 100 mm with thickness of metal 5 mm. Calculate the change in the volume of the vessel when it is subjected to an internal pressure of 15 MPa. E = 200 GPa and Poisson's ratio = 0.3.*

Solution :　　　　　$d = \text{Internal diameter} = 100 - 2 \times 5 = 90$ mm

Length of the cylindrical portion $= 500 - 90 = 410$ mm.

1.　Cylindrical portion :

$$\delta V_1 = \frac{pd}{4 \, t \, E} \, (5 - 4\mu) \left[\frac{\pi}{4} \times (90)^2 \times 410 \right]$$

$$= \frac{15 \times 90}{4 \times 5 \times 200 \times 10^3} \, (5 - 1.2) \left(\frac{\pi}{4} \times (90)^2 \times 410 \right)$$

$$= 1064.80 \text{ mm}^3$$

2.　End portion : two hemispheres, i.e. one sphere

$$\frac{\delta V}{V} = 3 \frac{\delta d}{d} \quad 3e_c$$

$$\delta V_2 = \frac{3 \, pd}{4 \, t \, E} \, (1 - \mu) \left(\frac{\pi}{6} \times d^3 \right)$$

$$= \frac{3 \times 15 \times 90}{4 \times 5 \times 200 \times 10^3} \, (1 - 0.3) \left(\frac{\pi}{6} \times 90^3 \right)$$

$$= 270.53 \text{ mm}^3$$

$\therefore$ 　　　　　　$\delta V = \text{change in the volume of the vessel}$

$$= \delta V_1 + \delta V_2 = 1064.80 + 270.53$$

$$= \textbf{1335.33 mm}^3$$

Example 2.13 : *A copper tube having 45 mm internal diameter and 1.5 mm thick wall thickness is closed at its ends by plugs which are 450 mm apart. The tube is subjected to an internal fluid pressure of 3 MPa and at the same time pulled in axial direction with a force of 3 kN. Compute : (i) the change in the length between the plugs and (ii) change in internal diameter of the tube.*

$$E_{cu} = 100 \text{ GPa and } \mu_{cu} = 0.3$$

Solution : 1. Due to the fluid inside :

$$f_L = \frac{pd}{4t} = \frac{3 \times 45}{4 \times 1.5} = 22.50 \text{ MPa}$$

$$e_c = \frac{f_L}{E}(2 - \mu)$$

$$= \frac{22.50}{100 \times 10^3} \times 1.70$$

$$= 3.825 \times 10^{-4}$$

$$e_L = \frac{f_L}{E}(1 - 2\mu)$$

$$= \frac{22.50}{100 \times 10^3} \times 0.40$$

$$= 9 \times 10^{-5}$$

$$\delta d = e_c \cdot d = 3.825 \times 10^{-4} \times 45$$

$$= + 0.01721 \text{ mm (increase)}$$

$$\delta L = e_L \cdot L = 9 \times 10^{-5} \times 450$$

$$= + 0.0405 \text{ mm (increase)}$$

2. Due to the pull of 3 kN :

We neglect the fall in water pressure due to applied tensile force. Area of cross-section of the copper tube,

$$A_C = \pi d t = \pi \times 45 \times 1.5 = 212.06 \text{ mm}^2$$

$$\sigma = \frac{P}{A_C} = \frac{3000}{212.06} = 14.15 \text{ MPa}$$

$$e_L = \text{Longitudinal strain}$$

$$= \frac{\sigma}{E} = \frac{14.15}{100 \times 10^3} = 1.415 \times 10^{-4}$$

$$e_c = \text{Lateral strain}$$

$$= -\mu\, e_L = -0.3 \times 1.415 \times 10^{-4} = -4.245 \times 10^{-5}$$

$$\delta L = e_L \cdot L = 1.415 \times 10^{-4} \times 450$$

$$= + 0.06368 \text{ mm (increase)}$$

$$\delta d = e_c \cdot d = -4.245 \times 10^{-5} \times 45$$

$$= -1.91 \times 10^{-3} \text{ mm (decrease)}$$

3.   Due to the combined effect :

We will add these results in (1) and (2) to get the combined effect.

∴ δL = 0.0405 + 0.06368 = **0.104 mm (increase)**

                    δd = 0.01721 – 0.00191 = **+ 0.0153 mm (increase)**

Example 2.14 : *A steel cylinder is 2000 mm long, 1000 mm diameter and 10 mm thickness of plate. After being filled with water at atmospheric pressure, more water is pumped in until the pressure increases to 2.00 MPa. On relieving the pressure, the water let out measured 3×10^6 mm³. If E_{st} = 200 GPa and μ = 0.3, estimate the bulk modulus of water. Assume the ends to remain flat.*

Solution : 1. $V = \dfrac{\pi}{4} d^2 L$

                    $= \dfrac{\pi}{4} \times 10^6 \times 2000 = 1.571 \times 10^9 \, mm^3$

          $\dfrac{\delta V}{V} = \dfrac{pd}{4 \, t \, E} (5 - 4\mu)$

                    $= \dfrac{2 \times 1000}{4 \times 10 \times 200 \times 10^3} (5 - 1.2) = 0.00095$

∴ $\delta V = 0.00095 \times 1.571 \times 10^9 \, mm^3$

                    $= 1492450 \, mm^3$

This increase in the volume of cylinder is due to circumferential and longitudinal stresses induced in the cylinder due to internal fluid pressure of 2 MPa.

2.   The water in the cylinder will get compressed due to internal fluid pressure. The decrease in the volume of water is given by

          $\delta V_{(water)} = \dfrac{p}{K} V$

where K is the bulk modulus of water.

∴ $\delta V_{(water)} = \dfrac{2}{K} \times 1.571 \times 10^9 \, mm^3$

3.   On relieving the pressure, the increased volume of the cylinder will come back to its original volume and the compressed water will be decompressed and will be under atmospheric pressure. Thus the quantity of water let out on relieving the pressure will be the sum of the above two quantities. Thus,

          $3 \times 10^6 = 1492450 + \dfrac{2}{K} \times 1.571 \times 10^9$

∴ $K = 2084.18 \, MPa$

∴ $K = $ **2.08 GPa**

Example 2.15 : A copper tube 25 mm bore and 2.5 mm thick is plugged at its ends and just filled with water at atmospheric pressure. If an axial compressive load of 5 kN is applied at the plugs, find by how much the water pressure will rise. Assume the plugs rigid and fixed to the tube. Neglect the end effects.

$$E_{cu} = 103 \text{ GPa}, \quad K_{water} = 2.2 \text{ GPa} \quad \text{and} \quad \mu = 0.35$$

Solution : Let p be the rise in the pressure due to the applied compressive force.

$$\sigma_C = \text{Rise in the circumferential stress}$$

$$= \frac{pd}{2t} = \frac{p \times 25}{2 \times 2.5} = +5p \text{ (Tensile)}$$

and $-\sigma_L \pi \, 25 \times 2.5 - p\frac{\pi}{4} \cdot 25^2 = -5000$

$\therefore \qquad \sigma_L = -(25.46 - 2.5\, p) \quad \text{(Compressive)}$

$$e_C = \text{Circumferential strain}$$

$$= \frac{5\,p}{E} + \frac{0.35}{E}(25.46 - 2.5\,p)$$

$$= \frac{4.125\,p}{E} + \frac{8.911}{E}$$

$$e_L = -\left(\frac{25.46 - 2.5\,p}{E}\right) - \frac{0.35 \times 5p}{E}$$

$$= -\frac{25.46}{E} + \frac{0.75\,p}{E}$$

$$\frac{\delta V}{V} = 2\,e_C + e_L = -\frac{7.638}{E} + \frac{9\,p}{E}$$

But $\qquad \dfrac{-p}{K} = \dfrac{\delta V}{V}$

$\therefore \qquad -\dfrac{7.638}{E} + \dfrac{9\,p}{E} = \dfrac{-p}{K}$

$\therefore \qquad -7.638 + 9p = \dfrac{-p}{K} \cdot E$

$\therefore \qquad -7.638 + 9\,p = \dfrac{-p\,103}{2.2} = -46.82\,p$

$\therefore \qquad p\,(55.82) = 7.638$

$\therefore \qquad p = 0.133683 \text{ MPa}$

$$= \textbf{133.68 kPa}$$

Note : In the above solution, the rise in the longitudinal stress due to the applied compressive force is neglected.

Example 2.16 : *A boiler made up of 20 mm thick plates is 1000 mm in diameter and 5000 mm long. It is subjected to an internal pressure of 10 MPa. Find (i) hoop stresses, (ii) longitudinal stress, (iii) change in volume, (iv) absolute maximum shear stress.*

Take E = 200 GPa and $\mu = \dfrac{1}{3}$.

Solution : (i) Hoop stress, $\quad \sigma_1 = \dfrac{pd}{2t} = \dfrac{10 \times 1000}{2 \times 20} =$ **250 MPa**

(ii) Longitudinal stress, $\quad \sigma_2 = \dfrac{\sigma_1}{2} =$ **125 MPa**

(iii) $\qquad\qquad\qquad\qquad \delta V = \dfrac{pd}{4tE}\,(5 - 4\mu)\left(\dfrac{\pi}{4} \times d^2 \times L\right)$

∴ $\qquad\qquad\qquad\qquad \delta V = \dfrac{10 \times 1000}{4 \times 20 \times 200 \times 10^3}\left(5 - \dfrac{4}{3}\right)\left(\dfrac{\pi}{4} \times 1000^2 \times 3000\right)$

$\qquad\qquad\qquad\qquad\qquad = $ **5399612.4 mm³**

(iv) Absolute maximum shear stress

$$= \dfrac{\sigma_1 - \sigma_2}{2} = \dfrac{250 - 125}{2}$$

$$= \textbf{62.50 MPa}$$

Example 2.17 : *A cylindrical shell is 3 m long, 1 m internal diameter and 15 mm metal thickness. Calculate the maximum intensity of shear stress induced and the change in the dimensions of the shell. The shell is subjected to an internal pressure of 1.5 MPa. Take E = 204 GPa and $\mu = 0.3$.*

Solution :

(i) $\qquad\qquad \tau_{max} = \dfrac{pd}{8t} = \dfrac{1.5 \times 1000}{8 \times 15} =$ **12.5 MPa**

(ii) $\qquad\qquad \delta d = \varepsilon_d \times d$

∴ $\qquad\qquad \delta d = \dfrac{pd}{4tE}\,(2 - \mu)\,d$

$\qquad\qquad\qquad = \dfrac{25}{204 \times 10^3} \times 1.7 \times 1000$

$\qquad\qquad\qquad = $ **0.208 mm (increase)**

(iii) $\qquad\qquad \delta L = \dfrac{pd}{4tE}\,(1 - 2\mu)\,L$

∴ $\qquad\qquad \delta L = \dfrac{25}{204 \times 10^3} \times 0.4 \times 3000$

$$= \textbf{0.147 mm (increase)}$$

(iv) δt = change in the thickness

∴ $\delta t = -\dfrac{3\mu pd}{4tE} \; t = -\dfrac{3\mu pd}{4E}$

∴ $\delta t = -\dfrac{3 \times 0.3 \times 1.5 \times 1000}{4 \times 20 \times 10^3}$

$$= \textbf{– 0.00165 mm (decrease)}$$

Example 2.18 : *A steel cylinder is 20 mm long, 1000 mm in diameter and 10 mm in thickness. After being filled with water at atmospheric pressure, more water is pumped in until the pressure becomes 2 MPa. On relieving the pressure, the water let out measured 2.9 × 10⁶ mm³. If E_{st} = 200 GPa and μ = 0.3, estimate the bulk modulus of water. Assume the ends remain flat.*

Solution : For thin cylinder

$$\delta V_c = \frac{pd}{4tE}(5 - 4\mu)\frac{\pi}{4}d^2 L$$

$$= \frac{2 \times 1000}{4 \times 10 \times 200 \times 10^3}(5 - 1.2)\frac{\pi}{4} \times 1000^2 \times 2000$$

$$= 1492256.5 \text{ mm}^3$$

$$\delta V_{water} = \frac{P}{K} \times V = \frac{2}{K} \times \frac{\pi}{4} \times 1000^2 \times 2000 = \frac{3.14 \times 10^9}{K}$$

$$2.9 \times 10^6 = 1492256.5 + \frac{3.14 \times 10^9}{K}$$

∴ $K = 2230.52 \text{ MPa} = \textbf{2.23 GPa}$

Note : Refer to Example 2.14.

Example 2.19 : *A closed cylindrical vessel made up of steel plates, 8 mm thick is filled with a fluid under a pressure of 400 MPa. The internal diameter of the cylinder is 300 mm and length 2000 mm. The cylinder is closed at ends with flat plates. Determine (a) Hoop stress, (b) Longitudinal stress, (c) Change in diameter, (d) Change in length, (e) Change in volume. Given : E_{st} = 200 GPa; μ = 0.25.*

Solution : (a) $f_c = \dfrac{pd}{2t} = \dfrac{400 \times 300}{2 \times 8} = \textbf{7500 MPa}$

(b) $f_L = \dfrac{f_c}{2} = \textbf{3750 MPa}$

(c) $\delta d = \varepsilon_c \times d$

$$= \frac{pd}{4tE}(2 - \mu) \cdot d$$

$$= \frac{3750}{200 \times 10^3} \times 1.75 \times 300 = \mathbf{9.84 \ mm}$$

(d)

$$\delta L = \varepsilon_L \times L = \frac{pd}{4tE} \ (1 - 2\mu) \cdot L$$

$$= \frac{3750}{200 \times 10^3} \times 0.5 \times 2000 = \mathbf{18.75 \ mm}$$

(e)

$$\delta V = \varepsilon_v \cdot V = \frac{pd}{4tE} \ (5 - 4\mu) \times \left(\frac{\pi}{4} d^2 L\right)$$

$$= \frac{3750}{200 \times 10^3} \times 4 \times \frac{\pi}{4} \times 300^2 \times 2000$$

$$= \mathbf{10602875 \ mm^3}$$

Example 2.20 : *A cylindrical shell 160 mm internal diameter, 1000 mm long and wall thickness 5 mm is completely filled with fluid. Additional 15 c.c. of incompressible fluid is pumped into the cylinder.*

Determine the internal pressure developed and corresponding hoop stress and longitudinal stress taking E = 200 GPa and μ = 0.3.

Solution : Substituting in the expression,

$$dV = \frac{pd}{4 \ t \ E} \ (5 - 4\mu) \left(\frac{\pi}{4} d^2 L\right)$$

∴

$$15 \times 10^3 \ (mm^3) = \frac{p \times 160}{4 \times 5 \times 200 \times 10^3} \ (5 - 1.2) \left(\frac{\pi}{4} \times 160^2 \times 1000\right)$$

∴

$$p = \mathbf{4.91 \ MPa}$$

$$\sigma_C = \text{Hoop stress} = \frac{pd}{2 \ t}$$

$$= \frac{4.91 \times 160}{2 \times 5}$$

$$= \mathbf{78.56 \ MPa}$$

$$\sigma_L = \text{Longitudinal stress} = \frac{pd}{4 \ t} = \frac{\sigma_C}{2}$$

$$= \mathbf{39.28 \ MPa}$$

2.7 THIN SPHERICAL SHELL UNDER INTERNAL PRESSURE

Let d be the internal diameter and t be the thickness of the thin spherical shell. Let it contain a fluid under pressure p. Any diametrical plane cutting the sphere offers a hollow circular section. Therefore, both the principal stresses have the same magnitude, $\frac{pd}{4 \ t}$. Both these stresses are tensile. As both principal stresses are equal, the shear stress is absent. Following equations hold good :

1. $$f_{C_1} = f_{C_2} = \frac{pd}{4t} \qquad \text{... (2.16)}$$

2. $$e_{C_1} = e_{C_2} = \frac{pd}{4tE} - \mu \frac{pd}{4tE}$$

$$= \frac{pd}{4tE} (1 - \mu) \qquad \text{... (2.17)}$$

3. $$\delta d = \frac{pd}{4tE} (1 - \mu) \cdot d \qquad \text{... (2.18)}$$

4. $$\frac{\delta t}{t} = -\frac{\mu pd}{4tE} - \frac{\mu pd}{4tE} = -\frac{\mu pd}{2tE}$$

$$\therefore \qquad \delta t = -\frac{\mu pd}{2tE} \cdot t = -\frac{\mu pd}{2E} \qquad \text{... (2.19)}$$

5. Due to symmetry in all directions

$$\frac{\delta V}{V} = 3e_c = \frac{3pd}{4tE} (1 - \mu)$$

$$\therefore \qquad \delta V = \frac{3pd}{4tE} (1 - \mu) \cdot V \qquad \text{... (2.20)}$$

Example 2.21 : A thin spherical shell of 1.2 m diameter and 6 mm metal thickness is filled with a liquid under pressure until its volume increases by 250 ml. Determine the pressure exerted by the liquid on the shell. E = 200 GPa, μ = 0.25.

Solution : For thin spherical shell,

$$\frac{\delta V}{V} = \frac{3pd}{4tE} (1 - \mu)$$

$$V = \frac{\pi}{6} d^3 = \frac{\pi}{6} \times 1200^3 = 9.05 \times 10^8 \text{ mm}^3$$

$$\frac{\delta V}{V} = \frac{250 \times 10^3 \text{ (mm}^3\text{)}}{9.05 \times 10^8} = 2.76 \times 10^{-4}$$

$$p = \frac{\delta V}{V} \cdot \frac{4tE}{3d(1 - \mu)}$$

$$\therefore \qquad p = 2.76 \times 10^{-4} \left[\frac{4 \times 6 \times 200 \times 10^3}{3 \times 1200 \times 0.75} \right]$$

$$= \mathbf{0.49 \ MPa}$$

Example 2.22 : A spherical shell of 1000 mm internal diameter, 20 mm thick is subjected to an internal pressure of 40 MPa. Find the circumferential stress and change in the volume. E = 210 GPa, Poisson's ratio = 0.30.

Solution : 1. $\quad f_C = \dfrac{pd}{4t}$

$$= \dfrac{40 \times 1000}{4 \times 20} = \textbf{500 MPa}$$

2. $\quad \delta V = \dfrac{3\,pd}{4\,t\,E}\,(1 - \mu)\ V,\ \text{where}\ V = \dfrac{\pi}{6}\,d^3$

∴ $\quad \delta V = \dfrac{3}{4} \times \dfrac{40 \times 1000}{20 \times 210 \times 10^3} \times 0.70 \times \dfrac{\pi}{6} \times 10^9$

$$= \textbf{26179939 mm}^3$$

Example 2.23 : *A thin spherical shell of 450 mm diameter is subjected to internal pressure of 12 MPa. The change in the diameter was observed to be 0.15 mm. Find the percentage change in the volume of the shell.*

Solution : $\quad \delta d = 0.15 = \dfrac{pd}{4\,t\,E}\,(1 - \mu) \times 450$

$$\dfrac{\delta V}{V} = \dfrac{3\,pd}{4\,t\,E}\,(1 - \mu) = 3 \times \dfrac{0.15}{450}$$

∴ % change in the volume $= \dfrac{\delta V}{V} \times 100$

$$= \dfrac{3 \times 0.15}{450} \times 100$$

$$= \textbf{0.1\%}$$

Example 2.24 : *A spherical shell 1000 mm in diameter is 10 mm thick. It is being filled with a fluid under pressure until its volume increases by 2 × 10⁵ mm³. Calculate the pressure exerted by the fluid on the shell. E for the shell = 210 GPa, μ = 0.25.*

Solution : $\quad V = \dfrac{\pi}{6}\,d^3 = \dfrac{\pi}{6} \times 10^9 = 5.24 \times 10^8\ mm^3$

$$\delta V = 2 \times 10^5\ mm^3$$

∴ $\quad \dfrac{\delta V}{V} = \dfrac{2 \times 10^5}{5.24 \times 10^8} = 3.82 \times 10^{-4}$

But, $\quad \dfrac{\delta V}{V} = \dfrac{3\,pd}{4\,t\,E}\,(1 - \mu)$

∴ $\quad 3.82 \times 10^{-4} = \dfrac{3p \times 1000}{4 \times 10 \times 210 \times 10^3} \times 0.75$

∴ $\quad p = \textbf{1.426 MPa, say 1.43 MPa}$

Example 2.25 : *A spherical steel vessel with 600 mm internal diameter and 10 mm wall thickness is filled with water under a pressure of 5 MPa. The pressure is gradually reduced by letting out some water. To reduce the pressure to atmospheric, the volume of the water let out was 3.7×10^5 mm^3. If bulk modulus of water, K is 2.00 GPa and E for steel is 210 GPa, find the value of Poisson's ratio.*

Solution :

$$V = \frac{\pi}{6} d^3$$

$$= \frac{\pi}{6} \times 600^3 = 1.131 \times 10^8 \text{ mm}^3$$

1.

$$\delta V_{(sphere)} = \frac{3 \, pd}{4 \, t \, E} (1 - \mu) \, V$$

$$= \frac{3 \times 5 \times 600}{4 \times 10 \times 210 \times 10^3} (1 - \mu) \times 1.131 \times 10^8$$

$$= 121178.57 \, (1 - \mu) \text{ (increase)}$$

2.

$$\delta V_{(water)} = \frac{p}{K} \cdot V$$

$$= \frac{5}{2 \times 10^3} \times (1.131 \times 10^8)$$

$$= 282750 \text{ mm}^3 \text{ (decrease)}$$

3.

$$\delta V = 3.7 \times 10^5 = \delta V_{(sphere)} + \delta V_{(water)}$$

$$\therefore \quad 3.7 \times 10^5 = 121178.57 \, (1 - \mu) + 282750$$

$$\therefore \quad \mu = \textbf{Poisson's ratio = 0.28}$$

Example 2.26 : *A spherical shell having 1250 mm mean diameter is manufactured by using 4 mm thick plates. It is filled with non-compressible fluid under pressure of magnitude 10 MPa. Determine : (1) Surface stress, (2) Surface strain, (3) Change in diameter and (4) Change in volume. Take E = 200 GPa.*

Solution : 1. Surface stress $= f_{C_1} = f_{C_2} = \dfrac{pd}{4 \, t}$

d, internal diameter $= 1250 - t = 1250 - 4 = 1246$ mm

$\therefore \quad$ Surface stress $= \dfrac{10 \times 1246}{4 \times 4} = \textbf{778.75 MPa}$

2. $\quad$ Surface strain $= \dfrac{pd}{4 \, t \, E} (1 - \mu)$

Assuming $\mu = 0.25$

Surface strain $= \dfrac{778.75}{200 \times 10^3} (1 - 0.25)$

$= \textbf{0.00292}$

3.

$$\delta d = \frac{pd}{4 t E} (1 - \mu) \cdot d = 0.00292 \times 1246$$

$$= \mathbf{3.64 \ mm}$$

4.

$$\delta V = 3 \frac{pd}{4 t E} (1 - \mu) \cdot V$$

$$= 3 \times 0.00292 \times \frac{\pi}{6} \ 1246^3$$

$$= \mathbf{8872721.6 \ mm^3}$$

2.8 THICK CYLINDERS

The thickness of the thick cylinder is large as compared to that of the thin cylinder. In case of the thin cylinder, the circumferential stress was 'assumed' uniform because the variation in it was negligible across the small thickness. In case of the thick cylinder, however, this assumption fails. The circumferential stress is not uniform across the thickness of the thick cylinder.

2.8.1 Lame's Assumption

The theory of thick cylinders is based on Lame's assumption. It states that *sections perpendicular to the central axis of the cylinder, which are plane before the pressure comes in, remain plane after the shell is under pressure.* In other words, *the longitudinal strain at any point in the thickness of the metal is constant and is independent of the position of the point.*

2.8.2 Derivation of Lame's Formulae for Radial Pressure and Circumferential Stress

Consider a thick cylinder of external radius r_1 and internal radius r_2 as shown in (a) of Fig. 2.4. It contains the liquid under pressure p inside the shell. Let its length be L. Consider an elemental ring of the shell of radius x and thickness δx. Let p_x and $(p_x + \delta p_x)$ be the intensities of radial pressure at the inner and outer sides of the ring and let f_x be the intensity of circumferential or hoop stress induced in the ring. Consider the longitudinal section XX of the ring (diametrical) as shown in (b) of Fig. 2.4. The bursting force is evaluated based on the projected area which is 2xL for inner surface and 2 (x + δx) L for outer surface. The bursting force $P = p_x (2xL) - (p_x + \delta p_x) \cdot 2 (x + \delta x) L$. If f_x is the intensity of hoop stress induced in the ring, the resisting force $= f_x (2 \delta x L)$.

Equating the bursting force to the resisting force,

$$f_x (2\delta x \ L) = p_x (2x \ L) - (p_x + \delta p_x) \cdot 2 (x + \delta x) L$$

$$\therefore \qquad f_x \ \delta x = p_x \ \delta x - x \ \delta p_x - \delta p_x \ \delta x$$

Neglecting small quantities of the higher order,

$$f_x = - p_x - x \ \frac{\delta p_x}{\delta x} \qquad\qquad ... (i)$$

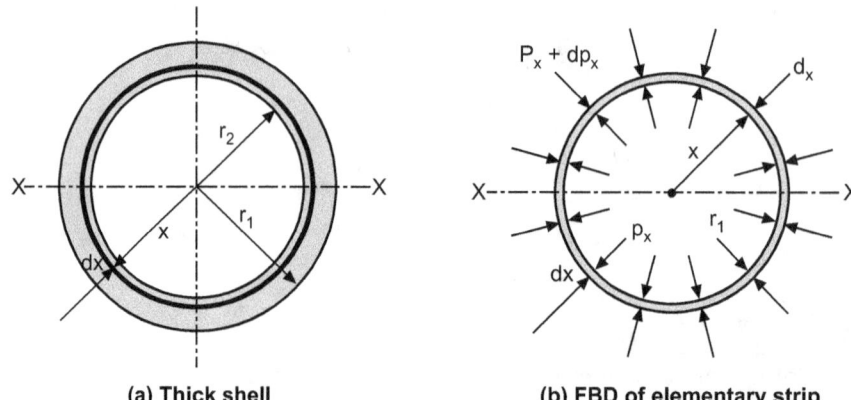

(a) Thick shell   **(b) FBD of elementary strip**

Fig. 2.4

At any point in the section of the elemental ring, the three principal stresses are :

(i)   The radial pressure p_x, (ii) the hoop stress f_x, and (iii) the longitudinal tensile stress p_L which may be assumed uniform across the thickness of the shell.

$$p_L = \frac{p\,\pi\,r_2^2}{\pi\left(r_1^2 - r_2^2\right)} = \frac{p\,r_2^2}{\left(r_1^2 - r_2^2\right)}$$

The longitudinal strain at any point in the ring of radius x and thickness δx is obviously equal to

$$\frac{p_L}{E} - \frac{\mu\,f_x}{E} + \frac{\mu\,p_x}{E}$$

which is independent of x.

$$\frac{p_L}{E} - \frac{\mu\,f_x}{E} + \frac{\mu\,p_x}{E} = \text{a constant}$$

As p_L, μ and E are all constants.

$$(f_x - p_x) = \text{a constant} = 2a, \text{ where a is a constant.} \qquad \ldots \text{(ii)}$$

Substituting f_x (= $2a + p_x$) in (i), we get

$$p_x + 2a = -p_x - x\,\frac{\delta p_x}{\delta x}$$

∴ $$\frac{\delta p_x}{\delta x} = \frac{-2\,(p_x + a)}{x}$$

∴ $$\frac{\delta p_x}{(p_x + a)} = \frac{-2\delta x}{x}$$

Integrating

$$\ln\,(p_x + a) = -2\ln x + \ln b, \text{ where ln b is the constant of integration.}$$

$$p_x + a = \frac{b}{-x^2}$$

$\therefore$ $$p_x = \frac{b}{x^2} - a \qquad \qquad \text{... (2.21)}$$

and from (ii), $$f_x = \frac{b}{x^2} + a \qquad \qquad \text{... (2.22)}$$

These are Lame's formulae for the radial pressure and hoop stress at any specified point in the section of a thick cylindrical shell. The variation across the thickness is parabolic and is shown in Fig. 2.5.

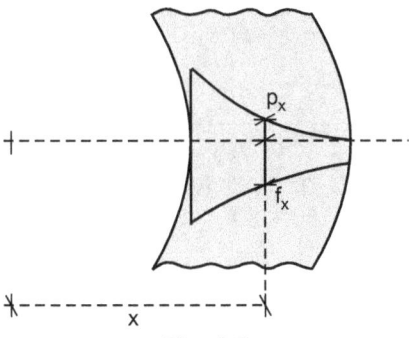

Fig. 2.5

2.8.3 Evaluation of 'a' and 'b' in Lame's Equations

The radial pressure at inner surface where $x = r_2$ is p and at outer surface where $x = r_1$ is zero (i.e. atmospheric).

$\therefore$ $$p = \frac{b}{r_2^2} - a$$

$$0 = \frac{b}{r_1^2} - a$$

Solving these equations simultaneously, we get

$$a = \frac{p}{K^2 - 1} \quad \text{where,} \qquad \qquad \text{... (2.23)}$$

$$K = \frac{r_1}{r_2}$$

$$b = \frac{r_1^2\, p}{K^2 - 1} \qquad \qquad \text{... (2.24)}$$

2.8.4 Evaluation of f_{max} and f_{min} when $p_{min} = 0$

$$f_{max} = \frac{b}{r_2^2} + a$$

$$= \frac{r_1^2}{r_2^2} \frac{1}{K^2 - 1}\, p + \frac{p}{K^2 - 1}$$

$$= \frac{K^2}{K^2 - 1} \, p + \frac{p}{K^2 - 1}$$

$$= \left(\frac{K^2 + 1}{K^2 - 1} \right) p \qquad\qquad ... (2.25)$$

$$f_{min} = \frac{b}{r_1^2} + a$$

$$= \frac{p}{K^2 - 1} + \frac{p}{K^2 - 1}$$

$$= \left(\frac{2}{K^2 - 1} \right) p \qquad\qquad ... (2.26)$$

Example 2.27 : *A C.I. pipe 160 mm in radius, thickness of metal 80 mm carries water under a pressure of 8 MPa. Calculate the maximum and minimum intensities of hoop stress.*

Solution : $\varepsilon_2 = 160$ mm, $\varepsilon_1 = 160 + 80 = 240$ mm

$$K = \frac{\varepsilon_1}{\varepsilon_2} = \frac{240}{160} = 1.5, \ K^2 = 2.25$$

$$f_{max} = \left(\frac{K^2 + 1}{K^2 - 1} \right) p$$

$$= \left(\frac{3.25}{1.25} \right) \times 8 = \textbf{20.80 MPa}$$

$$f_{min} = \left(\frac{2}{K^2 - 1} \right) p = \frac{2}{1.25} \times 8 = \textbf{12.80 MPa}$$

Example 2.28 : *A steel cylindrical shell of internal diameter 120 mm carries water having pressure 45 MPa. If maximum possible tensile stress in the section is 120 MPa, determine the thickness of the shell.*

Solution : $f_{max} = 120$ MPa

$$= \frac{K^2 + 1}{K^2 - 1} \, p = \frac{K^2 + 1}{K^2 - 1} \times 45$$

$\therefore$ $\dfrac{K^2 + 1}{K^2 - 1} = 2.67$

$\therefore$ $K^2 + 1 = 2.67 \ K^2 - 2.67$

$\therefore$ $1.67 \ K^2 = 3.67$

$\therefore$ $K = 1.48 = \dfrac{r_1}{r_2} = \dfrac{r_1}{60}$

$\therefore$ $r_1 = 88.80$ mm

$\therefore$ $t = 88.80 - 60 = \textbf{28.80 mm}$ say 30 mm

$\therefore$ External diameter $= 120 + 2 \times 30 = \textbf{180 mm}$

Example 2.29 : *A thick cylinder whose external diameter is K times the internal diameter is subjected to an internal pressure. If the ratio of maximum to minimum hoop stress is n, find the relation between n and K – 2b. The maximum hoop stress is 45 MPa and the value of n is 2.5. Also find the internal radial pressure exerted and the necessary thickness of the metal if the diameter of the bore is 150 mm.*

Solution : 　　　　　$r_1 = Kr_2$,　$\dfrac{f_{max}}{f_{min}} = n$

$$\frac{f_{max}}{f_{min}} = \frac{K^2 + 1}{2} = n$$

∴　　　$K^2 + 1 = 2n$　is the required relation

$$\frac{f_{max}}{f_{min}} = 2.5$$

∴　　　$f_{min} = \dfrac{45}{2.5} = 18$

　　　$K^2 + 1 = 2n = 5$

∴　　　　$K^2 = 4,$　$K = 2$

$$f_{max} = 45 = \frac{K^2 + 1}{K^2 - 1}\, p$$

∴　　　$p = 45 \times \dfrac{3}{5} = $ **27.0 MPa**

　　　$r_2 = 75$ mm

　　　$r_1 = Kr_2 = 150$ mm

　　　$t = r_1 - r_2 = 150 - 75 = $ **75 mm**

Example 2.30 : *A pipe of 400 mm internal diameter and 100 mm thickness contains a fluid at a pressure of 8 MPa. Find the maximum and minimum hoop stresses induced across the section.*

Solution : $\varepsilon_2 = 200$ mm, $\varepsilon_1 = 200 + 100 = 300$ mm,　$p = 8$ MPa.

$$f_{max} = \left(\frac{K^2 + 1}{K^2 - 1}\right) p, \quad K = \frac{\varepsilon_1}{\varepsilon_2} = \frac{300}{200} = 1.5$$

∴　　　$f_{max} = \dfrac{3.25}{1.25} \times 8 = $ **20.8 MPa**

　　　$f_{min} = \left(\dfrac{2}{K^2 - 1}\right) p$

　　　　$= \dfrac{2}{1.25} \times 8 = $ **12.8 MPa**

Example 2.31 : *Find the thickness of the metal of a steel cylindrical shell of internal diameter 150 mm to withstand an internal pressure of 50 MPa. The maximum hoop stress is limited to 150 MPa.*

Solution :
$$f_{max} = \left(\frac{K^2 + 1}{K^2 - 1}\right) p$$

$\therefore$
$$150 = \left(\frac{K^2 + 1}{K^2 - 1}\right) 50$$

$\therefore$
$$\frac{K^2 + 1}{K^2 - 1} = 3$$

$$K^2 + 1 = 3K^2 - 3$$

$\therefore$
$$2K^2 = 4$$

$$K = \sqrt{2} = 1.414$$

$$r_2 = \frac{150}{2} = 75 \text{ mm}$$

$$r_1 = K \varepsilon_2 = 75 \times 1.414 = 106.06 \text{ mm}$$

$\therefore$
$$t = 106.06 - 75 = 31.06 \text{ mm}$$

$$t = \text{say } \mathbf{31 \text{ mm}}$$

Example 2.32 : *A thick cylindrical shell has internal diameter 500 mm and metal thickness 100 mm. If it contains a liquid under a pressure of 6 MPa, find f_{max} and f_{min}.*

Solution :
$$r_2 = \frac{500}{2} = 250 \text{ mm}$$

$$r_1 = 250 + 100 = 350 \text{ mm}$$

$$K = \frac{\varepsilon_1}{\varepsilon_2} = \frac{350}{250} = 1.4$$

$$K^2 = 1.96$$

$$f_{max} = \left(\frac{K^2 + 1}{K^2 - 1}\right) p$$

$$= \frac{2.96}{0.96} \times 6$$

$$= \mathbf{18.50 \text{ MPa}}$$

$$f_{min} = \left(\frac{2}{K^2 - 1}\right) p$$

$$= \frac{2}{0.96} \times 6 = \mathbf{12.5 \text{ MPa}}$$

EXERCISE

1. A thin cylindrical shell 1200 mm in diameter is subjected to an internal water pressure of 3 MPa. Find the thickness of the plate if the permissible stress for wall plate is 120 MPa.   (t = 15 mm)

2. Calculate the minimum wall thickness of a thin cylindrical vessel 1000 mm in diameter to withstand an internal pressure of 2 MPa. The limiting values of circumferential and longitudinal stresses are 40 MPa and 25 MPa respectively.
                                    (t = 25 mm)

3. A water main 1000 mm in diameter contains water at a pressure head of 100 m. Find the thickness of the wall required if the permissible stress in the pipe material is 30 MPa. The unit weight of the water is 10 kN/m³.   (t = 16.67 mm)

4. A boiler of 1 m diameter contains fluid at a pressure of 2.5 MPa. If the safe stress in tension for boiler material is 100 MPa, find the thickness of the boiler plate.

                                                                                    (t = 12.5 mm)

5. A cylindrical compressed air drum is 2 m in diameter with plate thickness 12 mm. If the tensile stress in the plate is limited to 100 MPa, find the maximum safe air pressure inside the drum.   (p = 1.2 MPa)

6. A thin cylindrical shell of internal diameter 1200 mm and length 3000 mm has plate thickness of 12 mm. It is subjected to an internal fluid pressure of 2 MPa. Calculate circumferential, longitudinal and shear stress induced in the material, circumferential and longitudinal strains, and increase in diameter, length and capacity of the shell. Take   E = 200 GPa and μ = 0.25.

                (f_c = 100 MPa, f_L = 50 MPa, τ = 25 MPa, e_c = 0.0004375, e_L = 0.000125,
                          δd = 0.525 mm, δL = 0.375 mm, δV = 3392920.1 mm³)

7. A gravity main is 2000 mm in diameter and 15 mm in thickness. It is subjected to an internal pressure of 1.5 MPa. Calculate the hoop and longitudinal stresses induced in the pipe material. If the factor of safety 4 was used in design, what is ultimate tensile stress of the pipe material ?   (f_c = 100 MPa, f_L = 50 MPa, U = 400 MPa)

8. Calculate the circumferential and longitudinal strains for a boiler shell of 1000 mm diameter, when it is subjected to an internal pressure of 1 MPa. The wall thickness is such that the safe maximum tensile stress in the boiler material is 35 MPa. E = 200 GPa, μ = 0.25.   (e_c = 0.0001531, e_L = 0.00004375)

9. A thin cylindrical shell 1500 mm in diameter and 8000 mm long is subjected to an internal fluid pressure to produce a hoop stress of 80 MPa. Find
   (a) increase in the diameter,
   (b) increase in the length, and
   (c) increase in the volume.
   Take E = 210 GPa and μ = 0.28
                ((a) δd = 0.0004914 mm, (b) δL = 0.6705 mm, (c) δV = 3325714.3 mm)

10. A factory boiler shell of length 10 m and diameter 4 m is subjected to a uniform internal pressure of 2 MPa. The thickness of plate is 20 mm.
    Calculate :
    (a) hoop stress, (b) longitudinal stress, (c) change in the volume.
    Take E = GPa, μ = 0.25.
                ((a) f_c = 200 MPa, (b) f_L = 100 MPa, (c) δV = 2.51327 × 10⁸ mm)

11. A cylindrical shell, 600 mm diameter, 10 mm thickness and 2500 mm long is subjected to an internal fluid pressure of 1.5 MPa. Calculate the change in (a) length, (b) diameter. Take E = 200 GPa, μ = 0.25.   ((a) δL = 0.1406 mm, (b) δd = 0.1181 mm)

12. A steel cylinder having 1 m diameter and 10 mm thickness is filled with water under a pressure of 2 MPa. Calculate :

    (a) Circumferential stress and strain

    (b) Longitudinal stress and strain. E = 200 GPa, μ = 0.3.

    ((a) f_C = 100 MPa, e_C = 0.000425, (b) f_L = 50 MPa, e_L = 0.0001)

13. The cylinder of a hydraulic press has internal diameter of 500 mm and wall thickness of 20 mm. If it has to sustain a pressure of 6 MPa, find

    (a) the maximum tensile stress developed in the wall of the cylinder, and

    (b) maximum shear stress, if any.   ((a) $f_{t\ max}$ = f_C = 75 MPa, (b) τ = 18.75 MPa)

14. In a thin cylindrical shell under internal pressure p, the hoop strain is 0.035 and the longitudinal strain is 0.010. Find the percentage change in the volume.   (8%)

15. In a thin cylinder, with usual notations, show that the increase in the capacity due to internal pressure is given by –

$$\frac{\pi\,p\,d^3\,L}{4\,t\,E}$$

    provided Poisson's ratio is 0.25.

16. In a thin cylindrical shell under some internal pressure, if the maximum shear stress is 25 MPa, find the hoop and longitudinal stresses.   (100 MPa, 50 MPa)

17. A thin cylindrical container has 2000 mm diameter and 20 mm thickness of plate. If it contains a liquid under the pressure of 2 MPa, find (i) hoop stress, (ii) longitudinal stress and (iii) shear stress.   (100 MPa, 50 MPa, 25 MPa)

18. Calculate the minimum wall thickness of a thin cylinder 1200 mm in diameter to withstand an internal pressure of 2 MPa. The hoop stress should not exceed 42 MPa and the longitudinal stress should not exceed 30 MPa.   (28.57 mm)

19. A water main 1000 mm in diameter contains water at a pressure head of 120 m. Find the thickness of metal if the unit weight of water is 10 kN/m³. The working stress in the pipe metal is 30 MPa.

20. At a point in a thin cylindrical shell subjected to internal radial pressure, the value of hoop strain was 600 × 10⁻⁶ tensile. Compute the values of hoop and longitudinal stresses. How much is the percentage change in the volume of the cylinder ?
    Take E = 200 GPa and μ = 0.2857.   (140 MPa, 70 MPa, 0.135%)

21. The change in the volume of a thin walled cylinder : 1200 mm long, 150 mm diameter, 5 mm thickness is 15000 mm³ when the internal pressure is p. If Poisson's ratio for the material is 0.28 and E = 210 GPa, find the value of p.   (15.84 MPa)

22. A thin cylindrical vessel of 1500 mm diameter and 4000 mm length is subjected to an internal fluid pressure of 3 MPa. If the maximum principal stress is not to exceed 150 MPa, find the minimum thickness of the vessel. Also find the increase in diameter, length and volume of the vessel. Take E = 200 GPa and Poisson's ratio = 0.25.   (t = 15 mm, δd = 0.9844 mm, δL = 0.75 mm, δV = 10602875 mm³)

23. Calculate the circumferential and longitudinal strains for a boiler shell of 1000 mm diameter when it is subjected to an internal pressure of 2 MPa. The wall thickness is such that the maximum tensile stress in the shell material is limited to 50 MPa. Take E = 200 GPa and μ = 0.25.   (e_c = 0.000219, e_L = 0.0000625)

24. A thin cylindrical shell 1200 mm in diameter and 6000 mm in length is subjected to an internal pressure to produce a hoop stress of 40 MPa. At this pressure in the cylinder, find : (a) increase in the diameter, (b) increase in the length, (c) increase in the capacity. Take E = 205 GPa and μ = 0.30.

$$(δd = 0.199 \text{ mm}, δL = 0.2341 \text{ mm}, δV = 2515726.1 \text{ mm}^3)$$

25. A steel cylinder 150 mm in diameter and 1200 mm long is made from the plates of 6 mm thickness. It is subjected to an internal pressure of 12 MPa. If the increase in the volume of the cylinder is 31.809 × 10^3, find the value of Poisson's ratio. Also calculate the corresponding changes in diameter and length of the cylinder. Take E = 200 GPa.   (μ = 0.25, δd = 0.098 mm, δL = 0.225 mm)

26. A steel cylinder 250 mm internal diameter is to withstand an internal pressure of 5 MPa. The increase in the area of the bore due to resulting radial expansion is limited to 0.1% of the original area. Calculate the necessary thickness of the cylinder and the hoop stress induced. Take E = 200 GPa and μ = 0.25

$$(t = 5.47 \text{ mm}, f_c = 114.28 \text{ MPa})$$

27. A cylindrical shell, 150 mm diameter, thickness of metal 5 mm, 900 mm long, is filled with an incompressible fluid at atmospheric pressure. If an additional quantity of 10,000 mm³ of fluid is pumped into the cylinder, calculate the pressure exerted by the fluid on the wall of the cylinder. Also calculate the hoop stress induced. Take E = 210 GPa and μ = 0.25.   (p = 4.40 MPa, f_c = 66 MPa)

28. A thin cylinder of 150 mm internal diameter and 2.5 mm thick has its ends closed by rigid plates and is then filled with water. When an external axial pull of 37150 N is applied to the ends, the water pressure is observed to fall by 0.101 MPa. If E for material of cylinder is 140 GPa and K for water 2.2 GPa, compute the value of Poisson's ratio, if the structural behaviour is in the elastic range. (μ = 0.3075 say 0.31)

29. A spherical steel container has internal diameter of 600 mm and wall thickness of 10 mm. It is being filled with a fluid under a pressure of 5 MPa. The pressure is reduced gradually by letting out some water. To reduce the pressure to atmospheric, find the quantity of fluid required to be let out if K, the bulk modulus for the fluid is 2 GPa. Take E, the modulus of elasticity of steel as 200 GPa and Poisson's ratio = 0.30.   (371806.39 mm³)

30. A seamless spherical shell 1200 mm in diameter is subjected to an internal pressure of 4 MPa. If the permissible stress in tension for the material of shell is 120 MPa, find the thickness of plate.   (10 mm)

31. A spherical shell is 600 mm diameter and has wall thickness 6 mm. If the tensile stress is limited to 60 MPa, calculate the safe working pressure of the inside fluid. Also find the increase in volume of the sphere due to this pressure. E = 210 GPa, μ = 0.3. (2.40 MPa, 6758.40 mm³)

32. A spherical shell 1000 mm in diameter is 10 mm thick. It is being filled with water under pressure until its volume increases by 10^6 mm³. Calculate the pressure exerted by the water on the shell. E = 200 GPa, μ = 0.30. (7.28 MPa)

33. A spherical shell 1000 mm in diameter and 5 mm thick is filled with a fluid under a pressure of 1 MPa. If E = 210 GPa and Poisson's ratio = 0.28, find the increase in the capacity of the shell. (269279.37 mm³)

34. A pipe of 150 mm internal diameter with the thickness of metal 50 mm transmits water under a pressure of 6 MPa. Calculate the maximum and minimum intensities of circumferential stress induced. (12.75 MPa, 6.75 MPa)

35. The cylinder of a hydraulic press is 400 mm in diameter and has to sustain a pressure of 8 MPa. If the safe stress for the material is 72 MPa, calculate the necessary thickness. **Ans.** 24 mm

36. Show that the maximum shear stress in the wall of a thick cylinder subjected to internal pressure occurs at the inner face and is $\frac{1}{2}$ $(p_1 + f_1)$, where p_1 and f_1 are the maximum radial and hoop stresses respectively.

37. A pipe of 400 mm internal diameter and 600 mm external diameter contains a fluid at a pressure of 10 MPa. Find the maximum and minimum hoop stresses across the section. **Ans.** 26 MPa, 16 MPa

38. Find the thickness of the metal of a cylindrical shell of internal diameter 200 mm to withstand an internal pressure of 50 MPa if the maximum hoop stress is limited to 150 MPa. (42 MPa)

◈ ◈ ◈

STRAIN ENERGY

3.1 INTRODUCTION

When a load is applied on any elastic member, there is deformation. The kind of deformation, that the member undergoes, depends on the type of load applied. For example, axial load causes elongation or contraction of the member depending on whether the axial load is tensile or compressive in nature. Similarly, torsional moment causes angular deformation called as twist. Bending moment also causes angular deformation. Thus, the applied load does some work on a member. When the external loads are removed, member has a capacity to regain its original shape, provided the loads were applied within elastic limit. Thus, the work done on a member is stored in the body as energy and that is why body has capacity to regain its original size and shape. This stored energy, which is by virtue of strain, is called as *strain energy*. Our main interest in this chapter is to study strain energy due to axial force.

3.2 STRAIN ENERGY DUE TO AXIAL FORCE

When a member is subjected to axial load, it undergoes axial deformation i.e. change in length. Also, resistance is set up in the member gradually. Within the limit of proportionality, the relation between resistance set up and deformation is always linear as shown in Fig. 3.1.

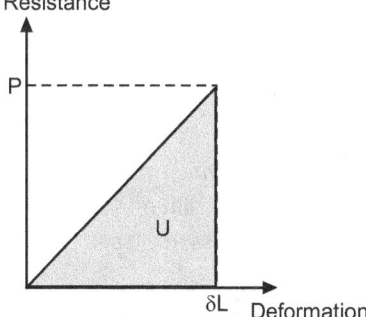

Fig. 3.1 : Relation between resistance and deformation within elastic limit

Symbols :

R	=	Resistance
σ	=	Normal stress
A	=	Cross sectional area
δL	=	Axial deformation
L	=	Length of member
E	=	Young's modulus of elasticity
P	=	Applied load

$$U = \text{Strain energy}$$

From Fig. 3.1, area under resistance deformation diagram indicates strain energy U.

$$\therefore \qquad U = \frac{1}{2} R \cdot \delta L$$

$$= \frac{1}{2} (\sigma A) \, \delta L \qquad\qquad (\because R = \sigma A)$$

$$= \frac{1}{2} (\sigma A) \left(\frac{\sigma L}{E} \right) \qquad\qquad \left(\because \delta L = \frac{\sigma L}{E} \right)$$

$$= \frac{\sigma^2}{2E} \cdot (AL)$$

$$= \frac{\sigma^2}{2E} \cdot \text{Volume} \qquad\qquad (\because \text{Volume} = AL)$$

OR

$$U = \frac{1}{2} \sigma A \cdot \delta L \times \frac{L}{L} \qquad\qquad \text{(multiply and divide by L)}$$

$$= \frac{1}{2} \cdot \sigma \cdot \varepsilon \cdot AL \qquad\qquad \left(\because \text{linear strain} = \varepsilon = \frac{\delta L}{L} \right)$$

$$= \frac{1}{2} \sigma \cdot \varepsilon \cdot \text{Volume}$$

Thus, various forms of expression of strain energy are,

$$U = \frac{1}{2} \sigma A \cdot \delta L \qquad\qquad \dots \text{(3.1 a)}$$

OR

$$U = \frac{\sigma^2}{2E} \cdot \text{Volume} \qquad\qquad \dots \text{(3.1 b)}$$

OR

$$U = \frac{1}{2} \sigma \cdot \varepsilon \cdot \text{Volume} \qquad\qquad \dots \text{(3.1 c)}$$

Unit of strain energy is Nm.

3.3 PROOF RESILIENCE

It is defined as the *maximum strain energy which can be stored by a body without undergoing permanent deformation*. Obviously, it is the strain energy at elastic limit.

Let $\qquad\qquad F_y = \text{Stress at elastic limit}$

$$\therefore \qquad \textbf{Proof resilience} = \frac{F_y^2}{2E} \cdot \textbf{Volume} \qquad\qquad \dots \text{(3.2)}$$

Unit of proof resilience is same as that of strain energy i.e. Nm.

3.4 MODULUS OF RESILIENCE

It is defined as *proof resilience per unit volume*.

$$\therefore \qquad \textbf{Modulus of resilience} = \frac{F_y^2}{2E} \qquad\qquad \dots \text{(3.3)}$$

Unit of Modulus of resilience is MPa.

3.5 STRESS DUE TO VARIOUS TYPES OF AXIAL LOADS

3.5.1 Gradually Applied Load

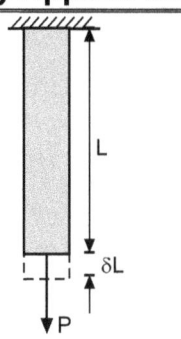

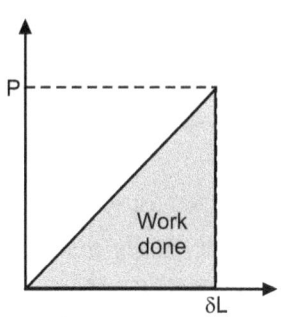

(a) Gradually applied axial load

(b) Relation between gradual load and deformation within elastic limit

Fig. 3.2

Let the load P be gradually applied to a member of uniform cross-sectional area A and length L which means magnitude of P increases from zero to final value P. Initially, when load P is zero, the corresponding deformation is also zero. When the magnitude of load is equal to P, the corresponding deformation is δL. Fig. 3.2 (b) shows this relation of gradually applied load and corresponding deformation.

Equating work done to strain energy,

$$\frac{1}{2} \, P \cdot \delta L \;=\; \frac{1}{2} \, \sigma A \cdot \delta L$$

$$\therefore \qquad\qquad \sigma \;=\; \frac{P}{A} \qquad\qquad\qquad\qquad \ldots (3.4)$$

3.5.2 Suddenly Applied Load

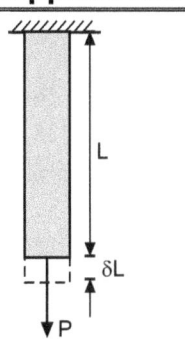

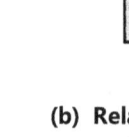

(a) Suddenly applied axial load

(b) Relation between suddenly applied load and deformation within elastic limit

Fig. 3.3

Let, the load P be suddenly applied to a member of uniform cross-sectional area A and length L. In this case, magnitude of load P is constant throughout the process of extension. Fig. 3.3 (b) shows this relation of gradually applied load and corresponding deformation.

Equating work done to strain energy,

$$\therefore \quad P \cdot \delta L = \frac{1}{2} \sigma \cdot A \cdot \delta L$$

$$\therefore \quad \sigma = \frac{2P}{A} \qquad \qquad \text{... (3.5)}$$

It is important here to note that stress produced by suddenly applied load is twice that of gradually applied load. After the instantaneous extension due to suddenly applied load, the state of equilibrium is not reached. As the force of resistance is double the applied load, it sets the motion of vibration into a member like suddenly loaded spring. The equation (3.5) gives maximum instantaneous stress developed in a member due to suddenly applied load.

3.5.3 Impact Load

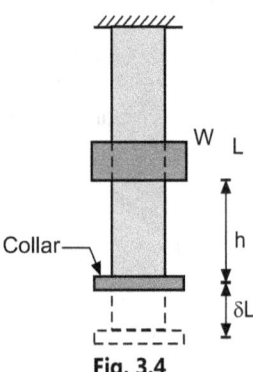

Fig. 3.4

Let the load W fall freely through a distance h before it strikes the rigid collar attached at the bottom of the bar as shown in Fig. 3.4. This is the case of impact loading.

$$\text{Work done} = W (h + \delta L)$$

$$\text{Strain energy} = \frac{1}{2} \sigma A \cdot \delta L$$

Equation of instantaneous stress produced by impact load can be derived by equating work done to strain energy and substituting $\delta L = \frac{\sigma L}{E}$.

$$W \left(h + \frac{\sigma L}{E} \right) = \frac{1}{2} \sigma A \cdot \frac{\sigma L}{E}$$

$$\therefore \quad \frac{\sigma^2}{2E} \cdot AL - \left(\frac{WL}{E} \right) \sigma = Wh$$

$$\sigma^2 - \left(\frac{2W}{A} \right) \sigma = \frac{2WhE}{AL}$$

$$\therefore \quad \left(\sigma - \frac{W}{A} \right)^2 = \frac{2WhE}{AL} + \frac{W^2}{A^2}$$

$$\therefore \quad \sigma - \frac{W}{A} = \pm \sqrt{\frac{2WhE}{AL} + \frac{W^2}{A^2}}$$

$$\therefore \quad \sigma = \frac{W}{A} \pm \sqrt{\frac{2WhE}{AL} + \frac{W^2}{A^2}} \qquad \text{... (3.6)}$$

Other form of equation (3.6) can be derived as,

$$\sigma = \frac{W}{A} \pm \sqrt{\frac{2\,WhE}{AL} \cdot \frac{WA}{WA} + \frac{W^2}{A^2}}$$

$$= \frac{W}{A} \pm \sqrt{\frac{2\,h}{WL/AE} \cdot \frac{W^2}{A^2} + \frac{W^2}{A^2}}$$

$$= \frac{W}{A}\left[1 \pm \sqrt{\frac{2\,h}{\delta_{st}} + 1}\right] \qquad \text{... (3.7)}$$

where, δ_{st} = Axial deformation produced by gradually applied load called

as axial deformation produced by static load = $\dfrac{WL}{AE}$

It should be noted that, in equation (3.7) if h = 0,

$$\sigma = \frac{2W}{A} = \text{Instantaneous stress produced by suddenly applied load.}$$

SOLVED EXAMPLES

Example 3.1 : *A vertical steel bar 1.5 m long is fixed at top. A weight can slide freely along the rod and its fall is arrested at the bottom by collar. When weight falls through 40 mm, the maximum instantaneous stress developed in the bar is 200 MPa. Determine the stress in the same bar when same weight is (i) gradually applied; (ii) suddenly applied; (iii) with free fall of 50 mm.*

Data   : L = 1.5 m = 1500 mm ; h = 40 mm which produces σ_{max} = 200 MPa ;

E = 200 GPa.

Required : Maximum stress for gradually applied; suddenly applied load and maximum stress with the same weight falling through height of 50 mm.

Concept : Knowing instantaneous stress σ_{max} = 200 MPa for h = 40 mm, find $\dfrac{W}{A}$

and then evaluate stresses for different types of loads applied.

Solution : (i) For   h = 40 mm ; σ_{max} = 200 MPa

$$\sigma_{max} = \frac{W}{A} \pm \sqrt{\frac{2\,WhE}{AL} + \frac{W^2}{A^2}}$$

$$200 = \frac{W}{A} \pm \sqrt{\frac{2 \times W \times 40 \times 200 \times 10^3}{A \times 1500} + \frac{W^2}{A^2}}$$

Let, $\dfrac{W}{A}$ = x

∴ $200 = x \pm \sqrt{10.67 \times 10^3\,(x) + x^2}$

$(200 - x)^2 = 10.67 \times 10^3\,(x) + x^2$

$40 \times 10^3 - 400\,x + x^2 = 10.67 \times 10^3\,(x) + x^2$

$40 \times 10^3 - 400\,x = 10.67 \times 10^3\,(x)$

∴   x   = 3.62 MPa

$$\frac{W}{A} = 3.62 \text{ MPa}$$

(ii) σ_{max} when load is gradually applied :

$$\sigma_{max} = \frac{W}{A} = 3.62 \text{ MPa}$$

(iii) σ_{max} when load is suddenly applied :

$$\sigma_{max} = \frac{2W}{A} = 2 \times 3.62$$

$$= 7.24 \text{ MPa}$$

(iv) σ_{max} when load falls through height of 50 mm :

$$\sigma_{max} = \frac{W}{A} \pm \sqrt{\frac{2\,WhE}{AL} + \frac{W^2}{A^2}}$$

$$= 3.62 \pm \sqrt{\frac{2 \times 3.62 \times 50 \times 200 \times 10^3}{(1500)} + (3.62)^2}$$

$$= \mathbf{223.35 \ MPa}$$

Example 3.2 : *Water under pressure of 10 MPa is suddenly admitted on to a plunger of 100 mm diameter, attached to a rod 28 mm diameter, 3 m long. Find the maximum instantaneous stress and deformation of the rod if E = 210 GPa.*

Data   :   Water pressure p = 10 MPa ; Diameter of plunger = 100 mm; Diameter of rod = 28 mm ; Length of rod = L = 3000 mm ; E = 210 GPa.

Required :   Maximum instantaneous stress and elongation for rod.

Concept :   Knowing pressure intensity and area of plunger, find force on the rod.

Stress due to suddenly applied load = $\sigma = \dfrac{2\,P}{A}$.

Solution :   (i) Geometric properties :

Cross-sectional area of plunger $= \dfrac{\pi}{4} (100)^2 = 7853.98 \text{ mm}^2$

Cross-sectional area of rod $= \dfrac{\pi}{4} (28)^2 = 615.75 \text{ mm}^2$

(ii)   Force on rod 'P'   P   = Water pressure × C/s area of plunger

$$= 10 \times 7853.98$$

$$= 78539.8 \text{ N}$$

(iii) Maximum instantaneous stress for rod,

$$\sigma_{max} = \frac{2\,P}{A} \qquad \text{... (\textbf{Note :} Sudden application of force)}$$

$$= \frac{2 \times 78539.8}{615.75}$$

$$= 255.1 \text{ MPa}$$

(iv) Maximum instantaneous elongation,

$$\delta L = \frac{\sigma \cdot L}{E} = \frac{255.1 \times 3000}{210 \times 10^3}$$

$$= \textbf{3.64 mm}$$

Example 3.3 : *A bar 50 mm in diameter, 2 m long has to transmit shock energy of 100 joules. Calculate maximum instantaneous stress developed and maximum elongation if E = 200 GPa.*

Data   : d = 50 mm ; L = 2000 mm ; U = 100 joules

$\therefore$ U = 100 Nm = 100×10^3 Nmm;   E = 200 GPa

Required : σ_{max} and δL_{max}.

Concept : Equate shock energy to strain energy and find maximum instantaneous stress and hence elongation.

Solution : (i) Maximum instantaneous stress :

$$\text{Strain energy} = \frac{\sigma_{max}^2}{2\,E} \times \text{Volume}$$

$$100 \times 10^3 = \frac{\sigma_{max}^2}{2 \times 200 \times 10^3} \times \frac{\pi}{4}\,(50)^2 \times 2000$$

$$\therefore \qquad\qquad \sigma_{max} = 100.9 \text{ MPa}$$

(ii) Maximum elongation :

$$\delta L_{max} = \frac{\sigma_{max} \cdot L}{E}$$

$$= \frac{100.9 \times 2000}{200 \times 10^3}$$

$$= \textbf{1 mm}$$

Example 3.4 : *A vertically suspended steel bar, circular in cross section, is subjected to load of 5 kN which falls by 20 mm on rigid collar provided at lower end of bar. If maximum allowable strain for bar is $\frac{1}{1250}$, find suitable diameter of rod.*

Assume E = 200 GPa and length of bar = 2 m.

Data : $W = 5 \, kN$; $h = 20 \, mm$; $Strain = \dfrac{1}{1250}$;

$E = 200 \, GPa$; $L = 2000 \, mm$ as shown in Fig. 3.5

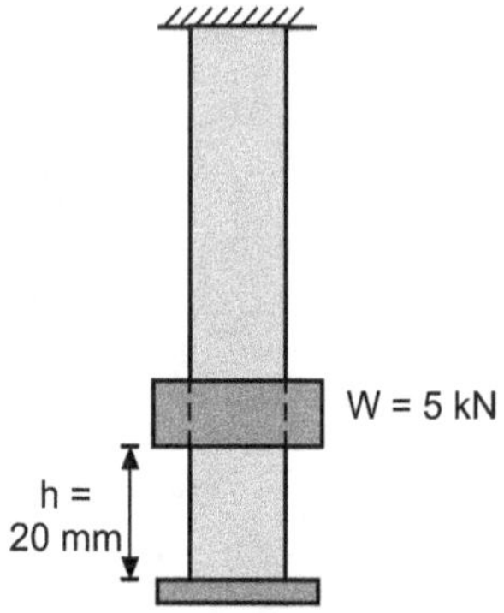

Required : Diameter of bar.

Concept : Knowing strain, elongation and stress for the bar can be obtained, then use basic work equation.

Solution : (i) Work equation :

$$W \, (h + \delta L) = \frac{\sigma^2}{2 \, E} \times Volume$$

where $\delta L = Strain \times L$

$$= \frac{1}{1250} \times 2000$$

$$= 1.6 \, mm$$

$$\sigma = Strain \times E$$

$$= \frac{1}{1250} \times 200 \times 10^3 = 160 \, MPa$$

Substituting,

$$5 \times 10^3 \times (20 + 1.6) = \frac{(160)^2}{2 \times 200 \times 10^3} \times \frac{\pi}{4} \, (\phi)^2 \times 2000$$

$$\phi = \textbf{32.78 mm}$$

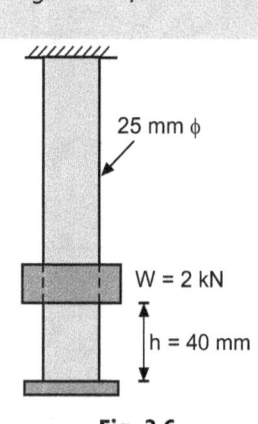

W = 5 kN

h = 20 mm

Fig. 3.5

Example 3.5 : *A bar of 25 mm diameter stretches 2 mm under gradually applied load of 65 kN. If a weight of 2 kN is dropped on to a collar at the lower end of this bar, through a height of 40 mm, calculate maximum instantaneous stress and elongation of bar. Assume E = 200 GPa.*

Data : $\phi = 25 \, mm$; $\delta L = 2 \, mm$ for gradually applied load of 65 kN; $W = 2 \, kN$; $h = 40 \, mm$; $E = 200 \, GPa$ as shown in Fig. 3.6.

Required : Maximum instantaneous stress and elongation.

Concept : Length of bar can be obtained by knowing elongation due to gradually applied load ; then use standard formulae for impact loading.

25 mm ϕ

W = 2 kN

h = 40 mm

Fig. 3.6

Solution : (i) Geometric properties

$$A = \frac{\pi}{4} (25)^2 = 490.87 \text{ mm}^2$$

(ii) Gradually applied load

$$\delta L = \frac{PL}{AE}$$

$$2 = \frac{65 \times 10^3 \times L}{490.87 \times 200 \times 10^3}$$

∴　　　　$$L = 3020.76 \text{ mm}$$

(iii) Stress for impact loading,

$$\sigma = \frac{W}{A} \pm \sqrt{\frac{2 WhE}{AL} + \frac{W^2}{A^2}}$$

$$= \frac{2 \times 10^3}{490.87} \pm \sqrt{\frac{2 \times 2 \times 10^3 \times 40 \times 200 \times 10^3}{490.87 \times 3020.76} + \left(\frac{2000}{490.87}\right)^2}$$

$$= 151.03 \text{ MPa}$$

(iv) Elongation for impact loading,

$$\delta L = \frac{\sigma L}{E} = \frac{151.03 \times 3020.76}{200 \times 10^3}$$

$$\delta L = \mathbf{2.281 \text{ mm}}$$

Example 3.6 : *A vertical steel bar 16 mm diameter; 1.5 m long is provided with a collar at lower end. Find the maximum weight that can be dropped through a height of 100 mm over the collar if maximum permissible tensile stress is 150 MPa. Assume E = 200 GPa.*

Data : $\phi = 16$ mm ; $L = 1500$ mm ; $h = 100$ mm

$\sigma_{max} = 150$ MPa ; $E = 200$ GPa

as shown in Fig. 3.7.

Required : Weight W.

Concept : Standard formulae.

Solution : (i) Geometric properties :

$$A = \frac{\pi}{4} (16)^2 = 201.06 \text{ mm}^2$$

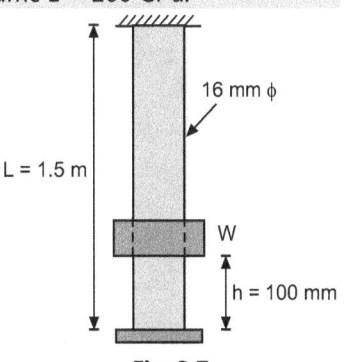

L = 1.5 m

16 mm φ

W

h = 100 mm

Fig. 3.7

(ii) Maximum weight : $\sigma_{max} = \frac{W}{A} \pm \sqrt{\frac{2 WhE}{AL} + \frac{W^2}{A^2}}$

Let　　　　$$\frac{W}{A} = x$$

$$150 \ = \ x \pm \sqrt{\frac{2x \times 100 \times 200 \times 10^3}{1500} + x^2}$$

$$150 \ = \ x \pm \sqrt{26.67 \times 10^3 x + x^2}$$

$$(150 - x)^2 \ = \ 26.67 \times 10^3 x + x^2$$

$$22500 - 300 x + x^2 = 26.67 \times 10^3 x + x^2$$

$$x \ = \ 0.834 \ = \ \frac{W}{A}$$

$\therefore$

$$W \ = \ 0.834 \times 201.06$$

$$W \ = \ \textbf{167.75 N}$$

Example 3.7 : *A steel specimen 16 mm ϕ stretches by 0.12 mm over 150 mm length under an axial load of 35 kN. Calculate the strain energy stored in the specimen at this stage. If the load at the elastic limit for the specimen is 50 kN, calculate the elongation at elastic limit and the proof resilience.*

Data   : $\phi = 16$ mm ; for W = 35 kN; δL = 0.12 mm ;

L = 150 mm ; for elastic limit W = 50 kN.

Required : Strain energy of bar for W = 35 kN; elongation at elastic limit; proof resilience.

Concept   : Standard formula.

Solution : (i) Geometric properties :

$$A \ = \ \frac{\pi}{4} \ (16)^2 = 201.06 \ mm^2$$

(ii) Strain energy of bar for W = 35 kN :

$$U \ = \ \frac{1}{2} \ W \cdot \delta L$$

$$= \frac{1}{2} \times 35 \times 10^3 \times 0.12$$

$$= \ 2100 \ \ Nmm$$

$$= \ 2.1 \ Nm$$

$$= \ 2.1 \ J$$

(iii) Elongation at elastic limit :

Elongation due to 35 kN load = 0.12 mm

$\therefore$ Elongation due to 50 kN load $= 0.12 \times \dfrac{50}{35}$

$$= \ 0.171 \ mm$$

(iv)   Proof resilience = Maximum strain energy stored in the member at elastic limit

$$= \frac{1}{2} \cdot W \cdot \delta L$$

$$= \frac{1}{2} \times 50 \times 10^3 \times 0.171$$

$$= 4275 \text{ Nmm}$$

$$= \textbf{4.275 Nm} = \textbf{4.275 J}$$

Example 3.8 : *A uniform bar of cross-sectional area 500 mm² is 2.5 m long. Find the proof resilience and modulus of resilience, if the elastic limit for the bar material is 250 MPa. Also find maximum value of suddenly applied load that the member can carry.*

Assume E = 200 GPa.

Data   :   A = 500 mm² ; L = 2.5 m = 2500 mm ; F_y = 250 MPa ; E = 200 GPa.

Required :   Proof resilience, modulus of resilience and suddenly applied load.

Concept :   Standard formulae.

Solution :   (i) Proof resilience :

$$U_{max} = \frac{\sigma_{max}^2}{2E} \times \text{Volume}$$

$$= \frac{(250)^2}{2 \times 200 \times 10^3} (500 \times 2500)$$

$$= 195312.5 \text{ Nmm}$$

$$= 195.312 \text{ Nm}$$

$$= 195.312 \text{ J}$$

(ii)   Modulus of resilience = Maximum strain energy per unit volume

$$= \frac{\sigma_{max}^2}{2E}$$

$$= \frac{(250)^2}{2 \times 200 \times 10^3}$$

$$= 0.156 \text{ MPa}$$

(iii) Maximum suddenly applied load,

$$\sigma_{max} = \frac{2P}{A}$$

$$250 = \frac{2P}{500}$$

$\therefore$ P = 62500 N

= **62.5 kN**

Example 3.9 : Show that for a member subjected to principal stresses σ_1 and σ_2, the strain energy per unit volume is given by $\dfrac{1}{2E}\left(\sigma_1^2 + \sigma_2^2 - 2\mu\,\sigma_1\,\sigma_2\right)$

where E = Young's modulus

and μ = Poisson's ratio

Data : Principal stresses are σ_1 and σ_2.

Required : Strain energy per unit volume.

Concept : Generalised Hook's law and $U = \dfrac{1}{2}\,\sigma \cdot E$

Solution : (i) Principal strains :

$$\varepsilon_1 = \frac{1}{E}\,(\sigma_1 - \mu\,\sigma_2)$$

$$\varepsilon_2 = \frac{1}{E}\,(\sigma_2 - \mu\,\sigma_1)$$

(ii) Strain energy per unit volume :

$$U = \frac{1}{2}\,\sigma_1\,\varepsilon_1 + \frac{1}{2}\,\sigma_2\,\varepsilon_2$$

$$= \frac{1}{2}\,\sigma_1\left[\frac{1}{E}\,(\sigma_1 - \mu\,\sigma_2)\right] + \frac{1}{2}\,\sigma_2\left[\frac{1}{E}\,(\sigma_2 - \mu\,\sigma_1)\right]$$

$$U = \frac{1}{2E}\left[\sigma_1^2 + \sigma_2^2 - 2\mu\,\sigma_1\,\sigma_2\right]$$

Example 3.10 : Determine the diameter of aluminium shaft designed to store same amount of strain energy per unit volume as that of 50 mm ϕ steel bar of same length, when both shafts are subjected to same axial load.

Take $E_S = 200$ GPa and $E_A = 67$ GPa.

Also find the ratio of stresses developed in two bars.

Data : Diameter of steel shaft = 50 mm ; E_S = 200 GPa ; E_A = 67 GPa ; $U_A = U_S$

Required : Diameter of aluminium shaft and ratio of stresses developed.

Concept : Equate strain energy of aluminium and steel shaft and get relation between stresses and then find diameter of aluminium shaft.

Solution : (i) Ratio of stresses :

$$U_A = U_S \text{ for unit volume}$$

$\therefore$
$$\left(\frac{\sigma_{max}^2}{2E}\right)_A = \left(\frac{\sigma_{max}^2}{2E}\right)_S$$

$$\frac{\left(\sigma_{max}^{2}\right)_A}{2 \times 67 \times 10^3} = \frac{\left(\sigma_{max}^{2}\right)_S}{2 \times 200 \times 10^3}$$

$$(\sigma_{max})_A = (0.578)\,(\sigma_{max})_S$$

$\therefore$

$$\frac{(\sigma_{max})_A}{(\sigma_{max})_S} = 0.578$$

OR

$$\frac{(\sigma_{max})_S}{(\sigma_{max})_A} = 1.727$$

(ii) Diameter of aluminium shaft :

$$\left(\frac{P}{A}\right)_A = 0.578 \left(\frac{P}{A}\right)_S \qquad\qquad (\because\ P_A = P_S)$$

$\therefore$

$$\frac{1}{\frac{\pi}{4}\,(\phi)_A^2} = 0.578 \left(\frac{1}{\frac{\pi}{4}\,(50)^2}\right)$$

$\therefore$　　　　　　　　ϕ_A = **65.76 mm**

Example 3.11 : *A copper rod 30 mm diameter is enclosed in a steel tube 45 mm internal diameter and 5 mm thickness. The length of composite member is 2 m. It is fixed at top and provided with a rigid collar at bottom. A body of mass 50 kg is allowed to slide down freely through a height (h). If maximum instantaneous stress developed in copper is not to exceed 75 MPa, find height and elongation of composite bar. Take E_S = 200 GPa and E_C = 120 GPa.*

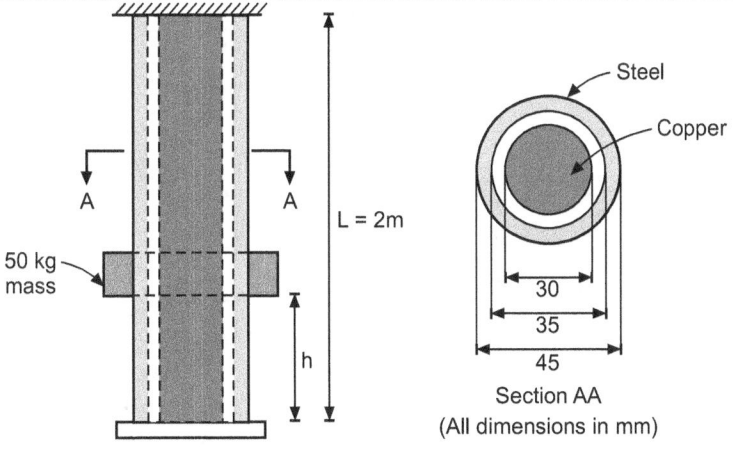

Fig. 3.8

Data　　　: As shown in Fig. 3.8.

Required : h and δL.

Concept : Use basic work equation along with compatibility as $(\delta L)_S = (\delta L)_C$.

Solution : (i) Geometric properties :

$$A_c = \frac{\pi}{4} (30)^2 = 706.85 \text{ mm}^2$$

$$A_s = \frac{\pi}{4} [(45)^2 - (35)^2] = 628.32 \text{ mm}^2$$

(ii) Work equation :

$$W (h + \delta L) = \left(\frac{\sigma_{max}^2}{2 E} \times \text{Volume}\right)_c + \left(\frac{\sigma_{max}^2}{2 E} \times \text{Volume}\right)_s$$

We have, $(\delta L)_c = (\delta L)_s$

$\therefore$ $\sigma_s = \dfrac{E_s}{E_c} \times \sigma_c$

$$= \frac{200}{120} \times 75$$

$$= 125 \text{ MPa}$$

Also, $W = 50 \text{ kg}$

$$= 50 \times 9.81 = 490.5 \text{ N}$$

Instantaneous elongation $= \delta L = \left(\dfrac{\sigma L}{E}\right)_c = \left(\dfrac{\sigma L}{E}\right)_s$

$$= \frac{75 \times 2000}{120 \times 10^3} = 1.25 \text{ mm}$$

Substituting,

$$490.5 (h + 1.25) = \frac{(75)^2}{2 \times 120 \times 10^3} \times 706.85 \times 2000 + \frac{(125)^2}{2 \times 200 \times 10^3} \times 628.32 \times 2000$$

$$490.5 (h + 1.25) = 82.22 \times 10^3$$

$\therefore$ $h = \textbf{166.37 mm}$

Example 3.12 : *A vertical steel rod 1.5 m long is fixed at top and provided with collar at bottom. The upper 900 mm length of bar is 28 mm φ, while the lower 600 mm bar is 16 mm φ. A weight of magnitude 150 N falls freely through a height of 60 mm. Find*

(i) *Maximum instantaneous stress,*

(ii) *Maximum elongation,*

(iii) *Total strain energy stored.*

Assume E = 200 GPa

Data   :   As shown in Fig. 3.9.

Required : σ_{max}, δL_{max} and U

Concept :   Use of equation (3.7) where,

$$\delta_{st} = \left(\frac{PL}{AE}\right)_1 + \left(\frac{PL}{AE}\right)_2$$

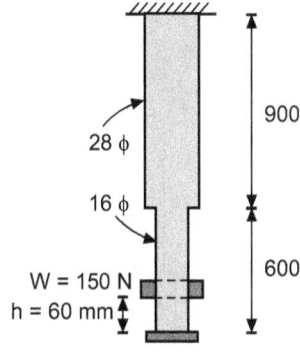

900

28 ϕ

16 ϕ

W = 150 N
h = 60 mm

600

(All dimensions in mm)

Fig. 3.9

Solution :   (i)   Geometric properties :

Let, $A_1 = \frac{\pi}{4}(28)^2 = 615.75$ mm^2

$A_2 = \frac{\pi}{4}(16)^2 = 201.06$ mm^2

(ii)   Maximum instantaneous stress,

$$\sigma_{max} = \frac{W}{A}\left[1 \pm \sqrt{1 + \frac{2h}{\delta_{st}}}\right]$$

where $\delta_{st} = \left(\frac{PL}{AE}\right)_1 + \left(\frac{PL}{AE}\right)_2$

$$= \left[\frac{150 \times 900}{615.75} + \frac{150 \times 600}{201.06}\right] \times \frac{1}{200 \times 10^3}$$

$$= 3.33 \times 10^{-3} \text{ mm}$$

∴ $\sigma_{max} = \frac{150}{201.06}\left[1 \pm \sqrt{1 + \frac{2 \times 60}{3.33 \times 10^{-3}}}\right]$

$$= 142.28 \text{ MPa}$$

Note : Maximum stress occurs in the portion of relatively smaller area.

(iii)   Maximum instantaneous elongation :

We have, $\sigma_1 A_1 = \sigma_2 A_2$

$\sigma_1 \times 615.75 = 142.28 \times 201.06$

$\sigma_1 = 46.46$ MPa

Now, $\delta L = \frac{1}{E}(\sigma_1 L_1 + \sigma_2 L_2)$

$$= \frac{1}{200 \times 10^3}(46.46 \times 900 + 142.28 \times 600) = 0.6359 \text{ mm}$$

(iv)   Total strain energy U :

$$U = W(h + \delta L)$$

$$= 150(60 + 0.6359) = 9095.3 \text{ Nmm}$$

$$= \textbf{9.09 J}$$

Example 3.13 : *A hammer of weight 75 N falls freely through a distance of 100 mm on a bar as shown in Fig. 3.10. Assuming E = 200 GPa, find instantaneous stress developed in bar at top and bottom.*

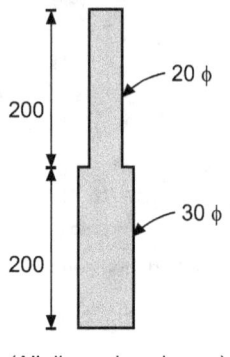

200

20 φ

30 φ

200

(All dimensions in mm)

Fig. 3.10

Data : W = 75 N ; h = 100 mm ;

E = 200 GPa

Required : Instantaneous stress at top and bottom.

Concept : Same as Example 3.12.

Solution : (i) Geometric properties :

$$A_1 = \frac{\pi}{4} (20)^2$$

$$= 314.16 \text{ mm}^2$$

$$A_2 = \frac{\pi}{4} (30)^2 = 706.86 \text{ mm}^2$$

(ii)   Stresses :

$$\sigma_{max} = \sigma_1 = \frac{W}{A}\left[1 + \sqrt{1 + \frac{2h}{\delta_{st}}}\right] \quad \{\textbf{Note :} \ \sigma_1 > \sigma_2\}$$

where

$$\delta_{st} = \left(\frac{WL}{AE}\right)_1 + \left(\frac{WL}{AE}\right)_2$$

$$= \frac{75}{200 \times 10^3}\left[\frac{200}{314.16} + \frac{200}{706.86}\right]$$

$$= 3.448 \times 10^{-4}$$

∴　　　　　$$\sigma_{max} = \sigma_1 = \frac{75}{314.16}\left[1 + \sqrt{1 + \frac{2 \times 100}{3.448 \times 10^{-4}}}\right]$$

$$\sigma_1 = 182 \text{ MPa}$$

Also　　　　　$$\sigma_1 A_1 = \sigma_2 A_2$$

$$182 \times 314.16 = \sigma_2 \times 706.86$$

∴　　　　　$$\sigma_2 = \textbf{80.91 MPa}$$

Example 3.14 : *A uniform rod of cross-sectional area = A ; length = L is held vertically as shown in Fig. 3.11. Derive the expression for strain energy due to self weight. Assume Young's modulus of elasticity 'E' and mass density 'ρ'.*

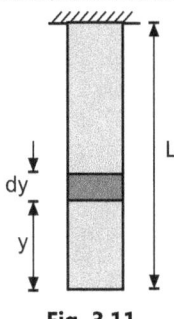

Data : A, L, E, ρ.

Required : Expression for strain energy due to self weight.

Concept : Strain energy due to self weight by integration.

Fig. 3.11

Solution : Consider an elementary strip of thickness 'dy' at a distance 'y' from bottom as shown in Fig. 3.11.

$$\text{Axial force on elementary strip} = F = \text{Volume below the strip} \times \text{Weight density}$$

$$= A \cdot y \cdot \rho \cdot g$$

$$\text{Normal stress on elementary strip} = \sigma = \frac{F}{\text{Cross-sectional area of strip}} = \frac{A \cdot y \cdot \rho \cdot g}{A}$$

$$\sigma = y \cdot \rho \cdot g$$

$$\text{Strain energy of strip} = dU = \frac{\sigma^2}{2\,E} \times \text{Volume of strip}$$

$$= \frac{(y\,\rho \cdot g)^2}{2\,E} \times (A \cdot dy)$$

$$\text{Strain energy of member} = U = \int_0^L dU = \int_0^L \frac{y^2\,\rho^2\,g^2 \cdot A}{2\,E} \cdot dy$$

$$= \frac{\rho^2 \cdot g^2 \cdot A \cdot L^3}{6\,E}$$

Example 3.15 : *A solid right circular cone is held vertically as shown in Fig. 3.12. Derive the expression for strain energy stored in it due to self weight using standard notation.*

Data   : As shown in Fig. 3.12.

Required : Expression for strain energy due to self weight.

Concept : Same as Example 3.14.

Solution : Consider an elementary strip of thickness 'dy' at a distance 'y' from bottom as shown in Fig. 3.12.

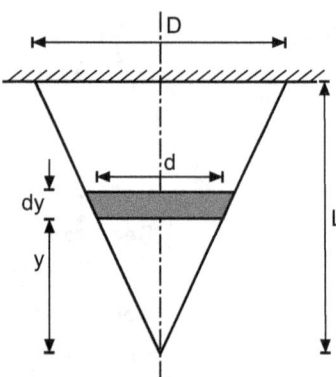

Fig. 3.12

Let,   D = Diameter of cone at fixed end

d = Diameter of cone at 'y' from bottom

L = Height of cone

ρ = Mass density of cone material

g = Gravitational acceleration

E = Modulus of elasticity

Axial force on elementary strip = Volume below the strip × Weight density

$$= \left(\frac{1}{3} A_y \cdot y\right) \cdot \rho \cdot g$$

where A_y = Area of cross section at 'y' from bottom.

$\therefore$ Normal stress on elementary strip $= \sigma = \dfrac{F}{A_y} = \dfrac{y \cdot \rho \cdot g}{3}$

$\therefore$ Strain energy of elementary strip $= dU = \dfrac{\sigma^2}{2E} \times$ Volume of strip

$\therefore$ $dU = \left(\dfrac{y \cdot \rho \cdot g}{3}\right)^2 \cdot \dfrac{1}{2E} \cdot (A_y \cdot dy)$

$\therefore$ $dU = \dfrac{y^2 \cdot \rho^2 \cdot g^2}{18E} \cdot (A_y \cdot dy)$

where, $A_y = \dfrac{\pi}{4} d^2 = \dfrac{\pi}{4} \left[\dfrac{D}{L} \cdot y\right]^2$

Total strain energy for cone $= U = \displaystyle\int_0^L dU$

$\therefore$ $U = \displaystyle\int_0^L \dfrac{y^2 \rho^2 g^2}{18E} \left[\dfrac{\pi}{4}\left(\dfrac{D}{L} \cdot y\right)^2\right] dy = \dfrac{\rho^2 g^2 \pi D^2}{72 E L^2} \cdot \left[\dfrac{L^5}{5}\right]$

$\qquad\qquad = \dfrac{\rho^2 g^2 \cdot \pi D^2}{360 E} \cdot L^3$

Example 3.16 : *A load of 500 N falls freely through a height of 150 mm onto a coller attached to end of vertical rod of 50 mm diameter and 2 m long, the upper end of rod being fixed to the ceiling. Calculate the maximum instantaneous extension of the bar. Also calculate the maximum stress in the bar. Assume E = 200 GPa.*

Data : W = 500 N, h = 150 mm, D = 50 mm, E = 200 GPa

Required : Maximum instantaneous extension and stress.

Concept : Standard formula.

Solution :

$$\sigma_{max} = \frac{W}{A} \pm \left[\sqrt{\left(\frac{2WhE}{AL}\right)^2 + \frac{W^2}{A^2}} \right]$$

∴

$$\sigma_{max} = \frac{500}{19635} \pm \left[\sqrt{\left(\frac{2 \times 500 \times 150 \times 200 \times 10^3}{1963.5 \times 2000}\right)^2 + \frac{500^2}{1963.5^2}} \right]$$

$$\sigma_{max} = 0.255 \pm \sqrt{(7639.42 + 0.065)}$$

$$\sigma_{max} = 0.255 + 87.40 = 87.655 \text{ N/mm}^2$$

$$\delta l = \frac{\sigma l}{E} = \frac{87.655 \times 2000}{200 \times 10^3} = \textbf{0.88 mm}$$

3.6 COMBINED ACTIONS

3.6.1 Bending and Torsion

In practice, members are generally subjected to combined bending and torsion. In this article, we shall discuss the evaluation of principal stresses and maximum shear stress for such combined action.

Consider a solid circular shaft subjected to bending moment and torsion as shown in Fig. 3.13.

Let, M = Bending moment (sagging)

T = Torsional moment

D = Diameter of shaft

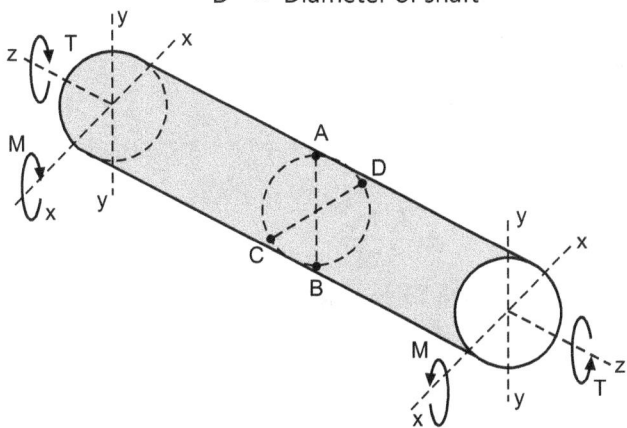

Fig. 3.13 : Combined bending and torsion

Consider an intermediate cross section of shaft as shown in Fig. 3.13.

Shear stress due to torque $T = \tau = \dfrac{16\,T}{\pi D^3}$ ... (3.8 a)

Bending stress due to $M = \sigma = \dfrac{32M}{\pi D^3}$ ... (3.8 b)

It should be noted that shear stress τ is uniform at all elements A, B, C and D while bending stress σ is compressive in nature at A, tensile in nature at B while zero at elements C and D. Hence, elements C and D are subjected to state of pure shear while principal stresses will occur at elements A and B. Principal stresses σ_1 and σ_2 at any of these two points are given by

$$\sigma_1 ; \sigma_2 = \frac{\sigma}{2} \pm \sqrt{\left(\frac{\sigma}{2}\right)^2 + \tau^2} \qquad \text{... (3.9)}$$

Substituting equations (3.7) and (3.8) in equation (3.9), we get

$$\sigma_1 ; \sigma_2 = \frac{32M}{2\pi D^3} \pm \sqrt{\left(\frac{32M}{2\pi D^3}\right)^2 + \left(\frac{16T}{\pi D^3}\right)^2}$$

$$= \frac{16M}{\pi D^3} \pm \sqrt{\left(\frac{16M}{\pi D^3}\right)^2 + \left(\frac{16T}{\pi D^3}\right)^2}$$

$$\sigma_1 ; \sigma_2 = \frac{16}{\pi D^3} \left[M \pm \sqrt{M^2 + T^2} \right] \qquad \text{... (3.10)}$$

Principal planes can be located by using

$$\tan(2\theta_1) = \frac{2\tau}{\sigma} = \frac{T}{M} \qquad \text{... (3.11)}$$

and $\theta_2 = \theta_1 + 90^\circ$

Maximum shear stress is given by,

$$\tau_{max} = \frac{\sigma_1 - \sigma_2}{2} = \frac{16}{\pi D^3} \sqrt{M^2 + T^2} \qquad \text{... (3.12)}$$

Equivalent bending and torsional moment

Let M_e = Equivalent bending moment which acting alone produces the same maximum normal stress.

Bending stress due to $M_e = \sigma = \dfrac{32\,M_e}{\pi D^3}$ ... (3.13)

Equating equations (3.10) and (3.13), we get

$$M_e = \frac{1}{2} \left[M + \sqrt{M^2 + T^2} \right] \qquad \text{... (3.14)}$$

Let T_e = Equivalent torsional moment which acting alone produces the same maximum shear stress.

Shear stress due to $T_e = \tau = \dfrac{16\,T_e}{\pi D^3}$ ... (3.15)

Equating equations (3.12) and (3.15), we get

$$T_e = \sqrt{M^2 + T^2}$$ ... (3.16)

3.6.2 Axial Force and Torsion

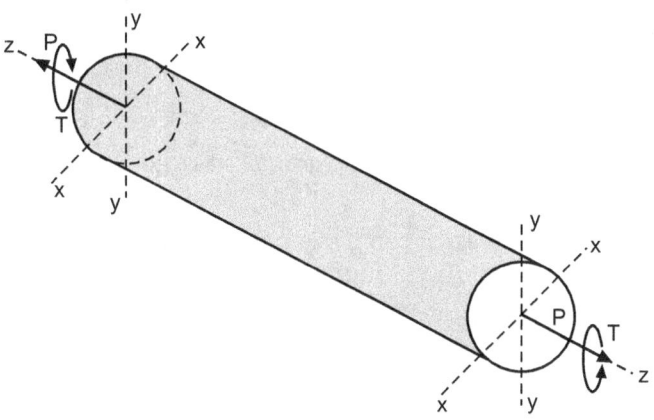

Fig. 3.14 : Combined axial force and torsion

Consider a solid circular shaft subjected to axial force and torsional moment as shown in Fig. 3.14.

Let   P = Axial force (tensile)

            T = Torsional moment

            D = Diameter of shaft

Normal stress due to axial force P = $\sigma = \dfrac{4P}{\pi D^2}$ ... (3.17)

Shear stress due to torque T is obtained from equation (3.8 a).

It should be noted that normal stress 'σ' due to axial force is uniform over the entire cross section, while shear stress τ due to torque is same at any point on the surface of the shaft.

Principal stresses can be evaluated by equation (3.9) and principal planes can be located by

$$\tan 2\theta_1 = \frac{2\tau}{\sigma} \quad \text{and} \quad \theta_2 = \theta_1 + 90^\circ$$

3.6.3 Axial force, Bending and Torsion

When a shaft is subjected to all these three actions, for elements farthest from neutral axis of bending; normal stresses due to bending and axial force will get added algebraically and shear stress due to torque is same on all the elements at surface of the shaft. Nature of normal stresses on various elements will depend on nature of axial force and bending moment. Algebraic addition of normal stresses is possible within elastic behaviour of the material, since principle of superpositions is valid till then. Principal stresses can then be obtained by using same equations discussed earlier.

SOLVED EXAMPLES

Example 3.17 : *A shaft section 80 mm in diameter is subjected to bending moment of 3 kNm and torque of 8 kNm. Find the maximum normal stresses induced on section and locate the plane on which it acts. Find also what stress acting alone can produce the same maximum strain. Take $\mu = 0.3$.*

Data   : $D = 80$ mm; $M = 3$ kNm; $T = 8$ kNm; $\mu = 0.3$

Required : Principal stresses and single normal stress to produce equivalent principal strain.

Concept : Principal stresses for combined bending and torsion using equations (3.10), and (3.11).

Solution : (i) Principal stresses :

$$\sigma_1 ; \sigma_2 \;=\; \frac{16}{\pi D^3}\left(M \pm \sqrt{M^2 + T^2}\right)$$

$$=\; \frac{16}{\pi \times (80)^3}\left(3 \pm \sqrt{3^2 + 8^2}\right) \times 10^6$$

$$=\; 9.95\,(3 \pm 8.54)$$

$$\sigma_1 \;=\; \mathbf{114.82\ MPa}$$

$$\text{and}\ \ \sigma_2 \;=\; \mathbf{-\,55.12\ MPa}$$

(ii)   Principal planes :

$$\tan(2\theta_1) \;=\; \frac{T}{M} \;=\; \frac{8}{3}$$

∴ $\theta_1 = \mathbf{34.72^o}$ and $\theta_2 = \theta_1 + 90^o = 34.72 + 90 = \mathbf{124.72^o}$

(iii)   Major principal strain :

$$\varepsilon_1 = \frac{1}{E}\,(\sigma_1 - \mu\,\sigma_2) \;=\; \frac{1}{E}\,(114.82 - 0.3\,(-55.12))$$

$$=\; \frac{131.36}{E}$$

(iv)   Single normal stress to produce major principal strain :

Let σ = Normal stress to produce major principal strain

∴ $\dfrac{\sigma}{E} = \dfrac{131.36}{E}$

∴ $\sigma = \mathbf{131.36\ MPa}$

Example 3.18 : *A steel shaft is subjected to torque of 15 kNm and bending moment of 12 kNm. Calculate the principal stresses and maximum shear stress if diameter of shaft is 100 mm.*

Data   :   T = 15 kNm;   M = 12 kNm;   D = 100 mm

Required   :   Principal stresses, maximum shear stress.

Concept   :   Same as Example (3.17).

Solution   :   (i) Principal stresses :

$$\sigma_1 ; \sigma_2 \;=\; \frac{16}{\pi D^3}\left(M \pm \sqrt{M^2 + T^2}\right)$$

$$=\; \frac{16}{\pi \times (100)^3}\left(12 \pm \sqrt{(12)^2 + (15)^2}\right) \times 10^6$$

$$=\; 5.09\,(12 \pm 19.2)$$

$$\sigma_1 \;=\; \mathbf{158.8\ MPa}$$

and $\qquad\qquad \sigma_2 \;=\; \mathbf{-\,36.65\ MPa}$

(ii)   Position of principal planes :

$$\tan(2\theta_1) \;=\; \frac{T}{M} \;=\; \frac{15}{12}$$

$\therefore \qquad\qquad\qquad \theta_1 \;=\; \mathbf{25.67^o} \text{ and } \theta_2 = \theta_1 + 90^o = 25.67 + 90^o = \mathbf{115.67^o}$

(iii)   Maximum shear stress :

$$\tau_{max} \;=\; \frac{16}{\pi D^3}\sqrt{M^2 + T^2}$$

$$=\; \frac{16}{\pi \times (100)^3}\left(\sqrt{(12)^2 + (15)^2}\right) \times 10^6$$

$$\tau_{max} \;=\; \mathbf{97.83\ MPa}$$

Example 3.19 : *A hollow shaft is subjected to torque of 400 kNm and bending moment of 200 kNm. Internal diameter of shaft is 0.6 times the external diameter. If maximum normal stress is not to exceed 150 MPa and shear stress is not to exceed 80 MPa, design the cross section of shaft.*

Data   :   T = 400 kNm; M = 200 kNm; d = 0.6 D; $\sigma_{max} \le 150$ MPa; $\tau_{max} \le 80$ MPa.

Required   :   Design of cross section of shaft.

Concept   :   Design of shaft based on maximum normal stress and maximum shear stress criteria. Governing dimensions will be greater of that obtained for above two conditions.

Solution   :   (i) Cross section based on maximum normal stress :

Principal stresses : $\qquad \sigma_1 ; \sigma_2 \;=\; \frac{16D}{\pi\,(D^4 - d^4)}\left(M \pm \sqrt{M^2 + T^2}\right)$

Major principal stress : $\qquad \sigma_1 \;=\; 150$ MPa

$$\sigma_1 = \frac{16D}{\pi\,[D^4 - (0.6\,D)^4]}\left(200 + \sqrt{(200)^2 + (400)^2}\right) \times 10^6$$

$$= \frac{3.296 \times 10^9\,D}{0.8704\,D^4}$$

∴　　　　　　$D = \textbf{293.36 mm}$ and $d = \textbf{176.02 mm}$　　　　... (1)

(ii)　Cross section based on maximum shear stress :

$$\tau_{max} = \frac{16\,D}{\pi\,(D^4 - d^4)}\cdot\sqrt{M^2 + T^2}$$

Substituting,　　$80 = \frac{16\,D}{\pi\,[D^4 - (0.6\,D)^4]}\cdot\left(\sqrt{(200)^2 + (400)^2}\right) \times 10^6$

$$= \frac{2.278 \times 10^9}{0.8704\,D^3}$$

∴　　　　　　$D = \textbf{319.8 mm}$ and $d = \textbf{191.89 mm}$　　　　... (2)

∴　Use　　　　$D = \textbf{320 mm}$ and $d = 0.6 \times 320 = \textbf{192 mm}$

(Greater of (1) and (2))

Example 3.20 : *A flywheel weighing 4 kN is mounted on a shaft 50 mm ϕ, 600 mm long. Shaft is free to rotate at ends and flywheel is mounted on centre of shaft. If shaft is transmitting 44 kW at 300 rpm, calculate the principal stresses and maximum shear stresses in the shaft at the ends of horizontal and vertical diameter of cross-section close to that of flywheel.*

Data　　: 　Weight of flywheel = W = 4 kN;　diameter of shaft = D = 50 mm;
　　　　　　　L = 600 mm; Power = 44 kW;　N = 300 r.p.m.

Required : 　Principal stresses and maximum shear stresses in the shaft at the ends of horizontal and vertical diameter of cross section close to flywheel.

Concept : 　(i)　Self weight of flywheel will produce bending moment and shear force for shaft and knowing power and speed of shaft, torque can be obtained.

　　　　　　(ii)　Stresses at the ends of horizontal diameter (AB) :

　　　　　　　　(a)　Shear stresses due to shear force.

　　　　　　　　(b)　Shear stresses due to torque.

　　　　Normal stresses due to bending moment are zero at horizontal diameter.

　　　　　　(iii)　Stresses at the ends of vertical diameter (CD) :

　　　　　　　　(a)　Shear stresses due to torque.

　　　　　　　　(b)　Normal stresses due to bending moment.

　　　　Shear stresses due to shear force are zero at the ends of vertical diameter.

Solution : 　(i) Analysis of forces :

　　Reactions at supports due to self weight of flywheel = 2 kN (↑)

　　Maximum BM at centre = $\dfrac{WL}{4} = \dfrac{4 \times 0.6}{4} = 0.6$ kNm.

SF and BM diagrams are drawn as shown in Fig. 3.14.

Also $P = \dfrac{2\pi NT}{60}$ ∴ $44 \times 10^3 = \dfrac{2\pi \times 300 \times T}{60}$

∴   T = **1400.56 Nm**

(ii)   Geometric properties of shaft :

$$I_x = \frac{\pi}{64} \cdot D^4 = \frac{\pi}{64} (50)^4 = 306.796 \times 10^3 \text{ mm}^4$$

$$J = \frac{\pi}{32} \cdot D^4 = \frac{\pi}{32} (50)^4 = 613.592 \times 10^3 \text{ mm}^4$$

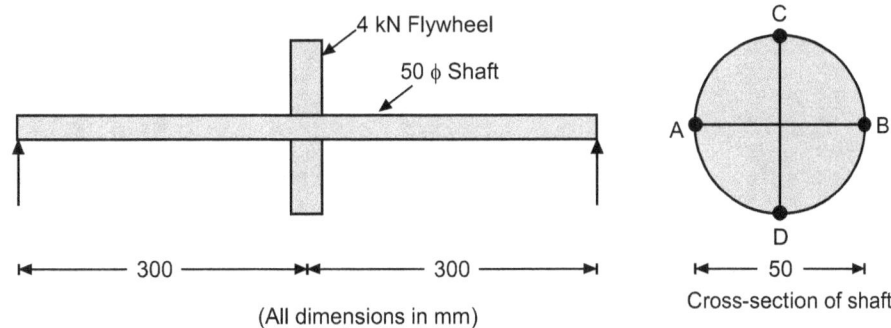

(a) Flywheel arrangement

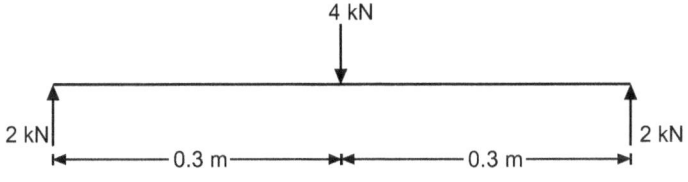

(b) FBD of shaft

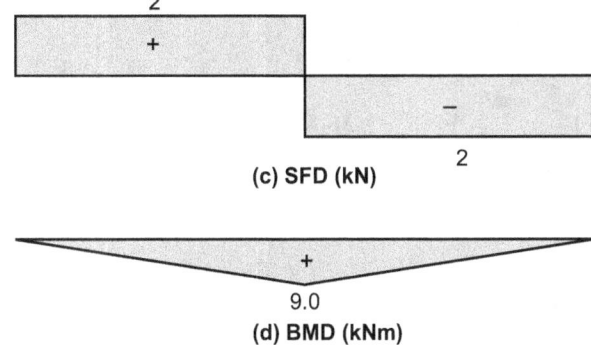

(c) SFD (kN)

(d) BMD (kNm)

Fig. 3.14

Section modulus @ x axis = Z_x = $\dfrac{I_x}{y_{max}}$

$$= \dfrac{306.796 \times 10^3}{50/2} = \mathbf{12.27 \times 10^3 \ mm^3}$$

Polar section modulus = $\dfrac{J}{R}$ = $\dfrac{613.592 \times 10^3}{50/2} = \mathbf{24.54 \times 10^3 \ mm^3}$

$$A = \dfrac{\pi}{4} \cdot D^2 = \dfrac{\pi}{4} (50)^2 = \mathbf{1963.49 \ mm^2}$$

(iii) Evaluation of different stresses :

Shear stresses due to torque,

$$\tau_1 = \dfrac{T}{J/R} = \dfrac{1400.56 \times 10^3}{24.54 \times 10^3}$$

$$= \mathbf{57.07 \ MPa}$$

[**Note :** $\tau_1 = 57.07$ MPa is same at all elements A, B, C and D.]

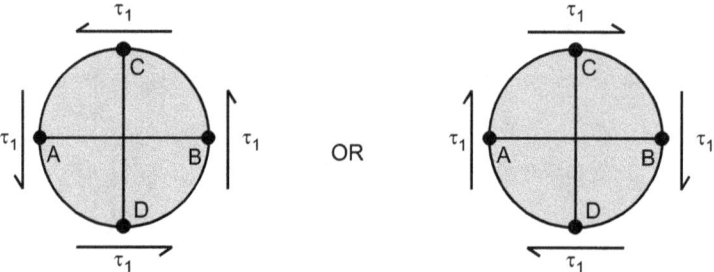

Fig. 3.15 : Shear stresses due to torque

Shear stresses due to shear force :

$$\tau_2 = \dfrac{4}{3} \tau_a$$

where τ_a = Average shear stress = $\dfrac{\text{Shear force}}{\text{c/s area}}$

$$= \dfrac{2 \times 10^3}{1963.49} = \mathbf{1.02 \ MPa}$$

∴ $\tau_2 = \dfrac{4}{3} \times 1.02 = \mathbf{1.36 \ MPa}$

[**Note :** $\tau_2 = 1.36$ MPa is at A and B only]

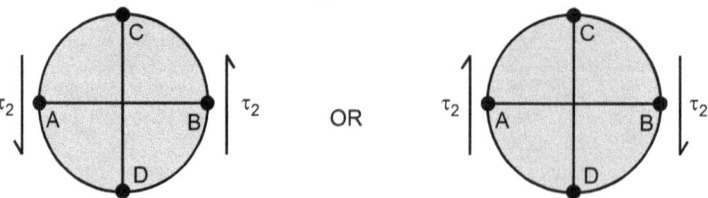

Fig. 3.16 : Shear stresses due to shear force

Bending stresses, $\sigma = \dfrac{B.M.}{Z_x}$

$$= \dfrac{0.6 \times 10^6}{12.27 \times 10^3}$$

$$= \mathbf{48.9 \ MPa}$$

[**Note :** $\sigma = 48.9$ MPa is at C and D only]

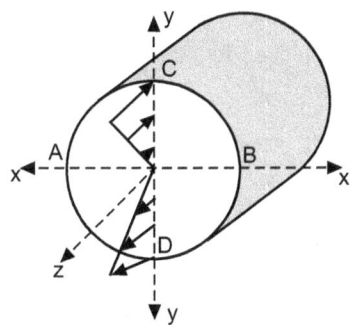

Bending compression at C.

Bending tension at D.

Fig. 3.17 : Bending stresses

(iv)   Analysis of stresses at elements A and B :

Out of A and B, one element will have resultant shear stress

$$= \tau_1 + \tau_2$$
$$= 57.07 + 1.36$$
$$= \mathbf{58.43 \ MPa}$$

While other elements will have resultant shear stress

$$= \tau \ = \ -\tau_1 + \tau_2$$
$$= -57.07 + 1.36$$
$$= \mathbf{-55.71 \ MPa}$$

Note : Because the direction of torque is not specified and position of cross section of shaft whether on left or on right of flywheel is not defined, no comment can be made about whether the maximum shear stress is at element A or B. However, both these elements are subjected to state of pure shear.

Selecting maximum shear stress

$$\tau_{max} \ = \ \mathbf{58.43 \ MPa}$$

∴   Principal stresses $\sigma_1 = \sigma_2 \ = \ \mathbf{\pm 58.43 \ MPa}$

Note : For element subjected to state of pure shear stress 'τ' principal stresses $\sigma_1 = \sigma_2 = \tau$ out of the two, one principal stress is tensile in nature while other is compressive.

(v)   Analysis of stresses C and D :

$$\sigma_1 \ ; \ \sigma_2 \ = \ \dfrac{\sigma}{2} \pm \sqrt{\left(\dfrac{\sigma}{2}\right)^2 + \tau_1^2}$$

$$= \frac{48.9}{2} \pm \sqrt{\left(\frac{48.9}{2}\right)^2 + (57.07)^2}$$

$$= 24.45 \pm 62.08$$

$$\sigma_1 = \textbf{86.53 MPa} \text{ and } \sigma_2 = \textbf{– 37.63 MPa.}$$

Maximum shear stress = τ_{max} = $\dfrac{\sigma_1 - \sigma_2}{2}$ = $\dfrac{86.53 + 37.63}{2}$ = **62.08 MPa**

However, principal stresses at elements C and D subjected to stresses due to bending and torsion can be worked out by standard expression as ;

$$\sigma_1 ; \sigma_2 = \frac{16}{\pi D^3} \left(M \pm \sqrt{M^2 + T^2} \right)$$

$$= \frac{16}{\pi \times (50)^3} \left(0.6 \pm \sqrt{(0.6)^2 + (1.4)^2} \right) \times 10^6$$

$$\sigma_1 = \textbf{86.5 MPa} \text{ and } \sigma_2 = \textbf{– 37.6 MPa}$$

Note : + ve sign of σ_1 OR σ_2 indicates that it is of the same nature as that of normal stress produced by B.M. Thus, normal stress of 86.53 MPa is compressive at 'C' and tensile at 'D' while normal stress of 37.63 MPa is tensile at 'C' and compressive at 'D' because bending moment produces compression at 'C' and tension at 'D'.

Example 3.21 : *A cantilever steel rod 25 mm diameter is supporting force 'F' as shown in Fig. 3.18. Determine the maximum force 'F' that can be applied if (a) the bending stress is not to exceed 125 MPa and (b) resultant shear stress due to bending and torsion is not to exceed 100 MPa.*

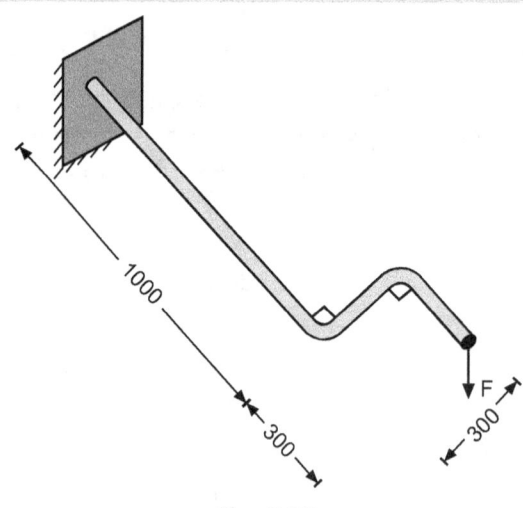

Fig. 3.18

Data   :   As shown in Fig. 3.18; bending stress $\leq$ 125 MPa and maximum shear stress $\leq$ 100 MPa.

Required :   Safe value of F.

Concept   :   Maximum bending moment is at fixed end; Bending stresses; Shear stresses due to bending and torsion.

Solution   :   (i) Analysis :

Let 'F' be the force in newtons.

Maximum bending moment at fixed end = **1300 F Nmm**

Maximum torque at fixed end = **300 F Nmm**

(ii)   From bending stress criteria,

$$I_x = \frac{\pi}{64} D^4 = \frac{\pi}{64} \times (25)^4 = 19.17 \times 10^3 \text{ mm}^4$$

$$y_{max} = \frac{25}{2} = 12.5 \text{ mm}$$

$\therefore$ Section modulus $= Z_x = \dfrac{I_x}{y_{max}} = \dfrac{19.17 \times 10^3}{12.5} = 1533.98 \text{ mm}^3$

$$\text{Bending stress} = \sigma = 125 = \frac{BM}{Z_x}$$

$$= \frac{1300 \, F}{1533.98}$$

$\therefore$ F = **147.49 N**   ... (1)

(iii)   From resultant shear stress due to bending and torsion,

$$\tau_{max} = \frac{16}{\pi D^3} \sqrt{M^2 + T^2}$$

$$100 = \frac{16}{\pi \times (25)^3} \left(\sqrt{(1300 \, F)^2 + (300 \, F)^2} \right)$$

$\therefore$ F = **229.95 N**   ... (2)

$\therefore$ Safe value of F = Least of (1) and (2)

$$= \textbf{147.49 N}$$

Example 3.22 : *A solid circular shaft 20 mm ϕ is loaded as shown in Fig. 3.19.*

Determine (i) maximum shear stress on horizontal diameter AB and (ii) principal stresses at element C of vertical diameter.

Data   :   As shown in Fig. 3.19.

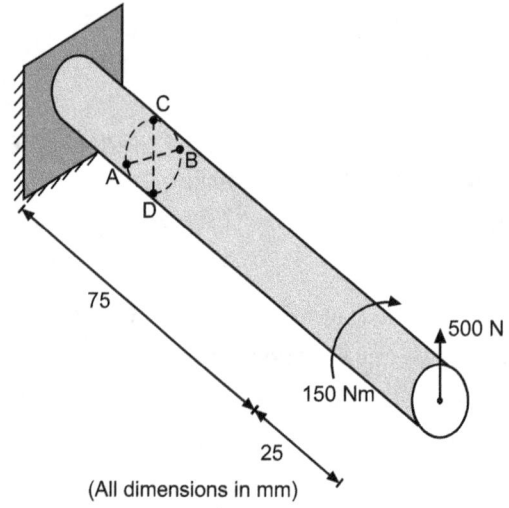

(All dimensions in mm)

Fig. 3.19

Required : Maximum shear stress on AB and principal stresses at element C.

Concept : Combined stresses : Normal stresses due to bending moment and shear stresses due to torque and shear force.

Solution : (i) Geometric properties.

$$A = \frac{\pi}{4}(20)^2 = 314.16 \text{ mm}^2$$

$$I_x = \frac{\pi}{64}(20)^4 = 7853.98 \text{ mm}^4$$

$$y_{max} = \frac{20}{2} = \textbf{10 mm}$$

∴ $\quad$ Section modulus $= Z_x = \dfrac{I_x}{y_{max}} = \dfrac{7853.98}{10} = \textbf{785.39 mm}^3$

$$J = \frac{\pi}{32}(20)^4 = 15.71 \times 10^3 \text{ mm}^4$$

$$\frac{J}{R} = \frac{15.71 \times 10^3}{10} = \textbf{1.57} \times \textbf{10}^3 \textbf{ mm}^3$$

(ii) Evaluation of different stresses :

$$\text{Shear stress due to torque} = \tau_1 = \frac{T}{J/R} = \frac{150 \times 10^3}{1.57 \times 10^3}$$

$$= \textbf{95.54 MPa}$$

$$\text{Shear stress due to shear force} = \tau_2 = \frac{4}{3}\left(\frac{SF}{A}\right)$$

∴ $$\tau_2 = \frac{4}{3} \times \frac{500}{314.16} = 2.14 \text{ MPa}$$

Bending stresses due to B.M. (σ)

$$\sigma = \frac{B.M.}{Z_x} \quad \text{where} \quad BM = 500 \times 100 \text{ Nmm}$$

$\therefore$

$$\sigma = \frac{500 \times 100}{785.39} = \textbf{63.66 MPa}$$

Compressive at C and tensile at D.

(iii) Maximum shear stress on horizontal diameter :

$$\tau_{max} = \tau_1 + \tau_2 = 95.54 + 2.14 = \textbf{97.68 MPa}$$

(iv) Principal stresses at C :

$$\sigma_1 ; \sigma_2 = \frac{\sigma}{2} \pm \sqrt{\left(\frac{\sigma}{2}\right)^2 + \tau_1^2}$$

$$= \frac{63.66}{2} \pm \sqrt{\left(\frac{63.66}{2}\right)^2 + (95.54)^2}$$

$$= 31.83 \pm 100.7$$

$$\sigma_1 = \textbf{132.53 MPa i.e. compressive at C.}$$

$$\sigma_2 = \textbf{– 68.87 MPa i.e. tensile at C.}$$

Note : + ve sign of σ_1 or σ_2 indicates that principal stress is of same nature as that of σ.

Principal planes :

$$\tan(2\theta_1) = \frac{2\tau_1}{\sigma} = \frac{2 \times 95.54}{63.66}$$

$$\theta_1 = \textbf{35.78°}$$

and

$$\theta_2 = \theta_1 + 90° = 35.78 + 90$$

$$= \textbf{125.78°}$$

Example 3.23 : *A solid shaft of 100 mm diameter transmits 500 kW at 500 r.p.m. and is also subjected to an axial thrust of 200 kN. If the maximum principal stress is not to exceed 100 MPa, find what additional bending moment may safely be carried ?*

Data   :   D = 100 mm; Power = 500 kW; N = 500 rpm;

P = 200 kN; Maximum principal stress = 100 MPa.

Required :   Additional bending moment carrying capacity.

Concept   :   Combined stresses : Normal stresses due to bending moment and axial force and shear stresses due to torsion.

Solution :   (i) Geometric properties :

$$A = \frac{\pi}{4} D^2 = \frac{\pi}{4} (100)^2 = 7.85 \times 10^3 \text{ mm}^2$$

$$I_x = \frac{\pi}{64}(D)^4 = \frac{\pi}{64}(100)^4 = 4.91 \times 10^6 \text{ mm}^4$$

$$y_{max} = \frac{100}{2} = 50 \text{ mm}$$

$$Z_x = \frac{I_x}{y_{max}} = \frac{4.91 \times 10^6}{50} = 98.17 \times 10^3 \text{ mm}^3$$

$$J = \frac{\pi}{32}(D)^4 = \frac{\pi}{32}(100)^4 = 9.82 \times 10^6 \text{ mm}^4$$

$$\frac{J}{R} = \frac{9.82 \times 10^6}{50} = \mathbf{196.4 \times 10^3 \text{ mm}^3}$$

(ii)   Evaluation of different stresses :

Normal stress due to axial force :

$$\sigma_a = \frac{P}{A} = \frac{200 \times 10^3}{7.85 \times 10^3} = 25.48 \text{ MPa}$$

$$\text{Power} = \frac{2\pi \, NT}{60}$$

$$500 \times 10^3 = \frac{2\pi \times 500 \times T}{60}$$

∴ $T = 9.55 \times 10^3 \text{ Nm} = \mathbf{9.55 \times 10^6 \text{ Nmm}}$

∴   Shear stresses due to torque $= \dfrac{T}{J/R} = \dfrac{9.55 \times 10^6}{196.4 \times 10^3} = \mathbf{48.62 \text{ MPa}}$

(iii) Additional maximum bending moment :

For an element subjected to normal stress in one direction and shear stress,

Principal stresses $\sigma_1 ; \sigma_2 = \dfrac{\sigma}{2} \pm \sqrt{\left(\dfrac{\sigma}{2}\right)^2 + \tau^2}$

∴   Maximum principal stress $= \sigma_1 = \dfrac{\sigma}{2} + \sqrt{\left(\dfrac{\sigma}{2}\right)^2 + \tau^2}$

$$100 = \frac{\sigma}{2} + \sqrt{\left(\frac{\sigma}{2}\right)^2 + (48.62)^2}$$

∴ $\sigma = \mathbf{76.36 \text{ MPa}}$

$= $ Stress due to axial force $+$ Stress due to bending moment

$= \sigma_a + \sigma_b$

$= 25.48 + \sigma_b$

∴ σ_b = 50.88 MPa = Maximum additional normal stress.

∴   Additional maximum BM = $\sigma_b \times Z_x$ = 50.88 × 98.17 × 10³

$$= 4.99 \times 10^6 \, \text{Nmm}$$

$$= \textbf{4.99 kNm}$$

Example 3.24 : *A solid shaft in a small hydraulic turbine is 100 mm in diameter. It supports an axial compressive load of 440 kN. Determine the maximum power that will be developed at a speed of 240 r.p.m. without exceeding maximum shear stress of 70 MPa and maximum normal stress of 90 MPa.*

Data   : D = 100 mm; Axial compressive load = P = 440 kN; N = 240 r.p.m.;
                 τ_{max} = 70 MPa and Maximum normal stress = 90 MPa.

Required : Safe power P.

Concept : Combined stresses : Normal stress due to axial force and shear stress due to torsion.

Solution : (i) Geometric properties :

$$A = \frac{\pi}{4} D^2 = \frac{\pi}{4} (100)^2 = 7853.98 \text{ mm}^2$$

$$J = \frac{\pi}{32} (D)^4 = \frac{\pi}{32} (100)^4 = 9.82 \times 10^6 \text{ mm}^4$$

$$R = \frac{100}{2} = 50 \text{ mm}$$

$$\frac{J}{R} = \frac{9.82 \times 10^6}{50} = \textbf{196.35} \times \textbf{10}^3 \textbf{ mm}^3$$

(ii)   Normal stress due to axial force (σ) :

$$\sigma = \frac{P}{A} = \frac{440 \times 10^3}{7853.98} = \textbf{56.02 MPa}$$

(iii)   From maximum normal stress criteria,

$$\sigma_1 = \frac{\sigma}{2} + \sqrt{\left(\frac{\sigma}{2}\right)^2 + \tau^2}$$

$$90 = \frac{56.02}{2} + \sqrt{\left(\frac{56.02}{2}\right)^2 + \tau^2}$$

∴ τ = **55.3 MPa**   ... (1)

(iv)   From maximum shear stress criteria,

$$\tau_{max} = \sqrt{\left(\frac{\sigma}{2}\right)^2 + \tau^2}$$

$$70 = \sqrt{\left(\frac{56.02}{2}\right)^2 + \tau^2}$$

τ = **64.15 MPa**   ... (2)

(v)   Safe torque : Shear stress due to torque to be allowed for safety = 55.3 MPa.

(Least of (1) and (2))

$$\therefore \qquad \tau = \frac{T}{(J/R)}$$

$$55.3 = \frac{T}{196.35 \times 10^3}$$

$$\therefore \qquad T = 10.86 \times 10^6 \, Nmm = \mathbf{10.86 \times 10^3 \, Nm}$$

(vi)   Safe power, $\qquad P = \dfrac{2\pi \, NT}{60} = \dfrac{2\pi \times 240 \times 10.86 \times 10^3}{60}$

$$= 272.94 \times 10^3 \, W = \mathbf{272.94 \, kW}$$

3.7 STRAIN ENERGY DUE TO TORSION

Refer to Fig. 3.20. Total strain energy of a shaft of length L, under the action of torque T is the work done in twisting i.e. for gradually applied torque,

$$U = \frac{1}{2} \, T\theta \qquad \qquad \text{... (3.18)}$$

Expressed in terms of maximum shear stress,

$$U = \frac{1}{2} \left(\frac{J}{R} \, \tau_{max} \right) \left(\frac{\tau_{max}}{R} \cdot \frac{L}{G} \right) \qquad \qquad \text{... (3.19)}$$

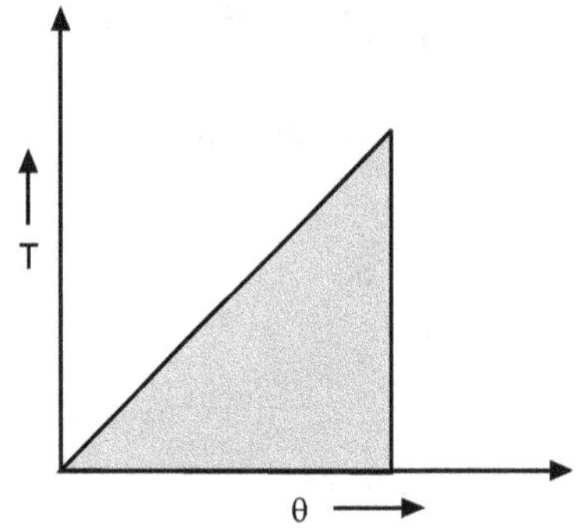

Fig. 3.20

(a)   For solid circular shaft,

$$U = \frac{1}{2} \left[\frac{\pi D^3}{16} \times \tau_{max} \right] \left[\frac{\tau_{max}}{D/2} \times \frac{L}{G} \right] = \frac{\tau_{max}^2}{4G} \times \frac{\pi}{4} \, D^2 L$$

$$= \frac{\tau_{max}^2}{4G} \times \mathbf{(Volume)} \qquad \qquad \text{... (3.20)}$$

(b)   For hollow circular shaft,

$$U = \frac{1}{2} \cdot \left[\frac{\pi}{16 \, D} \cdot (D^4 - d^4) \times \tau_{max} \right] \left[\frac{\tau_{max}}{D/2} \times \frac{L}{G} \right]$$

$$= \frac{\tau_{max}^2}{4G} \cdot \left[\frac{D^2 + d^2}{D^2} \right] \times \mathbf{(Volume)} \qquad \qquad \text{... (3.21)}$$

Example 3.25 : *A hollow shaft subjected to a pure torque, attains maximum shear stress τ. Given that strain energy per unit volume is τ²/3G.*

   (i)   Calculate the ratio of shaft diameters.

   (ii)   Determine the actual diameters of such a shaft to transmit 4 MW at 100 r.p.m. when energy stored is 25 kN.m/m³ and G = 80 GPa.

Data   **:**   Power = 4 MW, N = 100 r.p.m.; $U = 25\ kNm/m^3$, G = 80 GPa.

Required : (i) Ratio of shaft diameters, (ii) Diameter of shaft.

Concept : Strain energy due to torsion.

Solution : (i) Let, 'D' and 'd' be the external and internal diameters respectively.

From equation (3.21),

$$\frac{U}{Volume} = \frac{\tau^2}{4G}\left(\frac{D^2}{D^2+d^2}\right) = \frac{\tau^2}{3G}$$

∴
$$\frac{D^2+d^2}{D^2} = \frac{4}{3}$$

∴
$$1 + \frac{d^2}{D^2} = \frac{4}{3}$$

$$\frac{d}{D} = \sqrt{\frac{1}{3}}$$

∴
$$\frac{D}{d} = \mathbf{1.732}$$

(ii)   Diameters of shaft,   P = 4 MW = 4×10^6 N.m/sec.

             N = 100 r.p.m.

$$P = \frac{2\pi\ NT_a}{60}$$

$$4 \times 10^6 = \frac{2\pi \times 100 \times T_a}{60}$$

$$T_a = 381971.86\ Nm = 381971.86 \times 10^3\ N.mm$$

Also, it is given that,   G = 80×10^3 MPa

      Energy stored = 25 kN.m/m³ = 25×10^{-3} N.mm/mm³

i.e.
$$\frac{\tau^2}{3G} = 25 \times 10^{-3}$$

$$\frac{\tau^2}{3 \times 80 \times 10^3} = 25 \times 10^{-3}$$

$$\tau = \mathbf{77.46\ MPa}$$

Using
$$\frac{T}{J} = \frac{\tau}{R}$$

$$\frac{J}{R} = \frac{T}{\tau} = \frac{381971.86 \times 10^3}{77.46} = \mathbf{4931214.3\ mm^3}$$

$$\therefore \qquad \frac{J}{R} = \frac{\pi}{16\,D}\,(D^4 - d^4) = 4931214.3$$

$$\frac{\pi}{16 \times 1.732\,d}\,[(1.732\,d)^4 - d^4] = 4931214.3$$

$$d = \mathbf{175.85\ mm}$$

$$D = \mathbf{304.57\ mm}$$

3.8 THEORIES OF FAILURE

Following are the theories of failure adopted for design of structural members.

    (i)   **Maximum Principal Stress Theory :** As per this theory, maximum principal stress shall not exceed the working stress for the material. i.e. $\sigma_1 \le \sigma_{safe}$. This theory is known as Rankine's theory.

    (ii)   **Maximum Principal Strain Theory :** If σ_1 and σ_2 are the principal stresses at a point in the strained material, the major principal strain is given by

$$\varepsilon_1 = \frac{1}{E}\,(\sigma_1 - \mu\,\sigma_2)$$

Let σ be the stress which acting alone produces the same principal strain, then

$$\frac{\sigma}{E} = \frac{1}{E}\,(\sigma_1 - \mu\,\sigma_2)$$

$$\therefore \qquad \sigma = \sigma_1 - \mu\,\sigma_2$$

The criteria of design will therefore be

$$\sigma = \sigma_1 - \mu\,\sigma_2 \le \sigma_{safe}$$

This theory was given by St. Venant.

    (iii)   **Maximum Shear Stress Theory :** If σ_1 and σ_2 are the principal stresses, maximum shear stress

$$\tau_{max} = \frac{\sigma_1 - \sigma_2}{2}$$

This maximum shear stress shall not exceed the working stress in shear for the material i.e. $\tau_{max} \le \tau_{safe}$. This theory was given by Sir J. J. Guest.

    (iv)   **Maximum Strain Energy Theory :** If σ_1 and σ_2 are the principal stresses, then the strain energy stored per unit volume

$$= \frac{1}{2\,E}\left(\sigma_1^2 + \sigma_2^2 - 2\,\mu\,\sigma_1\,\sigma_2\right)$$

Let σ be the stress acting alone, to store the same amount of strain energy per unit volume, then

$$\frac{\sigma^2}{2E} = \frac{1}{2E}\left(\sigma_1^2 + \sigma_2^2 - 2\,\mu\,\sigma_1\,\sigma_2\right)$$

$$\therefore \qquad \sigma = \sqrt{\sigma_1^2 + \sigma_2^2 - 2\,\mu\,\sigma_1\,\sigma_2} \le \sigma_{safe}$$

This theory was given by Beltrami and Haigh.

Example 3.26 : *A member, solid circular in cross section is subjected to an axial pull of 13 kN and a shear force of 5 kN. Design the cross section of member based on (i) the maximum principal stress theory, (ii) the maximum principal strain theory, (iii) the maximum shear stress theory, (iv) the maximum strain energy theory. For the material of member, elastic limit in axial tension is 250 MPa, Poisson's ratio = 0.3. Use factor of safety = 2.5.*

Data   :   Axial pull = 13 kN, shear force = 5 kN, Elastic limit in axial tension = 250 MPa, μ = 0.3, factor of safety = 2.5.

Required :   Design of cross section based on various theories of failure.

Concept :   Failure theories.

Solution :   (i) Geometric properties and allowable stresses :

Let 'a' be the cross-sectional area of member in mm².

$$\text{Safe stress in axial tension} = \sigma_{safe} = \frac{250}{2.5} = 100 \text{ MPa}$$

$$\text{Safe stress in shear} = \tau_{safe} = \frac{100}{2} = \textbf{50 MPa}$$

(ii)   Maximum principal stress theory,

$$\text{Direct stress on cross section} = \sigma = \frac{P}{A} = \frac{13 \times 10^3}{a} \text{ MPa}$$

$$\text{Shear stress on cross section} = \tau = \frac{SF}{A} = \frac{5 \times 10^3}{a} \text{ MPa}$$

Principal stresses are,

$$\sigma_1, \sigma_2 = \frac{\sigma}{2} \pm \sqrt{\left(\frac{\sigma}{2}\right)^2 + \tau^2}$$

$$= \frac{13 \times 10^3}{2a} \pm \sqrt{\left(\frac{13 \times 10^3}{2a}\right)^2 + \left(\frac{5 \times 10^3}{a}\right)^2}$$

$$= \frac{6500}{a} \pm \frac{8200.6}{a}$$

$$\therefore \qquad \sigma_1 = \frac{14700.6}{a} \text{ MPa}$$

$$\sigma_2 = -\frac{1700.6}{a} \text{ MPa}$$

As per this theory ; $\sigma_1 \le \sigma_{safe}$

$$\therefore \qquad \frac{14700.6}{a} \le 100$$

$$\therefore \qquad a \ge 147 \text{ mm}^2$$

$$\therefore \qquad \text{Diameter of the cross section} = d = \sqrt{\frac{4 \times 147}{\pi}} = \textbf{13.68 mm}$$

(iii)   Maximum principal strain theory :

Let, σ be the stress alone which produces same maximum strain.

$$\sigma = \sigma_1 - \mu\,\sigma_2 = \frac{14700.6}{a} - 0.3\left(-\frac{1700.6}{a}\right)$$

$$= \frac{15210.78}{a}\ \text{MPa}$$

As per this theory ; $\sigma \le \sigma_{safe}$ i.e. $\dfrac{15210.78}{a} \le 100$

$\therefore$ $a \ge 152.1\ \text{mm}^2$

$\therefore$ Diameter of the cross section $= d = \sqrt{\dfrac{4 \times 152.1}{\pi}} = \textbf{13.91 mm}$

(iv)   Maximum shear stress theory :

$$\tau_{max} = \frac{\sigma_1 - \sigma_2}{2} = \frac{1}{2}\left[\frac{14700.6}{a} - \left(\frac{-1700.6}{a}\right)\right]$$

$$= \frac{8200.6}{a}\ \text{MPa}$$

As per this theory, $\tau_{max} \le \tau_{safe}$

$\therefore$ $\dfrac{8200.6}{a} \le 50$

$\therefore$ $a \ge 164.01\ \text{mm}^2$

$\therefore$ Diameter of the cross section $= d = \sqrt{\dfrac{4 \times 164.01}{\pi}} = \textbf{14.45 mm}$

(v)   Maximum strain energy theory :

Strain energy stored per unit volume

$$= \frac{1}{2E}\left(\sigma_1^2 + \sigma_2^2 - 2\mu\,\sigma_1\sigma_2\right)$$

$$= \frac{1}{2E}\left[\left(\frac{14700.6}{a}\right)^2 + \left(-\frac{1700.6}{a}\right)^2 - 2 \times 0.3\left(\frac{14700.6}{a}\right)\left(-\frac{1700.6}{a}\right)\right]$$

$$= \frac{116.99 \times 10^6}{a^2\,E}$$

As per this theory, $\dfrac{1}{2E}\left(\sigma_1^2 + \sigma_2^2 - 2\mu\,\sigma_1\sigma_2\right) \le \dfrac{(\sigma_{safe})^2}{2E}$

$$\frac{116.99 \times 10^6}{a^2\,E} \le \frac{(100)^2}{2E}$$

$\therefore$ $a \ge 152.97\ \text{mm}^2$

$\therefore$ Diameter of the cross section $= d = \sqrt{\dfrac{4 \times 152.97}{\pi}} = \textbf{13.95 mm}$

Example 3.27 : *A shaft of hollow circular section with outside diameter 200 mm and inside diameter 160 mm is subjected to simultaneously a torque of 12 kNm and an axial compressive load of 300 kN. Determine the maximum tensile stress, maximum compressive stress and maximum shear stress in the shaft.*

Data   : D = 200 mm, d = 160 mm, T = 12 kN-m, P = 300 kN

Required : Maximum tensile stress, maximum compressive stress and maximum shear stress.

Concept : Standard formula.

Solution :

$$A = \frac{\pi}{4}(200^2 - 160^2) = 11309.73 \text{ mm}^2$$

$$J = \frac{\pi}{32}(200^4 - 160^4) = 92.7 \times 10^6 \text{ mm}^4$$

$$\sigma = \frac{P}{A} = \frac{300000}{11309.73} = 26.53 \text{ N/mm}^2$$

$$\tau = \frac{T}{J} \times R = \frac{12 \times 10^6}{92.74 \times 10^6} \times 100 = \textbf{12.94 N/mm}^2$$

$$\sigma_1; \sigma_2 = \frac{\sigma}{2} \pm \left[\left(\frac{\sigma}{2}\right)^2 + \tau^2\right]$$

$$\sigma_1; \sigma_2 = \frac{26.53}{2} \pm \left[\left(\frac{26.53}{2}\right)^2 + 12.94^2\right]$$

$$\sigma_1 = \textbf{31.8 N/mm}^2 \textbf{ (T)}$$

$$\sigma_2 = -5.27 \text{ N/mm}^2$$

$$\sigma_2 = \textbf{5.27 N/mm}^2 \textbf{ (C)}$$

Example 3.28 : *A solid shaft of 60 mm diameter has to resist a bending moment of 450 kN-mm accompanied by a torque of 360 kN-mm. Calculate the maximum principal stress induced in the shaft, also calculate the maximum shear stress induced.*

Data   : D = 60 mm, T = 360 kN-mm, M = 450 kN-mm

Required : Maximum principal stress and maximum shear stress.

Concept : Standard formula.

Solution :

$$P = \frac{2\pi NT}{60}$$

$$\sigma_1; \sigma_2 = \frac{16}{\pi D^3}\left[M \pm \sqrt{M^2 + T^2}\right]$$

$$\sigma_1; \sigma_2 = \frac{16 \times 10^3}{\pi(60)^3}\left[450 + \sqrt{332100}\right]$$

$$\sigma_1 = \textbf{24.20 N/mm}^2 \textbf{ (T)}$$

$$\sigma_2 = -2.98 \text{ N/mm}^2 = \textbf{2.98 N/mm}^2 \textbf{ (C)}$$

$$\tau_{max} = \frac{24.20 - (-2.98)}{2} = \textbf{13.55 N/mm}^2$$

Example 3.29 : *In a circular shaft subjected to twisting moment 'T' and bending moment 'M', show that when M = 1.2T, the ratio of maximum shear stress to the greater principal stress is nearly 0.566.*

Data   :   M = 1.2T

Required   :   Ratio of maximum shear stress to the greater principal stress is nearly 0.566.

Concept   :   Standard formula.

Solution   :

$$\sigma_1; \sigma_2 = \frac{16}{\pi D^3}\left[M \pm \sqrt{M^2 + T^2}\right]$$

$$\sigma_1 = \frac{16}{\pi D^3}\left[M + \sqrt{M^2 + T^2}\right]$$

$$\sigma_1 = \frac{16}{\pi D^3}\left[1.2T + \sqrt{(1.2T)^2 + T^2}\right]$$

$$\sigma_1 = \frac{16T}{\pi D^3}\left[1.2 + \sqrt{(1.2)^2 + 1}\right] = \frac{44.19T}{\pi D^3}$$

$$\sigma_1 = \frac{16}{\pi D^3}\left[M - \sqrt{M^2 - T^2}\right]$$

$$T_{max} = \frac{\sigma_1 - \sigma_2}{2} = \frac{25M}{\pi D^3} = \frac{25T}{\pi D^3}$$

$$\frac{T_{max}}{\sigma_1} = \frac{\dfrac{25T}{\pi D^3}}{\dfrac{44.19T}{\pi D^3}}$$

$$= \mathbf{0.566}$$

EXERCISE

1. A bar 75 mm in diameter, 3.2 m long has to transmit shock energy of 175 joules. Calculate maximum instantaneous stress developed and maximum elongation if E = 200 GPa.   (σ_{max} = 70.36 MPa ; δL_{max} = 1.125 mm)

2. A vertical steel bar 1.75 m long is fixed at top. A weight can slide freely along the rod and its fall is arrested at the bottom by collar. When weight falls through 50 mm, the maximum instantaneous stress developed in the bar is 200 MPa. Determine the stress in the same bar when weight is (i) gradually applied, (ii) suddenly applied, (iii) applied with free fall of 60 mm.

     ((i) σ_{max} = 3.38 MPa, (ii) σ_{max} = 6.76 MPa, (iii) σ_{max} = 218.706 MPa)

3. A uniform bar of cross-sectional area 485 mm² is 8.85 m long. Find the proof resilience and modulus of resilience if the elastic limit for the bar material is 250 MPa. Also find the maximum value of suddenly applied load, the member can carry. Assume E = 200 GPa.

     (Proof resilience = 215.976 joules, Modulus of resilience = 0.156 MPa, Suddenly applied load = 60.625 kN)

4. A vertical steel rod 1.7 m long is fixed at top and provided with collar at bottom. The upper 1000 mm length of bar is 30 mm ϕ, while the lower 700 mm is of 15 mm ϕ. A weight of magnitude 175 N falls freely through a height of 75 mm. Find (i) maximum instantaneous stress, (ii) maximum elongation, (iii) total strain energy stored. Assume   E = 200 GPa.

   ((i) σ_{max} = 177.84 MPa, (ii) δL = 0.848 mm (iii) U = 13.273 joules)

5. A vertical steel bar 15 mm diameter, 1.4 m long is provided with a collar at lower end. Find the maximum weight that can be dropped through a height of 95 mm over the collar if maximum permissible tensile stress is 150 MPa. Assume E = 200 GPa.

   (W = 144.88 N)

6. A bar of 20 mm diameter stretches 1 mm under gradually applied load of 50 kN. If a weight of 1.5 kN is dropped on to a collar at the lower end of this bar through a height of 35 mm, calculate the maximum instantaneous stress and elongation of the bar.

   Take E = 200 GPa.   (σ_{max} = 235.46 MPa ; δL = 1.479 mm)

7. Water under pressure of 10 MPa is suddenly admitted on to a plunger of 125 mm diameter attached to a rod 30 mm diameter, 4 m long. Find the maximum instantaneous stress and deformation of the rod if E = 210 GPa.

   (σ_{max} = 347.22 MPa ; δL = 6.9 mm)

8. A steel specimen 15 mm ϕ stretches by 0.1 mm over 175 mm length under an axial load of 40 kN. Calculate the strain energy stored in the specimen at this stage. If the load at the elastic limit for the specimen is 50 kN, calculate the elongation at elastic limit and proof resilience.

   (U = 2 joules ; δL = 0.125 mm, Proof resilience = 3.125 joules)

9. A vertically suspended steel bar, circular in cross section, is subjected to load of 7.5 kN, which falls by 15 mm on rigid collar provided at lower end of the bar. If maximum allowable strain for the bar is $\dfrac{1}{1300}$, find suitable diameter of bar. Assume E = 200 GPa and length of bar = 3 m.   (30.512 mm)

10. A wagon weighing 25 kN is attached to a wire rope and is moving at the speed of 5.5 kmph. The rope suddenly jams and the wagon is brought to rest. If length of the rope is 45 m and diameter 40 mm, find maximum instantaneous stress and elongation of rope assuming E = 200 GPa. (σ_{max} = 145.04 MPa ; δL_{max} = 32.63 mm)

11. A lift weighing 22 kN is connected by 24 mm diameter and 42 m long rope. If yield stress for the rope material is 300 MPa and factor of safety = 2.1, E = 200 GPa, find the safe working speed for the lift.   (0.9 m/s)

12. A copper rod 25 mm diameter is enclosed in a steel tube 30 mm internal diameter and 3 mm thickness. The length of composite member is 2.4 m. It is fixed at top and provided with a rigid collar at bottom. A body of mass 44 kg is allowed to slide down

freely through a height 'h'. If maximum instantaneous stress developed in copper is not to exceed 70 MPa, find height and elongation of composite bar.
Take E_s = 200 GPa, E_c = 120 GPa.   (h = 113.17 mm ; δL = 1.4 mm)

13. A copper bar 18 mm ϕ is enclosed in a steel tube 28 mm external diameter and 3.2 mm thickness. The composite bar is held vertically and provided with a rigid collar at bottom. A weight of 1.75 kN falls freely through a height of 22 mm. If length of the bar is 2.5 m, find (i) Maximum instantaneous stress developed in each material and (ii) Maximum instantaneous elongation. Take E_s = 200 GPa, E_c = 110 GPa.
(σ_s = 130.36 MPa, σ_c = 71.7 MPa, δL = 1.629 mm)

14. A vertical steel bar is fixed at top and provided with rigid collar at bottom as shown in Fig. 3.21. Compute maximum stress induced in a member if 30 N weight falls through a height of 200 mm. E = 200×10^3 MPa.   (σ_{max} = 107.4 MPa)

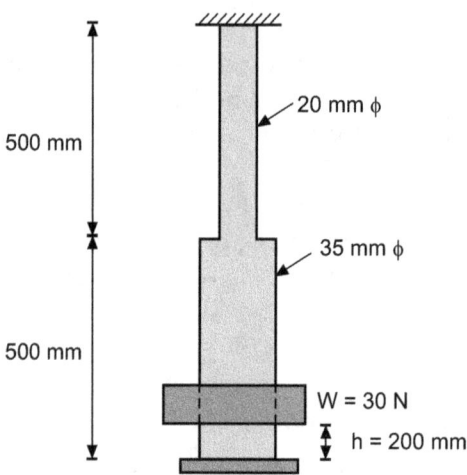

500 mm

20 mm ϕ

35 mm ϕ

500 mm

W = 30 N

h = 200 mm

Fig. 3.21

15. A copper tube is enclosed in a steel tube 35 mm external diameter and 5 mm thickness. This composite bar is held vertically fixed at top and provided with a rigid collar at bottom. A weight of 3 kN falls freely through a height of 25 mm. Length of composite member is 3 m. Find diameter of copper bar if maximum instantaneous stress developed in steel is 150 MPa. Assume E_c = 100 GPa, E_s = 200 GPa. (21.1 mm)

16. A 500 mm long stepped bar 'A' has a diameter of 25 mm for a length of 200 mm and a diameter of 45 mm for the remaining length. Another bar 'B' made of same material has a diameter of 30 mm throughout the entire length of 500 mm. Compare the values of maximum strain energy stored in them if permissible stress for the material is same.   (1 : 2.46)

17. An unknown weight 'W' falls through a height of 10 mm on a collar rigidly attached to the lower end of a vertical bar 5 m long and 600 mm² in section. If the maximum extension of the rod is to be 3 mm, what is the corresponding stress and magnitude of unknown weight ? E = 200 GPa.   (W = 8.3 kN)

18. A vertical steel rod of 25 mm diameter checks the fall on its end of weight 2.5 kN which drops through a distance of 4 mm before it strikes the rod. Find the shortest length of rod which will bear the impact if the stress is not to exceed 150 MPa. E = 210 GPa.

(407.9 mm)

19. A bar 1 m long as shown in Fig. 3.22 is subjected to an axial pull such that the maximum stress is equal to 160 MPa. If E = 200 GPa, calculate the strain energy stored in the bar.

(3.359 Nm)

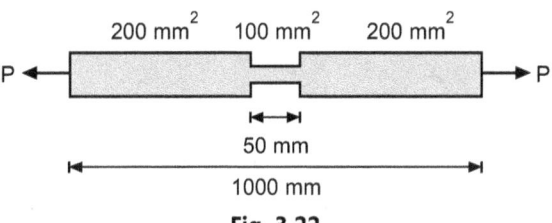

Fig. 3.22

20. Two circular bars of some material have the same length L. One bar has diameter 'd' for a length $\frac{L}{3}$ and diameter '2d' for the remaining length. The other bar has a diameter '2d' for a length $\frac{2L}{3}$ and the diameter '3d' for the remaining length. The bars are subjected to same axial loads. Compare the amount of strain energy in the bar. Compare also the amount of strain energy in them when the maximum stress induced in both the bars is the same, the stress being within elastic limit. $\left(\frac{27}{11}, \frac{27}{176}\right)$

21. A propeller shaft of 240 mm external diameter and 180 mm internal diameter has to transmit 1000 kW at 100 rpm. It is additionally subjected to bending moment of 10 kN/m and an end thrust of 200 kN. Determine : (i) principal stresses and their planes, (ii) maximum shear stress.   (σ_1 = 62.94 MPa (compressive),

σ_2 = 42.05 MPa (tensile), θ_1 = 39.26°, θ_2 = 129.26°, Z_{max} = 52.49 MPa)

22. A propeller shaft 200 mm in diameter transmits 2250 kW at 240 rev/min. The propeller weighing 50 kN is carried by the shaft overhanging the support by 400 mm. If the propeller thrust is 150 kN, calculate the maximum direct stress induced in the cross-section of the propeller shaft.   (τ = 74 N/mm²)

23. A solid shaft 127 mm diameter transmits 600 kW at 300 r.p.m. It is also subjected to a bending moment of 9.1 kN/m and an end thrust. If the maximum principal stress is limited to 77 N/mm², find the end thrust.   (End thrust = 39 kN)

24. In a shaft subjected to bending moment and twisting moment, the greater principal stress is numerically 5 times the lesser one. Find the ratio of M : T and the angle which the plane of greater principal stresses makes with plane of bending stress.

$$(2/\sqrt{5}, \ 24°5')$$

25. At a certain section of a shaft of 80 mm diameter, there is a bending moment of 35 kN-m and a twisting moment of 50 kN-m. Determine the principal stresses and the plane where they act.   (σ_1 = 95.5 N/mm² (compression),

$$\sigma_2 = 26.0 \text{ N/mm}^2 \text{ (tension)}, \ \theta_1 = 27°30' \text{ and } \theta_2 = 117° 30')$$

26. A shaft section 75 mm in diameter is subjected to bending moment of 5 kNm and torque of 10 kNm. Find the maximum normal stresses induced on section and locate the plane on which it acts. Find also what stress acting along can produce the same maximum strain ? Take $\mu = 0.3$.

(Max. normal stresses σ_1 = 195.33 MPa; σ_2 = – 74.61 MPa;

$$\theta_1 = 31.717°, \quad \theta_2 = 121.717°, \quad \sigma = 217.713 \text{ MPa})$$

27. A steel shaft is subjected to torque of 20 kNm and bending moment 15 kNm. Calculate the principal stresses and maximum shear stress if diameter of shaft is 115 mm.

(σ_1 = 133.948 MPa; σ_2 = – 33.487 MPa; θ_1 = 26.56°, θ_2 = 116.56°, τ_{max} = 83.717 MPa)

28. A hollow shaft is subjected to torque of 500 kNm and bending moment of 250 kNm. Internal diameter of shaft is 0.75 times the external diameter. If maximum normal stress is not to exceed 150 MPa and shear stress is not to exceed 80 MPa, design the cross section of shaft.   (D = 373.395 mm,   d = 280 mm)

29. A solid shaft in a small hydraulic turbine is 125 mm in diameters, it supports an axial compressive load of 500 kN. Determine the maximum power that will be developed at a speed of 250 rpm without exceeding maximum shear stress of 70 MPa and maximum normal stress of 90 MPa.

(σ = 40.74 MPa, τ = 66.58 MPa,   T = 25.53 × 10³ Nm, Safe power = 668.455 kW)

UNIT II

CHAPTER
4

SHEAR FORCE AND BENDING MOMENT (PART – A)

4.1 INTRODUCTION

We have so far studied stresses set up in a member due to axial force. The axial force may or may not be constant along the length of member. When axial force is not constant along the length of member, we had used method of section to evaluate the axial force at a section of our interest and axial force diagrams were drawn to study the variation of axial force along the length of member. In this chapter, our interest is to study the effect of transverse loading on the member.

Beam is a structural member which carries lateral or transverse forces i.e. forces at right angles to the axis of the member. The study of these transverse loads, however, is complicated by the fact that the loading effects vary from section to section of the beam. As a preliminary to study the stresses in beams, we shall study the variation of shear and bending moment at various cross sections of the beam. Beams may be straight or curved, but we shall study only straight beams in this chapter. Also the forces applied to the beam will be assumed to lie in the same plane. All the beams discussed will be *statically determinate* i.e. unknown reactions can be determined by applying equations of static equilibrium.

4.2 TYPES OF SUPPORTS

In making sketches of structures or structural members it will be convenient to make use of symbols to show the manner in which it is supported. The various types of supports commonly employed in structural arrangements and their description are given in Table 4.1.

From the above discussion of various types of supports, it must be clear that, a hinged or a pinned support is capable of resisting a force acting in any direction of the plane. Hence, in general, the reaction at such a support may have two components, one in the horizontal and one in the vertical direction. The roller or link support is capable of resisting a force only in the direction normal to the plane on which it is supported. The fixed support is capable of resisting a force in any direction and is also capable of resisting a couple or a moment.

Thus, two reaction components are possible at hinged end, one reaction component is possible at roller end and three reaction components are possible at the fixed end as shown in Fig. 4.1.

Table 4.1

Sr. No.	Support type	Symbol	Description
1.	Hinged or pinned		Horizontal or vertical movement of the point of support, A, is prevented, but free rotation about the point of support is possible.
2.	Roller/Link	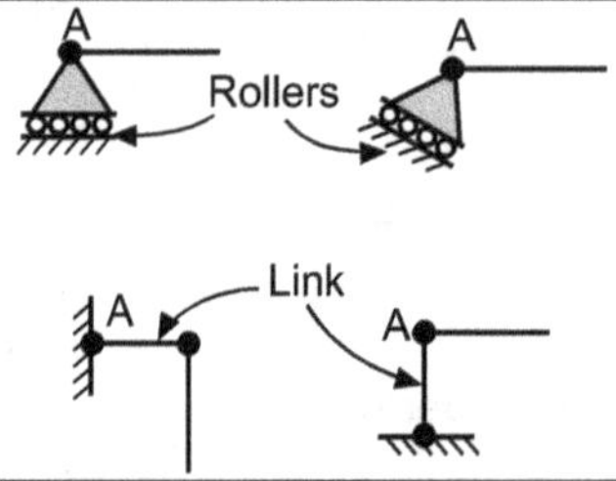	Movement normal to the plane on which rollers are supported is prevented, but movement parallel to the surface of support and rotation about the point of support is possible.
3.	Fixed	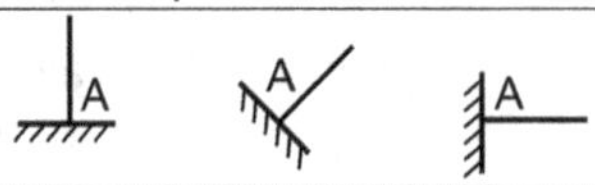	Movement or rotation in any direction is absolutely prevented.

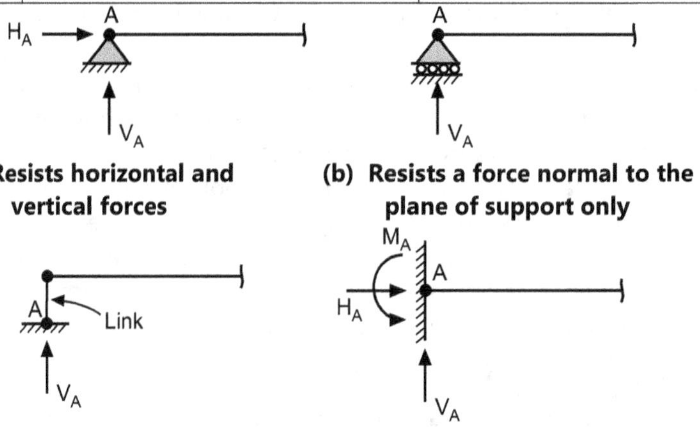

(a) **Resists horizontal and vertical forces**

(b) **Resists a force normal to the plane of support only**

(c) **Resists a force normal to the plane of support only**

(d) **Resists horizontal, vertical forces and a moment**

Fig. 4.1

4.3 TYPES OF LOADS

A beam may be subjected to the following types of loads :

(i) **Concentrated or Point Loads :** These loads act on a very small area and hence it can be assumed to act at a point as shown in Fig. 4.2 (a). Magnitude of the point load is expressed in **N** or **kN.**

(ii) **Uniformly Distributed Load (UDL) :** A load which is spread over a length of beam such that, each unit length is loaded to the same extent is known as uniformly distributed load (UDL), as shown in Fig. 4.2 (b). The intensity of UDL is expressed in **N/m** or **kN/m.**

(iii) **Uniformly Varying Load (UVL) :** A load which is spread over a length of beam such that, its extent varies uniformly on each unit length is known as uniformly varying load (UVL); as shown in Fig. 4.2 (c), (d). The intensity of UVL is expressed in **N/m** or **kN/m**.

(iv) **Couple or Moment :** A beam may be subjected to couple or moment at a point as shown in Fig. 4.2 (d). The magnitude of couple or moment is expressed in **Nm** or **kNm**.

(v) **Bracket Loads :** A beam may be subjected to a bracket load as shown in Fig. 4.2 (g) which ultimately result in **point load** and **couple** at the point of attachment of bracket with the beam.

The reactions from secondary beams, columns, brackets etc. are generally idealized as concentrated or point loads. The self weight of beam, live load etc. are generally uniformly distributed over the length of beam. Loading on side walls of water tanks, lintels, retaining walls etc. is uniformly varying load. Point loads on brackets or point loads eccentric to the axis of the member result in couples.

There may also be various combinations of these loadings. All these loads are assumed to act in one plane, called as plane of loading. To get the reactions set up by various *distributed loads,* one needs only to consider the load replaced by an *equivalent concentrated load acting at its centre of gravity.*

4.4 REACTIONS

If a body, subjected to forces acting in a plane, is at rest, there are three conditions of equilibrium which must be satisfied.

$$\Sigma F_x = 0 ; \quad \Sigma F_y = 0 \quad \text{and} \quad \Sigma M_z = 0$$

It follows that, in determining the reactions acting on the body, the loads being known, not more than three unknown quantities can be found. There are three things which must be known about each force in order to have it fully determined : *its magnitude, its direction, and its point of application or line of action.* If knowledge of all these concerning one reaction is lacking, then the magnitude, direction and point of application or line of action of all other forces acting on the structure must be known. This reaction would then hold the body at equilibrium.

It must be remembered that, the number of unknowns which can be determined is fixed by the number of equations available, and it makes no difference whether they pertain to one reaction or to several reactions as long as the unknown quantities do not exceed in number of independent equations.

To find the reactions of given beam or structure, first of all we remove the supports and show the respective reaction components in their places and draw complete free body diagram (FBD). Then apply laws of statics to get the required unknown reactions. *Sign convention* used for applying laws of *statics* is as under :

- All horizontal forces to the right are considered positive.
- All vertical forces acting upwards are considered positive.
- All anticlockwise moments are considered positive.

Forces, moments, opposite of above are considered negative.

4.5 TYPES OF BEAMS

Beams are basically classified as statically determinate and statically indeterminate beams. When unknown reactions can be obtained by use of equations of static equilibrium alone, it is called as statically determinate. The various types of statically determinate beams are (i) Simply supported beam, (ii) Simple beam, (iii) Cantilever beam, (iv) Overhanging beam etc. While the various types of statically indeterminate beams are (i) Fixed beams, (ii) Continuous beams, (iii) Propped cantilevers, etc. These various types of beams are shown in Fig. 4.2.

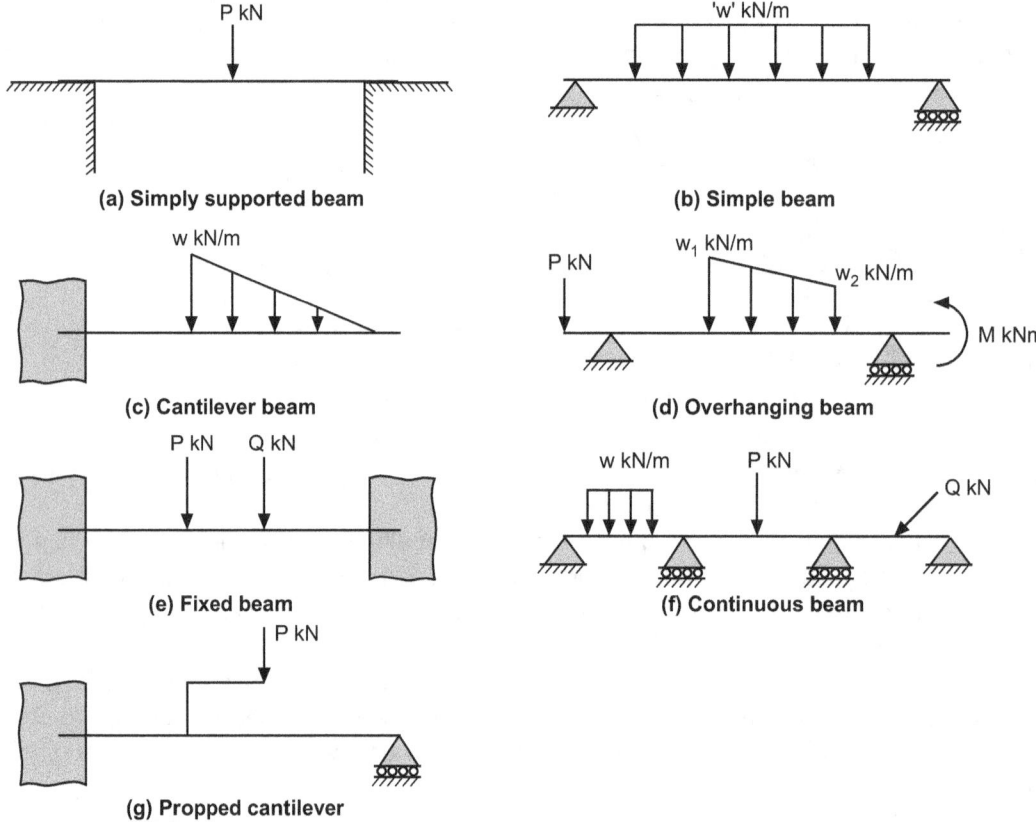

Fig. 4.2 : Various types of beams

4.6 SHEAR FORCE AND BENDING MOMENT

Consider a FBD of beam as shown in Fig. 4.3 (a). The unknown reactions are determined by equations of laws of statics and having obtained the unknown reactions, *method of section* is used to find shear force and bending moment at a cross section.

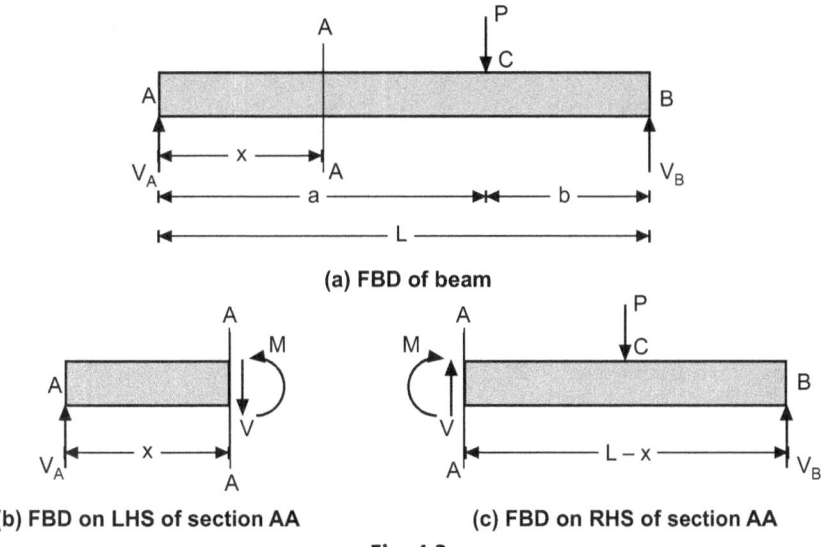

(a) FBD of beam

(b) FBD on LHS of section AA   **(c) FBD on RHS of section AA**

Fig. 4.3

Fig. 4.3 (b) shows the FBD of part of the beam on left hand side of the section considered at a distance x from A. Since the beam and all its parts are in equilibrium, this section of the beam must be in equilibrium. First consider the equilibrium of the vertical forces i.e. $\sum F_y = 0$. This equation shows that, there must be a downward vertical force equal in magnitude to the reaction at left support. The only surface on which such a force can act is that on the right end of the free body. This downward force is called as the shear force and is designated as V or SF. Since, there are no horizontal forces, a moment equation is all that remains to be satisfied for equilibrium of the element shown. We can, of course, write a moment equation about any point in the plane of the diagram, but it is convenient to write it with respect to the right hand end of the section. Assuming unknown couple at this section of magnitude M, we have

$$M - V_A(x) = 0$$
$$\therefore \qquad M = V_A(x)$$

This quantity is known as the bending moment and is designated as M or BM.

Fig. 4.3 (c) shows FBD of part of the beam on right hand side of the section considered. *It should be noted that magnitude and nature of the shear force and bending moment at a section whether computed from left or right hand side of the section remains the same.* The side to be chosen for calculation is that side on which fewer external forces are acting and the *section is to be considered normal to the axis of the beam.*

Thus, shear force and bending moment at a section can be defined as follows :

Shear force : It is the algebraic sum of all the external forces acting parallel to the section, on any one side of the section.

Bending moment : It is the algebraic sum of the moments of all the external forces acting on any one side of the section taken about the centre of gravity of section.

4.6.1 Sign Conventions for Shear force and Bending Moment

(a) Shear Force : An upward shear force to the left of the section or downward shear force to the right of the section is considered as positive; otherwise it will be negative. See Fig. 4.4 (a).

This sign convention of shear force leads to the shear effect as shown in Fig. 4.4 (b).

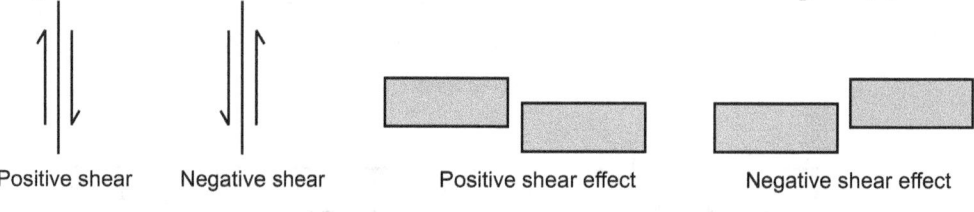

| Positive shear | Negative shear | Positive shear effect | Negative shear effect |

(a) Sign convention for shear force   **(b) Effect of shear force**

Fig. 4.4

(b) Bending Moment : The bending moment which produces the deformation of the beam **concave upwards** is called **sagging** bending moment and it is considered **positive**. The bending moment which produces the deformation of the beam **convex upwards** is called **hogging** bending moment and it is considered **negative**. See Fig. 4.5 (a). This sign convention of bending moment leads to the bending effect as shown in Fig. 4.5 (b).

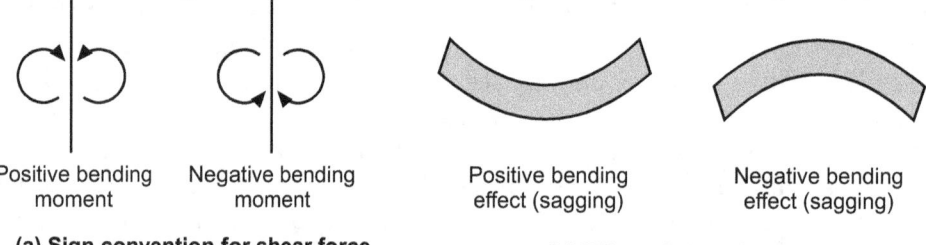

| Positive bending moment | Negative bending moment | Positive bending effect (sagging) | Negative bending effect (sagging) |

(a) Sign convention for shear force   **(b) Effect of shear force**

Fig. 4.5

It should be noted that, for a horizontal beam, upward external forces cause positive bending moments with respect to any section, while the downward external forces cause negative bending moments.

4.7 SHEAR FORCE AND BENDING MOMENT DIAGRAMS (SFD AND BMD)

The shear force and bending moment can be calculated numerically at any particular section. But from the design point of view, we are interested in knowing the manner in which these values vary, along the length of beam. This can be done by plotting the shear force or the bending moment as ordinate and the position of the cross section as abscissa to give shear force diagram (SFD) and bending moment diagram (BMD) respectively. While plotting these diagrams, positive values are plotted above the reference line and negative values below it. The shear force and bending moment diagrams can be plotted from shear force and bending moment equations written for respective zones. The nature of these curves depends on the type of loading the beam is subjected to. This is illustrated in following simple examples.

Note : (i)   SFD is parallel to the reference line.

(ii)   Bending moment variation is linear along the length of beam.

(iii)   At a section where couple is acting, shear force does not change.

(iv)   Section where bending moment changes its sign is called as point of *contraflexure*. Since change of sign is possible, only when bending moment at point of contraflexure is zero, it is also called as point of zero bending moment or point of **inflection**. It should be understood that a point of contraflexure is necessarily a point of inflection, but point of inflection need not be a point of contraflexure. *For locating point of contraflexure, bending moment equation in the respective zone shall be equated to zero.*

(v)   Vertical drop in the BMD indicates sudden change in the value of bending moment at a section. The magnitude of drop in the BM diagram is equal to the magnitude of couple acting at a section.

4.8 RELATIONSHIP BETWEEN LOAD, SHEAR AND BENDING MOMENT

The relationship between load, shear and bending moment can be derived as under. Consider a beam supported and loaded as shown in Fig. 4.6 (a).

Let V_x and M_x be the shear and bending moment on a section at a distance 'x' from A. Likewise $V_x + dV_x$ and $M_x + dM_x$ are the shear and bending moment on a section at a distance x + dx from A. The free body diagram of the segment of the beam which is dx in length is shown in Fig. 4.6 (b).

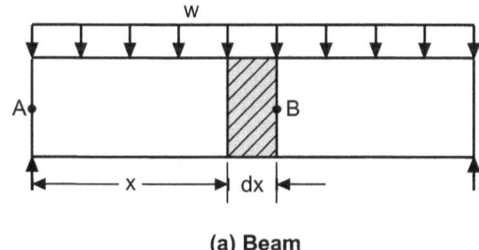

(a) Beam	(b) FBD of beam segement

Fig. 4.6

Applying equations of equilibrium to FBD of segment as under :

$\Sigma F_y = 0 \Rightarrow V_x - (V_x + dV_x) - w \cdot dx = 0$

$dV_x = -w \cdot dx$

$\therefore \quad \dfrac{dV_x}{dx} = -w$ ... (4.1)

Thus, *the rate of decrease of shear force with respect to x, on any section at a distance 'x' from left end of the beam is equal to the intensity of load at the section.*

$\Sigma M_B = 0 \Rightarrow \qquad V_x \cdot dx + M_x = M_x + dM_x + w \dfrac{dx^2}{2}$

The term $w\dfrac{dx^2}{2}$ being very small; can be neglected.

$$dM_x = V_x \cdot dx$$

$$\frac{dM_x}{dx} = V_x \qquad\qquad \text{... (4.2)}$$

Thus, *the rate of increase of bending moment with respect to 'x', on any section at a distance 'x' from left end of the beam, is equal to shear at the section.*

SOLVED EXAMPLES

Example 4.1 : *The beam is supported and loaded as shown in Fig. 4.7 (a). Draw SFD and BMD indicating all the important values.*

Data   :   As shown in Fig. 4.7 (a).

Required :   SFD, BMD.

Solution :   (i) Reactions :

$\sum F_y = 0;$ $V_A - 20 - 30 = 0$ $\therefore$ $V_A = 50$ kN $(\uparrow)$

$\sum M_A = 0;$ $M_A - 20 \times 1 - 30 \times 2.5 = 0$ $\therefore$ $M_A = 95$ kNm $(\circlearrowleft)$

$\sum F_x = 0;$ $H_A = 0$

FBD of beam is as shown in Fig. 4.7 (b).

(ii)   SF calculations :

$$SF_A = 50 \text{ kN}$$
$$SF_B \text{ (just to the left)}$$
$$= 50 \text{ kN}$$
$$SF_B \text{ (just to the right)}$$
$$= 50 - 20 = 30 \text{ kN}$$
$$SF_C = 30 \text{ kN}$$

SFD is as shown in Fig. 4.7 (c).

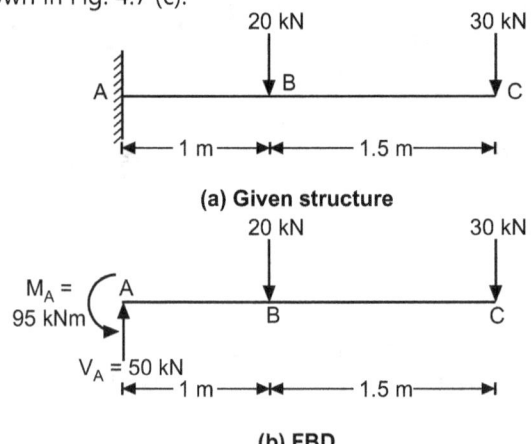

(a) Given structure

(b) FBD

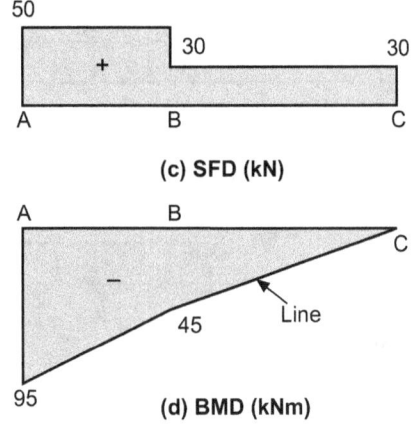

(c) SFD (kN)

(d) BMD (kNm)

Fig. 4.7

(iii)   BM calculations :

$$BM_A = -95 \text{ kNm}$$

$$BM_B = -30 \times 1.5$$

$$= -45 \text{ kNm}$$

$$BM_C = 0$$

BMD is as shown in Fig. 4.7 (d).

Example 4.2 : *The beam is supported and loaded as shown in Fig. 4.8 (a). Draw SFD and BMD indicating all important values.*

Data   :   As shown in Fig. 4.8 (a).

Required :   SFD, BMD.

Solution :   (i) Reactions :

$$\sum F_y = 0 ; \qquad V_A - 2 \times 1.5 - 6 = 0$$

$$\therefore \qquad V_A = 9 \text{ kN } (\uparrow)$$

$$\sum M_A = 0 ; \qquad M_A - 2 \times 1.5 \times 2.25 - 6 \times 3 = 0$$

$$M_A = 24.75 \text{ kN.m } (\circlearrowleft)$$

$$\sum F_x = 0 ; \qquad H_A = 0$$

FBD of beam is as shown in Fig. 4.8 (b).

(ii)   SF calculations :

$$SF_A = SF_B = 9 \text{ kN}$$

$$SF_C = 6 \text{ kN}$$

SFD is as shown in Fig. 4.7 (c).

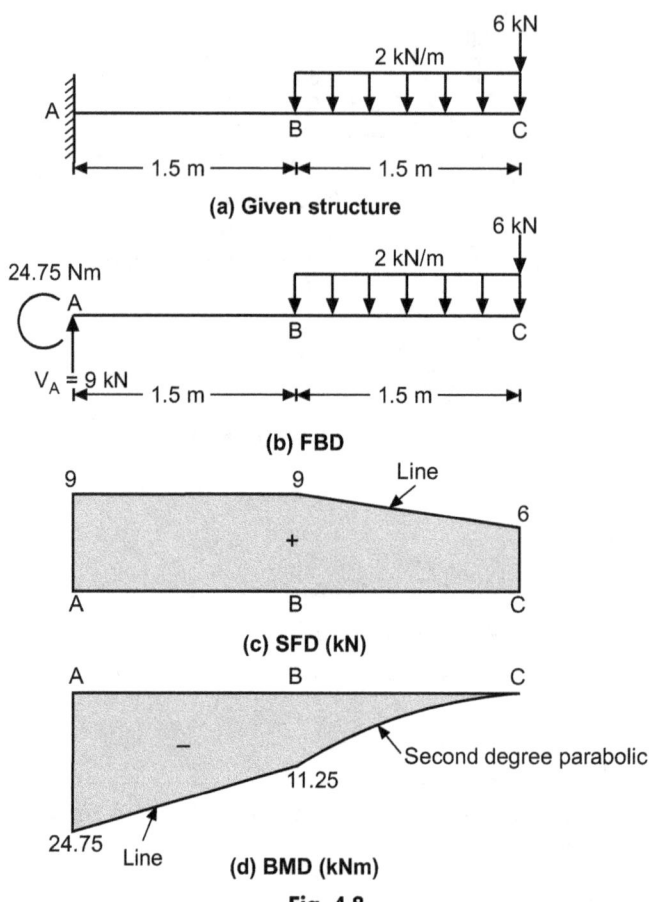

(a) Given structure

(b) FBD

(c) SFD (kN)

(d) BMD (kNm)

Fig. 4.8

(iii)   BM calculations :

$$BM_A = -24.75 \text{ kN.m}$$
$$BM_B = -24.75 + 9 \times 1.5 = -11.25 \text{ kN.m}$$
$$BM_C = 0$$

BMD is as shown in Fig. 4.8 (d).

Example 4.3 : *The beam is supported and loaded as shown in Fig. 4.9 (a). Draw SFD and BMD indicating all the important values.*

Data   :   As shown in Fig. 4.9 (a).

Required :   SFD, BMD.

Solution :   (i) Reactions :

$$\sum F_y = 0 ; \quad V_A - 25 = 0 \qquad\qquad \therefore \; V_A = 25 \text{ kN } (\uparrow)$$
$$\sum M_A = 0 ; \quad M_A - 50 - 25 \times 2 = 0$$
$$\therefore \qquad\qquad M_A = 100 \text{ kN.m } (\circlearrowleft)$$

$$\sum F_X = 0 \; ; \quad H_A = 0$$

FBD of beam is as shown in Fig. 4.9 (b).

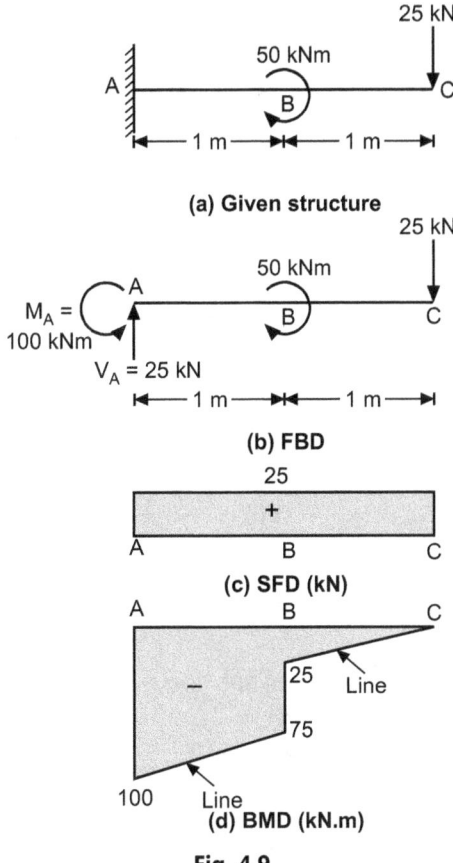

(a) Given structure

(b) FBD

(c) SFD (kN)

(d) BMD (kN.m)

Fig. 4.9

(ii)   SF calculations :

$$SF_A = SF_B = SF_C = 25 \text{ kN}$$

SFD is as shown in Fig. 4.9 (c).

(iii)   BM calculations :

$$BM_A = -100 \text{ kN.m}$$

$$BM_B \text{ (just to the left)} = -100 + 25 \times 1 = -75 \text{ kN.m}$$

$$BM_B \text{ (just to the right)} = -75 + 50 = -25 \text{ kN.m}$$

$$BM_C = 0$$

BMD is as shown in Fig. 4.9 (d).

Example 4.4 : *The beam is supported and loaded as shown in Fig. 4.10 (a). Draw SFD and BMD indicating all the important values.*

Data   :   As shown in Fig. 4.10 (a).

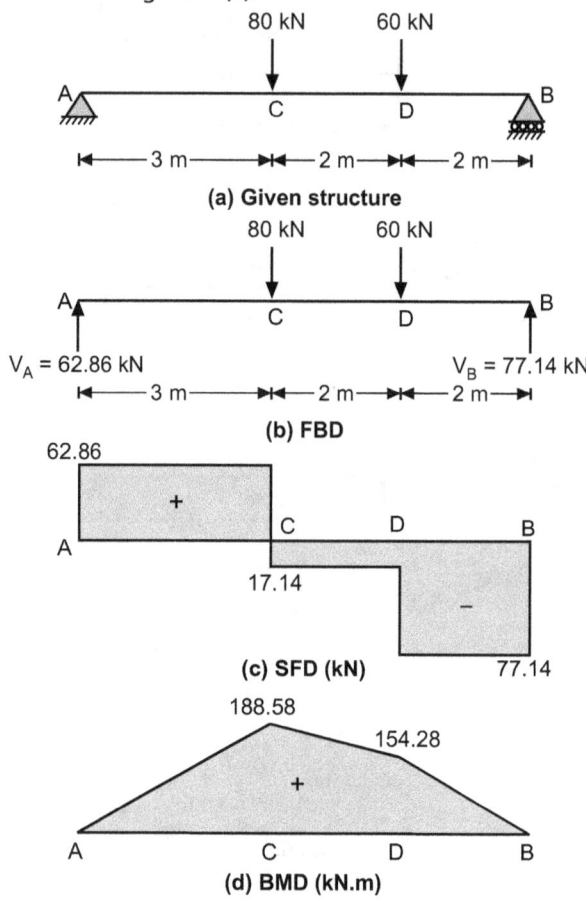

(a) Given structure

(b) FBD

(c) SFD (kN)

(d) BMD (kN.m)

Fig. 4.10

Required : SFD, BMD.

Solution : (i) Reactions :

$\Sigma M_A = 0$; $V_B \times 7 - 60 \times 5 - 80 \times 3 = 0$

$\therefore$ $V_B = 77.14$ kN ($\uparrow$)

$\Sigma F_y = 0$; $V_A + V_B - 80 - 60 = 0$

$\therefore$ $V_A = 62.86$ kN ($\uparrow$)

$\Sigma F_x = 0$; $H_A = 0$

FBD of beam is as shown in Fig. 4.10 (b).

(ii)   SF calculations : SF_A = 62.86 kN

SF_C (just to the left) = 62.86 kN

SF_C (just to the right) = 62.86 – 80

= – 17.14 kN

SF_D (just to the left) = – 17.14 kN

SF_D (just to the right) = – 17.14 – 60

= – 77.14 kN

SF_B = – 77.14 kN

SFD is as shown in Fig. 4.10 (c).

(iii)   BM calculations : BM_A = BM_B = 0

BM_C = 62.86 × 3

= 188.58 kN.m

BM_D = 77.14 × 2

= 154.28 kN.m

BMD is as shown in Fig. 4.10 (d).

Example 4.5 : *The beam is supported and loaded as shown in Fig. 4.11 (a). Draw SFD and BMD indicating all the important values.*

Data   :   As shown in Fig. 4.11 (a).

Required :   SFD, BMD.

Solution   :   (i) Reactions :

Couple at D = 5 × 2 × 0.375 = 3.75 kN.m ($\circlearrowleft$)

$\sum M_A = 0$; $V_B × 3 – 5 × 2.625 – 3.75 – 5 × 0.375 = 0$

∴ V_B = 6.25 kN (↑)

$\sum F_y = 0$; $V_A + V_B – 5 – 5 = 0$

V_A = 3.75 kN (↑)

$\sum F_x = 0$ $H_A = 0$

FBD of beam is as shown in Fig. 4.11 (b).

(ii)   SF calculations : SF_A = 3.75 kN

SF_C = 3.75 – 5

=   – 1.25 kN

SF_B = – 6.25 kN.

To locate point of zero SF, consider a section at a distance 'x' from A in zone AC.

SF_x = 3.75 – 6.67 x = 0

∴   x = 0.5625 m from A

SFD is as shown in Fig. 4.11 (c).

(iii) BM calculations :

$$BM_A = BM_B = 0$$

$$BM_C = 3.75 \times 0.75 - 5 \times \frac{0.75}{2} = 0.9375 \text{ kN.m}$$

BM at point of zero SF $= BM_F = 3.75 \times 0.5625 - 6.67 \times \dfrac{(0.5625)^2}{2}$

$$= 1.05 \text{ kN.m}$$

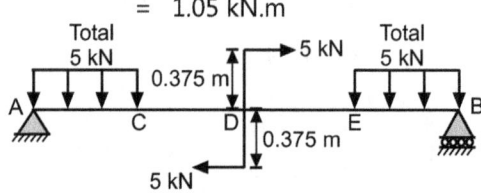

(a) Given structure

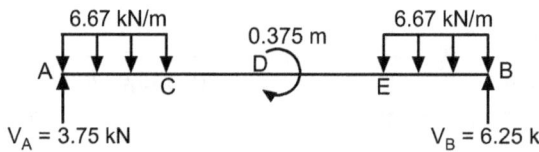

(b) FBD

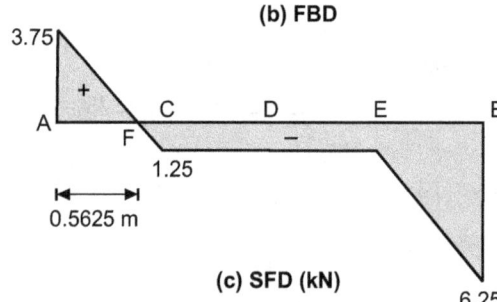

(c) SFD (kN)

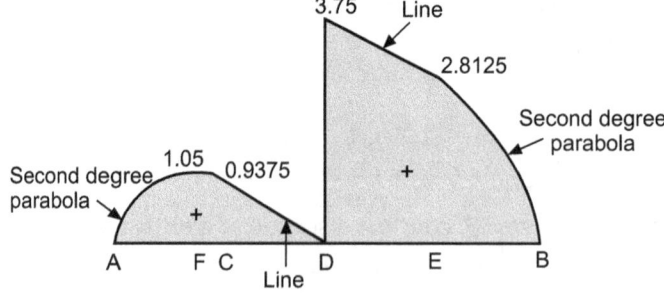

(d) BMD (kN.m)

Fig. 4.11

BM$_D$ (just to the left) $= 3.75 \times 1.5 - 5 \times 1.125 = 0$

BM$_D$ (just to the right) $= 0 + 3.75 = 3.75$ kN.m

$$BM_E = 6.25 \times 0.75 - 5 \times \frac{0.75}{2} = 2.8125 \text{ kN.m}$$

Example 4.6 : *The beam is supported and loaded as shown in Fig. 4.12 (a). Draw SFD, BMD indicating all important values.*

Data   :   As shown in Fig. 4.12 (a).

Required :   SFD, BMD.

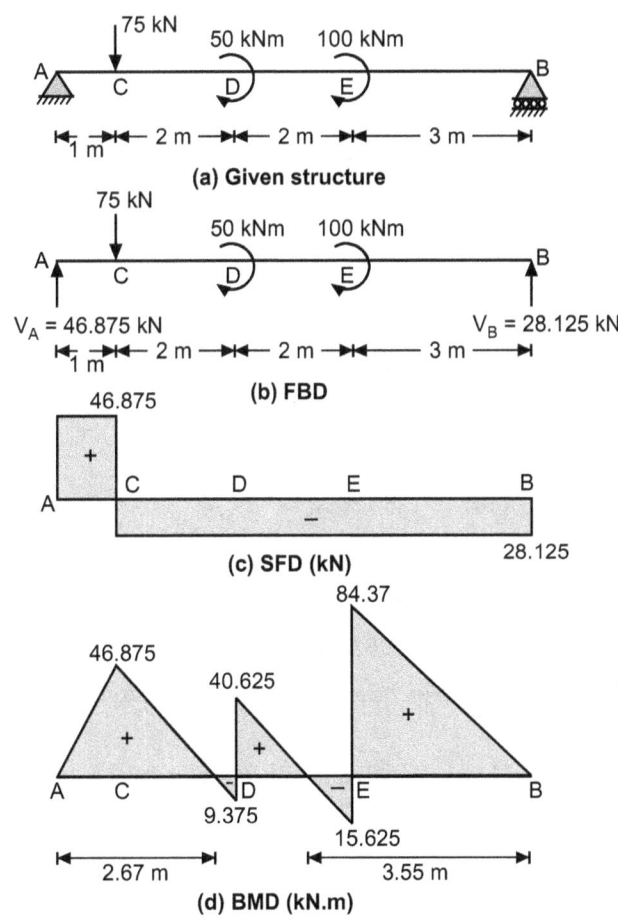

(a) Given structure

(b) FBD

(c) SFD (kN)

(d) BMD (kN.m)

Fig. 4.12

Solution   :   (i) Reactions :

$\Sigma M_A = 0$; $V_B \times 8 - 100 - 50 - 75 \times 1 = 0$

$$V_B = 28.125 \text{ kN } (\uparrow)$$

$\Sigma F_y = 0;$ $\qquad V_A + V_B - 75 = 0$

$$V_A = 46.875 \text{ kN } (\uparrow)$$

$\Sigma F_x = 0;$ $\qquad H_A = 0$

FBD of beam is as shown in Fig. 4.12 (b).

(ii)　SF calculations :　$SF_A = 46.875$ kN

$$SF_C \text{ (just to the left) } = 46.875 \text{ kN}$$

$$SF_C \text{ (just to the right) } = 46.875 - 75 = -28.125 \text{ kN}$$

$$SF_D = SF_E = SF_B = -28.125 \text{ kN}$$

SFD is as shown in Fig. 4.12 (c).

(iii)　BM calculations :

$$BM_A = BM_B = 0$$

$$BM_C = 46.875 \times 1$$

$$= 46.875 \text{ kN.m}$$

$$BM_D \text{ (just to the left) } = 46.875 \times 3 - 75 \times 2$$

$$= -9.375 \text{ kN.m}$$

$$BM_D \text{ (just to the right) } = -9.375 + 50$$

$$= 40.625 \text{ kN.m}$$

$$BM_E \text{ (just to the right) } = 28.125 \times 3$$

$$= 84.375 \text{ kN.m}$$

$$BM_E \text{ (just to the left) } = 84.375 - 100$$

$$= -15.625 \text{ kN.m}$$

To locate point of contraflexure in zone CD, consider a section at a distance 'x' from 'A' in zone CD.

$$BM_x = 46.875 \, x - 75 \, (x - 1) = 0$$

$\therefore$ $\qquad x = 2.67$ m from 'A'

To locate point of contraflexure in zone DE, consider a section at a distance 'x' from B in zone DE.

$$BM_x = 28.125 \, x - 100 = 0$$

$\therefore$ $\qquad x = 3.55$ m from B

BMD is as shown in Fig. 4.12 (d).

Example 4.7 : *The beam is supported and loaded as shown in Fig. 4.13 (a). Draw SFD and BMD indicating all the important values.*

Data   :   As shown in Fig. 4.13 (a).

Required :   SFD, BMD.

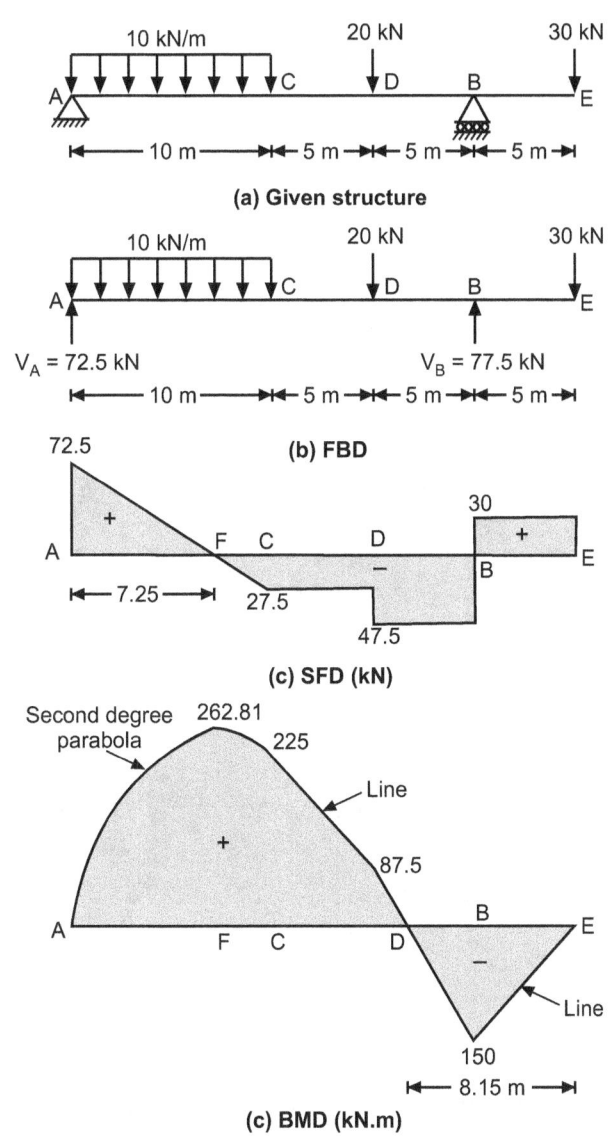

(a) Given structure

$V_A = 72.5$ kN $V_B = 77.5$ kN

(b) FBD

(c) SFD (kN)

(c) BMD (kN.m)

Fig. 4.13

Solution   :   (i) Reactions :

$$\Sigma M_A = 0 ; \qquad V_B \times 20 - 10 \times \frac{10^2}{2} - 20 \times 15 - 30 \times 25 = 0$$

$\therefore$ V_B = 77.5 kN ($\uparrow$)

$\Sigma F_y = 0$; $V_A + V_B - 10 \times 10 - 20 - 30 = 0$

$\therefore$ V_A = 72.5 kN ($\uparrow$)

$\Sigma F_x = 0$; $H_A = 0$

FBD of beam is as shown in Fig. 4.13 (b).

(ii)   SF calculations :

$SF_A = 72.5$ kN

$SF_C = 72.5 - 10 \times 10 = -27.5$ kN

SF_D (just to the left) = -27.5 kN

SF_D (just to the right) = $-27.5 - 20 = -47.5$ kN

SF_B (just to the right) = 30 kN

SF_B (just to the left) = $30 - 77.5 = -47.5$ kN

SF_E = 30 kN

To locate point of zero SF, consider a section at a distance x from A in zone AC.

$SF_x = 72.5 - 10 \, x = 0$

$\therefore$ x = 7.26 m from A

SFD is as shown in Fig. 4.13 (c).

(iii)   BM calculations :

$BM_A = BM_E = 0$

$BM_C = 72.5 \times 10 - 10 \times \dfrac{10^2}{2} = 225$ kN.m

BM at a point of zero SF $= BM_F = 72.5 \times 7.25 - 10 \times \dfrac{(7.25)^2}{2}$

$= 262.81$ kN.m

$BM_D = 77.5 \times 5 - 30 \times 10 = 87.5$ kN.m

$BM_B = -30 \times 5 = -150$ kN.m

To locate point of contraflexure, consider a section at a distance 'x' from E in zone DB.

$BM_x = -30 \, x + 77.5 \, (x - 5) = 0$

$\therefore$ x = 8.15 m from E

BMD is as shown in Fig. 4.13 (d).

Example 4.8 : *The beam is supported and loaded as shown in Fig. 4.14 (a). Draw SFD and BMD indicating all the important values.*

Data   :   As shown in Fig. 4.14 (a).

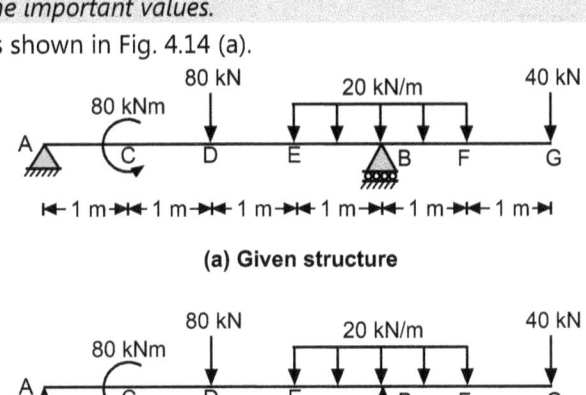

(a) Given structure

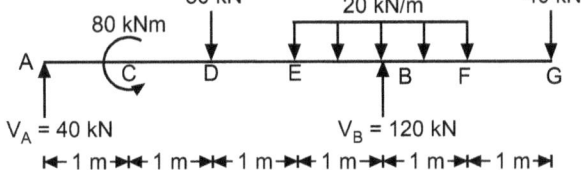

(b) FBD

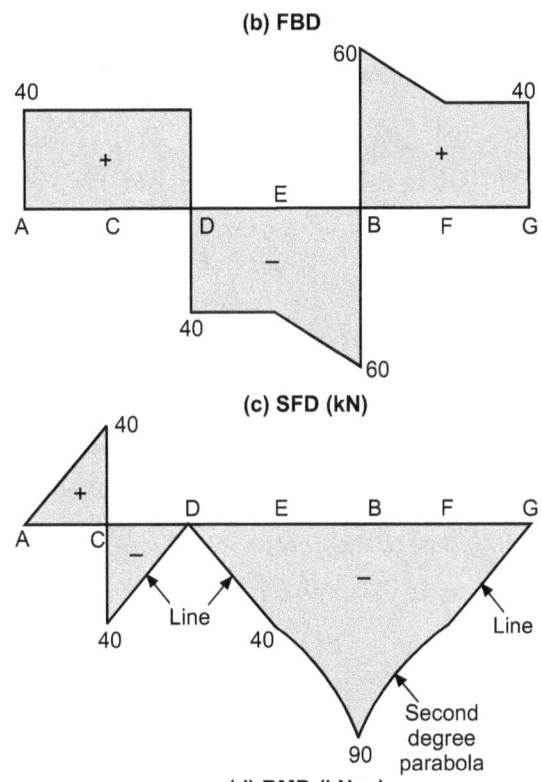

(c) SFD (kN)

(d) BMD (kN.m)

Fig. 4.14

Required : SFD, BMD.

Solution : (i) Reactions :

$$\Sigma M_A = 0 \; ; \qquad V_B \times 4 - 40 \times 6 - 20 \times 2 \times 4 - 80 \times 2 + 80 = 0$$

$$V_B = 120 \text{ kN } (\uparrow)$$

$$\Sigma F_y = 0 \; ; \qquad V_A + V_B - 80 - 20 \times 2 - 40 = 0$$

$$\therefore \qquad V_A = 40 \text{ kN } (\uparrow)$$

$$\Sigma F_x = 0 \; ; \qquad H_A = 0.$$

FBD of beam is as shown in Fig. 4.14 (b).

(ii) SF calculations :

$$SF_A = 40 \text{ kN}$$

$$SF_C = 40 \text{ kN}$$

$$SF_D \text{ (just to the left)} = 40 \text{ kN}$$

$$SF_D \text{ (just to the right)} = 40 - 80 = -40 \text{ kN}$$

$$SF_E = 40 - 80 = -40 \text{ kN}$$

$$SF_B \text{ (just to the left)} = 40 - 80 - 20 \times 1 = -60 \text{ kN}$$

$$SF_B \text{ (just to the right)} = -60 + 120 = 60 \text{ kN}$$

$$SF_F = SF_G = 40 \text{ kN}$$

SFD is as shown in Fig. 4.14 (c).

(iii) BM calculations :

$$BM_A = BM_G = 0$$

$$BM_C \text{ (just to the left)} = 40 \times 1 = 40 \text{ kN.m}$$

$$BM_C \text{ (just to the right)} = 40 - 80 = -40 \text{ kN.m}$$

$$BM_D = 40 \times 2 - 80 = 0$$

$$BM_E = 40 \times 3 - 80 - 80 \times 1 = -40 \text{ kN.m}$$

$$BM_B = -40 \times 2 - 20 \times \frac{1^2}{2} = -90 \text{ kN.m}$$

$$BM_F = -40 \times 1 = -40 \text{ kN.m}$$

BMD is as shown in Fig. 4.14 (d).

Example 4.9 : *The beam is supported and loaded as shown in Fig. 4.15 (a). Draw AFD, SFD and BMD for beam ABC indicating all the important values.*

Data   :   As shown in Fig. 4.15 (a).

Required :   AFD, SFD, BMD.

Solution :   (i) Reactions :

Vertical component of 50 kN force at D

$$= 50 \times \frac{3}{5} = 30 \text{ kN} \ (\uparrow)$$

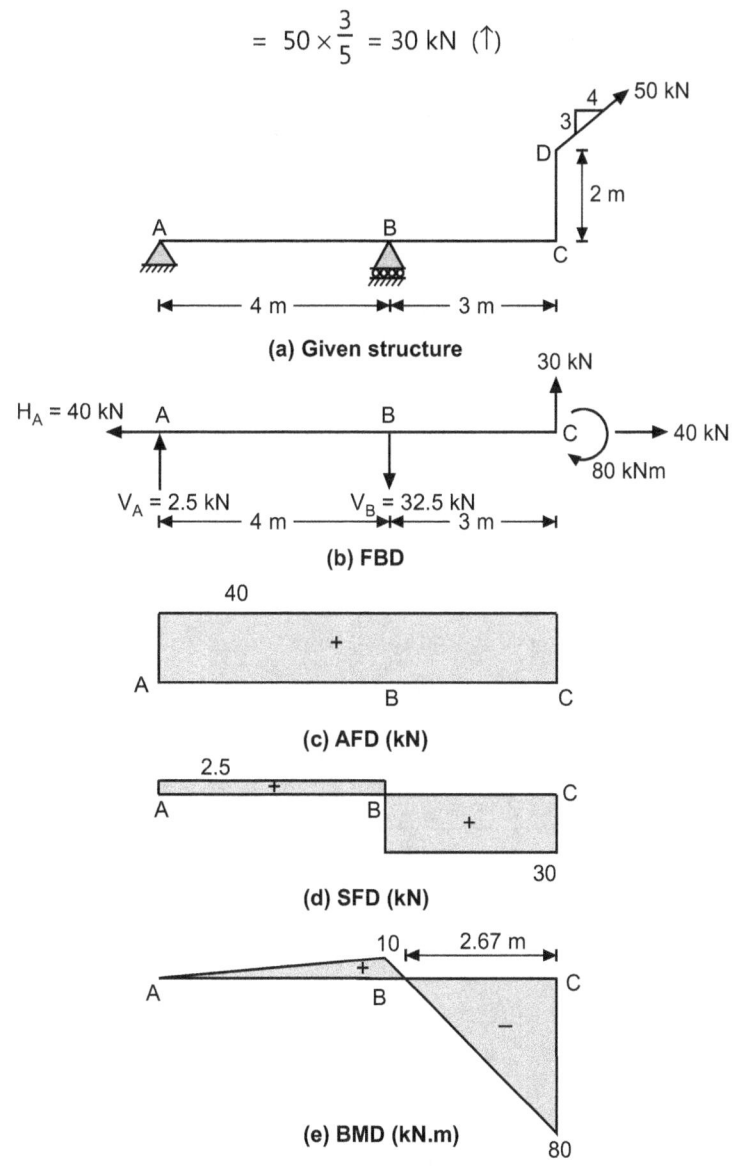

(a) Given structure

(b) FBD

(c) AFD (kN)

(d) SFD (kN)

(e) BMD (kN.m)

Fig. 4.15

Horizontal component of 50 kN force at D

$$= 50 \times \frac{4}{5} = 40 \text{ kN } (\rightarrow)$$

Force components at D are transferred at C as shown in Fig. 4.15 (b).

$\sum M_A = 0;$ $V_B \times 4 - 80 + 30 \times 7 = 0$

$\therefore$ $V_B = -32.5 \text{ kN } = 32.5 \text{ kN } (\downarrow)$

$\sum F_y = 0;$ $V_A + V_B + 30 = 0$

$\therefore$ $V_A = 2.5 \text{ kN } (\uparrow)$

$\sum F_x = 0;$ $H_A = 40 \text{ kN } (\leftarrow)$

FBD of beam is as shown in Fig. 4.15 (b).

(ii)   Axial force :

Member ABC is subjected to axial tension of 40 kN. AFD is as shown in Fig. 4.15 (c).

(iii)   SF calculations :

$$SF_A = 2.5 \text{ kN}$$

$$SF_B \text{ (just to the left) } = 2.5 \text{ kN}$$

$$SF_B \text{ (just to the right) } = 2.5 - 32.5 = -30 \text{ kN}$$

$$SF_C = -30 \text{ kN}$$

SFD is as shown in Fig. 4.15 (d).

(iv)   BM calculations :

$$BM_A = 0$$

$$BM_B = 2.5 \times 4 = 10 \text{ kN.m}$$

$$BM_C = -80 \text{ kN.m}$$

To locate point of contraflexure, consider a section at a distance 'x' from 'C' in zone BC.

$$BM_X = 30 x - 80 = 0$$

$$x = 2.67 \text{ m from C.}$$

BMD is as shown in Fig. 4.15 (e).

Example 4.10 : *The beam is supported and loaded as shown in Fig. 4.16 (a). Draw SFD and BMD indicating all the important values.*

Data   :   As shown in Fig. 4.16 (a).

Required :   SFD, BMD.

Solution :   (i) Reactions :

$\sum M_A = 0;$ $V_B \times 7 - 10 \times \dfrac{3^2}{2} + 50 - 30 \times 1 \times 7.5 = 0$

$\therefore$ $V_B = 31.43 \text{ kN } (\uparrow)$

$\sum F_y = 0;$ $V_A + V_B - 10 \times 3 - 30 \times 1 = 0$

$$V_A = 28.57 \text{ kN } (\uparrow)$$

$$\sum F_X = 0 ; \qquad H_A = 0$$

FBD of beam is as shown in Fig. 4.16 (b).

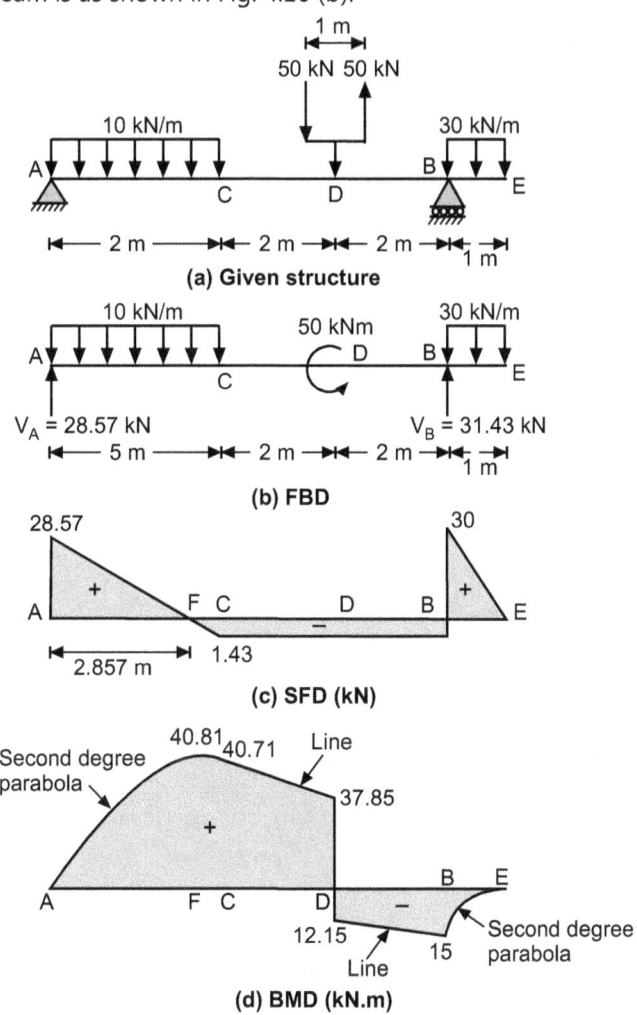

(a) Given structure

(b) FBD

(c) SFD (kN)

(d) BMD (kN.m)

Fig. 4.16

(ii)   SF calculations :

$$SF_A = 28.57 \text{ kN}$$

$$SF_C = 28.57 - 10 \times 3 = -1.43 \text{ kN}$$

$$SF_B \text{ (just to the right)} = 30 \text{ kN}$$

$$SF_B \text{ (just to the left)} = 30 - 31.43 = -1.43 \text{ kN}$$

$$SF_E = 0$$

To locate point of zero SF, consider a section at a distance 'x' from A in zone AC.

$$SF_x = 28.57 - 10\,x = 0$$

$$\therefore \qquad x = 2.857 \text{ m from A.}$$

SFD is as shown in Fig. 4.16 (c).

(iii) BM calculations :

$$BM_A = BM_E = 0$$

BM at point of zero SF $= BM_F$

$$= 28.57 \times 2.857 - 10 \times \frac{(2.857)^2}{2}$$

$$= 40.81 \text{ kN.m}$$

$$BM_C = 28.57 \times 3 - 10 \times \frac{3^2}{2} = 40.71 \text{ kN.m}$$

$$BM_D \text{ (just to the left)} = 28.57 \times 5 - 10 \times 3 \times 3.5$$

$$= 37.85 \text{ kN.m}$$

$$BM_D \text{ (just to the right)} = 37.85 - 50$$

$$= -12.15 \text{ kN.m}$$

$$BM_B = -30 \times \frac{1^2}{2} = -15 \text{ kN.m}$$

BMD is as shown in Fig. 4.16 (d).

Example 4.11 : *The beam is supported and loaded as shown in Fig. 4.17 (a). Draw AFD, SFD, BMD indicating all the important values.*

Data   : As shown in Fig. 4.17 (a).

Required : AFD, SFD, BMD.

Solution : (i) Reactions :

$$\sum M_A = 0 \,; \ \ V_D \times 3.4 - 21.21 \times 1 + 21.21 - 20 \times 2.2 \ - 15 \times 2.4 \times 3.4 = 0$$

$$\therefore \qquad V_D = 48.94 \text{ kN } (\uparrow)$$

$$\sum F_y = 0 \,; \qquad V_A + V_D - 21.21 - 20 - 15 \times 2.4 = 0$$

$$V_A = 28.27 \text{ kN } (\uparrow)$$

$$\sum F_x = 0 \,; \qquad H_A = 21.21 \text{ kN } (\rightarrow)$$

(ii) Axial force :

Portion AB has axial compressive force of 21.21 kN.

AFD is as shown in Fig. 4.17 (c).

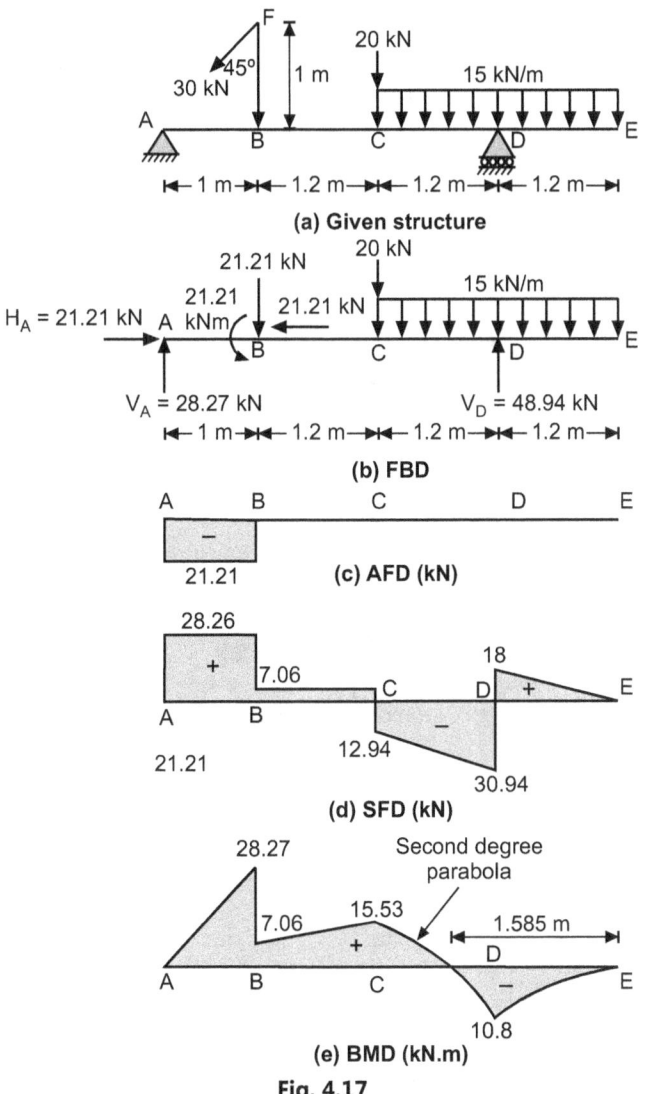

(a) Given structure

(b) FBD

(c) AFD (kN)

(d) SFD (kN)

(e) BMD (kN.m)

Fig. 4.17

(iii)   SF calculations :

$$SF_A = 28.27 \text{ kN}$$

SF_B (just to the left) = 28.27 kN

SF_B (just to the right) = 28.27 – 21.21 = 7.06 kN

SF_C (just to the left) = 7.06 kN

SF_C (just to the right) = 7.06 – 20 = – 12.94 kN

SF_D (just to the right) = 15 × 1.2 = 18 kN

SF_D (just to the left) = 18 – 48.94 = – 30.94 kN

SFD is as shown in Fig. 4.17 (d).

(iv) BM calculations : $BM_A = BM_E = 0$

BM_B (just to the left) $= 28.27 \times 1 = 28.27$ kN.m

BM_B (just to the right) $= 28.27 - 21.21 = 7.06$ kN.m

$BM_C = 28.27 \times 2.2 - 21.21 - 21.21 \times 1.2 = 15.53$ kN.m

$$BM_D = -15 \times \frac{(1.2)^2}{2} = -10.8 \text{ kN.m}$$

To locate point of contraflexure, consider a section at a distance 'x' from 'E' in zone CD,

$$BM_x = -15 \frac{x^2}{2} + 48.94 (x - 1.2) = 0$$

Solving, $x = 1.585$ m from E.

BMD is as shown in Fig. 4.17 (e).

Example 4.12 : *The beam is supported and loaded as shown in Fig. 4.18 (a). Draw SFD and BMD indicating all the important values.*

Data   : As shown in Fig. 4.18 (a).

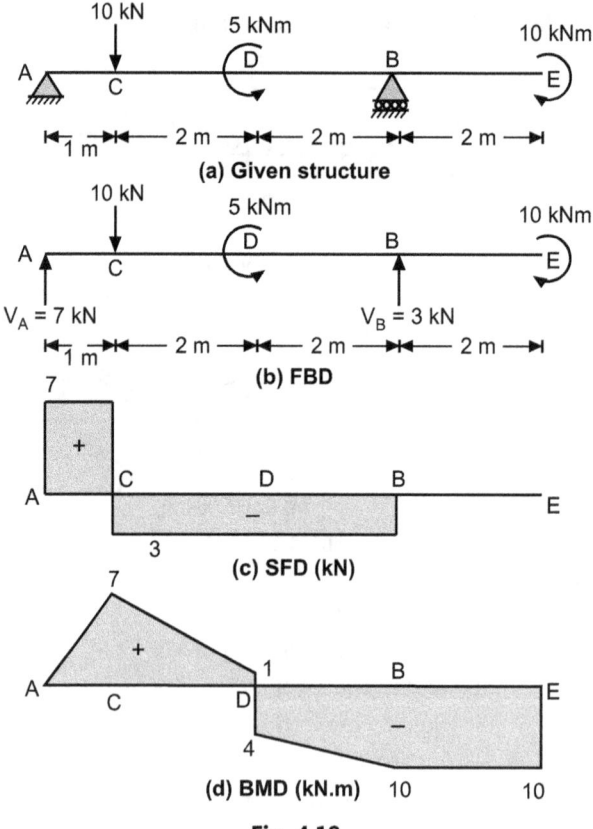

(a) Given structure

(b) FBD

(c) SFD (kN)

(d) BMD (kN.m)

Fig. 4.18

Required : SFD, BMD.

Solution : (i) Reactions :

$\sum M_A = 0$; $V_B \times 5 - 10 \times 1 + 5 - 10 = 0$

$\therefore$ V_B $= 3$ kN ($\uparrow$)

$\sum F_y = 0$; $V_A + V_B - 10 = 0$

$\therefore$ V_A $= 7$ kN ($\uparrow$)

$\sum F_x = 0$; H_A $= 0$

FBD of beam is as shown in Fig. 4.18 (b).

(ii)   SF calculations :

$SF_A = 7$ kN

SF_C (just to the left) $= 7$ kN

SF_C (just to the right) $= 7 - 10 = -3$ kN

SF_B (just to the left) $= -3$ kN

SF_B (just to the right) $= -3 + 3 = 0$

$SF_E = 0$

SFD is as shown in Fig. 4.18 (c).

(iii)   BM calculations :

$BM_A = 0$

$BM_C = 7 \times 1 = 7$ kN.m

BM_D (just to the left) $= 7 \times 3 - 10 \times 2 = 1$ kN.m

BM_D (just to the right) $= 1 - 5 = -4$ kN.m

$BM_D = BM_E = -10$ kN.m

BMD is as shown in Fig. 4.18 (d).

Example 4.13 : *The beam is supported and loaded as shown in Fig. 4.19 (a). Find the magnitude of couple 'M' such that reaction at A will be* $\dfrac{1}{4}$ *th of the reaction at B. Draw SFD and BMD indicating all the important values.*

Data   **:** As shown in Fig. 4.19 (a).

Required : Magnitude of couple 'M' and SFD, BMD.

Solution : (i) Magnitude of couple 'M' and reactions :

Let V_A and V_B be the vertical reaction components at A and B respectively.

We have,

$$V_A = \frac{1}{4} V_B \qquad\qquad \text{... (i)}$$

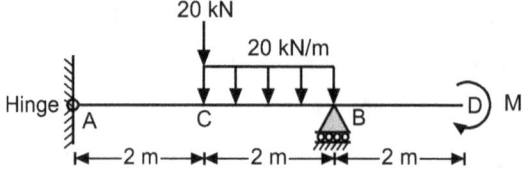

(a) Given structure

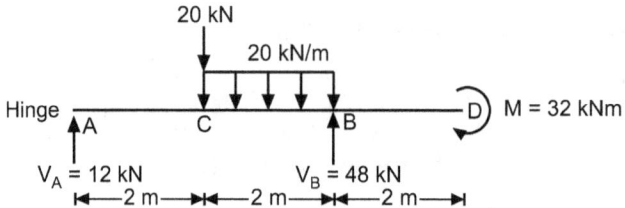

(a) Given structure

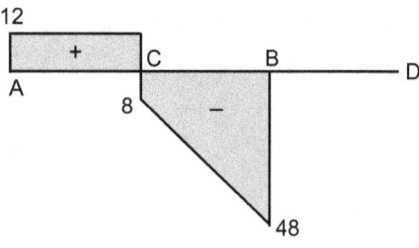

(c) SFD (kN)

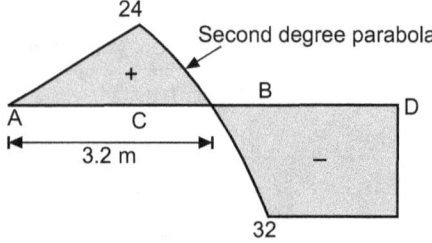

(d) BMD (kN.m)

Fig. 4.19

$\sum M_A = 0;$ $V_B \times 4 - M - 20 \times 2 \times 3 - 20 \times 2 = 0$

$$V_B = \frac{M}{4} + 40 \qquad \qquad \text{... (ii)}$$

$\sum F_y = 0;$ $V_A + V_B - 20 \times 2 - 20 = 0$

$$V_A + V_B = 60 \qquad \qquad \text{... (iii)}$$

Put equation (i) in equation (ii),

$$\frac{1}{4} V_B + V_B = 60$$

∴ $V_B = 48 \text{ kN}$ (↑)

∴ $V_A = 12 \text{ kN}$ (↑)

∴ $M = 32 \text{ kN.m}$ (↺)

$\Sigma F_X = 0$; $H_A = 0$

FBD of beam is as shown in Fig. 4.19 (b).

(ii)   SF calculations :

$$SF_A = 12 \text{ kN}$$

$$SF_D = 0$$

SF_B (just to the right) = 0

SF_B (just to the left) = 0 – 48 = – 48 kN

SF_C (just to the left) = 12 kN

SF_C (just to the right) = 12 – 20 = – 8 kN

SFD is as shown in Fig. 4.19 (c).

(iii)   BM calculations :

$$BM_A = 0$$

$$BM_B = BM_D = -32 \text{ kN.m}$$

$$BM_C = 12 \times 2 = 24 \text{ kN.m}$$

To locate point of contraflexure, consider a section at a distance 'x' from A in zone CB.

$$BM_x = 12x - 20(x-2) - \frac{20(x-2)^2}{2} = 0$$

∴ $x^2 - 3.2x = 0$

∴ $x = 3.2 \text{ m}$ from A.

BMD is as shown in Fig. 4.19 (d).

Example 4.14 : *The beam is supported and loaded as shown in Fig. 4.20 (a). Draw SFD and BMD indicating all the important values.*

Data   :   As shown in Fig. 4.20 (a).

Required :   SFD, BMD.

Solution :   (i) Reactions :

$\Sigma M_A = 0$; $V_B \times 3.5 - 4 \times 2 \times 2.5 - 6 \times 4 - \frac{1}{2} \times 4 \times 1.5 \times \frac{1}{3} \times 1.5 = 0$

$V_B = 13 \text{ kN}$ (↑)

$\Sigma F_y = 0$; $V_A + V_B - \frac{1}{2} \times 4 \times 1.5 - 4 \times 2 - 6 = 0$

$\therefore$ $V_A = 4$ kN ($\uparrow$)

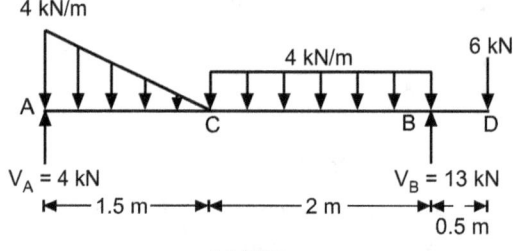

(a) Given structure

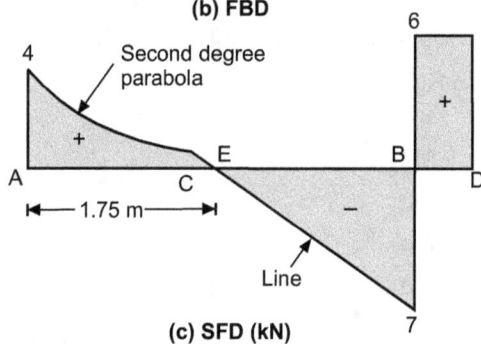

(b) FBD

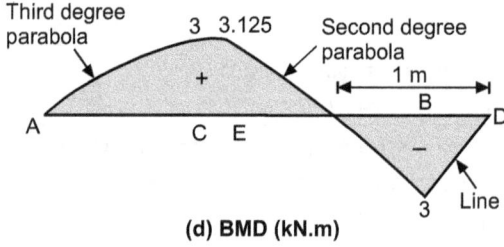

(c) SFD (kN)

(d) BMD (kN.m)

Fig. 4.20

$\Sigma F_x = 0$; $H_A = 0$

FBD of beam is as shown in Fig. 4.20 (b).

(ii)   SF calculations :

             $SF_A = 4$ kN

$$SF_C = 4 - \frac{1}{2} \times 4 \times 1.5 = 1 \text{ kN}$$

$$SF_D = 6 \text{ kN}$$

$$SF_B \text{ (just to the right)} = 6 \text{ kN}$$

$$SF_B \text{ (just to the left)} = 6 - 13 = -7 \text{ kN}$$

To locate point of zero SF, consider a section at a distance x from A in zone CB.

$$SF_X = 4 - \frac{1}{2} \times 4 \times 1.5 - 4 \times (x - 1.5) = 0$$

$$\therefore \qquad x = 1.75 \text{ m from A}$$

SFD is as shown in Fig. 4.20 (c).

(iii)   BM calculations :

$$BM_A = BM_D = 0$$

$$BM_C = 4 \times 1.5 - \frac{1}{2} \times 4 \times 1.5 \times \frac{2}{3} \times 1.5 = 3 \text{ kN.m}$$

$$BM \text{ at point of zero SF} = BM_E = 4 \times 1.75 - \frac{1}{2} \times 4 \times 1.5 \times \left(\frac{2}{3} \times 1.5 + 0.25\right) - 4 \times \frac{(0.25)^2}{2}$$

$$= 3.125 \text{ kN.m}$$

$$BM_B = -6 \times 0.5 = -3 \text{ kN.m}$$

To locate point of contraflexure, consider a section at a distance x from D in zone BC.

$$BM_X = -6x + 13 (x - 0.5) - 4 \frac{(x - 0.5)^2}{2} = 0$$

$$\therefore \qquad x^2 - 4.5 x + 3.5 = 0$$

Solving, x = 1 m > 0.5 m and < 2.5 m, OK

or x = 3.5 m > 2.5 m, hence neglected.

EXERCISE

Draw shear force and bending moment diagrams for the following beams indicating all the important values :

1.

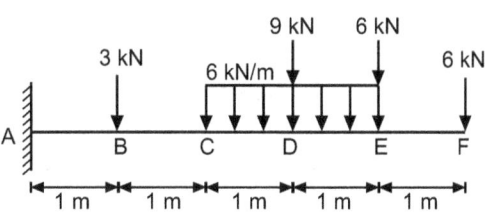

Fig. 4.21

$$(BM_A = -120 \text{ kNm}, \quad BM_B = -84 \text{ kNm}, \quad BM_C = -51 \text{ kNm},$$
$$BM_D = -21 \text{ kNm}, \quad BM_E = -6 \text{ kNm}, \quad BM_F = 0)$$

2.

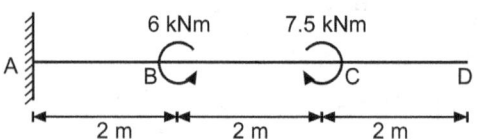

Fig. 4.22

$(BM_A = -1.5$ kNm, $BM_{B\,(L)} = -1.5$ kNm, $BM_{B\,(R)} = -7.5$ kNm,

$BM_{C\,(L)} = -7.5$ kNm, $BM_{C\,(R)} = 0$, $BM_D = 0$)

3.

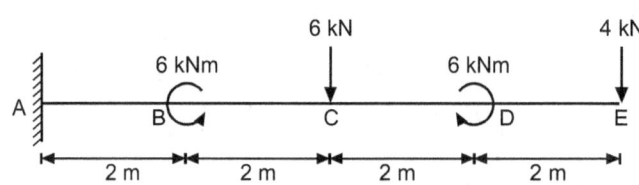

Fig. 4.23

$(BM_A = -58$ kNm, $BM_{B\,(L)} = -38$ kNm, $BM_{B\,(R)} = -42$ kNm, $BM_C = -22$ kNm,

$BM_{D\,(L)} = -14$ kNm, $BM_{D\,(R)} = -8$ kNm, $BM_E = 0$)

4.

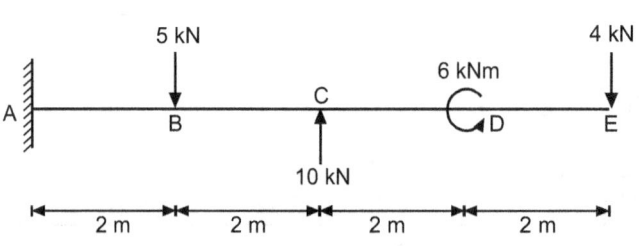

Fig. 4.24

$(BM_A = 10$ kNm, $BM_B = 20$ kNm, $BM_C = 20$ kNm, $BM_{D\,(L)} = 40$ kNm,

$BM_{D\,(R)} = -20$ kNm, $BM_E = 0$)

5.

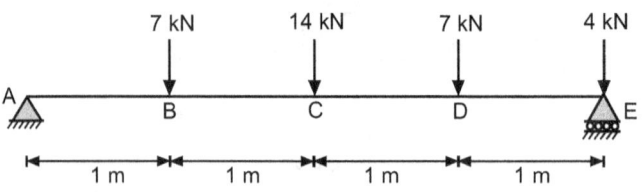

Fig. 4.25

$(BM_A = BM_E = 0$, $BM_B = 14$ kNm, $BM_C = 21$ kNm, $BM_D = 14$ kNm)

6.

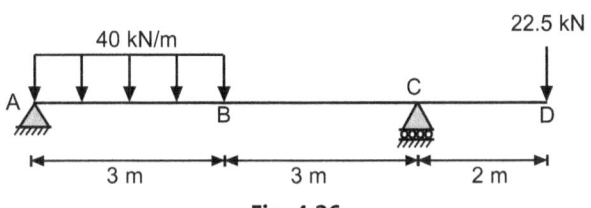

Fig. 4.26

(BM$_A$ = BM$_D$ = 0, BM$_B$ = 67.5 kNm, BM$_C$ = – 45 kNm, BM$_{max}$ = 84.93 m at 2.06 m

from A)

7.

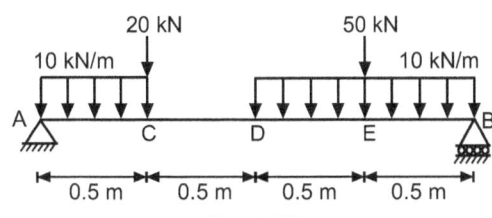

Fig. 4.27

(BM$_A$ = BM$_B$ = 0, BM$_C$ = 16.5 kNm, BM$_D$ = 21 kNm, BM$_E$ = 24.25 kNm)

8.

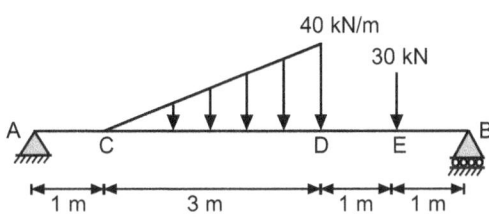

Fig. 4.28

(BM$_A$ = BM$_B$ = 0, BM$_C$ = 35 kNm, BM$_D$ = 80 kNm, BM$_E$ = 55 kNm,

BM$_{max}$ = 88.46 kNm at 3.29 m from A)

9.

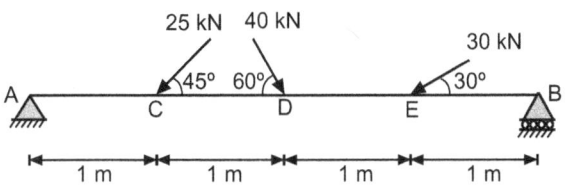

Fig. 4.29

(BM$_A$ = BM$_B$ = 0,   BM$_C$ = 34.33 kNm,   BM$_D$ = 50.985 kNm, BM$_E$ = 32.995 kNm)

10.

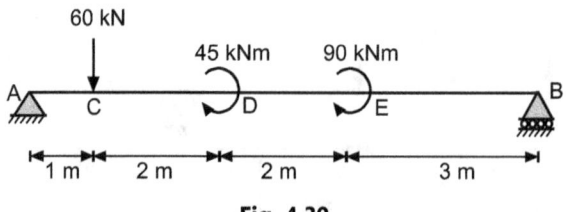

Fig. 4.30

$(BM_A = BM_B = 0, \ BM_C = 35.625 \text{ kNm}, \ BM_{D\ (L)} = -13.125 \text{ kNm},$

$BM_{D\ (R)} = 31.875 \text{ kNm}, \ BM_{E\ (L)} = -16.875 \text{ kNm}, \ BM_{E\ (R)} = 73.125 \text{ kNm})$

◈ ◈ ◈

SHEAR FORCE AND BENDING MOMENT
(PART – B)

5.1 RELATIONSHIP BETWEEN LOAD, SHEAR AND BENDING MOEMNT

The relationship between load, shear and bending moment can be derived as under. Consider a beam supported and loaded as shown in Fig. 5.1 (a).

Let V_x and M_x be the shear and bending moment on a section at a distance 'x' from A. Likewise $V_x + dV_x$ and M_x and dM_x are the shear and bending moment at a section at a distance x + dx from A. The free body diagram of the segment of the beam which is dx in length is shown in Fig. 5.1 (b).

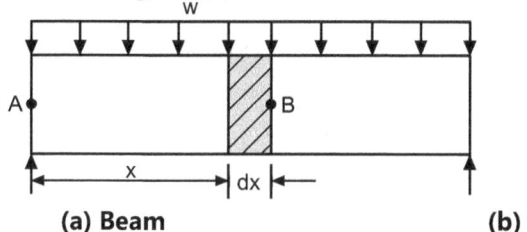

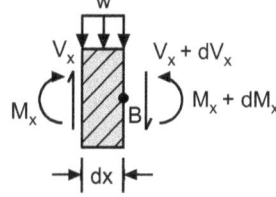

(a) Beam   (b) FBD of beam segment

Fig. 5.1

Applying equations of equilibrium to FBD of segment as under :

$$\sum F_y = 0 \implies V_x - (V_x + dV_x) - w \cdot dx = 0$$

$$dV_x = -w \cdot dx$$

$$\therefore \quad \frac{dV_x}{dx} = -w \qquad \qquad ... (5.1)$$

Thus, the rate of decrease of shear force with respect to x, on any section at a distance 'x' from left end of the beam is equal to the intensity of load at the section.

$$\sum M_B = 0 \implies V_x \cdot dx + M_x = M_x + dM_x + w\frac{dx^2}{2}$$

The term $w\dfrac{dx^2}{2}$ being very small, can be neglected.

$$dM_x = V_x \cdot dx$$

$$\frac{dM_x}{dx} = V_x \qquad \qquad ... (5.2)$$

Thus, the rate of increase of bending moment with respect to 'x', on any section at a distance 'x' from left end of the beam, is equal to shear at the section.

SOLVED EXAMPLES

Example 5.1 : *A beam ABCD is simply supported at A and fixed at D. Shear force diagram for the beam is as shown in Fig. 5.2 (a). Obtain the load diagram and hence construct BMD.*

Data   : Given SFD as shown in Fig. 5.2 (a).

Required : Load diagram and BMD.

Solution : (i) Load diagram :

Rise in SFD at A indicates upward point force of magnitude 40 kN at A.

Drop in SFD at B indicates downward point force of magnitude 20 kN at B.

Drop in SFD at C indicates downward point force of magnitude 15 kN at C.

Rise in SFD at D indicates upward point force of magnitude 35 kN at D.

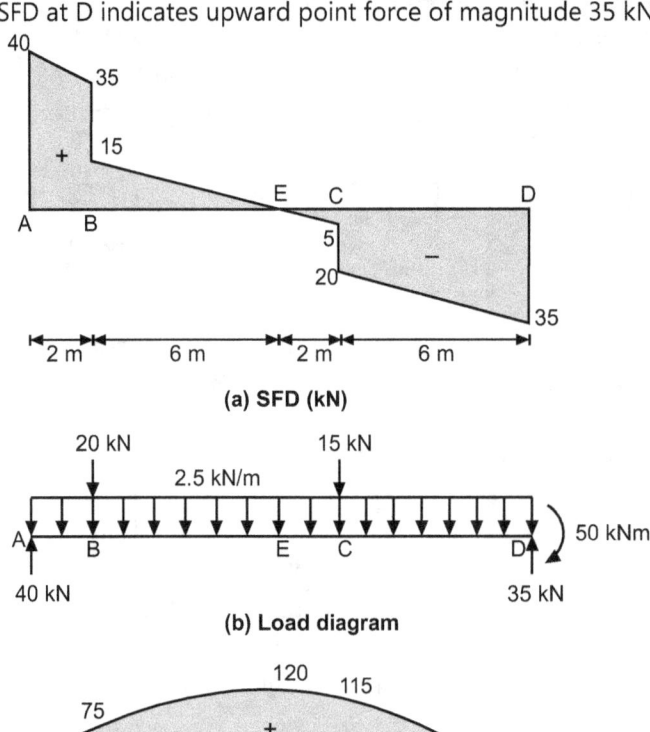

(a) SFD (kN)

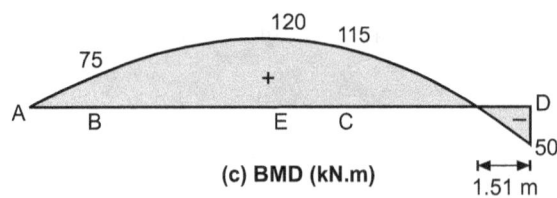

(b) Load diagram

(c) BMD (kN.m)

Fig. 5.2

Zone AB : Intensity of udl $= \dfrac{dV}{dx} = \dfrac{35 - 40}{2} = -2.5$ kN/m.

Zone BC : Intensity of udl $= \dfrac{dV}{dx} = \dfrac{-5 - 15}{8} = -2.5$ kN/m.

Zone CD : Intensity of udl $= \dfrac{dV}{dx} = \dfrac{-35 - (-20)}{6} = -2.5$ kN/m.

Thus, there is downward udl of intensity 2.5 kN/m throughout the length of beam.

(ii)   Equilibrium of beam from load diagram :

$$\Sigma F_y = 40 + 35 - 20 - 15 - 2.5 \times 16 = 0$$

$$\Sigma M_A = 35 \times 16 - 2.5 \times \dfrac{(16)^2}{2} - 15 \times 10 - 20 \times 2 = 50 \text{ kN.m}$$

Moment equilibrium is not satisfied.

Hence, moment at fixed end D = – 50 kN.m = 50 kN.m (↻)

Load diagram is as shown in Fig. 5.2 (b).

(iii)   BMD is as shown in Fig. 5.2 (c).

Example 5.2 : *A beam ABC is simply supported at A and B. Supports at A and B are 3 m apart and overhang BC = 1 m. The shear force diagram for the beam is as shown in Fig. 5.3 (a). Obtain the load diagram and hence construct BMD. Assume that there is no couple acting on the beam.*

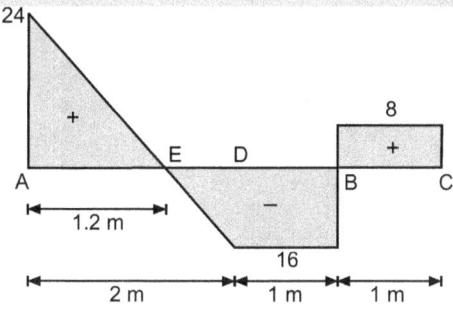

(a) SFD (kN)

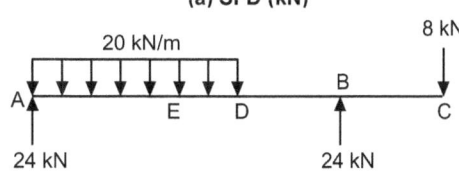

(b) Load diagram

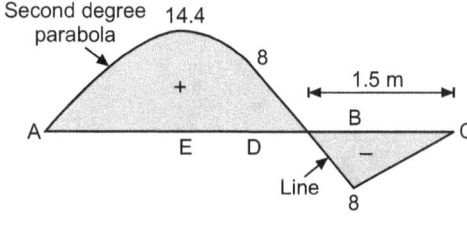

(c) BMD (kN.m)

Fig. 5.3

Data :   Given SFD as shown in Fig. 5.3 (a).

Required :   Load diagram and BMD.

Solution :   (i) Load diagram :

Rise in SFD at A indicates upward point force of 24 kN at A.

Zone AD, intensity of udl $= \dfrac{dV}{dx} = \dfrac{-16 - (24)}{2} = -20$ kN/m

Thus, there is a downward udl from A to D of intensity 20 kN/m.

Rise in SFD at B indicates upward point force of 24 kN at B.

Drop in SFD at C indicates downward point force of 8 kN at C.

Load diagram is as shown in Fig. 5.3 (b).

(ii)   Equilibrium of beam from load diagram :

$$\Sigma F_y = 24 + 24 - 20 \times 2 - 8 = 0$$

$$\Sigma M_A = -8 \times 4 + 24 \times 3 - 20 \times \frac{2^2}{2} = 0$$

Thus the load diagram obtained is justified.

(iii)   BMD as shown in Fig. 5.3 (c).

Example 5.3 : *A beam ABC is simply supported at A and B. Supports at A and B are 6 m apart and overhang BC = 1 m. The bending moment diagram for the beam is as shown in Fig. 5.4 (a). Construct SFD and load diagram.*

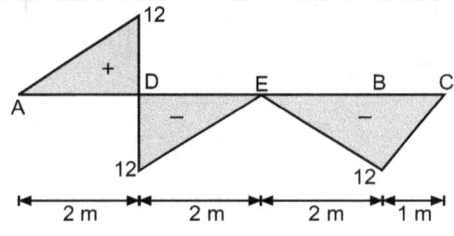

(a) BMD (kN.m)

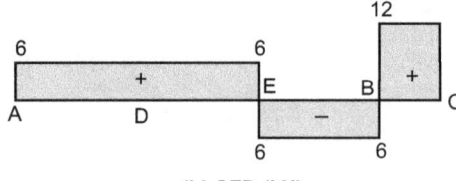

(b) SFD (kN)

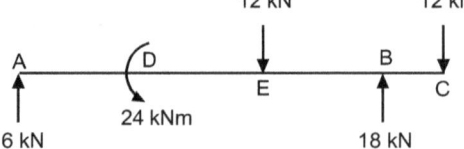

(c) Load diagram

Fig. 5.4

Data : Given BMD as shown in Fig. 5.4 (a).

Required : SFD and load diagram.

Solution : (i) SFD :

Zone AD : $\qquad SF = \dfrac{dM}{dx} = \dfrac{12-0}{2} = 6 \text{ kN}$

Zone DE : $\qquad SF = \dfrac{dM}{dx} = \dfrac{0-(-12)}{2} = 6 \text{ kN}$

Zone EB : $\qquad SF = \dfrac{dM}{dx} = \dfrac{-12-0}{2} = -6 \text{ kN}$

Zone BC : $\qquad SF = \dfrac{dM}{dx} = \dfrac{0-(-12)}{1} = 12 \text{ kN}$

SFD is as shown in Fig. 5.4 (b).

(ii) Load diagram :

Rise in SFD at A indicates upward point force of magnitude 6 kN at A.

Drop in SFD at E indicates downward point force of magnitude 12 kN at E.

Rise in SFD at B indicates upward point force of magnitude 18 kN at B.

Drop in SFD at C indicates downward point force of magnitude 12 kN at C.

Also, at D, drop in BM diagram = 24 kN.m and BM changes from sagging to hogging from left of D to right of D, hence there must be an anticlockwise couple of magnitude 24 kN.m at D.

The load diagram for the beam is as shown in Fig. 5.4 (c).

Note : Having obtained the load diagram, check the equilibrium of beam to justify the results.

Example 5.4 : *A beam ABC is supported on roller at A and hinged at C. The bending moment diagram for the beam ABC is as shown in Fig. 5.5 (a). Construct SFD and load diagram.*

Data   : Given BMD as shown in Fig. 5.5 (a).

Required : SFD and load diagram.

Solution : (i) SFD :

Zone AB : $\text{SF} = \dfrac{dM}{dx} = \dfrac{5 - (-10)}{1} = 15 \text{ kN}$

Zone BC : $\text{SF} = \dfrac{dM}{dx} = \dfrac{10 - (-5)}{1} = 15 \text{ kN}$

SFD is as shown in Fig. 5.5 (b).

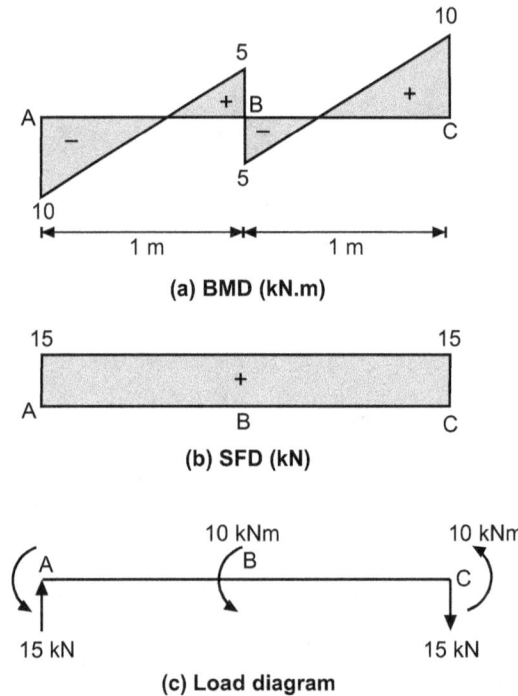

(a) BMD (kN.m)

(b) SFD (kN)

(c) Load diagram

Fig. 5.5

(ii)   Load diagram :

In zone AC, constant SF = 15 kN.

∴   Upward reaction at A = 15 kN and downward reaction at C = 15 kN.

At A, BM = – 10 kN.m which indicates anticlockwise couple of magnitude 10 kN.m at A.

At B, drop in BM diagram = 10 kN.m and BM changes from sagging to hogging from left of B to right of B, hence there must be an anticlockwise couple of magnitude 10 kN.m at B.

At C, BM = 10 kN.m which indicates anticlockwise couple of magnitude 10 kN.m at C.

The load diagram for the beam is as shown in Fig. 5.5 (c).

Note : Having obtained the load diagram, check the equilibrium of beam to justify the results.

Example 5.5 : *Fig. 5.6 shows SFD for a simply supported beam AB. Draw BMD for the beam.*

Data : Given SFD as shown in Fig. 5.6.

Required : BMD.

Solution : (i) Load diagram : Rise in SFD at A indicates upward point force 12.5 kN at A.

Horizontal line between A to C shows no load between A to C.

Rise in SFD at B indicates upward point force of 7.5 kN at B.

Zone CD : Intensity of UDL $= \dfrac{dV}{dx} = \dfrac{-7.5 - 12.5}{4} = -5$ kN.m.

Load diagram is as shown in Fig. 5.6 (b).

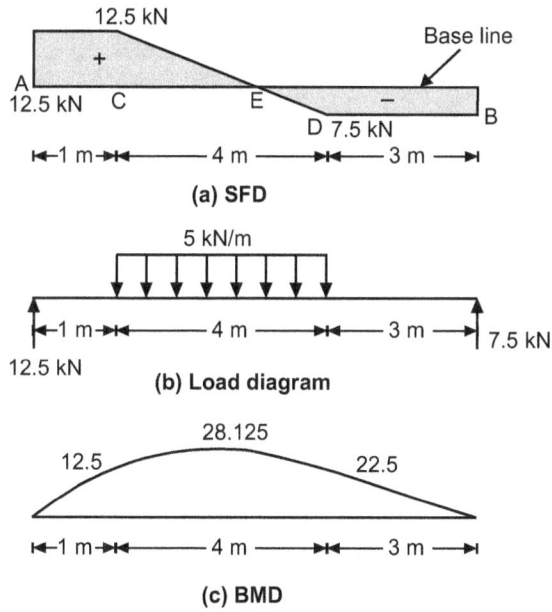

(a) SFD

(b) Load diagram

(c) BMD

Fig. 5.6

(ii)   BMD : Bending moment, maximum at SF is zero.

$\therefore$ $x = \dfrac{12.5}{5} = 2.5$ m (from starting point of UDL)

BMD is as shown in Fig. 5.6 (c).

Example 5.6 : *The SFD of a 4 m long beam is a second degree curve as shown in Fig. 5.7 (a), with the maximum –ve SF of 3 kN at the beam centre. Assuming that no couples act on the beam, draw the loading and BMD. Locate the position of maximum BM and their magnitudes. Points of contraflexure if any, too, should be located.*

Data : SFD as shown in Fig. 5.7 (a).

Required : Loading diagram and BMD.

Solution :

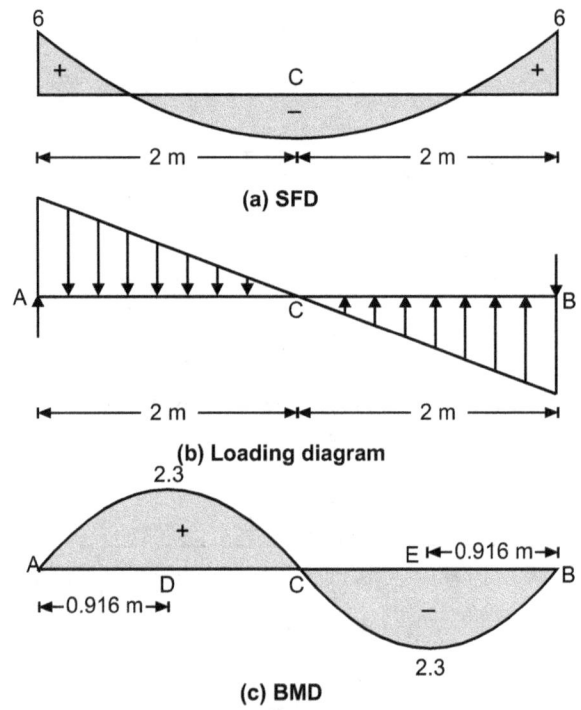

(a) SFD

(b) Loading diagram

(c) BMD

Fig. 5.7

(i)   **Loading diagram :** Rise in SFD at A indicates upward point force of 6 kN at A. Drop in SFD at B indicates downward point force of 6 kN at B.

Zone A to C : Intensity of UVL $= (-3 - 6) = \dfrac{1}{2}$ w $\times l$

$$-9 = \frac{1}{2} \times w \times 2$$

∴   w $= -9$ kN.m

Zone C to B : Intensity of UVL $= 6 - (-3) = \dfrac{1}{2}$ w $\times l$

$\therefore$ $\qquad\qquad$ $w = 9$ kN.m

To locate point of zero SF, consider a section at a distance x from A in zone AC.

$$SF_x = 6 - (\text{Area of trapezoidal load diagram}) = 0$$

$$\frac{9}{2} = \frac{y}{x} \qquad \therefore\ y = 4.5\,x$$

$\therefore$ $\qquad$ $6 - \dfrac{(9 + 4.5\,x)}{2} \times x = 0$

$$9x + 4.5x^2 - 12 = 0$$

$\therefore$ $\qquad$ $x^2 + 2x - 2.67 = 0$

$$x = -2 \pm \frac{\sqrt{(2)^2 - 4 \times 1\,(-2.67)}}{2}$$

$$= 0.916 \text{ m from A and B.}$$

(As beam is symmetrical, so points of zero SF are at same distance from both ends.)

Loading diagram is as shown in Fig. 5.7 (b).

(ii) BM calculations :

$$BM_A = BM_B = 0$$

BM at zero SF : $BM_D = 6 \times 0.916 - \text{Moment due to trapezoidal loading diagram}$

$$= 6 \times 0.916 - \frac{(9 + 4.5 \times 1.084)}{2} \times 0.916 \times \left(\frac{4.878 + 9 \times 2}{4.878 + 9}\right) \times \frac{0.916}{3}$$

$$= 2.3 \text{ kN.m}$$

$$BM_C = 6 \times 2 - \frac{1}{2} \times 9 \times 2 \times \frac{2}{3} \times 2$$

$$= 0$$

$$BM_E = -2.3 \text{ kN.m}$$

BMD is as shown in Fig. 5.7 (c).

Example 5.7 : *The BMD of a simply supported beam is linear in the 1.5 m long portion AC and parabolic in the 3 m long portion CDEB. There is no slope discontinuity anywhere in the BMD. The moments of D and E are 28.125 kN.m and 22.5 kN.m respectively. Draw the SFD and loading diagrams for the beam and highlight all the significant values.*

Data : BMD as shown in Fig. 5.8 (a).

Required : Loading diagram and SFD.

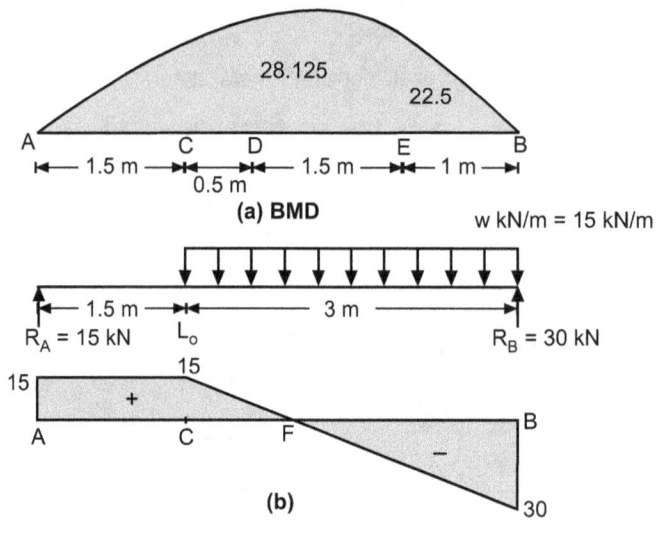

(a) BMD

(b)

Fig. 5.8

(i)   w and reactions :

$$M_E = R_B \times 1 - \frac{w \times 1^2}{2}$$

$$= 22.5$$

$$R_B - 0.5\,w = 22.5 \qquad\qquad \dots \text{(i)}$$

$$M_D = R_B \times 2.5 - \frac{w \times (2.5)^2}{2}$$

$$= 28.125$$

$$\therefore \qquad R_B - 1.25\,w = 11.25 \qquad\qquad \dots \text{(ii)}$$

Solving equations (i) and (ii),

$$w = 15 \text{ kN/m}, \quad R_B = 30 \text{ kN } (\uparrow)$$

$$\Sigma F_y = 0; \quad R_A + R_B - w \times 3 = 0$$

$$R_A = 15 \text{ kN } (\uparrow)$$

(ii)   Loading diagram as shown in Fig. 5.8 (b).

(iii) SF calculations :

$$SF_A = 15 \text{ kN}$$

$$SF_C = 15 \text{ kN}$$

$$SF_B = 15 - 15 \times 3 = -30 \text{ kN}$$

To locate point of SF, consider a section at a distance x from B in portion BC.

$\therefore$ $$SF_x = 30 - 15 \times x = 0$$

$\therefore$ $$x = 2 \text{ m from B.}$$

(iv) Maximum BM is at 2 m from B.

$\therefore$ $$BM_F = 30 \times 2 - 15 \times 2 \times 1$$

$$= 30 \text{ kN.m}$$

SFD is as shown in Fig. 5.8 (c).

Example 5.8 : *The bending moment diagram for a beam ABCDE is as shown in Fig. 5.9. Portions AB, CD and DE have linear curves whereas portion BC has a second degree curve with a peak located at 1.8 m from B and enjoys slope continuity at C. Draw the shear force and loading diagrams for the beam. Hence or otherwise locate the points of contraflexure.*

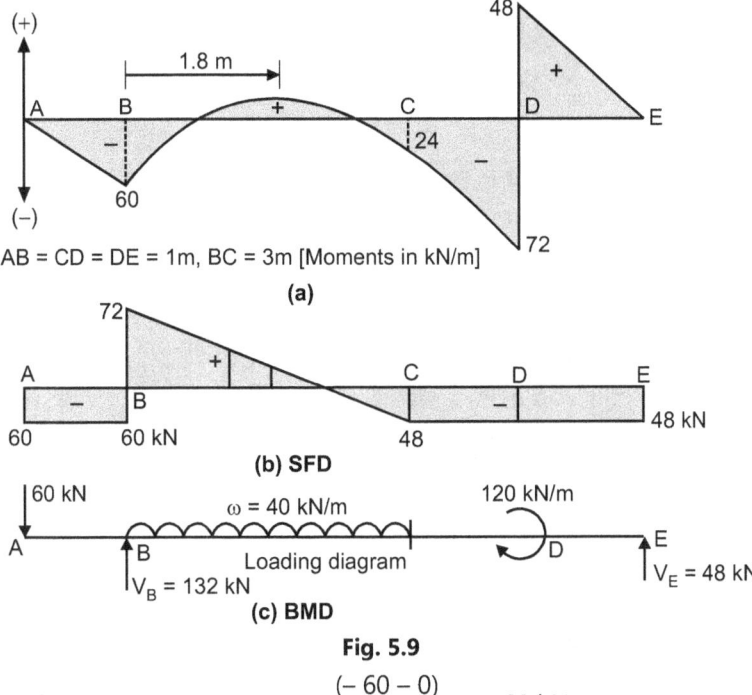

AB = CD = DE = 1m, BC = 3m [Moments in kN/m]

(a)

(b) SFD

Loading diagram

(c) BMD

Fig. 5.9

Solution : (i) $$SF_{(AB)} = \frac{(-60 - 0)}{1} = -60 \text{ kN}$$

Let BM equation in zone BC be,

$$M_x = Ax^2 + Bx + C \qquad \text{(B as origin)}$$

When x = 0, $$BM = -60 \text{ kN-m}$$

$\therefore$ $$C = -60$$

When x = 3 m,   BM = – 24

∴   – 24 = 9A + 3B – 60   ... (i)

                                  36 = 9A + 3B

Also SF_X = 2Ax + B

$$SF_{(CD)} = \frac{[-72 - (-24)]}{1}$$

                                      = – 48 kN

When x = 3 m, SF_C = – 48 kN Put in SF equation

                                 – 48 = 6 A + B   ... (ii)

Solving (i) and (ii),   A = – 20, B = 72

∴ M_X = – 20x² + 72x – 60

                                SF_X = – 40x + 72

                                 w_X = – 40

At x = 0, SF_B = 72 kN

At x = 3 m, SF_C = – 48 kN

$$SF_{(DE)} = \frac{(0-48)}{1} = -48 \text{ kN}$$

SFD is as shown in Fig. 5.9 (b).

(ii)   Point load at A = 60 kN (↓)

                       Point load at B = 60 + 72

                                       = 132 kN (↑)

                   UDL in zone BC = 40 kN/m (↑)

                       Couple at D = 120 kN/m (↻)

                   Point load at E = 48 kN (↑)

Load diagram is shown in Fig. 5.9 (c).

Example 5.9 : *Fig. 5.10 shows the shear force for beam ABCD. Draw the loading diagram and bending moment diagram.*

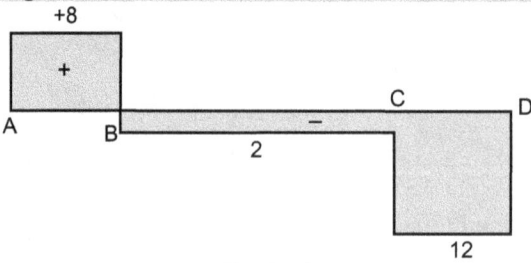

Fig. 5.10

Data : As shown in Fig. 5.10.

Required : Loading diagram and bending moment diagram.

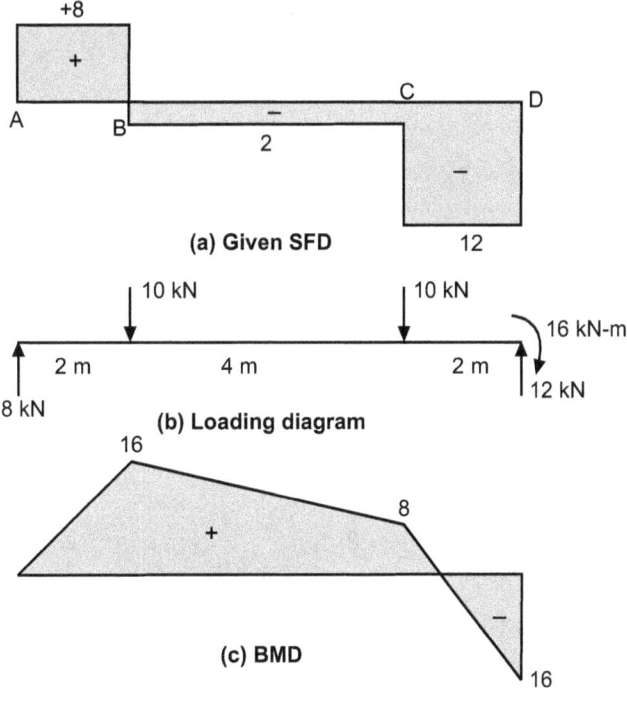

(a) Given SFD

(b) Loading diagram

(c) BMD

Fig. 5.11

Example 5.10 : *Shown in Fig. 5.12 is the shear force diagram of a beam. The curve in portion AB is a second-degree curve that has zero slope at 'A'. Draw completely the loading diagram of the beam.*

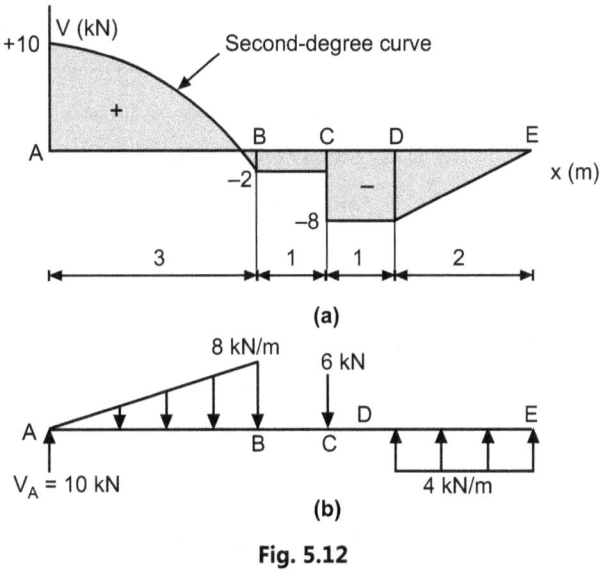

(a)

(b)

Fig. 5.12

Solution : At 'A' upward point load of 10 kN.

SF equation in zone AB $= Ax^2 + B$

When x = 0,   SF = 10 kN,   ∴   B = 10

When x = 3 m,   SF = − 2 kN   ∴   A = − 1.33

∴ $SF_{(x)}$ = − 1.33 x² + 10   ... (i)

∴ $w_{(x)}$ = − 2.67 x   ... (ii)

When x = 0,   w = 0

When x = 3 m,   w = 8 kN/m

Thus in zone AB, we have triangular load with zero intensity at A and 8 kN/m at B.

At 'C' downward point load of 6 kN is present.

Intensity of UDL from D to E $= \dfrac{0 - (- 8)}{2}$ = 4 kN/m (↑)

Load diagram is as shown in Fig. 5.12.

EXERCISE

1.   Draw the bending moment diagram and loading diagram from the given shear force diagram. (Refer Fig. 5.13)

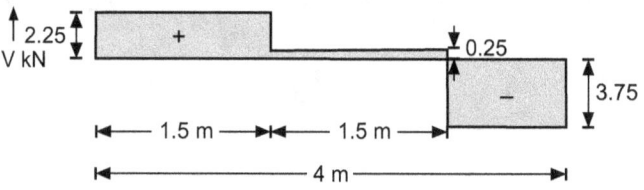

Fig. 5.13 : Shear force diagram

2.   The shear force diagram for a simple beam is shown in Fig. 5.14. Determine the loading on the beam and draw the bending moment diagram, assuming that no couples act as loads on the beam.

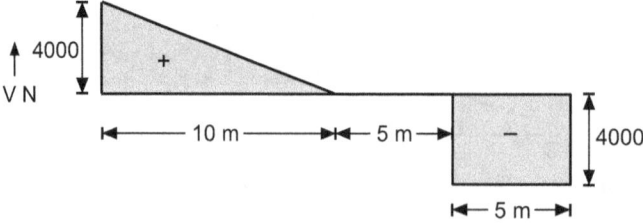

Fig. 5.14 : Shear force diagram

3. The shear force diagram for a beam is as shown in Fig. 5.15. Assuming that no couples act as load on the beam, draw the bending moment diagram and also show the loading diagram.

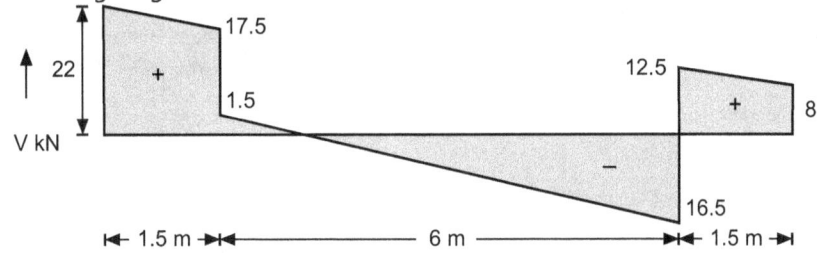

Fig. 5.15 : Shear force diagram

4. Construct the loading and shear force diagram for the beam with an overhang as shown in Fig. 5.16.

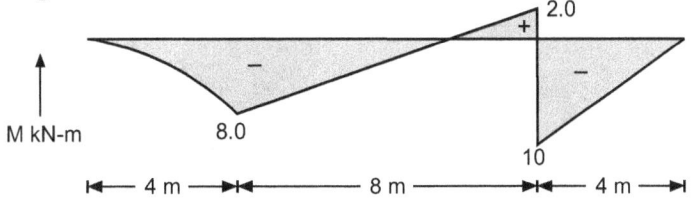

Fig. 5.16 : Bending moment diagram

5. Construct the shear force diagram and loading diagram for the cantilever beam shown in Fig. 5.17.

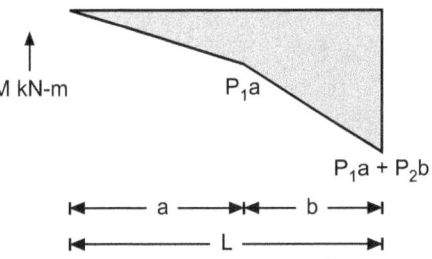

Fig. 5.17 : Bending moment diagram

6. Construct the bending moment diagram and loading diagram for the simply supported beam as shown in Fig. 5.18.

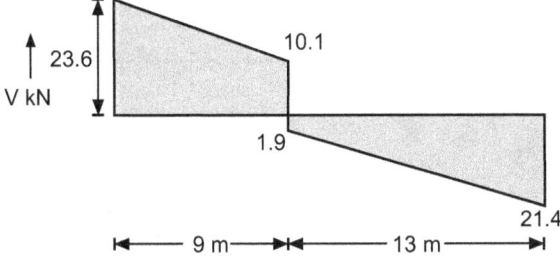

Fig. 5.18 : Shear force diagram

7. Draw the bending moment diagram and loading diagram from shear for the simply supported beam as shown in Fig. 5.19.

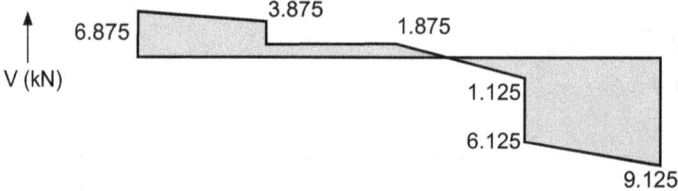

Fig. 5.19 : Shear force diagram

8. Draw bending moment diagram and loading diagram from shear force diagram for simply supported beam as shown in Fig. 5.20.

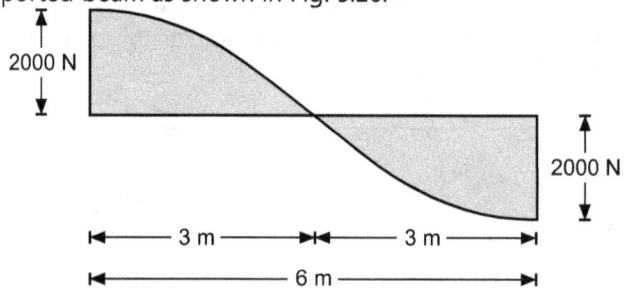

Fig. 5.20 : Shear force diagram

9. Construct bending moment diagram and loading diagram for the overhanging beam shown in Fig. 5.21.

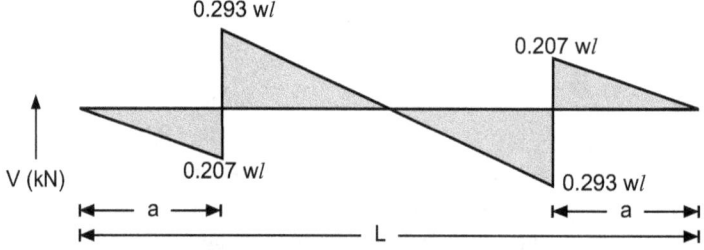

Fig. 5.21 : Shear force diagram

10. Construct the shear force diagram and loading diagram for the beam shown in Fig. 5.22.

Fig. 5.22 : Bending moment diagram

◈ ◈ ◈

CHAPTER

6

DEFLECTION OF BEAMS AND CONJUGATE METHOD

6.1 INTRODUCTION

Under the action of external loads the beam deflects from its initial position. Exact values of deflections are required in many designs. For example, in buildings, floor beams shall not deflect beyond the specified limit to maintain the sense of security of the occupants. Also study of deflection is necessary to check the dimensional accuracy of various machine elements, under the action of variety of loads.

Basically, beam is subjected to flexure and shear. Both of these actions are responsible for causing deflection. However, deflections due to shear are generally neglected, being smaller in magnitude as compared to that due to bending.

When the cross section of beam is designed to resist bending stresses safely, it is called as design for *strength criterion*. And when the cross section of beam is designed such that deflection is within specified limit, it is called as *stiffness criterion* of design. Practically, design of flexure member is required for strength as well as stiffness criteria.

6.2 ASSUMPTIONS

When line members are subjected to bending without twisting (i.e. the plane of the external forces acting on member must pass through the shear centre of the cross section) their axis does not elongate and their cross sections do not twist. Moreover, because the dimensions of the cross sections of line members are small compared to their length, the following assumptions as to the geometry of their deformed configuration can be made.

   (i) Plane sections normal to the axis of a line member prior to the deformation can be considered plane subsequent to deformation, that is the warping of cross section of a line member is assumed negligible.

   (ii) Plane sections normal to the axis of a line member before deformation can be considered normal to its deformed axis subsequent to deformation. This implies that, the effect of shearing components of strain on transverse components of translation of cross sections is negligible.

6.3 SLOPE, DEFLECTION AND RADIUS OF CURVATURE

A segment of initially straight beam is shown in a deformed state in Fig. 6.1. The deflected axis of the beam is called *elastic curve*, which bends into an arc of a circle with radius of curvature R as shown in Fig. 6.1. The elastic curve is very flat and its slope at any point is very small.

$$\tan \theta = \frac{dy}{dx}$$

∴ $$\theta = \frac{dy}{dx} \qquad \qquad ... (6.1)$$

∴ $$\frac{d\theta}{dx} = \frac{d^2y}{dx^2} \qquad \qquad ... (6.2)$$

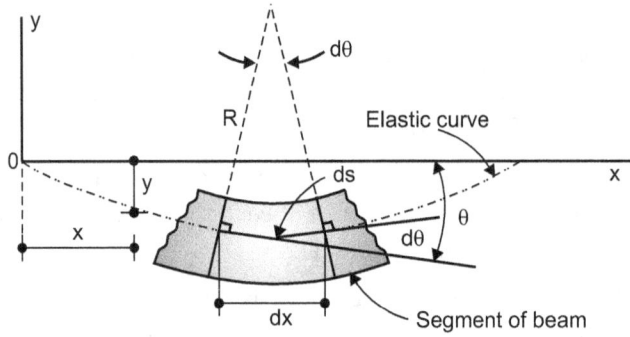

Fig. 6.1

From Fig. 6.1,

$$ds = R\, d\theta \qquad \qquad ... (6.3)$$

where,   R = radius of curvature for arc of length ds

∴ $$\frac{1}{R} = \frac{d\theta}{ds} \approx \frac{d\theta}{dx} = \frac{d^2y}{dx^2} \qquad \qquad ... (6.4)$$

In deriving the flexure formula, we have obtained

$$\frac{1}{R} = \frac{M}{EI} \qquad \qquad ... (6.5)$$

Equating values of $\frac{1}{R}$ from equations (6.4) and (6.5), we get

$$EI\frac{d^2y}{dx^2} = M \qquad \qquad ... (6.6)$$

Equation (6.6) is known as differential equation of the elastic curve of a beam. The product EI is called *flexural rigidity* of the beam.

The exact value of $\dfrac{1}{R}$ is given by

$$\frac{1}{R} = \frac{\dfrac{d^2y}{dx^2}}{\left[1 + \left(\dfrac{dy}{dx}\right)^2\right]^{3/2}} \qquad \text{... (6.7)}$$

However, $\dfrac{dy}{dx}$ being very small its square is still smaller compared to unity and hence neglected.

Assuming EI = constant along the length of beam and integrating equation (6.6), we get

$$EI\frac{dy}{dx} = \int M\,dx + C_1 \qquad \text{... (6.8)}$$

Equation (6.8) is a slope equation, where M represents the bending moment equation in terms of x and C_1 is the constant of integration to be evaluated knowing the boundary conditions.

Integrating equation (6.8), we get

$$EIy = \int \int M\,dx + C_1 x + C_2 \qquad \text{... (6.9)}$$

Equation (6.9) is a deflection equation, where C_2 is another constant of integration to be evaluated knowing the boundary conditions.

6.4 METHODS OF DISPLACEMENT ANALYSIS

Several methods are available for determining slopes and deflections of beams. Although based on the same principles, they differ in technique and their immediate objective. The three methods that are discussed in detail are :

   (i) Macaulay's method

   (ii) Moment area method and

   (iii) Conjugate beam method.

6.5 MACAULAY'S METHOD

This is a convenient method of displacement analysis particularly when the beam is subjected to different loading conditions. In this method, single bending moment equation is written such that it becomes continuous for the entire length of beam inspite of the discontinuity of loading.

For example, consider a beam AB supported and loaded as shown in Fig. 6.2.

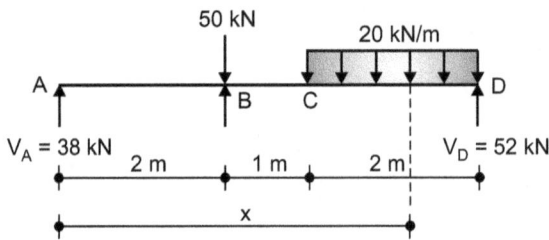

Fig. 6.2

Reactions V_A and V_D are obtained from statics as shown in Fig. 6.2.

Bending moment equations for different zones can be written as under;

$$M_{AB} = 38 x$$

$$M_{BC} = 38 x - 50 (x - 2)$$

$$M_{CD} = 38 x - 50 (x - 2) - \frac{20 (x - 3)^2}{2}$$

It should be noted that bending moment equation of zone CD is valid for zones AB and BC also provided that the terms $(x - 2)$ and $(x - 3)^2$ are neglected for values of x less than 2 m and 3 m respectively. For the ease of working, the section shall be considered in the last zone and bending moment equation for it shall be written with vertical lines of division as shown

$$EI \frac{d^2y}{dx^2} = M_x = 38 x \left| - 50 (x - 2) \right| - \frac{20 (x - 3)^2}{2} \qquad \text{... (a)}$$

$$\underset{AB}{\longleftrightarrow}$$

$$\underset{BC}{\longleftrightarrow}$$

$$\underset{CD}{\longleftrightarrow}$$

The above equation is valid for the complete length of beam if we neglect the negative values of terms in brackets.

Thus, equation (a) is the general equation of bending moment for the beam considered.

Integrating equation (a) with respect to x, we get

$$EI \cdot \frac{dy}{dx} = 38 \frac{x^2}{2} + C_1 \left| - \frac{50 (x - 2)^2}{2} \right| - \frac{20 (x - 3)^3}{6}$$

$$= 19x^2 + C_1 \left| - 25 (x - 2)^2 \right| - 3.33 (x - 3)^3 \qquad \text{... (b)}$$

Equation (b) is general equation of slope for the beam considered. Integrating this equation further with respect to x, we get

$$EI \cdot y = \frac{19x^3}{3} + C_1 x + C_2 \left| \frac{-25 (x-2)^3}{3} \right| - \frac{3.33 (x-3)^4}{4}$$

$$= 6.33 \, x^3 + C_1 x + C_2 \left| -8.33 (x-2)^3 \right| - 0.83 (x-3)^4 \qquad \text{... (c)}$$

Equation (c) is general equation of deflection for the beam considered.

In equations (b) and (c) C_1, C_2 are constants of integrations which can be evaluated using boundary conditions. Then substituting different values of x and considering proper terms from equations (b) and (c) slope and deflection at desired sections can be obtained.

Following points must be noted regarding slope and deflection equations :

 (i) Constants of integration C_1 and C_2 must be written before the first vertical line of division.

 (ii) Terms in the bracket shall be integrated as a whole. For example,

$$\int (x-a) \, dx = \frac{(x-a)^2}{2}$$

6.6 BOUNDARY CONDITIONS

For the solution of beam deflection problems, in addition to the differential equations, boundary conditions must be prescribed. Several types of homogeneous boundary conditions are as shown in Table 6.1.

Table 6.1 : Boundary conditions

Support type	Displacements restrained	Displacements allowed
Fixed	$\cdot$ x , $\cdot$ y , $\cdot$ z	NIL
Hinged	$\cdot$ x, $\cdot$ y	$\cdot$ z
Horizontal Roller	$\cdot$ y	$\cdot$ x, $\cdot$ z
Horizontal Guide	$\cdot$ y, $\cdot$ z	$\cdot$ x

 Note 1 : Δ_x ; Δ_y indicate translations in x and y directions respectively while θ_z represents rotation @ z-axis.

 Note 2 : All the supports are assumed in x-y plane.

6.7 SIGN CONVENTIONS

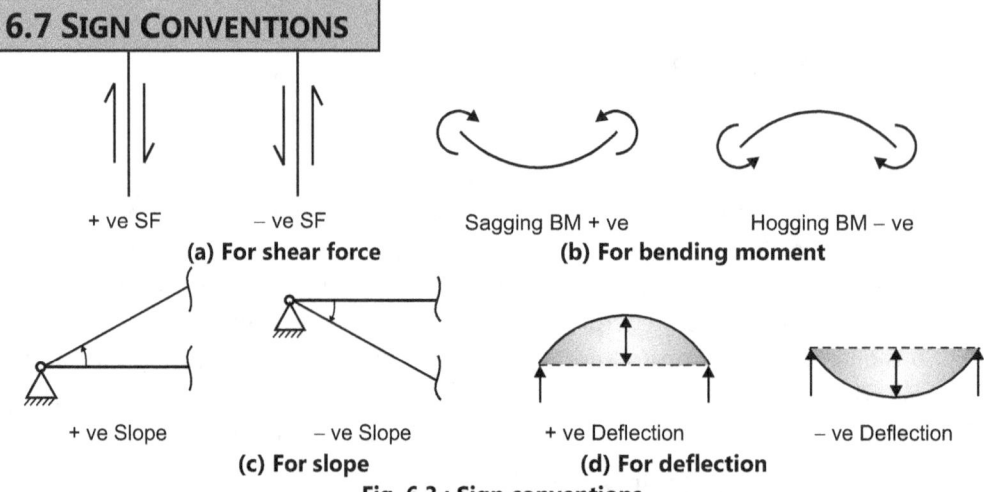

+ ve SF   – ve SF   Sagging BM + ve   Hogging BM – ve
(a) For shear force   **(b) For bending moment**

+ ve Slope   – ve Slope   + ve Deflection   – ve Deflection
(c) For slope   **(d) For deflection**

Fig. 6.3 : Sign conventions

6.8 BENDING MOMENT EQUATIONS FOR MACAULAY'S METHOD

Following are some of the variety of loadings that we generally come across for displacement analysis. Bending moment equations are written after each type of loading considering extreme left end of the beam as origin. Few cases of simply supported beams are discussed, while cantilever beams and beams with overhangs can be analysed based on same principles.

Case (i) : Beam with point loads :

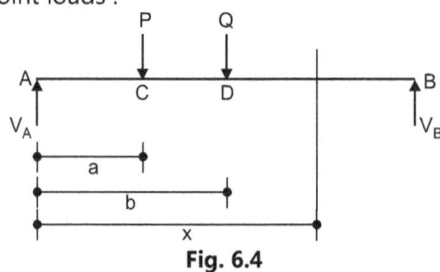

Fig. 6.4

$$EI \frac{d^2y}{dx^2} = V_A(x) \Big| - P(x-a) \Big| - Q(x-b)$$

Case (ii) : Beam with partial UDL and point load :

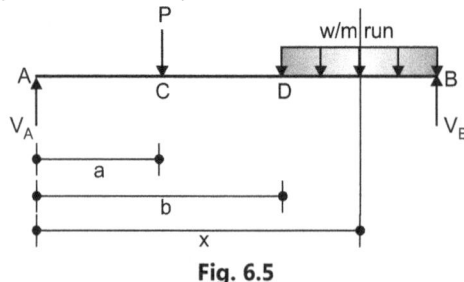

Fig. 6.5

$$EI \cdot \frac{d^2y}{dx^2} = V_A(x) \Big| -P(x-a) \Big| -\frac{w}{2}(x-b)^2$$

Case (iii) : Beam with partial UDL and point load :

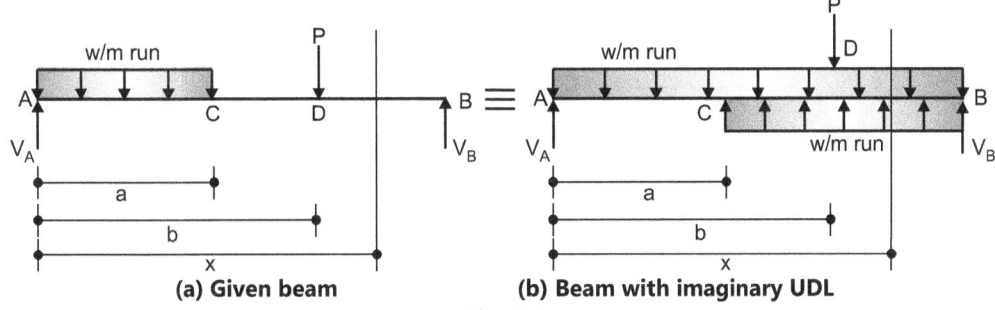

(a) Given beam　　　　　(b) Beam with imaginary UDL

Fig. 6.6

In case if partial UDL does not continue upto last zone i.e. DB as shown in Fig. 6.6 (a); an imaginary UDL is required to be considered to maintain the continuity of bending moment equation as shown in Fig. 6.6 (b). Bending moment equation for the above case now can be

written as,　　　$$EI \cdot \frac{d^2y}{dx^2} = V_A(x) -\frac{w}{2}(x)^2 \Big| +\frac{w}{2}(x-a)^2 \Big| -P(x-b)$$

Case (iv) : Beam with point load and couple :

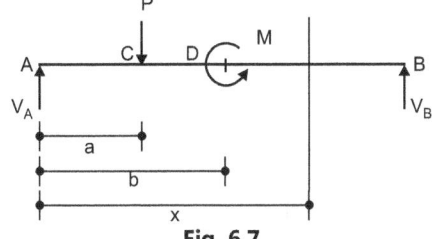

Fig. 6.7

$$EI \cdot \frac{d^2y}{dx^2} = V_A(x) \Big| -P(x-a) \Big| -M(x-b)^0$$

SOLVED EXAMPLES

Example 6.1 : *Derive expressions for slope and deflection at free end of cantilever beam carrying point load 'P' at free end.*

Solution :

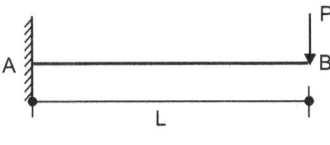

(a) Given beam

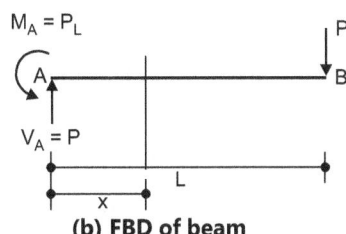

(b) FBD of beam

Fig. 6.8

(i) Reactions for equilibrium :

$\sum M_A = 0$; $M_A - PL = 0$ $\therefore$ $M_A = PL$ (↺)

$\sum F_y = 0$; $V_A - P = 0$ $\therefore$ $V_A = P$ (↑)

$\sum F_x = 0$; $H_A = 0$

(ii) Equations of BM; slope and deflection :

Consider section at a distance 'x' from 'A'.

$$EI \left(\frac{d^2y}{dx^2}\right) = P(x) - PL(x)^0 \qquad \qquad ... \text{(I)}$$

$$EI \left(\frac{dy}{dx}\right) = \frac{P}{2}(x)^2 - PL(x) + C_1 \qquad \qquad ... \text{(II)}$$

$$EI(y) = \frac{P}{6}(x)^3 - \frac{PL}{2}(x)^2 + C_1(x) + C_2 \qquad \qquad ... \text{(III)}$$

Note : For simplicity of equations; BM at a distance 'x' from 'A' can be written from RHS as

$$EI \frac{d^2y}{dx^2} = -P(L-x)$$

$$EI \left(\frac{dy}{dx}\right) = \frac{-P}{2}(L-x)^2 + C_1$$

$$EI(y) = \frac{-P}{6}(L-x)^3 + C_1(x) + C_2$$

However, now values of C_1 and C_2 will not be zero as obtained in the present analysis.

(iii) Boundary conditions :

At A i.e. x = 0; $\frac{dy}{dx} = 0$ put in equation (II) $\therefore$ $C_1 = 0$

At A i.e. x = 0; y = 0 put in equation (III) $\therefore$ $C_2 = 0$

Substituting C_1 and C_2, equations (II) and (III) are written as

$$EI \left(\frac{dy}{dx}\right) = \frac{P}{2}(x)^2 - PL(x) \qquad \qquad ... \text{(II)}$$

$$EI(y) = \frac{P}{6}(x)^3 - \frac{PL}{2}(x)^2 \qquad \qquad ... \text{(III)}$$

(iv) Slope and deflections :

For slope and deflection at free end put x = L in equations (II) and (III) respectively.

$$EI \left(\frac{dy}{dx}\right)_B = \frac{P}{2}(L)^2 - PL(L) \qquad \therefore \left(\frac{dy}{dx}\right)_B = \frac{-PL^2}{2\,EI} = \frac{PL^2}{2\,EI}\ (↺)$$

$$EI(y)_B = \frac{P}{6}(L)^3 - \frac{PL}{2}(L)^2 \qquad \therefore (y)_B = \frac{-PL^3}{3\,EI} = \frac{PL^3}{3\,EI}\ (↓)$$

Example 6.2 : *Derive expressions for slope and deflections at free end of cantilever beam carrying couple 'M' at free end.*

Solution :

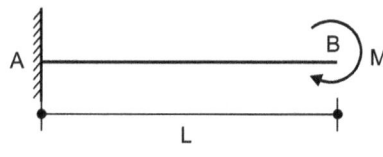

(a) Given beam　　　　　　　　　(b) FBD of beam

Fig. 6.9

(i)　Reactions for equilibrium. $M_A = M$ (↺)

(ii)　Equations of BM ; slope and deflection.

$$EI\left(\frac{d^2y}{dx^2}\right) = -M (x)^0 \qquad\qquad ... (I)$$

$$EI\left(\frac{dy}{dx}\right) = -M (x) + C_1 \qquad\qquad ... (II)$$

$$EI (y) = \frac{-M (x)^2}{2} + C_1 (x) + C_2 \qquad\qquad ... (III)$$

(iii) Boundary conditions.

At $x = 0$; $\frac{dy}{dx}$ and $y = 0$ ∴ $C_1 = C_2 = 0$

(iv) Slope and deflections.

Substituting $x = L$ in equations (II) and (III)

$$\left(\frac{dy}{dx}\right)_B = \frac{ML}{EI} \text{ (↺)}$$

$$(y)_B = \frac{ML^2}{2\ EI} \text{ (↓)}$$

Example 6.3 : *Find slope and deflection at 'C' for cantilever beam shown in Fig. 6.10.*

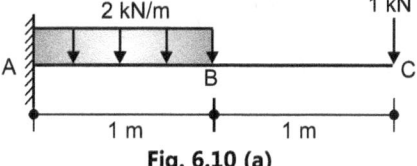

Fig. 6.10 (a)

Solution : Using principle of superposition and standard results.

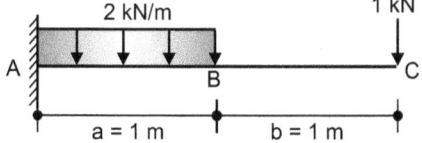 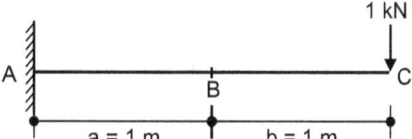

Fig. 6.10 (b) : Beam with UDL　　　**Fig. 6.10 (c) : Beam with point load**

$$\left(\frac{dy}{dx}\right)_C = \frac{-wa^3}{6\ EI} = \frac{-2\ (1)^3}{6\ EI} \qquad\qquad \left(\frac{dy}{dx}\right)_C = \frac{-PL^2}{2\ EI} = \frac{-1\ (2)^2}{2\ EI}$$

$$= \frac{-1}{3\ EI} \qquad\qquad\qquad\qquad = \frac{-2}{EI}$$

$$(\because a + b = L = 2m)$$

$$(y)_C = \frac{-wa^3}{EI}\left(\frac{a}{8} + \frac{b}{6}\right) \qquad\qquad (y)_C = \frac{-PL^3}{3\ EI} = \frac{-1 \times 2^3}{3\ EI}$$

$$= \frac{-2 \times 1^3}{EI}\left(\frac{1}{8} + \frac{1}{6}\right) \qquad\qquad = \frac{-2.67}{EI}$$

$$= \frac{-0.583}{EI}$$

$$\therefore \qquad \text{Slope at C} \;=\; \frac{-1}{EI}\left(\frac{1}{3} + 2\right) = \frac{-2.33}{EI} = \frac{2.33}{EI}\ (\circlearrowleft)$$

$$\text{Deflection at C} \;=\; \frac{-1}{EI}(0.583 + 2.67) = \frac{-3.25}{EI} = \frac{3.25}{E\ I}\ (\downarrow)$$

Example 6.4 : *Derive the expressions for slope at supports and maximum deflection for the simply supported beam carrying UDL throughout the span.*

Solution :

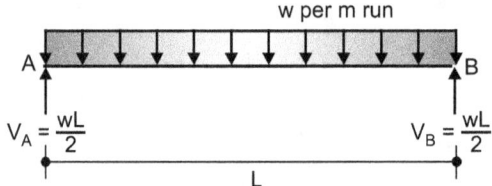

Fig. 6.11 : FBD of beam

Let;   w = Intensity of UDL

                        L = Span of the beam

(i) Reactions for equilibrium :

$$V_A \;=\; V_B = \frac{wL}{2}\ (\uparrow) \qquad\qquad\qquad (\because \text{symmetry})$$

(ii) Equations of BM; slope and deflection :

$$EI\left(\frac{d^2y}{dx^2}\right) \;=\; \frac{wL}{2}\,(x) - \frac{w\,(x)^2}{2} \qquad\qquad\qquad\text{... (I)}$$

$$EI\left(\frac{dy}{dx}\right) \;=\; \frac{wL}{4}\,(x)^2 - \frac{w}{6}\,(x)^3 + C_1 \qquad\qquad\text{... (II)}$$

$$EI\,(y) \;=\; \frac{wL}{12}\,(x)^3 - \frac{w}{24}\,(x)^4 + C_1\,(x) + C_2 \qquad\text{... (III)}$$

(iii) Boundary conditions :

At A i.e. x = 0 ; y = 0 put in equation (III) ∴ $C_2 = 0$

At B i.e. x = L ; y = 0 put in equation (III)

$$0 = \frac{wL}{12}(L)^3 - \frac{w(L)^4}{24} + C_1(L)$$

$$\therefore \qquad C_1 = -\frac{wL^3}{24}$$

Substituting values of C_1 and C_2, equations (II) and (III) are written as

$$EI\left(\frac{dy}{dx}\right) = \frac{wL}{4}(x)^2 - \frac{w}{6}(x)^3 - \frac{wL^3}{24} \qquad \qquad ... \text{(II)}$$

$$EI(y) = \frac{wL}{12}(x)^3 - \frac{w}{24}(x)^4 - \frac{wL^3}{24}(x) \qquad \qquad ... \text{(II)}$$

(iv) Slope and deflections :

For slope at support A put x = 0 in equation (II).

$$EI\left(\frac{dy}{dx}\right)_A = -\frac{wL^3}{24} \qquad \therefore \quad \left(\frac{dy}{dx}\right)_A = \frac{wL^3}{24\,EI} \ (\circlearrowright)$$

$$\left(\frac{dy}{dx}\right)_B = \frac{wL^3}{24\,EI} \ (\circlearrowleft)$$

Maximum deflection will occur at midspan due to symmetry ; put $x = \dfrac{L}{2}$ in equation (III).

$$EI(y)_{max} = \frac{wL}{12}\left(\frac{L}{2}\right)^3 - \frac{w}{24}\left(\frac{L}{2}\right)^4 - \frac{wL^3}{24}\left(\frac{L}{2}\right)$$

$$\therefore \qquad y_{max} = -\frac{5}{384} \cdot \frac{wL^4}{EI}$$

Example 6.5 : *Find the magnitude of 'W' for the beam shown in Fig. 6.12 such that deflection at free end A of the beam is zero.*

Data   :   As shown in Fig. 6.12.

Required   :   Magnitude of W for deflection at 'A' to be zero.

Concept   :   Principle of superposition.

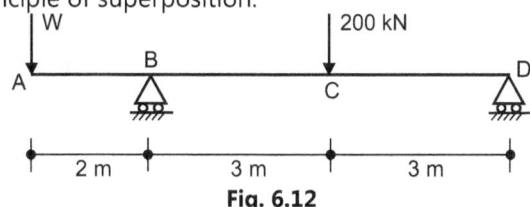

Fig. 6.12

Solution :

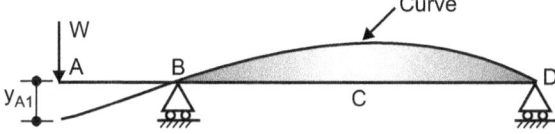

Fig. 6.13 : Elastic curve due to W

$$y_{A_1} = \frac{Wa^2}{3\,EI}(L + a)$$

$$= \frac{W\,(2)^2}{3\,EI}(6 + 2) = \frac{10.67}{EI}W\;(\downarrow)$$

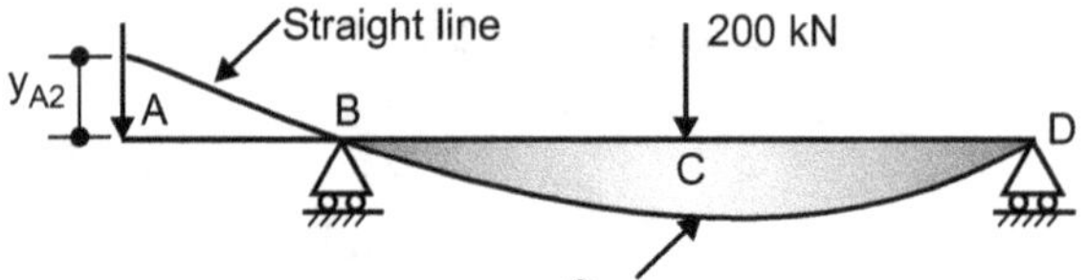

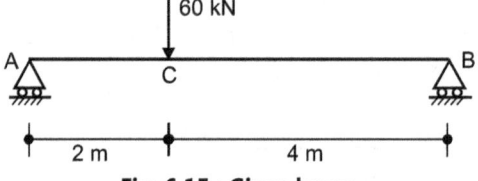

Fig. 6.14 : Elastic curve due to 200 kN load

$$y_{A_2} = \text{slope at } B \times l\,(AB)$$

$$= \frac{PL^2}{16\,EI} \times l\,(AB)$$

$$= \frac{200 \times 6^2}{16\,EI} \times 2$$

$$= \frac{900}{EI}\;(\uparrow)$$

For $y_A = 0$;

$$y_{A_1} = y_{A_2}$$

$$\frac{10.67\,W}{EI} = \frac{900}{EI}$$

$\therefore$ $W = 84.375$ kN

Example 6.6 : *For the beam shown in Fig. 6.15, find slope at supports; deflection under the load and maximum deflection.*

60 kN

Fig. 6.15 : Given beam

Data   : As shown in Fig. 6.15.

Required   : Slope at A; B; deflection at C and maximum deflection.

Concept   : Consider 'A' as origin and section at a distance 'x' from A in zone CB for BM equation.

Solution   : (i) Reactions for equilibrium :

$\sum M_A = 0$; $V_B \times 6 - 60 \times 2 = 0$ $\therefore$ $V_B = 20$ kN $(\uparrow)$

$\sum F_y = 0$; $V_A + V_B - 60 = 0$ $\therefore$ $V_A = 40$ kN $(\uparrow)$

$\sum F_x = 0$; $H_A = 0$

FBD of beam is as shown in Fig. 6.50.

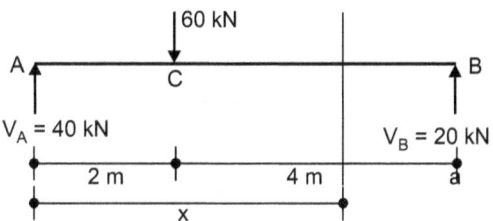

Fig. 6.16 : FBD of beam

(ii) Equations of BM, slope and deflection :

$$EI \left(\frac{d^2y}{dx^2}\right) = 40\,(x) \left| -60\,(x-2) \right. \qquad \text{... (I)}$$

$$\underset{AC}{\vdash\!\!-\!\!\dashv}$$

$$\underset{CB}{\vdash\!\!-\!\!\!-\!\!\dashv}$$

$$EI \left(\frac{dy}{dx}\right) = 20\,(x)^2 + C_1 \left| -30\,(x-2)^2 \right. \qquad \text{... (II)}$$

$$EI\,(y) = \frac{20}{3}\,(x)^3 + C_1\,(x) + C_2 \left| -10\,(x-2)^3 \right. \qquad \text{... (III)}$$

(iii) Boundary conditions :

At A i.e. x = 0 ; y = 0 put in equation (III).

$$0 = 0 + 0 + C_2 \qquad \therefore \quad C_2 = 0$$

At B i.e. x = 6 m ; y = 0 put in equation (III).

$$0 = \frac{20}{3}\,(6)^3 + C_1\,(6) + C_2 - 10\,(6-2)^3 \quad (\because C_2 = 0)$$

$$0 = 1440 + 6\,C_1 - 640$$

$$\therefore \qquad\qquad C_1 = -133.33$$

Substituting values of C_1 and C_2, equations (II) and (III) are written as

$$EI \left(\frac{dy}{dx}\right) = 20\,(x)^2 - 133.33 \left| -30\,(x-2)^2 \right. \qquad \text{... (II)}$$

$$EI\,(y) = \frac{20}{3}\,(x)^3 - 133.33\,(x) \left| -10\,(x-2)^3 \right. \qquad \text{... (III)}$$

(iv) Slopes and deflections :

For slope at 'A' put x = 0 in equation (II).

$$EI \left(\frac{dy}{dx}\right)_A = 0 - 133.33 \quad \therefore \quad \left(\frac{dy}{dx}\right)_A = \frac{-133.33}{EI} = \frac{133.33}{EI}\ (\circlearrowleft)$$

For slope at 'B' put x = 6 m in equation (II).

$$EI \left(\frac{dy}{dx}\right)_B = 20\,(6)^2 - 133.33 - 30\,(6-2)^2$$

$$\therefore \quad \left(\frac{dy}{dx}\right)_B = \frac{106.67}{EI} = \frac{106.67}{EI} \, (\circlearrowleft)$$

For deflection at 'C' put x = 2 m in equation (III).

$$EI\,(y)_C = \frac{20}{3}\,(2)^3 - 133.33\,(2)$$

$$\therefore \quad y_C = \frac{-213.33}{EI} = \frac{213.33}{EI} \, (\downarrow)$$

For maximum deflection;

let maximum deflection occurs in zone CB i.e. (2 < x < 6)

Equating slope equation (II) for zone CB to zero.

$$0 = 20\,(x)^2 - 133.33 - 30\,(x-2)^2$$

$$0 = 10x^2 - 120x + 253.33$$

Solving　　　　x = 2.73 m Assumption is OK.

Put x = 2.73 m in equation (III) to get maximum deflection.

$$EI\,(y)_{max} = \frac{20}{3}\,(2.73)^3 - 133.33\,(2.73) - 10\,(2.73-2)^3$$

$$(y)_{max} = \frac{-232.24}{EI} = \frac{232.24}{EI} \, (\downarrow)$$

Example 6.7 : *Find slope at 'B', 'C' and deflection at 'C' and 'D' for the beam shown in Fig. 6.17. Assume E = 200 GPa ; I = 2 ×10⁸ mm⁴.*

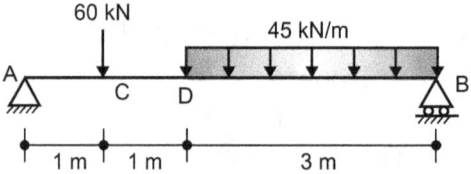

Fig. 6.17 : Given beam

Data　　: As shown in Fig. 6.17 ; EI = 4×10^4 kN.m².

Required : Slope at 'B', 'C' and deflection at 'C' and 'D'.

Concept : Consider 'A' as origin and section at a distance 'x' from 'A' in zone DB for BM equation.

Solution : (i) Reactions for equilibrium :

$\sum M_A = 0;$ 　　$V_B \times 5 - 45 \times 3 \times 3.5 - 60 \times 1 = 0$ 　$\therefore$ 　$V_B = 106.5$ kN ($\uparrow$)

$\sum F_y = 0;$ 　　　$V_A + V_B - 60 - 45 \times 3 = 0$ 　　$\therefore$ 　$V_A = 88.5$ kN ($\uparrow$)

$\sum F_x = 0;$ 　　　　　　$H_A = 0$

FBD of beam is as shown in Fig. 6.18.

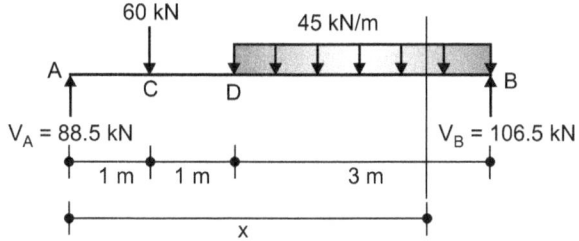

Fig. 6.18 : FBD of beam

(ii) Equations of BM ; slope and deflection.

$$EI\left(\frac{d^2y}{dx^2}\right) = 88.5\,(x)\bigg| - 60\,(x-1)\bigg| - 45\,\frac{(x-2)^2}{2} \qquad \ldots \text{(I)}$$

AC

CD

DB

$$EI\left(\frac{dy}{dx}\right) = 44.25\,(x)^2 + C_1\bigg| - 30\,(x-1)^2\bigg| - 7.5\,(x-2)^3 \qquad \ldots \text{(II)}$$

$$EI\,(y) = 14.75\,(x)^3 + C_1\,(x) + C_2\bigg| - 10\,(x-1)^3\bigg| - 1.875\,(x-2)^4 \qquad \ldots \text{(III)}$$

(iii) Boundary conditions :

At A i.e. $x = 0$; $y = 0$ put in equation (III).

$$C_2 = 0$$

At B i.e. $x = 5$ m ; $y = 0$ put in equation (III).

$$0 = 14.75\,(5)^3 + C_1\,(5) - 10\,(5-1)^3 - 1.875\,(5-2)^4$$

∴ $$C_1 = -210.375$$

Substituting values of C_1 and C_2, equations (II) and (III) are written as

$$EI\left(\frac{dy}{dx}\right) = 44.25\,(x)^2 - 210.375\bigg| - 30\,(x-1)^2\bigg| - 7.5\,(x-2)^3 \qquad \ldots \text{(II)}$$

$$EI\,(y) = 14.75\,(x)^3 - 210.375\,(x)\bigg| - 10\,(x-1)^3\bigg| - 1.875\,(x-2)^4 \qquad \ldots \text{(III)}$$

(iv) Slopes and deflections : For slope at 'B' put $x = 5$ m in equation (II).

$$EI\left(\frac{dy}{dx}\right)_B = 44.25\,(5)^2 - 210.375 - 30\,(5-1)^2 - 7.5\,(5-2)^3$$

∴ $$\left(\frac{dy}{dx}\right)_B = \frac{213.375}{EI} = 5.33 \times 10^{-3}\,\text{rad} \;(\circlearrowleft)$$

For slope at 'C' put $x = 1$ m in equation (II)

$$EI\left(\frac{dy}{dx}\right)_C = 44.25\,(1)^2 - 210.375$$

$$\left(\frac{dy}{dx}\right)_C = \frac{-166.125}{EI} = 4.153 \times 10^{-3} \text{ rad } (\circlearrowleft)$$

For deflection at 'C' put $x = 1$ m in equation (III).

$$EI\,(y)_C = 14.75\,(1)^3 - 210.375\,(1)$$

$$\therefore \quad y_C = \frac{-195.625}{EI} = 4.89 \text{ mm } (\downarrow)$$

For deflection at 'D' put $x = 2$ m in equation (III).

$$EI\,(y)_D = 14.75\,(2)^3 - 210.375\,(2) - 10\,(2-1)^3$$

$$\therefore \quad y_D = \frac{-312.75}{EI} = 7.82 \text{ mm } (\downarrow)$$

6.9 MOMENT AREA METHODS – MOHR'S THEOREMS

The moment area method provides convenient means of determining slopes and deflections in beams. The method is especially suitable when it is desired to find the slope or deflection at a given point of the beam instead of the complete equation of the deflection curve. Depending on geometry of elastic curve, the moment area method emphasizes the physical significance of slope and deflection. We first discuss the two basic theorems of the method.

Consider a simply supported beam shown in Fig. 6.20 (a). The elastic curve and $\frac{M}{EI}$ diagram is also shown in Fig. 6.20 (b) and Fig. 6.20 (c) respectively. Consider portion AB of the elastic curve of the beam. The tangents to the curve at two cross sections C and D of the beam at a distance ds apart, will intersect at angle dθ which is the change in slope from C to D.

From flexural formula, we have

$$\frac{1}{R} = \frac{M}{EI}$$

Since

$$ds = R \cdot d\theta$$

$$\frac{1}{R} = \frac{M}{EI} = \frac{d\theta}{ds} \quad \therefore d\theta = \frac{M}{EI} \cdot ds$$

Assuming the length ds to be equal to its projection dx,

$$d\theta = \frac{M}{EI} \cdot dx \qquad \qquad \dots (6.10)$$

From Fig. 6.20 (d), it is clear that tangents drawn to elastic curve at C and D are separated by the same angle dθ by which sections OC and OD rotate relative to each other. Hence, change in slope between tangents drawn to the elastic curve at any two points A and B will be equal to the sum of such small angles.

$$\theta_{AB} = \int_{\theta_A}^{\theta_B} d\theta = \frac{1}{EI} \int_{x_A}^{x_B} M \cdot dx \qquad \dots (6.11)$$

Thus, we obtain the following theorem.

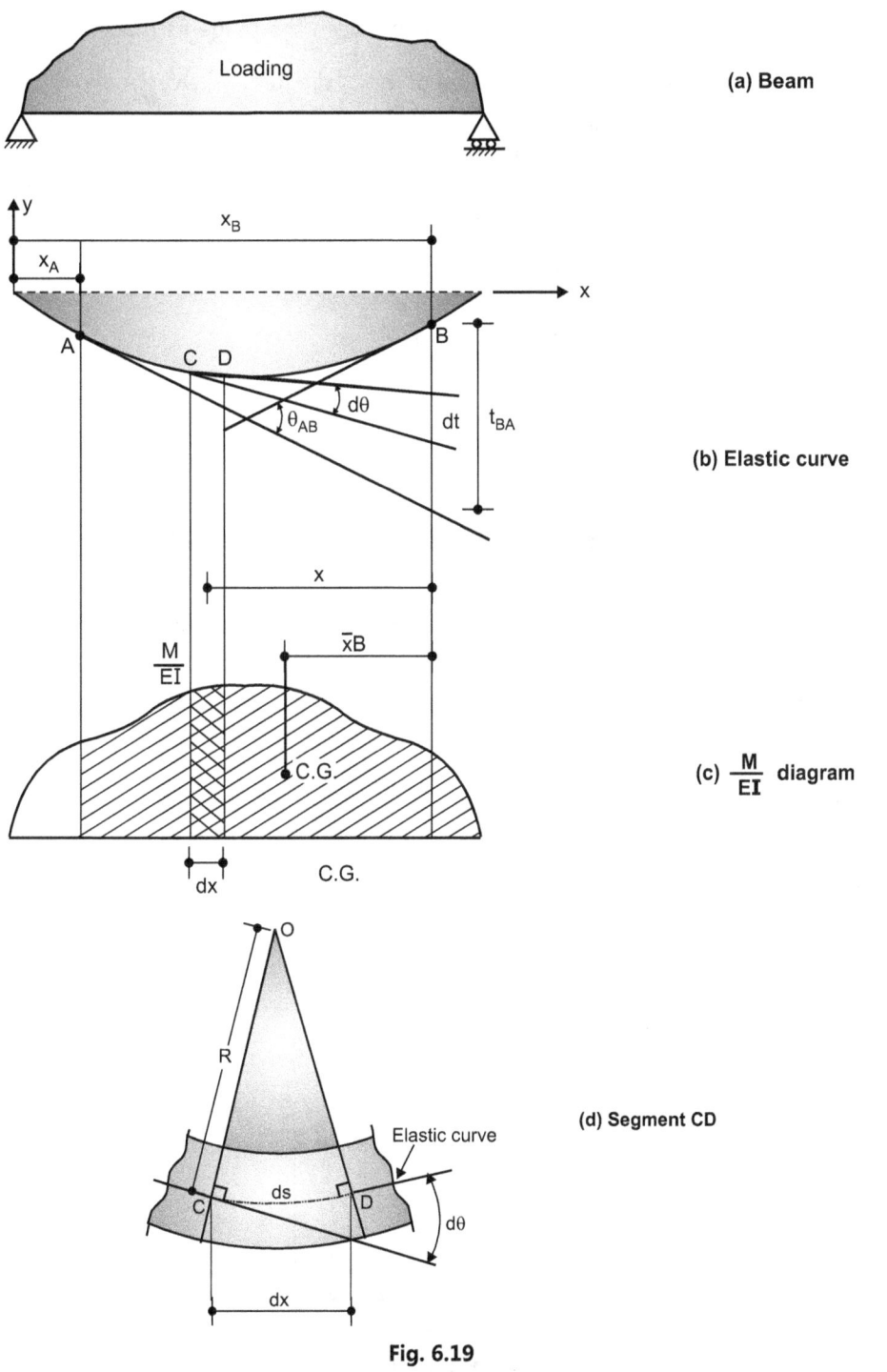

Fig. 6.19

First Moment - Area Theorem : The angle between the tangents drawn at two points A and B of an elastic curve is equal to the area of the $\frac{M}{EI}$ diagram between A and B.

From Fig. 6.20 (b), it can also be noted that, the distance from B on the elastic curve (measured perpendicular to the original position of the beam) that will intersect a tangent drawn to this curve at any other point A is the sum of intercepts dt created by tangents to the curve at adjacent points. Each of these intercepts may be considered as the arc of a circle of radius x subtended by angle dθ.

$$dt = x \cdot d\theta$$

$$t_{BA} = \int dt = \int x \cdot d\theta$$

From equation (6.10), substituting for dθ,

$$t_{BA} = \frac{1}{EI} \int_{x_A}^{x_B} x \cdot (M \cdot dx) \qquad \qquad ...(6.12)$$

Second Moment-Area Theorem : The displacement of any point B on elastic curve relative to a tangent drawn to the elastic curve at any other point A, in a direction perpendicular to the original position of beam, is equal to the moment of area of $\frac{M}{EI}$ diagram between A and B taken about B.

Thus, $$t_{BA} = (Area)_{BA} \cdot \bar{x}_B \qquad \qquad ...(6.13)$$

Thus, in Fig. 6.20,

and

$$\left.\begin{array}{l} t_{AB} = (Area)_{AB} \cdot \bar{x}_A \\[2mm] t_{BA} = (Area)_{BA} \cdot \bar{x}_B \end{array}\right\} \qquad ...(6.14)$$

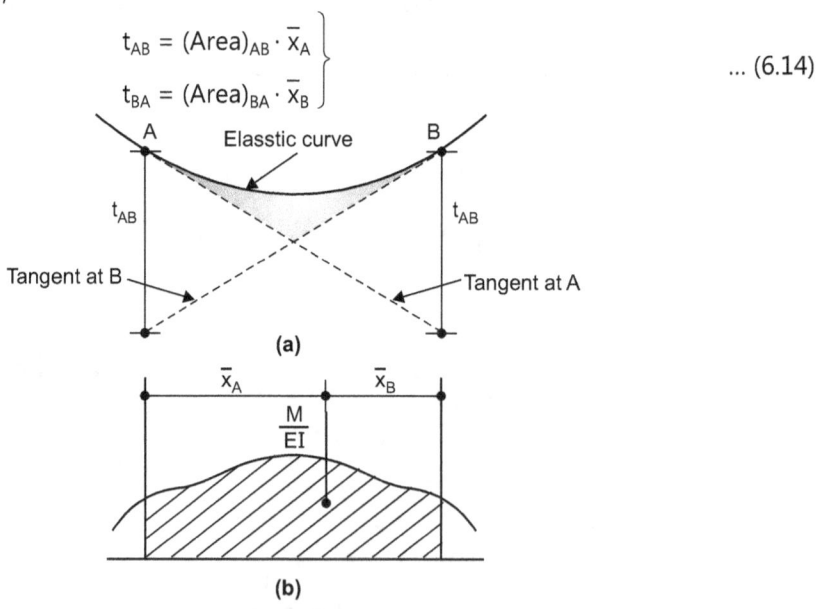

Fig. 6.20

6.9.1 Sign Conventions

For slope and deflection

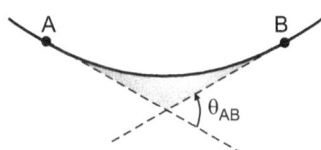

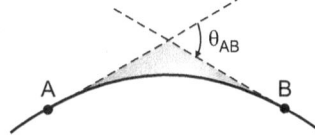

(a) Positive change of slope; θ_{AB} is anticlockwise from left tangent

(b) Negative change of slope; θ_{AB} is clockwise from left tangent

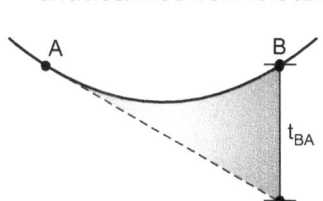

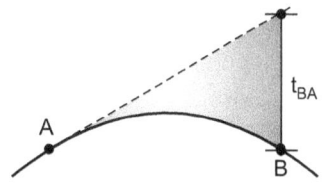

(c) Positive displacement; B is located above tangent at A

(d) Negative displacement; B is located below tangent at A

Fig. 6.21

Fig. 6.21 (a) and (b) show that; positive value of change in slope θ_{AB} between points A and B on elastic curve means that the angle measured from left tangent (at A) to right tangent (at B) is anticlockwise and vice versa.

Fig. 6.21 (c) and (d) show that; displacement at any point is positive if the point lies above the tangent drawn at reference point from which the displacement is measured; and negative if the point lies below tangent drawn at reference point.

Moment area method thus involves computing area of $\dfrac{M}{EI}$ diagram between the two points of interest; and also to find moment of area of $\dfrac{M}{EI}$ diagram between two points about any of the point. A method of doing this from calculus is to integrate the two expressions $\displaystyle\int \dfrac{M}{EI}\,dx$ and $\displaystyle\int \left(\dfrac{M}{EI}\right)\cdot x \cdot dx$ between proper limits; where bending moment M is expressed in terms of x. For replacing integration by simple numerical calculations, $\dfrac{M}{EI}$ diagram is divided into parts whose areas and centroids are known. Geometric properties of such several figures are shown in Table 6.2.

Table 6.2

Sr. No.	Diagram	Degree of curve	Area	$\bar{x}$
1.		zero	bh	$\dfrac{b}{2}$
2.		one	$\dfrac{1}{2}bh$	$\dfrac{b}{3}$
3.		two	$\dfrac{1}{3}bh$	$\dfrac{b}{4}$
4.		three	$\dfrac{1}{4}bh$	$\dfrac{b}{5}$
5.		two	$\dfrac{2}{3}bh$	$\dfrac{3}{8}b$
6.		one	$\dfrac{1}{2}\cdot Lh$	$\dfrac{L+b}{3}$

6.10 APPLICATION OF MOMENT-AREA METHOD
TO CANTILEVER BEAMS

Consider cantilever beam AB of constant flexural rigidity (EI) throughout and let it is required to find slope and deflection at C.

Fig. 6.22 (b) shows $\frac{M}{EI}$ diagram and Fig. 6.22 (c) shows elastic curve.

Slope at C = θ = Angle between tangents drawn at A and C' since the tangent drawn at A to elastic curve is horizontal.

∴ By first theorem of moment area,

$$\theta = \text{Area (PQST)}$$

Due to hogging bending moment above area will be negative which indicates that angle measured from tangent drawn at A to tangent drawn at C' is clockwise and θ is treated negative i.e. (↻).

Also deflection at C = y_C = Displacement of C' with respect to tangent drawn at A = t_{CA}.

$$= \text{Moment of area of } \frac{M}{EI} \text{ diagram between A and C' about C'}.$$

∴ By second theorem of moment area, y_C = Area (PQST) $\bar{x}$.

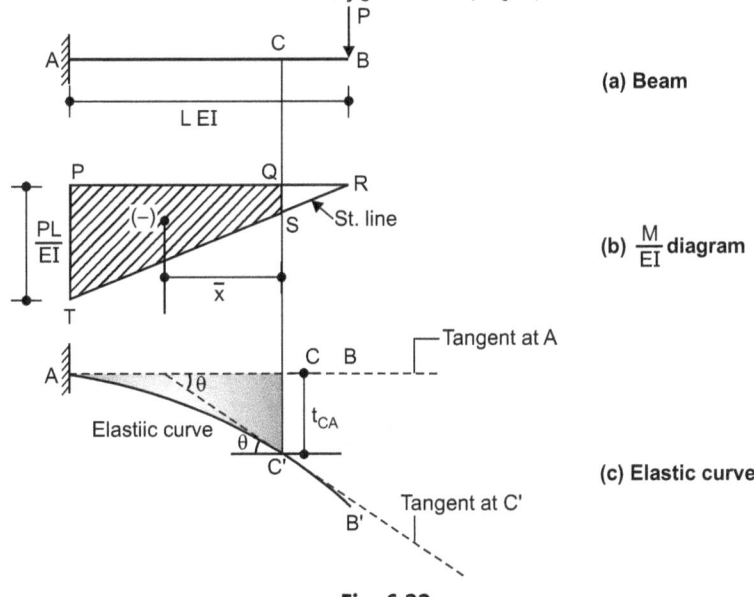

(a) Beam

(b) $\frac{M}{EI}$ **diagram**

(c) Elastic curve

Fig. 6.22

Due to hogging bending moment, the moment of above area will also be negative which indicates that C' is located below the tangent drawn at reference point. A. In this case, t_{CA}

directly gives the value of deflection at C since the tangent drawn at A to elastic curve is horizontal. The above deflection is treated negative i.e. ($\downarrow$). Thus, for finding slope and deflection at any point on cantilever beam, moment area method is very simple to apply. Application of method to cantilever beams is illustrated in the following examples.

SOLVED EXAMPLES

Example 6.8 : *Determine slope and deflection at free end of cantilever. Take W = 10 kN; L = 5 m; I = 6.5 × 10⁷ mm⁴; E = 2 × 10⁵ MPa. Use moment area method. Assume uniform flexural rigidity. [Refer Fig. 6.23 (a)].*

Solution :

(i) $\theta_B = \theta_A + \Delta\theta_{AB}$

where; $\Delta\theta_{AB}$ = Change of slope from A to B

$\qquad\qquad$ = Angle between tangents drawn at A and B.

$\qquad\qquad$ = Area of $\dfrac{M}{EI}$ diagram between A and B

$$= \frac{1}{2}\left[\frac{-50 \text{ kN.m}}{EI}\right] \times 5 = -\frac{125 \text{ kN.m}^2}{EI}$$

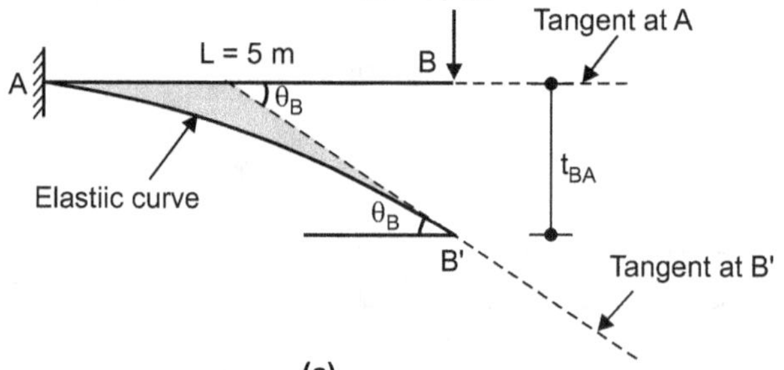

(a)

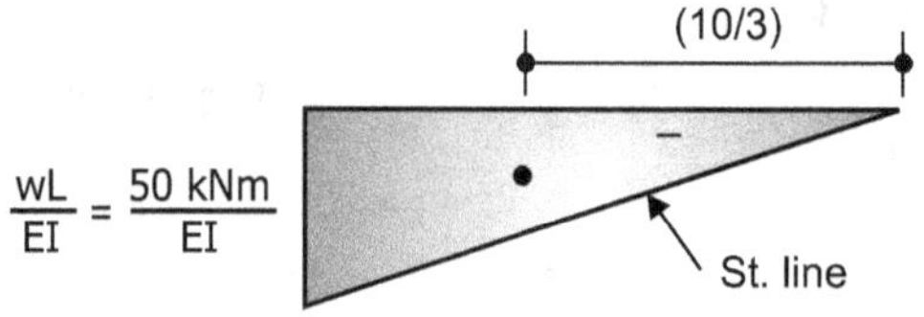

(b) $\dfrac{M}{EI}$ **diagram**

Fig. 6.23

$$EI = 2 \times 10^5 \times 6.5 \times 10^7 = 13 \times 10^{12} \text{ N.mm}^2$$
$$= 13 \times 10^3 \text{ kN.m}^2$$

Also $\qquad\qquad \theta_A = 0$

∴ $\qquad\qquad \theta_B = \Delta\theta_{AB} = -\frac{125 \text{ kN.m}^2}{EI} = -\frac{125}{13 \times 10^3}$

$$= - \, 0.00961 \text{ rad}$$

$$= 0.55^\circ \text{ (↻)}$$

(–ve sign indicates that angle made by tangent drawn at A with tangent drawn at B' is clockwise.)

(ii) Displacement of B' with respect to tangent drawn at A = t_{BA}

∴ t_{BA} = Moment of area of $\dfrac{M}{EI}$ diagram between A and B' about B'.

∴ $t_{BA} = y_B = \left[\dfrac{1}{2} \times \dfrac{-50 \text{ kN.m}}{EI} \right] \times 5 \times \dfrac{2}{3}$ (5)

$$= -\dfrac{416.67 \text{ kN.m}^3}{EI}$$

$$= -\dfrac{416.67 \times 10^3}{13 \times 10^3} = 32.051 \text{ mm (↓)}$$

(– ve sign indicates that, B' is below tangent drawn at A)

Example 6.9 : *Find slope and deflections at B and C for cantilever shown in Fig. 6.24 (a); using moment area method. Take E = 2 × 10⁵ MPa, I = 4 × 10⁷ mm⁴, l (AB) = 2 m, l (BC) = 1 m.*

Solution :

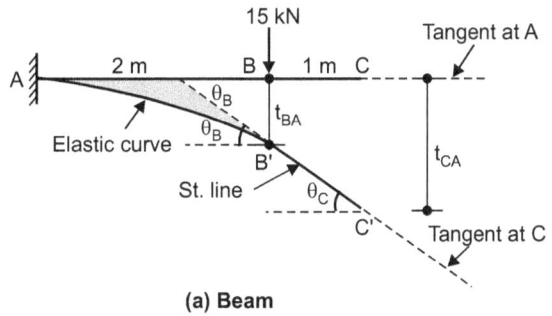

(a) Beam

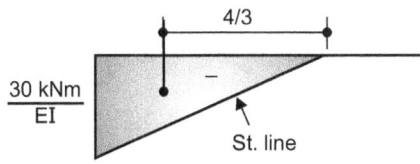

(b) $\dfrac{M}{EI}$ **diagram**

Fig. 6.24

(i) θ_B = Angle between tangent drawn at A and B' as tangent at A is horizontal

$= $ Area of $\dfrac{M}{EI}$ diagram between A and B'

$$= \left[\dfrac{1}{2} \times (-30)\ \dfrac{kN.m}{EI}\right] \times 2 = \dfrac{-30\ kN.m^2}{EI}$$

$$EI = 2 \times 10^5 \times 4 \times 10^7 = 8 \times 10^{12}\ Nmm^2$$

$$= 8 \times 10^3\ kN.m^2$$

$$\theta_B = \dfrac{-30\ kN.m^2}{EI} = \dfrac{-30}{8 \times 10^3}$$

$$= -0.00375\ rad$$

$$= 0.214^\circ\ (\circlearrowleft)$$

$$\theta_C = \theta_B = 0.214^\circ\ (\circlearrowleft)$$

$$y_B = t_{BA}$$

$= $ Displacement of B' with respect to tangent drawn at A

$= $ Moment of area of $\dfrac{M}{EI}$ diagram between A and B' about B'

$$= \left[\dfrac{-30\ kN.m^2}{EI}\right] \times \dfrac{4}{3}$$

$$= -\dfrac{40\ kN.m^3}{EI}$$

$$= -\dfrac{40 \times 10^3}{8 \times 10^3} = 5\ mm\ (\downarrow)$$

$$y_C = t_{CA}$$

$= $ Displacement of C' with respect to tangent drawn at A

$= $ Moment of area of $\dfrac{M}{EI}$ diagram between A and C' about C'

$$= \left[-\dfrac{30\ kN.m^2}{EI}\right]\left(1 + \dfrac{4}{3}\right)$$

$$= -\dfrac{70\ kN.m^3}{EI} = -\dfrac{70 \times 10^3}{8 \times 10^3}$$

$$= 8.75\ mm\ (\downarrow)$$

Example 6.10 : *Using moment area method, derive expression for slope and deflection at free end of cantilever of uniform section carrying uniformly distributed load of intensity 'w' per unit run, throughout the span.*

Solution : [Refer Fig. 6.25 (a)]

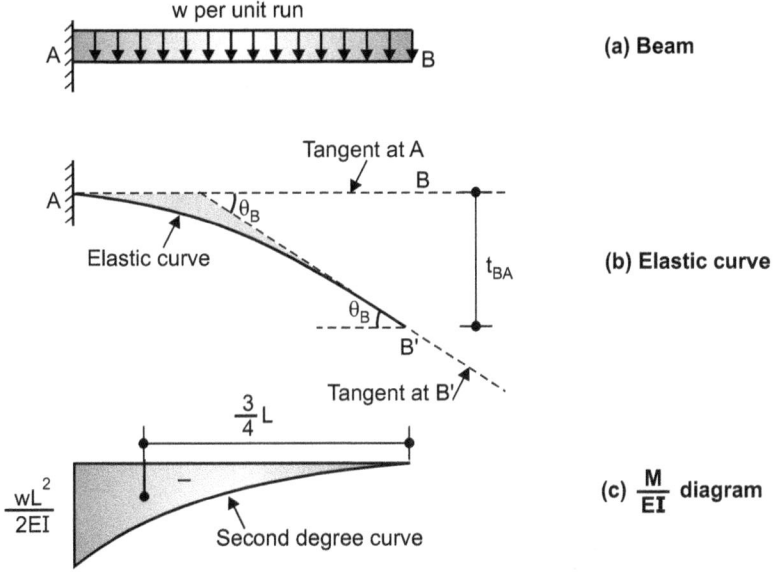

Fig. 6.25

θ_B = Angle between tangents drawn at A and B'; as tangent at A is horizontal

= Area of $\dfrac{M}{EI}$ diagram between A and B'

= $-\left(\dfrac{1}{3} \times L \times \dfrac{wL^2}{2\ EI}\right) = \dfrac{wL^3}{6\ EI}$ (↻)

$y_B = t_{BA}$ = Displacement of B' with respect to tangent drawn at A

= Moment of area of $\dfrac{M}{EI}$ diagram between A and B' about B'

= $-\left(\dfrac{wL^3}{6\ EI}\right)\dfrac{3}{4}\ (L) = \dfrac{wL^4}{8\ EI}$ (↓)

Example 6.11 : *For the cantilever beam shown in Fig. 6.26 (a), find slope and deflection at free end using moment area method. Take EI = Constant.*

Solution :

Slope at free end = θ_C = Angle between tangents drawn at A and C' as tangent at A is horizontal.

= Area of $\dfrac{M}{EI}$ diagram between A and C'

= $-\left[\dfrac{1}{3} \times 90\ \dfrac{kN.m}{EI} \times 3\right]$ = 90 kN.m²/EI (↻)

$y_C = t_{CA}$ = Displacement of C' with respect to tangent drawn at A

= Moment of area of $\dfrac{M}{EI}$ diagram between A and C' about C'

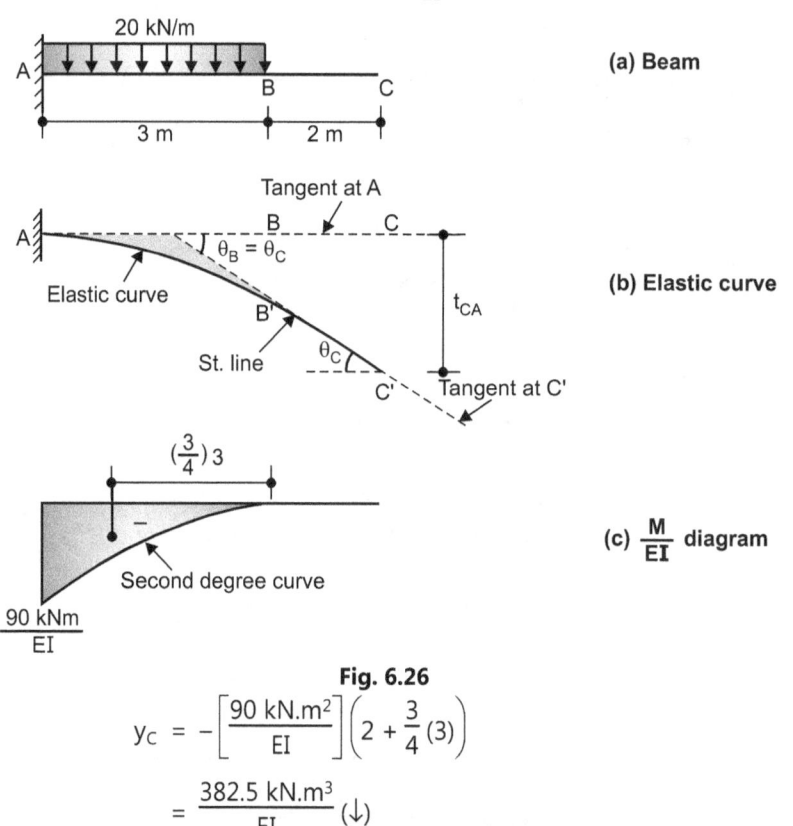

(a) Beam

(b) Elastic curve

(c) $\dfrac{M}{EI}$ **diagram**

Fig. 6.26

$$y_C = -\left[\frac{90 \text{ kN.m}^2}{EI}\right]\left(2 + \frac{3}{4}(3)\right)$$

$$= \frac{382.5 \text{ kN.m}^3}{EI} \ (\downarrow)$$

6.11 APPLICATION OF MOMENT-AREA METHOD TO SIMPLY SUPPORTED AND OVERHANGING BEAMS

Consider a simply supported beam AB as shown in Fig. 6.27 (a). Assuming the beam has constant flexural rigidity and let, it be required to find slope at supports A and B and deflection under load point.

$$\theta_A = \frac{t_{BA}}{L}$$

and

$$\theta_B = \frac{t_{AB}}{L}$$

where,

t_{BA} = Displacement of B with respect to tangent drawn at A and

t_{AB} = Displacement of A with respect to tangent drawn at B

Here, t_{AB} and t_{BA} will be positive due to sagging bending moments; indicating that A and B are located above the tangents drawn at B and A respectively. By second theorem of moment area;

$$t_{AB} = \text{Area (PQR)} \ \bar{x}_A \ \text{and}$$

$$t_{BA} = \text{Area (PQR)} \ \bar{x}_B$$

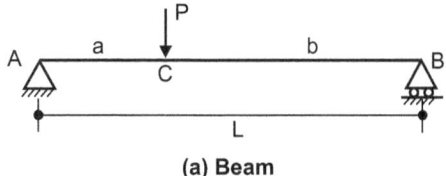

(a) Beam

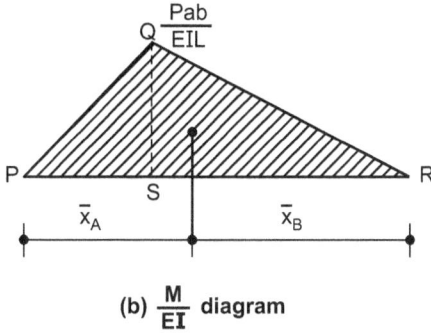

(b) $\dfrac{M}{EI}$ **diagram**

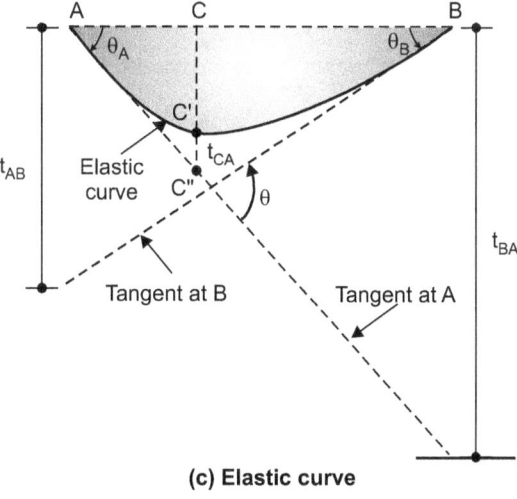

(c) Elastic curve

Fig. 6.27

From Fig. 6.27 (c).

Deflection under load = y_C = CC' = CC" – C' C"

where   CC" = $(\theta_A) \cdot a$ and C'C" = t_{CA}

= Displacement of C' with respect to tangent drawn at A to elastic curve.

= Moment of area of $\dfrac{M}{EI}$ diagram between A and C' about C'

= Area (PQS) × Distance of C.G. of area (PQS) from S i.e. (C')

Here, t_{CA} will be positive indicating that C' is above tangent at A. Note that, slope and deflection at various points of simply supported beam cannot be determined directly as in case of cantilevers. Application of moment-area method to determine slope and deflection at various points of simply supported and overhanging beams is illustrated in the following examples.

SOLVED EXAMPLES

Example 6.12 : *Using moment-area method, find deflection at centre and slope at supports for simply supported beam of uniform section carrying concentrated load P at centre. [Refer Fig. 6.28 (a)].*

Solution :

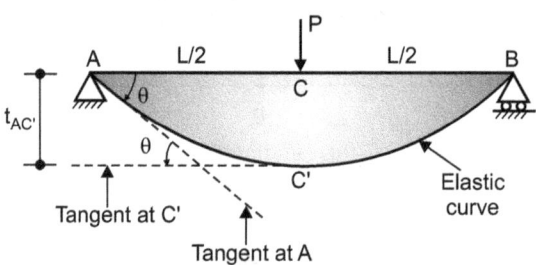

(a) Beam and Elastic curve

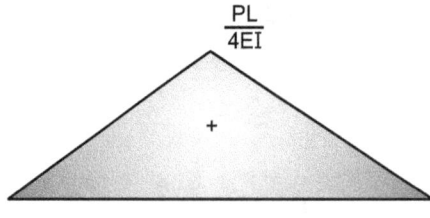

(b) $\dfrac{M}{EI}$ **diagram**

Fig. 6.28

Due to symmetry; maximum deflection occurs at centre and tangent drawn to elastic curve at centre is horizontal.

∴ Angle between tangents drawn at A and C'

$$= \theta = \text{Slope at A} = \text{Area of } \frac{M}{EI} \text{ diagram between A and C'}$$

$$= \frac{1}{2}\left(\frac{L}{2}\right) \times \frac{PL}{4\,EI} = \frac{PL^2}{16\,EI} \,(\circlearrowleft)$$

+ve sign indicates that angle made by tangent drawn at A with tangent drawn at C' is anticlockwise.

By symmetry, slope at B = $\theta = \dfrac{PL^2}{16\,EI} \,(\circlearrowright)$

Displacement of A with respect to tangent drawn at C' = t_{AC}

$$= \text{Moment of area of } \frac{M}{EI} \text{ diagram between A and C' about A}$$

∴ $t_{AC'} = \left[\dfrac{1}{2}\left(\dfrac{L}{2}\right)\dfrac{PL}{4\,EI}\right]\dfrac{2}{3}\left(\dfrac{L}{2}\right)$

$$= \frac{PL^3}{48\,EI}$$

Point A is above the tangent at C', hence $t_{AC'}$ is + ve.

$$y_C = y_{max} = t_{AC'} = \frac{PL^3}{48\,EI} \,(\downarrow)$$

Example 6.13 : *For simply supported beam shown in Fig. 6.29 (a), find slope and deflection at centre of beam. Use moment-area method and assume uniform flexural rigidity. Also find position and amount of maximum deflection.*

Solution :

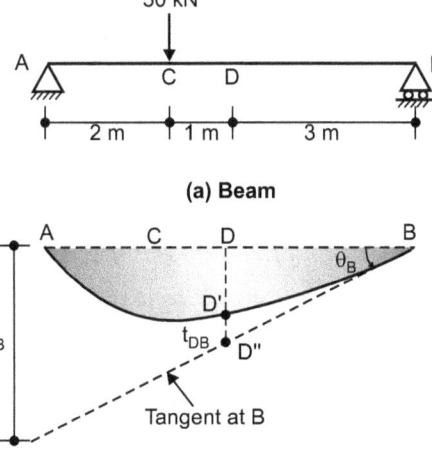

(a) Beam

(b) Elastic curve

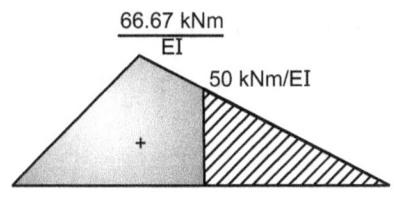

(c) $\dfrac{M}{EI}$ **diagram**

Fig. 6.29

(i) From elastic curve :

$$y_D = \text{Deflection at centre} = DD' = DD'' - D'D''$$

where, $DD'' = (\theta_B) \times 3$ and

$D'D'' = $ Displacement of D' with respect to tangent drawn at B $= t_{D'B}$

$\quad\quad\quad = $ Moment of area of $\dfrac{M}{EI}$ diagram between D' and B about D'

To find DD'', $DD'' = (\theta_B) \times 3$

where, $\theta_B = \dfrac{t_{AB}}{6}$

$t_{AB} = $ Displacement of A with respect to tangent drawn at B

$\quad\quad\quad = $ Moment of area of $\dfrac{M}{EI}$ diagram between A and B about A

$$= \left[\dfrac{1}{2} \times 6 \times 66.67 \dfrac{kN.m}{EI}\right] \times \left(\dfrac{6+2}{3}\right)$$

$$= \dfrac{533.33 \ kN.m^3}{EI}$$

∴. $\theta_B = \dfrac{t_{AB}}{6} = \dfrac{533.33}{6}\dfrac{kN.m^3}{EI} = \dfrac{88.88 \ kN.m^2}{EI}$

∴. $DD'' = \left(\dfrac{88.88 \ kN.m^2}{EI}\right) \times 3 = 266.67 \ \dfrac{kN.m^3}{EI}$

To find $D'D'' = t_{D'B}$

$$= \dfrac{1}{2} \times \dfrac{50 \ kN.m}{EI} \times (3) \times \dfrac{1}{3} \times (3) = \dfrac{75 \ kN.m^3}{EI}$$

∴. $y_D = DD'' - D'D'' = (266.67 - 75) \ kN.m^3/EI$

$$y_D = \dfrac{191.67 \ kN.m^3}{EI} \ (\downarrow)$$

The positive sign of t_{AB} and $t_{D'B}$ indicates that, points A and D' are above the tangent at B.

(ii) To find slope at centre (θ_D) :

We have, $\theta_B = \theta_D + \Delta\theta_{DB}$

where, $\Delta\theta_{DB}$ = Change of slope from D to B

= Angle between the tangents drawn at D and B to elastic curve

= Area of $\dfrac{M}{EI}$ diagram between D and B

$= \dfrac{1}{2} \times 3 \times 50 \ \dfrac{kN.m}{EI} = \dfrac{75 \ kN.m^2}{EI}$

∴ $\theta_D = \theta_B - \Delta\theta_{DB} = (88.88 - 75)\dfrac{kN.m^2}{EI} = \dfrac{13.88 \ kN.m^2}{EI}$ radians (↺)

(iii) To locate point of maximum deflection :

Tangent drawn to elastic curve at a point where maximum deflection occurs will be horizontal i.e. slope will be zero at that point. Let the point be at a distance 'x' from B. [As l (CB) > l (AC)]

∴ $\theta_x = 0$

$\theta_B = \theta_x + \Delta\theta_{xB}$

∴ $\theta_B = \Delta\theta_{xB}$

where, $\Delta\theta_{xB}$ = Change of slope between x and B

= Area of $\dfrac{M}{EI}$ diagram between x and B

$= \dfrac{1}{2}(x)\dfrac{66.67 \ kN.m}{EI}\left(\dfrac{x}{4}\right) = \dfrac{66.67}{8}(x^2)\dfrac{kN.m^2}{EI}$

∴ $\theta_B = \theta_{xB}$

$88.88 \ \dfrac{kN.m^2}{EI} = \dfrac{66.67}{8}(x^2)\dfrac{kN.m^2}{EI}$

∴ $x = 3.265$ m from B

∴   Maximum deflection at 3.265 m from B

$= y_{max} = xx' = xx'' - x'x''$ [Refer Fig. 6.30]

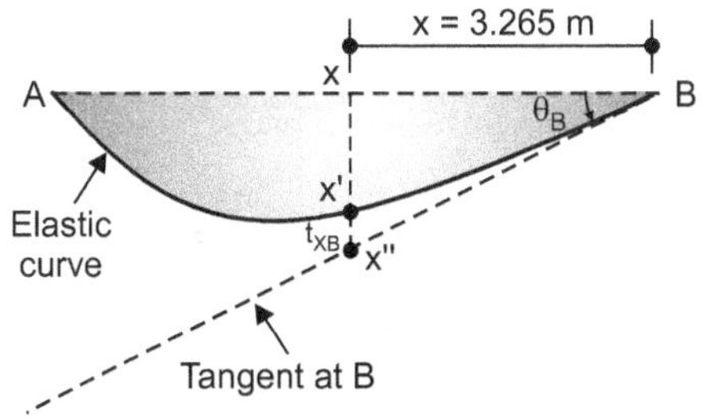

Fig. 6.30

$xx'' = (\theta_B) \times 3.265 = 88.88 \ \dfrac{kN.m^2}{EI} \times 3.265$

$= 290.22 \ \dfrac{kN.m^3}{EI}$

x' x" = Displacement of x' with respect to tangent drawn at B = t_{XB}

$= $ Moment of area of $\dfrac{M}{EI}$ diagram between x and B about x

$= \dfrac{1}{2} (3.265)(66.67)\dfrac{kN.m}{EI} \times \left(\dfrac{3.265}{4}\right) \times \dfrac{3.265}{3}$

x' x" $= 96.68$ kN.m³/EI

$y_{max} = $ xx" – x' x" $= (290.22 – 96.68)$ kN.m³/EI

$y_{max} = 193.54 \dfrac{kN.m^3}{EI}$ (↓)

Example 6.14 : *Determine the central deflection and slope at supports for simply supported beam shown in Fig. 6.31 (a). Take E = 2.1 $\times10^5$ MPa and I = 3 $\times10^7$ mm⁴.*

Solution :

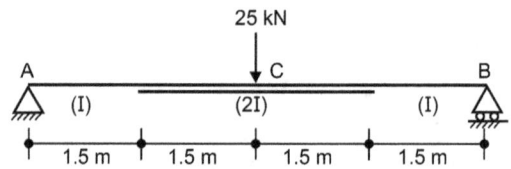

(a) Beam

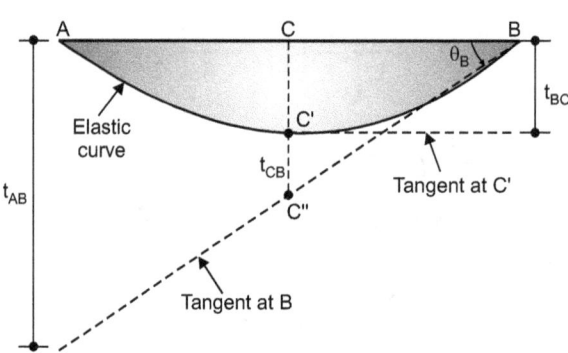

(b) Elastic curve

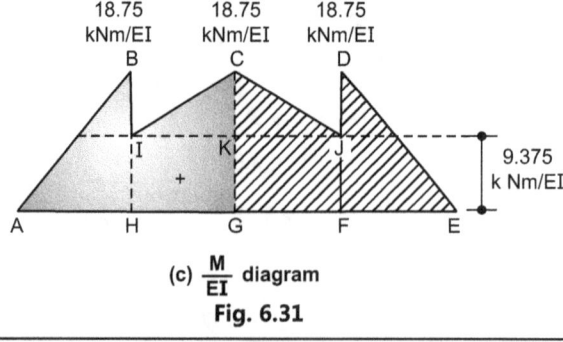

(c) $\dfrac{M}{EI}$ **diagram**

Fig. 6.31

(i) To find slope at supports :

t_{AB} = Displacement of A with respect to tangent drawn at B

= Moment of area of $\dfrac{M}{EI}$ diagram between A and B about A

Table 6.3

Area	Distances of C.G. from A (m)	Moment of area @ A
$ABH = \dfrac{1}{2} \times 1.5 \times \dfrac{18.75 \text{ kN.m}}{EI}$ $= \dfrac{14.0625 \text{ kN.m}^2}{EI}$	$\dfrac{2}{3}(1.5)$	$\dfrac{14.0625 \text{ kN.m}^3}{EI}$
$ICJ = \dfrac{1}{2} \times 3 \times \dfrac{9.375 \text{ kN.m}}{EI}$ $= \dfrac{14.0625 \text{ kN.m}^2}{EI}$	3	$\dfrac{42.1875 \text{ kN.m}^3}{EI}$
$IJHF = 3 \times \dfrac{9.375 \text{ kN.m}}{EI}$ $= 28.125 \dfrac{\text{kN.m}^2}{EI}$	3	$\dfrac{84.375 \text{ kN.m}^3}{EI}$
$DFE = \dfrac{1}{2} \times 1.5 \times \dfrac{18.75 \text{ kN.m}}{EI}$ $= \dfrac{14.0625 \text{ kN.m}^2}{EI}$	$4.5 + \dfrac{1}{3}(1.5) = 5$	$\dfrac{70.3125 \text{ kN.m}^3}{EI}$
	Total	$210.9375 \text{ kN.m}^3/EI$

$\therefore$ t_{AB} = 210.9375 kN.m³/EI

$\therefore$ $\theta_B = \dfrac{t_{AB}}{6} = \dfrac{210.9375 \text{ kN.m}^3/EI}{6} = 35.156 \dfrac{\text{kN.m}^2}{EI}$

$EI = 2.1 \times 10^5 \times 3 \times 10^7 \text{ Nmm}^2$

$= 6.3 \times 10^{12} \text{ N.mm}^2$

$= 6.3 \times 10^3 \text{ kN.m}^2$

$\therefore$ $\theta_B = \dfrac{35.156}{6.3 \times 10^3} = 0.00558 \text{ rad} = 0.319° \; (\circlearrowleft)$

Due to symmetry,

$\theta_A = \theta_B = 0.319° \; (\circlearrowright)$

(ii) To find central deflection : Due to symmetry, central deflection is the maximum deflection, hence tangent drawn to elastic curve at C will be horizontal.

$\therefore$ $\quad\quad\quad\quad\quad\quad\quad\quad\quad y_C = t_{BC'}$

$\quad\quad\quad\quad\quad\quad = $ Displacement of B with respect to tangent drawn at C'

$\quad\quad\quad\quad\quad\quad = $ Moment of area of $\dfrac{M}{EI}$ diagram between B and C about B

Table 6.4

Area	Distances of C.G. from B (m)	Moment of area @ B
$CKJ = \dfrac{1}{2} \times \dfrac{9.375 \text{ kN.m}}{EI} \times 1.5$ $= \dfrac{7.03125 \text{ kN.m}^2}{EI}$	$1.5 + \dfrac{2}{3} \times 1.5 = 2.5$	$\dfrac{17.578 \text{ kN.m}^3}{EI}$
$KJGF = 9.375 \dfrac{\text{kN.m}}{EI} \times 1.5$ $= 14.0625 \dfrac{\text{kN.m}^2}{EI}$	$1.5 + \dfrac{1.5}{2} = 2.25$	$\dfrac{31.64 \text{ kN.m}^3}{EI}$
$DFE = \dfrac{1}{2} \times 1.5 \times 18.75 \dfrac{\text{kN.m}}{EI}$ $= 14.0625 \dfrac{\text{kN.m}^2}{EI}$	$2/3 (1.5) = 1$	$14.0625 \text{ kN.m}^3/EI$
	Total	$63.2806 \text{ kN.m}^3/EI$

$\therefore$ $\quad\quad\quad y_{max} = 63.2806 \dfrac{\text{kN.m}^3}{EI} = \dfrac{63.2806 \times 10^3}{6.3 \times 10^3} = 10.04 \text{ mm } (\downarrow)$

6.12 CONJUGATE BEAM METHOD

The conjugate beam method is another alternate method for finding slopes and deflections in beams. Successive differentiation of the deflection equation gives the following relations :

$\quad\quad\quad\quad E.I. (y) = $ Deflection $\quad\quad\quad\quad\quad\quad\quad\quad\quad$ ... (a)

$\quad\quad\quad\quad E.I. \left(\dfrac{dy}{dx}\right) = $ Slope $\quad\quad\quad\quad\quad\quad\quad\quad\quad$ ... (b) $\quad\quad$ ... (6.14)

$\quad\quad\quad\quad E.I. \left(\dfrac{d^2y}{dx^2}\right) = $ Moment $= M \quad\quad\quad\quad\quad$ ... (c)

$\quad\quad\quad\quad E.I. \left(\dfrac{d^3y}{dx^3}\right) = $ Shear $= V = \dfrac{dM}{dx} \quad\quad\quad$ ... (d)

$\quad\quad\quad\quad E.I. \left(\dfrac{d^4y}{dx^4}\right) = $ Rate of loading $= \dfrac{dV}{dx} = \dfrac{d^2M}{dx^2} \quad$ ... (e)

The validity of these relationships depend on the sign convention used for various quantities. The co-ordinate systems that satisfy these relationships are : y upward and x to the right are positive. Shear and bending moment sign convention is the same as explained earlier. Load is positive when it acts upwards and negative when it acts downwards.

Consider the cantilever beam as shown in Fig. 6.32 (a). Assume that beam has uniform flexural rigidity. Fig. 6.32 (b) shows $\dfrac{M}{EI}$ diagram for the beam. Consider fictitious beam as shown in Fig. 6.32(c) wherein free end of real beam is changed to fixed end and fixed end of real beam is changed to free end. Let, fictitious beam be loaded with load diagram corresponding to $\dfrac{M}{EI}$ diagram for real beam.

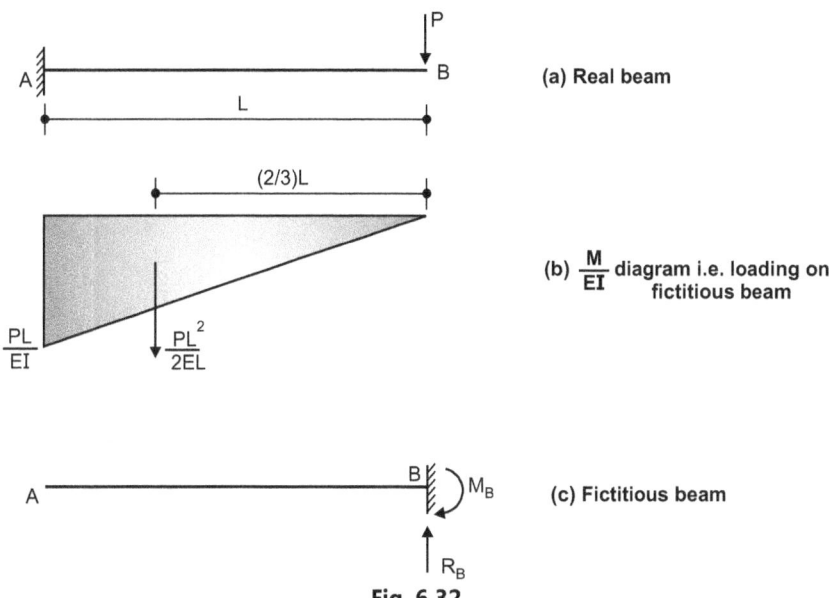

(a) Real beam

(b) $\dfrac{M}{EI}$ diagram i.e. loading on fictitious beam

(c) Fictitious beam

Fig. 6.32

Due to hogging bending moment, negative sign is shown for $\dfrac{M}{EI}$ diagram. Thus due to this negative sign, when $\dfrac{M}{EI}$ diagram is treated as load diagram for fictitious beam, it implies downward load. To maintain static equilibrium of fictitious beam; reaction components at B can be found out as,

$$\Sigma F_y = 0; \qquad\qquad R_B = \frac{PL^2}{2\,EI}\,(\uparrow)$$

$$\Sigma M_B = 0; \qquad\qquad M_B = \frac{PL^2}{2\,EI}\left(\frac{2}{3}L\right) = \frac{PL^3}{3\,EI}\,(\circlearrowleft)$$

Shear force at B for fictitious beam $= V_B = \dfrac{-PL^2}{2\,EI}$

(Upward force on R.H.S. of cross section means negative shear.)

Bending moment at B for fictitious beam = $M_B = \dfrac{PL^3}{3\,EI}$ (Hogging)

$$M_B = \dfrac{-PL^3}{3\,EI}$$

(–ve sign is due to hogging bending moment)

Little consideration will show that shear force at B for fictitious beam is nothing but slope at B for real beam.

i.e. $\qquad\qquad\qquad \theta_B = V_B = \dfrac{-PL^2}{2\,EI}$

$\therefore \qquad\qquad\qquad \theta_B = \dfrac{PL^2}{2\,EI}\ (\circlearrowright)$ $\qquad\qquad$ (due to negative shear, slope is clockwise)

Also bending moment at B for fictitious beam is equal to deflection at B for real beam.

$\therefore \qquad\qquad\qquad y_B = M_B = -\dfrac{PL^3}{3\,EI}$

$\therefore \qquad\qquad\qquad y_B = \dfrac{PL^3}{3\,EI}\ (\downarrow)$

(due to negative sign for moment, deflection is in negative y direction i.e. downwards).

The fictitious beam thus created is known as *conjugate beam*. We may now define the conjugate beam as follows :

Definition : A conjugate beam is a fictitious beam, which has the same length as the real beam, but is supported in such a manner that when it is loaded with $\dfrac{M}{EI}$ diagram of the real beam, the shear and bending moment at a section in the conjugate beam gives the slope and deflection (in sign and value) for the corresponding section of the real beam.

6.13 SUPPORT CONDITIONS

To apply conjugate beam method correctly, the supports of the conjugate beam shall be so changed that correct slopes and deflections are obtained for real beam. These support conditions are discussed below :

(1) At the fixed end of real beam, slope and deflection both are zero. Shear force and bending moment must be zero for conjugate beam at corresponding section which is possible only if fixed end of real beam is made free end for conjugate beam.

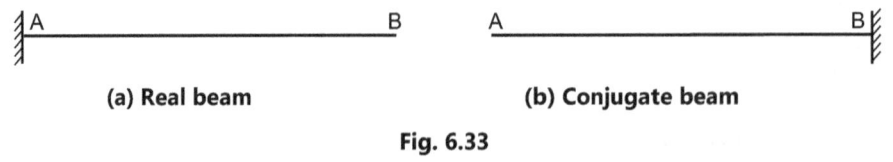

(a) Real beam $\qquad\qquad\qquad\qquad$ (b) Conjugate beam

Fig. 6.33

At the free end of the real beam, there exist slope and deflection both. In a corresponding conjugate beam, at this end, there should be shear force and bending moment both. This requirement is satisfied only by fixed support.

Thus, fixed end of real beam becomes free end of conjugate beam and free end of real beam becomes fixed end for conjugate beam. [Refer Fig. 6.34].

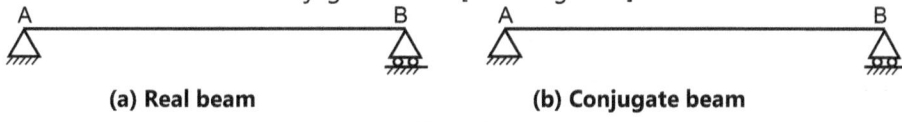

(a) Real beam   **(b) Conjugate beam**

Fig. 6.34

(2) At hinge or roller end of the real beam, slope is present but deflection is zero. Therefore, in a corresponding conjugate beam at this end there must be shear force but no moment; which is satisfied by hinge or roller support.

Thus, hinge or roller end of real beam remains as hinge or roller end in corresponding conjugate beam. [Refer Fig. 6.35].

(3) At interior roller support, there is continuity of slope i.e. $\theta_{BA} = \theta_{BC}$. Also there is no deflection at interior roller support. Thus in a corresponding conjugate beam, there must be a support which gives shear force but no bending moment which is obtained by internal hinge which gives equal and opposite shear force on two sides but no moment.

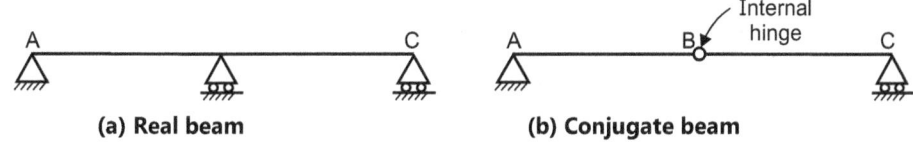

(a) Real beam   **(b) Conjugate beam**

Fig. 6.35

Thus, interior support in real beam becomes an internal hinge in a conjugate beam [Refer Fig. 6.36].

(4)

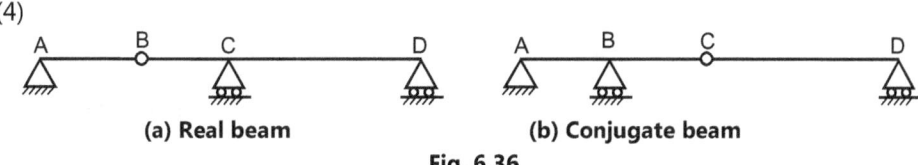

(a) Real beam   **(b) Conjugate beam**

Fig. 6.36

At the unsupported internal hinge of a real beam there exist slope and deflection both. Thus, a simple support would be required in a corresponding conjugate beam.

Thus, an unsupported internal hinge in a real becomes interior roller support in a conjugate beam. [Refer Fig. 6.36]

The foregoing conjugate beam support conditions are to be carefully applied while using the method.

It is very important to note that conjugate beam is always statically determinate even though the real beam is indeterminate. Conjugate beam may sometimes appear to be unstable, however, the loading would be so balanced as to give zero reactions if any support is there. For a real fixed beam, conjugate beam is supportless. It should be remembered that conjugate beam is an imaginary beam.

Conjugate beam method is illustrated in the following examples. Following points shall be noted regarding sign convention.

1. Sagging bending moment for real beam gives positive $\frac{M}{EI}$ diagram and hogging bending moment for real beam gives negative $\frac{M}{EI}$ diagram.

2. Positive $\frac{M}{EI}$ diagram means upward loading for conjugate beam and negative $\frac{M}{EI}$ diagram means downward loading for conjugate beam.

3. Positive shear for conjugate beam means anticlockwise rotation of tangent drawn to elastic curve with respect to original position at corresponding point in a real beam and vice versa.

4. Positive bending moment for conjugate beam means upward deflection of a corresponding point in a real beam and vice versa.

SOLVED EXAMPLES

Example 6.15 : *Using the conjugate beam method, calculate the slope and deflection at B. Take E = 2.1 × 10⁵ MPa and I = 117.7 × 10⁶ mm⁴. [Refer Fig. 6.37 (a)].*

Solution :

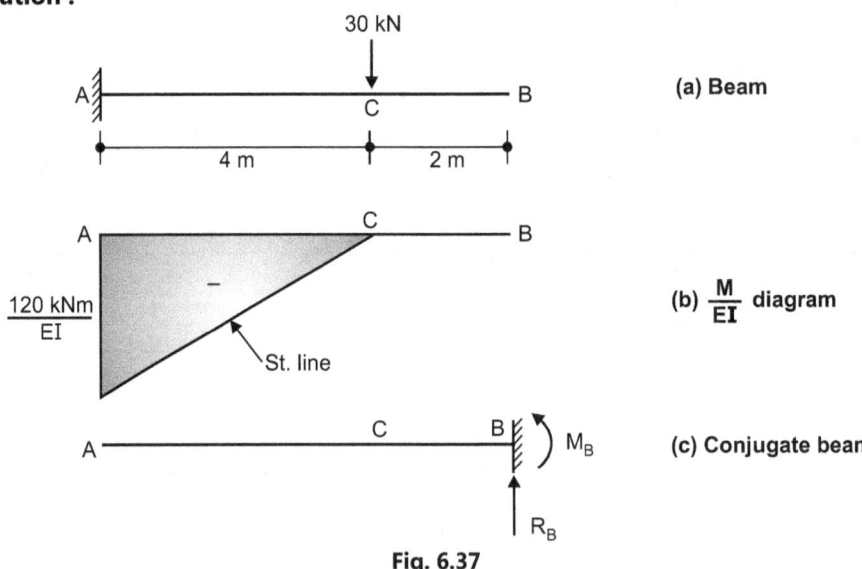

Fig. 6.37

Analysis of conjugate beam :

$\sum F_y = 0$ gives Reaction at B = $R_B = \frac{1}{2} \times 4 \times \frac{120}{EI}$

$$R_B = \frac{240}{EI} \text{ kN.m}^2 \ (\uparrow)$$

$$\Sigma M_B = 0; \quad \text{Moment at B} = \left[\frac{1}{2} \times 4 \times \frac{120}{EI}\right] \times \left[2 + \frac{2}{3} \times 4\right]$$

$$M_B = \frac{1120}{EI} \text{ kN.m}^3 \ (\circlearrowleft)$$

Slopes : Slope at B = Shear at B = $V_B = -\dfrac{240 \text{ kN.m}^2}{EI}$

∴

$$\theta_B = \frac{240 \times 10^3 \times (10^3)^2}{2.1 \times 10^5 \times 117.7 \times 10^6} = 0.009709 \text{ rad} \ (\circlearrowleft) = 0.556° \ (\circlearrowleft)$$

$$y_B = \text{Deflection at B} = \text{B.M. at B}$$

$$M_B = \frac{1120 \text{ kN.m}^3}{EI} \text{ (Hogging)}$$

∴

$$y_B = -\frac{1120 \times 10^3 \times (10^3)^3}{2.1 \times 10^5 \times 117.7 \times 10^6} \qquad \binom{\text{–ve sign due to}}{\text{hogging moment}}$$

$$= 45.312 \text{ mm} \ (\downarrow)$$

Example 6.16 : *For the cantilever beam shown below compute the deflection and slope at free end. Take E = 2.1 × 10⁵ MPa; I = 300 × 10⁶ mm⁴. Use conjugate beam method. [Refer Fig. 6.38 (a)].*

Solution :

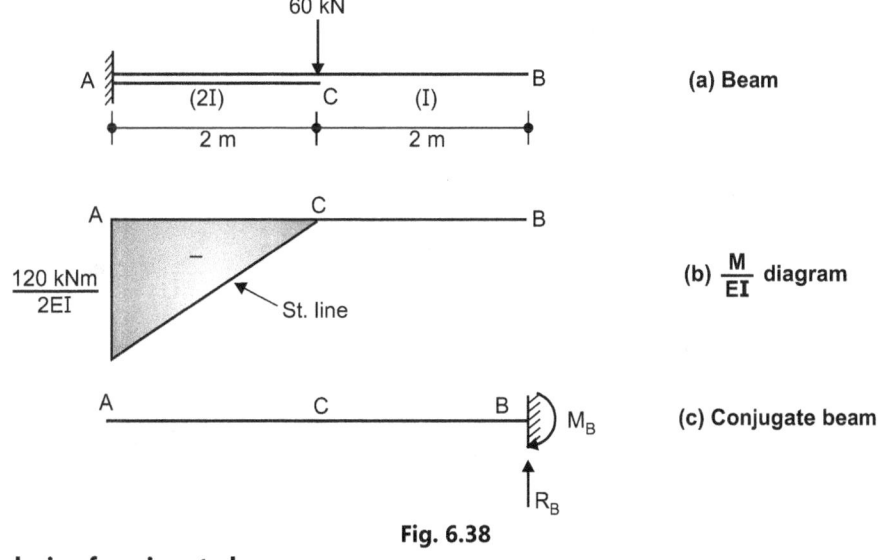

(a) Beam

(b) $\dfrac{M}{EI}$ diagram

(c) Conjugate beam

Fig. 6.38

Analysis of conjugate beam :

$$\Sigma F_y = 0; \qquad \text{Vertical reaction at B} = \frac{1}{2} \times 2 \times \left[\frac{120}{2\,EI}\right]$$

$$R_B = \frac{60}{EI} \text{ kN.m}^2 (\uparrow)$$

$\sum M_B = 0;$ Moment at B = $M_B = \left[\frac{1}{2} \times 2 \times \frac{120}{2\,EI}\right] \times \left(2 + \frac{2}{3} \times 2\right) = \frac{200}{E} \text{ kN.m}^3 (\circlearrowright)$

$$\text{Shear force at B} = V_B = -\frac{60}{EI} \text{ kN.m}^2$$

$$\text{Bending moment at B} = M_B = \frac{200}{EI} \text{ kN.m}^3 \text{ (Hogging)}$$

$\therefore$ Slope at B = $\theta_B = V_B$

$$= \frac{-60 \times 10^3 \times (10^3)^2}{2.1 \times 10^5 \times 300 \times 10^6}$$

$$= 0.00095 \text{ rad} = 0.0545° (\circlearrowright)$$

$$\text{Deflection at B} = y_B = \frac{-200 \text{ kN.m}^3}{EI}$$

$$= \frac{-200 \times (10^3)(10^3)^3}{2.1 \times 10^5 \times 300 \times 10^6} = 3.174 \text{ mm} (\downarrow)$$

Example 6.17 : *Using conjugate beam method, compute slope and deflection at free end of cantilever shown in Fig. 6.39 (a). Take E = 2.1 $\times 10^5$ MPa; I = 117.7 $\times 10^8$ mm^4.*

Solution :

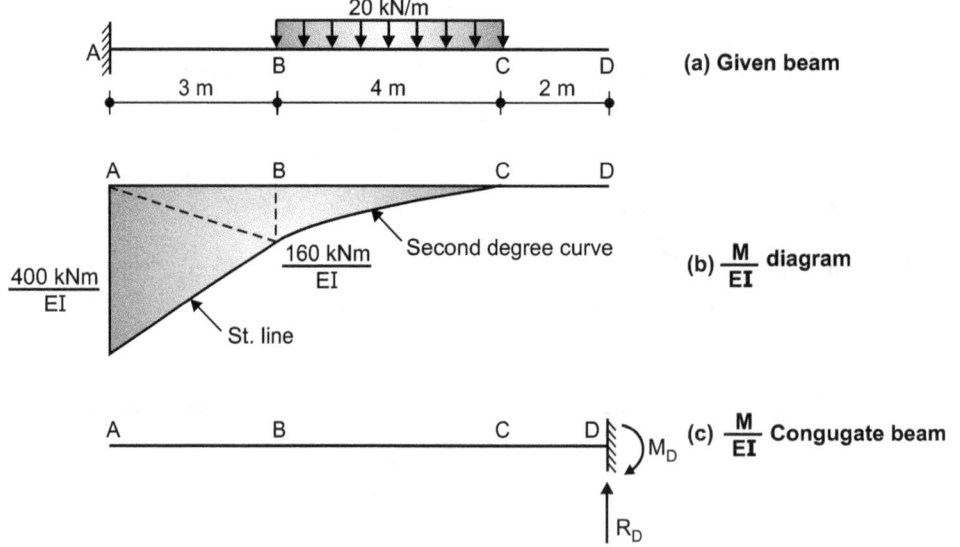

(a) Given beam

(b) $\frac{M}{EI}$ diagram

(c) $\frac{M}{EI}$ Conjugate beam

Fig. 6.39

Analysis of conjugate beam :

$\sum F_y = 0;$

$$R_D - \left(\frac{1}{2} \times 400 \times 3 + \frac{1}{2} \times 160 \times 3 + \frac{1}{3} \times 4 \times 160 \right) \frac{kN.m^2}{EI} = 0$$

$$\therefore \qquad R_D = (600 + 240 + 213.33) \frac{kN.m^2}{EI}$$

$$R_D = (1053.33) \frac{kN.m^2}{EI} \ (\uparrow)$$

$$\Sigma M_D = 0; - M_D + \left[600 \left(2 + 4 + \frac{2}{3} \times 3 \right) + 240 \left(2 + 4 + \frac{1}{3} \times 3 \right) + (213.33) \left(2 + \frac{3}{4} \times 4 \right) \right] \frac{kN.m^3}{EI} = 0$$

$$\therefore \qquad M_D = 7546.67 \frac{kN.m^3}{EI} \ (\circlearrowright)$$

$$\text{Shear force at D} = V_D = -\frac{1053.33}{EI} \ kN.m^2$$

$$\text{Bending moment at D} = M_D = \frac{7546.67}{EI} \ kN.m^2 \ \text{(Hogging)}$$

$$\text{Slope at D} = \theta_D = -\frac{1053.33 \ kN.m^2}{EI} = -\frac{1053.33 \times (10^3)(10^3)^2}{2.1 \times 10^5 \times 117.7 \times 10^8}$$

$$= 0.000426 \ \text{rad} \ (\circlearrowright) = 0.024^\circ \ (\circlearrowright)$$

$$\text{Deflection at D} = y_D = -\frac{7546.67 \ kN.m^3}{EI}$$

$$= -\frac{7546.67 \times (10)^3 (10^3)^3}{2.1 \times 10^5 \times 117.7 \times 10^8} = 3.05 \ \text{mm} \ (\downarrow)$$

Example 6.18 : *Determine the deflection and slope at free end of cantilever beam shown in Fig. 6.40 (a).*

Solution : Analysis of conjugate beam :

$$\Sigma F_y = 0 \Rightarrow R_C + 2 \times \frac{2 \ kN.m}{EI} - \frac{1}{2} \times 4 \times \frac{1 \ kN.m}{EI} = 0; \ \text{i.e.} \ R_C = -\frac{2 \ kN.m^2}{EI}$$

$$\therefore \qquad R_C = \frac{2 \ kN.m^2}{EI} \ (\downarrow)$$

$$\Sigma M_C = 0 \Rightarrow - M_C - 2 \times 2 \frac{kN.m}{EI} \times (2 + 1) + \frac{1}{2} \times \frac{1 \ kN.m}{EI} \times 4 \times \left(\frac{2}{3} \times 4 \right)$$

$$\therefore \qquad M_C = (-12 + 5.33) \frac{kN.m^3}{EI}$$

$$\therefore \qquad M_C = -6.67 \frac{kN.m^3}{EI}$$

$$= 6.67 \frac{kN.m^3}{EI} \ (\circlearrowright)$$

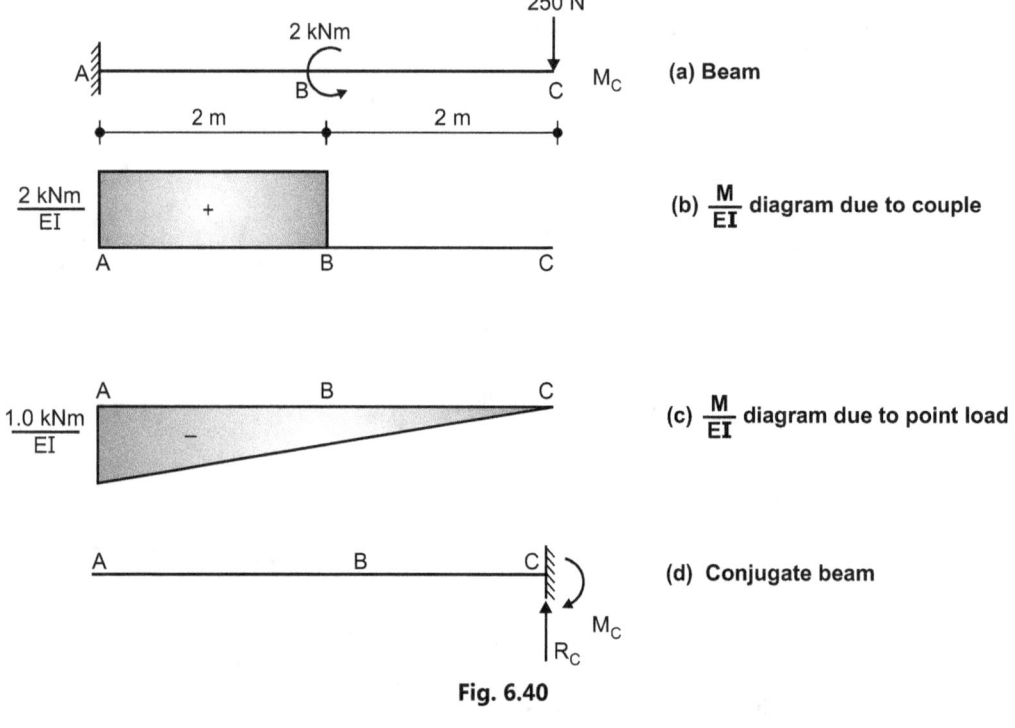

Fig. 6.40

Assumed directions of reaction components at C for conjugate beam are wrong.

$$\text{Shear force at C } = V_C = \frac{2 \text{ kN.m}^2}{EI}$$

$$\text{Bending moment at C } = M_C = \frac{6.67 \text{ kN.m}^3}{EI} \text{ (sagging)}$$

$$\therefore \qquad \text{Slope at C } = \theta_C = \frac{2 \text{ kN.m}^2}{EI} \text{ (↺)}$$

$$\text{Deflection at C } = y_C = \frac{6.67 \text{ kN.m}^3}{EI} \text{ (Upwards)}$$

Example 6.19 : *Find slope at supports and deflection at centre for simply supported beam of span 'L' and carrying UDL of intensity 'w' per unit run throughout. Assume uniform flexural rigidity. [Refer Fig. 6.41 (a)]. Use conjugate beam method.*

Solution :

Analysis of conjugate beam :

By symmetry,　　　　　　$R_A = R_B = \dfrac{1}{2}\left[\dfrac{2}{3} \times L \times \dfrac{wL^2}{8 \, EI}\right]$

$$= \frac{wL^3}{24 \, EI} \text{ (↓)}$$

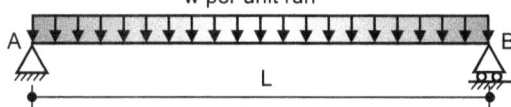

(a) Beam

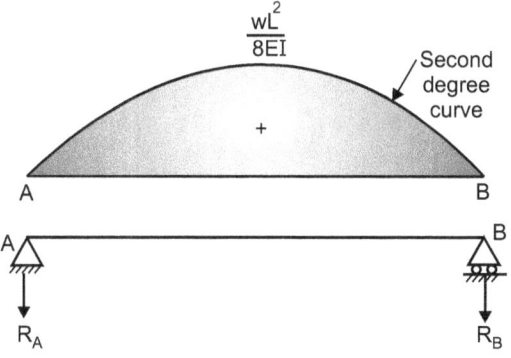

(b) $\dfrac{M}{EI}$ diagram

(c) Conjugate beam

Fig. 6.41

Shear force and bending moment for conjugate beam :

$$V_A = -\frac{wL^3}{24\,EI}$$

$$V_B = \frac{wL^3}{24\,EI}$$

Maximum bending moment will occur at centre.

$$M_{max} = -\frac{wL^3}{24\,EI}\left(\frac{L}{2}\right) + \frac{wL^3}{24\,EI}\cdot\left(\frac{3}{8}\times\frac{L}{2}\right)$$

$$= -\frac{wL^4}{48\,EI} + \frac{3\,wL^4}{384\,EI} = -\frac{5}{384}\cdot\left(\frac{wL^4}{EI}\right)$$

$$= \frac{5}{384}\cdot\frac{wL^4}{EI}\ \text{(Hogging)}$$

Slope and deflections :　　$\theta_A = V_A = -\dfrac{wL^3}{24\,EI} = \dfrac{wL^3}{24\,EI}\ (\circlearrowright)$

$$\theta_B = V_B = \frac{wL^3}{24\,EI}\ (\circlearrowleft)$$

$$y_{max} = M_{max} = \frac{5}{384}\cdot\frac{wL^4}{EI}\ (\downarrow)$$

Example 6.20 : *For a simply supported beam shown in Fig. 6.42 (a), find slope at supports and deflection at the point of application of couple. Also find maximum deflection. Take EI = 40,000 kN.m². Use conjugate beam method.*

Solution :

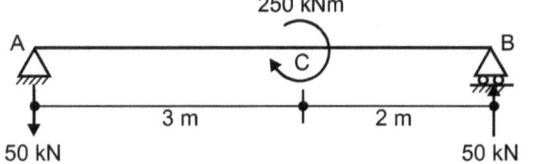

(a) Beam

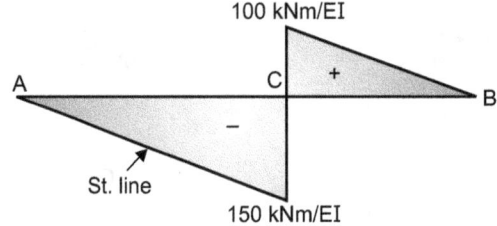

(b) $\dfrac{M}{EI}$ diagram

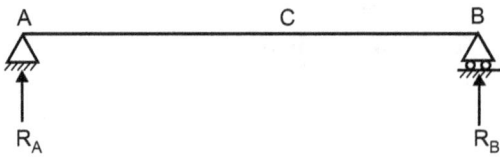

(c) Conjugate beam

Fig. 6.42

Analysis of conjugate beam :

$$R_B \times (5) + \frac{1}{2} \times (2) \times \frac{100 \text{ kN.m}}{EI}\left[3 + \frac{1}{2}(2)\right] - \frac{1}{2}(3)\frac{150 \text{ kN.m}}{EI}\left(\frac{2}{3} \times 3\right) = 0$$

$$\therefore \qquad R_B = \left[\frac{450 - 366.67}{5}\right]\frac{\text{kN.m}^2}{EI}$$

$$= 16.67 \text{ kN.m}^2/EI \ (\uparrow)$$

$$\Sigma F_y = 0 \ ; \ R_A + R_B + \frac{1}{2} \times \frac{100 \text{ kN.m}}{EI} \times 2 - \frac{1}{2} \times \frac{3 \times 150 \text{ kN.m}}{EI} = 0$$

$$R_A = \frac{108.33 \text{ kN.m}^2}{EI} = \frac{108.33 \text{ kN.m}^2}{EI} \ (\uparrow)$$

Shear force and bending moment for conjugate beam :

$$V_A = \frac{108.33 \text{ kN.m}^2}{EI}$$

$$V_B = \frac{-16.67 \text{ kN.m}^2}{EI}$$

$$M_C = \frac{108.33 \text{ kN.m}^2}{EI} \times (3) - \frac{1}{2} \times (3) \times \frac{150 \text{ kN.m}}{EI} \times \left(\frac{1}{3}(3)\right)$$

$$= \frac{100 \text{ kN.m}^3}{EI} \text{ (Sagging)}$$

To locate the point of maximum bending moment. As AC > CB, a point of zero shear force occurs in span AC. Consider a section at a distance 'x' from A.

$$V_x = 108.33 \frac{\text{kN.m}^2}{EI} - \frac{1}{2}(x) \times \frac{150 \text{ kN.m}}{EI}\left(\frac{x}{3}\right) = 0$$

$$\therefore \qquad \frac{150x^2}{6} = 108.33$$

$$\therefore \qquad x = 2.082 \text{ m from A}$$

Maximum bending moment $= M_{max}$

$$= 108.33 \frac{\text{kN.m}^2}{EI}(2.082) - \frac{1}{2}\frac{(2.082)^2}{3} \times \frac{150 \text{ kN.m}}{EI}\left(\frac{2.082}{3}\right)$$

$$= \frac{150.39 \text{ kN.m}^3}{EI} \text{ (Sagging)}$$

Slope and deflections : $\theta_A = V_A = \dfrac{108.33}{40000} = 0.0027 \text{ rad} = 0.155° \text{ (↻)}$

$$\theta_B = V_B = \frac{16.67}{40000}$$

$$= 0.00041 \text{ rad} = 0.0238° \text{ (↻) (Note the direction)}$$

$$y_C = M_C = \frac{100}{40000} \times 10^3$$

$$= 2.5 \text{ mm (↑)}$$

$$y_{max} = \frac{150.39 \times 10^3}{40000}$$

$$= 3.759 \text{ mm (↑)}$$

Example 6.21 : *For a simply supported beam shown in Fig. 6.43 (a), find slope at supports and deflection at centre using conjugate beam method.*

Solution :

Analysis of conjugate beam :

By symmetry,

$$R_A = R_B = \frac{1}{2} \times a \times \frac{Pa}{2 EI} + \frac{Pa}{3 EI} \times a + \frac{1}{2}(a)\frac{Pa}{3 EI}$$

$$= \frac{Pa^2}{4 EI} + \frac{Pa^2}{3 EI} + \frac{Pa^2}{6 EI} = \frac{9}{12}\frac{Pa^2}{EI} = \frac{9}{12}\frac{Pa^2}{EI} \text{ (↓)}$$

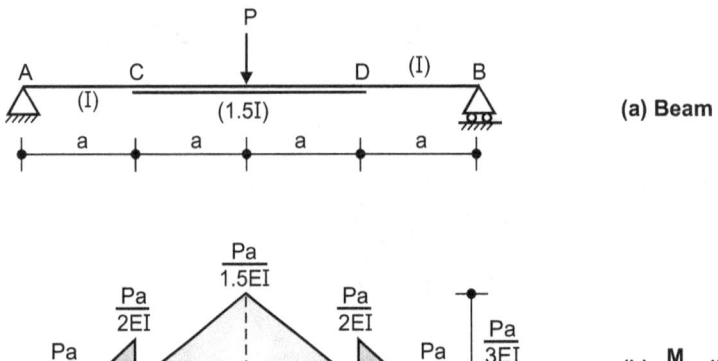

(a) Beam

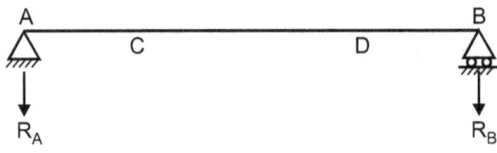

(b) $\dfrac{M}{EI}$ diagram

(c) Conjugate beam

Fig. 6.43

Shear force and bending moment for conjugate beam :

$$V_A = -\frac{9}{12}\frac{Pa^2}{EI}$$

$$V_B = \frac{9}{12}\frac{Pa^2}{EI}$$

By symmetry, maximum B.M. will occur at centre.

$$M_{max} = -\frac{9}{12}\frac{Pa^2}{EI}(2a) + \frac{Pa^2}{4EI}\left(a+\frac{a}{3}\right) + \frac{Pa^2}{3EI}\left(\frac{a}{2}\right) + \frac{Pa^2}{6EI}\left(\frac{a}{3}\right)$$

$$= -\frac{9}{6}\left(\frac{Pa^3}{EI}\right) + \frac{Pa^3}{4EI} + \frac{Pa^3}{12EI} + \frac{Pa^3}{6EI} + \frac{Pa^3}{18EI}$$

$$= -\frac{34}{36}\left(\frac{Pa^3}{EI}\right)$$

$$= \frac{17}{18}\frac{Pa^3}{EI} \text{ (Hogging)}$$

Slope and deflections :

$$\theta_A = V_A = -\frac{9}{12}\frac{Pa^2}{EI} = \frac{9\,Pa^2}{12\,EI}\,(\circlearrowright)$$

$$\theta_B \; = \; V_B = \frac{9}{12}\frac{Pa^2}{EI}$$

$$= \; \frac{9}{12}\frac{Pa^2}{EI}\;(\circlearrowleft)$$

$$y_{max} \; = \; M_{max} = -\left(\frac{17}{18}\right)\frac{Pa^3}{EI}$$

$$= \; \frac{17}{18}\frac{Pa^3}{EI}\;(\downarrow)$$

Example 6.22 : *Using conjugate beam method, determine slope at supports and deflection at centre for the simply supported beam shown in Fig. 6.44 (a). Tak E = 2.1 ×10⁵ MPa; I = 250 ×10⁶ mm⁴.*

Solution :

Analysis of conjugate beam :

By symmetry, $R_A = R_B \; = \; \dfrac{1}{2}(4)\left(\dfrac{200 \text{ kN.m}}{EI}\right) + (2)\left(\dfrac{100 \text{ kN.m}}{EI}\right) + \dfrac{1}{2}\times(2)\times\dfrac{20 \text{ kN.m}}{EI}$

$$= \; \frac{620 \text{ kN.m}^2}{EI}\;(\downarrow)$$

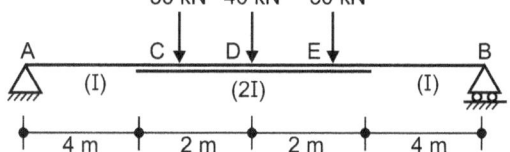

(a) Beam

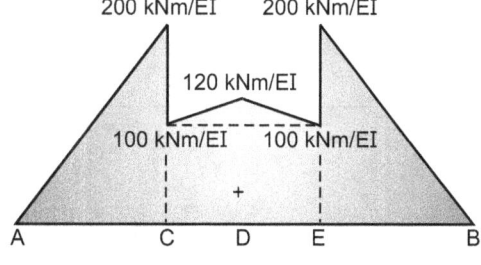

(b) $\dfrac{M}{EI}$ diagram

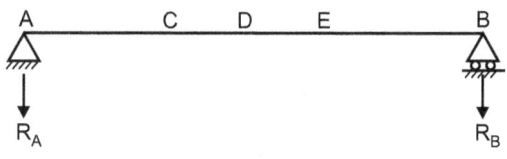

(c) Conjugate beam

Fig. 6.44

Shear force and bending moment for conjugate beam :

$$V_A = \frac{-620 \text{ kN.m}^2}{EI}$$

$$V_B = \frac{620 \text{ kN.m}^2}{EI}$$

Maximum B.M. will occur at centre.

$$M_{max} = \frac{-620 \text{ kN.m}^2}{EI}(6) + \frac{1}{2}(4)\frac{200 \text{ kN.m}}{EI}\left(2 + \frac{1}{3} \times 4\right)$$

$$+ 2 \times \frac{100 \text{ kN.m}}{EI}\left(\frac{2}{2}\right) + \frac{1}{2} \times 2 \times \frac{20 \text{ kN.m}}{EI}\left(\frac{1}{3} \times 2\right)$$

$$= \frac{-2174 \text{ kN.m}^3}{EI}$$

$$= \frac{2174 \text{ kN.m}^3}{EI} \text{ (Hogging)}$$

Slope and deflections :

$$\theta_A = V_A = -\frac{620 \text{ kN.m}^2}{EI}$$

$$= -\frac{620 \times 10^3 \times (10^3)^2}{2.1 \times 10^5 \times 250 \times 10^6}$$

$$= -0.0118 \text{ rad}$$

$$= 0.677° \text{ (↻)}$$

$$\theta_B = 0.677° \text{ (↺)}$$

$$y_{max} = M_{max} = -\frac{2174 \text{ kN.m}^3}{EI}$$

$$= \frac{-2174 \times 10^3 \times (10^3)^3}{2.1 \times 10^5 \times 250 \times 10^6}$$

$$= 41.4 \text{ mm (↓)}$$

Example 6.23 : *Find slope and deflections at A, B, C and D for a beam shown in Fig. 6.45 (a) using conjugate beam method. Take E = 2 × 10⁵ MPa; I = 3 × 10⁸ mm⁴.*

Solution : Analysis of given beam :

$$\Sigma M_A = 0; \qquad V_B \times 6 = 20 \times 3 \times \frac{3}{2} + 60 \times 4 \qquad \therefore \qquad V_B = 55 \text{ kN (↑)}$$

$$\Sigma F_y = 0; \qquad V_A + V_B = 20 \times 3 + 60 \qquad \therefore \qquad V_A = 65 \text{ kN (↑)}$$

Bending moments, $\quad M_A = M_B = 0$

$$M_C = 65 \times 3 - 20 \times 3 \times \frac{3}{2} = 105 \text{ kN.m (Sagging)}$$

$$M_D = 55 \times 2 = 110 \text{ kN.m (Sagging)}$$

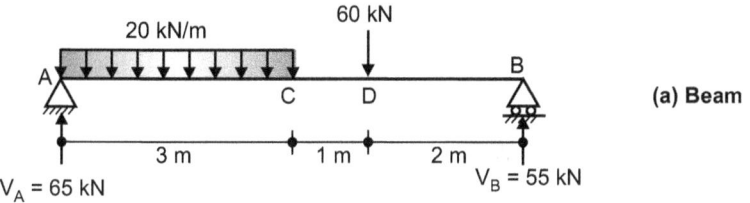

(a) Beam

$V_A = 65$ kN $V_B = 55$ kN

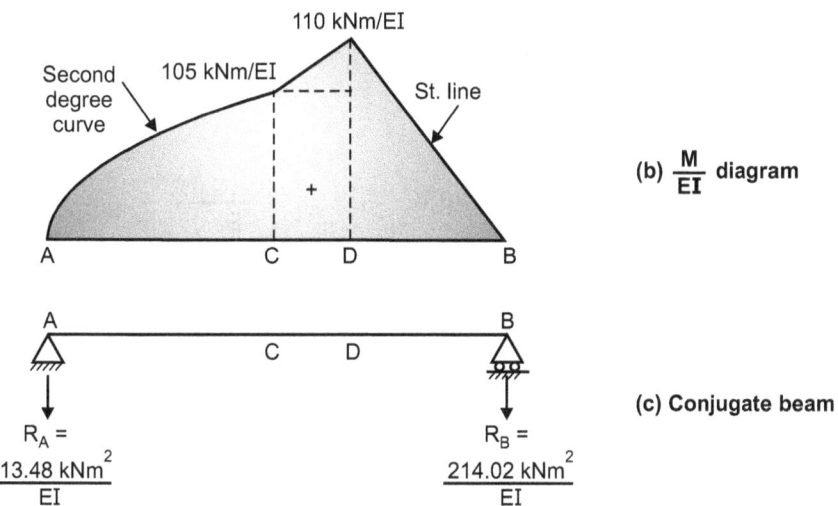

(b) $\dfrac{M}{EI}$ diagram

(c) Conjugate beam

$R_A = \dfrac{213.48 \text{ kNm}^2}{EI}$ $R_B = \dfrac{214.02 \text{ kNm}^2}{EI}$

Fig. 6.45

Analysis of conjugate beam :

Table 6.5

Load component	Magnitude of load	Distance from A (m)	Moment about A
Load on AC $\dfrac{2}{3} \times 3 \times \dfrac{105 \text{ kN.m}}{EI}$	$\dfrac{210 \text{ kN.m}^2}{EI}$	$\dfrac{5}{8}(3) = \dfrac{15}{8}$	$\dfrac{393.75 \text{ kN.m}^3}{EI}$
Load on CD $1 \times 105 \dfrac{\text{kN.m}}{EI}$ $\dfrac{1}{2} \times 1 \times \dfrac{5 \text{ kN.m}}{EI}$	$\dfrac{105 \text{ kN.m}^2}{EI}$ $\dfrac{2.5 \text{ kN.m}^2}{EI}$	$3 + \dfrac{2}{3}(1) = 3.67$	$\dfrac{367.5 \text{ kN.m}^3}{EI}$ $\dfrac{9.175 \text{ kN.m}^3}{EI}$
Load on DB $\dfrac{1}{2} \times 2 \times \dfrac{110 \text{ kN.m}}{EI}$	$\dfrac{110 \text{ kN.m}^2}{EI}$	$4 + \dfrac{1}{3}(2) = 4.67$	$\dfrac{513.7 \text{ kN.m}^3}{EI}$
Total :	$427.5 \dfrac{\text{kN.m}^2}{EI}$		$1284.125 \dfrac{\text{kN.m}^3}{EI}$

To find reactions :

$$\sum M_A = 0; \qquad R_B \times 6 = 1284.125 \frac{kN.m^3}{EI}$$

$$\therefore \qquad R_B = \frac{214.02 \; kN.m^2}{EI}$$

$$\sum F_y = 0; \qquad R_A + R_B = 427.5 \frac{kN.m^2}{EI}$$

$$\therefore \qquad R_A = \frac{213.48 \; kN.m^2}{EI}$$

Bending moments :

$$M_C = \left(-213.48 \frac{kN.m^2}{EI}\right) 3 + \left(\frac{210 \; kN.m^2}{EI}\right)\frac{3}{8} \cdot (3)$$

$$= -404.19 \frac{kN.m^3}{EI} = 404.19 \frac{kN.m^3}{EI} \; \text{(Hogging)}$$

$$M_D = \left(-\frac{214.02 \; kN.m^2}{EI}\right)(2) + \left(\frac{110 \; kN.m^2}{EI}\right)\left(\frac{1}{3}(2)\right)$$

$$= -354.7 \frac{kN.m^3}{EI} = 354.7 \frac{kN.m^3}{EI} \; \text{(Hogging)}$$

$$EI = 2 \times 10^5 \times 3 \times 10^8 \; N.mm^2$$
$$= 6 \times 10^{13} \; N.mm^2 = 6 \times 10^4 \; kN.m^2$$

Slope and deflections :

$$\theta_A = V_A = -213.48 \frac{kN.m^2}{EI} = -\frac{213.48}{6 \times 10^4} = -0.0035 \; \text{rad}$$

$$= 0.203^\circ \; (\circlearrowleft)$$

$$\theta_B = V_B = \frac{214.02 \; kN.m^2}{EI} = \frac{214.02}{6 \times 10^4}$$

$$= 0.003567 \; \text{rad} = 0.204^\circ \; (\circlearrowright)$$

$$\theta_C = (-213.48 + 210) \frac{kN.m^2}{EI}$$

$$= -\frac{3.48 \; kN.m^2}{EI} = -\frac{3.48}{6 \times 10^4} = -0.000058 \; \text{rad}$$

$$= 0.0033^\circ \; (\circlearrowright)$$

$$\theta_D = V_D = (214.02 - 110) \frac{kN.m^2}{EI}$$

$$= \frac{104.02 \; kN.m^2}{EI} = \frac{104.02}{6 \times 10^4} = 0.0017 \; \text{rad}$$

$$= 0.099^\circ \ (\circlearrowleft)$$

$$y_C = M_C = -\frac{404.19 \text{ kN.m}^3}{EI} = -\frac{404.19}{6 \times 10^4} \times (10^3) = 6.73 \text{ mm} \ (\downarrow)$$

$$y_D = M_D = -\frac{354.7 \text{ kN.m}^3}{EI}$$

$$= -\frac{354.7}{6 \times 10^4} (10^3)$$

$$= 5.91 \text{ mm} \ (\downarrow)$$

$$y_A = y_D = 0$$

Example 6.24 : *Determine vertical deflection and slope at B for a beam shown in Fig. 6.46 (a). Use conjugate beam method. Take E = 2 × 10⁵ MPa; I = 180 × 10⁶ mm⁴.*

Solution :

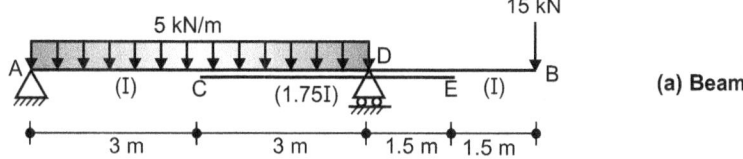

(a) Beam

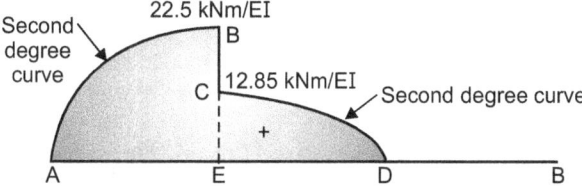

(b) $\dfrac{M}{EI}$ diagram for UDL

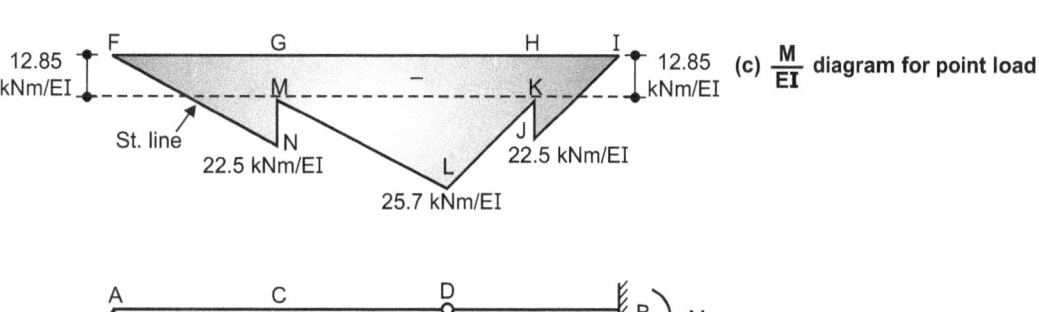

(c) $\dfrac{M}{EI}$ diagram for point load

(d) Conjugate beam

Fig. 6.46

Table 6.6

Component of load	Load magnitude
$ABE = \dfrac{2}{3}(3)\,22.5\,\dfrac{kN.m}{EI}$	$45\,\dfrac{kN.m^2}{EI}\,(\uparrow)$
$BED = \dfrac{2}{3}(3)\,12.85\,\dfrac{kN.m}{EI}$	$25.7\,\dfrac{kN.m^2}{EI}\,(\uparrow)$
$FGN = \dfrac{1}{2}(3)\,22.5\,\dfrac{kN.m}{EI}$	$33.75\,\dfrac{kN.m^2}{EI}\,(\downarrow)$
$GHMK = 12.85\,\dfrac{kN.m}{EI}\,(4.5)$	$57.825\,\dfrac{kN.m^2}{EI}\,(\downarrow)$
$MKL = \dfrac{1}{2}\times 4.5 \times \dfrac{12.85\ kN.m}{EI}$	$28.9125\,\dfrac{kN.m^2}{EI}\,(\downarrow)$
$HIJ = \dfrac{1}{2}\times (3) \times \dfrac{22.5\ kN.m}{EI}$	$33.75\,\dfrac{kN.m^2}{EI}\,(\downarrow)$

Analysis of conjugate beam :

$\sum M_D = 0;$ (L.H.S.)

$$R_A \times 6 + \frac{45\ kN.m^2}{EI}\left(3 + \frac{3}{8}(3)\right) + 25.7\,\frac{kN.m^2}{EI}\left(\frac{5}{8}(3)\right)$$

$$-\frac{33.75\ kN.m^2}{EI}\left(3 + \frac{1}{3}(3)\right) - \frac{57.825 \times 3}{4.5}\,\frac{kN.m^2}{EI}\left(\frac{3}{2}\right)$$

$$-\frac{1}{2}\times\frac{12.85\ kN.m}{EI}\times (3)\times\left(\frac{1}{3}\right)3 = 0$$

$$\therefore \quad R_A \times 6 + 185.625\,\frac{kN.m^3}{EI} + 48.1875\,\frac{kN.m^3}{EI} - \frac{135\ kN.m^3}{EI} - 57.825\,\frac{kN.m^3}{EI}$$

$$- 19.275\,\frac{kN.m^3}{EI} = 0$$

$$\therefore \qquad\qquad\qquad R_A = -3.6187\,\frac{kN.m^2}{EI} = \frac{3.6187\ kN.m^2}{EI}\,(\downarrow)$$

$\sum F_y = 0$; (Part AD)

$$\left(-3.6187 + 45 + 25.7 - 33.75 - \frac{57.825 \times 3}{4.5} - 19.275 + R_D\right)\frac{kN.m^2}{EI} = 0$$

$$R_D = 24.5\,\frac{kN.m^2}{EI}\,(\uparrow)$$

$\sum F_y = 0$; (Part DB)

$$-24.5\,\frac{kN.m^2}{EI} - 12.85\,\frac{kN.m}{EI}\times 1.5 - \frac{1}{2}\times 1.5 \times 12.85\,\frac{kN.m}{EI} - 33.75\,\frac{kN.m^2}{EI} + R_B = 0$$

$\therefore$ $\qquad\qquad R_B = 87.1625 \dfrac{\text{kN.m}^2}{EI}$ ($\uparrow$)

$\sum M_B = 0$;

$\quad M_B - \left(\dfrac{24.5 \text{ kN.m}^2}{EI}\right) 3 - 19.275 \dfrac{\text{kN.m}^2}{EI}\left(1.5 + \dfrac{1.5}{2}\right)$

$\qquad - 9.6375 \dfrac{\text{kN.m}^2}{EI}\left(1.5 + \dfrac{2}{3}(1.5)\right) - 33.75 \dfrac{\text{kN.m}^2}{EI}\left(\dfrac{2}{3}(1.5)\right) = 0$

$\therefore$ $\qquad\qquad M_B = (-73.5 - 43.368 - 24.093 - 33.75)\dfrac{\text{kN.m}^3}{EI}$

$\qquad\qquad\qquad = -174.71 \dfrac{\text{kN.m}^3}{EI} = \dfrac{174.71 \text{ kN.m}^3}{EI}$ ($\circlearrowleft$)

$\therefore$ $\qquad\qquad \theta_B = V_B = -\dfrac{87.1625 \text{ kN.m}^2}{EI}$

$\qquad\qquad\qquad = -\dfrac{87.1625 \times 10^3 \times (10^3)^2}{2 \times 10^5 \times 180 \times 10^6} = -0.00242 \text{ rad}$

$\qquad\qquad\qquad = 0.138° $ ($\circlearrowleft$)

$\qquad\qquad y_B = M_B = -\dfrac{174.71 \text{ kN.m}^3}{EI} = \dfrac{-174.71 \times (10^3)(10^3)^3}{2 \times 10^5 \times 180 \times 10^6}$

$\qquad\qquad\qquad = 4.85 \text{ mm}$ ($\downarrow$)

Example 6.25 : *Using conjugate beam method, find the slope and deflection at the free end of a cantilever of span 3 m carrying a load of 75 kN/m over the entire length. Refer Fig. 6.47 (a). Take E = 200 GPa, I = 10⁸ mm⁴.*

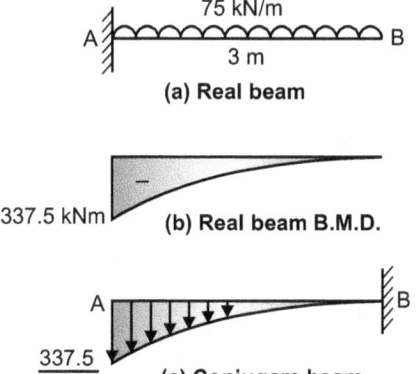

75 kN/m

A ⌒⌒⌒⌒⌒⌒⌒⌒⌒ B
3 m

(a) Real beam

337.5 kNm

(b) Real beam B.M.D.

A

B

$\dfrac{337.5}{EI}$

(c) Conjugare beam

Fig. 6.47

Solution : (i) $EI = 200 \times 10^8 \times 10^{-6} = 2 \times 10^4 \, kNm^2$

(ii)   Slope at B $= SF_B = -\dfrac{1}{3} \times \dfrac{337.5}{EI} \times 3 = \dfrac{-337.5}{EI} = 0.0168 \, rad \, (\circlearrowright)$

(iii)   Deflection at B $= BM_B = -\left\{\dfrac{1}{3} \times \dfrac{337.5}{EI} \times 3\right\} \dfrac{3}{4} \times 3$

$= -0.0379 \, m = 37.9 \, mm \, (\downarrow)$

Example 6.26 : *A beam 8 m long is simply supported at its ends and carries concentrated loads of 20 kN each at points 2 m, from the ends. Calculate by moment-area method, the maximum slope and deflection under each load. EI = 50,000 kN/m³.*

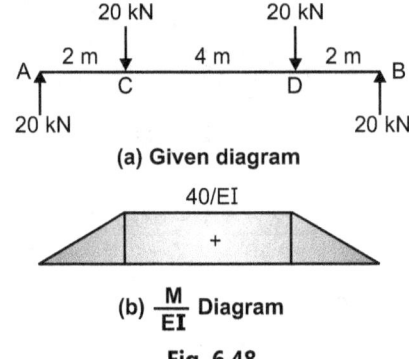

(a) Given diagram

(b) $\dfrac{M}{EI}$ Diagram

Fig. 6.48

Solution : (i) $\dfrac{M}{EI}$ diagram.

(ii)   Due to symmetry,

$$t_{AB} = t_{BA} = (A)_{AB} \cdot \bar{x}_A = (A)_{AB} \cdot \bar{x}_B$$

$$= \left\{40 \times \dfrac{(4+8)}{2}\right\} \dfrac{4}{EI} = \dfrac{960}{EI}$$

$$\theta_A = \theta_B = \dfrac{t_{AB}}{8} = \dfrac{120}{EI} = 0.0024 \, rad$$

(iii) $CC'' = 2\theta_A = \dfrac{240}{EI}$

$C'C'' = t_{CA} = (A)_{CA} \cdot \bar{x}_C$

$= (1/2 \times 2 \times 40) \, 2/3EI = 26.67/EI$

Deflection at C $= CC'' - C'C''$

$= (240 - 26.67)/EI$

$= 4.26 \, mm \, (\downarrow)$ $(\because y_C = y_D)$

Example 6.27 : *Determine the ratio P/Q, that will make the deflection at C equal to zero.*

Solution :

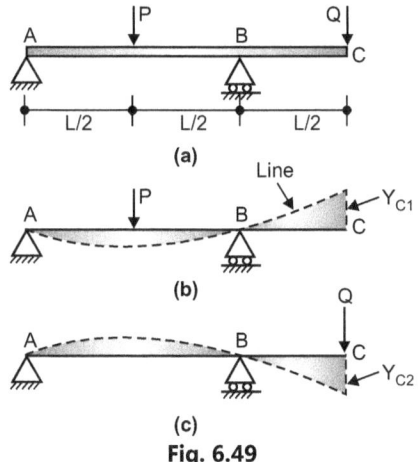

(a)

(b)

(c)

Fig. 6.49

$$y_{C1} + y_{C2} = 0$$

$$\left[\frac{dy}{dx}\right]_B \times 1\ (BC) - Qa^2\frac{(2 + a)}{3EI} = 0$$

$$\left(\frac{PL^2}{16EI}\right)\frac{L}{2} = Q\left[\frac{L}{2}\right]^2\frac{(1.5L)}{3EI}$$

$\therefore$ $P/Q = 4$

Example 6.28 : *Find the maximum deflection for the beam shown in Fig. 6.50 (a) by conjugate beam method.*

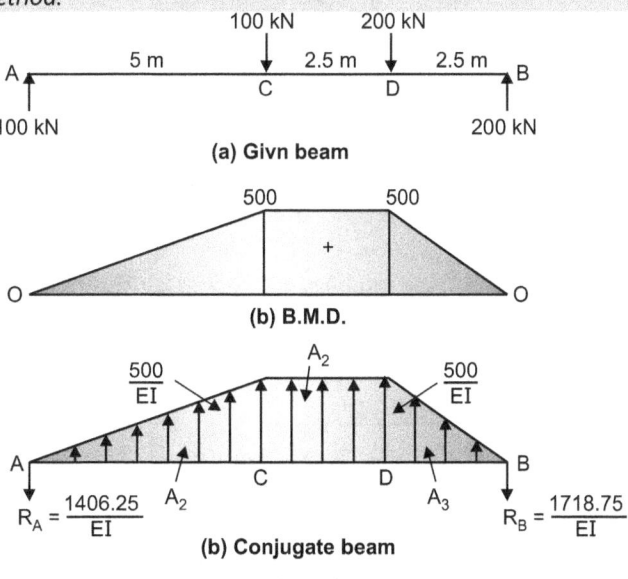

(a) Givn beam

(b) B.M.D.

(b) Conjugate beam

Fig. 6.50

Solution : (i) Analysis of given beam : BMD and conjugate beam is as shown in Fig. 6.50.

(ii) Analysis of conjugate beam :

$A_1 = 1250/EI, \quad A_2 = 1250/EI, \quad A_3 = 625/EI.$

$$\Sigma M_A = -R_B (10) + (625/EI) (8.33) + (1250/EI) (8.25) + (1250/EI) (3.33) = 0$$

∴ $R_B = 1718.75/EI$

∴ $R_A = 1406.25/EI$

For maximum deflection (BM), SF for conjugate beam = 0.

∴ $SF_{(x)}$ (zone CD) $= (-1406.25/EI) + (1250/EI) + (500/EI) (x - 5) = 0$

∴ $x = 5.3125$ m from A

∴   Maximum deflection $= BM_{(5.3125)}$

$$= \{-1406.25 \times 5.3125 + 1250 \times 1.979 + 500 \times (0.31)^2/2\} \, 1/EI$$

$$= -4973/EI$$

$$= 20.72 \text{ mm} (\downarrow)$$

EXERCISE

1. A 2 m long cantilever made of steel tube 150 mm external diameter and 10 mm thickness is loaded as shown in Fig. 6.51. Determine the maximum deflection. Assume E = 200 GPa.   (13.98 mm ($\downarrow$))

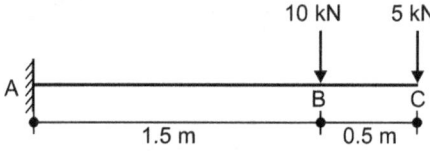

Fig. 6.51

2. A 2 m long cantilever is of rectangular section 100 mm wide and 200 mm deep. It is loaded as shown in Fig. 6.52. Find deflection at free end assuming E = 10 GPa.
                                                                                  (19.39 mm ($\downarrow$))

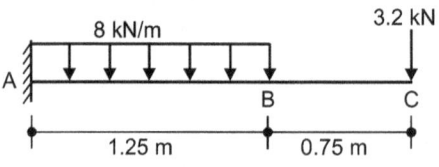

Fig. 6.52

3. A horizontal cantilever of uniform section and span 'L' is loaded as shown in Fig. 6.53. Find the deflection at free end. $\left(\dfrac{26.76}{EI}\;(\uparrow)\right)$

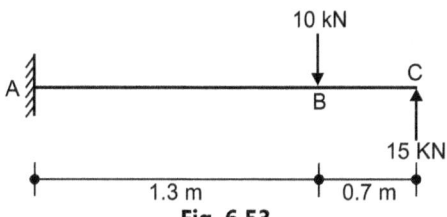

Fig. 6.53

4. A cantilever of uniform section is loaded as shown in Fig. 6.54. Find the deflection at B. If the cantilever is propped at B, find the reaction at prop assuming there is no deflection at B. $\left(y_B = \dfrac{33.75}{EI}\;(\downarrow)\,;\;V_B = 30\;kN\;(\uparrow)\right)$

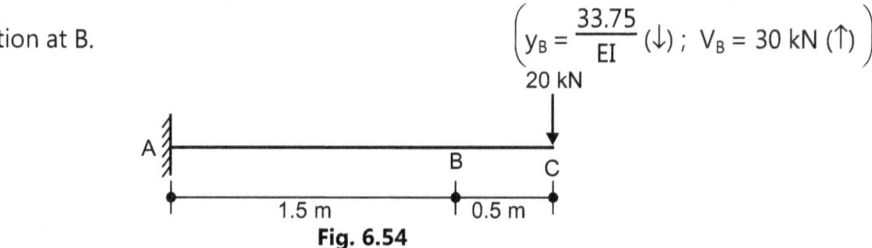

Fig. 6.54

5. A vertical post AB of constant flexural rigidity 4000 kNm² is fixed at the base A and subjected to a horizontal load of 20 kN at C as shown in Fig. 6.55. Determine the necessary force in horizontal tie at B such that the deflection at B is limited to 20 mm to the left. (5.13 kN)

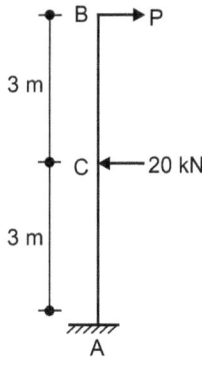

Fig. 6.55

6. Two equal steel beams are built in at one end and connected by a steel rod as shown in Fig. 6.56. Show that the pull in the rod is

$$P \;=\; \frac{5\,WL^3}{32\left(\dfrac{6\,aI}{\pi d^2} + L^3\right)}$$

where ;   d = diameter of the rod and

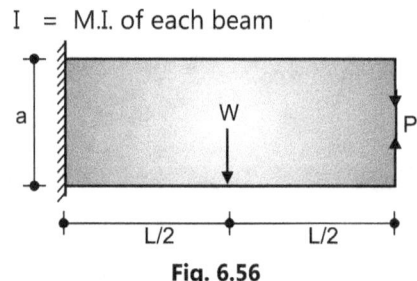

Fig. 6.56

7. For the beam shown in Fig. 6.57, show that the deflection under load is $\dfrac{W}{3.2\,EI}$.

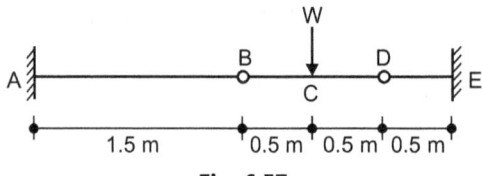

Fig. 6.57

8. A timber beam carries a UDL of 10 kN/m over a span of 6 m. The ends of the beam are simply supported. Determine the section of the beam if the central deflection is limited to 15 mm and the maximum bending stress to 10 MPa. Take E = 12 GPa.

(b = 154 mm, d = 417 mm)

9. The beam is supported and loaded as shown in Fig. 6.58. Find (i) the deflection under the load, (ii) the position and amount of maximum deflection.

Assume E = 200 GPa and I = 50×10^6 mm⁴

(y_C = 6 mm (↓); y_{max} = 6.53 mm (↓) at 2.45 m from A)

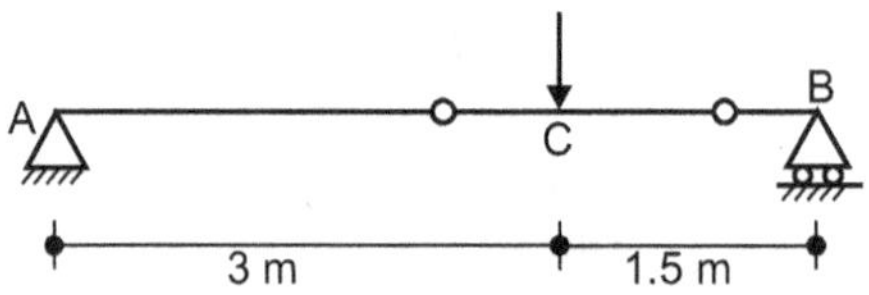

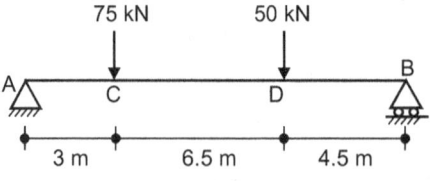

Fig. 6.58

10. The beam is supported and loaded as shown in Fig. 6.59. Find (i) the deflection under loads, (ii) the maximum deflection. Assume E = 200 GPa, I = 70×10^8 mm⁴.

(y_C = 2.34 mm (↓) ; y_D = 2.98 mm (↓) ; y_{max} = 3.54 mm (↓) at 6.87 m from A)

Fig. 6.59

11. The beam is supported and loaded as shown in Fig. 6.60. Determine the position and amount of maximum deflection. $EI = 1.39 \times 10^{11}$ kNmm².

$(y_{max} = 6.82$ mm $(\downarrow)$ at 4.97 m from A)

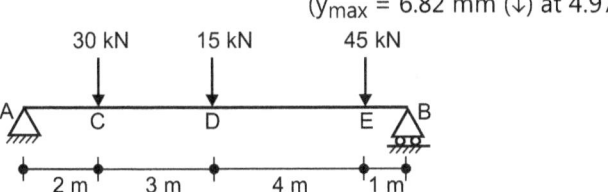

Fig. 6.60

12. The beam is supported and loaded as shown in Fig. 6.61. Find deflection at C.

$$\left(y_C = \frac{3.75}{EI}\ (\downarrow)\right)$$

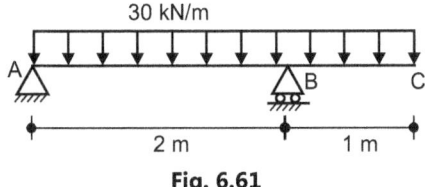

Fig. 6.61

13. The beam is supported and loaded as shown in Fig. 6.62. Assuming $E = 200$ GPa, $I = 40 \times 10^6$ mm⁴, find (i) the deflection at C; (ii) the maximum deflection, and (iii) slope at end A.

$(y_C = 8.74$ mm $(\downarrow)$; $y_{max} = 8.75$ mm $(\downarrow)$ at 1.958 m from A; $\theta_A = 0.417°$ $(\circlearrowright))$

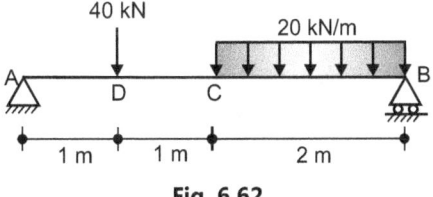

Fig. 6.62

14. The beam is supported and loaded as shown in Fig. 6.63. Calculate slope and deflection at point C.

$$\left(\theta_C = \frac{12.67}{EI}\ (\circlearrowright)\ ;\ y_C = \frac{20.85}{EI}\ (\downarrow)\right)$$

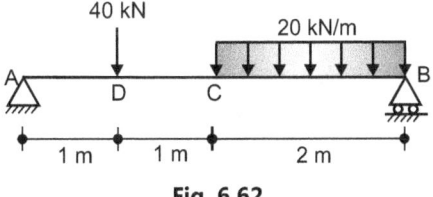

Fig. 6.63

15. A beam of constant section, symmetric about neutral axis is simply supported over a span of 8 m. The beam has to carry a concentrated load of 40 kN at the midspan and a UDL of 15 kN/m over the entire span. If the central deflection is limited to $\dfrac{1\text{th}}{480}$ of the span and the maximum fibre stresses due to bending are not to exceed 118 MPa, determine the required depth of the beam and moment of inertia.

$$(d = 435 \text{ mm}; \ I_{xx} = 3.686 \times 10^8 \text{ mm}^4)$$

16. The beam is supported and loaded as shown in Fig. 6.64. Determine the deflections at C and D and maximum deflection assuming $EI = 3 \times 10^{10}$ kNmm^2.

$$(y_C = 12.09 \text{ mm} (\downarrow); \ y_D = 13.81 \text{ mm} (\downarrow); \ y_{max} = 16.19 \text{ mm} (\downarrow) \text{ at } 3.55 \text{ m from A})$$

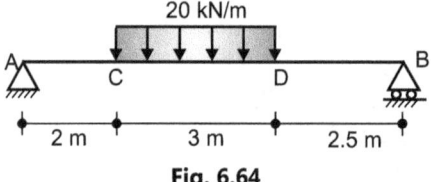

Fig. 6.64

17. Find slope and deflection at C and E for the beam supported and loaded as shown in Fig. 6.65. Assume $E = 200$ GPa, $I = 2 \times 10^7$ mm^4.

$$(\theta_C = 0.0047^\circ (\circlearrowright); \ y_C = 12.5 \text{ mm} (\downarrow); \ \theta_E = 0.568^\circ (\circlearrowright); \ y_E = 9.916 \text{ mm} (\uparrow))$$

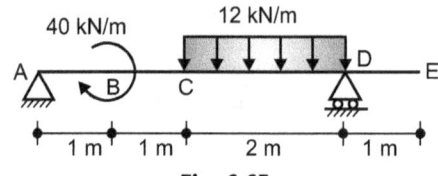

Fig. 6.65

18. A simply supported beam AB of length 'L' just touches a spring of midspan in unloaded condition. Find the stiffness k of the spring that will make the forces on the supports and on the spring equal for a uniformly distributed load. Assume EI = constant.

$$(54.857 \ EI/L^3)$$

19. The beam is supported and loaded as shown in Fig. 6.66. Determine (i) the deflection at C and (ii) the maximum deflection between A and B. Assume $EI = 2700$ kNm^2.

$$(y_C = 10.08 \text{ mm} (\downarrow); \ y_{max} \text{ in zone AB} = 11.4 \text{ mm} (\downarrow) \text{ at } 2.46 \text{ m from A})$$

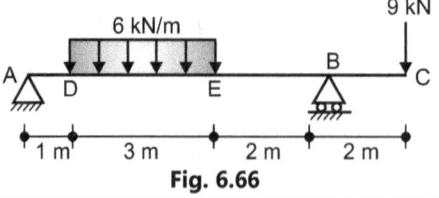

Fig. 6.66

20. Determine slope and deflection at free end of cantilever shown in Fig. 6.67. Assume uniform flexural rigidity. Take $E = 2 \times 10^5$ MPa; $I = 8.5 \times 10^7$ mm^4.

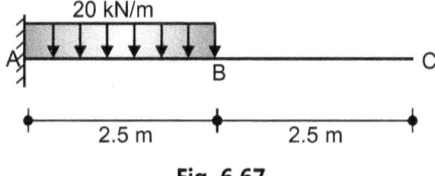

Fig. 6.67

$[\theta_C = 0.175^o \;(\circlearrowleft), \; y_C = 13.40$ mm $(\downarrow)]$

21. Find slope and deflection at free end of cantilever shown in Fig. 6.68. Assume uniform flexural rigidity. Take $E = 2 \times 10^5$ MPa; $I = 2.5 \times 10^8$ mm^4.

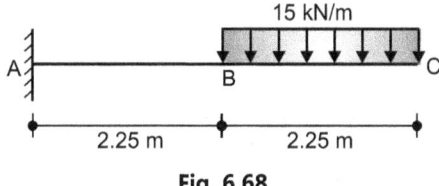

Fig. 6.68

$\left[\theta_C = 0.228^o \;(\circlearrowleft), \; y_C = 13.13$ mm $(\downarrow)\right]$

22. Find midspan and maximum deflection for cantilever beam of uniform section shown in Fig. 6.69. Take $EI = 7560$ kNm^2.

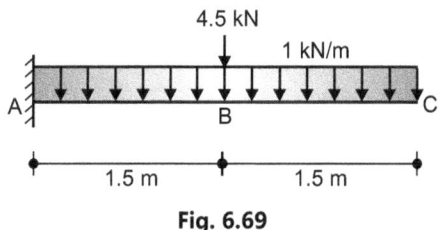

Fig. 6.69

$\left[y_B = 11.44$ mm $(\downarrow), y_{max} = 30.1$ mm $(\downarrow)\right]$

23. Find θ_B; θ_C; y_B; y_C for the cantilever beam shown in Fig. 6.70. Take $E = 2 \times 10^5$ MPa. $I = 5 \times 10^8$ mm^4.

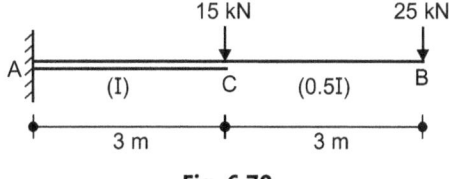

Fig. 6.70

$[\theta_B = 0.36^o \;(\circlearrowleft); \; \theta_C = 0.23^o \;(\circlearrowleft); y_B = 23.63$ mm $(\downarrow); \; y_C = 6.98$ mm $(\downarrow)]$

24. Find θ_B; θ_C; y_B; y_C for the cantilever beam shown in Fig. 6.71. Take E = 2×10^5 MPa. I = 5×10^8 mm^4.

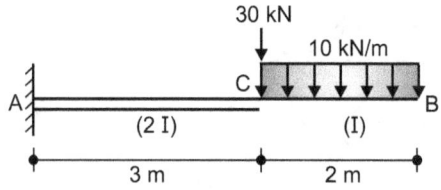

Fig. 6.71

$[\theta_B = 0.09^\circ$ (↺); $\theta_C = 0.08^\circ$ (↺) $y_B = 5.75$ mm (↓); $y_C = 2.7$ mm (↓)]

25. Find slope and deflection at free end of aluminium cantilever shown in Fig. 6.72. Take E = 70,000 MPa, $I_1 = 2 \times 10^6$ mm^4, $I_2 = 0.4 \times 10^6$ mm^4.

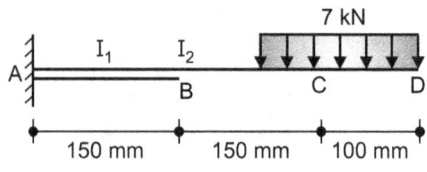

Fig. 6.72

$\left[\theta_D = 0.2575^\circ$ (↺) ; $y_D = 1.124$ mm (↓) $\right]$

UNIT IV

CHAPTER 7

TORSION

7.1 INTRODUCTION

In this chapter, study is aimed at evaluation of stresses and deformation within elastic range due to torque applied on solid and hollow circular shafts. In practice, members that transmit torque, such as shafts of motors or power equipments etc. are predominantly circular or tubular in cross-section. Hence the scope is restricted to circular sections only. Various situations for statically determinate and indeterminate shafts subjected to pure torque are illustrated. But in practice, members are generally subjected to bending and torsion or bending, torsion and axial force which involve evaluation of stresses and strains due to each of these actions and then by using principle of superposition, resultant stresses are obtained. Evaluation of principal stresses and strains for such combined actions is of prime importance from practical design point of view.

7.2 BASICS OF TORSION

Torsion is defined as the *resultant moment on any one side of the section about longitudinal or polar axis of the member*. It is also called as torque or torsional moment or twisting moment. Deformation corresponding to torque is rotation about polar axis called as twist.

Thus, various cross-sections of shaft subjected to torque tend to rotate relatively with respect to each other; about polar axis which developes shear stresses normal to shaft within elastic limit, magnitude of angle of twist and shear stresses are proportional to the magnitude of torque section is subjected to.

7.3 METHOD OF SECTION

For analysis of members subjected to torques, the basic approach of method of section is used. First the system as a whole is examined for equilibrium. Section is considered perpendicular to the axis of the member and then equilibrium of any one side of the section is examined. Internal torque necessary for equilibrium of isolated part on any one side of the section is then evaluated by using equation of statics viz. $\sum$ M @ polar axis = 0. This is illustrated in following example :

Note : Sign convention

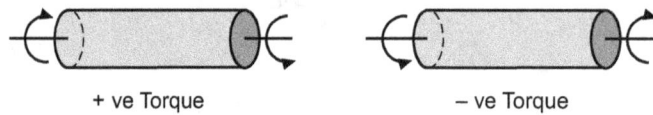

+ ve Torque   − ve Torque

Fig. 7.1 : Sign convention

Consider a shaft ABC subjected to torques T_A = 30 kNm, T_B = 80 kNm and T_C = 50 kNm as shown in Fig. 7.2 (a). Let, it be required to find torque for portions AB and BC. Consider sections 1-1 and 2-2 in segments AB and BC respectively as shown.

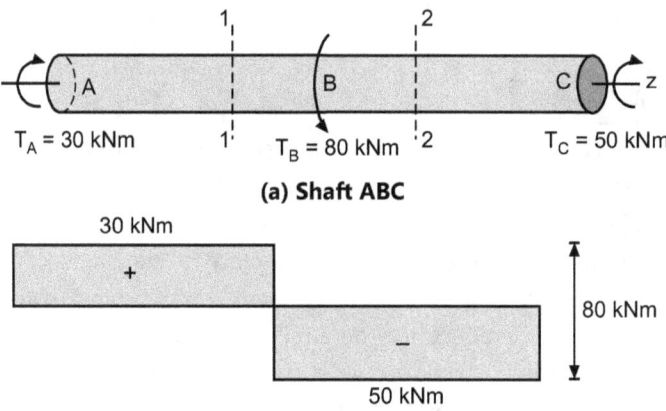

(a) Shaft ABC

(b) Torsional moment diagram

Fig. 7.2

$\sum M_z$ on LHS of section 1-1 = 30 kNm, OR

$\sum M_z$ on RHS of section 1-1 = − 50 + 80 = 30 kNm

$\sum M_z$ on LHS of section 2-2 = 30 − 80 = − 50 kNm OR

$\sum M_z$ on RHS of section 2-2 = − 50 kNm

Thus, the torque of 30 kNm is constant in portion AB and torque of − 50 kNm is constant in portion BC. It should be noted that, torque just to the left of cross-section B is + 30 kNm and just to the right of cross-section B is − 50 kNm.

7.3.1 Torsional Moment Diagram

It is the diagram which shows variation of torsional moment along the length of member. With above discussion, torsional moment diagram for the shaft ABC is drawn as shown in Fig. 7.2 (b).

Note : There is a vertical drop or rise in torsional moment diagram at a section of application of torque and magnitude of drop or rise in the diagram is equal to magnitude of torque acting at that section.

Above example illustrates drawing of torsional moment diagram for shaft subjected to concentrated torques. However, torque can be uniformly distributed over the length of a member as shown in Fig. 7.3 (a). Torsional moment diagram for such a shaft will vary linearly as shown in Fig. 7.3 (b).

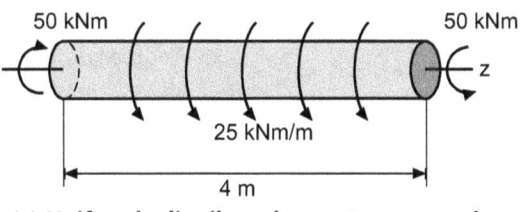

(a) Uniformly distributed torque on a member

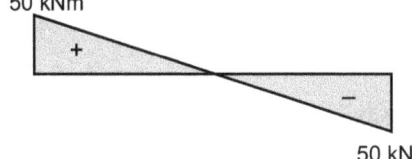

(b) Torsional moment diagram

Fig. 7.3

However, intensity of torque along the length of member can be varying. Such situations are not discussed in the present text.

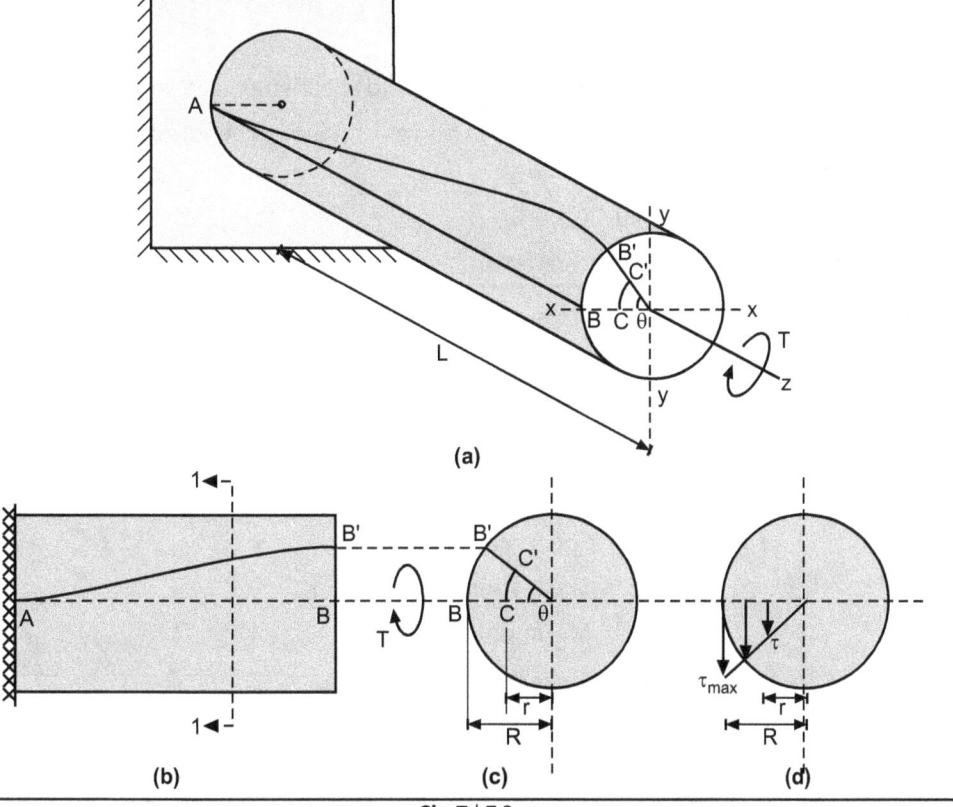

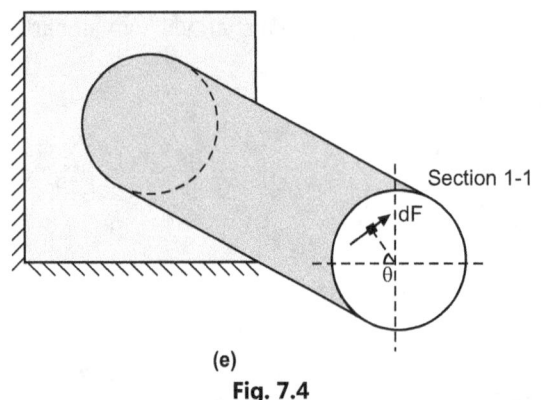

(a) Shaft subjected to torque
(b) Side view of shaft
(c) Angular deformation in cross-section
(d) Shear stress variation over the cross-section
(e) Section 1-1

Fig. 7.4

7.4 THEORY OF TORSION

7.4.1 Assumptions in Deriving the Torsion Formulae

- Plane sections remain plane and do not warp.

- Stresses do not exceed the limit of proportionality.

- Radial lines remain radial after twisting.

- Material is elastic and obeys Hook's law.

  i.e. Shear stress at any point is proportional to shear strain at that point.

- Shaft is loaded by twisting couples in planes that are perpendicular to the axis of the shaft.

- Circular sections remain circular.

7.4.2 Derivation of Torsion Formula

Symbols :

T = Torsional moment

L = Length of shaft

R = Radius of shaft

r = Radial distance

θ = Angle of twist

G = Shear modulus

τ = Shear stress

τ_{max} = Maximum shear stress

J = Polar moment of inertia

T_a = Average torque

P = Power transmitted by shaft

Consider a circular shaft subjected to pure torque as shown in Fig. 7.4 (a). Imagine the shaft to consist of infinite number of circular laminas which individually are rigid and joined to each other by elastic fibres. Thus, due to the application of torque each lamina rotates with respect to each other.

Consider now any internal fibre located at radial distance 'r' from origin. The deformation of such a fibre is marked by CC' in the Fig. 7.4 (c). It should be noted that deformation is maximum at outermost periphery marked by BB' and zero at the centre of the shaft. Thus, axis passing through centre of the shaft and normal to the cross-section is neutral axis (polar axis). It is clearly seen from Fig. 7.4 that deformation of a fibre is directly proportional to its distance from polar axis and hence the stress. The shear stress variation over the cross-section when loaded within elastic limit is also shown in Fig. 7.4 (a).

Thus, $\qquad$ BB' $= R\theta$ and   CC' $= r\,\theta$ $\hspace{3cm}$ ... (7.1)

Shear deformation per unit length of fibre at a distance 'r'

$$= \frac{CC'}{L} = \frac{r\,\theta}{L}$$

$\therefore \qquad$ Shear strain $= \gamma = \dfrac{r\theta}{L}$

$\qquad$ Shear stress $= \tau = \dfrac{Gr\theta}{L} = \left(\dfrac{G\theta}{L}\right) r$ $\hspace{2cm}$ ... (7.2)

"Thus, shear stress along any radius varies linearly with the radial distance of the shaft."

$\therefore \qquad \dfrac{\tau}{r} = \dfrac{\tau_{max}}{R} = \dfrac{G\theta}{L}$ $\hspace{3cm}$ ... (7.3)

Torsional Resistance :

Consider FBD of section 1-1 as shown in Fig. 7.4 (e). An elementary area dA is considered at a distance r from axis of the shaft on which shear stress is equal to τ. By considering area to be infinitely small, we can assume stress to be uniform over area dA. Shear force acting on elementary area $= dF = dA\cdot\tau$. This force dF must be normal to the radius vector as it has to resist the applied torque as efficiently as possible so that energy is conserved.

Small twisting moment produced by dF about polar axis $= dT = dF\cdot r$

$$\therefore \qquad T = \int_{0}^{R} dF\cdot r$$

$$= \int_{0}^{R} (dA\cdot\tau)\, r$$

$$= \int_0^R dA \cdot \frac{G\theta}{L} \cdot r^2 = \frac{G\theta}{L} \int_0^R dA \cdot r^2$$

$$\therefore \qquad T = \frac{G\theta}{L} J \qquad\qquad \ldots (7.4)$$

Since $\qquad J = \int_0^R dA \cdot r^2 = $ polar moment of inertia of cross-section

From equations (7.3) and (7.4),

$$\frac{T}{J} = \frac{\tau_{max}}{R} = \frac{G\theta}{L} \qquad\qquad \ldots (7.5)$$

7.5 IMPORTANT TERMS

7.5.1 Torsional Stiffness

It is the torque required to produce unit angle of twist.

Thus, $\qquad$ Torsional stiffness $= \dfrac{GJ}{L}$

Unit of torsional stiffness is Nm/radian.

7.5.2 Torsional Flexibility

It is the angle of twist produced by unit torque applied.

Thus, $\qquad$ Torsional flexibility $= \dfrac{L}{GJ}$

Unit of torsional flexibility is radian/Nm.

It should be noted that stiffness and flexibility coefficients are reciprocal of each other.

7.5.3 Torsional Rigidity

Product of shear modulus and polar moment of inertia of cross-section is called as torsional rigidity (GJ).

Unit of torsional rigidity is Nm^2.

7.5.4 Torsional Section Modulus

Ratio of polar moment of inertia of cross-section to its radius is called as torsional section modulus (J/R).

Unit of torsional section modulus is m^3.

Torsional Section Modulus for Solid Circular Shaft :

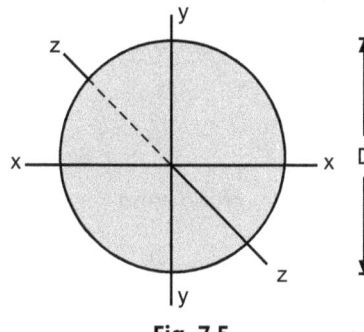

Fig. 7.5

$$I_{xx} = I_{yy} = \frac{\pi}{64} D^4$$

$$J = I_{zz} = I_{xx} + I_{yy}$$

$$= 2 \times \frac{\pi}{64} D^4$$

$$= \frac{\pi}{32} D^4$$

$$R = \frac{D}{2}$$

$$\therefore \quad \frac{J}{R} = \frac{\pi}{32} D^4 \times \frac{2}{D} = \frac{\pi}{16} D^3 \quad ... (7.6)$$

Torsional Section Modulus For Hollow Circular Shaft :

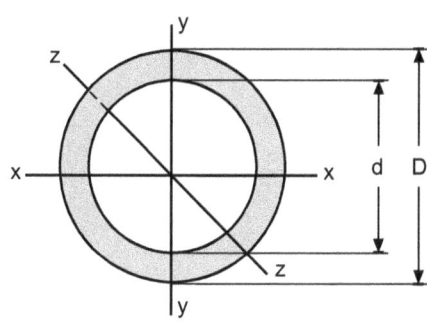

Fig. 7.6

$$I_{xx} = I_{yy} = \frac{\pi}{64} (D^4 - d^4)$$

$$J = I_{zz} = I_{xx} + I_{yy}$$

$$= 2 \times \frac{\pi}{64} (D^4 - d^4)$$

$$= \frac{\pi}{32} (D^4 - d^4)$$

$$R = \frac{D}{2}$$

$$\therefore \quad \frac{J}{R} = \frac{\pi}{32} (D^4 - d^4) \times \frac{2}{D}$$

$$= \frac{\pi}{16 D} (D^4 - d^4) \quad ... (7.7)$$

7.5.5 Power Transmitted by Shaft

It is the product of average torque and corresponding angle turned per unit duration of time.

$$\text{Power} = \text{Average torque} \times \text{Angle of rotation/sec.}$$

$$= T_a \times \frac{2\pi N}{60}$$

$$\therefore \quad \mathbf{P = Power} = \frac{2\pi N\, T_a}{60} \quad ... (7.8)$$

where N = No. of revolutions per minute (RPM). Unit of power is Nm/s or watts.

However, power can also be expressed in Horse power (H.P.) unit.

$$1 \text{ H.P.} = \frac{2\pi N\, T_a}{4500} \quad ... (7.9)$$

SOLVED EXAMPLES

Example 7.1 : Find power transmitted by a shaft having 60 mm diameter rotating at 150 rpm, if maximum permissible shear stress = 80 MPa.

Data :   D = 60 mm;   N = 150 rpm; τ_{max} = 80 MPa

Required :   Power transmitted.

Concept :   Find the value of torque based on shear stress criteria and then use equation of power.

Solution :   (i)   Geometric properties :

$$J = \frac{\pi}{32} \cdot D^4 = \frac{\pi}{32} (60)^4 = 1.272 \times 10^6 \text{ mm}^3$$

$$R = \frac{D}{2} = \frac{60}{2} = 30 \text{ mm}$$

(ii)   Torque corresponding to shear stress :

$$T = \frac{J}{R} \cdot \tau_{max}$$

$$= \frac{1.272 \times 10^6}{30} \times 80$$

$$= 3.392 \times 10^6 \text{ N.mm}$$

$$= 3.392 \times 10^3 \text{ N.m.}$$

(iii)   Power transmitted : $P = \dfrac{2\pi N\, T_a}{60}$

$$= \frac{2 \times \pi \times 150 \times 3.392 \times 10^3}{60}$$

$$= 53281.41 \text{ W}$$

$$= \mathbf{53.281 \text{ kW}}$$

Example 7.2 : A hollow circular shaft of 150 mm external diameter; thickness of metal 20 mm is rotating at 200 rpm. The angle of twist on 3 m length was found to be 0.7°. Calculate the power transmitted and maximum shear stress induced in the material. Assume G = 80 GPa.

Data   :   D = 150 mm ;   t = 20 mm ;   N = 200 rpm ;   θ = 0.7° = 0.0122 rad.; G = 80 GPa ;   L = 3000 mm.

Required :   Power transmitted (P) and maximum shear stress (τ_{max}).

Concept :   Find torque based on angle of twist criteria and then use equation of power.

Solution :   (i)   Geometric properties :

$$d = \text{Internal diameter of shaft}$$

$$= 150 - 2 \times 20$$

$$= 110 \text{ mm}$$

$$J = \frac{\pi}{32} (D^4 - d^4) = \frac{\pi}{32} [(150)^4 - (110^4)]$$

$$= 35.32 \times 10^6 \text{ mm}^4$$

$$R = \frac{150}{2} = 75 \text{ mm}$$

$\therefore$
$$\frac{J}{R} = \frac{35.32 \times 10^6}{75} = 471.03 \times 10^3 \text{ mm}^3$$

(ii) Torque corresponding to angle of twist :

$$T = \left(\frac{G \cdot \theta}{L}\right) \cdot J$$

$$= \frac{80 \times 10^3 \times 0.0122}{3000} \times 35.32 \times 10^6$$

$$= 11.49 \times 10^6 \text{ Nmm}$$

$$= 11.49 \times 10^3 \text{ Nm}$$

(iii) Power transmitted (P) :

$$P = \frac{2\pi N\, T_a}{60} = \frac{2 \times \pi \times 200 \times 11.49 \times 10^3}{60}$$

$$= 240.66 \times 10^3 \text{ W}$$

$$= \mathbf{240.66\ kW}$$

(iv) Maximum shear stress (τ_{max}) :

$$\tau_{max} = \frac{T}{J/R} = \frac{11.49 \times 10^6}{471.03 \times 10^3}$$

$$= \mathbf{24.39\ MPa}$$

Example 7.3 : A hollow circular shaft has external diameter of 100 mm and internal diameter of 80 mm. Find the safe power that can be transmitted if allowable shear stress is 100 MPa and maximum angle of twist is 3° for 2 m length. Take speed of shaft = 2.5 revolutions per second and maximum torque to exceed by mean torque by 20%. Take G = 80 GPa.

Data : D = 100 mm ; d = 80 mm ; τ_{max} = 100 MPa ; θ = 3° = 0.0524 rad ;

L = 2000 mm ; N = 2 r.p.s. ; G = 80 GPa ; T = 1.2 T_a

Required : Safe power.

Concept : Safe torque is the least of that obtained from shear stress and angle of twist criteria.

Solution : (i) Geometric properties :

$$J = \frac{\pi}{32} (D^4 - d^4)$$

$$= \frac{\pi}{32} [(100)^4 - (80)^4]$$

$$= 5.796 \times 10^6 \text{ mm}^4$$

$$R = \frac{100}{2} = 50 \text{ mm}$$

∴
$$\frac{J}{R} = \frac{5.796 \times 10^6}{50} = 115.93 \times 10^3 \text{ mm}^3$$

(ii) Torque based on strength criteria :

$$T = \left(\frac{J}{R}\right) \cdot \tau_{max}$$

$$= 115.93 \times 10^3 \times 100$$

$$= 11.59 \times 10^6 \text{ Nmm} \qquad \qquad \text{... (A)}$$

(iii) Torque based on stiffness criteria :

$$T = \left(\frac{G\theta}{L}\right) J$$

$$= \frac{80 \times 10^3 \times 0.0524}{2000} \times 5.796 \times 10^6$$

$$= 12.15 \times 10^6 \text{ Nmm} \qquad \qquad \text{... (B)}$$

(iv) Safe maximum torque (T) :

$$T = \text{Least of (A) and (B)}$$

$$= 11.59 \times 10^6 \text{ Nmm}$$

$$= \mathbf{11.59 \times 10^3 \text{ Nm}}$$

∴ Safe average torque, T_a
$$= \frac{T}{1.2}$$

$$= \frac{11.59 \times 10^3}{1.2}$$

$$= \mathbf{9.66 \times 10^3 \text{ Nm}}$$

(v) Safe power (P) :

$$P = 2\pi N T_a \qquad \text{... (\textbf{Note} : N = 2.5 revolutions per second)}$$

$$= 2\pi \times 2.5 \times 9.66 \times 10^3$$

$$= 151.74 \times 10^3 \text{ W}$$

$$= \mathbf{151.74 \text{ kW}}$$

Example 7.4 : A steel bar 38 mm diameter and 450 mm long, when tested under an axial tensile load of 100 kN found to stretch by 0.2 mm. The same bar when subjected to a torque of 1.27 kNm is found to twist by 1.922º. Determine the values of four elastic constants.

Data   :   D = 38 mm ;   L = 450 mm ;   P = 100 kN ; δL = 0.2 mm ;

                T = 1.27 kNm ; θ = 1.922º.

Required   :   E ; G ; K and μ.

Concept   :   Standard formulae,

Solution   :   (i) Geometric properties :

$$A = \frac{\pi}{4} (D)^2 = \frac{\pi}{4} (38)^2 = 1134.12 \text{ mm}^2$$

$$J = \frac{\pi}{32} (D^4) = \frac{\pi}{32} (38)^4 = 204.7 \times 10^3 \text{ mm}^4$$

(ii)   Modulus of elasticity (E)

$$\delta L = \frac{PL}{AE}$$

$$0.2 = \frac{100 \times 10^3 \times 450}{1134.12 \text{ E}}$$

$\therefore$ E = 198.39 $\times 10^3$

                 = **198.39 GPa**

(iii)   Modulus of rigidity (G) :

$$\theta = \frac{TL}{GJ} \quad \therefore \quad 1.922 \times \frac{\pi}{180} = \frac{1.27 \times 10^6 \times 450}{G \times 204.7 \times 10^3}$$

$\therefore$ G = 83.23 $\times 10^3$ MPa = **83.23 GPa.**

(iv)   Poisson's ratio (μ) :

             E = 2G (1 + μ)

       198.39 = 2 $\times$ 83.23 (1 + μ)

             μ = **0.19**

(v)   Bulk modulus (K) :

             E = 3K (1 – 2μ)

       198.39 = 3K (1 – 2 $\times$ 0.19)

$\therefore$ K = **106.66 GPa**

Example 7.5 : A metal bar 16 mm ϕ, subjected to a pull of 35 kN, elongates by 0.40 mm over a gauge length of 500 mm. In a torsion test on the same material, maximum shear stress of 45 MPa was measured on a bar of 40 mm ϕ and angle of twist over a length of 400 mm was measured to be 0.6º. Determine Poisson's ratio for the material.

Data   :   For axial pull : P = 35 kN ; δL = 0.40 mm; D = 16 mm ;   L = 500 mm

            For torsion test : τ = 45 MPa; D = 40 mm; θ = 0.6º = 0.01047;

            L = 400 mm.

Required : Poisson's ratio (μ)

Concept : Standard formulae.

Solution : (i) For axial pull :

$$\delta L = \frac{PL}{AE}$$

$$0.40 = \frac{35 \times 10^3 \times 500}{\frac{\pi}{4} (16)^2 \times E}$$

$\therefore$ $\qquad E = 217.59 \times 10^3$ MPa = **217.59 GPa**

(ii) For torsion test : $\dfrac{\tau}{R} = \dfrac{G\theta}{L}$

$\therefore$ $\qquad G = \dfrac{\tau L}{R\theta} = \dfrac{45 \times 400}{0.01047 \times 20}$

$\qquad\qquad = 85.96 \times 10^3$ MPa

$\qquad\qquad = $ **85.96 GPa**

(iii) Poisson's ratio (μ) : $\quad E = 2G(1 + \mu)$

$\qquad\qquad 217.59 = 2 \times 85.96 (1 + \mu)$

$\qquad\qquad\qquad \mu = $ **0.266**

7.6 DESIGN OF SHAFTS

For the design of circular shafts (solid or hollow), following are the two criteria :

(i) **Strength Criteria :** It means, with the designed diameter, shear stress shall not exceed the allowable value.

(ii) **Stiffness Criteria :** It means, with the designed diameter, angle of twist shall not exceed the allowable value.

Diameter of the shaft is obtained using above two conditions and greater of the two is to be used.

7.7 SOLID AND HOLLOW CIRCULAR SHAFTS FOR THE SAME TORQUE

When solid shaft is replaced by hollow shaft, there is saving in material. This is due to the fact that for solid shaft, material very near to the polar axis contributes very little for resisting the applied torque, while the same material placed away from polar axis provides greater

polar moment of inertia and section modulus in case of hollow shaft $\left(\because J = \int\limits_{0}^{R} dar^2 \right)$.

However, the hollow circular shaft requires more space to accommodate as compared to solid shaft.

Example 7.6 : Design the diameter of solid circular shaft to transmit 50 kW power rotating at 150 rpm. Maximum torque is likely to exceed mean torque by 25%. Permissible shear stress = 60 MPa. Also calculate angle of twist for 2 m length. Assume G = 85 GPa.

Data : $P = 50$ kW ; $N = 150$ r.p.m. ; $T = 1.25\, T_a$;

$\tau_{max} = 60$ MPa ; $L = 2000$ mm ; $G = 85$ GPa.

Required : Diameter of shaft (D) and angle of twist (θ).

Concept : Design based on strength criteria.

Solution : (i) Average torque (T_a) :

We have, $P = \dfrac{2\pi N\, T_a}{60}$

$50 \times 10^3 = \dfrac{2\pi \times 150 \times T_a}{60}$

$T_a = 3183.1$ Nm

$= \mathbf{3183.1 \times 10^3\ Nmm}$

(ii) Maximum torque (T), $T = 1.25\, T_a$

$= 1.25 \times 3183.1 \times 10^3$

$= \mathbf{3978.87 \times 10^3\ Nmm}$

(iii) Diameter based on strength criteria :

$T = \dfrac{J}{R} \cdot \tau_{max}$

$3978.87 \times 10^3 = \dfrac{\pi}{16}\, (D)^3 \times 60$

$\therefore$ $D = \mathbf{69.64\ mm,\ say\ 70\ mm.}$

(iv) Angle of twist (θ) :

$\dfrac{T}{J} = \dfrac{G\theta}{L}$ $\therefore$ $\theta = \dfrac{T L}{G J}$

where $J = \dfrac{\pi}{32}\, (70)^4 = 2.357 \times 10^6\ mm^4$

$\therefore$ $\theta = \dfrac{3978.87 \times 10^3 \times 2000}{85 \times 10^3 \times 2.357 \times 10^6}$

$= 0.0397$ rad.

$\theta = \mathbf{2.27^o}$

Example 7.7 : A steel shaft of solid circular cross-section has to transmit 200 kW at 180 r.p.m. The maximum shear stress is not to exceed 50 MPa and the angle of twist must not be more than 1.6^o in a length of 2.6 m. Design suitable diameter of shaft. Take G = 80 GPa.

Data : $P = 200$ kW; $N = 180$ r.p.m.; $\tau_{max} = 50$ MPa;

$\theta = 1.6^o = 0.0279$ rad; $L = 2600$ mm; $G = 80$ GPa.

Required : Design of cross-section of shaft.

Concept : Design based on strength and stiffness criteria. Diameter to be used is greater of that obtained from above two conditions.

Solution : (i) Average torque (T_a) :

We have, $$P = \frac{2\pi N\, T_a}{60}$$

$$200 \times 10^3 = \frac{2\pi \times 180 \times T_a}{60}$$

$$T_a = \mathbf{10.61 \times 10^3\ Nm}$$

Assuming maximum torque, $\quad T = T_a = 10.61 \times 10^3\ Nm$

$$= \mathbf{10.61 \times 10^6\ Nmm}$$

(**Note :** Relation between maximum torque and average torque is not given.)

(ii)　Diameter based on strength criteria :

$$T = \left(\frac{J}{R}\right) \cdot \tau_{max}$$

$$10.61 \times 10^6 = \left(\frac{\pi}{16} \cdot D^3\right) \cdot 50$$

$\therefore \qquad\qquad D = \mathbf{102.62\ mm}$　　　　　　　　　　　　... (1)

(iii)　Diameter based on stiffness criteria :

$$\frac{T}{J} = \frac{G\theta}{L} \quad \therefore \quad J = \frac{T\,L}{G\theta}$$

$$\frac{\pi}{32} \cdot D^4 = \frac{10.61 \times 10^6 \times 2600}{80 \times 10^3 \times 0.0279}$$

$\therefore \qquad\qquad D = 105.92\ mm$　　　　　　　　　　　　... (2)

$\therefore \qquad\qquad D = \mathbf{105.92\ mm}$

$\qquad\qquad\qquad$ **say 106 mm**　　　　　(Greater of (1) and (2))

Example 7.8 : Design the cross-section of hollow shaft for which internal diameter is $\frac{3}{4}$ th of its external diameter to resist a torque of 1600 Nm, such that shear stress does not exceed 60 MPa and angle of twist does not exceed 2° for 1.8 m length. Assume G = 80 GPa.

Data : $d = \frac{3}{4}\ D$;　$T = 1600\ Nm$;　$\tau_{max} = 60\ MPa$;

$\qquad\qquad \theta = 2° = 0.0349\ rad$;　$L = 1800\ mm$;　$G = 80\ GPa$.

Required : Design of cross-section of shaft.

Concept : Same as Example (7.7).

Solution : (i) Diameter based on strength criteria :

$$T = \left(\frac{J}{R}\right) \tau_{max}$$

$$1600 \times 10^3 = \frac{\pi}{16\,D} (D^4 - d^4)\ 60$$

$$1600 \times 10^3 = \frac{\pi}{16\,D} \left[D^4 - \left(\frac{3}{4}D\right)^4\right]\ 60$$

$$D = 58.35 \text{ mm}$$

(ii) Diameter based on stiffness criteria :

$$\frac{T}{J} = \frac{G\theta}{L} \qquad \therefore\ J = \frac{TL}{G\theta}$$

$$\frac{\pi}{32}(D^4 - d^4) = \frac{1600 \times 10^3 \times 1800}{80 \times 10^3 \times 0.0349}$$

$$\frac{\pi}{32}\left[D^4 - \left(\frac{3}{4}D\right)^4\right] = 1.031 \times 10^6$$

$$D = 62.61 \text{ mm}$$

∴ Use $\qquad D = 62.61 \text{ mm} \cong \mathbf{63\ mm}$

and $\qquad d = \dfrac{3}{4}(63) = 47.25 \text{ mm} \cong \mathbf{47\ mm}$

Example 7.9 : A hollow steel shaft 2.5 m long transmits a torque of 15 kNm. Total angle of twist is not to exceed 2.5º and permissible shear stress = 80 MPa. Determine inside and outside diameter of shaft. G = 82 GPa.

Data : L = 2500 mm; T = 15 kNm; θ = 2.5º = 0.0436 rad; τ_{max} = 80 MPa; G = 82 GPa

Required : Design of cross-section of shaft.

Concept : Generally cross-section of shaft is designed for strength and stiffness criteria and dimensions to be provided are governed by greater of the requirement for above two conditions. For the design of hollow shaft, relation between external and internal diameter must be known to use the conventional procedure. In this example, this relation is not given.

Solution : (i) External diameter of shaft (D)

Using $\qquad \dfrac{\tau_{max}}{R} = \dfrac{G\theta}{L}$

$$\frac{80}{D/2} = \frac{82 \times 10^3 \times 0.0436}{2500}$$

∴ $\qquad D = \mathbf{111.9\ mm\ \ say\ 112\ mm.}$

(ii)   Polar M.I. of shaft :

$$\frac{T}{J} = \frac{G\theta}{L}$$

∴

$$J = \frac{TL}{G\theta} = \frac{15 \times 10^6 \times 2500}{82 \times 10^3 \times 0.0436}$$

$$J = \textbf{10.49} \times \textbf{10}^\textbf{6}\ \textbf{mm}^\textbf{4}$$

(iii)   Internal diameter of shaft :

$$J = \frac{\pi}{32}\ (D^4 - d^4)$$

$$10.49 \times 10^6 = \frac{\pi}{32}\ [(112)^4 - d^4] = \textbf{84.3 mm}\quad \textbf{say 84 mm}$$

Thus;   D = **112 mm** and **d = 84 mm**

(**Note :** Internal diameter shall be rounded off on lower side.)

Example 7.10 : A hollow shaft has 60 mm external diameter and 50 mm internal diameter. Determine the twisting moment it can resist if permissible shear stress is 100 MPa. Determine the diameter of solid circular shaft made of the same material which can transmit same twisting moment. Hence, compare their weights per metre length. Take G = 80 GPa.

Data   :   D = 60 mm; d = 50 mm for hollow shaft, τ_{max} = 100 MPa; G = 80 GPa.

Required :   Twisting moment, Diameter of solid shaft; Comparison of weights.

Concept   :   Hollow shaft is economical as compared to solid shaft.

Solution :   (i) Geometric properties :

For hollow shaft, $J = \dfrac{\pi}{32}\ (D^4 - d^4) = \dfrac{\pi}{32}\ [(60)^4 - (50)^4]$

$$= 658.75 \times 10^3\ mm^4$$

$$R = \frac{60}{2} = 30\ mm$$

∴

$$\frac{J}{R} = \frac{658.75 \times 10^3}{30} = \textbf{21.96} \times \textbf{10}^\textbf{3}\ \textbf{mm}^\textbf{3}$$

(ii) Torque based on shear stress (T) :

$$T = \left(\frac{J}{R}\right)\ \tau_{max}$$

$$= 21.96 \times 10^3 \times 100$$

$$= \textbf{2.196} \times \textbf{10}^\textbf{6}\ \textbf{Nmm}$$

(iii)   Diameter of solid shaft (D_1) :

$$T = \left(\frac{J}{R}\right) \tau_{max}$$

$$2.196 \times 10^6 = \left(\frac{\pi}{16} D_1^3\right) 100$$

$$D_1 = 48.18 \text{ mm} \cong \mathbf{49 \text{ mm}}$$

(iv) Comparison of weights :

$$(A)_{solid} = \frac{\pi}{4} D_1^2 = \frac{\pi}{4} (49)^2 = \mathbf{1885.74 \text{ mm}^2}$$

$$(A)_{hollow} = \frac{\pi}{4} (D^2 - d^2) = \frac{\pi}{4} [(60)^2 - (50)^2] = \mathbf{863.94 \text{ mm}^2}$$

$$\therefore \quad \frac{\text{Weight of solid shaft}}{\text{Weight of hollow shaft}} = \frac{(A)_{solid}}{(A)_{hollow}} = \frac{1885.74}{863.94} = \mathbf{2.18}$$

Example 7.11 : Design diameter of solid shaft for resisting torque of 2500 Nm. Also design cross-section of hollow shaft made of same material assuming internal diameter as 0.7 times the external diameter for the same torque. Hence, comment on percentage saving in weight and shear stress for shaft. Assume allowable angle of twist 2º for 1 m length of both shafts. Take G = 80 GPa.

Data : T = 2500 Nm; d = 0.7 D for hollow shaft;

θ = 2º = 0.0349 rad; L = 1000 mm; G = 80 GPa.

Required : Comparison of hollow and solid shaft.

Concept : Design of shafts based on stiffness criteria.

Solution : (i) Design of solid shaft :

Let $\qquad D_1$ = Diameter of solid shaft

$$\frac{T}{J} = \frac{G\theta}{L} \quad \therefore \quad J = \frac{TL}{G\theta}$$

$$\therefore \quad \frac{\pi}{32} D_1^4 = \frac{2500 \times 10^3 \times 1000}{80 \times 10^3 \times 0.0349}$$

$$= 895.41 \times 10^3 \text{ mm}^4$$

$$\therefore \quad D_1 = \mathbf{54.95 \text{ mm}}$$

(ii) Design of hollow shaft :

$$J = \frac{TL}{G\theta}$$

$$\therefore \quad \frac{\pi}{32} (D^4 - d^4) = 895.41 \times 10^3 \text{ mm}^4$$

$$\frac{\pi}{32} [D^4 - (0.7\,D)^4] = 895.41 \times 10^3$$

$$D = \mathbf{58.85\ mm}$$

$\therefore \qquad\qquad\qquad\qquad d = \mathbf{41.19\ mm}$

(iii)   Comparison of weights :

$$A_s = \frac{\pi}{4}\left(D_1^2\right) = \frac{\pi}{4} \times (54.95)^2 = \mathbf{2.37 \times 10^3\ mm^2}$$

$$A_h = \frac{\pi}{4}(D^2 - d^2) = \frac{\pi}{4}[(58.85)^2 - (41.19)^2]$$

$$= \mathbf{1.387 \times 10^3\ mm^2}$$

$\therefore$ Percentage saving in weight $= \dfrac{A_s - A_h}{A_s} \times 100$

$$= \frac{(2.37 - 1.387) \times 10^3}{2.37 \times 10^3} \times 100$$

$$= \mathbf{41.47\ \%}$$

(iv)   Comparison of shear stresses :

For solid shaft, $\qquad \dfrac{J}{R} = \dfrac{895.41 \times 10^3}{\dfrac{54.95}{2}} = \mathbf{32.59 \times 10^3\ mm^3}$

$$\tau_s = \frac{T}{J/R} = \frac{2500 \times 10^3}{32.59 \times 10^3} = \mathbf{76.71\ MPa}$$

For hollow shaft, $\qquad \dfrac{J}{R} = \dfrac{895.41 \times 10^3}{58.85/2}$

$$= \mathbf{30.43 \times 10^3\ mm^3}$$

$$\tau_h = \frac{T}{J/R} = \frac{2500 \times 10^3}{30.43 \times 10^3} = \mathbf{82.15\ MPa}$$

Thus; $\qquad\qquad \dfrac{\tau_s}{\tau_h} = \dfrac{76.71}{82.15} = 0.93$

$\therefore \qquad\qquad\qquad \tau_s = 0.93\,\tau_h$

i.e. $\qquad\qquad\qquad \tau_h = \mathbf{1.075\,\tau_s}$

Note : For the same torque when solid and hollow shafts are designed from stiffness criteria, there is saving in weight when hollow shaft is used. However, shear stress developed for hollow shaft is of higher magnitude than that of solid shaft. If this stress of comparatively higher magnitude for hollow shaft is less than permissible stress, then only replacement of solid shaft by hollow shaft will be possible.

It should also be noted that for stress criteria of design, polar section modulii (J/R) of solid and hollow shafts are same; while for stiffness criteria of design, polar moment of inertia (J) of solid and hollow shafts are same.

Example 7.12 : Design diameter of solid shaft for resisting torque of 2500 Nm. Also design cross-section of hollow shaft made of same material assuming internal diameter as 0.7 times the external diameter for the same torque. Hence, comment on percentage saving in weight and angle of twist per unit length of shafts. Assume permissible shear stress = 60 MPa.

Data : $T = 2500$ Nm; $d = 0.7$ D for hollow shaft; $\tau_{max} = 60$ MPa.

Required : Comparison of hollow and solid shaft.

Concept : Design of shafts based on strength criteria.

Solution : (i) Design of solid shaft :

Let $\qquad D_1$ = Diameter of solid shaft

$$T = \left(\frac{J}{R}\right) \tau_{max}$$

$\therefore \qquad\qquad 2500 \times 10^3 = \left[\frac{\pi}{16}\left(D_1^3\right)\right] 60$

$\therefore \qquad\qquad\qquad D_1 = \textbf{59.64 mm}$

(ii) Design of hollow shaft :

$$T = \left(\frac{J}{R}\right) \tau_{max}$$

$$2500 \times 10^3 = \frac{\pi}{16\,D}\,(D^4 - d^4) \times 60$$

$$= \frac{\pi}{16\,D}\,(D^4 - (0.7\,D)^4) \times 60$$

$\therefore \qquad\qquad\qquad D = \textbf{65.36 mm}$

$\therefore \qquad\qquad\qquad d = 0.7\,D$

$$= 0.7 \times 65.36 = \textbf{45.75 mm}$$

(iii) Comparison of weights :

$$A_{solid} = \frac{\pi}{4}\,D_1^2 = \frac{\pi}{4}\,(59.64)^2 = 2.79 \times 10^3 \text{ mm}^2$$

$$A_{hollow} = \frac{\pi}{4}(D^2 - d^2) = \frac{\pi}{4}[(65.36)^2 - (45.75)^2]$$

$$= 1.71 \times 10^3 \text{ mm}^2$$

$$\text{Percentage saving in weight} = \frac{A_{solid} - A_{hollow}}{A_{solid}} \times 100$$

$$= \frac{(2.79 - 1.71) \times 10^3}{2.79 \times 10^3} \times 100$$

$$= 38.7\%$$

(iv)   Comparison of angle of twist :

For solid shaft, $J = \frac{\pi}{32} \cdot D_1^4 = \frac{\pi}{32}(59.64)^4$

$$= 1.242 \times 10^6 \text{ mm}^4$$

For hollow shaft, $J = \frac{\pi}{32}(D^4 - d^4) = \frac{\pi}{32}[(65.36)^4 - (45.75)^4]$

$$= 1.36 \times 10^6 \text{ mm}^4$$

Angle of twist for solid shaft :

$$\theta_s = \frac{TL}{GJ_s}$$

$$= \frac{TL}{G \times 1.242 \times 10^6}$$

Angle of twist for hollow shaft $= \theta_h = \frac{TL}{GJ_h}$

$$\theta_h = \frac{TL}{G \times 1.36 \times 10^6}$$

$\therefore$ $\dfrac{\theta_s}{\theta_h} = \dfrac{TL}{G \times 1.242 \times 10^6} \times \dfrac{G \times 1.36 \times 10^6}{TL}$

$$\frac{\theta_s}{\theta_h} = 1.095$$

$\therefore$ $\theta_s = 1.095\,\theta_h$

i.e. $\theta_h = 0.913\,\theta_s$

Note : For the same torque when solid and hollow shafts are designed from strength criteria, there is saving in weight if hollow shaft is used. Also angle of twist for hollow shaft is smaller than that of solid shaft. Hence, if stress is the criteria of design, hollow shaft has advantage over solid shaft.

Example 7.13 : Compare the weights of equal lengths of hollow and solid shaft to resist same torsional moment for same maximum shear stress. Assume internal diameter 0.8 times the external diameter for hollow shaft.

Data   : $d = 0.8\,D$ for hollow shaft.

Required :   Ratio of weights for hollow and solid shaft.

Concept   :   Design based on strength criteria and then comparison of weights.

Solution   :   (i) For solid shaft :

Let D_1 = Diameter of solid shaft

$$\tau_{max} = \left(\frac{T}{J}\right) \cdot R = \frac{T}{J/R}$$

$$= \frac{T}{\left(\frac{\pi}{16}\right) D_1^3} \qquad \text{... (1)}$$

(ii)   For hollow shaft :

Let D = External diameter

d = $0.8\,D$ = Internal diameter

$\therefore$ $\tau_{max} = \left(\frac{T}{J}\right) \cdot R = \frac{T}{(J/R)}$

$$= \frac{T}{\left(\frac{\pi}{16\,D}\right)(D^4 - d^4)}$$

$$= \frac{T}{\left(\frac{\pi}{16\,D}\right)[D^4 - (0.8\,D)^4]}$$

$$= \frac{T}{\left(\frac{\pi}{16}\right) \cdot (0.59\,D^3)} \qquad \text{... (2)}$$

(iii)   Relation between diameter of solid and hollow shaft :

Equating (1) and (2),

$$\frac{T}{\left(\frac{\pi}{16}\right) D_1^3} = \frac{T}{\left(\frac{\pi}{16}\right)(0.59\,D^3)}$$

we get, D_1 = **0.84 D**

(iv)   Comparison of weights :

Cross-sectional area of solid shaft $= A_S = \dfrac{\pi}{4} \cdot D_1^2$

$$= \frac{\pi}{4} \ (0.84 \ D)^2$$

$$= (0.7056) \cdot \frac{\pi}{4} \ D^2$$

Cross-sectional area of hollow shaft $= A_h = \frac{\pi}{4} \ (D^2 - d^2)$

$$= \frac{\pi}{4} \ [D^2 - (0.8 \ D)^2]$$

$$= (0.36) \cdot \frac{\pi}{4} \cdot D^2$$

$\therefore$ $\dfrac{\text{Weight of hollow shaft}}{\text{Weight of solid shaft}} = \dfrac{A_h}{A_s} = \dfrac{0.36}{0.7056} = \mathbf{0.51}$

Example 7.14 : A solid shaft of 200 mm diameter has the same cross-sectional area as that of hollow shaft of the same materials of inside diameter 150 mm.

   (i)   Find the ratio of power transmitted by the two shafts of same angular velocity.

   (ii)   Compare angle of twist in equal lengths of these shafts when stressed equally.

Data : $d = 150$ mm for hollow shaft, $D_1 = 20$ mm for solid shaft

Required : Comparison of hollow and solid shaft.

Concept : Design of shafts based on stiffness criteria.

Solution : (i) Outside diameter of hollow shaft :

$$\frac{\pi}{4} \ (D^2 - d^2) \quad = \quad \frac{\pi}{4} \ D_1^2$$

$$[D^2 - (150^2)] \quad = \quad (200)^2$$

$$D \quad = \quad 250 \ mm$$

(ii)   Ratio of power transmitted :

$$\frac{\text{Power transmitted by hollow shaft}}{\text{Power transmitted by solid shaft}} = \frac{\text{Torque transmitted by hollow shaft}}{\text{Torque transmitted by solid shaft}}$$

Torque transmitted by hollow shaft $= \left(\dfrac{J}{R}\right) \tau_{max}.$

$\therefore$ $T = \pi \ \dfrac{[(250^4 - 150^4)]}{16 \times 250} \times \tau_{max}$

$$= 2.67 \times 10^6 \ \tau_{max}$$

$$T_1 = \frac{\pi}{16} \ D^3 \ \tau_{max}$$

$$= \frac{\pi}{16} \times (200)^3 \times \tau_{max}$$

$$= 1.57 \times \tau_{max}$$

$$\therefore \quad \frac{T}{T_1} = \frac{2.67 \times 10^6 \times \tau_{max}}{1.57 \times \tau_{max}}$$

$$\therefore \quad \frac{P}{P_1} = \frac{T}{T_1} = 1.7$$

(iii) Comparison of angle of twist :

$$\frac{\tau_{max}}{R} = \frac{G\theta}{l}$$

$$\therefore \qquad \theta_{hollow} = \frac{\tau_{max} \times l}{G \times 125}$$

$$\therefore \qquad \theta_{solid} = \frac{\tau_{max} \times l}{G \times 100}$$

$$\therefore \qquad \frac{\theta_{hollow}}{\theta_{solid}} = \frac{100}{125} = 0.8$$

$$\therefore \qquad \boldsymbol{\theta_{hollow}} = \boldsymbol{0.8 \; \theta_{solid}}$$

Example 7.15 : A hollow circular shaft having internal diameter 50% of its external diameter transmits 600 kW at 150 rpm. Determine the external diameter of the shaft if the shear stress is not to exceed 65 N/mm^2 and a twist in a length of 3 m should not exceed 1.4°. Assume T_{max} = 1.2 times T_{mean}, G = 100 GPa.

Data : d = $\frac{D}{2}$, τ_{max} = 65 N/mm^2, θ = 1.4° = 0.0244 rad, l = 3000 mm, G = 100 GPa,

P = 600 kW, N = 150 rpm.

Required : External diameter.

Concept : Design based on strength and stiffness criteria.

Solution : (i) Torque calculation :

$$P = \frac{2\pi NT}{60}$$

$$T = \frac{P \times 60}{2\pi N} = \frac{600 \times 10^3 \times 60}{2\pi \times 150}$$

$$= 38.197 \times 10^3 \text{ N-m}$$

$$T_{max} = 1.2 \times T = 1.2 \times 38.197 \times 10^6 = 45.384 \times 10^6 \text{ N-mm}$$

(ii) Diameter based on strength criteria :

$$T = \frac{J}{R} \tau_{max}$$

Substituting,

$$45.384 \times 10^6 \ = \ \frac{\pi}{16D} \ (D^4 - d^4) \ 65$$

$$45.384 \times 10^6 \ = \ \frac{\pi}{16D} \left(D^4 - \frac{D^4}{16}\right) 65$$

$$D \ = \ 156.47 \ mm$$

(iii) Diameter based on stiffness criteria :

$$\frac{T}{J} \ = \ \frac{G\theta}{l} \qquad\qquad \therefore \ J \ = \ \frac{T\,L}{G\theta}$$

$$\frac{\pi}{32} \ (D^4 - d^4) \ = \ \frac{45.384 \times 10^6 \times 3000}{100 \times 10^3 \times 0.0244}$$

$$D \ = \ \mathbf{156.92 \ \ mm, \ \ say \ 160 \ mm}$$

7.8 SHAFTS IN SERIES

When two or more shafts are connected length-wise, they are said to be in series. It is also called as compound shaft. For the analysis of shafts in series, following points are to be noted :

(i) All the component shafts are co-axially connected i.e. polar axis is common for all the shafts.

(ii) Joint between the components is rigid i.e. there is no relative rotation between the two adjacent shafts at a joint.

Consider a compound shaft ABC subjected to torque 'T' as shown in Fig. 7.7.

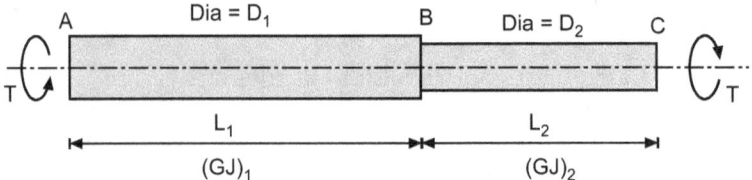

Fig. 7.7 : Shafts in series

Shear stress for portion AB = $\tau_1 = \dfrac{T}{J_1}\left(\dfrac{D_1}{2}\right)$

Shear stress for portion BC = $\tau_2 \ = \ \dfrac{T}{J_2}\left(\dfrac{D_2}{2}\right)$

Total angle of twist at C relative to A :

$$(\theta)_{AC} \ = \ (\theta)_{AB} + (\theta)_{BC}$$

$$= \left(\frac{TL}{GJ}\right)_{AB} + \left(\frac{TL}{GJ}\right)_{BC}$$

$$= T \left[\frac{L_1}{(GJ)_1} + \frac{L_2}{(GJ)_2}\right] \qquad \text{... (7.10 a)}$$

$$= T \text{ [Sum of flexibility coefficients for components]}$$

If material for shafts AB and BC is same,

$$(\theta)_{AC} = \frac{T}{G} \left[\frac{L_1}{J_1} + \frac{L_2}{J_2}\right] \qquad \text{... (7.10 b)}$$

Example 7.16 : A compound shaft ABCD has details as shown in Fig. 7.8. Determine inside diameter of portion AB such that shear stresses developed in portions AB and CD are equal. Also find total angle of twist if shaft is subjected to torque of 1.1 kNm. Assume G = 80 GPa.

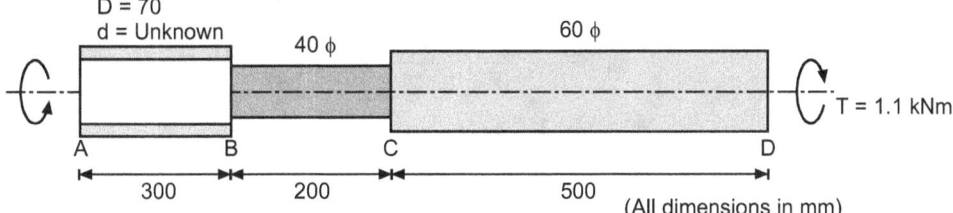

Fig. 7.8

Data   : As shown in Fig. 7.8, T = 1.1 kNm; G = 80 GPa, $\tau_{AB} = \tau_{CD}$.

Required : Inside diameter (d) for AB and total angle of twist.

Concept   : (i)   Equating shear stress for portions AB and CD, get the diameter of portion AB.

  (ii) Total angle of twist at D relative to A = $\theta_{AD} = \theta_{AB} + \theta_{BC} + \theta_{CD}$.

Solution : (i)   Geometric properties :

Component	J (mm⁴)	R (mm)	(J/R) (mm³)
AB	$\frac{\pi}{32} [(70)^4 - d^4]$	$\frac{70}{2} = 35$	$\frac{\pi}{1120} [(70)^4 - d^4]$
BC	$\frac{\pi}{32} (40)^4 = 251.33 \times 10^3$	$\frac{40}{2} = 20$	12.57×10^3
CD	$\frac{\pi}{32} (60)^4 = 1272.35 \times 10^3$	$\frac{60}{2} = 30$	42.41×10^3

(ii)   Inside diameter for AB :

$$\tau_{AB} = \tau_{CD}$$

$$\left(\frac{T}{J/R}\right)_{AB} = \left(\frac{T}{J/R}\right)_{CD}$$

$$\therefore \quad \left(\frac{J}{R}\right)_{AB} = \left(\frac{J}{R}\right)_{CD}$$

Substituting, $\dfrac{\pi}{1120}\,[(70)^4 - d^4] = 42.41 \times 10^3$

$\therefore \quad d = 54.605$ mm

$\therefore \quad (J)_{AB} = \dfrac{\pi}{32}\,[(70)^4 - (54.605)^4]$

$\qquad\qquad = \mathbf{1.484 \times 10^6\ mm^4}$

(iii)　Total angle of twist : $\theta = \theta_{AB} + \theta_{BC} + \theta_{CD}$

$$= \left(\frac{T}{G}\right)\left[\left(\frac{L}{J}\right)_{AB} + \left(\frac{L}{J}\right)_{BC} + \left(\frac{L}{J}\right)_{CD}\right]$$

$$= \frac{1.1 \times 10^6}{80 \times 10^3}\left[\frac{300}{1.484 \times 10^6} + \frac{200}{251.33 \times 10^3} + \frac{500}{1272.35 \times 10^3}\right]$$

$$= 0.01912 \text{ rad.}$$

$$\theta = \mathbf{1.095^o}$$

Example 7.17 : A compound shaft consists of brass and steel components coaxially attached; fixed at one end and subjected to torque T at free end as shown in Fig. 7.9. Find the safe value of torque T at free end subjected to following conditions :

(i) $\tau_{brass} \leq 40$ MPa　(ii) $\tau_{steel} \leq 60$ MPa　(iii) $\theta \leq 2.5^o$.

Assume $G_s = 80$ GPa and $G_b = 35$ GPa.

Also find actual stresses developed in each part.

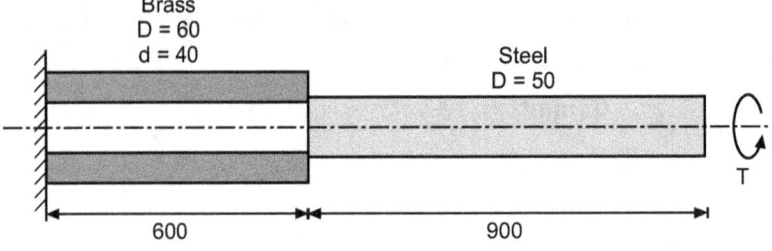

Fig. 7.9

Data　　:　As shown in Fig. 7.9, $\tau_B \leq 40$ MPa, $\tau_s \leq 60$ MPa, $\theta \leq 2.5^o$, $G_s = 80$ GPa,

$G_b = 35$ GPa.

Required :　Safe torque (T) at free end and shear stresses.

Concept : Safe torque (T) is the least of that obtained from given conditions of strength and stiffness.

Solution : (i) Geometric properties :

Component	J (mm⁴)	R (mm)	$\left(\dfrac{J}{R}\right)$ (mm³)
Brass	$\dfrac{\pi}{32}\,[(60)^4 - (40)^4] = 1.021 \times 10^6$	$\dfrac{60}{2} = 30$	34.03×10^3
Steel	$\dfrac{\pi}{32}\,(50)^4 = 613.59 \times 10^3$	$\dfrac{50}{2} = 25$	24.54×10^3

(ii) Torque based on strength criteria :

(a) $\tau_B \le 40$ MPa.

∴
$$T = \left(\frac{J}{R}\right)_B \times \tau_B = 34.03 \times 10^3 \times 40$$

$$= \mathbf{1361.2 \times 10^3 \ Nmm} \qquad\qquad \dots (1)$$

(b) $\tau_S \le 60$ MPa

∴
$$T = \left(\frac{J}{R}\right)_S \cdot \tau_S$$

$$= 24.54 \times 10^3 \times 60 = \mathbf{1472.4 \times 10^3 \ Nmm} \qquad \dots (2)$$

(iii) Torque based on stiffness criteria ($\theta \le 2.5°$) :

Maximum angle of twist at free end = $\theta_B + \theta_S$

$$2.5 \times \frac{\pi}{180} = T\left[\left(\frac{L}{GJ}\right)_B + \left(\frac{L}{GJ}\right)_S\right]$$

$$= T\left[\frac{600}{35 \times 10^3 \times 1.021 \times 10^6} + \frac{900}{80 \times 10^3 \times 613.59 \times 10^3}\right]$$

∴
$$T = \mathbf{1242.227 \times 10^3 \ Nmm} \qquad\qquad \dots (3)$$

∴ Safe torque, $T = \mathbf{1242.227 \times 10^3 \ Nmm}$ (Least of 1, 2, and 3)

(iv) Shear stresses :

$$\tau_B = \frac{T}{(J/R)_B} = \frac{1242.227 \times 10^3}{34.03 \times 10^3} = \mathbf{36.50 \ MPa}$$

$$\tau_S = \frac{T}{(J/R)_S} = \frac{1242.227 \times 10^3}{24.54 \times 10^3} = \mathbf{50.62 \ MPa}$$

Example 7.18 : A compound shaft consists of steel and aluminium segments acted upon by two torques as shown in Fig. 7.10. Determine maximum permissible value of 'T' subjected to following conditions.

(i) $\tau_S \le 80$ MPa (ii) $\tau_a \le 55$ MPa (iii) $\theta \le 6°$

Assume $G_s = 83$ GPa and $G_a = 28$ GPa.

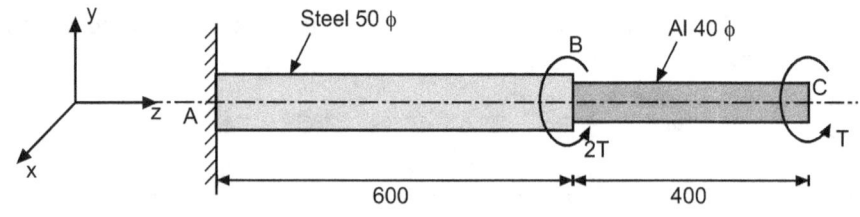

(All dimensions in mm)

Fig. 7.10

Data   :   As shown in Fig. 7.10, $\tau_s \le 80$ MPa, $\tau_a \le 55$ MPa;

                 $\theta \le 6^\circ$, $G_s = 83$ GPa, $G_a = 28$ GPa.

Required :   Safe value of torque 'T'.

Concept   :   Reactive torque at fixed end, torsional moment diagram, strength criteria, stiffness criteria.

Solution   :   (i)   Analysis :

         From statistics;

                 $\sum M_z = 0$ gives reactive torque at fixed end   A $= 3\,T$ (↺)

FBD of shaft and torsional moment diagram is as shown in Fig. 7.11.

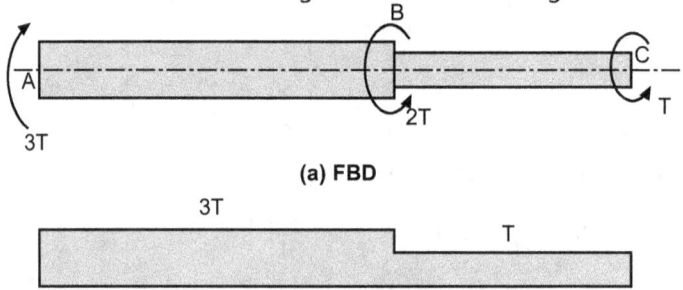

(a) FBD

(b) TMD

Fig. 7.11

(ii)   Geometric properties :

Component	J (mm⁴)	R (mm)	$\left(\dfrac{J}{R}\right)$ (mm³)
Steel	$\dfrac{\pi}{32}(50)^4 = 613.59 \times 10^3$	$\dfrac{50}{2} = 25$	24.54×10^3
Aluminium	$\dfrac{\pi}{32}(40)^4 = 251.33 \times 10^3$	$\dfrac{40}{2} = 20$	12.57×10^3

(iii)   Strength criteria :

         (a) $\tau_s \le 80$ MPa

$$3T = \left(\frac{J}{R}\right)_s \cdot \tau_s = 24.54 \times 10^3 \times 80$$

∴ $T = \mathbf{654.4 \times 10^3}$ **Nmm**   ... (1)

(b)　　$\tau_a \le 55$ MPa

$$T = \left(\frac{J}{R}\right)_a \cdot \tau_a = 12.57 \times 10^3 \times 55$$

∴　　　　　　　　$T = \mathbf{691.35 \times 10^3\ Nmm}$　　　　　　　... (2)

(iv)　Stiffness criteria ($\theta \le 6^\circ$) :

　　θ_{max} at free end $= 6^\circ = \theta_{AB} + \theta_{BC}$

$$6 \times \frac{\pi}{180} = \left(\frac{TL}{GJ}\right)_{AB} + \left(\frac{TL}{GJ}\right)_{BC}$$

$$= \frac{3T \times 600}{83 \times 10^3 \times 613.59 \times 10^3} + \frac{T \times 400}{28 \times 10^3 \times 251.33 \times 10^3}$$

$$T = \mathbf{1135.98 \times 10^3\ Nmm}\qquad\qquad... (3)$$

　　Safe value of $T = \mathbf{654.4 \times 10^3\ Nmm}$　　　　(Least of (1), (2) and (3))

Example 7.19 : The shaft shown in Fig. 7.12 below rotates at 200 rpm with 40 H.P. and 20 H.P. taken off at A and B respectively and 60 H.P. applied at C. Find the maximum shear stress developed in the shaft and angle of twist of gear 'A' relative to gear 'C'. G = 85 GPa.

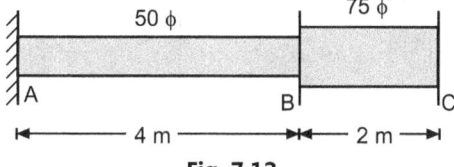

Fig. 7.12

Data　　:　N = 200 r.p.m.; at A and B 40 H.P. and 20 H.P. taken off, while at C 60 HP applied; G = 85 GPa.

Required :　Maximum shear stress and angle of twist at A w.r.t. C.

Concept　:　From the given power, find torques at A, B and C, draw torsional moment diagram and then analyse for stresses and angle of twist.

Solution　:　(i) Analysis and T.M.D. :

$$P_A = 40\ \text{H.P.} = \frac{2\pi\ NT_A}{4500} = \frac{2\pi \times 200 \times T_A}{4500}$$

∴　　　　　　　　$T_A = \mathbf{143.24\ Nm}\ (\circlearrowleft)$

$$P_B = 20\ \text{H.P.} = \frac{2\pi\ NT_B}{4500} = \frac{2\pi \times 200 \times T_B}{4500}$$

∴　　　　　　　　$T_B = \mathbf{71.62\ Nm}\ (\circlearrowleft)$

$$P_C = 60\ \text{H.P.} = \frac{2\pi\ NT_C}{4500} = \frac{2\pi \times\ 200 \times T_C}{4500}$$

∴　　　　　　　　$T_C = \mathbf{214.86\ Nm}\ (\circlearrowleft)$

Fig. 7.13 (a) below shows FBD and Fig. 7.13 (b) shows torsional moment diagram for the shaft.

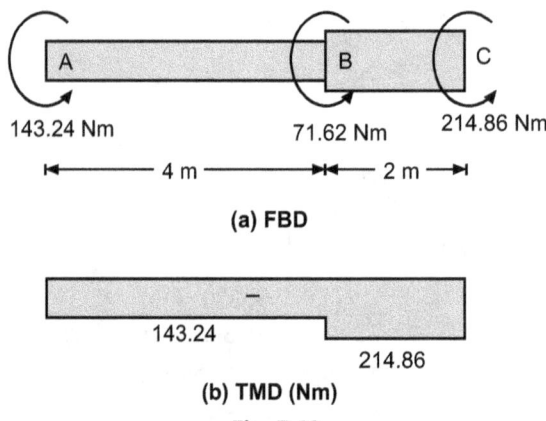

143.24 Nm   71.62 Nm   214.86 Nm

|← 4 m →|← 2 m →|

(a) FBD

143.24

214.86

(b) TMD (Nm)

Fig. 7.13

(ii)   Geometric properties :

Component	J (mm⁴)	R (mm)	$\left(\dfrac{J}{R}\right)$ (mm³)
AB	$\dfrac{\pi}{32}\,(50)^4 = 613.59 \times 10^3$	$\dfrac{50}{2} = 25$	24.54×10^3
BC	$\dfrac{\pi}{32}\,(75)^4 = 3106.31 \times 10^3$	$\dfrac{75}{2} = 37.5$	82.83×10^3

(iii)   Shear stresses :

$$\tau_{AB} = \frac{T_{AB}}{(J/R)_{AB}} = \frac{143.24 \times 10^3}{24.54 \times 10^3} = \textbf{5.83 MPa}$$

$$\tau_{BC} = \frac{T_{BC}}{(J/R)_{BC}} = \frac{214.86 \times 10^3}{82.83 \times 10^3} = \textbf{2.59 MPa}$$

∴ $\qquad\qquad \tau_{max} = \textbf{5.83 MPa}$

(iv)   Angle of twist of gear 'A' w.r.t. gear 'C' :

$$\theta_{AC} = \theta_{AB} + \theta_{BC} = \left(\frac{TL}{GJ}\right)_{AB} + \left(\frac{TL}{GJ}\right)_{BC}$$

$$= \frac{1}{85 \times 10^3}\left[\frac{143.24 \times 10^3 \times 4000}{613.59 \times 10^3} + \frac{214.86 \times 10^3 \times 2000}{3106.31 \times 10^3}\right]$$

$$= 0.0126 \text{ rad} = \textbf{0.7219°}$$

Example 7.20 : An aluminium shaft of constant diameter 80 mm is loaded by torques applied to gears attached to it, as shown in Fig. 7.14. Determine the angle of twist of gear A relative to gear D. Take G = 30 GPa.

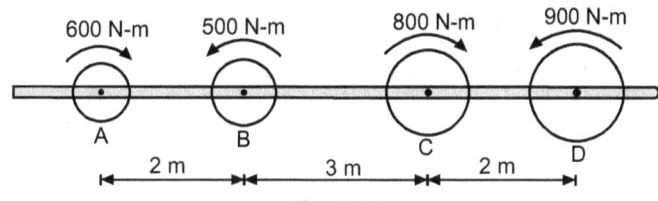

Fig. 7.14

Data : As shown in Fig. 7.14,   D = 80 mm, G = 30 GPa.

Required : Twist at D w.r. to A.

Concept : $\theta_{A/D} = \theta_A + \theta_B + \theta_C + \theta_D$.

Solution : (i) Geometric properties :

$$J = \frac{\pi}{32} D^4 = \frac{\pi}{32} \times (80)^4 = 4.02 \times 10^6 \text{ mm}^4$$

(ii)   Calculation for $\theta_{A/D}$:

$$\theta_{A/D} = \theta_A + \theta_B + \theta_C + \theta_D = \left(\frac{TL}{JG}\right)_{AB} + \left(\frac{TL}{JG}\right)_{BC} + \left(\frac{TL}{JG}\right)_{CD}$$

$$= \frac{1}{JG} \left[(TL)_{AB} + (TL)_{BC} + (TL)_{CD}\right]$$

$$= \frac{[- 600 \times 10^3 \times 2000 - 100 \times 10^3 \times 3000 - 900 \times 10^3 \times 2000]}{4.02 \times 10^6 \times 30 \times 10^3}$$

$$\theta_{A/D} = \textbf{0.027 radians} = \textbf{1.57°}$$

Example 7.21 : A stepped shaft is subjected to the couples (in the same direction) at change in section at the free end as shown in Fig. 7.15 (a). The length of each section is 0.5 m and diameters are 80 mm, 60 mm and 40 mm. If G = 80 GPa, find the angle of twist θ in degrees at the free end.

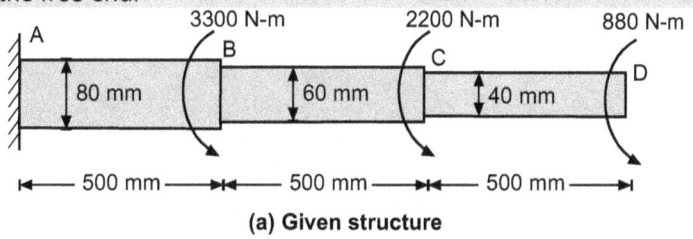

(a) Given structure

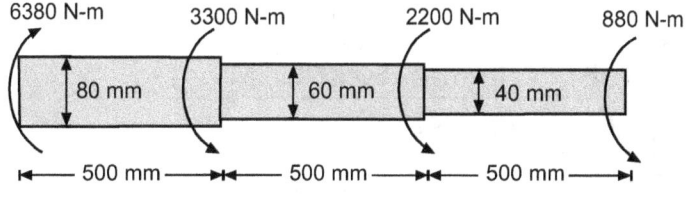

(b) FBD

Fig. 7.15

Data : As shown in Fig. 7.15 (a), G = 80 GPa.

Required : Angle of twist 'θ' at the free end.

Concept : $\theta = \theta_{AB} + \theta_{BC} + \theta_{CD}$.

Solution : (i) Geometric properties :

$$J_{AB} = \frac{\pi}{32} D^4 = \frac{\pi}{32} \times (80)^4$$

$$= 4.02 \times 10^6 \, \text{mm}^4$$

$$J_{BC} = \frac{\pi}{32} D^4 = \frac{\pi}{32} \times (60)^4$$

$$= 1.27 \times 10^6 \, \text{mm}^4$$

$$J_{CD} = \frac{\pi}{32} D^4 = \frac{\pi}{32} \times (40)^4$$

$$= 251.33 \times 10^3 \, \text{mm}^4$$

(ii)　　Torsion in members :

$$T_{AB} = 3300 + 2200 + 880 = 6380 \, \text{Nm}$$

$$= 6.38 \times 10^6 \, \text{Nmm}$$

$$T_{BC} = 2200 + 880 = 3080 \, \text{Nm}$$

$$= 3.08 \times 10^6 \, \text{Nmm}$$

$$T_{CD} = 880 \, \text{N-m}$$

$$= 880 \times 10^3 \, \text{Nmm}$$

Now,　　　　　　　$$\theta = \theta_{AB} + \theta_{BC} + \theta_{CD}$$

$$= \left(\frac{TL}{GJ}\right)_{AB} + \left(\frac{TL}{GJ}\right)_{BC} + \left(\frac{TL}{GJ}\right)_{CD}$$

$$= \frac{L}{G}\left[\left(\frac{T}{J}\right)_{AB} + \left(\frac{T}{J}\right)_{BC} + \left(\frac{T}{J}\right)_{CD}\right]$$

$$= \frac{500}{80 \times 10^3}\left[\frac{6.38 \times 10^6}{4.02 \times 10^6} + \frac{3.08 \times 10^6}{1.27 \times 10^6} + \frac{880 \times 10^3}{251.33 \times 10^3}\right]$$

$$\theta = \textbf{0.047 radians = 2.69°}$$

7.9 STATICALLY INDETERMINATE PROBLEMS

7.9.1 Shafts Fixed at Both Ends

When equations of statics are not sufficient to evaluate the unknown forces, it is called as statically indeterminate problem. For example, consider a shaft fixed at two ends and subjected to torque T as shown in Fig. 7.16.

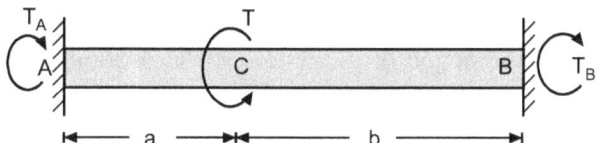

Fig. 7.16 : Shaft fixed at both ends

Unknown reactions = T_A and T_B i.e. resistive torques at A and B.

Equation of statics : $\sum M_z = 0$ gives

$$T_A + T_B = T \qquad \text{... (7.11)}$$

Second equation can be formulated using the fact that angle of twist of C (θ_{CA}) due to torque 'T_A' acting over length AC is equal to angle of twist at C (θ_{CB}) due to torque 'T_B' acting over length CB.

$$\theta_{CA} = \theta_{CB}$$

$$\left(\frac{TL}{GJ}\right)_{CA} = \left(\frac{TL}{GJ}\right)_{CB} \qquad \text{... (7.12)}$$

Substituting geometric properties for portions CA and CB in equation (7.12), relation between T_A and T_B can be obtained. Then by using equation (7.11), T_A and T_B can be evaluated.

Note : Equation (7.12) is the condition of deformation called as equation of **compatibility** wherein member deformation is assumed continuous.

The above situation will be called as externally indeterminate because equations of statics are not sufficient enough to evaluate external reactive torques T_A and T_B. However, member can be internally indeterminate also as discussed below.

7.9.2 Shafts in Parallel

When one shaft is surrounded by other shaft, the two shafts are said to be in parallel.

Consider two shafts placed in parallel as shown in Fig. 7.17.

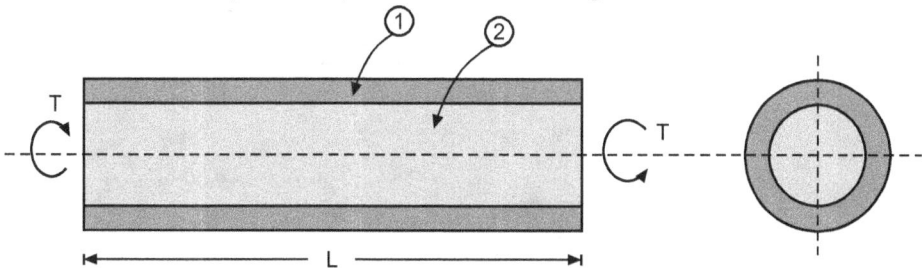

Fig. 7.17 : Shafts in parallel

Let,   T = Total torque acting on the shaft

T_1, T_2 = Torque resisted by individual components 1 and 2 respectively.

Unknown torques are T_1 and T_2, while the equation of statics available is only one i.e.

$$\sum M_z = 0 \quad \Rightarrow \quad T = T_1 + T_2 \qquad \text{... (7.13)}$$

Second equation can be formulated using the fact that the angle of twist for both the shafts for a given length under the action of given torque, is constant. This is the equation of **compatibility** here.

Thus, $\quad\quad\quad\quad\quad\quad\quad\quad \theta_1 = \theta_2$

$$\left(\frac{TL}{GJ}\right)_1 = \left(\frac{TL}{GJ}\right)_2 \quad\quad\quad\quad\quad\quad ...(7.14\ a)$$

Lengths of both components being same for the shaft considered in Fig. 7.17,

$$\left(\frac{T}{GJ}\right)_1 = \left(\frac{T}{GJ}\right)_2 \quad\quad\quad\quad\quad\quad ...(7.14\ b)$$

Solving equations (7.13) and (7.14), values of T_1 and T_2 can be obtained.

The above situation will be called as internally indeterminate because equations of statics are not sufficient enough to evaluate internal resistive torques T_1 and T_2.

Note : In the above analysis, it is assumed that the shafts are co-axially fitted and there is no relative rotation between the two components.

Example 7.22 : A uniform bar AB of length 'L' is fixed at A and B. It is subjected to torque 'T' at 'C' at a distance 'a' from left end and 'b' from right end. Derive expressions for reactive torques developed at A and B and draw torsional moment diagram.

Data   :   As shown in Fig. 7.18 (a).

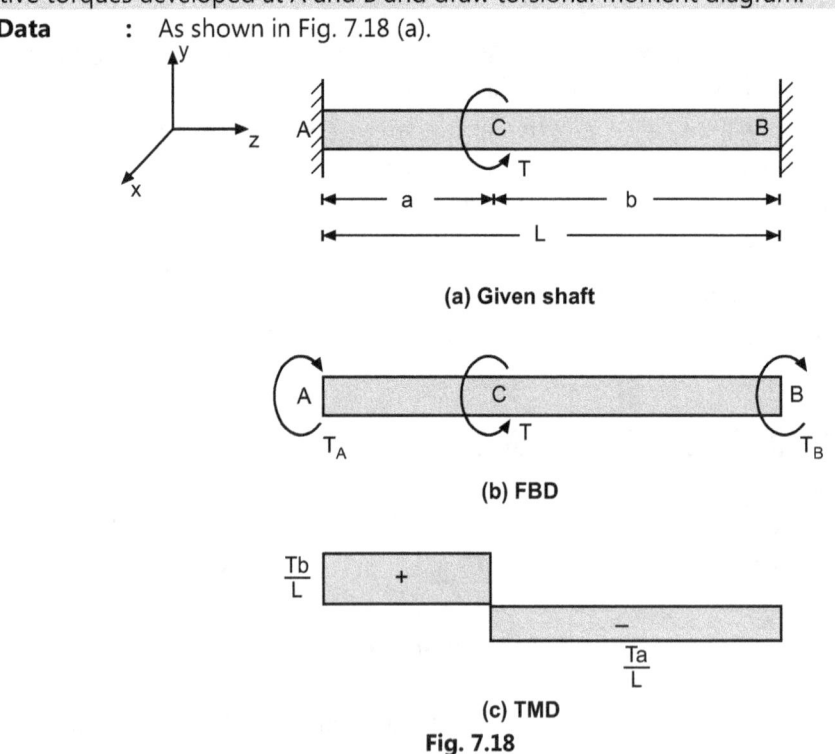

(a) Given shaft

(b) FBD

(c) TMD

Fig. 7.18

Required   :   Expressions for reactive torques.

Concept : Statically indeterminate; equation of statics and compatibility.

Solution : (i) Equation of statics :

$$\sum M_z = 0 ; \qquad T_A + T_B = T \qquad \qquad ...(1)$$

(ii) Equation of compatibility :

$$\theta_{CA} = \theta_{CB}$$

$$\left(\frac{TL}{GJ}\right)_{CA} = \left(\frac{TL}{GJ}\right)_{CB}$$

$$T_A \cdot a = T_B \cdot b \qquad \therefore \qquad T_A = \frac{b}{a} T_B \qquad \qquad ...(2)$$

(iii) Solution of equations :

Solving (1) and (2),

$$T_A = \frac{Tb}{L} \; (\circlearrowleft) \; \text{ and } \; T_B = \frac{Ta}{L} \; (\circlearrowleft)$$

Example 7.23 : A steel shaft ABCD is subjected to torques as shown in Fig. 7.19. (i) Determine reactive torques at fixed ends, (ii) Draw torsional moment diagram, (iii) Find maximum shear stress and angle of twist. Assume G = 80 GPa.

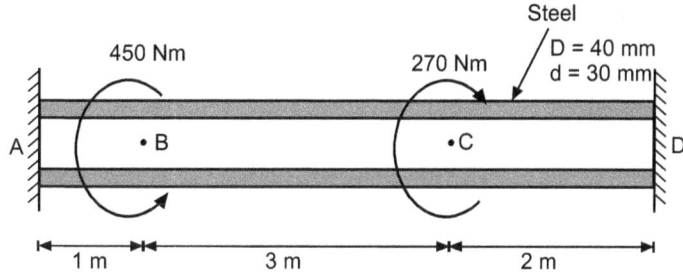

Fig. 7.19

Data : As shown in Fig. 7.19, G = 80 GPa.

Required : Reactive torques at A and D, TMD, Maximum shear stress and angle of twist.

Concept : Statically indeterminate problem, use of standard results and principle of superposition.

Solution : (i) Reactive torques :

Using standard result and principle of superposition.

Reactions due to 450 Nm ($\circlearrowleft$), $T_A = \dfrac{450 \times 5}{6} = $ **375 Nm** ($\circlearrowleft$)

$$T_D = \frac{450 \times 1}{6} = \textbf{75 Nm } (\circlearrowleft)$$

Reactions due to 270 Nm (↺),

$$T_A = \frac{270 \times 2}{6} = \textbf{90 Nm } (\circlearrowleft)$$

$$T_D = \frac{270 \times 4}{6}$$

$$= \textbf{180 Nm } (\circlearrowleft)$$

Final reactions, $T_A = 375 - 90$

$$= \textbf{285 Nm } (\circlearrowleft)$$

$$T_B = 75 - 180$$

$$= -105 \text{ Nm} = \textbf{105 Nm } (\circlearrowleft)$$

(ii)   FBD and torsional moment diagram :

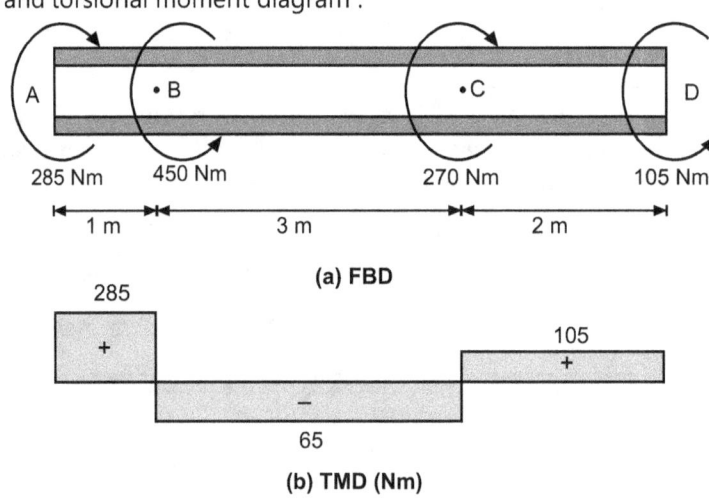

(a) FBD

(b) TMD (Nm)

Fig. 7.20

(iii)   Geometric properties :

$$J = \frac{\pi}{32} [(40)^4 - (30)^4] = 171.8 \times 10^3 \text{ mm}^4$$

$$R = \frac{40}{2} = 20 \text{ mm}$$

$$\frac{J}{R} = \frac{171.8 \times 10^3}{20} = \textbf{8.59} \times \textbf{10}^3 \textbf{ mm}^3$$

(iv)   Maximum shear stress (τ_{max}) :

Maximum shear stress will occur in portion AB.

$$\therefore \qquad \tau_{max} = \frac{T_{AB}}{(J/R)} = \frac{285 \times 10^3}{8.59 \times 10^3} = \textbf{33.18 MPa}$$

(v)   Maximum angle of twist :

$$\theta_{AB} = \left(\frac{TL}{GJ}\right)_{AB} = \frac{285 \times 10^3 \times 1000}{80 \times 10^3 \times 171.8 \times 10^3} = \textbf{0.0207 rad} \; (\circlearrowleft)$$

$$\theta_{BC} = \left(\frac{TL}{GJ}\right)_{BC} = \frac{165 \times 10^3 \times 3000}{80 \times 10^3 \times 171.8 \times 10^3} = \textbf{0.036 rad} \quad (\circlearrowleft)$$

$$\theta_{CD} = \left(\frac{TL}{GJ}\right)_{CD} = \frac{105 \times 10^3 \times 2000}{80 \times 10^3 \times 171.8 \times 10^3} = \textbf{0.0153 rad} \; (\circlearrowleft)$$

∴   Maximum angle of twist = 0.036 rad = 2.063° which occurs in portion BC.

Note : Total angle of twist from A to D

$$= \theta_{AB} + \theta_{BC} + \theta_{CD}$$
$$= -0.0207 + 0.036 - 0.0153$$
$$= 0 \;\; \text{(Ends A and D are fixed)}.$$

Example 7.24 : A compound shaft shown in Fig. 7.21 is attached to rigid supports. Determine the ratio of lengths 'b' to 'a' so that each material is stressed to its permissible limit. What torque T is applied ? Assume G_b = 42 GPa; G_s = 84 GPa; $\tau_b \leq$ 70 MPa; $\tau_s \leq$ 100 MPa.

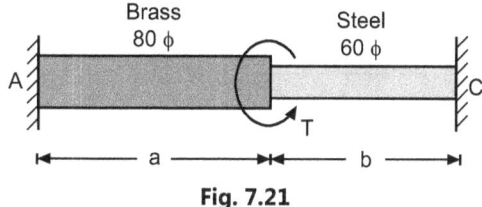

Fig. 7.21

Data   :   As shown in Fig. 7.21.

Required :   Ratio $\dfrac{b}{a}$ and T.

Concept   :   Both materials brass and steel are stressed to their permissible limit, hence torques on portions AB and BC are known. Equation of equilibrium and compatibility.

Solution :   (i) Geometric properties :

Component	J (mm⁴)	R (mm)	$\left(\dfrac{J}{R}\right)$ (mm³)
Brass	$\dfrac{\pi}{32}$ (80)⁴ = 4.02 × 10⁶	$\dfrac{80}{2}$ = 40	100.5 × 10³
Steel	$\dfrac{\pi}{32}$ (60)⁴ = 1.27 × 10⁶	$\dfrac{60}{2}$ = 30	42.41 × 10³

(ii)   Torque for components :

$$T_{brass} \; = \; \text{Reactive torque at A} = T_A$$

$$= \; \left(\frac{J}{R}\right)_b \cdot \tau_b$$

$$= \; 100.5 \times 10^3 \times 70$$

$$= \; \textbf{7.035} \times \textbf{10}^6 \; \textbf{Nmm}$$

$$T_{steel} \; = \; \text{Reactive torque at C} = T_C$$

$$= \; \left(\frac{J}{R}\right)_s \cdot \tau_s$$

$$= \; 42.41 \times 10^3 \times 100$$

$$= \; \textbf{4.241} \times \textbf{10}^6 \; \textbf{Nmm}$$

(iii)   FBD and torsional moment diagram :

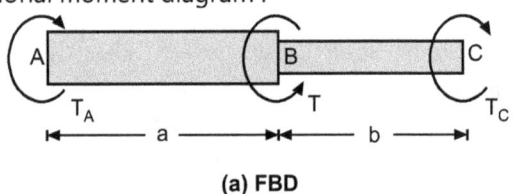

(a) FBD

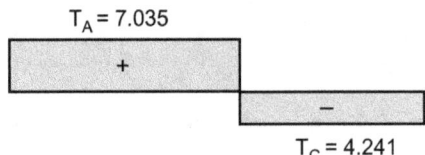

$T_A = 7.035$

$T_C = 4.241$

(b) TMD (kNm)

Fig. 7.22

(iv)   Compatibility :

$$\theta_{BA} \; = \; \theta_{BC}$$

$$\left(\frac{TL}{GJ}\right)_{BA} \; = \; \left(\frac{TL}{GJ}\right)_{BC}$$

Substituting, $\dfrac{7.035 \times 10^6 \times a}{42 \times 10^3 \times 4.02 \times 10^6} \; = \; \dfrac{4.241 \times 10^6 \times b}{84 \times 10^3 \times 1.27 \times 10^6}$

∴ $\dfrac{b}{a} \; = \; \textbf{1.048}$

(v)   Equilibrium : $T \; = \; T_A + T_C$

$$= \; (7.035 + 4.241) \times 10^6$$

$$= \; \textbf{11.276} \times \textbf{10}^6 \; \textbf{Nmm}$$

Example 7.25 : A shaft ABC fixed at 'A' and 'B' is subjected to torque of 42.5 Nm at 'C' as shown in Fig. 7.23. Calculate the end reactions and shear stresses in both components. Also find angle of twist at junction 'C'.

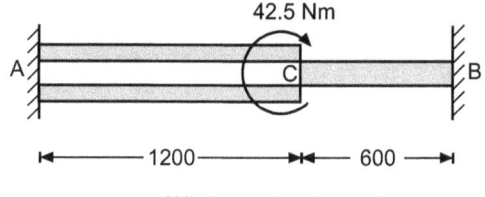

42.5 Nm

|←———— 1200 ————→|←— 600 —→|

(All dimensions in mm)

Fig. 7.23

Data : As shown in Fig. 7.23.

Required : End reactions, shear stresses, and angle of twist at 'C'.

Concept : Equations of equilibrium and compatibility.

AC	CB
Brass	**Steel**
D = 30 mm	D = 20 mm
d = 20 mm	
G_b = 39 GPa	G_s = 79 GPa

Solution : (i) Geometric properties :

Component	J (mm⁴)	R (mm)	$\left(\dfrac{J}{R}\right)$ (mm³)
Brass	$\dfrac{\pi}{32}$ [(30)⁴ – (20)⁴] = 63.81 × 10³	$\dfrac{30}{2}$ = 15	4.254 × 10³
Steel	$\dfrac{\pi}{32}$ (20)⁴ = 15.71 × 10³	$\dfrac{20}{2}$ = 10	1.571 × 10³

(ii) Equation of statics :

$$T = T_A + T_B$$
$$42.5 = T_A + T_B \qquad \ldots (1)$$

(iii) Equation of compatibility :

$$\theta_{CA} = \theta_{CB}$$
$$\left(\frac{TL}{GJ}\right)_{CA} = \left(\frac{TL}{GJ}\right)_{CB}$$

Substituting, $\dfrac{T_A \times 1200}{39 \times 10^3 \times 63.81 \times 10^3} = \dfrac{T_B \times 600}{79 \times 10^3 \times 15.71 \times 10^3}$

$$T_A = T_B \qquad \ldots (2)$$

(iv) Solution of equations :

Solving equations (1) and (2),

$$\mathbf{T_A = T_B = 21.25 \ Nm}$$

(v)   Shear stresses :

$$\tau_{brass} = \left(\frac{T}{J/R}\right)_{brass} = \frac{21.25 \times 10^3}{4.254 \times 10^3} = \textbf{4.99 MPa}$$

$$\tau_{steel} = \left(\frac{T}{J/R}\right)_{steel} = \frac{21.25 \times 10^3}{1.571 \times 10^3} = \textbf{13.52 MPa}$$

(vi)   Angle of twist at C :

$$\theta_{CA} = \theta_{CB} = \left(\frac{TL}{GJ}\right)_{brass} \quad OR \quad \left(\frac{TL}{GJ}\right)_{steel}$$

$$= \frac{21.25 \times 10^3 \times 1200}{39 \times 10^3 \times 63.81 \times 10^3}$$

$$= 0.0102 \text{ rad.}$$

$$= \textbf{0.587}^\circ$$

Example 7.26 : For a compound shaft ABC shown in Fig. 7.24 if allowable shear stress is 70 MPa, find the safe value of torque T at C.

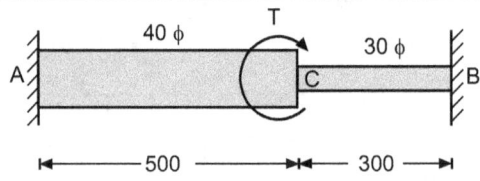

(All dimensions in mm)

Fig. 7.24

Data   :   As shown in Fig. 7.24; τ_{max} = 70 MPa.

Required :   Safe value of torque T at C.

Concept   :   Equations of statics and compatibility.

Solution   :   (i) Geometric properties :

Component	J (mm⁴)	R (mm)	$\left(\dfrac{J}{R}\right)$ (mm³)
AC	$\dfrac{\pi}{32}(40)^4 = 251.33 \times 10^3$	$\dfrac{40}{2} = 20$	12.57×10^3
CB	$\dfrac{\pi}{32}(30)^4 = 79.52 \times 10^3$	$\dfrac{30}{2} = 15$	5.3×10^3

(ii)   Equation of compatibility :

$$\theta_{CA} = \theta_{CB}$$

$$\left(\frac{TL}{GJ}\right)_{CA} = \left(\frac{TL}{GJ}\right)_{CB}$$

$$\frac{T_A \times 500}{251.33 \times 10^3} = \frac{T_B \times 300}{79.52 \times 10^3} \qquad (\because \ G = \text{constant})$$

$$\therefore \qquad T_A = \textbf{1.896 } T_B \qquad \qquad \dots (1)$$

(iii)   Equation of equilibrium :

$$T = T_A + T_B$$

Let, stress in portion CB reaches to allowable value of 70 MPa.

$$\therefore \qquad T_B = \left(\frac{J}{R}\right)_{CB} \tau_{CB} = 5.3 \times 10^3 \times 70$$

$$= \textbf{371} \times \textbf{10}^3 \textbf{ Nmm}$$

Put T_B in equation (1)

$$T_A = 1.896 \times 371 \times 10^3 = \textbf{703.416} \times \textbf{10}^3 \textbf{ Nmm}$$

$$\therefore \qquad \tau_{AC} = \frac{T_A}{(J/R)_{AC}} = \frac{703.416 \times 10^3}{12.57 \times 10^3} = 55.96 \text{ MPa} < 70 \text{ MPa (OK)}$$

$$\therefore \qquad T = (703.416 + 371) \times 10^3$$

$$= 1074.416 \times 10^3 \text{ Nmm}$$

$$= \textbf{1074.416 Nm}$$

Note : If stress calculated for portion AC is greater than 70 MPa, allow portion AC to get stressed to 70 MPa and find corresponding stress in portion CB. Stress calculated for portion CB will then be less than 70 MPa.

Example 7.27 : A composite shaft consists of copper rod 40 mm ϕ enclosed in a steel tube of 50 mm external diameter and 5 mm thickness. There is no relative motion between the two and shafts are coaxially fixed. Determine shear stresses developed in copper and steel rods if both the shafts have equal lengths. Assume G_c = 40 GPa; G_s = 80 GPa and torque = 1400 Nm.

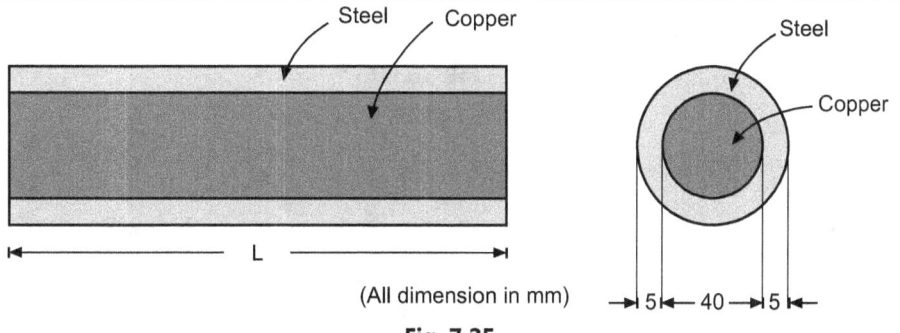

(All dimension in mm)

Fig. 7.25

Data : As shown in Fig. 7.25, $G_c = 40$ GPa, $G_s = 80$ GPa, $T = 1400$ Nm.

Required : Shear stresses for steel and copper.

Concept : Statically indeterminate problem; Equation of statics : $T_s + T_c = T$.

Equation of compatibility : $\theta_s = \theta_c$.

Solution : (i) Geometric properties :

For copper, $J_c = \dfrac{\pi}{32} (40)^4 = 251.33 \times 10^3$ mm^4

$R = \dfrac{40}{2} = 20$ mm

$\therefore$ $\left(\dfrac{J}{R}\right)_c = \dfrac{251.33 \times 10^3}{20} = 12.56 \times 10^3$ mm^3

For steel, $J_s = \dfrac{\pi}{32} [(50)^4 - (40)^4] = 362.26 \times 10^3$ mm^4

$R = \dfrac{50}{2} = 25$

$\left(\dfrac{J}{R}\right)_s = \dfrac{362.26 \times 10^3}{25} = 14.49 \times 10^3$ mm^3

(ii) Equation of statics :

$T = T_c + T_s$

$1400 = T_c + T_s$ ... (1)

(iii) Equation of compatibility :

$\theta_c = \theta_s$

$\left(\dfrac{TL}{GJ}\right)_c = \left(\dfrac{TL}{GJ}\right)_s$ $[\because L_c = L_s]$

$\dfrac{T_c}{40 \times 10^3 \times 251.33 \times 10^3} = \dfrac{T_s}{80 \times 10^3 \times 362.26 \times 10^3}$

$\therefore$ $T_c = 0.3469\, T_s$ ... (2)

(iv) Solution of equations :

Solving (1) and (2), $T_c = 360.58$ Nm

$T_s = 1039.42$ Nm

(v) Shear stresses :

For copper, $\tau_c = \dfrac{T_c}{(J/R)_c} = \dfrac{360.58 \times 10^3}{12.56 \times 10^3} = 28.7$ MPa

For steel, $\tau_s = \dfrac{T_s}{(J/R)_s} = \dfrac{1039.42 \times 10^3}{14.49 \times 10^3} = 71.73$ MPa

Example 7.28 : A composite shaft is made of 40 mm φ steel core enclosed in alloy tube of 60 mm external diameter and 10 mm thickness. There is no relative motion between the two and shafts are coaxially fitted. Permissible shear stress for steel and alloy are 60 MPa and 40 MPa respectively. Find maximum power transmitted by composite shaft at 500 rpm. Assume G_s = 80 GPa and G_a = 44 GPa.

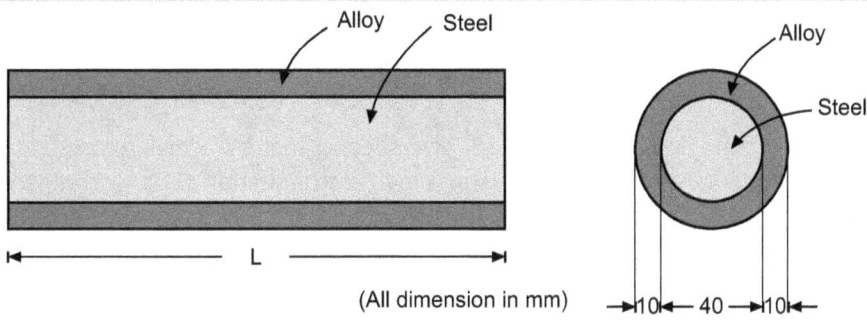

(All dimension in mm)

Fig. 7.26

Data   : τ_s = 60 MPa; τ_a = 40 MPa; G_s = 80 GPa; G_a = 44 GPa;   N = 500 rpm.

Required : Power transmitted by composite shaft.

Concept   : Permissible shear stresses for the two materials are given. It does not mean that both the materials are subjected to given values of stresses. Hence governing stresses shall be found out from angle of twist which is constant for both the shafts.

Solution : (i) Geometric properties :

For steel, $J_s = \dfrac{\pi}{32}(40)^4 = 251.33 \times 10^3 \text{ mm}^4$

$R = \dfrac{40}{2} = 20 \text{ mm}$

∴ $\left(\dfrac{J}{R}\right)_s = \dfrac{251.33 \times 10^3}{20} = \mathbf{12.57 \times 10^3 \text{ mm}^3}$

For alloy, $J_a = \dfrac{\pi}{32}[(60)^4 - (40)^4] = 1021.01 \times 10^3$

$R = \dfrac{60}{2} = 30 \text{ mm}$

∴ $\left(\dfrac{J}{R}\right)_a = \dfrac{1021.01 \times 10^3}{30} = \mathbf{34.03 \times 10^3 \text{ mm}^3}$

(ii)   Governing stresses using compatibility :

$$\theta_s = \theta_a$$

$$\left(\frac{\tau L}{GR}\right)_s = \left(\frac{\tau L}{GR}\right)_a \qquad \left(\because \text{using } \frac{\tau}{R} = \frac{G\theta}{L}\right)$$

$$\frac{\tau_s}{80 \times 10^3 \times 20} = \frac{\tau_a}{44 \times 10^3 \times 30}$$

$$\tau_s = \mathbf{1.21\ \tau_a} \qquad \qquad \dots (1)$$

Let stress in alloy is allowed to reach to 40 MPa.

$$\text{Stress in steel} = \tau_s = 1.21 \times 40 = \mathbf{48.4\ MPa < 60\ MPa} \qquad \dots \text{(OK)}$$

Note : If this condition is not satisfied, give second trial by allowing stress in steel to reach its permissible value and find stress in alloy using equation (1) and compare it with permissible stress.

Thus, in our case, $\tau_a = 40$ MPa and $\tau_s = 48.4$ MPa

(iii)   Torque by composite shafts from statics :

$$T_a = \left(\frac{J}{R}\right)_a \times \tau_a = 34.03 \times 10^3 \times 40 = \mathbf{1.36 \times 10^6\ Nmm}$$

$$T_s = \left(\frac{J}{R}\right)_s \times \tau_s = 12.57 \times 10^3 \times 48.4 = \mathbf{0.608 \times 10^6\ Nmm}$$

$$\therefore \qquad T = T_a + T_s = (1.36 + 0.608) \times 10^6 = \mathbf{1.968 \times 10^6\ Nmm}$$

$$= \mathbf{1.968 \times 10^3\ Nm.}$$

(iv)   Power transmitted (P) :

$$P = \frac{2\pi\ NT}{60} = \frac{2\pi \times 500 \times 1.968 \times 10^3}{60}$$

$$= 103.04 \times 10^3\ W$$

$$= \mathbf{103.04\ \ kW}$$

Example 7.29 : A shaft of 80 mm diameter transmits 150 kN power at 180 r.p.m. A flanged coupling is keyed to the shaft by means of a key 100 mm long and 30 mm wide. The coupling has 6 bolts of 20 mm diameter symmetrically arranged along a bolt circle of 200 mm diameter. Calculate the shear stress in the shaft, the key and the bolts of the coupling.

Solution : (i) For shaft, $J = (\pi/32)\,(80)^4 = 4.02 \times 10^6\ mm^4$

$$P = \frac{(2\pi NT)}{60}$$

$$150 \times 10^3 = \frac{2\pi \times 180 \times T}{60} \qquad \therefore\ T = \mathbf{7957.74\ Nm}$$

$$\tau = (T/J) \times R = \frac{7957.74 \times 10^3}{4.02 \times 10^6} \times 40 = \mathbf{79.18\ MPa}$$

(ii) For key,   Shear force $= \dfrac{T}{R} = \dfrac{7957.74 \times 10^3}{40} = $ **198943.5 N**

Shear stress $= \dfrac{198943.5}{100 \times 30} = $ **66.31 MPa**

(iii) For bolts, $\tau = (T/J) \times R'$

$= \dfrac{7957.74 \times 10^3}{6 \times (\pi/4) \times (20)^2 \times (100)^2} (100) = $ **42.21 MPa**

Example 7.30 : A bar of steel is 40 mm in diameter and 450 mm long. A tensile load of 100 kN is found to stretch the bar by 0.25 mm. The same bar when subjected to a torque of 1.2 kNm, is found to twist through 2°. Find the values of four elastic constants.

Solution : (i) $A = 1256.63 \text{ mm}^2$

$J = 251.32 \times 10^3 \text{ mm}^4$

(ii) $\delta_L = \dfrac{PL}{AE}$

$\therefore$ $0.25 = \dfrac{100 \times 450}{1256.63 \, E}$

$\therefore$ $E = $ **143.24 GPa**

(iii) $\theta = \dfrac{TL}{GJ}$

$\dfrac{2\pi}{180} = \dfrac{1.2 \times 10^3 \times 450}{G \times 251.32 \times 10^3}$ $\therefore G = $ **61.55 GPa**

(iv) $E = 2G(1 + \upsilon) = 3K(1 - 2\upsilon)$

$\therefore$ $\nu = 0.163; \; K = 70.96 \text{ GPa}$

Example 7.31 : A steel shaft (G = 80 GPa) of total length 4 m is encased over half its length by a brass tube (40 GPa) that is securely bonded to the steel as shown in Fig. 7.27. The diameters of the shaft and tube are 70 mm and 90 mm respectively.

(i)   Determine the allowable torque T_1 if the angle of twist θ between ends A and C is limited to $\theta = 12°$.

(ii) Determine the allowable torque T_2 if the shear stress in brass is limited to $\tau_b = 100$ MPa.

(iii) Determine the allowable torque T_3 if the shear stress in steel is limited to $\tau_s = 80$ MPa.

(iv) What is the allowable torque T, if all three of the preceding conditions must be satisfied ?

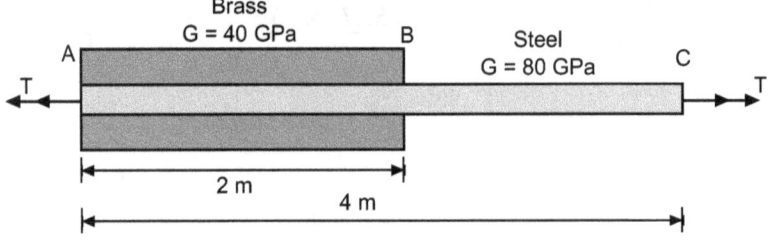

Fig. 7.27

Solution : (i) J_{AB} = J_{Brass} = $4.084 \times 10^6 \, mm^4$

            J_{BC} = J_{steel} = $2.35 \times 10^6 \, mm^4$

Apparent shear modulus for portion AB

$$G' = \frac{G_S J_S + G_B J_B}{J_S + J_B} = 54.609 \, GPa$$

(ii)   For $\theta \leq 12°$,

        $\theta_{A/C}$ = $\{TL/GJ\}_{AB + BC}$

$\dfrac{12\pi}{180}$ = $(T \times 2000) \{(1/54.609 \times 10^3 \times 6.434 \times 10^6) + (1/80 \times 10^3 \times 2.35 \times 10^6)\}$

        T = **12.82×10^6 Nmm**   ... (i)

(iii)   For $\tau_B \leq 100$ MPa,

∴ τ_S = 155.55 MPa (equating angle of twist)

        T = $\{(J/R) \cdot \tau\}_B + \{(J/R) \cdot \tau\}_S$ = 19.51×10^6

            = **19.51×10^6 Nmm**   ... (ii)

(iv)   For $\tau_S \leq 80$ MPa,

        T = $\{(J/R) \tau\}_S$ = $2.35 \times 10^6 \times 80/35$

            = **5.37×10^6 Nmm**   ... (iii)

If all above conditions are to be satisfied, safe torque = **5.37 kN/m.**

Example 7.32 : A 2.5 m long solid steel shaft of 30 mm diameter rotates at a frequency of 30 Hz. Determine the maximum power that the shaft may transmit, knowing that the allowable shearing stress is 50 MPa and that the angle of twist must not exceed 7.5°. Take G = 80 GPa.

Solution : (i)   J = $79.52 \times 10^3 \, mm^4$

(ii)   Strength criteria :

$$\frac{T}{J} = \frac{\tau_{max}}{R}$$

            T = $79.52 \times 10^3 \times \dfrac{50}{15}$ = **265.07×10^3 Nmm**   ... (i)

(iii) Stiffness criteria : $\dfrac{T}{J} = \dfrac{G\theta}{L}$

$$T = \dfrac{79.52 \times 10^3 \times 80 \times 10^3 \times 7.5\pi}{180 \times 2500} = \mathbf{333.1 \times 10^3 \ Nmm} \quad ...(ii)$$

Safe torque $= 265.07 \times 10^3 \, \text{Nmm} = \mathbf{265.07 \ Nm}$

(iv)   Power $= 2\pi \, NT$

$$= 2\pi \times 30 \times 265.07 = 49.96 \times 10^3 \, \text{watts}$$

Example 7.33 : A tube of 50 mm outside diameter and 2 mm thickness is attached to a solid shaft of 25 mm diameter as shown in Fig. 7.28. If both the tube and the shaft are of the same material, what percentage of applied torque T is carried by the tube ?

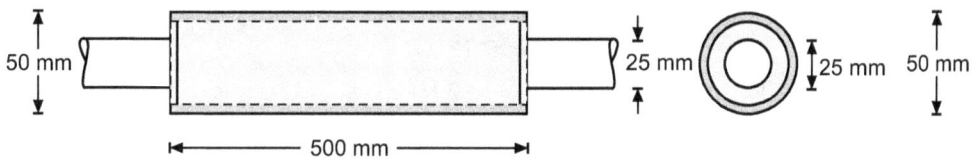

Fig. 7.28

Data : As shown in Fig. 7.28.

Required : Torque carried by the tube.

Solution :

$$T = T_t + T_s$$

$$J_t = \dfrac{\pi}{32} \left[(50)^4 - (46)^4 \right]$$

$$= 174.02 \times 10^3 \, \text{mm}^4$$

$$J_s = \dfrac{\pi}{32} D^4 = \dfrac{\pi}{32} \times (25)^4$$

$$= 38.35 \times 10^3 \, \text{mm}^4$$

$$Q_t = Q_s$$

∴ $$\left(\dfrac{TL}{GJ} \right)_t = \left(\dfrac{TL}{GJ} \right)_s$$

$$\dfrac{T_t \times 500}{G \times 174.02 \times 10^3} = \dfrac{T_s \times 500}{G \times 38.35 \times 10^3}$$

$$T_t = 4.54 \, T_s$$

∴ $$T = T_t + 0.22 \, T_t$$

∴ $$T_t = \dfrac{T}{1.22} = 0.820 \, T$$

∴   82% torque is carried by the tube.

Example 7.34 : Modulus of rigidity of steel and brass are respectively G_s = 80 GPa and G_b = 36 GPa for the shaft shown in Fig. 7.29. If the allowable shear stresses in steel and brass are respectively τ_s = 82 MPa and τ_b = 50 MPa, determine the maximum permissible torque T that may be applied to the shaft.

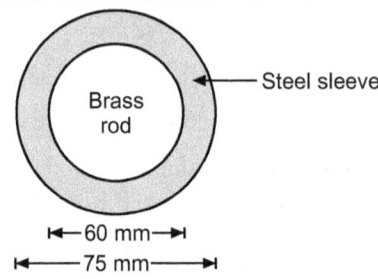

Fig. 7.29

Data : G_s = 80 GPa, G_b = 36 GPa, τ_s = 82 MPa, τ_b = 50 MPa.

Required : Torque.

Solution : (i) Geometric properties :

$$A_b = \frac{\pi}{4} \times (60)^2 = 2827.43 \text{ mm}^2$$

$$A_s = \frac{\pi}{4} [(75)^2 - (60)^2] = 1590.43 \text{ mm}^2$$

$$J_b = \frac{\pi}{32} \times (60)^4 = 1.27 \times 10^6 \text{ mm}^4$$

$$J_s = \frac{\pi}{32} [(75)^4 - (60)^4] = 18.68 \times 10^6 \text{ mm}^4$$

(ii)   Governing stresses using compatibility :

$$\theta_b = \theta_s$$

$$\left(\frac{\tau L}{GR}\right)_b = \left(\frac{\tau L}{GR}\right)_s$$

$$\frac{\tau_b \times L}{36 \times 10^3 \times 30} = \frac{\tau_s \times L}{80 \times 10^3 \times \left(\frac{75}{2}\right)}$$

$\therefore$ $\tau_b = 0.36 \, \tau_s$

Let us assume stress in steel is 82 MPa.

$\therefore$ $\tau_b = 29.52$ MPa < 50 MPa

$\therefore$ $\tau_b = 29.52$ MPa and $\tau_s = 82$ MPa

We have $\quad\quad T = T_b + T_s$

$$= \left(\frac{J}{R}\right)_b \times \tau_b + \left(\frac{J}{R}\right)_s \times \tau_s$$

$$= \frac{1.27 \times 10^6}{30} \times 29.52 + \frac{1.83 \times 10^6}{37.5} \times 82$$

$$= 4.01 \times 10^6 \text{ Nmm}$$

$$= 4.01 \text{ kNm}$$

Example 7.35 : A hollow cylindrical shaft is 1.5 m long. It has inner and outer diameter respectively equal to 40 mm and 60 mm. What is the largest torque that can be applied to the shaft if the shearing stress is not to exceed 120 MPa ? What is corresponding minimum value of shearing stress in the shaft ?

Data   : $l = 1.5$ m, $D = 60$ mm, $d = 40$ mm, $\tau_{max} = 120$ MPa

Required : Largest torque and corresponding minimum value of shearing stress.

Concept : Standard formula.

Solution :
$$T = \frac{\tau \times J}{R}$$

$$J = \frac{\pi}{32} (D^4 - d^4)$$

$$= \frac{\pi}{32} (60^4 - 40^4)$$

$$= 1.02 \times 10^6 \text{ mm}^4$$

$$T = \frac{120 \times 1.02 \times 10^6}{30} = \mathbf{4.08 \times 10^6 \text{ N-mm}}$$

$$T_{min} = \frac{4.08 \times 10^6 \times 20}{1.02 \times 10^6} = \mathbf{80 \text{ N/mm}^2}$$

Example 7.36 : A hollow circular steel shaft has external and internal diameters as 75 mm and 30 mm respectively, while the shaft rotates at 120 rpm, its twist was observed as 2 in 4 m length. Using G = 77 GPa, determine the power being transmitted.

Data   : D = 75 mm, d = 30 mm, N = 120 rpm, $\theta = 2°$, $l = 4$ m, G = 77 GPa

Required : Transmitted power.

Concept : Standard formula.

Solution :
$$T = \frac{G \times \theta \times J}{L}$$

$$= \frac{77 \times 10^3 \times 0.0349 \times 3.027 \times 10^6}{4000}$$

$$= 2.034 \times 10^6 \text{ N-mm}$$

$$P = \frac{2\pi NT}{60}$$

$$= \frac{2\pi \times 120 \times 2.034 \times 10^3}{60}$$

$$P = \mathbf{25.56 \times 10^3 \ watt}$$

Example 7.37 : A shaft transmits 75 kW power at 120 rpm. Determine the diameter of shaft if allowable shear stress is 50 N/mm^2. The twist in the shaft shall not exceed 1.5° in 5 m length. Take G = 85 kN/mm^2.

Data   :   Power transmitted = 75 kW = 75×10^3 W,   Speed = 120 rpm,

               $\tau_{allowable}$ = 50 N/mm^2, θ = 1.5,   L = 5 m,   G = 85×10^3 N/mm^2

Required :   Diameter of shaft.

Concept   :   Standard formula.

Solution   :

$$P = \frac{2\pi NT}{60}$$

$$75 \times 10^3 = \frac{2\pi\,(120) \times T}{60}$$

$$T = 5968.31 \text{ N-m}$$

$$T = 5.97 \times 10^6 \text{ N-mm}$$

$$\frac{T}{J} = \frac{\tau_{max}}{R}$$

$$\frac{J}{R} = \frac{T}{\tau_{max}}$$

$$\frac{\pi}{32} \times \frac{D^4}{\frac{D}{2}} = \frac{5.97 \times 10^6}{50}$$

$$\frac{\pi}{18} D^3 = 119400$$

$$D^3 = 684111.61$$

$$D = 88.11 \text{ mm}$$

$$\frac{T}{J} = \frac{G\theta}{L}$$

$$\frac{5.97 \times 10^6}{J} = \frac{85 \times 10^3 \times 1.5}{5000}$$

$$J = \frac{5.97 \times 10^6 \times 5000}{85 \times 10^3 \times 1.5}$$

$$J = 234117.65$$

$$\frac{\pi}{32} D^4 = 234117.65$$

$$D^4 = 2384702.77$$

$$D = \textbf{39.30 mm}$$

Example 7.38 : A hollow shaft whose internal diameter is 0.55 times its external diameter and is to replace a solid shaft of the same material to transmit the same power at the same speed. Find the ratio of external diameter of hollow shaft to diameter of shaft. Find also the % saving in the weight.

Data   : Let the external diameter be D.

                ∴ internal diameter = 0.55 D

Required : Ratio of external diameter of hollow shaft to diameter of solid shaft and % saving in the weight.

Concept : Standard formula.

Solution : $T_h = T_s$

But, $\dfrac{T}{J} = \dfrac{\tau_{max}}{R}$

∴ $T = \dfrac{J\tau_{max}}{R}$

∴ $T_h = T_s$

$$\left[\frac{J\tau_{max}}{R}\right]_h = \left[\frac{J\tau_{max}}{R}\right]_s$$

$$\frac{\pi}{32}\left[\frac{D^4 - (0.55D)^4}{0.5D}\right] = \frac{\pi}{32}\frac{D_s^4}{0.5D_s}$$

$$\frac{0.91\,D^4}{0.5\,D} = 2\,D_s^3$$

$$1.82\,D^3 = 2D_s^3$$

$$0.91\,D^3 = D_s^3$$

$$D_s = 0.97\,D$$

Cross-sectional area of solid shaft, $A_s = \dfrac{\pi}{4}(D_s)^2$

$$= \frac{\pi}{4}(0.97D)^2$$

$$= \frac{\pi}{4}D^2(0.94)$$

Cross-sectional area of hollow shaft,

$$A_h = \frac{\pi}{4}[D^2 - (0.55D)^2]$$

$$= \frac{\pi}{4}D^2(0.70)$$

$$\frac{D_h}{D_s} = \frac{D}{0.91D} = \mathbf{1.098}$$

$$\text{Saving in weight} = \frac{A_s - A_h}{A_s} \times 100$$

$$= \frac{\frac{\pi}{4}D^2(0.97 - 0.70)}{\frac{\pi}{4}D^2(0.94)} \times 100$$

$$= \mathbf{38.57\%}$$

Example 7.39 : A composite shaft consists of a steel rod 100 mm in diameter surrounded by a closely fitting tube of brass fixed to it. Find the outer diameter of the tube so that when a torque is applied to the composite shaft, it will be shared equally by both the materials. If the torque is 20 kNm, calculate maximum shear stress in each material and angle of twist in length of 4 m. Take G_{ST} = 80 GPa, G_{BR} = 40 GPa.

Data   :   Diameter of steel rod = 100 mm, d_{tube} = 100 mm, T = 20 kN-m,

l = 4 m, G_{ST} = 80 GPa, G_{Br} = 40 GPa

Required :   Maximum shear stress and angle of twist.

Concept :   Standard formula.

Solution :

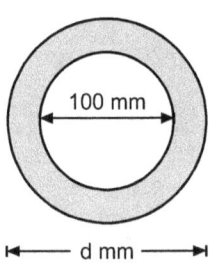

Fig. 7.30

$$J_{St} = \frac{\pi}{32}100^4 = 9.82 \times 10^6$$

$$\theta_{St} = \theta_{Br}$$

$$\left[\frac{TL}{GJ}\right]_{St} = \left[\frac{TL}{GJ}\right]_{Br}$$

$$\left[\frac{1}{80 \times 10^3 \times 9.82 \times 10^6}\right]_{St} = \left[\frac{1}{40 \times 10^3 \times (\pi \times (D^4 - 100^4)/32)}\right]_{Br}$$

$$(D^4 - 100^4) = 2 \times 100^4$$

$$D = 131.6 \text{ mm}$$

$$J_{St} = \frac{\pi}{32}(131.6^4 - 100^4) = 19.63 \times 10^6$$

$$\tau_{St} = \frac{T_{St} \times R}{J}$$

$$= 50.92$$

$$\tau_{St} = \frac{10 \times 10^6 \times (100/2)}{9.82 \times 10^6} = 50.92 \text{ N/mm}^2$$

$$\tau_{br\,max} = \frac{10 \times 10^6 \times (131.2/2)}{19.63 \times 10^6} = 33.42 \text{ N/mm}^2$$

$$\theta_{St} = \left[\frac{TL}{GJ}\right]_{St}$$

$$= \left[\frac{10 \times 10^6 \times 4000}{80 \times 10^3 \times 9.82 \times 10^6}\right] = \mathbf{0.051 \text{ rad}}$$

Example 7.40 : A solid steel rod, 6 m long is fixed at both ends. A torque of 12 kNm is applied at 2.4 m from left end. What are the fixing torques if diameter of shaft is 40 mm ? Find maximum shear stress in two portions. Also calculate angle of twist from the section where torque is applied. Assume G = 80 GPa.

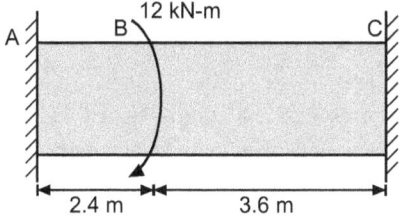

Fig. 7.31

Data   : $l = 6$ m, T = 12 kN-m, D = 40 mm, G = 80 GPa

Required :   Maximum shear stress and angle of twist.

Concept :   Standard formula.

Solution : $\theta_{BA} = \theta_{BC}$

$$\left[\frac{TL}{GJ}\right]_{BA} = \left[\frac{TL}{GJ}\right]_{BC}$$

$$T_{BA} \times 2400 = T_{BC} \times 3600$$

$$T_{BA} = 1.5 \, T_{BC}$$

$$T_{BA} + T_{BC} = 12$$

$$T_{BC} = 4.8 \text{ kN-m}$$

$$T_{BA} = 7.2 \text{ kN-m}$$

$$\tau_B = \frac{T_{AB} \times R}{J}$$

$$\tau = \frac{4.8 \times 10^6 \times (40/2)}{\frac{\pi}{32} \times (40)^4} = \textbf{381.97 N/mm}^2$$

$$\tau_{BC} = \frac{T_{BC} \times R}{J} = \frac{7.2 \times 10^6 \, (40/2)}{\frac{\pi}{32} \times (40)^4} = \textbf{572.96 N/mm}^2$$

$$\theta_{BA} = \left[\frac{TL}{GJ}\right]_{BA}$$

$$\theta_{BA} = \left[\frac{4.8 \times 10^6 \times 2400}{80 \times 10^3 \times 251.33 \times 10^3}\right] = \textbf{0.57 rad}$$

EXERCISE

1. Find the power transmitted by a shaft having 50 mm diameter at 150 rpm if maximum permissible shear stress is 80 MPa. (P = 30.834 kW)

2. A hollow circular shaft of 125 mm external diameter thickness of metal 25 mm is rotating at 150 rpm. The angle of twist on 5 m length was found to be 0.8°. Calculate the power transmitted and maximum shear stress induced in the material. Assume G = 80 GPa. (P = 73.19 kW, τ_{max} = 13.96 MPa)

3. A hollow circular shaft has external diameter of 125 mm and internal diameter of 100 mm. Find the safe power that can be transmitted if allowable shear stress is 100 MPa and maximum angle of twist is 4° for 3.5 m length. Take speed of shaft = 3 revolutions per second and maximum torque to exceed by mean torque by 25%. Take G = 80 MPa.

(P = 340.498 kW)

4. Design the diameter of solid circular shaft to transmit 40 kW power rotating at 120 rpm. Maximum torque is likely to exceed mean torque by 20%. Permissible shear stress = 60 MPa. Also calculate angle of twist for 2.5 m length, assume G = 85 GPa.

(D = 68.698 mm, θ = 2.9435°)

5. A steel shaft of solid circular cross-section has to transmit 220 kW at 200 rpm. The maximum shear stress is not to exceed 50 MPa and angle of twist must not be more than 1.5° in a length of 2.5 m. Design suitable diameter of shaft. Take G = 80 MPa.

    (D (based on strength criteria) = 102.278 mm ,
    D (based on stiffness criteria) = 86.798 mm ∴ D = 102.278 mm)

6. Design the cross-section of hollow shaft for which internal diameter is 3/4th of its external diameter to resist a torque of 2000 Nm such that shear stress does not exceed 60 MPa and angle of twist does not exceed 2° for 2 m length.
    Assume G = 80 GPa.

    (D (based on strength criteria) = 62.85 mm, D (based on stiffness criteria) = 67.96 mm
    ∴ D = 67.96 mm, d = 50.977 mm)

7. A hollow steel shaft 3 m long transmits a torque of 2 kNm. Total angle of twist is not to exceed 3° and permissible shear stress = 80 MPa. Determine inside and outside diameters of shaft, G = 85 MPa.   (D = 107.85 mm, d = 105.05 mm)

8. A hollow shaft has 75 mm external diameter and 50 mm internal diameter. Determine the twisting moment it can resist if permissible shear stress is 110 MPa. Determine the diameter of solid circular shaft made of same material which can transmit same twisting moment. Hence compare their weights per metre length. Take G = 80 GPa.

    (T = 7.312 × 10^6 N.mm, D$_{(solid\ shaft)}$ = 69.69 mm, $\dfrac{\text{Weight of solid shaft}}{\text{Weight of hollow shaft}}$ = 1.55)

9. Design diameter of solid shaft for resisting torque of 3000 Nm. Also design cross-section of hollow shaft made of same material assuming internal diameter as 0.75 times the external diameter for the same torque. Hence comment on percentage saving in weight and shear stress for shaft. Assume allowable angle of twist 2.5° for 2 m length of both shafts. Take G = 80 GPa.

    (D$_{solid}$ = 64.686 mm, (D$_{ext}$)$_{hollow}$ = 71.139 mm, (D$_{int}$)$_{hollow}$ = 53.354 mm
    % saving in weight = 47.085%
    τ_{solid} = 0.909 τ_{hollow} or τ_{hollow} = 1.099 τ_{solid})

10. Design diameter of solid shaft for resisting torque of 3000 Nm. Also design cross-section of hollow shaft made of same material assuming internal diameter 0.75 times the external diameter for the same torque. Hence comment on percentage saving in weight and angle of twist per unit length of shafts. Assume permissible shear stress as 60 MPa.

    (D$_{solid}$ = 63.384 mm, (D$_{ext}$)$_{hollow}$ = 71.952 mm, (D$_{int}$)$_{hollow}$ = 53.965 mm
    % saving in wt. = 43.625%, θ_s = 1.135 θ_h or θ_h = 0.88 θ_s)

11. Compare the weights of equal lengths of hollow and solid shaft to resist same torsional moment for same maximum shear stress. Assume internal diameter 0.75 times the external diameter for hollow shaft. $\left(\dfrac{\text{wt. of hollow shaft}}{\text{wt. of solid shaft}} = 0.564 \right)$

12. The shaft shown in Fig. 7.32 below rotates at 250 rpm with 40 H.P. and 20 HP taken off at A and B respectively and 60 HP applied at C. Find the maximum shear stress developed in the shaft and angle of twist of gear A relative to gear C.

Take G = 85 GPa.   (τ_{max} = 11.399 MPa, θ = 2.034°)

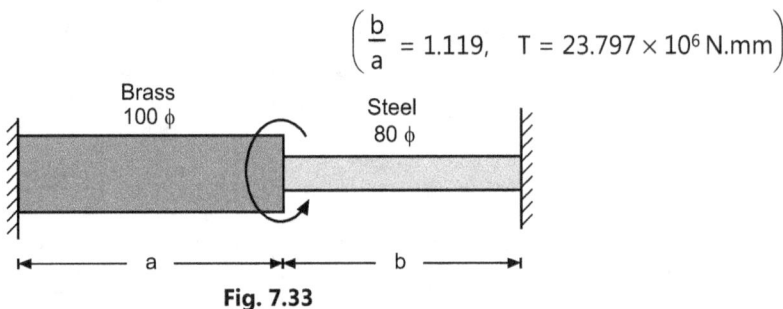

Fig. 7.32

13. A compound shaft as shown in Fig. 7.33 is attached to rigid supports. Determine the ratio of lengths 'b' to 'a' so that each material is stressed to its permissible limit. What torque T is applied ? Assume G_b = 42 GPa, G_s = 84 GPa, $\tau_b \leq$ 70 MPa, $\tau_s \leq$ 100 MPa.

$$\left(\frac{b}{a} = 1.119, \quad T = 23.797 \times 10^6 \text{ N.mm} \right)$$

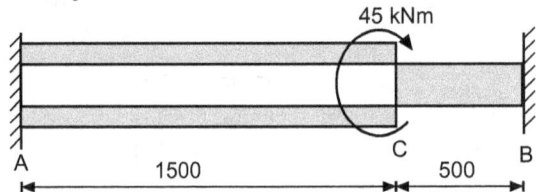

Fig. 7.33

14. A shaft ABC fixed at A and B is subjected to torque of 45 Nm at C as shown in Fig. 7.34. Calculate the end reactions and shear stresses in both components. Also find angle of twist at junction C.

Fig. 7.34

AC	CB
Brass	**Steel**
D = 50 mm	D = 25 mm
d = 25 mm	
G_b = 40 GPa	G_s = 80 GPa

(T_A = 32.142 kNm; T_B = 12.857 kNm; θ_C = 0.12°)

15. A steel bar 40 mm diameter and 500 mm long when tested under an axial tensile load of 150 kN is found to stretch by 0.24 mm. The same bar when subjected to a torque of 1.5 kN.m is found to twist by 2°. Determine the values of four elastic constants.

$$(E = 248.67 \text{ GPa}; \quad G = 85.48 \text{ GPa}; \quad \mu = 0.4545; \quad K = 910.912 \text{ GPa})$$

16. A metal bar 15 mm ϕ subjected to a pull of 40 kN elongates by 0.5 mm over a gauge length of 500 mm. In a torsion test on the same material, maximum shear stress of 45 MPa was measured on a bar of 50 mm ϕ and angle of twist over a length of 300 mm was measured to be 0.4°. Determine Poisson's ratio for the material.

$$(\mu = 0.463)$$

17. A circular shaft supported on bearings 5 m apart transmits 80 kW power at 130 rpm. A pulley provided at 2m from one bearing exerts a transverse load of 50 kN on the shaft. Determine the suitable diameter of shaft if

    (i)   Maximum normal stress is not to exceed 90 MPa.

    (ii) Maximum intensity of shear stress is not to exceed 40 MPa.

$$((i) \text{ D} = 189.52 \text{ mm}, \text{ D} = 197.26 \text{ mm}, \text{ Select D} = 197.26 \text{ mm})$$

18. Fig. 7.35 shows a horizontal shaft AB subjected to torques at C and D. Determine (i) the end fixing couples in magnitude and direction, (ii) the diameter of the shaft if the maximum shear stress is not to exceed 80 MPa, (iii) the position of section where the shaft suffers no angular twist.

$$(T_A = 12.25 \text{ kNm}; \quad T_B = 13.75 \text{ kNm}; \quad D = 95.7 \text{ mm}; \quad 1.182 \text{ m})$$

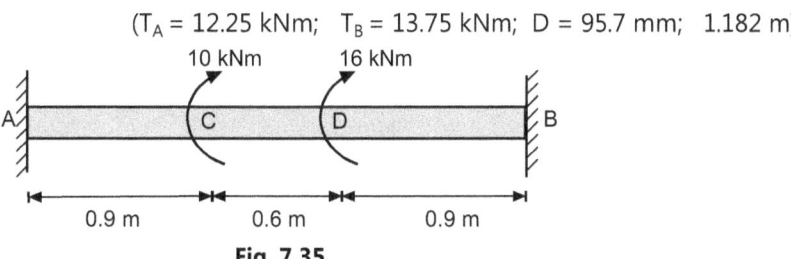

Fig. 7.35

19. A circular shaft supported on bearings 4 m apart transmits 75 kW power at 120 rpm. A pulley provided at 1.5 m from one bearing exerts a transverse load of 40 kN on the shaft. Determine the suitable diameter of shaft if (i) maximum normal stress is not to exceed 90 MPa, (ii) maximum shear stress is not to exceed 40 MPa.

$$((i) \text{ D} = 162 \text{ mm}, \quad (ii) \text{ D} = 169 \text{ mm} \quad \therefore \quad \text{use D} = 169 \text{ mm})$$

20. A solid alloy shaft of 50 mm diameter is to be coupled in series with a hollow steel shaft of the same external diameter. If the angle of twist per unit length of the steel shaft is to be 70% of that of alloy shaft, find the diameter of the steel shaft. Also find the speed at which the shaft should be driven to transmit 20 kW if allowable shear stresses in alloy and steel are 56 MPa and 80 MPa respectively. Assume $G_{steel} = 2.25 \, G_{alloy}$.

$$(38.87 \text{ mm}; \quad 153.3 \text{ rpm})$$

21. Two shafts are of length 'L' and outside diameter D. The first one is solid while the second one is hollow with inside diameter D/2. What is the ratio of strain energies that two steel shafts can absorb without exceeding the allowable shear stress ?

$$\left(\frac{\mu_S}{\mu_H} = \frac{16}{15}\right).$$

22. A hollow circular shaft 20 mm thick transmits 294 kW at 200 rpm. Determine the diameters of the shaft if shear strain due to torsion is not to exceed 8×10^{-4}. Assume G = 80 GPa.   (D = 110 mm; d = 70 mm)

◈ ◈ ◈

HELICAL AND LEAF SPRINGS

8.1 INTRODUCTION

Spring are elastic members whose function is to distort under loads and regain its original dimensions when load is removed.

The springs are made up of high carbon steel or medium carbon alloy steel. Springs are broadly classified into two types as

1. Helical springs : These springs are made up from wire of circular, rectangular or square cross section. They are made of wire coiled into a helical form. Load is applied along the axis of the helix. Helical springs are further classified in to following four types.

    (a) Compression helical springs

    (b) Tension helical spring

    (c) Close-coiled helical springs

    (d) Open-coiled helical spring

2. Leaf springs : Leaf springs are also known as laminated springs. They consist of flat bars of varying lengths clamed together at the centre. Depending upon the shape of the spring, they are classified as elliptical, semi-elliptical spring or cantilever types.

The close-coiled helical spring :

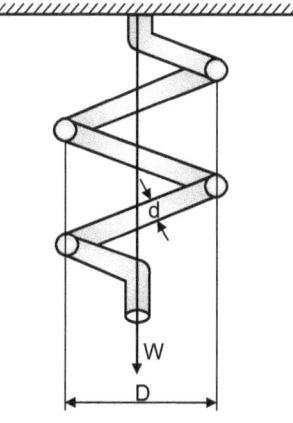

Fig. 8.1

8.2 CLOSED-COILED HELICAL SPRING WITH AXIAL LOAD

Fig. 8.1 shows a closed-coiled helical spring W be the load applied to spring.

r : Radius of the coil.

D : Mean coil diameter

d : Diameter of the wire of the coil

G : Modulus of rigidity

n : no. of coils or turns

θ : Angle of twist

e : length of wire

t : shear stress

J : polar moment of inertia

When the spring is subjected to an axial load, it gets twisted like a shaft. The bending and shear stresses developed at each section are small and hence neglected.

Applying the torsion formula to spring,

$$\frac{T}{J} = \frac{G\theta}{l} = \frac{\tau}{r}$$

$$\therefore \qquad \theta = \frac{Tl}{GJ}$$

$$T = WR, \, l = (2\pi r)n, \, J = \frac{\pi}{32}D^4$$

$$\therefore \qquad \theta = \frac{WR \times 2\pi rn}{G \times \frac{\pi}{32}D^4} = \frac{64\,Wr^2n}{Gd^4}$$

We have, energy stored

$$U = \frac{1}{2}T \cdot \theta = \frac{1}{2} \times \frac{W \times 64 \times W\,r^3n}{Gd^4}$$

$$U = \frac{32\,W^2r^3n}{Gd^4}$$

$$\therefore \qquad \frac{\partial U}{\partial W} = \delta_w = \frac{64\,Wr^3n}{Gd^4}$$

Rectangular And Square Section Wire Springs

We have angle of twist for non-circular solid section as

$$\theta = \left(\frac{\beta}{bh^3}\right)\left(\frac{Tl}{G}\right)$$

$$\beta = 3.5\left[1 + \left(\frac{h}{b}\right)^2\right]$$

(a) Rectangular section : Deflection of spring is given by

$$\delta = r \cdot \theta = \left(\frac{r \times \beta}{bh^3}\right)\left[\frac{Wr \times 2\pi r \times n}{G}\right]$$

∴
$$\delta = \frac{2\pi Wr^3 n}{Gbh^3}\left[3.5\left(\frac{b^2 + h^2}{b^2}\right)\right]$$

$$\boxed{\delta = 7\pi\,\frac{Wr^3 n}{G}\left(\frac{b^2 + h^2}{b^3 h^3}\right)}$$

(b) Square section : In case of square section, substitute h = b.

∴
$$\delta = 7\pi\frac{Wr^3 n}{G}\left[\frac{b^2 + b^2}{b^6}\right]$$

$$\boxed{\delta = \frac{14\pi Wr^3 n}{Gb^4}}$$

8.3 CLOSE-HELICAL SPRING WITH AXIAL TWIST

When the material is subjected to twist causes bending effect. Due to bending effect radius of the coil reduces. In this case bending moment is constant throughout and is equal to axial torque T.

Applying flexural formula

$$\frac{M}{I} = \frac{\sigma}{y}$$

∴
$$\sigma_{max} = \frac{M}{I} \cdot y = \frac{T\,(d/2)}{\dfrac{\pi d^4}{64}} = \frac{32T}{\pi d^3}$$

We have
$$\phi = \frac{Ml}{EI}$$

$$= \frac{M \times \pi Dn}{E \times \dfrac{\pi}{64}\,d^4}$$

$$= \frac{64\,MDn}{Ed^4} = \frac{64\,TDn}{Ed^4}$$

Now energy stored

$$U = \frac{1}{2}M \cdot \phi = \frac{T}{2} \times \frac{64\ TDn}{Ed^4} \quad (M = T)$$

$$U = \frac{32\ T^2Dn}{Ed^4}$$

$\therefore$
$$\frac{\partial U}{\partial T} = \theta = \frac{64\ TDn}{Ed^4}$$

$\therefore$
$$\boxed{\theta = \frac{64\ TDn}{Ed^4}}$$

8.4 OPEN-COILED HELICAL SPRING

With axial load Fig. shows a open coiled helical spring subjected to axial load W causes couple WR along the axis of the spring. This couple may be resoled in the two components as shown in Fig.

The couple producing torsion. T = WR cos α

The couple producing bending M = WR sin α.

Deflection of the spring can be calculated easily using energy method.

$\therefore$
$$U = U_T + U_M$$

$$U_T = \text{Strain energy due to moment} = M^2l/2EI$$

$$U_M = \text{Strain energy due to torsion} = T^2l/2GJ$$

$\therefore$
$$\frac{1}{2}W \cdot \delta = \frac{T^2l}{2GT} + \frac{M^2l}{2EI}$$

$$W \cdot \delta = \left[\frac{W^2r^2\cos_2\alpha}{1GJ} + \frac{W^2r^2\ \sin^2\alpha}{EI}\right] 2\pi\ rn\ \sec\ \alpha$$

$\therefore$
$$\delta = 2Wr^3n\pi\ \sec\ \alpha \left[\frac{\cos^2\alpha}{GJ} + \frac{\sin^2\alpha}{EI}\right]$$

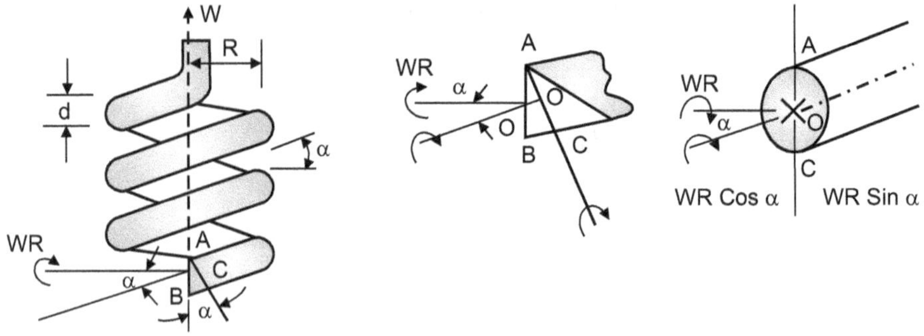

Fig. 8.2 : Open coiled helical spring

Open-coiled helical spring with axial thrust. Let the torque 'T' applied to open coiled spring. This torque may be resoled into two components.

$$T_1 = T \sin \alpha$$

$$M = T \cos \alpha$$

ϕ be the angle of twist.

$\therefore$
$$\frac{1}{2} T \cdot \phi = \frac{T_1^2 l}{2GT} + \frac{M^2 l}{2EI}$$

$\therefore$
$$T\phi = \left[\frac{T^2 \sin^2 \alpha}{GJ} + \frac{T^2 \cos^2 \alpha}{EI} \right] 2\pi \ rn \sec \alpha$$

$\therefore$
$$\phi = 2Trn \, \pi \sec \alpha \left[\frac{\sin^2 \alpha}{GJ} + \frac{\cos^2 \alpha}{EI} \right]$$

Axial deformation is given by

$$\delta = Trl \ \sin \alpha \cos \alpha \left[\frac{1}{GJ} - \frac{1}{EI} \right]$$

$\therefore$
$$\delta = Tr \cdot 2\pi \, rn \sec \alpha \sin \alpha \cos \alpha \left[\frac{1}{GJ} - \frac{1}{EI} \right]$$

$$\delta = 2Tr^2 n\pi \sin \alpha \left[\frac{1}{GJ} - \frac{1}{EI} \right]$$

8.5 LAMINATED SPRING

These springs are called lead or carriage spring.

(a) Semi-elliptical spring :

b : Width of each plate

t : Thickness of each plate

a : Overlap at each end

No. : No. of plates in the spring

l : Spring span length

δ : Initial deflection of plate

R_c : Radius of curvature of plate

The maximum moment occurs at the centre of spring.

$\therefore$
$$\text{Max. B. M.} = \frac{Wl}{4}$$

$\therefore$ Moment resisted by each plate $= \dfrac{Wl}{4N}$

From Fig.

$$R_c^2 = \left(\frac{l}{2}\right)^2 + (R_c - \delta)^2$$

$$R_c^2 = \left(\frac{l}{2}\right)^2 (R_c)^2 - 2R_c\delta + \delta^2$$

Neglecting term δ^2

$\therefore$

$$2R_c\delta = \left(\frac{l}{2}\right)^2$$

$\therefore$

$$\delta = \frac{l^2}{8R_c}$$

$$\frac{M}{I} = \frac{E}{R_c}$$

$\therefore$

$$R_c = \frac{EI}{M} = \frac{E \cdot bt^3}{12 \times \dfrac{Wl}{4N}} = \frac{ENbt^3}{3Wl}$$

$\therefore$

$$\delta = \frac{l^2}{8R_c} = \frac{l^2}{\dfrac{8ENbt^3}{2W_e}} = \frac{2Wl^3}{8ENbt^3}$$

$\therefore$

$$\boxed{\delta = \frac{3Wl^3}{8ENbt^3}}$$

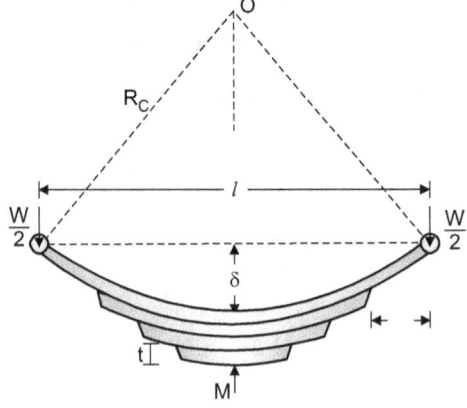

Fig. 8.3 : Laminated semi-elliptical spring

(b) Quarter elliptical spring : These are also called as cantilever laminated spring. This spring is equivalent to semi-elliptical laminated spring considering W = 2W and e = 2e.

$$\therefore \qquad \delta = \frac{3(2W)\,(2l)^3}{8ENbt^3}$$

$$\boxed{\delta = \frac{6Wl^3}{ENbt^3}}$$

Solved Examples

Example 8.1 : *A closely spaced helical spring of 15 mm diameter steel wire wound on a 120 mm mandrel. If there are to active coils, what is spring constant. What force must be applied to the spring to elongate it by 60 mm. Take G = 80 GN/m².*

Solution :

d = 15 mm = 0.015 m

D = 120 mm. r = 0.06 m

n = 10

G = 80 GN/m² = 80 × 10⁹ N/m²

Spring constant = stiffness of spring (k)

$$k = \frac{W}{8} = \frac{Gd^4}{64r^3n}$$

$$= \frac{80 \times 10^9 \times (0.015)^4}{64 \times (0.06)^3 \times 10}$$

$$= 29296.875 \text{ N/m}$$

∴ Force to be applied to elongate 50 mm.

$$\frac{W}{\delta} = k$$

W = k · 8 = 29296.875 × 0.005

W = 1464.84 N

Example 8.2 : *A helical coil spring is made of round steel wire 5.85 mm in diameter. Mean radius of helix is 34.25 mm, no. of complete turns, 15. The spring is closed coil. If G = 82 GN/m², find the pull required to extend the spring by 21.30 mm.*

Solution : Pull required to elongate spring :

$$\delta = \frac{64Wr^3n}{Gd^4}$$

$\therefore$　　　　$$W = \frac{6d^4 \cdot \delta}{64R^3n}$$

$$= \frac{82 \times 10^3 \times (0.00585)^4 \times 0.0213}{64 \times (0.03425)^3 \times 14}$$

$$W = 56.82 \text{ N}$$

Example 8.3 : *A close-coiled spring of 120 mm mean diameter is made of 12 mm diameter and has 18 turns. The spring carries an axial load of 200 N. Determine the deflection. Take G = 85 GN/m².*

Solution : Deflection of spring :

$$\delta = \frac{64\,Wr^3n}{Gd^4}$$

$$= \frac{64 \times 200 \times (0.06)^3 \times 18}{85 \times 10^3 \times (0.012)^4}$$

$$= 0.02824 \text{ m}$$

$\therefore$　　　　$$\delta = 28.24 \text{ mm}$$

Example 8.4 : *For a closed coiled helical spring subjected to an axial load of 300 N having 10 cols of wire diameter 20 mm and made with coil diameter of 225 mm, find*

　(i) *Axial deformation*

　(ii) *strain energy store. Take G = 85 MN/m²*

Solution :

　Wire diameter d = 20 mm

　Coil diameter D = 225 mm

　W = 300 N, G = 85 MN/m²

$\therefore$　Axial deformation

$$\delta = \frac{64\,Wr^3n}{Gd^4} = \frac{64 \times 300 \times \left(\frac{0.225}{2}\right)^3 \times 10}{85 \times 10^9 \times (0.020)^4}$$

$$= 0.0201 \text{ m}$$

$\therefore$　　　　$$\delta = 20.10 \text{ mm}$$

Strain energy stored.

$$U = \frac{1}{2} W \cdot \delta$$

$$= \frac{1}{2} \times 300 \times 0.020$$

$$= 3 \text{ N-m} = 3J$$

Example 8.5 : A closely coiled helical spring having 12 coils each of 100 mm mean diameter and wire of 10 mm diameter is held at one end and twisting moment of 6N-m applied axially about the other end determine the angle of twist. Take E = 200 GN/m².

Solution : Angle of twist

$$\phi = \frac{128 \text{ Mrn}}{Ed^4} = \frac{128 \times 6 \times \left(\dfrac{0.100}{2}\right) \times 12}{200 \times 10^9 \times (0.01)^4}$$

$$= 0.23 \text{ radians}$$

Example 8.6 : An open-coiled helical spring made form wire of circular cross section is required to carry a l;oad of 100 N. The wire diameter is 8 mm and the mean coil radius is 40 mm. If the helix angle of the spacing is 30° and number of turns is 12, calculate : (a) axial deflection (ii) Angular rotation at free end. Take G = 826 Pa, E$_{steel}$ = 200 GPa.

Solution : Axial deflection :

$$\delta = 2Wr^3n\,\pi \sec \alpha \left[\frac{\cos^2\alpha}{GJ} + \frac{\sin^2\alpha}{EI}\right]$$

$$= 2 \times 100 \times (0.04)^3 \times 12 \times \pi \sec 30$$

$$\times \left[\frac{\cos^2 30}{82 \times 10^9 \times \dfrac{\pi}{32}(0.008)^4} + \frac{\sin^2 30}{200 \times 10^9 \times \dfrac{\pi}{64}(0.008)^4}\right]$$

$$= 0.5572\,[0.02275 + 6.217 \times 10^{-3}]$$

$$= 0.01614 \text{ m}$$

$$= 16.14 \text{ mm}$$

Angular rotation :

$$\psi = 2\,Wr^2n\,\pi \sin \alpha \left[\frac{1}{GJ} - \frac{1}{EI}\right]$$

$$= 2 \times 100 \times (0.04)^2 \times 12 \times \pi \sin 30$$

$$\left[\frac{1}{82 \times 10^9 \times \dfrac{\pi}{32} \times (0.008)^4} - \frac{1}{200 \times 10^9 \times \dfrac{\pi}{64}(0.008)^4}\right]$$

$$= 6.032\,[0.03033 - 0.02487]$$

$$= 0.033 \text{ radian.}$$

Example 8.7 : *An open coiled spring consists of 10 coils, each of mean diameter 50 mm, the wire forming the coil being 6 mm the diameter. Each coil makes an angle of 30° with the plane perpendicular to the axis of spring. Determine the load required to elongate the spring by 20 mm. Take G = 82 GN/m², E = 20 GN/m².*

Solution : Load required for elongation :

$$\delta = 2Wr^3m\,\pi\,\sec\alpha\left[\frac{\cos^2\alpha}{GJ} + \frac{\sin^2\alpha}{EI}\right]$$

$$0.020 = 2 \times W \times \left(\frac{0.05}{2}\right)^3 \times 90 \times \sec 30 \times \pi$$

$$\left[\frac{\cos^2 30}{82 \times 10^9 \times \frac{\pi}{32}(0.006)^4} + \frac{\sin^2 30}{200 \times 10^9 \times \frac{\pi}{64} \times 0.0064}\right]$$

$$0.020 = 1.1336 \times 10^{-3}\,W\,[0.07188 + 0.01965]$$

∴ $$W = 192.76\,N$$

Example 8.8 : *A carriage spring made of lamination each 100 mm wide and 8 mm thick and 0.8 m long. The no. of plates when the spring is designed for a maximum central load of 6 kN. What would be deflection under the load when E = 200 GN/m².*

Solution : Central deflection δ :

$$\delta = \frac{2E l^3}{8ENbt^3}$$

$$= \frac{3 \times 6 \times 10^3 \times (0.8)^3}{8 \times 200 \times 10^9 \times 6 \times 0.1 \times (0.008)^3}$$

$$= 0.01875\,m$$

$$= 18.75\,mm$$

EXERCISE

1. Explain open coiled helical spring and close coiled helical spring.

2. Write short notes on laminated spring.

3. Define helical springs and leaf springs.

COMPLEX STRESSES AND PLANE TRUSSES

9.1 INTRODUCTION

The problems studied so far include direct tension, compression and shear separately, but there are many structures in which these various stresses occur in combination. Hence, it is of practical importance to find the resultant stresses which may be greater than the applied ones and also the planes on which they act when subjected to complex stress system.

In general, a three dimensional state of stress is as shown in Fig. 9.1 (a) which indicates nine stress components.

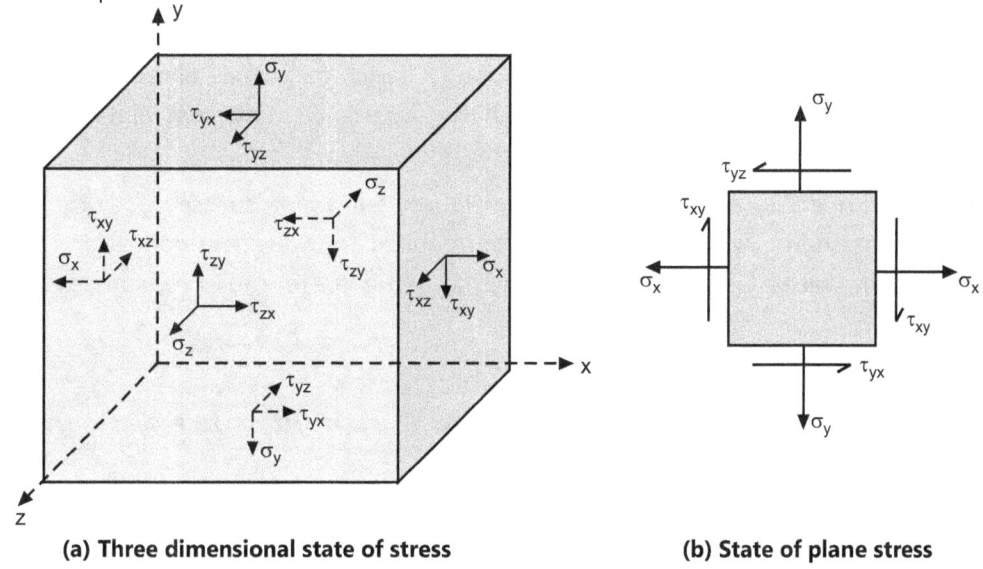

(a) Three dimensional state of stress   **(b) State of plane stress**

Fig. 9.1

The notation used here defines a normal stress by means of single subscript corresponding to the face on which it acts. A face takes the name of the axis normal to it; for example, the x face is perpendicular to x-axis. A shear stress is indicated by double subscript, the first letter corresponding to the face on which it acts and second indicating its direction. Thus, the shear stress on x face acting in the y direction is denoted by τ_{xy}. It should be noted that $\tau_{xy} = \tau_{yx}$ since, the shear stresses on perpendicular planes are equal.

In this text, we consider only plane stress i.e. state of stress that can be represented by components that act parallel to a single plane i.e. stress components normal to the plane of body are zero. State of plane stress is shown in Fig. 9.1 (b).

9.2 Transformation Of Plane Stress

The stress acting at a point is represented by the stresses acting on the faces of the element enclosing the point. These stresses will change as a function of the inclination of the planes passing through that point. Thus, the stresses on the faces of the element vary as the angular position of the element changes.

Two algebraic expressions, one for the normal stress and one for the shear stress, can be developed to give these stresses in terms of the initially known stresses and of an angle of inclination of the plane being investigated. These equations are called equations of *stress transformation.* The derivatives of these algebraic equations with respect to the angle of inclination, when equated to zero, locate the planes on which either the normal or the shear stress reaches maximum or minimum values.

Stress components are vectorial in nature but mathematically they do not obey the laws of vector addition and subtraction, since in addition to having magnitude and direction, they are also associated with unit of area over which they act. Hence, stress components are first converted to forces and then added or subtracted vectorially.

Consider an elementary area of uniform thickness isolated from a stressed body on which stresses are as shown in Fig. 9.2 (a). Let, it be required to investigate normal and shear stresses on any plane AC making an angle θ as shown. Fig. 9.2 (b) shows the stresses acting on wedge ABC.

Let $\qquad$ A = Area of wedge face AC

∴ $\qquad$ A cos θ, A sin θ = Areas of vertical face AB and horizontal face BC respectively.

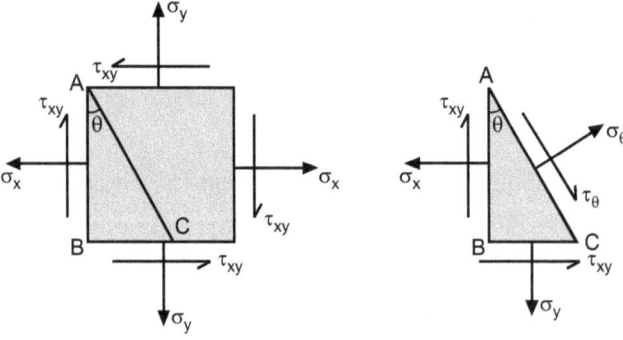

(a) State of plane stress   (b) Stresses on wedge ABC

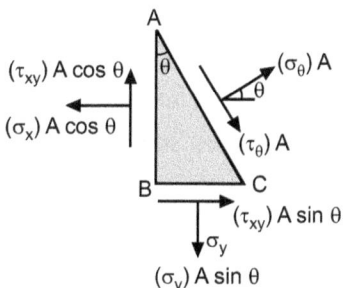

(c) FBD of wedge ABC

Fig. 9.2

Stresses acting on the wedge having converted to forces, FBD of wedge ABC can be drawn as shown in Fig. 9.2 (c).

Using equations of statics ;

Algebraic sum of all the forces acting normal to the face $AC = \sum F_\theta = 0$

$\therefore \qquad (\sigma_\theta)\, A = (\sigma_x\, A \cos\theta)\cos\theta + (\sigma_y\, A \sin\theta)\sin\theta$

$\qquad\qquad\qquad - (\tau_{xy} \cdot A \cos\theta)\sin\theta - (\tau_{xy}\, A \sin\theta)\cos\theta$

$\therefore \qquad \sigma_\theta = \sigma_x \cdot \cos^2\theta + \sigma_y \cdot \sin^2\theta - 2\,\tau_{xy}\sin\theta\cos\theta \qquad\qquad \text{... (9.1)}$

Algebraic sum of all the forces acting tangential to the face $AC = \sum F_t = 0$

$\therefore \qquad (\tau_\theta)\, A = (\sigma_x\, A \cos\theta)\sin\theta - (\sigma_y\, A \sin\theta)\cos\theta$

$\qquad\qquad\qquad + (\tau_{xy}\, A \cos\theta)\cos\theta - (\tau_{xy}\, A \sin\theta)\sin\theta$

$\therefore \qquad \tau_\theta = (\sigma_x - \sigma_y)\sin\theta\cos\theta + \tau_{xy}\,(\cos^2\theta - \sin^2\theta) \qquad\qquad \text{... (9.2)}$

We have, $\qquad \cos^2\theta = \dfrac{1 + \cos 2\theta}{2}$

$\qquad\qquad\qquad \sin^2\theta = \dfrac{1 - \cos 2\theta}{2}$

$\qquad\qquad \sin\theta\cos\theta = \dfrac{\sin 2\theta}{2}$

Using these relations for equations (9.1) and (9.2),

$$\sigma_\theta = \frac{\sigma_x + \sigma_y}{2} + \frac{\sigma_x - \sigma_y}{2}\cos(2\theta) - \tau_{xy}\sin(2\theta) \qquad\qquad \text{... (9.3)}$$

$$\tau_\theta = \frac{\sigma_x - \sigma_y}{2}\sin(2\theta) + \tau_{xy}\cos(2\theta) \qquad\qquad \text{... (9.4)}$$

These equations (9.3) and (9.4) are called as the *equations of stress transformation.*

The angle that the line of action of resultant stress makes with the normal to the plane is called the *obliquity (ϕ).*

$$\tan\phi = \frac{\tau_\theta}{\sigma_\theta} \qquad\qquad \text{... (9.5)}$$

9.3 PRINCIPAL STRESSES

The planes on which maximum or minimum normal stresses occur, there is no shear stress. These planes are called as **principal planes** and the stresses acting on these planes - the maximum and minimum normal stresses – are called as the **principal stresses.** To locate the planes of maximum and minimum normal stresses, differentiate equation (9.3) with respect to 'θ' and equate it to zero

i.e.
$$\frac{d}{d\theta}(\sigma_\theta) = -\frac{\sigma_x - \sigma_y}{2} \cdot 2 \cdot \sin(2\theta) - 2\tau_{xy} \cdot \cos(2\theta) = 0$$

$$\therefore -(\sigma_x - \sigma_y)\sin(2\theta) - 2\tau_{xy}\cos(2\theta) = 0$$

$$\therefore \quad -(\sigma_x - \sigma_y)\tan(2\theta) = 2\tau_{xy}$$

$$\therefore \quad \tan(2\theta_n) = -\frac{2\tau_{xy}}{\sigma_x - \sigma_y} \qquad \ldots (9.6)$$

where, θ_n = Orientation of plane of maximum normal stress.

Note : These planes can also be located by setting τ_θ equal to zero from equation (9.4) which indicates that there is no shear stress on the plane of maximum or minimum normal stress. Equation (9.6) gives two values of ($2\theta_n$) that differ by 180°, hence *principal planes are 90° apart.*

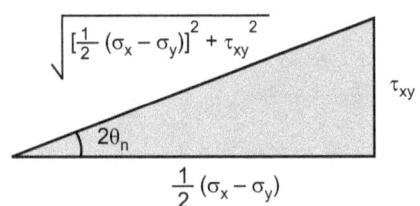

Fig. 9.3

From equation (9.6), we can write

$$\left.\begin{array}{l} \sin(2\theta_n) = \dfrac{\tau_{xy}}{\sqrt{\left[\dfrac{1}{2}(\sigma_x - \sigma_y)\right]^2 + (\tau_{xy})^2}} \\[5ex] \cos(2\theta_n) = \dfrac{\dfrac{1}{2}(\sigma_x - \sigma_y)}{\sqrt{\left[\dfrac{1}{2}(\sigma_x - \sigma_y)\right]^2 + (\tau_{xy})^2}} \end{array}\right\} \qquad \ldots (9.7)$$

Substituting these values of sin $(2\theta_n)$ and cos $(2\theta_n)$ from equation (9.7) in equation (9.3), we get principal stresses as,

$$\sigma_1, \sigma_2 = \frac{\sigma_x + \sigma_y}{2} \pm \sqrt{\left(\frac{\sigma_x - \sigma_y}{2}\right)^2 + (\tau_{xy})^2} \qquad \text{... (9.8)}$$

where; σ_1, σ_2 = Major and minor principal stresses.

Note : + ve sign shall be used to get major principal stress, while – ve sign shall be used to get minor principal stress.

9.4 MAXIMUM SHEAR STRESS

To locate the plane of maximum shear stress, differentiate equation (9.4) with respect to θ and equate it to zero.

i.e. $\dfrac{d}{d\theta}\ (\tau_\theta) = \left(\dfrac{\sigma_x - \sigma_y}{2}\right) 2 \cdot \cos(2\theta) - (\tau_{xy})\ 2 \sin(2\theta) = 0$

$\therefore$ $(\sigma_x - \sigma_y) \cos(2\theta) = 2\ \tau_{xy} \sin(2\theta)$

$\therefore$ $\tan(2\theta_s) = \dfrac{\sigma_x - \sigma_y}{2\ \tau_{xy}}$ ... (9.9)

where, θ_s = Orientation of plane of maximum shear stress.

Equation (9.9) is a negative reciprocal of equation (9.6). That means values of $(2\theta_n)$ defined by equation (9.6) and that of $(2\theta_s)$ defined by equation (9.9) differ by 90°. In other words, *planes of maximum shear stress are inclined at 45° to the principal planes.*

From equation (9.8), we can write,

$$\left. \begin{aligned} \sin(2\theta_s) &= \frac{\frac{1}{2}(\sigma_x - \sigma_y)}{\sqrt{\left[\frac{1}{2}(\sigma_x - \sigma_y)\right]^2 + (\tau_{xy})^2}} \\[2em] \cos(2\theta_s) &= \frac{\tau_{xy}}{\sqrt{\left[\frac{1}{2}(\sigma_x - \sigma_y)\right]^2 + (\tau_{xy})^2}} \end{aligned} \right\} \qquad \text{... (9.10)}$$

Substituting these values of sin $(2\theta_s)$ and cos $(2\theta_s)$ from equation (9.10) in equation (9.4), we get

$$\tau_{max}\ ;\ \tau_{min} = \pm \sqrt{\left(\frac{\sigma_x - \sigma_y}{2}\right)^2 + (\tau_{xy})^2} \qquad \text{... (9.11)}$$

If σ_x and σ_y are principal stresses of σ_1 and σ_2 then τ_{xy} is zero and equation (9.11) simplifies to

$$\tau_{max} = \pm \frac{\sigma_1 - \sigma_2}{2} \qquad \text{... (9.12)}$$

Thus, the maximum shear stress differs from minimum shear stress only in sign.

On the principal planes, shear stresses are zero but on the planes of maximum shear stress, normal stress is not zero. Substituting equation (9.10) in equation (9.3), the magnitude of normal stress (σ') on the plane of maximum shear stress is obtained as ;

$$\sigma' = \frac{\sigma_x + \sigma_y}{2} \qquad \text{... (9.13)}$$

Therefore, normal stress (σ') acts simultaneously with the maximum shear stress.

SOLVED EXAMPLES

Example 9.1 : *A circular bar 40 mm diameter carries an axial tensile load of 100 kN. What is the value of shear stress on the plane on which normal stress has value of 50 MPa, tensile ?*

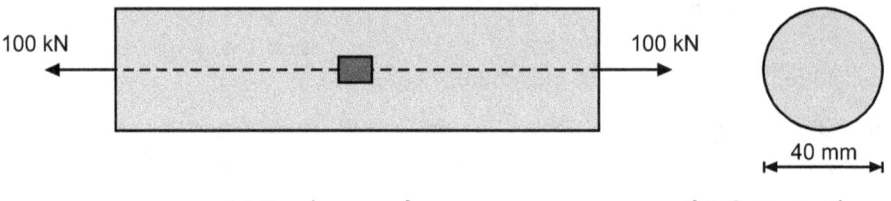

100 kN   100 kN

40 mm

(a) Tension member   (b) Cross-section

Fig. 9.4

Data   :   As shown in Fig. 9.4.

Required   :   Value of shear stress on the plane on which normal stress is 50 MPa, tensile.

Concept   :   Considering an element as shown in Fig. 9.4 find normal stress σ_x and then use standard formulae.

Solution   :   (i) State of stress :

$$\text{Normal stress} = \sigma_x = \frac{P}{A} = \frac{100 \times 10^3}{\frac{\pi}{4}(40)^2}$$

$$= 79.57 \text{ MPa} \quad \text{(Tensile)}$$

State of stress is as shown in Fig. 9.5.

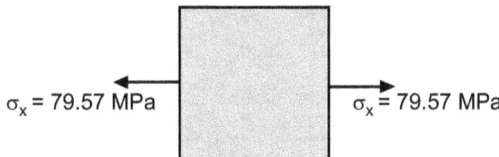

$\sigma_x = 79.57$ MPa $\sigma_x = 79.57$ MPa

Fig. 9.5 : State of stress on element

(ii) Plane on which normal stress is 50 MPa, tensile :

$$\sigma_\theta \;=\; \frac{\sigma_x}{2} + \frac{\sigma_x}{2}\,\cos(2\theta) \qquad\qquad (\because\ \sigma_y = \tau_{xy} = 0)$$

$$50 \;=\; \frac{79.57}{2} + \frac{79.57}{2}\,\cos(2\theta)$$

$$\theta \;=\; 37.56^\circ$$

(iii) Shear stress : $\tau_\theta \;=\; \dfrac{\sigma_x}{2}\,\sin(2\theta)$ $\qquad\left(\because\ \sigma_y = \tau_{xy} = 0\right)$

$$\tau_{37.56^\circ} \;=\; \frac{79.57}{2} \cdot \sin(2 \times 37.56)$$

$$= \mathbf{38.45\ MPa}$$

Example 9.2 : *If an element is subjected to state of stress as shown in Fig. 9.6, find the principal stresses. Also find the stress components on a plane at 30° anticlockwise from x face.*

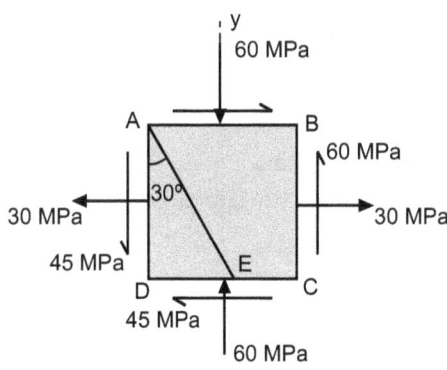

Fig. 9.6 : Given state of stress

Data   :   As shown in Fig. 9.6.

Required :   Principal stresses, stress components on plane AE.

Concept :   Standard formulae.

Solution : (i) Principal stresses :

$$\sigma_1, \sigma_2 = \frac{\sigma_x + \sigma_y}{2} \pm \sqrt{\left(\frac{\sigma_x - \sigma_y}{2}\right)^2 + (\tau_{xy})^2}$$

$$= \frac{30 - 60}{2} \pm \sqrt{\left[\frac{30 - (-60)}{2}\right]^2}$$

$$= -15 \pm 63.63$$

$$\sigma_1 = -78.63 \text{ MPa} = \textbf{78.63 MPa (Compressive)}$$

$$\sigma_2 = \textbf{48.63 MPa (Tensile)}$$

(ii) Stress components on plane AE :

$$\sigma_\theta = \frac{\sigma_x + \sigma_y}{2} + \frac{\sigma_x - \sigma_y}{2} \cos(2\theta) - \tau_{xy} \sin(2\theta)$$

$$= \frac{30 - 60}{2} + \frac{30 - (-60)}{2} \cos(2 \times 30) - (-45) \sin(2 \times 30)$$

$$\sigma_{30°} = 46.47 \text{ MPa (Tensile)}$$

$$\tau_\theta = \frac{\sigma_x - \sigma_y}{2} \sin(2\theta) + \tau_{xy} \cos(2\theta)$$

$$= \frac{30 - (-60)}{2} \sin(2 \times 30) + (-45) \cos(2 \times 30)$$

$$\tau_{30°} = \textbf{16.47 MPa}$$

Example 9.3 : *The principal tensile stresses at a point on two perpendicular planes are 60 MPa and 30 MPa. Find normal, tangential and resultant stress and its obliquity on a plane at 20° with the major principal plane as shown in Fig. 9.7. Also find the intensity of stress which acting alone can produce the same maximum strain. Assume Poisson's ratio $\mu = 0.3$.*

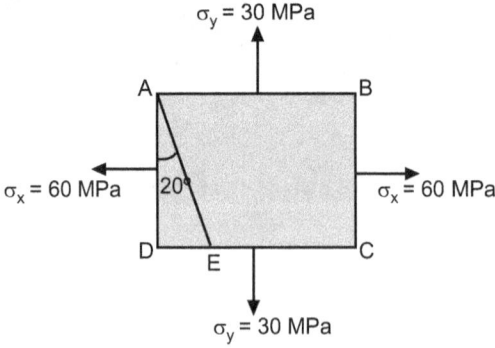

Fig. 9.7 : Given state of stress

Data   :   As shown in Fig. 9.7.

Required :   Normal, tangential, resultant stress and its obliquity on a plane at 20° to major principal plane.

Concept :   Transformation of stress.

Solution :   (i) Normal stress on plane AE :

$$\sigma_\theta = \frac{\sigma_x + \sigma_y}{2} + \frac{\sigma_x - \sigma_y}{2} \cos(2\theta) - \tau_{xy} \sin 2\theta$$

$$= \frac{60 + 30}{2} + \frac{60 - 30}{2} \cos(2 \times 20) - 0$$

$$\sigma_{20°} = \textbf{56.49 MPa} \quad \textbf{(Tensile)}$$

(ii) Shear stress on plane AE :

$$\tau_\theta = \frac{\sigma_x - \sigma_y}{2} (\sin 2\theta) + \tau_{xy} \cos(2\theta)$$

$$= \frac{60 - 30}{2} \sin(2 \times 20) + 0$$

$$\tau_{20°} = \textbf{9.64 MPa}$$

(iii) Resultant stress and its obliquity :

$$\text{Resultant stress} = \sqrt{\sigma_\theta^2 + \tau_\theta^2}$$

$$= \sqrt{(56.49)^2 + (9.64)^2}$$

$$= 57.30 \text{ MPa}$$

$$\text{Obliquity} = \phi = \tan^{-1}\left(\frac{\tau_\theta}{\sigma_\theta}\right)$$

$$= \tan^{-1}\left(\frac{9.64}{56.49}\right)$$

$$= \textbf{9.68°}$$

(iv) Stress (σ) which produces the same principal strain :

$$\text{Principal strain} = \varepsilon_1 = \frac{1}{E} (\sigma_1 - \mu\, \sigma_2)$$

$$= \frac{1}{E} (60 - 0.3 \times 30) = \frac{51}{E}$$

$$\therefore \qquad \frac{\sigma}{E} = \frac{51}{E}$$

$$\therefore \qquad \sigma = \textbf{51 MPa}$$

Example 9.4 : *At a point in a strained material, the state of stress is as shown in Fig. 9.8. Determine : (i) principal stresses, (ii) principal planes, (iii) maximum shear stress and plane on which it acts, (iv) the tensile stress which acting alone will produce same maximum shear stress, and (v) the shear stress which acting alone will produce same maximum tensile principal stress.*

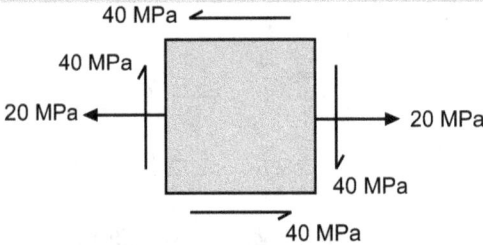

40 MPa

40 MPa

20 MPa ←   → 20 MPa

40 MPa

40 MPa

Fig. 9.8 : Given state of stress

Data   :   As shown in Fig. 9.8.

Required :   As given above in the example.

Concept :   Standard formulae.

Solution :   (i) Principal stresses (σ_1, σ_2) :

$$\sigma_1, \sigma_2 = \frac{\sigma_x}{2} \pm \sqrt{\left(\frac{\sigma_x}{2}\right)^2 + (\tau_{xy})^2} \qquad\qquad (\because \sigma_y = 0)$$

$$\sigma_1, \sigma_2 = \frac{20}{2} \pm \sqrt{\left(\frac{20}{2}\right)^2 + (40)^2}$$

$$= 10 \pm 41.23$$

$$\sigma_1 = \textbf{51.23 MPa (Tensile)}$$

$$\sigma_2 = -31.23 \text{ MPa} = \textbf{31.23 MPa (Compressive)}$$

(ii) Principal planes :

$$\tan (2\theta) = -\frac{2\,\tau_{xy}}{\sigma_x} \qquad\qquad \left(\because \sigma_y = 0\right)$$

$$\tan (2\theta) = -\frac{2 \times 40}{20} = -4$$

$$\theta = \textbf{–37.98°} \text{ and } \textbf{–127.98°}$$

(iii) Maximum shear stress (τ_{max}) :

$$\tau_{max} = \frac{\sigma_1 - \sigma_2}{2} = \frac{51.23 - (-31.23)}{2} = \textbf{41.23 MPa}$$

(iv) Planes of maximum shear :

$$\tan(2\theta) = \frac{\sigma_x}{2\,\tau_{xy}} \qquad (\because \sigma_y = 0)$$

$$= \frac{20}{2 \times 40} = 0.25$$

∴ $\theta = 7°$ and $97°$

(v) The tensile stress which acting alone will produce same maximum shear stress :

$$\tau_{max} = \frac{\sigma_1 - \sigma_2}{2} = \frac{\sigma_1}{2} \qquad (\because \sigma_2 = 0)$$

$$41.23 = \frac{\sigma_1}{2} \qquad \therefore \sigma_1 = 82.46 \text{ MPa (Tensile)}$$

(vi) The shear stress which acting alone will produce same maximum principal tensile stress :

$$\sigma_1 = \frac{\sigma_x + \sigma_y}{2} \pm \sqrt{\left(\frac{\sigma_x - \sigma_y}{2}\right)^2 + (\tau_{xy})^2}$$

$$51.23 = 0 + \tau_{xy}$$

∴ $\tau_{xy} = 51.23$ MPa

Example 9.5 : At a point in a piece of strained material, there are two planes at right angles on which the shear stress intensity is 'τ' along with normal stress intensity of 40 MPa, tensile on one plane and 24 MPa, compressive on the other. If the major principal stress is 56 MPa, tensile, evaluate the smaller principal stress and shear stress τ. Also evaluate maximum shear stress τ_{max} and normal stress on plane of maximum shear.

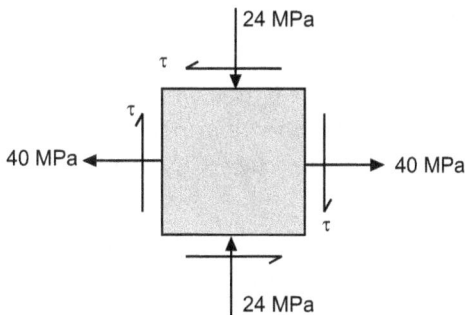

Fig. 9.9 : Given state of stress

Data   : As shown in Fig. 9.9 ; $\sigma_1 = 56$ MPa, tensile

Required   : Shear stress (τ) ; minor principal stress (σ_2) ; τ_{max} and normal stress (σ) on the plane of maximum shear.

Concept   : Standard formulae.

Solution   : (i) Shear stress (τ) :

$$\sigma_1 = \frac{\sigma_x + \sigma_y}{2} + \sqrt{\left(\frac{\sigma_x - \sigma_y}{2}\right)^2 + (\tau_{xy})^2}$$

$$56 = \frac{40 + (-24)}{2} + \sqrt{\left(\frac{40 - (-24)}{2}\right)^2 + (\tau_{xy})^2}$$

$\therefore$ τ_{xy} = **35.78 MPa**

(ii) Minor principal stress (σ_2) :

$$\sigma_2 = \frac{\sigma_x + \sigma_y}{2} - \sqrt{\left(\frac{\sigma_x - \sigma_y}{2}\right)^2 + (\tau_{xy})^2}$$

$$= \frac{40 + (-24)}{2} - \sqrt{\left(\frac{40 - (-24)}{2}\right)^2 + (35.78)^2}$$

$$= -40 \text{ MPa}$$

$$= 40 \text{ MPa} \quad \textbf{(Compressive)}$$

(iii) Maximum shear stress (τ_{max}) :

$$\tau_{max} = \frac{\sigma_1 - \sigma_2}{2} = \frac{56 - (-40)}{2} = \textbf{48 MPa}$$

(iv) Normal stress (σ) on the plane of maximum shear :

$$\sigma = \frac{\sigma_x + \sigma_y}{2} = \frac{40 - 24}{2} = \textbf{8 MPa (tensile)}$$

Example 9.6 : *At a point in a strained material subjected to two dimensional state of stress, one of the principal stress is 78 MPa, tensile on a plane at 60° to this principal plane, the normal stress is zero. Determine : (i) the other principal stress, (ii) the shear stress on the plane of zero normal stress, and (iii) the planes on which the normal and shear stresses are equal in magnitude.*

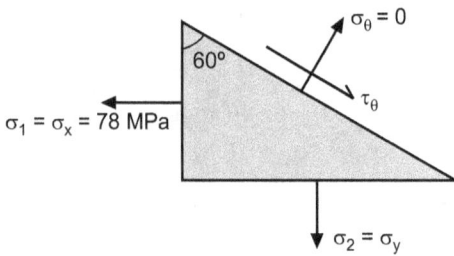

Fig. 9.10 : Given state of stress

Data   :   As shown in Fig. 9.10.

Required : (i)   Other principal stress (σ_2)

          (ii)   Shear stress (τ_θ)

          (ii)   Plane on which $\sigma_\theta = \tau_\theta$.

Concept : Standard formulae.

Solution : (i)   Principal stress σ_2 :

Let, other principal stress σ_2 be tensile in nature. See Fig. 9.10.

We have,

$$\sigma_\theta = 0 = \frac{\sigma_x + \sigma_y}{2} + \frac{\sigma_x - \sigma_y}{2} \cos(2\theta) \qquad (\because \tau_{xy} = 0)$$

$$\therefore \qquad 0 = \frac{78 + \sigma_2}{2} + \frac{78 - \sigma_2}{2} \cdot \cos(2 \times 60)$$

$$0 = 39 + 0.5\,\sigma_2 + 0.25\,\sigma_2 - 19.5$$

$$\therefore \qquad \sigma_2 = -26 \text{ MPa} = \textbf{26 MPa}\ \textbf{(Compressive)}$$

(ii) Shear stress (τ_θ) :

$$\tau_\theta = \frac{\sigma_x - \sigma_y}{2} \cdot \sin(2\theta)$$

$$= \frac{78 - (-26)}{2} \sin(2 \times 60)$$

$$\therefore \qquad \tau_{60} = \textbf{45 MPa}$$

(iii) The inclination of plane for which normal and shear stresses are equal in magnitude :
Equating σ_θ and τ_θ from equations (9.1) and (9.2),

$$\sigma_x \cdot \cos^2\theta + \sigma_y \cdot \sin^2\theta = (\sigma_x - \sigma_y)\sin\theta\cos\theta$$

$$78 \cdot \cos^2\theta - 26\sin^2\theta = (78 - (-26)) \cdot \sin\theta \cdot \cos\theta$$

$$78\cos^2\theta - 26\sin^2\theta = 104 \cdot \sin\theta\cos\theta$$

$$\frac{78}{\tan\theta} - 26\tan\theta = 104$$

$$78 - 26\tan^2\theta = 104\tan\theta$$

$$\tan^2\theta + 4\tan\theta - 3 = 0$$

Solving, $\tan\theta = 0.646$ or -4.646

$$\therefore \qquad \theta = \textbf{32.87°} \text{ or } \textbf{-77.87°}$$

Example 9.7 : *At a point in a stressed elastic plate the following information is known :*

(i) *Maximum shearing strain = $\phi_{max} = 5 \times 10^{-4}$.*

(ii) *The sum of the normal stresses on two perpendicular planes passing through the point = 27.5 MPa.*

(iii) *Modulus of elasticity E = 200 GPa and Poisson's ratio μ = 0.25. Compute the magnitude of principal stresses at the point.*

Data   : $\phi_{max} = 5 \times 10^{-4}$; E = 200 GPa; μ = 0.25 ; $\sigma_1 + \sigma_2 = 27.5$ MPa.

Required :   Principal stresses σ_1 and σ_2.

Concept :   (i)   Knowing maximum shear strain, find τ_{max}.

(ii) $\tau_{max} = \dfrac{\sigma_1 - \sigma_2}{2}$ and $\sigma_1 + \sigma_2 = 27.5$.

Solving these two equations, principal stresses can be obtained.

Solution :   (i)   Maximum shear stress (τ_{max}).

$$E = 2\,G\,(1 + \mu)$$
$$200 = 2G\,(1 + 0.25)$$
$\therefore$
$$G = 80 \text{ GPa}$$
$$\tau_{max} = \phi_{max} \cdot G = 5 \times 10^{-4} \times 80 \times 10^3 = 40 \text{ MPa}$$

(ii) Principal stresses (σ_1, σ_2).

$$\sigma_1 - \sigma_2 = 2 \times 40 \qquad\qquad \text{... (i)}$$
$$\sigma_1 + \sigma_2 = 27.5 \qquad\qquad \text{... (ii)}$$

Solving equations (i) and (ii),

$$\sigma_1 = \textbf{53.75 MPa (Tensile)}$$

$$\sigma_2 = \textbf{– 26.25 MPa = 26.25 MPa (Compressive)}$$

Example 9.8 : *At certain element; plane AB carries direct tensile stress of 30 MPa and shear stress of 20 MPa while other plane BC carries direct tensile stress of 20 MPa and a shear stress as shown in Fig. 9.11 (a). If the planes AB and BC are inclined at 30° and plane AC at right angles to plane AB which carries direct stress of unknown magnitude and nature, find : (i) shear stress on BC, (ii) magnitude and nature of direct stress on AC and (iii) principal stresses.*

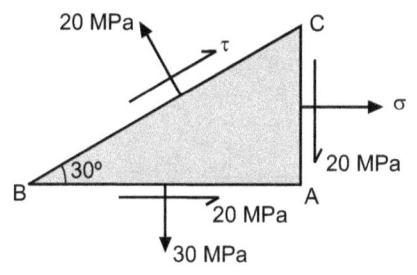

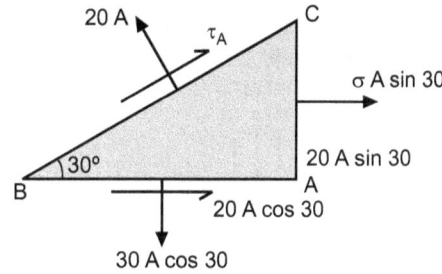

(a) Given state of stress   **(b) Forces on element ABC**

Fig. 9.11

Data   :   As shown in Fig. 9.11 (a).

Required :   (i) Shear stress (τ) on BC, (ii) Magnitude and nature of direct stress (σ) on AC and (iii) Principal stresses.

Concept   :   Equilibrium and standard formulae.

Solution :   (i) Equilibrium : Let A be the area along the plane BC.

∴   Area of plane AC = A sin 30 and area of plane AB = A cos 30. Forces on element ABC are as shown in Fig. 9.11 (b).

$\Sigma F_x = 0$;

$$\sigma A \sin 30 + 20 \, A \cos 30 + \tau A \cos 30 - 20 \, A \sin 30 = 0$$

$$0.5 \, \sigma + 0.86 \, \tau + 7.32 = 0 \qquad\qquad \text{... (i)}$$

$\Sigma F_y = 0$;

$$- 20 \, A \sin 30 - 30 \, A \cos 30 + \tau A \sin 30 + 20 \, A \cos 30 \; = 0 \qquad\qquad \text{... (ii)}$$

∴ $\tau = 37.32$ MPa   put this value in equation (i)

∴ $\sigma = - 79.28$ MPa = **79.28 MPa (Compressive)**

(ii) Principal stresses (σ_1, σ_2) :

$$\sigma_1, \sigma_2 = \frac{\sigma_x + \sigma_y}{2} \pm \sqrt{\left(\frac{\sigma_x - \sigma_y}{2}\right)^2 + (\tau_{xy})^2}$$

$$= \frac{-79.28 + 30}{2} \pm \sqrt{\left(\frac{-79.28 - 30}{2}\right)^2 + (20)^2}$$

$$= - 24.64 \pm 58.18$$

$$\sigma_1 = - 82.82 \text{ MPa}$$

$$= \textbf{82.82 MPa (Compressive)}$$

$$\sigma_2 = \textbf{33.54 MPa (Tensile)}$$

Example 9.9 : *At a point in a strained material, the state of stress is as shown in Fig. 9.12 (a). Locate the principal planes and evaluate the principal stresses.*

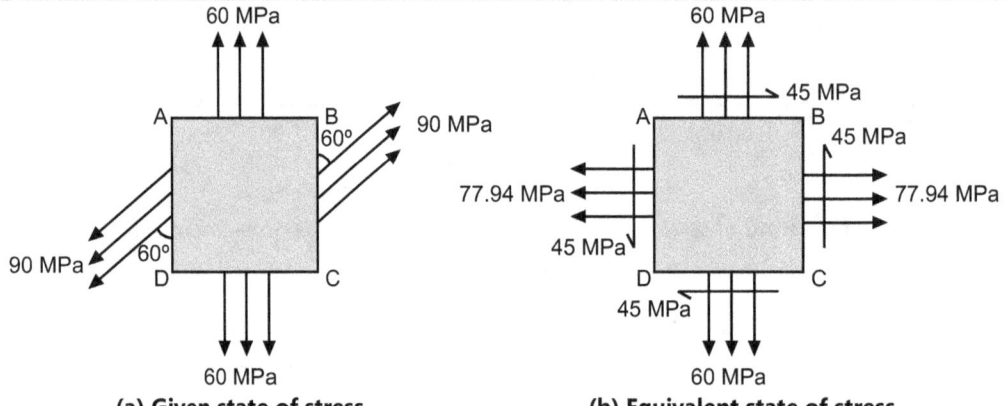

(a) Given state of stress   (b) Equivalent state of stress

Fig. 9.12

Data   : As shown in Fig. 9.12 (a).

Required : Principal planes and principal stresses.

Concept   : Standard formulae.

Solution : (i) Equivalent state of stress :

   Stress normal to faces BC and AD = $90 \times \sin 60 = 77.94$ MPa

   and shear stress = $90 \times \cos 60 = 45$ MPa

Equivalent state of stress is as shown in Fig. 9.12 (b).

(ii) Principal stresses (σ_1, σ_2) :

$$\sigma_1, \sigma_2 = \frac{\sigma_x + \sigma_y}{2} \pm \sqrt{\left(\frac{\sigma_x - \sigma_y}{2}\right)^2 + (\tau_{xy})^2}$$

$$\sigma_1, \sigma_2 = \frac{77.94 + 60}{2} \pm \sqrt{\left(\frac{77.94 - 60}{2}\right)^2 + (45)^2}$$

$$= 68.97 \pm 45.88$$

$$\sigma_1 = \textbf{114.85 MPa (Tensile)}$$

$$\sigma_2 = \textbf{23.09 MPa (Tensile)}$$

(iii) Principal planes :

$$\tan (2\theta) = -\frac{2\,\tau_{xy}}{\sigma_x - \sigma_y}$$

$$= \frac{2 \times 45}{77.94 - 60} \qquad \left(\because \tau_{xy} \text{ is } - \text{ve}\right)$$

$$= 5.016$$

$\therefore$ $\theta_1 = \textbf{39.36}^\circ$, $\theta_2 = \theta_1 + 90^\circ = \textbf{129.36}^\circ$

Example 9.10 : *At a point in a strained material under two-dimensional stress condition, the normal stress on a certain plane is 80 MPa compressive and the shear stress is 56 MPa. On a plane at right angles to this plane, there is no normal stress. If the maximum permissible stresses for the material are 150 MPa in compression, 130 MPa in tension and 65 MPa in shear; examine the safety of section giving reasons.*

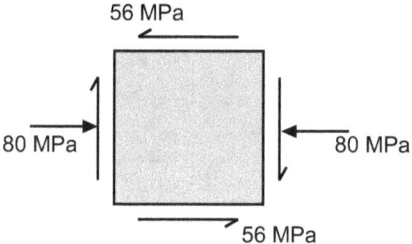

Fig. 9.13 : Given state of stress

Data   :   State of stress as shown in Fig. 9.13.

Allowable stresses : In compression : 150 MPa, In tension : 130 MPa

In shear : 65 MPa.

Required :   To check safety of the section.

Concept :   If actual stresses induced are less than respective allowable stresses, section is safe.

Solution :   (i) Principal stresses (σ_1, σ_2) :

$$\sigma_1, \sigma_2 \;=\; \frac{\sigma_x}{2} \pm \sqrt{\left(\frac{\sigma_x}{2}\right)^2 + (\tau_{xy})^2} \qquad\qquad \left(\because \sigma_y = 0\right)$$

$$\sigma_1, \sigma_2 \;=\; \frac{-80}{2} \pm \sqrt{\left(\frac{-80}{2}\right)^2 + (56)^2}$$

$$= -40 \pm 68.82 \text{ MPa}$$

$$\sigma_1 \;=\; -108.82 \text{ MPa}$$

= **108.82 MPa (Compressive) < 150 MPa**   ... (Safe)

σ_2 = **28.82 MPa (Tensile) < 130 MPa**   ... (Safe)

(ii) Maximum shear stress (τ_{max}) :

$$\tau_{max} \;=\; \frac{\sigma_1 - \sigma_2}{2} = \pm\,68.82 \text{ MPa} > 65 \text{ MPa} \qquad \textbf{... (Unsafe)}$$

∴   The section is unsafe in shear.

Example 9.11 : *At a point in a strained material, the resultant stress on vertical plane is 100 MPa, tensile, making 30° angle with normal. On horizontal plane through the point, the resultant compressive stress makes an angle of 60° with the normal as shown in Fig. 9.14 (a). Determine : (i) the principal stresses and principal planes, (ii) maximum shear stress and (iii) on properly oriented element, show principal stresses.*

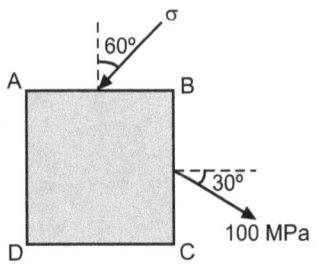

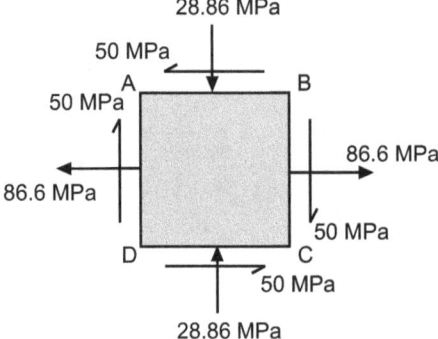

(a) Given state of stress   **(b) Equivalent state of stress**

Fig. 9.14

Data   :   As shown in Fig. 9.14 (a).

Required :   (i) Principal planes and principal stresses, (ii) Maximum shear stress.

Concept   :   Standard formulae.

Solution :   (i) Equivalent state of stress :

Normal stress on faces BC and AD = 100 cos 30 = 86.6 MPa (Tensile)

Shear stress = 100 sin 30 = 50 MPa (on all faces)

Compressive stress σ on face AB $= \dfrac{50}{\sin 60} = 57.73$ MPa.

Normal stress on faces AB and CD = 57.73 cos 60 = 28.86 MPa (Compressive)

Equivalent state of stress is as shown in Fig. 9.14 (b).

(ii) Principal stresses (σ_1, σ_2) :

$$\sigma_1, \sigma_2 \; = \; \frac{\sigma_x + \sigma_y}{2} \pm \sqrt{\left(\frac{\sigma_x - \sigma_y}{2}\right)^2 + (\tau_{xy})^2}$$

$$= \; \frac{86.6 - 28.86}{2} \pm \sqrt{\left(\frac{86.6 - (-28.86)}{2}\right)^2 + (50)^2}$$

$$= \; 28.87 \pm 76.37$$

σ_1 = **105.24 MPa (Tensile)**

σ_2 = – 47.50 MPa = **47.5 MPa (Compressive)**

(iii) Principal planes : $\tan (2\theta) = -\dfrac{2\,\tau_{xy}}{\sigma_x - \sigma_y} = -\dfrac{2 \times 50}{86.6 - (-28.86)}$

$= -0.866$

θ = **– 20.44°** and **– 110.44°**

(iv) Maximum shear stress (τ_{max}) :

$$\tau_{max} = \frac{\sigma_1 - \sigma_2}{2}$$

$$= \frac{105.24 - (-47.5)}{2} = 76.37 \text{ MPa}$$

σ2 = 47.5 MPa
20.44°
σ1
σ1 = 105.24 MPa
σ2

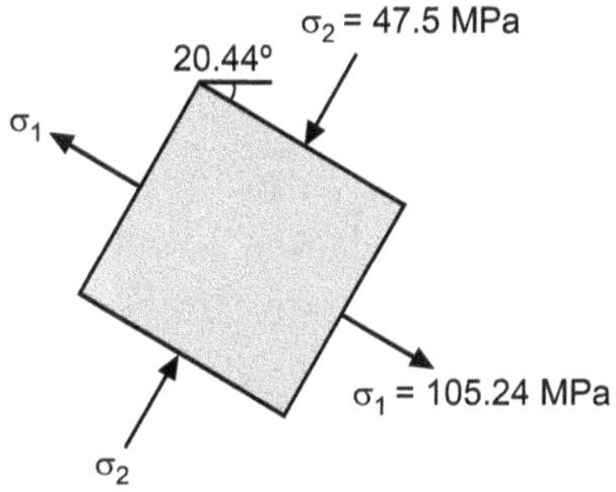

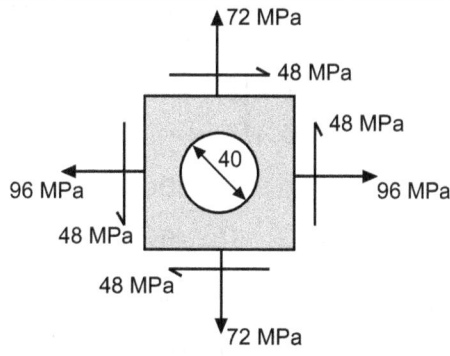

Fig. 9.14 (c) : Principal stresses on oriented element

Example 9.12 : *A circle 40 mm in diameter is marked on a steel plate before it is stressed as shown in Fig. 9.15. As a result of these stresses, the circle deforms to an ellipse. Calculate the lengths of the major and minor axes of the ellipse and their directions. Assume E = 200 GPa and μ = 0.25.*

72 MPa
48 MPa
48 MPa
40
96 MPa
96 MPa
48 MPa
48 MPa
72 MPa

Fig. 9.15 : State of stress on a plate

Data : State of stress as shown in Fig. 9.15.

Required : Lengths and directions of major and minor axes of the ellipse.

Concept : Principal stresses and principal strains.

Solution : (i) Principal stresses (σ_1, σ_2) :

$$\sigma_1, \sigma_2 = \frac{\sigma_x + \sigma_y}{2} \pm \sqrt{\left(\frac{\sigma_x - \sigma_y}{2}\right)^2 + (\tau_{xy})^2}$$

$$= \frac{96 + 72}{2} \pm \sqrt{\left(\frac{96 - 72}{2}\right)^2 + (48)^2}$$

$$= 84 \pm 49.47$$

$$\sigma_1 = \textbf{133.47 MPa (Tensile)}$$

$$\sigma_2 = \textbf{34.53 MPa (Tensile)}$$

(ii) Principal planes :

$$\tan(2\theta) = \frac{2\,\tau_{xy}}{\sigma_x - \sigma_y} \qquad (\because \tau_{xy} \text{ is } -ve)$$

$$= \frac{2 \times 48}{96 - 72} = 4$$

$$\theta = \textbf{37.98}° \text{ and } \textbf{127.98}°$$

(iii) Principal strains (ε_1, ε_2) :

$$\varepsilon_1 = \frac{1}{E}(\sigma_1 - \mu\,\sigma_2) = \frac{1}{200 \times 10^3}(133.47 - 0.25 \times 34.53)$$

$$= \textbf{6.24} \times \textbf{10}^{-4}$$

$$\varepsilon_2 = \frac{1}{E}(\sigma_2 - \mu\,\sigma_1) = \frac{1}{200 \times 10^3}(34.53 - 0.25 \times 133.47)$$

$$= \textbf{5.81} \times \textbf{10}^{-6}$$

Increase in diameter $= \delta d_1 = 6.24 \times 10^{-4} \times 40 = \textbf{0.0249 mm}$

∴ Length of major axis $= 40 + 0.0249 = \textbf{40.0249 mm}$

Increase in diameter $= \delta d_2 = 5.81 \times 10^{-6} \times 40 = \textbf{2.32} \times \textbf{10}^{-4} \textbf{mm}$

Length of minor axis $= 40 + 2.32 \times 10^{-4} = \textbf{40.000232 mm}$

Example 9.13 : *A small block is 60 mm long, 40 mm wide and 5 mm thick. It is subjected to uniformly distributed tensile forces having the resultant values as shown in Fig. 9.16. Compute the stress components developed along the diagonal AB.*

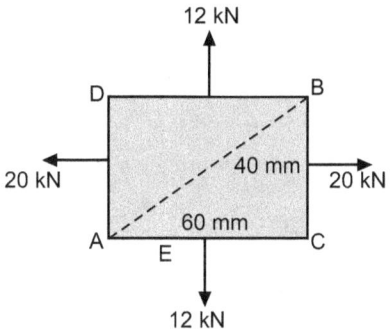

Fig. 9.16 : State of stress on a block

Data   : As shown in Fig. 9.16.

Required : Stress components on diagonal AB.

Concept : FBD and equations of statics.

Solution : (i) FBD of wedge ABC :

Let F_n and F_t be the forces normal and tangential to diagonal AB for equilibrium as shown in Fig. 9.17.

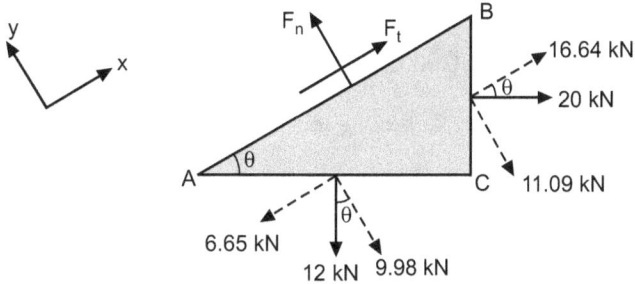

Fig. 9.17 : Forces on wedge ABC

$$\theta = \tan^{-1}\left(\frac{40}{60}\right) = 33.7^{\circ}$$

Resolving forces normal and tangential to plane AB, the components are obtained as shown in Fig. 9.17.

$\Sigma F_x = 0$;

$$F_t + 16.64 - 6.65 = 0$$

$\therefore$ $\qquad\qquad$ $F_t = 10$ kN

$\Sigma F_y = 0$; $\qquad\quad$ $F_n - 11.09 - 9.98 = 0$

$$F_n = 21.07 \text{ kN}$$

(ii) Stress components :

$$l\,(AB) = \sqrt{(60)^2 + (40)^2} = 72.11 \text{ mm}$$

∴   Area of plane AB = A   = $l\,(AB) \times$ Thickness

$$= 72.11 \times 5$$

$$A = 360.55 \text{ mm}^2$$

∴   Normal stress = $\sigma_n = \dfrac{F_n}{A} = \dfrac{21.07 \times 10^3}{360.55}$

$$= \textbf{58.43 MPa (Tensile)}$$

Shear stress = $\tau = \dfrac{F_t}{A} = \dfrac{10 \times 10^3}{360.55}$

$$= \textbf{27.73 MPa}$$

Example 9.14 : *The principal strains at a point in a two-dimensional stress system were observed to be 0.00035 extension and 0.00025 contraction. Determine the principal stresses. Also find the maximum shear stress.*

$$E = 200 \text{ GPa}, \quad \mu = \frac{1}{m} = 0.3$$

Data : $\varepsilon_1 = 0.00035$, $\varepsilon_2 = -0.00025$, $E = 200$ GPa, $\mu = \dfrac{1}{m} = 0.3$

Required : $\sigma_1,\ \sigma_2,\ \tau_{max}$ and plane on which maximum shear stress acts.

Concept : Generalised Hooke's law.

Solution : (i) Principal stresses :

We have, $\varepsilon_1 = \dfrac{1}{E}(\sigma_1 - \mu\,\sigma_2)$

$$0.00035 = \dfrac{1}{200 \times 10^3}(\sigma_1 - 0.3\,\sigma_2)$$

$$\sigma_1 - 0.3\,\sigma_2 = 70 \qquad\qquad \text{... (i)}$$

$$\varepsilon_2 = \dfrac{1}{E}(\sigma_2 - \mu\,\sigma_1)$$

$$-0.00025 = \dfrac{1}{200 \times 10^3}(\sigma_2 - 0.3\,\sigma_1)$$

$$\sigma_2 - 0.3\,\sigma_1 = -50 \qquad\qquad \text{...(ii)}$$

Solving equations (i) and (ii),

$$\sigma_1 = \textbf{60.44 MPa (Tensile)}$$

$$\sigma_2 = -31.87 \text{ MPa} = \textbf{31.87 MPa (Compressive)}$$

(ii) Maximum shear stress :

$$\tau_{max} = \frac{\sigma_1 - \sigma_2}{2}$$

$$= \frac{60.44 - (- 31.87)}{2}$$

∴ τ_{max} = **46.155 MPa (Tensile)**

Example 9.15 : *At a point in a strained material, direct stresses of 102 MPa (tensile) and 76.5 MPa (compressive) exist on two perpendicular planes. These planes also carry shear stresses. The major principal stress is 127.5 MPa. Find shear stresses on these planes. Also find the maximum shear stress.*

Data : $\sigma_x = 102$ MPa, $\sigma_y = - 76.5$ MPa, $\sigma_1 = 127.5$ MPa.

Required : τ_{xy}, τ_{max}.

Concept : Standard formulae.

Solution : (i) τ_{xy} :

$$\sigma_1 = \frac{\sigma_x + \sigma_y}{2} + \sqrt{\left(\frac{\sigma_x - \sigma_y}{2}\right)^2 + \tau_{xy}^2}$$

$$127.5 = \frac{102 - 76.5}{2} + \sqrt{\left(\frac{102 + 76.5}{2}\right)^2 + \tau_{xy}^2}$$

$$= 12.75 + \sqrt{7965.56 + \tau_{xy}^2}$$

$$13167.56 = 7965.56 + \tau_{xy}^2$$

∴ τ_{xy} = **72.12 MPa**

(ii) $$\sigma_2 = \frac{\sigma_x + \sigma_y}{2} - \sqrt{\left(\frac{\sigma_x - \sigma_y}{2}\right)^2 + \tau_{xy}^2}$$

$$= 12.75 - 114.74$$

$$\sigma_2 = - \textbf{101.99 MPa}$$

$$= \textbf{101.99 MPa   (Compressive)}$$

(iii) Maximum shear stress :

$$\tau_{max} = \frac{\sigma_1 - \sigma_2}{2} = \frac{127.5 - (- 101.99)}{2}$$

∴ τ_{max} = **114.745 MPa (Tensile)**

Example 9.16 : *A piece of material is subjected to a tensile stress of 80 MPa in one direction, a compressive stress of 60 MPa in a direction at right angle to the tensile stress, and a shearing stress of 50 MPa. Find the normal, tangential and resultant component of the stress on the plane, the normal of which makes an angle of 30° with the tensile stress.*

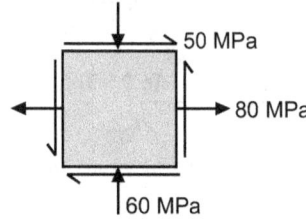

Fig. 9.18

Data : As shown in Fig. 9.18, θ = 60°.

Required : Normal, tangential and resultant component of the stress.

Concept : Standard formulae.

Solution : (i) Normal stress :

$$\sigma_\theta = \frac{\sigma_x + \sigma_y}{2} + \frac{\sigma_x - \sigma_y}{2} \cos 2\theta - \tau_{xy} \sin 2\theta$$

$$= \frac{80 - 60}{2} + \frac{80 - (-60)}{2} \cos 120 - 50 \sin 120$$

$$= 10 - 35 - 43.30$$

∴ σ_θ = **– 68.3 MPa = 68.3 MPa (Compressive)**

(ii)   Shear stress :

$$\tau_\theta = \frac{\sigma_x - \sigma_y}{2} \sin 2\theta + \tau_{xy} \cos 2\theta$$

$$= \frac{80 - (-60)}{2} \sin 120 + 50 \cos 120$$

$$= 60.62 - 25 = 35.62$$

τ_θ = **35.62 (Tensile)**

(iii) Resultant stress and its obliquity :

$$\text{Resultant stress} = \sqrt{\sigma_\theta^2 + \tau_\theta^2} = \sqrt{(-68.3)^2 + (35.62)^2}$$

$$= \textbf{77.03 MPa}$$

$$\text{Obliquity} = \phi = \tan^{-1}\left(\frac{\tau_\theta}{\sigma_\theta}\right)$$

$$= \tan^{-1}\left(\frac{35.62}{-68.3}\right) = \textbf{– 27.54°}$$

Example 9.17 : *A steel bolt of 30 mm diameter is subjected to direct tension of 20 kN and shearing force of 15 kN. Determine the intensities of normal and shear stresses across a plane at an angle of 70° to the axis of bolt. Also calculate the principal stresses.*

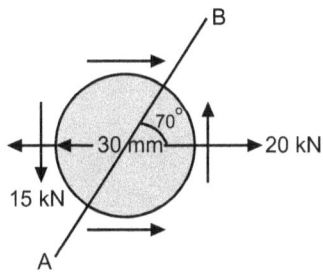

Fig. 9.19

Data : As shown in Fig. 9.19, $\theta = 20°$.

Required : Stress component on plane AB and principal stresses.

Concept : Standard formulae.

Solution : (i) State of stress :

$$\text{Normal stress} \;=\; \frac{P}{A} \;=\; \frac{20 \times 10^3}{\dfrac{\pi}{4} \times (30)^2} \;=\; 28.29 \text{ MPa}$$

$$\text{Shear stress} \;=\; \frac{S}{A} \;=\; \frac{15 \times 10^3}{\dfrac{\pi}{4} \times (30)^2} \;=\; 21.22 \text{ MPa}$$

(ii) Principal stresses :

$$\sigma_1, \sigma_2 \;=\; \frac{\sigma_x}{2} \pm \sqrt{\left(\frac{\sigma_x}{2}\right)^2 + \tau_{xy}^{\,2}}$$

$$=\; \frac{28.29}{2} \pm \sqrt{\left(\frac{28.29}{2}\right)^2 + (21.22)^2}$$

$$=\; 14.145 \pm 25.50$$

$$\sigma_1 \;=\; \textbf{39.645 MPa (Tensile)}$$

$$\sigma_2 \;=\; \textbf{– 11.355 MPa} \;=\; \textbf{11.355 (Compressive)}$$

(iii)   Stress component on plane AE :

$$\sigma_\theta \;=\; \frac{\sigma_x}{2} + \frac{\sigma_x}{2} \cos 2\theta - \tau_{xy} \sin 2\theta$$

$$= \frac{28.29}{2} + \frac{28.29}{2} \cos 40 - 21.22 \sin 40$$

$$\sigma_\theta = \textbf{11.34 MPa (Tensile)}$$

$$\tau_\theta = \frac{\sigma_x}{2} \sin 2\theta + \tau_{xy} \cos 2\theta$$

$$= \frac{28.29}{2} \sin 40 + 21.22 \cos 40$$

$$\tau_\theta = \textbf{25.35 MPa (Tensile)}$$

Example 9.18 : *An element in a plane stress is subjected to stresses as shown in Fig. 9.20. Obtain the principal stresses and show them on a properly oriented element.*

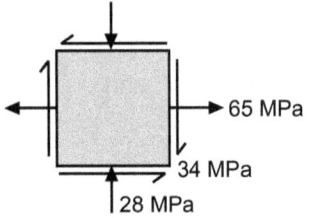

65 MPa

34 MPa

28 MPa

Fig. 9.20

Data : As shown in Fig. 9.20.

Required : σ_1, σ_2.

Concept : Standard formulae.

Solution : Principal stresses :

$$\sigma_1, \sigma_2 = \frac{\sigma_x + \sigma_y}{2} \pm \sqrt{\left(\frac{\sigma_x - \sigma_y}{2}\right)^2 + \tau_{xy}^2}$$

$$= \frac{65 - 28}{2} \pm \sqrt{\left(\frac{65 + 28}{2}\right)^2 + (34)^2}$$

$$= 18.5 \pm 57.60$$

$$\sigma_1 = \textbf{76.10 MPa (Tensile)}$$

$$\sigma_2 = \textbf{– 39.10 MPa} = \textbf{39.10 MPa \ (Compressive)}$$

$$\tan 2\theta = -\frac{2\tau_{xy}}{\sigma_x - \sigma_y} = \frac{-2 \times 34}{(65 - (-28))} = -0.73$$

$$\therefore \qquad \theta = -18.08, \ \theta = -108.09°$$

Example 9.19 : *At a particular point in a wooden member, the state of stress is as shown in Fig. 9.21. The direction of grain in the wood makes a 30° angle with the horizontal. If the allowable shearing stress parallel to the grain is 1 MPa, verify that, this state of stress is permissible.*

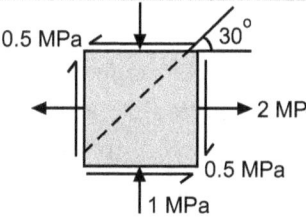

Fig. 9.21

Data : As shown in Fig. 9.21, $\tau_\theta = 1$ MPa, $\theta = 60°$.

Required : Check for shearing stress.

Solution : Standard formulae.

$$\tau_\theta = \frac{\sigma_x - \sigma_y}{2} \sin 2\theta + \tau_{xy} \cos 2\theta$$

$$= \frac{2 - (-1)}{2} \sin 120 + 0.5 \cos 120$$

$$= 1.3 + 0.25 = 1.55 \text{ MPa} > 1 \text{ MPa}$$

State of stress is not permissible.

9.5 MOHR'S CIRCLE

Mohr's circle is a graphical representation of a general state of stress at a point. It is a graphical method used for evaluation of principal stresses, maximum shear stress, normal and tangential stresses on any given plane.

Equations (9.3) and (9.4) are rewritten as

$$\sigma_\theta - \frac{\sigma_x + \sigma_y}{2} = \frac{\sigma_x - \sigma_y}{2} \cos(2\theta) - \tau_{xy} \cdot \sin(2\theta)$$

$$\tau_\theta = \frac{\sigma_x - \sigma_y}{2} \sin(2\theta) + \tau_{xy} \cdot \cos(2\theta)$$

Squaring and adding these equations we get,

$$\left(\sigma_\theta - \frac{\sigma_x + \sigma_y}{2}\right)^2 + \tau_\theta^2 = \left(\frac{\sigma_x - \sigma_y}{2}\right)^2 + (\tau_{xy})^2 \qquad \text{... (9.14)}$$

It should be noted that, σ_x, σ_y and τ_{xy} are constants for a given state of stress, while σ_θ and τ_θ are variables. Equation (9.13) is the equation of circle of the form

$$(\sigma_\theta - a)^2 + \tau_\theta^2 = R^2 \qquad \text{... (9.15)}$$

where,
$$a = \frac{\sigma_x + \sigma_y}{2}$$

and
$$R = \sqrt{\left(\frac{\sigma_x - \sigma_y}{2}\right)^2 + (\tau_{xy})^2}$$

The centre of Mohr's circle lies at (a, 0) i.e. $\left(\dfrac{\sigma_x + \sigma_y}{2}, 0\right)$.

Following important points must be noted for graphical analysis by Mohr's circle :

(1) The normal stresses σ_x, σ_y are plotted along the abscissa. The tensile stresses are considered positive and the compressive stresses are considered negative.

(2) The shear stress τ is plotted as ordinates. Shear stress which causes clockwise rotation of element is considered positive while the one which causes anticlockwise rotation is considered negative.

(3) Co-ordinates of various points on Mohr's circle represent the state of stress at different planes.

(4) The radius of the circle to any point on its circumference represents the axis directed normal to the plane whose stress components are given by the co-ordinates of that point.

(5) The angle between radii to points on Mohr's circle is twice the angle between the normals to the actual planes represented by these points. The rotational sense of this angle is same as that of rotational sense of the actual angle between the normals to the plane.

Example 9.20 : *At a certain point in a stressed body, the principal stresses are as shown in Fig. 9.22 (a). Determine normal and shear stress components on the planes whose normals are at 20° and 110° with x-axis. Show your result on properly oriented element.*

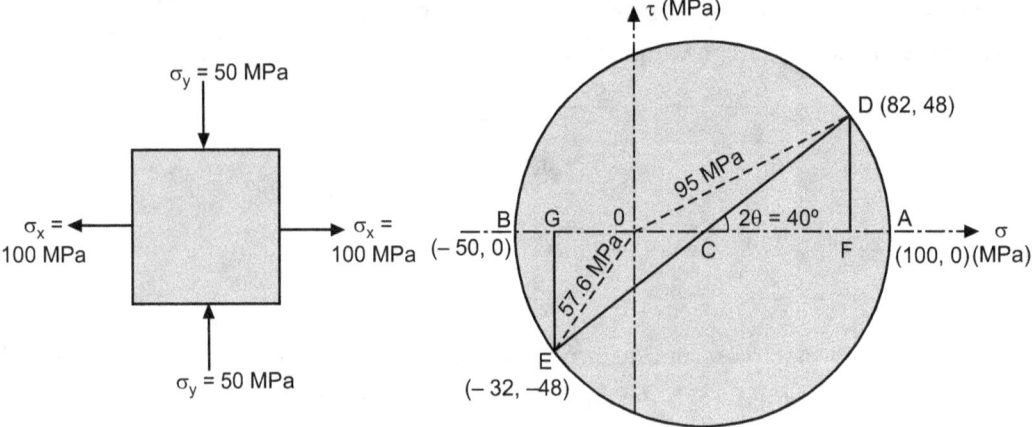

(a) State of stress at a given element   (b) Mohr's circle

Fig. 9.22

Data   :   State of stress as shown in Fig. 9.22 (a).

Required : Normal and shear stress components on the planes whose normals are at 20° and 110° with x-axis.

Concept : Mohr's circle.

Solution :

(i) Draw a set of rectangular axes and label them as σ and τ axes as shown in Fig. 9.22 (b).

(ii) Along the x-axis, OA and OB are set-off equal in length to σ_x and σ_y respectively. Please note that σ_x is + ve while σ_y is – ve.

(iii) AB represents the diameter of Mohr's circle. Mark centre 'C' of AB and with 'C' as centre and AC as radius, draw Mohr's circle.

(iv) Normal and tangential stress components are required on the planes whose normals are at 20° and 110° with x-axis. Hence, draw CD and CE at 40° and 220° anticlockwise as shown in Fig. 9.22 (b).

(v) The co-ordinates of points D and E represent state of stress on the planes whose normals are at 20° and 110° with x-axis respectively.

Ans. : On plane, whose normal is at 20° to x axis, σ = 82 MPa (Tensile) and τ = 48 MPa (clockwise)

On plane, whose normal is at 110° to x-axis, σ = – 32 MPa = 32 MPa (Compressive) and τ = – 48 MPa = 48 MPa (anticlockwise), as shown in Fig. 9.23.

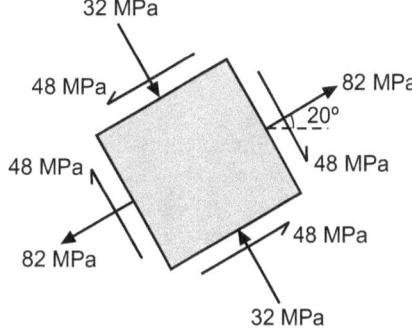

Fig. 9.23 : State of stress on oriented element

Note : It should be noted that OD and OE represent the resultant stresses on planes whose normals are at 20° and 110° with x-axis respectively. Thus, resultant stress on plane whose normal is at 20° = 95 MPa (Tensile) and resultant stress on plane whose normal is at 110° = 57.6 MPa (Compressive).

Example 9.21 : *At a point in a strained material, two-dimensional state of stress is as shown in Fig. 9.24 (a). Determine graphically : (i) Principal stresses, (ii) Principal planes, (iii) Maximum shear stress, (iv) Planes of maximum shear, (v) Normal and shear stress components on planes whose normals are at 35° and 125° with x-axis.*

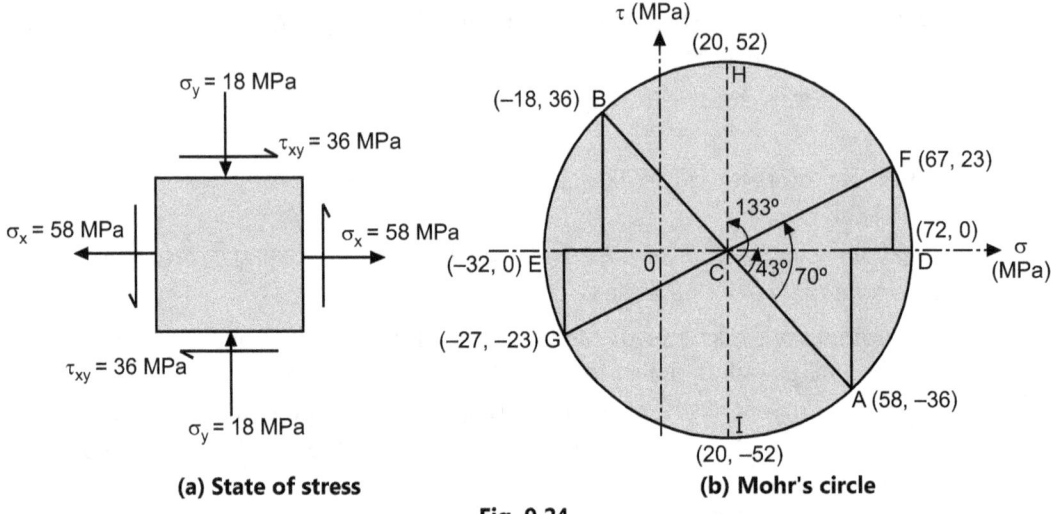

(a) State of stress   (b) Mohr's circle

Fig. 9.24

Data   : State of stress as shown in Fig. 9.24 (a).

Required : (i) Principal planes and principal stresses, (ii) Maximum shear stress and its plane, (iii) Normal and shear stress components on plane whose normals are at 35° and 125° with x-axis.

Concept : Mohr's circle.

Solution :

(i)   Draw a set of rectangular axes and label them as σ and τ axes.

(ii) Locate points A (58, – 36) and B (– 18, 36) representing state of stress on x and y planes respectively. It should be noted that shear on x plane is negative while that on y plane is positive.

(iii) AB is the diameter of Mohr's circle whose centre lies at C. With 'C' as centre and CA as radius draw Mohr's circle as shown in Fig. 9.24 (b); which cuts the x-axis at D and E. Measure and write the co-ordinates of points D and E which represent principal planes.

Thus, σ_1 = 72 MPa (Tensile) and σ_2 = – 32 MPa = 32 MPa (Compressive)

(iv) Measure $\angle$ ACD = $2\theta_n$ = 43°.

$\therefore$ θ_1 = 21.5° and θ_2 = 111.5° represent directions of principal planes. See Fig. 9.25 (a).

(v) Locate points H (20, 52) and I (20, – 52) on vertical diameter. These are the planes of maximum shear stress.

Thus, maximum shear stress = τ_{max} = ± 52 MPa and normal stress on the plane of maximum shear is 20 MPa (Tensile).

(vi) Measure $\angle$ ACH = 2 θ_s = 133°

∴ θ_3 = 66.5° and θ_4 = 156.5° represent the directions of planes of maximum shear. See Fig. 9.25 (b).

(vii) Normal and tangential stress components are required on planes whose normals are at 35° and 125° with x-axis. Hence, draw CF and CG at 70° and 250° anticlockwise with respect to CA as shown in Fig. 9.24 (b). The co-ordinates of points F and G represent the state of stress on planes whose normals are at 35° and 125° with x-axis, respectively.

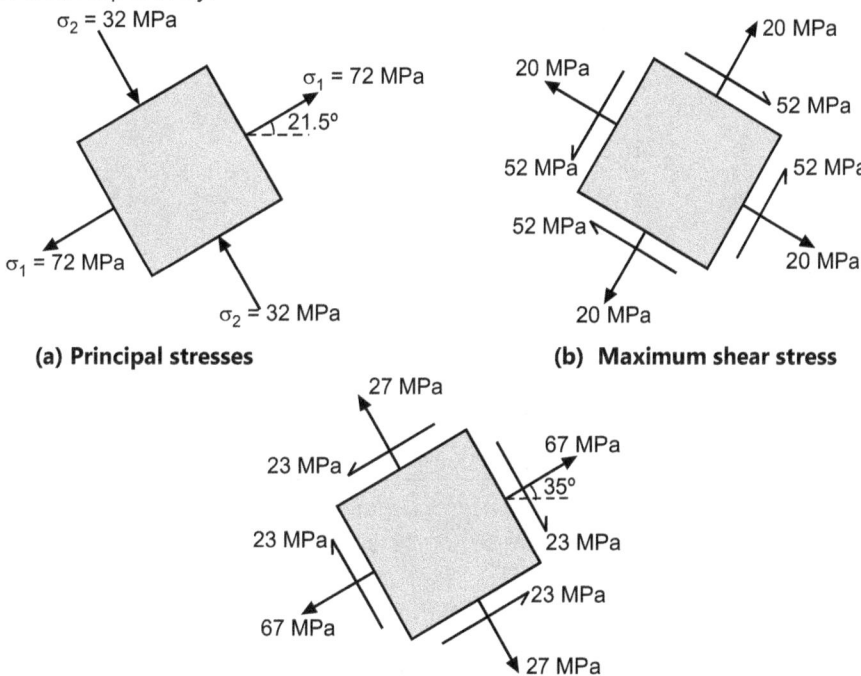

(a) **Principal stresses**

(b) **Maximum shear stress**

(c) **State of stress on element whose normals are at 35° and 125° to x-axis**

Fig. 9.25

Thus, on plane whose normal is at 35° with x-axis, normal stress = σ = 67 MPa (Tensile) and shear stress = τ = 23 MPa (clockwise).

On plane whose normal is at 125° with x-axis, normal stress = σ = – 27 MPa = 27 MPa (Compressive) and shear stress = τ = – 23 MPa = 23 MPa (anticlockwise). See Fig. 9.25 (c).

Example 9.22 : *At a point in a strained material, the normal and tangential stresses, on a plane inclined at 40° to the plane carrying major principal tensile stress, are 68 N/mm² tensile and 158 N/mm² respectively. Find the magnitude and nature of principal stresses. Also find the resultant stress on the given inclined plane.*

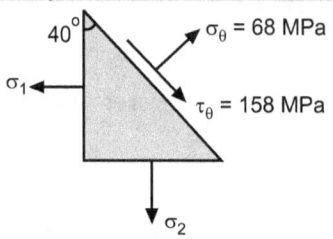

Fig. 9.26

Solution : (i)

$$\sigma_\theta = 68 = \frac{\sigma_1 + \sigma_2}{2} + \left\{\frac{\sigma_1 - \sigma_2}{2}\right\} \cos(2 \times 40)$$

∴

$$136 = 1.1736\,\sigma_1 + 0.8264\,\sigma_2 \qquad \ldots \text{(i)}$$

$$\tau_\theta = 156 = \left\{\frac{\sigma_1 - \sigma_2}{2}\right\} \sin(2 \times 40)$$

∴

$$316.81 = \sigma_1 - \sigma_2 \qquad \ldots \text{(ii)}$$

Solving (i) and (ii),

$$\sigma_1 = 198.9 \text{ MPa}, \quad \sigma_2 = 117.9 \text{ MPa}$$

(ii)   Resultant stress on inclined plane,

$$\sigma_R = \sqrt{(68)^2 + (156)^2}$$

$$= \textbf{170.17 MPa}$$

$$\phi = \tan^{-1}(\tau_\theta/\sigma_\theta)$$

$$= \textbf{66.41°}$$

Example 9.23 : *At a point in an strained material, stress pattern is as shown in Fig. 9.27. Determine (i) magnitude of principal stresses and their orientation, (ii) maximum shear stress and its orientation.*

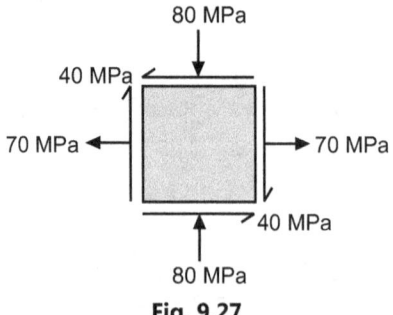

Fig. 9.27

Solution : (i) Principal stresses and its planes :

$$\sigma_1, \sigma_2 \;=\; \frac{\sigma_x + \sigma_y}{2} \;\pm\; \sqrt{\left(\frac{\sigma_x - \sigma_y}{2}\right)^2 + \tau_{xy}^{\,2}}$$

$$=\; \frac{70 - 80}{2} \;\pm\; \sqrt{\frac{(70 + 80)^2}{2} + (40)^2}$$

$$\sigma_1 \;=\; \mathbf{-\,90\ MPa} \ \text{ and } \ \sigma_2 = \mathbf{80\ MPa}$$

$$\tan(2\theta_1) \;=\; -\frac{2\tau_{xy}}{\sigma_x - \sigma_y}$$

$$\theta_1 \;=\; \mathbf{14.03°}, \ \ \theta_2 \;=\; \mathbf{104.03°}$$

(ii) Maximum shear stresses and its planes :

$$\tau_{max} \;=\; \pm\,(\sigma_1 - \sigma_2)/2 \;=\; \pm\,\mathbf{85\ MPa}$$

$$\theta_3 \;=\; \mathbf{-\,30.96°} \ \text{ and } \ \theta_4 = \mathbf{-\,120.96°}$$

Example 9.24 : σ_x, σ_y and τ_{xy} are the stress components along the rectangular axes x and y, whereas $\sigma_{x'}$, $\sigma_{y'}$ and τ_{xy}' are the components along the rectangular axes x' and y' as shown in Fig. 9.28. Prove that $\sigma_{x'} \cdot \sigma_{y'} - \tau_{x'y'}^{\,2}$ is independent of the orientation, as defined by θ, of x' and y'. Using this invariance property, express the shear stress τ_{xy} in terms of σ_x, σ_y and the principal stresses σ_1, σ_2.

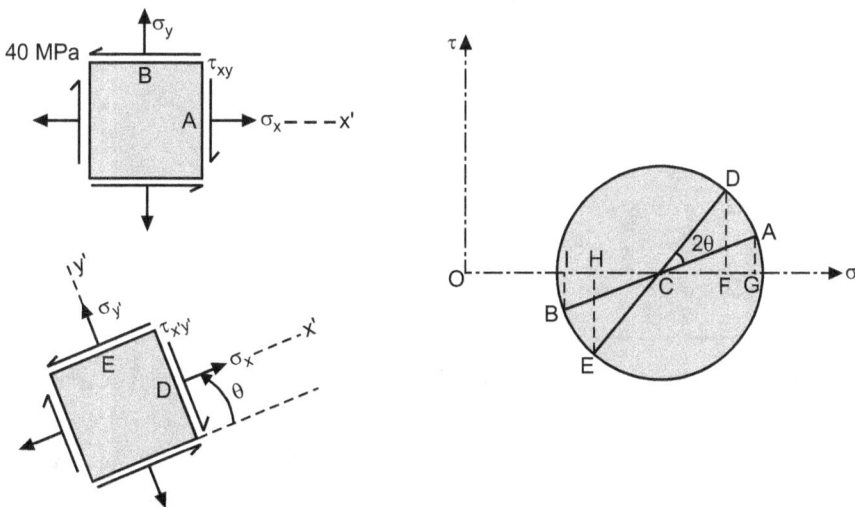

Fig. 9.28

Solution : Required : $\sigma_x \cdot \sigma_y - \sigma_{xy}^2 = \sigma_x' \cdot \sigma_y' - \tau_{x'y'}^2 = $ constant.

$$(OG)\,(OI) - AG^2 = (OF)\,(OH) - DF^2$$

$$(OC + CG)\,(OC - CI) - AG^2 = (OC + CF)\,(OC - CH) - DF^2$$

$$OC^2 - CG^2 - AG^2 = OC^2 - CF^2 - DF^2$$

$$CG^2 + AG^2 = CF^2 + DF^2$$

$$= R^2 = \text{constant. Hence proved.}$$

Also

$$\sigma_x \cdot \sigma_y - \tau_{xy}^2 = \sigma_1 \cdot \sigma_2$$

$$\tau_{xy} = \sqrt{\sigma_x \cdot \sigma_y - \sigma_1 \cdot \sigma_2}$$

Example 9.25 : *If σ_x = 60 MPa, σ_y = –120 MPa, τ_{xy} = 100 MPa and θ = 30°, obtain the values of σ_x', σ_y' and τ_{xy}'. Locate the planes of principal stresses and the planes of maximum shear stresses. Find the magnitude of these stresses.*

Solution :

$$\sigma_x' = \sigma_\theta = \frac{\sigma_x + \sigma_y}{2} + \frac{\sigma_x - \sigma_y}{2}\cos(2\theta) - \tau_{xy}\sin(2\theta)$$

$$= -71.6 \text{ MPa}$$

$$\sigma_y' = \frac{\sigma_x + \sigma_y}{2} + \frac{\sigma_x - \sigma_y}{2}\cos[2(\theta + 90)] - \tau_{xy}\sin[2(\theta + 90)]$$

$$= 11.6 \text{ MPa}$$

$$\tau_{xy}' = \frac{\sigma_x - \sigma_y}{2}\sin(2\theta) + \tau_{xy}\cos(2\theta)$$

$$= \pm 127.94 \text{ MPa}$$

$$\sigma_1 = 104.5 \text{ MPa}, \ \sigma_2 = -164.5 \text{ MPa}$$

$$\theta_1 = 24°, \quad \theta_2 = 114°, \quad \theta_3 = -21°, \quad \theta_4 = -111°$$

$$\tau_{max} = \pm 134.5 \text{ MPa}$$

Example 9.26 : *At a point in a structure subjected to plane stress, the stresses have magnitude and directions shown acting on element A in the first part of Fig. 9.29. Element B, located at the same point, is rotated through an angle θ of such magnitude that the stresses have the values shown in the second part of Fig. 9.29. Calculate the normal stress σ and the angle θ.*

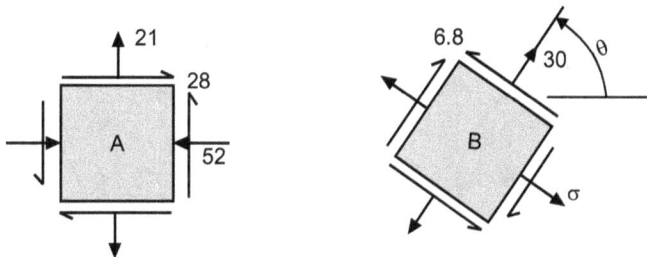

Fig. 9.29

Solution :

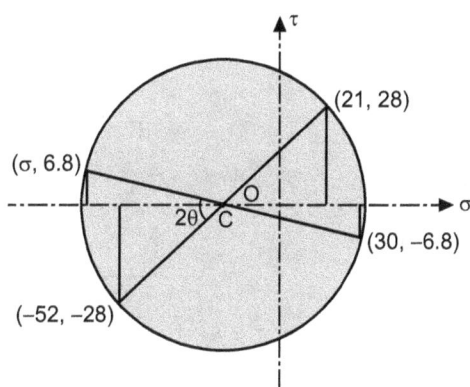

Fig. 9.30

From Mohr's circle, $\sigma = -61$ **MPa**, $\theta = 24°$.

Example 9.27 : *The state of stress at a point is the result of the three separate actions that produce the three states of stresses as shown in Fig. 9.31. Determine the principal stresses caused by the superposition of these three stress states.*

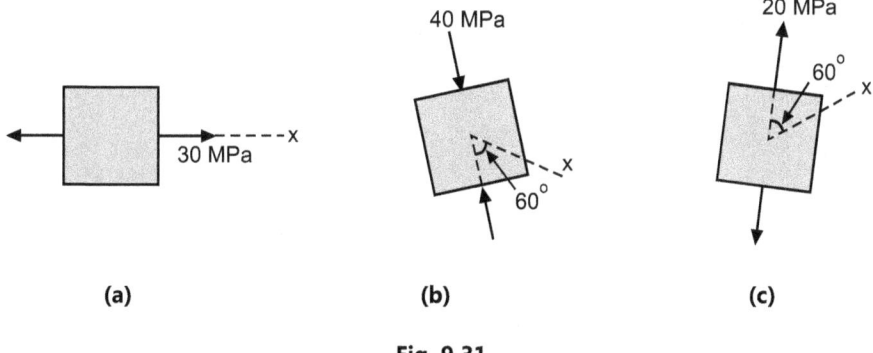

Fig. 9.31

Solution :

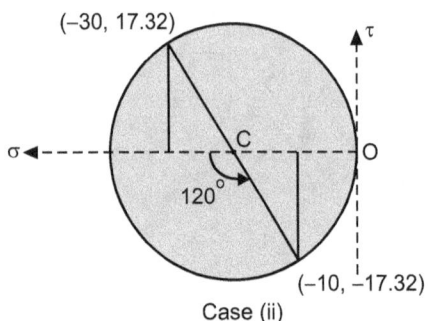

Case (ii)

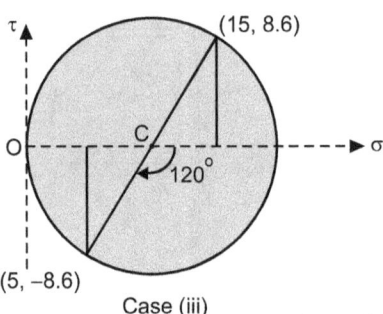

Case (iii)

Fig. 9.32

Case (i) : $\sigma_x = 30$ MPa, $\sigma_y = 0$, $\tau_{xy} = 0$

Case (ii) : $\sigma_x = -10$ MPa, $\sigma_y = -30$ MPa, $\tau_{xy} = -17.32$ MPa

Case (iii) : $\sigma_x = 5$ MPa, $\sigma_y = 15$ MPa, $\tau_{xy} = -8.6$ MPa

∴ Resultant, $\sigma_x = 25$ MPa, $\sigma_y = -15$ MPa, $\tau_{xy} = -25.92$ MPa

$$\sigma_1, \sigma_2 = \frac{\sigma_x + \sigma_y}{2} \pm \sqrt{\left(\frac{\sigma_x - \sigma_y}{2}\right)^2 + \tau_{xy}^2}$$

$$= (25 - 15)/2 \pm \sqrt{((25 + 15)/2)^2 + (25.92)^2}$$

$$\sigma_1 = \textbf{37.73 MPa} \quad \text{and} \quad \sigma_2 = \textbf{- 27.7 MPa}$$

Example 9.28 : *At a point in a strained material the normal and tangential stresses on a plane inclined at 40° to the vertical plane are 68 N/mm² and 158 N/mm² respectively. Find the magnitude and nature of principal stresses. Also find the resultant stresses on the given inclined plane.*

Data   : $\sigma_\theta = 68$ N/mm², $\tau_\theta = 158$ N/mm², $\theta = 40°$

Required   :   Principal stresses and resultant stresses.

Concept   :   Standard formula.

Solution   :
$$\sigma_\theta = \frac{\sigma_x + \sigma_y}{2} + \frac{\sigma_x - \sigma_y}{2} \cos 2\theta$$

$$68 = \frac{\sigma_x + \sigma_y}{2} + \frac{\sigma_x - \sigma_y}{2} \cos 80$$

$$\tau_\theta = \frac{\sigma_x - \sigma_y}{2} \sin 2\theta$$

$$158 = \frac{\sigma_x - \sigma_y}{2} \sin 80$$

$$\sigma_x - \sigma_y = 320.87$$

$$\sigma_x + \sigma_y = 80.28$$

$$\sigma_x = \textbf{200.58 N/mm}^2 \textbf{ (T)}$$

$$\sigma_y = -120.29 \text{ N/mm}^2$$

$$\sigma_y = \textbf{120.29 N/mm}^2 \textbf{ (C)}$$

$$\sigma_R = \sqrt{\sigma_\theta^2 + \tau_\theta^2} = \sqrt{68^2 + 158^2}$$

$$\sigma_R = \textbf{172 N/mm}^2$$

Example 9.29 : *Direct stresses of 160 N/mm^2 tensile and 120 N/mm^2 compressive, exist on two perpendicular planes at a certain point in a body. They are also accompanied by shear stresses on the planes. The greatest principal stress at the point is 200 N/mm^2. What must be the magnitude of shearing stresses on the two planes and what will be the maximum shearing stress at the point ?*

Data   : $\sigma_x = 160$ N/mm^2 (T), $\sigma_y = 120$ N/mm^2 (C), $\sigma_1 = 200$ N/mm^2

Required :   Shearing stress on planes and maximum shear stress.

Concept :   Standard formula

Solution : $$\sigma_1; \sigma_2 = \frac{\sigma_x + \sigma_y}{2} \pm \left[\sqrt{\left(\frac{\sigma_x - \sigma_y}{2}\right)^2 + \tau_{xy}^2} \right]$$

$$\sigma_1; \sigma_2 = \frac{160 - 120}{2} \pm \left[\sqrt{\left(\frac{160 - (-120)}{2}\right)^2 + \tau_{xy}^2} \right]$$

$$200 = 20 \pm \left[\sqrt{(140)^2 + \tau_{xy}^2} \right]$$

$$(140)^2 + \tau_{xy}^2 = 180^2$$

$$\tau_{xy} = \textbf{113.14 N/mm}^2$$

$$\sigma_2 = \textbf{ – 160 N/mm}^2$$

$$\tau_{max} = \frac{200 - (-160)}{2} = \textbf{180 N/mm}^2$$

Example 9.30 : *For the stress condition on an element as shown in Fig. 9.33, determine the principal planes and stresses. Also determine the maximum shear stress and the planes on which they act.*

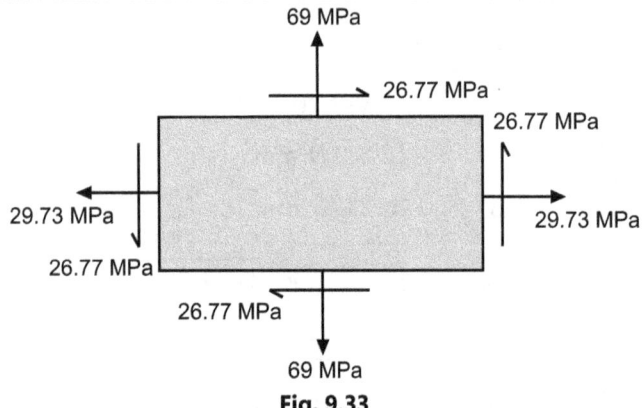

Fig. 9.33

Data   :   As shown in Fig. 9.33.

Required :   Principal stresses and their planes and maximum shear stress.

Concept :   Standard formula.

Solution :

$$\sigma_1; \sigma_2 = \frac{\sigma_x + \sigma_y}{2} \pm \left[\sqrt{\left(\frac{\sigma_x - \sigma_y}{2}\right)^2 + \tau_{xy}^2} \right]$$

$$\sigma_1; \sigma_2 = \frac{29.73 - (-69)}{2} \pm \left[\sqrt{\left(\frac{29.73 - 69}{2}\right)^2 + (26.67)^2} \right]$$

$$\sigma_1; \sigma_2 = 49.37 \pm \left[\sqrt{(-19.64)^2 + (26.67)^2} \right]$$

$$\sigma_1; \sigma_2 = 49.37 \pm 33.12$$

$$\sigma_1 = \mathbf{41.25\ N/mm^2}$$

$$\sigma_2 = \mathbf{8.13\ N/mm^2}$$

$$\tan 2\theta = \frac{-2\tau_{xy}}{(\sigma_x - \sigma_y)} = -\frac{2\,(26.77)}{(29.73) - (69)}$$

$$\theta_1 = 14.24, \qquad \theta_2 = 104.24$$

$$\tau_{max} = \frac{41.25 + 8.13}{2} = \mathbf{49.38\ N/mm^2}$$

$$\tan 2\theta_s = \frac{(\sigma_x - \sigma_y)}{2\tau_{xy}} = \frac{(29.73 - 69)}{2\,(26.77)}$$

$$\theta_{s_1} = \mathbf{-36.25}, \qquad \theta_{s_2} = \mathbf{53.75}$$

Example 9.31 : *The principal tensile stresses at a point are 100 N/mm² and 60 N/mm². Find normal, tangential and resultant stress on a plane at 30° with vertical plane. What is the angle of obliquity ?*

Data   : σ_x = 100 N/mm², σ_y = 60 N/mm², θ = 30°

Required :   Normal stress, tangential stress, resultant stress and angle of obliquity.

Concept :   Standard formula.

Solution :

Normal stress, $\sigma_n = \sigma_1 \cos^2 \theta + \sigma_2 \sin^2 \theta + \tau_{xy} \sin 2\theta$

$\qquad\qquad\qquad = 100 \cos^2 30 + 60 \sin^2 30 + 0$

$\qquad\qquad\qquad = 75 + 15 = \textbf{90 MPa}$

Tangential stress, $\sigma_t = \left[\dfrac{\sigma_1 - \sigma_2}{2}\right] \sin 2\theta - \tau_{xy} \cos 2\theta$

$\qquad\qquad\qquad = \left(\dfrac{100 - 60}{2}\right) \sin (2 \times 30) - 0$

$\qquad\qquad\qquad = \dfrac{40}{2} \sin 60$

$\qquad\qquad\qquad = \textbf{13.32 MPa}$

Resultant stress, $\sigma_R = \sqrt{\sigma_n^2 + \sigma_t^2}$

$\qquad\qquad\qquad = \sqrt{90^2 + 17.32^2}$

$\qquad\qquad \sigma_R = \textbf{91.65 MPa}$

Angle of obliquity, $\tan \theta = \dfrac{\sigma_t}{\sigma_n}$

$\qquad\qquad\quad \theta = \tan^{-1}\left[\dfrac{\sigma_t}{\sigma_n}\right]$

$\qquad\qquad\quad \theta = \textbf{10.76°}$

9.6 THEORIES OF FAILURE

Following are the theories of failure adopted for design of structural members.

  (i)   Maximum Principal Stress Theory : As per this theory, maximum principal stress shall not exceed the working stress for the material. i.e. $\sigma_1 \le \sigma_{safe}$. This theory is known as Rankine's theory.

  (ii)   Maximum Principal Strain Theory : If σ_1 and σ_2 are the principal stresses at a point in the strained material, the major principal strain is given by

$$\varepsilon_1 = \frac{1}{E}(\sigma_1 - \mu\,\sigma_2)$$

Let σ be the stress which acting alone produces the same principal strain, then

$$\frac{\sigma}{E} = \frac{1}{E}(\sigma_1 - \mu\,\sigma_2)$$

$\therefore$
$$\sigma = \sigma_1 - \mu\,\sigma_2$$

The criteria of design will therefore be

$$\sigma = \sigma_1 - \mu\,\sigma_2 \le \sigma_{safe}$$

This theory was given by St. Venant.

(iii) Maximum Shear Stress Theory : If σ_1 and σ_2 are the principal stresses, maximum shear stress

$$\tau_{max} = \frac{\sigma_1 - \sigma_2}{2}$$

This maximum shear stress shall not exceed the working stress in shear for the material i.e. $\tau_{max} \le \tau_{safe}$. This theory was given by Sir J. J. Guest.

(iv) Maximum Strain Energy Theory : If σ_1 and σ_2 are the principal stresses, then the strain energy stored per unit volume

$$= \frac{1}{2E}\left(\sigma_1^2 + \sigma_2^2 - 2\,\mu\,\sigma_1\sigma_2\right)$$

Let σ be the stress acting alone, to store the same amount of strain energy per unit volume, then

$$\frac{\sigma^2}{2E} = \frac{1}{2E}\left(\sigma_1^2 + \sigma_2^2 - 2\,\mu\,\sigma_1\sigma_2\right)$$

$\therefore$
$$\sigma = \sqrt{\sigma_1^2 + \sigma_2^2 - 2\,\mu\,\sigma_1\sigma_2} \le \sigma_{safe}$$

This theory was given by Beltrami and Haigh.

Example 9.32 : *A member, solid circular in cross section is subjected to an axial pull of 13 kN and a shear force of 5 kN. Design the cross section of member based on (i) the maximum principal stress theory, (ii) the maximum principal strain theory, (iii) the maximum shear stress theory, (iv) the maximum strain energy theory. For the material of member, elastic limit in axial tension is 250 MPa, Poisson's ratio = 0.3. Use factor of safety = 2.5.*

Data   : Axial pull = 13 kN, shear force = 5 kN, Elastic limit in axial tension = 250 MPa, μ = 0.3, factor of safety = 2.5.

Required : Design of cross section based on various theories of failure.

Concept : Failure theories.

Solution : (i) Geometric properties and allowable stresses :

Let 'a' be the cross-sectional area of member in mm^2.

Safe stress in axial tension $= \sigma_{safe} = \dfrac{250}{2.5} = 100$ MPa

Safe stress in shear $= \tau_{safe} = \dfrac{100}{2} = $ **50 MPa**

(ii) Maximum principal stress theory,

Direct stress on cross section $= \sigma = \dfrac{P}{A} = \dfrac{13 \times 10^3}{a}$ MPa

Shear stress on cross section $= \tau = \dfrac{SF}{A} = \dfrac{5 \times 10^3}{a}$ MPa

Principal stresses are,

$$\sigma_1, \sigma_2 = \frac{\sigma}{2} \pm \sqrt{\left(\frac{\sigma}{2}\right)^2 + \tau^2}$$

$$= \frac{13 \times 10^3}{2a} \pm \sqrt{\left(\frac{13 \times 10^3}{2a}\right)^2 + \left(\frac{5 \times 10^3}{a}\right)^2}$$

$$= \frac{6500}{a} \pm \frac{8200.6}{a}$$

$\therefore$ $\sigma_1 = \dfrac{14700.6}{a}$ MPa

$\sigma_2 = -\dfrac{1700.6}{a}$ MPa

As per this theory ; $\sigma_1 \leq \sigma_{safe}$

$\therefore$ $\dfrac{14700.6}{a} \leq 100$

$\therefore$ $a \geq 147$ mm^2

$\therefore$ Diameter of the cross section $= d = \sqrt{\dfrac{4 \times 147}{\pi}} = $ **13.68 mm**

(iii) Maximum principal strain theory :

Let, σ be the stress alone which produces same maximum strain.

$$\sigma = \sigma_1 - \mu\, \sigma_2$$

$$= \frac{14700.6}{a} - 0.3 \left(-\frac{1700.6}{a}\right)$$

$$= \frac{15210.78}{a} \text{ MPa}$$

As per this theory ; $\sigma \le \sigma_{safe}$ i.e. $\dfrac{15210.78}{a} \le 100$

$\therefore$ $a \ge 152.1$ mm²

$\therefore$ Diameter of the cross section $= d = \sqrt{\dfrac{4 \times 152.1}{\pi}} = \mathbf{13.91\ mm}$

(iv)   Maximum shear stress theory :

$$\tau_{max} = \dfrac{\sigma_1 - \sigma_2}{2} = \dfrac{1}{2}\left[\dfrac{14700.6}{a} - \left(-\dfrac{1700.6}{a}\right)\right]$$

$$= \dfrac{8200.6}{a}\ \text{MPa}$$

As per this theory, $\tau_{max} \le \tau_{safe}$

$\therefore$ $\dfrac{8200.6}{a} \le 50$

$\therefore$ $a \ge 164.01$ mm²

$\therefore$ Diameter of the cross section $= d = \sqrt{\dfrac{4 \times 164.01}{\pi}} = \mathbf{14.45\ mm}$

(v)   Maximum strain energy theory :

Strain energy stored per unit volume

$$= \dfrac{1}{2E}\left(\sigma_1^2 + \sigma_2^2 - 2\mu\,\sigma_1\,\sigma_2\right)$$

$$= \dfrac{1}{2E}\left[\left(\dfrac{14700.6}{a}\right)^2 + \left(-\dfrac{1700.6}{a}\right)^2 - 2 \times 0.3 \left(\dfrac{14700.6}{a}\right)\left(-\dfrac{1700.6}{a}\right)\right]$$

$$= \dfrac{116.99 \times 10^6}{a^2\,E}$$

As per this theory, $\dfrac{1}{2E}\left(\sigma_1^2 + \sigma_2^2 - 2\mu\,\sigma_1\,\sigma_2\right) \le \dfrac{(\sigma_{safe})^2}{2E}$

$$\dfrac{116.99 \times 10^6}{a^2\,E} \le \dfrac{(100)^2}{2E}$$

$\therefore$ $a \ge 152.97$ mm²

$\therefore$ Diameter of the cross section $= d = \sqrt{\dfrac{4 \times 152.97}{\pi}} = \mathbf{13.95\ mm}$

Example 9.33 : *A shaft of hollow circular section with outside diameter 200 mm and inside diameter 160 mm is subjected to simultaneously a torque of 12 kNm and an axial compressive load of 300 kN. Determine the maximum tensile stress, maximum compressive stress and maximum shear stress in the shaft.*

Data   : $D = 200$ mm, $d = 160$ mm, $T = 12$ kN-m, $P = 300$ kN

Required   :   Maximum tensile stress, maximum compressive stress and maximum shear stress.

Concept   :   Standard formula.

Solution   :

$$A = \frac{\pi}{4}(200^2 - 160^2) = 11309.73 \text{ mm}^2$$

$$J = \frac{\pi}{32}(200^4 - 160^4) = 92.7 \times 10^6 \text{ mm}^4$$

$$\sigma = \frac{P}{A} = \frac{300000}{11309.73} = 26.53 \text{ N/mm}^2$$

$$\tau = \frac{T}{J} \times R = \frac{12 \times 10^6}{92.74 \times 10^6} \times 100 = \textbf{12.94 N/mm}^2$$

$$\sigma_1; \sigma_2 = \frac{\sigma}{2} \pm \left[\left(\frac{\sigma}{2}\right)^2 + \tau^2\right]$$

$$\sigma_1; \sigma_2 = \frac{26.53}{2} \pm \left[\left(\frac{26.53}{2}\right)^2 + 12.94^2\right]$$

$$\sigma_1 = \textbf{31.8 N/mm}^2 \textbf{ (T)}$$

$$\sigma_2 = -5.27 \text{ N/mm}^2$$

$$\sigma_2 = \textbf{5.27 N/mm}^2 \textbf{ (C)}$$

Example 9.34 : *A solid shaft of 60 mm diameter has to resist a bending moment of 450 kN-mm accompanied by a torque of 360 kN-mm. Calculate the maximum principal stress induced in the shaft, also calculate the maximum shear stress induced.*

Data   : $D = 60$ mm, $T = 360$ kN-mm, $M = 450$ kN-mm

Required   :   Maximum principal stress and maximum shear stress.

Concept   :   Standard formula.

Solution   :

$$P = \frac{2\pi NT}{60}$$

$$\sigma_1; \sigma_2 = \frac{16}{\pi D^3}\left[M \pm \sqrt{M^2 + T^2}\right]$$

$$\sigma_1; \sigma_2 = \frac{16 \times 10^3}{\pi (60)^3}\left[450 + \sqrt{332100}\right]$$

$$\sigma_1 = \textbf{24.20 N/mm}^2 \textbf{ (T)}$$

$$\sigma_2 = -2.98 \text{ N/mm}^2$$

$$= \textbf{2.98 N/mm}^2 \textbf{ (C)}$$

$$\tau_{max} = \frac{24.20 - (-2.98)}{2} = \textbf{13.55 N/mm}^2$$

Example 9.35 : *In a circular shaft subjected to twisting moment 'T' and bending moment 'M', show that when M = 1.2 T, the ratio of maximum shear stress to the greater principal stress is nearly 0.566.*

Data   :   M = 1.2T

Required   :   Ratio of maximum shear stress to the greater principal stress is nearly 0.566.

Concept   :   Standard formula.

Solution   : $\sigma_1; \sigma_2 = \dfrac{16}{\pi D^3}\left[M \pm \sqrt{M^2 + T^2}\right]$

$$\sigma_1 = \frac{16}{\pi D^3}\left[M + \sqrt{M^2 + T^2}\right]$$

$$\sigma_1 = \frac{16}{\pi D^3}\left[1.2T + \sqrt{(1.2T)^2 + T^2}\right]$$

$$\sigma_1 = \frac{16T}{\pi D^3}\left[1.2 + \sqrt{(1.2)^2 + 1}\right] = \frac{44.19T}{\pi D^3}$$

$$\sigma_1 = \frac{16}{\pi D^3}\left[M - \sqrt{M^2 - T^2}\right]$$

$$T_{max} = \frac{\sigma_1 - \sigma_2}{2} = \frac{25M}{\pi D^3} = \frac{25T}{\pi D^3}$$

$$\frac{T_{max}}{\sigma_1} = \frac{\dfrac{25T}{\pi D^3}}{\dfrac{44.19T}{\pi D^3}} = \textbf{0.566}$$

EXERCISE

1. A circular bar is subjected to an axial pull of 80 kN. If the maximum intensity of shear stress on any oblique plane is not to exceed 50 MPa, determine the diameter of the bar.   (31.91 mm)

2. A short metallic column of 500 mm^2 cross-sectional area carries an axial compressive load of 80 kN. For a plane inclined at 60° with the direction of load, calculate (i) normal stress, (ii) shear stress, (iii) resultant stress, (iv) maximum shear stress, and (v) obliquity of the resultant stress.

   (σ_n = 120.08 MPa ; τ = 69.28 MPa, σ = 138.63 MPa, τ_{max} = 80 MPa, ϕ = 30°)

3. The principal tensile stresses at a point across two perpendicular planes are 100 MPa and 50 MPa. Find the normal and shear stresses and the resultant stress and its obliquity on a plane at 20° with the major principal plane. Find also the intensity of stress which acting alone can produce the same strain assuming μ = 0.25.

   (σ_n = 94.15 MPa, τ = 16.08 MPa ; Resultant σ = 95.51 MPa, ϕ = 9.68° ; σ = 87.5 MPa)

4. The principal stresses at a point are 150 MPa (tensile) and 75 MPa (compressive). Determine the resultant stress in magnitude and direction on a plane inclined at 60° to the axis of major principal stress. Also determine the maximum intensity of shear stress.   (σ_n = 93.75 MPa, τ = 97.425 MPa, Resultant σ = 135.2 MPa ;

   ϕ = 46.1°; τ_{max} = 112.5 MPa)

5. A prismatic bar carrying an axial tensile stress σ_x is cut by an oblique section. If the normal and shear stresses on this section are 73.8 MPa and 24.6 MPa respectively, find values of σ_x and angle θ defining the aspect of the section.

   (σ_x = 83.0 MPa; θ = 18.43°)

6. The principal stresses acting on an element subjected to plane stresses are 12 MPa and 4.5 MPa (both tensile) respectively. Find out the position of the plane AA when the resultant stress makes the maximum angle with the normal to the plane.(ϕ = 27°)

7. A piece of material is subjected to two compressive stresses at right angles, their values being 60 MPa and 90 MPa. Find the position of plane across which the resultant stress is most inclined to the normal and determine the value of this resultant stress.

   (θ = 39.14°; Resultant σ = 73.5 MPa)

8. At a point in a strained material, state of stress is as shown in Fig. 7.34. Find (i) The direction of principal planes, (ii) The magnitude of principal stresses, (iii) The magnitude of greatest shear stress.

   (σ_1 = 116.1 MPa ; σ_2 = 6.3 MPa ; θ_1 = 31.6° ; θ_2 = 121.6° ; τ_{max} = 54.9 MPa ;

   θ_3 = 76.6° , θ_4 = 166.6°)

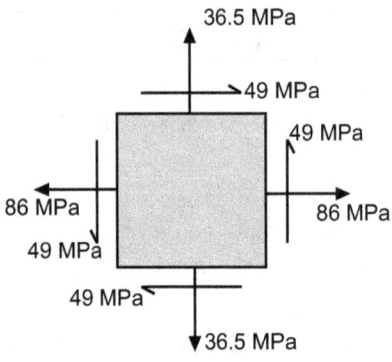

Fig. 9.34

9. State of stress at a point in a strained material is as shown in Fig. 9.35.

    Determine : (i) The resultant stress on plane AB.

    (ii)   The principal stresses and their directions.

    (iii) The maximum shear stresses and their planes.

    (Normal stress on AB = 86.6 MPa; shear stress on AB = 50 MPa, σ_1 = 131.13 MPa;

    σ_2 = 30.46 MPa, θ_1 = 41.69°, θ_2 = 131.69°, τ_{max} = 50.33 MPa, θ_3 = 86.69°,

    θ_4 = 176.69°)

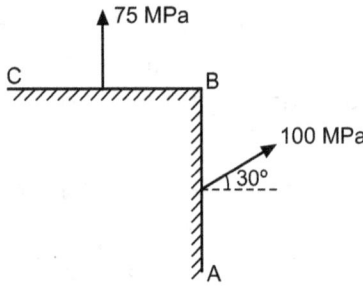

Fig. 9.35

10. Direct stresses of 102 MPa (tensile) and 76.5 MPa (compressive) exist on two perpendicular planes at a point in a strained material. These planes are also carrying shear stresses. The major principal stress is 127.5 MPa.

    (i)   Find the shear stresses on these planes.

    (ii) Find also the maximum shear stress.   (τ = 72.12 MPa, τ_{max} = 114.75 MPa)

11. Draw Mohr's circles for the elements subjected to state of stress as shown in Fig. 7.36.

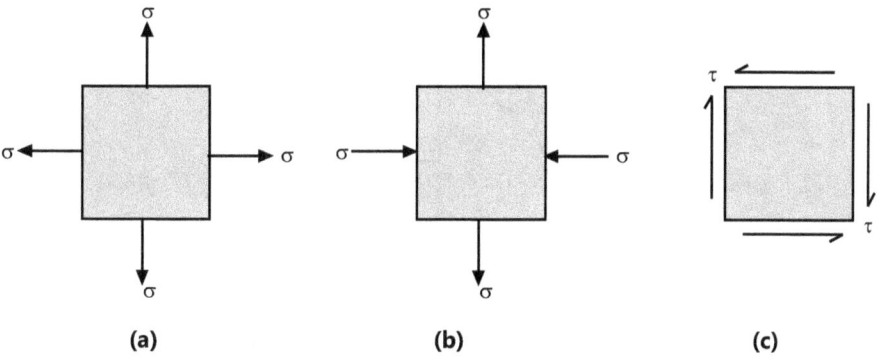

(a)   (b)   (c)

Fig. 9.36

(a) No Mohr's circle

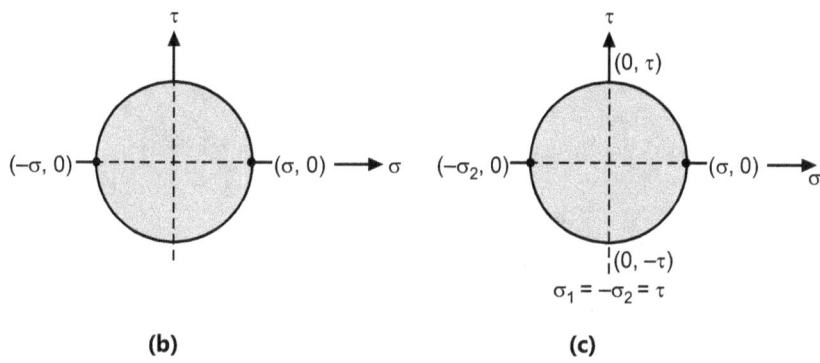

(b)   (c)

Fig. 9.37

12. At a point in a strained material, one of the principal stress is 60 MPa tensile. On a plane at 60° to this principal plane, the normal stress is zero. Determine (i) the other principal stress, (ii) the shear stress on the above plane of zero normal stress, (iii) the planes on which the normal and shear stresses are equal in magnitude.

   $(\sigma_2 = -20$ MPa $= 20$ MPa (compressive), $\tau_{60}° = 34.64$ MPa, $\theta = 32.85°)$

13. An element in a two-dimensional stress system is subjected to $\sigma_x = 150$ MPa tensile, $\sigma_y = 100$ MPa compressive and $\tau_{xy} = \tau_{yx} = 50$ MPa. Determine the planes of zero shear and maximum shear. Also find the normal and shear stress intensities on these planes. $(\theta_1 = 10.9°, \quad \theta_2 = 100.9°, \quad \theta_3 = 55.9°, \quad \theta_4 = 145.9°, \sigma_1 = 159.63$ MPa (tensile), $\sigma_2 = 109.63$ MPa (compressive), $\tau_{max} = 134.63$ MPa)

14. Fig. 9.38 shows the normal and tangential stresses on two planes. Determine the principal stresses. $(\sigma_1 = 53.73$ MPa, $\sigma_2 = 22.4$ MPa)

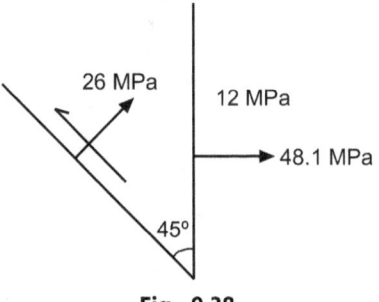

Fig. 9.38

15. At a point in a strained material, the principal stresses are 135 MPa and 54 MPa, both tensile. Locate graphically the planes for which the resultant stress is inclined at 15° to the normal. Find this resultant stress. Find also the planes for which the resultant stress is most inclined with the normal.

$(\theta_1 = 26°, \ \theta_2 = 79°, \ \theta_3 = 101°, \ \theta_4 = 154°,$ Resultant stresses = 92 MPa, 43.5 MPa,

Angular position of planes of maximum obliquity = 125°)

16. A thin plate is under a state of stress as shown in Fig. 9.39. Find the principal stresses and their directions by using the Mohr's circle method.

$(\sigma_1 = 121.42$ MPa (tensile), $\sigma_2 = 21.43$ MPa (compressive))

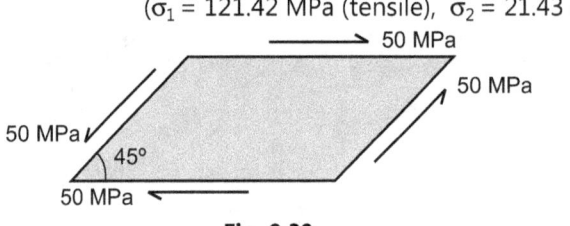

Fig. 9.39

17. A triangular prism of material is subjected to two-dimensional state of stress as shown in Fig. 9.40. Determine (i) the angle 'θ' between the planes AC and BC, (ii) the tangential, normal and resultant stress on BC, and (iii) other principal stress. [(i) θ = 33.34°; (ii) On plane BC; $\sigma_n = 69.7$ MPa (tensile), $\tau = 19.13$ MPa (clockwise), Resultant stress = 72.29 MPa, (iii) $\sigma_2 = 39.71$ MPa (tensile)].

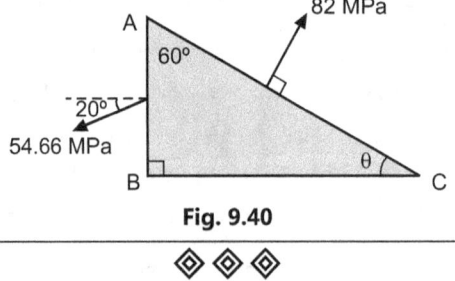

Fig. 9.40

◈ ◈ ◈

www.ingramcontent.com/pod-product-compliance
Lightning Source LLC
Chambersburg PA
CBHW081142020726
47504CB00009B/1962